The Last

Viking

A Novel by Jon Rant

*To my parents, who taught me to read
before I could tie my shoes.*

877 A.D.

SOUTHERN ENGLAND
IN THE NINTH CENTURY

CHAPTER I: Twilight Over Halfsfiord

"What exile from his country ever escaped from himself?"
—Horace, <u>Odes</u>

Mimir was his name. He was old and gnarled. His sinewy arms were like the roots of the great tree Yggdrasill, the World Ash that stretched from heavenly Asgard down into the depths of Niflheim, deep inside the bowels of the universe. His eyes had seen the light of the sun for some fifteen years until one winter's dawn he had awakened, on the verge of manhood, to a world that would remain as black as death forever.

For when he rose from his bed that fateful morning, he was blind. Such was the price for the gift he received from the All-Seeing Odin, who deemed in his infinite wisdom that Mimir should possess the ultimate vision, the future. And so he became a seer, and he lived in the village on the fiord, and no one else there had been born before him, nor had any of their fathers walked the land before Mimir did. He was the voice of the gods themselves.

His hands cradled the rocks of power, a set of smooth, small stones fashioned for magic. They were covered with ancient runes, keys that unlocked a thousand secrets that only an adept could perceive. Mimir ran his fingers over their contours and then down across the great rock on which he and the young man sat overlooking the village and the fiord. It had been a steep climb, scrambling up the narrow trail that snaked along the face of the rock. But while the young Viking labored for air as they rested on the ledge, Mimir's breath was even. He raised his face to the west, where the fiord curved one last time before merging with the sea.

"The fog rolls in."

The young man squinted. "It curls in around the southwest spur, across from the rocks guarding the harbor entrance." He looked questioningly at the old man. "But, Mimir…you're blind. How can you see it?"

"I smell it, boy. It cloaks that master of mischief, Loki. Listen!" He craned his head in the direction of the mist. Below them a wall of rock rose sharply from the water's edge, looming above the fiord that disappeared into the darkness. "Can you hear him...hissing in the fog?"

The young Viking shivered. "I can't hear a thing. But I know the fog, Mimir. Every sailor does."

"Never trust her, that She-wolf. She is cunning. She obscures." Mimir shifted his weight on the rock, turning his attention to his companion and shaking the stones in his cupped hands.

"So, young Sigli...you ask me to slice through the fog of your life and split the future open? You wish to dine on the entrails of the beast, child?" He cackled mischievously. "I warn you…you may not like the taste."

Sigli looked into Mimir's lifeless eyes. "It's my wedding day. It's time."

"And so it is."

Sigli shifted uncomfortably on the rock. He was tall, even for a Norseman, standing a full head above the other Vikings who sailed the seas aboard Lothar of Halfsfiord's dragon ships. Blonde hair cascaded onto his muscular shoulders, below which unfolded a body in the full flower of manhood. But a closer look at his face revealed a beard that was still undeveloped, struggling to fill the spaces across his rawboned face. His nose was aquiline and proud, and his mouth opened to reveal a long row of teeth yet to be spoiled by the unforgiving nature of the land of the northern lights. Most impressive of all were his eyes, two blue beacons that shone like stars, penetrating, perceptive. At nineteen years old he was the eldest son of Lothar, heir to the holdings of one of the fiercest of the Norse chieftains based on the coast of Norway.

"All is not as it seems, child," Mimir cautioned. "Keep your wits." He smiled, exposing a jagged line of teeth. "I have a gift, it's true, but there are limits. All is never revealed to me. I can only grasp at shadows that reflect the truth. Do you still want to read the runes?"

"My mind is set."

"Think twice...your guests fill Lothar's hall," Mimir smiled mischievously, "and the thighs of your young bride tremble."

Sigli blushed with pride. "Men would kill for Beolinde's hand."

"And more would kill for the treasure below her decks!" Mimir cackled. "You could fly to her now, and not bother with my idle fancies...."

But the Viking's mind was made up; that he could tell. The seer let out a sigh and then began to shake the rune stones in his hands, slowly at first and then faster, listening to their dissonant rattle before loosing them across the great slab of rock. They spun across the surface and clattered to a stop. He ran his fingers over them, breathing heavily and blinking with undivided concentration.

Sigli leaned forward. "What is it?"

"Be quiet!" Mimir raised his face toward the sky and began to moan softly, rolling back and forth on his haunches and fingering the stones, his half-closed eyelids fluttering as he swayed in the twilight. At last he began to speak.

"Oh, great Odin, All-Father, Wanderer and Wager of Battles, by your grace loosen the tongues of the Weird Sisters. Let me hear the song of the Norns as they spin the fates of man, drawing out the thread to be snipped suddenly, without warning. From the walls of Asgard, to Midgard, the land of men...from Valhalla's gates to the ends of the earth, from beyond Jotenheim and the mountains of the Frost Giants, let my prayer be heard!"

A gust of cold air rushed down the fiord. The screech of a hawk sounded far off in the distance, its cry fluttering in the wind and echoing against the cliff wall behind them. Mimir raised his arms and extended them. His eyes opened wide, exposing two empty windows without color, whiter than snow in the twilight. A shrill, hissing sound began to escape from his lips, a sound so serpentine and foul that Sigli began to shiver. The air grew heavy, and a strange voice growled hoarsely from the depths of Mimir's throat.

> *"Hearken to me, mortal man, and heed the Wanderer's call;*
> *'Neath Asgard's tow'ring ramparts, both friend and foe must fall.*
>
> *Prisoners we, of destiny...listen, and behold;*
> *I summon forth the Sisters three! Let Fortune's tale unfold!"*

A flash of lightning sheared through the fog, and the thunder rang out. Sigli felt his hair standing on end as he watched Mimir. The old man's eyes bulged from his head, glowing eerily, and he began to speak in a strange, gurgling tone. It was a sound altogether different from the whisper that had first sprung from his throat; now, the voices of three women could be distinguished, chanting in unison:

> *"Thunder, lightning, woe and worry, strife in Halfsfiord!*
> *He who lurks in Loki's womb shall conquer by the sword.*
>
> *Lothar's pride shall rise again upon a distant shore,*
> *To flourish in the setting sun, yet return...nevermore!*
>
> *Next to greatness, Sigli, stand! The dragon wields your fate.*
> *Lured by love of sovereign seed, yet driven hard by hate*
>
> *Vengeance at the twilight hour lies in wait for thee,*
> *Beneath the golden dragon's banner, far beyond the sea..."*

The light in Mimir's eyes began to dim. His shoulders sagged.

"My enemies!" Sigli shouted. "Mark them for me!"

The voice of the three women spoke again, fading deeper into Mimir's throat:

> *"Guard thee well...a hound from hell lies hard upon your scent.*
> *Sigli's bane, the one-eyed Dane, shall be your life's torment."*

Sigli grabbed the seer by the shoulders and shook him. "Mimir, his name! What is his name?"

> *"We can say no more...look to the west, where destiny beckons.*
> *Find your fortune beneath the setting sun!"*

Mimir's eyes shut and he slumped over into Sigli's arms. The Viking felt the sweat trickling down his face, cooling now as the heaviness in the air around them began to lift. The great weight of the future rolled over the crest of the surrounding cliffs, leaving all in the fiord as before. The sounds of feasting and revelry wafted up into the evening, reminding Sigli once again of the celebration going on in the great hall of Lothar on the hillside below them.

Off to the west, the fog continued to roll silently into the fiord.

*　　*　　*　　*　　*

"Your daughter's beauty is remarkable, Borstan. It's a miracle that someone as ugly as you could have produced such a fine treasure."

Lothar leaned his head back and roared with laughter. He thought himself clever, and it pleased him. He was not a man familiar with restraint; when he desired something he took it, and when even the beginning of a thought crossed his mind, he spoke it. His power and standing were in no way due to a superior intelligence, but rather were the products of an explosive energy, a singular sense of purpose. Nothing but ruin could come to anyone who dared stand between Lothar and his desires; in this, his fortieth year, he reigned over Halfsfiord with a will that could not be broken.

Lothar's dragon ships were the envy of many a rival chieftain, for to control the sea was to wield power. The rocky land of the north was poorly suited for farming, and what small benefits the soil provided were erased by long and cold winters. The people looked to the sea for life. Their settlements dotted the coastline, hugging fast to the scores of fiords that sliced into the land like so many bony fingers. The code of living was as harsh as the terrain itself. There was nothing gentle about the land; there was only the sea, and beyond it the promise of foreign shores and plunder for the taking.

The Norsemen were feared across northern Europe, wherever the sea provided access to unprotected beaches upon which their dragon ships could ground their keels and release their fury upon the land. These pagan raiders struck savagely and swiftly, fleeing seaward before resistance could materialize from the hamlets that dotted the Christian lands to the south and west. There were no strong central kingdoms to maintain order and civilization; the more savage and ruthless a society, the more power it wielded.

Lothar had not risen to his position by displaying weakness. For many years he had sailed the points of the compass at the helm of raiding fleets, to Frisia and the isles off Jutland, to the land of the Franks, to East Anglia and Northumbria on the island of the Britons and their Saxon overlords. He had passed through the Pillars of Hercules, far to the south, where the women were dark and smelled of strange perfumes anointed under the summer sun.

But he had been away from his hall on Halfsfiord too long, far longer than he had dwelt on the banks of the fiord, and now at last he was growing tired. A man of forty was not a young man; even the heartiest of Vikings was usually dead by that time, either by the sword, by sickness, or by the sea. Now, at least, he had two strong sons grown to fighting age who could lead his ships across the ocean. Sigli was already a proven warrior, and only the wolf Fenrir in his den in Hel could hope to hold the youthful Hathor from action any longer. The time had come to let his young lions roar.

He turned again to address the sinewy chieftain sitting beside him at the table in the great hall at Halfsfiord. "Come now, Borstan, answer me: how is it that Beolinde is so fine? It's a shame her mother's dead. Were she with us, she could name the true seed of her jewel...."

"The child is mine," Borstan winced, unamused. He had a long face, with pinched, narrow eyes. He had served under Lothar for many years, enjoying glory and profit, but over time a rift had developed between the two men. Borstan had been relegated to minding to affairs on the fiord during the past few years while his more privileged compatriots sailed off in the dragon fleets. As a result, his demeanor had deteriorated, leading Lothar to think that a marriage between the families would help consolidate matters and soothe old wounds.

But Borstan remained as sullen as ever. "Her looks were inherited from her mother," he said dryly, "but her good sense is mine."

Lothar's eyes narrowed. "Then she would be wise, Borstan, to remember her place and serve my house well."

Borstan felt Lothar's stare piercing into him, but he did not look up. "She'll obey, Warlord." His words were measured. "She'll do as I bid her."

"I have no doubt she'll serve my son, as the wife of a warrior should. But you, Borstan...what about you?"

Borstan raised his head slowly toward Lothar, and he could feel his mouth growing sour as their eyes met. There was so much he wanted to say, so many cutting remarks that he had rehearsed carefully while lying in his bed, eyes open, staring into the darkness and seeing Lothar laughing at him, a laughter that turned into a whine when Borstan in his fantasies reversed their positions and made Lothar the whipping boy.

But he, above all others, knew that could never be. Lothar bowed to no one. They had grown together from boyhood, and always Lothar had been the stronger, the braver, the more powerful. For years Borstan had not minded his fate; there had always been a bond between them, and he had been willing to settle for second best. There were spoils enough for everyone. But the passage of time had brought changes, and as one man's star rose, the other's fell. There had been disagreements between the two—a bit of plunder here, a woman there—and Borstan began to let his own ego and greed overcome him. He began, in his own quiet way, to despise Lothar.

They were interrupted by the approach of Hathor, Lothar's youngest son. He was almost as tall as his brother Sigli, with wide shoulders, a sharp, piercing glare, and a headstrong manner that could not be tamed.

"Father, my time has come," the young man implored. "I'm ready to command a raiding party. You can't deny me on this, my brother's wedding day."

Lothar laughed. "You're still a boy. Your time will come, soon enough."

"Would you have me stay here, tending to the women?"

"Don't be in such a rush, my son. You must be patient."

"I don't know the meaning of the word," Hathor grimaced. "You allowed Sigli the privilege when he was my age."

"You would do well to learn some of his restraint," Lothar replied. "There's more to leading men than just knowing how to use a sword. When you're old enough to marry, then you'll get your chance."

"But I must find a woman somewhere else. There are no more Beolindes left in Halfsfiord."

"True enough," Lothar agreed. "She is indeed a beauty. You'll do well to marry such a woman."

The mention of her name prompted the three men to turn toward the young bride, who stood off to one side of the hall, searching in vain for her husband. Beolinde wore her long blonde hair in a braid that reached below her waist, brushing lightly against her firm, rounded buttocks. Many a man had longed for her, but she only had eyes for Sigli. They had grown up together since the cradle, and only Lothar's disenchantment with Borstan had kept them apart. But there were many hidden crannies along Halfsfiord where lovers could steal away for an embrace, when the midnight sun slanted low across the land and licked the hills like a tongue of fire in the twilight. They had pledged their love to each other with the screams of the seagulls ringing in their ears, and now, finally, nothing could keep them apart.

"Don't look too hard for him, girl, or you'll forever be disappointed."

Beolinde swung around and found herself face to face with Sigli's mother Jorda, a tall woman who carried herself with an aging grace. The lines on her face had diminished her beauty, transforming her into a matronly, handsome woman. A lifetime with Lothar had left its mark.

"I miss him already," Beolinde said, looking down at the floor. "He's been gone from the feast for quite some time now."

"I saw him leave with Mimir. The seer keeps many secrets."

"We have no secrets."

"Ah, then you've much to learn," Jorda smiled sadly. "You'll keep him under your wing for a while, but he'll be gone, like all the others, when the sea breeze beckons. You'll wait here alone in your bed, with only the women to keep you company, and you'll wonder each night where he sleeps, hoping he's not in the arms of another—or worse, with Njord at the bottom of the sea." She looked across the room and sighed. "Most of the time they return, but they never come back the same."

"I'll bear it all, gladly."

"Come," Jorda offered warmly, placing her arm around Beolinde's shoulder, "I don't wish to alarm you. I'm happy today, happy for you and Sigli. May you live long and have many strong children."

Beolinde looked toward the door, and her eyes lit up. Jorda followed her line of sight until it led to the tall form of her son entering the hall. Sigli felt the eyes of the two women upon him and began to walk toward them, but Beolinde could not restrain herself. She rushed into his arms and embraced him.

"You've been gone so long," she whispered. "Do I displease you?"

Sigli looked into her eyes with affection. "Never, my love...not today, nor any other."

"Where have you been? You left me here alone."

"I'm sorry, Beolinde. I had to breathe in the night air," he said vacantly, looking away. His eyes met those of his mother; she moved closer, looking him over suspiciously.

"Where's Mimir? I saw him leave with you."

"He's coming, Mother. He moves slowly."

Jorda studied his face carefully. "Something troubles you. What's wrong?"

"It's nothing...nothing but a damp fog creeping in."

He was interrupted as Hathor bounded across the room, covering the distance between them in several long strides and leaping into his brother's arms. "Sigli! You must talk to Father! You must convince him I'm ready to lead the next expedition!"

"He'll know when the time is right. Trust him."

Hathor winked. "Now you'll grow soft in Beolinde's arms, and I'll be the swiftest and strongest of Lothar's sons."

"In my day, I could have beaten both of you on one leg!" Lothar's voice boomed out from behind the head table. "But never mind that! Come to me, my sons!" He beckoned to them, stretching his arms out as they strode forward to take their places at his side. "Vikings!" Lothar cried, "Raise your drinking horns to honor my sons!"

Their voices rang out and the mead flowed freely. Lothar's teeth glistened. He felt the power, and it consumed him. He looked over the heads of the assemblage and raised a fist in recognition. "The seer has come! Stand back, and make way for Mimir!"

All eyes swung toward the door of the hall, where the frail form of Mimir stood motionlessly. Without uttering a word, the men spread apart, leaving a path for the seer leading to the center of the room. He shuffled slowly past them and stopped in front of Lothar. "What does my lord require?"

"Entertain us. Tell us a story of the gods in Asgard."

Mimir turned slowly to the room, his sightless eyes glowing. "Bring me a cup of mead, and sit yourselves down, for I shall speak to you and fill your ears with matters great and glorious. Drink of my wisdom, borne on the eternal wings of time from the mouth of Odin, All-Father. Tonight, I shall tell you all a tale of Balder the Beautiful, and the twilight of the gods..."

*   *   *   *   *

The evening hung suspended in a quilt of gray over the hills surrounding Halfsfiord. Odo stared sullenly into his cup of mead, wondering at the bad turn of luck that had exiled him to the rock this night. Eagle's Nest, they called it. A cool wind always blew across the ledge, even when the waters of the fiord were still. The aerie commanded a stunning view of the harbor below, stretching from the rocks guarding the sea entrance beneath Odo's perch all the way inland and back across the fiord to Lothar's hall, and above it Mimir's rock and the forest that lay beyond. The hills rose sharply on all sides, culminating in a series of ridges that walled Halfsfiord off from the rest of the world.

When danger threatened, the warning call of Hrothgar's Horn—so named to honor Lothar's renowned father—could be heard from the rock. Hrothgar the Hardheart had returned with his prize one spring morning after a voyage of several years, a strange and perilous journey that had touched keel on many distant lands. The horn had been fashioned from some unknown and wondrous metal, and if a man of good wind put his lips to it and blew heartily, its blast could be heard in the most distant corners of Halfsfiord, reverberating between the rock walls and fading into an echo that dispersed into the air as it rose above the hillsides. It was the sentinel that watched over the village, manned at all times by a Viking who maintained an alert vigil atop Eagle's Nest.

Tonight, of all nights, Odo had been chosen for duty while his comrades feasted in the great hall below. He shivered as the wind licked at his legs, knowing it would only grow colder as darkness descended. It was a night to be warm and in the arms of a woman, not freezing like a fool, alone and untended on the ledge. He looked longingly behind him and down the trail that led from the aerie into the thickets that clung to the hillside. The path wended its way to the water far below, where a skiff docked there waited to eventually carry him back across the fiord to join in the celebration.

He could hear the distant sounds of laughter wafting up through the twilight. Lothar's fleet of dragon ships lay docked in the harbor, where nary a soul could be seen stirring on the decks. They were all celebrating, Odo scowled to himself, with heads swimming in mead as they drowned themselves in tales of valor or else knocked about with some pretty young thing in the bushes. None of the other sentinels who usually patrolled the harbor were about; they, too, had been permitted to partake in the festivities. He alone stood guard over Halfsfiord.

He took a long draught of mead and bemoaned his fortune. During the past week Lothar's captains had scouted the sea and the inlets along the shoreline, finding no reason to be alarmed. Raiding fleets were heading westward daily to the island of the Britons, where a number of loosely knit Viking armies feasted off the countryside. All eyes were riveted on their exploits, looking beyond the horizon and past the sleepy harbor of Halfsfiord. Even Sidroc, the Malevolent One, had been spotted sailing out to sea three days earlier to join the plunder seekers. There was no justice in being sentenced to Eagle's Nest tonight.

Odo refilled his drinking horn with mead. It was rich and full of flavor, a deep mixture that burned its way down his throat and settled roundly into his stomach. He swallowed another mouthful, aware for the first time of the lightness in his head. It took a considerable amount of drink to affect a man of his size, but Borstan at least had been generous, slipping a barrel into his skiff with a knowing wink as he pushed off for the rock. Odo had been drinking steadily for some hours now, and with every mouthful the breeze grew a little less harsh as the warmth in his body spread.

He stood up and ambled to the edge of the rock, to a point where all of Halfsfiord lay at his feet. An immense bank of fog, thick and impenetrable, curled through the harbor mouth directly below him. It moved like smoke across the water, creasing silently along the walls of the fiord and dancing in the twilight. Odo smiled, allowing his eyes to conjure up in its billowing folds visions of wraithlike horsemen riding in the sky, figures locked in a battle that frothed atop the cascading mist. It was peaceful and sensuous, a sharp contrast to the harsh walls of the surrounding rocks. The great cloud toyed with his imagination, tempting him to leap from the ledge and soar effortlessly into the heart of its secrets.

But what he next saw caused his eyes to grow wide with astonishment. There, knifing through the inner wall of fog, appeared the prow of a dragon ship. And then another, and after it a third, until the fiord was filled with a line of warships heading into the harbor.

Odo froze for a moment, until the realization of the immense danger that threatened Halfsfiord set in. He cast his drinking horn aside and dashed toward Hrothgar's Horn, mounted imperiously on the highest part of the ledge some twenty yards distant and up a flight of steps hewn out of the rock. He stumbled as he approached the horn, sprawling on his face and cutting his leg at the knee, but he paid no heed to the wound as he scrambled up the steps, one after the other, until the mouthpiece of the great horn was in his grasp. He filled his lungs with air to drive the blast that would awaken Halfsfiord.

Suddenly a hand emerged from behind him, covering his face and pulling his lips away from the horn. He caught a brief glimpse of a knife blade passing in front of his eyes before it dipped below his vision in a slashing motion. There was a moment of confusion, and then a convulsive shiver ran through his limbs as blood from his torn throat spurted into the air and down his chest. He sank to his knees with a horrible gurgling choke and keeled over at the foot of Hrothgar's Horn. And then his world dissolved into a dense and total darkness as his soul flew into the night and through the portals of Hel.

*   *   *   *   *

"Of all the gods in Asgard, none was as beautiful, nor as pure, as Balder the Beautiful," said Mimir.

The hall was filled with Vikings, and not a sound escaped them as they listened intently to the seer's words.

"But soon Balder began to have ominous dreams of doom. He spoke to the gods of these visions, and it was decided to seek protection for him from every conceivable kind of hurt. To this end, Frigg, the wife of Odin, exacted oaths from all things corporeal, from fire and water, to all metals and stones, to the beasts of the field, and all poisons and diseases—all agreed they would not harm Balder the Beautiful. Assured of this pledge, the gods made Balder an object of their sport, bidding him to stand unprotected while they hurled objects or thrust at him, because nothing in the universe could hurt him.

"After a time this sport came under the scrutiny of Loki, and the Mischief Maker plotted a course of deception. He disguised himself as an old crone and made his way to Frigg's palace. When the goddess learned that her fellows were engaged in their usual sport with Balder, she smiled. 'Neither weapon nor wand shall ever wound Balder,' she said, 'for I have their given word—all of them.'

"'Do you mean to say,' the old crone croaked, 'that every single thing in the world has taken your oath?'

"'Yes,' replied Frigg, 'all things except for one young sprout of mistletoe growing in a wood to the west of Valhalla. I thought it too insignificant to bother.'

"Loki immediately sought out the mistletoe and cut it down, and he fashioned it skillfully into a sharp, pointed missile. Upon returning to the meeting, he found the gods ringed around Balder, laughing as they hurled stones and lances that dropped harmlessly at his feet. Off to the side there stood Hodir, the blind god of night. Loki crept up behind him and innocently whispered, 'Why don't you join in the sport?'

"'Because I cannot see Balder,' Hodir replied, 'and I have nothing to cast at him.'

"'Show honor to Balder as the others do,' urged Loki. 'Come, and I shall guide you to where he stands, and you can pitch this shaft at him.'"

"So it was that Hodir took hold of the mistletoe and cast it at Balder, and no sooner had it struck the Beautiful One than he fell stone dead to the ground, and all the gods were dumbstruck with grief. But they were not ready to surrender their last hope, so Odin dispatched a messenger to Hel upon his warhorse. The messenger rode nine days and nights down ravines ever darker and deeper, meeting not a soul, living nor dead, until he encountered Modgurd, the terrible maiden who guards the bridge that leads to Hel.

"The messenger told her of his mission, but Modgurd would not allow him to pass, counseling that one thing still was needed for Balder to return from the dead. 'If Balder is beloved by all,' she said, 'then go forth into the world, and if every single creature in heaven and on earth mourns his loss, he shall be restored to the gods. But if even so much as one alone speaks against him, then Balder shall sleep eternally in Hel.'

"Armed with this news, the gods sent messengers to every corner of the world asking all to weep Balder undead, and everything did so, men and beasts, earth, stones, trees and every metal. As the messengers made their way homeward, they passed a cave where an old witch—Loki in disguise—was crouching. They asked her to mourn for Balder, but she scowled at them malevolently and refused to do so."

Mimir sighed and waved his hand in resignation. "And so Balder was lost forever. The gods flew into a blind rage and captured Loki, and they dragged him off to a deep and dark cavern. Once there, he was bound and bolted into place against the rocks, and above him was hung a poisonous snake that dripped venom into his open face. But Loki's wife stands beside him holding a basin to catch the poison drops. Whenever this basin fills with venom, she hurries away to empty it, and the poison dripping onto Loki's face throws him into great convulsions that shake the world. And these, men of Halfsfiord, are what we call earthquakes...."

Mimir allowed his voice to trail off, cocking his head to one side and listening to the silence that surrounded him. Slowly, he raised his hand and twisted it in a decisive gesture. "There Loki remains bound," he whispered ominously, "until the coming of Ragnarok...the Crack of Doom." His words hung in the air, hovering like a great cloud.

"Aye," he continued, "there shall come to pass three consecutive winters, during which the world will be at war. Brother shall slay brother, men will fornicate with beasts, and no quarter shall be shown to the meek or the pure of heart. And then the wolf Fenrir will break his fetter in Hel and swallow the Sun and Moon, and the World Serpent will boil forth from the sea, causing a great flood to cover the land. Loki shall rise again and join the Frost Giants and the dead from Hel, and this horrible host shall clamor forth and ride across the Rainbow Bridge to attack Asgard.

"There, Odin shall don his golden helmet and grab his great spear, and all of the gods and fallen warriors in Valhalla shall march forth with him. And Odin shall do battle with Fenrir the Wolf, while Thor charges the Serpent of the World, and all the gods and men and Frost Giants—all will perish. And Loki and the rest of the gods shall ignite as one flame, and all earth and heaven shall burn in a great conflagration, and nothing more of life shall remain after Ragnarok, the twilight of the gods...."

Mimir fell silent. A great stillness filled the hall as the Vikings absorbed the tale, reflecting soberly on their lives. Even Lothar was quiet, lost deep in thought, his eyes staring straight ahead without focus.

And then they heard it, a sound like no other sound, unmistakable as it drifted through the night air. It was faint at first, a muffled roar beyond the closed door of the hall, but there was not one among them who failed to recognize the familiar, rattling din of men at war.

In the next instant the door to the hall flew open, and a lone fighting man staggered into the room with an arrow embedded in his chest. "To arms, Vikings..." he gasped. "We're betrayed!"

He clutched frantically at the air and collapsed. One of the men standing near him sprang forward over his body to the threshold and peered outside, hurriedly closing the great door an instant before an arrow thudded into its oak front.

"Warlord!" he cried, "The harbor...it's filled with enemies!"

"How many?"

"Hundreds! It's hopeless!"

Lothar rose to his full height. "Bar the door! Vikings, flee through the rear and assemble in the hills, by the hermit's cave!"

"It's useless, Warlord," cried a man who peered out one of the narrow openings that faced the slope. "Men streak down from the forest. We're surrounded!"

"The gods be cursed!" Lothar grimaced. All eyes fixed upon him, waiting for the command that had so often spurred them on to victory. He was confused at first as he looked around the hall, but then all that was animal in him reasserted itself again, and he raised his mighty arms and shook his fists defiantly.

"If it's blood they want, then let them have it!" he growled hoarsely. "Listen to me, Vikings…barricade the openings and arm yourselves. We'll drive them back into the sea, or die trying!"

The men sprang to action, and within seconds the lone entrance and the few small windows in the rear were secured. The Vikings gathered up all manner of weapons—lances and battleaxes, bows, daggers and maces, great bucklers that stood as tall as a grown man—and formed an armored line behind a row of overturned tables in the center of the room. A file of archers knelt in the foreground, bows ready, while behind them the remaining warriors stood, their shields forming an unbroken wall facing forward. The women and children retreated to a far corner of the hall, huddling behind another half-circle of toppled tables.

Sigli and Hathor placed themselves in the center of the line on either side of their father, amidst a mass of Vikings that numbered some two hundred strong. They could hear the sounds of battle ranks forming outside the hall, but in the next few moments the noises mysteriously disappeared. Sigli craned an ear toward the door, listening for some sign of the enemy.

"It's too quiet. Something's going on."

"Maybe they're going to burn us out," a man said.

"Enough of that!" Lothar thundered. "They're Vikings, like us! They won't fight like women…it will be sword against sword! They make their prayers to Odin before the final rush."

As if in answer to his challenge, a great shout arose from behind the door. They could hear the rustling sound of feet, and then a terrible thud buckled the barricaded door on its hinges.

"Archers, get ready!" Lothar commanded, raising his gleaming ax on high. "Wait for the door to give way, and then let fly!"

The ramming process continued as all eyes remained fixed on the door. With each renewed effort on the part of the attackers the oak began to shred, until finally it ripped from its hinges and crashed to the floor. A wave of men poured into the hall, only to be met by a flock of arrows that buzzed through the air. The first line of attackers went down as the shafts embedded themselves in their targets, and before the last of the wounded and dead had fallen to the ground, Lothar's archers had already fitted another arrow to their bows. The next onslaught squeezed through the entrance, only to meet the same fate. But this time a few stragglers managed to lift the fallen door and hold it, extended, like a great shield in front of them. The attackers massed quickly behind the oak and surged forward with a bold war cry through the rain of arrows and spears, crashing into the center of the defense.

Lothar's men encircled the enemy, closing the line behind them and quickly cutting the opposition to pieces. But no longer could the defenders prevent reinforcements from entering the hall; as one warrior after another poured through the gap, heavy hand-to-hand combat ensued. The men fought like animals, hacking wildly at anything that moved. It grew difficult to maneuver in the close quarters, and the lodge soon became littered with fallen bodies. The men closest to Lothar's center managed to hold a united front, retreating toward one side of the hall and staving off the attempts of the enemy. Blow after blow rained down from their arms, swords and axes flashing in a dance of desperation. Sigli wielded his specialty, the double-headed axe, and his shield and arm were soaked with the blood of his enemies as he fought.

Meanwhile, the exuberant Hathor was everywhere, striking left and right and leaving a trail of destruction in his wake. Caught up in the euphoria of his battle lust, he sprang into the center of a cluster of enemies, dealing out death blows to several men in the first few seconds.

But the others were able to hold their ground and soon were joined by reinforcements, until suddenly Hathor found himself surrounded. A blow from a heavily studded mace crashed into the side of his head, knocking his helmet to the ground and stunning him long enough for a series of thrusts to find their way inside his relaxed defenses. He crumpled heavily to the same earth on which he had frolicked with squeals of delight as a child, a mighty tree felled in the forest before its time, and his spirit was gone before his body ever hit the ground. In spite of this his enemies did not desist, bludgeoning him repeatedly with their weapons until his features were mangled beyond recognition, leaving no doubt that the youngest son of Lothar, Hathor Hammerhand, was dead.

A roar went up from the invaders, who renewed their efforts with even greater confidence. By now the hall was choked with the dead and the dying, and the swollen ranks of attackers continued to press through the door, closing like a fist around the fate of Halfsfiord. The battle degenerated into a one-sided slaughter, for there was no escape from the confines of the hall through the entrance that led outside and down to the sea. Sensing the outcome, many of Lothar's men still standing dropped their arms and went over to the enemy.

Soon only two defenders remained, standing back-to-back in the center of the hall, refusing to surrender. Lothar and Sigli were the last to champion Halfsfiord. The attackers backed away from the father and son, leaving them breathing heavily in the center of a great circle of hostile faces, and then the Vikings began to jeer. But they did not advance, keeping their distance as their catcalls rang through the hall.

"Jackals! Women!" Lothar screamed. "Not one of you dares stand against me and my son!"

Sigli became aware of a movement behind the first line of warriors, which separated suddenly before him to reveal several men who ran toward them quickly. Lothar turned to help fend off the attack, but the men stopped abruptly and let fly with a dark mass that hovered overhead like a storm cloud before finally descending upon them. Father and son could do nothing to prevent the sturdy fishing net from engulfing them. As they struggled against its folds, they were swarmed over by a score of men, whose shouts echoed in triumph as the night descended on Halfsfiord.

Soon Sigli and Lothar were disarmed and trussed firmly to a pair of poles planted in the earth near the rear of the hall. Lothar's eyes raged with indignity. His ears rang with the wails of the women who still had not been gathered up as part of the spoils; they tore at their hair and wandered about the hall, weeping for the dead. Beolinde and Jorda were among them, clinging to each other as they attempted to force their way through the throng to the bound captives. No matter where they turned, they met with resistance from the men-at-arms who blocked their way.

The hall swelled with shouts of celebration, and scores of arms shot skyward with swords in hand. And then every eye focused on a swarthy figure moving slowly through the ranks and toward the captives. Lothar strained to make out the man's features, but his eyes could not pierce the darkness. As the figure slowly emerged from the shadows and into the flickering light from an overhead torch, the Warlord of Halfsfiord's expression contorted into a horrible mask of rage. He screamed with a mournful howl and bit his lips until they bled, straining at his bonds and gnashing his teeth.

There before him, leering with a hideous, mocking smile, stood the menacing figure of Sidroc, the Malevolent One.

"You!" Lothar's voice croaked out in a hoarse whisper.

Sidroc threw back his head, laughing hard and long until his eyes welled up with tears. His body began to shake with convulsive pleasure. He was an extremely ugly man, with a broad, flat nose and a malodorous tangle of matted black beard that only partially served to obscure a face pitted with a thousand pockmarks. His eyes were two thin slits not altogether unlike those of a pig, and when they opened wide enough to expose their character, there shone forth a singular and unmistakable sense of cruelty. He was by no means a tall man, but broad of beam, with massive arms that reputedly could break the back of an ox.

The Malevolent One, indeed. His name and reputation were well deserved, for at the tender age of seven, as an orphaned bastard, he had gouged the eyes out of a playmate who had teased him once too often about his ugliness. The incident was merely the start of a long series of brutal deeds, a lifetime of atrocities that had come to mark his existence. He was acknowledged to have the temperament of a wild animal, a noteworthy judgement in the land of the fiords, where tempers ran fierce and men were hard like the winter wind. Sidroc was a creature that evoked feelings of revulsion and disgust, from friend and foe alike.

He was almost a decade younger than Lothar, having risen to a position of eminence on the wings of a bloody power struggle some four years earlier. He had approached Lothar on several occasions to forge an alliance, but each of his advances had been repulsed. The Warlord of Halfsfiord had always been the more powerful of the two, with a superior fleet, a richer treasure trove and—most important of all—a birthright. There had never been any need to join forces with Sidroc, because the man's treachery was known to be all-consuming. He could not be trusted at close quarters. And so the Malevolent One had been rebuffed time and time again, and with each rejection the fires of hate and jealousy had burned all the brighter within him.

But there was no longer a need to pursue the alliance. Sidroc had destroyed Lothar in one bold sweep, and now at last all that the Warlord possessed was his. His laughter receded into the corners of the hall and he trained his sow's eyes on his captive.

"Yes, Lothar," he smirked, "it's Sidroc...the man you sent away with a backward wave of your hand when I humbly came to you seeking help."

"Humbly! Ugly lies, all of it!"

Sidroc brought the back of his hand across Lothar's face with a slap that wrenched the Warlord's head to one side. Lothar's eyes snapped back quickly, contemptuously. Blood flowed freely from his mouth and dripped onto the floor. Sigli struggled alongside him, straining to free himself from his bonds, burning to feel his fingers around the throat of their tormentor. His efforts attracted Sidroc's attention, and the Malevolent One sidled over to the pole where he was bound and looked him over closely.

"And you, young pup? Why do you struggle?" His eyes hardened. "I think the jackal who claims to be your father has taught you his ways, and..." he paused, noting Sigli's imposing physique, "a formidable force you would be, but for this night of the purging fire."

Sidroc turned to Lothar again, and the corners of his mouth stretched upward in a smile. "But, of course...none of this will come to pass. You'll both die, and the House of Lothar will be no more. I'll sail your ships, I'll tend your treasure, and I'll lay with your women. And when your souls have fled to Hel I'll cast your bodies upon the rocks, and the dogs will devour what's left and leave your bones to bleach in the sun!"

Lothar's eyes burned into the Malevolent One. "How did you find enough men to force my hall?"

"Many Viking fleets are bound for distant shores these days in search of plunder. I've dealt with those who command the best of them, and in exchange for men, I've promised them their share of your holdings. Your proud and unyielding ways have cut your throat, Lothar; he who does not join with the greater force must perish!

"But..." he paused, motioning to his men as an evil grin flickered across his face, "even this multitude of arms would not have been enough. There was one among you whose hate—whose utter loathing of you—was strong enough to slit your underbelly." He laughed and turned to face his army. "Show yourself, schemer! Let the conquering worm advance!"

There was a stirring from within the men, and a figure elbowed his way through the crowd and emerged into the forefront. The man's features were obscured by his helmet, so that only his eyes could be seen in the shadows; they bore into Lothar with grim purpose, a smirk of satisfaction perched in their dark centers. Slowly, the figure raised his hand to his head, pulling up the helmet to reveal his features in the firelight.

Sigli and Lothar gasped in disbelief. It was Borstan.

"Aye," Sidroc leered with delicious satisfaction, "Borstan was the one who betrayed you. Did you really believe him when he advised you that I was far out to sea? And did you not know, Lothar, that there was but a single guard who stood sentinel over Halfsfiord tonight, his head heavy with mead as he perched alone atop Eagle's Nest?" Sidroc smirked. "He sleeps now with Njord, the sea god, at the bottom of the fiord. But he won't sleep alone. The funeral fires shall burn for days as they devour the flesh of your most trusted men. Mark me, Warlord...all that you are and were is mine!"

Lothar's full attention had remained fixed on Borstan, and now he could no longer restrain himself. "Treachery!" he screamed. "Serpent, may you meet a horrible death, and writhe in hell! To defile all honor, on this, the wedding day of my son and your daughter!"

"*My* daughter!" Borstan sneered. "*My* daughter, indeed! Beolinde, the bastard child! All these years I've kept the secret, a truth that only I and her long dead mother have known, and it's burned inside me with every hot breath like a belly full of fire!" He leaped forward and spit full in Lothar's face. "Damn this unholy alliance! The whore-child is yours, Lothar! You marry your son to his own sister!"

A cry of anguish arose from off to the side as Beolinde swooned into Jorda's arms. Sigli looked back and forth from his father to Borstan, his eyes unbelieving. Lothar was speechless. A buzz of nervous energy rose from the ranks of Sidroc's mercenaries, punctuated by gasps of disbelief and wonderment from the remaining survivors of Halfsfiord at this strange, terrible news. Borstan rose to his full height, relishing the sweet moment of revenge that had been so many years in the making.

"I speak the truth, Lothar," he said. "She sprang from your seed. You were too drunk with mead to remember that night, when you forced your entry into my bedroom and had your way with my woman—all while I was off fighting your battles!" He paced back and forth before the bound captives, gesturing animatedly. "And you would have gotten away with it, too, but for fate's guiding hand. I spurned her bed upon my return, for my leg suffered from a painful sword wound. When the belly of the wench grew, I knew the child was not mine!

"At first she refused to confess to me, but I wrung the truth from her!" Borstan's brow creased, the remembrance of the disgrace once again fresh in his mind. "She begged my understanding, sobbing and pleading that it was rape. But I knew better...I'd seen her as she stole admiring looks at you from time to time, and I recognized the longing in her eyes, swept away as she was by your power.

"It was a mercy from the gods she died giving birth, for her life would have been forever miserable had she survived—I would have seen to that. But," he grinned maliciously, "the secret died with her. I knew in my heart that if I waited long enough, my chance would come. Your reign is over, Lothar! You're nothing. The birds will tear you apart by tomorrow!"

Lothar screamed in rage as Sidroc strode over to one of his warriors and relieved the man of his curved bow and quiver of arrows. "As painful as are the barbs that prick your heart, Lothar," the Malevolent One sneered, "they're nothing compared to what awaits you now. String the dog across those poles!" he motioned to a group of men. "We'll make blood sport of him!"

The conquering Vikings pounced upon Lothar and stretched him between two poles that served as roof supports in the hall. Sigli looked on helplessly, struggling in vain to break free and dive headlong into the throng surrounding his father. There was no hope. Sidroc waved for his men to part and paced off a distance of a dozen steps from the captive chieftain. He turned toward the assemblage and raised his arm.

"A contest of skill! Extra booty for each among you who can pierce one of Lothar's limbs...but death to him who strikes the body and kills the jackal! This must be slow, and the agony must linger!" A smile of satisfaction crossed his face. "You, Borstan, shall be the first."

The treacherous lieutenant moved without hesitation to Sidroc's side and grabbed eagerly for the bow. He fitted an arrow in place, drawing it back so that the fingers of his trigger hand brushed lightly against his cheek, and then he let the missile fly. It buzzed through the air and thudded into Lothar's left forearm, passing cleanly through the flesh without striking bone, its bloodied point protruding from the rear as the Warlord screamed out in pain.

Sidroc's men cheered as the lion of Halfsfiord writhed in agony. He struggled to muster his courage, fighting to preserve a sense of dignity in this, his final hour. Looking across the hall at Borstan, he laughed defiantly and spit onto the floor at Borstan's feet.

"I may die tonight, traitor, but I'll die a better man than you!" he yelled out hoarsely. "Nothing can ever take away from my glory...nothing! And as I speak, I swear to the gods that you'll meet an inglorious end! You'll find it was far better to be my dog than to trust Sidroc. As Odin is my witness, it shall come to pass!"

As Borstan eyed his nemesis hatefully, another eager Viking leaped to his side and grabbed the bow. The man drew forth an arrow and pulled it back upon the bow, propelling it into Lothar's bulging right thigh. The Warlord screamed out again, but his cry was absorbed by the shouts of the Vikings.

Suddenly the wall of men parted and Jorda broke through their ranks and dashed to Lothar's side. She dropped to her knees and attempted to loosen the bonds securing her husband, her teardrops mingling with Lothar's blood upon the ground as she tore frantically at the leather thongs around his ankles. Sidroc approached her from behind, waiting until she had almost succeeded in loosening one of the knots before grabbing her roughly by the hair and dragging her away across the lodge.

"On your feet, woman!" he commanded, pulling Jorda up by her hair. He cast her toward one of his warriors standing a few feet away. "Remove her from the hall, and take with her the pale bride, Beolinde. You can do what you want tonight with the old one, but save the beauty for me. I'll tend to her later."

The sport continued as each of the Viking archers lined up to take his turn, and for every arrow that flew astray, two others found their mark. Not a single shaft pierced Lothar's torso. The slow torture extended his agony, and the earth beneath him was soon drenched with blood. Before long a score of arrows protruded like pins from his ravaged arms and legs, and his breathing grew weaker by the minute. Sensing the end, Sidroc stepped into the open space before the bloodied chieftain and raised his hand to stop the contest.

"Hold fast!" he cried. "It is done!" He turned to the ebbing Lothar. "You stand on death's doorstep, Warlord. My victory is complete!"

Lothar's head lay buried on his chest. Without looking up he began to speak, the words escaping his mouth in a whisper.

"Sigli..." he hissed, "Sigli, my son...."

"I'm here, father! I hear you!" The voice betrayed a quiver.

"Promise me, Sigli, that I shall not go unavenged..."

"I promise it, father!!" Sigli choked, fighting back the tears. "Borstan and Sidroc shall die!"

Satisfied, Lothar summoned forth his remaining strength and raised his eyes to meet Sidroc's. "Now, Malevolent One, grant me the death of a warrior..." His words could barely be heard. "Give me a sword, so that I may take my place in Valhalla..."

Sidroc's eyes narrowed. "If it's a sword you want, so you'll have it," he grimaced, drawing forth a great blade from the scabbard that hung at his side. "Take this iron to Hel with you, Lothar, and rot forever!"

With a swift lunge he drove the sword deep into Lothar's belly, throwing his weight behind the thrust until the blade reappeared through the small of the chieftain's back. Blood exploded into the air and spattered onto several of the startled bystanders.

With a final convulsive shudder, the Warlord of Halfsfiord died.

Sigli squeezed his eyes shut tightly, as though he could somehow blot out the nightmare. A scream of rage tried to escape his throat, but he was unable to vent it. The blood pounded at his temples. He dimly became aware of Borstan as the traitor drew alongside Sidroc and gestured at Lothar.

"I've kept my part of our bargain, Sidroc," Borstan began, "an oath we swore in blood. Now, you must keep yours. Half of all that is Lothar's shall be mine." He reached for the limp right hand of the Warlord. "I claim the golden ring of Hrungnir, the symbol of power and sovereignty in Halfsfiord!"

"Not so fast!" Sidroc snarled, slapping Borstan's hand away from the spoils. "It's for me to decide what shall be!"

"You forget that, without my assistance, you'd still be far from unlocking the door to Lothar's hall." Borstan eyed the corpse greedily, reaching again for the Warlord's finger. "The ring! I must have it!"

Sidroc stepped in and rudely shoved Borstan away. "You dream if you think to cross me and live, traitor," he hissed.

For the first time, Borstan grew wary. He looked about the hall and was overwhelmed by a sea of unsympathetic faces, a rolling tide of men who recognized Sidroc as their sovereign. Danger dripped from their hollow smiles; Borstan, to his dismay, realized he was a beaten man. Adapting with chameleon quickness, he struck a conciliatory pose and turned back to the Malevolent One, speaking softly.

"I've waited a long time for this moment, Sidroc. Grant me what I deserve."

Sidroc's eyes crinkled into slits, and a jagged smile lit up his face. "But of course, my friend...there's no question you'll get exactly that." He motioned to his men. "Seize him!"

Four Vikings surrounded Borstan and pinned his arms to his sides. Realizing the futility of opposing them, he looked angrily instead at his captor. "You break the oath, Sidroc!

"You were broken from the beginning, you wretch," Sidroc leered. "If you were willing to betray a man you fought with for an entire lifetime, then what could I hope to expect from you? Fool, no ring of power will perch upon your crooked finger. Death shall be your reward...but it will be no ordinary flight into Hel. Instead, I'll grant you a taste of things to come." He grinned maliciously, delighted by this latest turn of events. "Take him outside and truss him like a pig upon the cooking spit! Roast him alive over Lothar's fire!"

The brutes in the hall were unable to contain their excitement. Borstan's eyes bulged with terror as he was dragged toward the door. "Sidroc! Sidroc..please!" he screamed. "I'll do anything...I swear allegiance to your will! Show me mercy!"

"I know not the word, jackal," the Malevolent One sneered. "Find your courage, and chew on what's left of it. The flames will melt it away like candle wax!"

Borstan was pulled through the door, followed by a bustle of warriors eager to witness his torture. As Sidroc watched the exodus, it occurred to him that one matter had yet to be decided. He turned and planted himself firmly in front of Sigli, the last surviving member of the House of Lothar, and smirked with disdain.

"And what are we to do with you?"

"I don't care about my own life," Sigli said defiantly. "Whether it ends tonight or endures till Ragnarok doesn't matter. But I warn you, Sidroc: if I survive this madness, I'll hunt you down like a wild beast, and tear the heart from your stinking body!"

"There will be no chance of that happening, my pup. It only remains to determine the method of your death...something entertaining, perhaps."

"What have you done with Beolinde?"

Sidroc smiled in anticipation. "Aye, and well you should ask, for a fine choice she is. Were she my sister, I'd plow her, too..."

He paused, hoping for a reaction, but got none. "I've already made plans for her," he continued. "It will be a fitting reward for a long night's work, to dine on her soft and supple breasts. I'll cleave her thighs and have at her until tomorrow's sun rises over Halfsfiord!"

"She'll never submit to you!"

"She'll have no choice," the Malevolent One sneered. "The more she resists, the greater your torture, the slower your death. Hear me, boy—she'll merely be the first. Before I'm done, I'll have sampled all of the women of Halfsfiord who catch my fancy, including your whore mother!"

"I'll have your head on a platter!!" Sigli's face was crimson.

Sidroc ignored him and turned to a nearby cluster of warriors. "Drag him down to the ships and lash him to a mast...perhaps that of the sorry looking hull that lists to one side, the one moored at the far end of Lothar's fleet. Tomorrow, we'll load all of the dead at his feet upon the deck, and set fire to the vessel. Let the whole lot be cast out to sea!" He turned to Sigli once again, a final glint of triumph shining in his eye. "You'll have the honor of dying at your own funeral— a Viking funeral!"

"Wretch! I'll kill you! I swear it!!!" Sigli screamed, struggling against his bonds.

A cordon of Vikings surrounded him, cutting him loose and dragging him toward the door. Sidroc watched as they receded, his eyes not leaving them until they disappeared into the night. Sigli's screams diminished into a faint echo that was masked by the clamor filling the hall. The conquering raiders feasted on the spoils of victory, consuming what was left of Lothar's banquet before breaking into the Warlord's fabled storehouse, rumored to be filled with provisions and all manner of riches.

Sidroc smiled to himself. It was only right that his men celebrated; the fight was over, the battle won. All of this, all of Lothar's might, now belonged to him. His eyes took in everything, absorbing the grandeur of the great hall. Its massive timbers spoke of strength and power, a worthy stronghold for a Viking king. But he knew in his heart that it was something not long for his enjoyment, for he was a wanderer and a fighting man. The time was ripe for plunder; fleets sailed in an unending stream to the continent, bound across the sea in a haste for distant shores. And he would be among them, for with his newly acquired armada nothing could stop him now. He was invincible.

His attention was diverted by a cry from the edge of the hall. His men had ripped the garments from one of Halfsfiord's women taken captive following the fight, and they prepared to mount her atop a great wooden table. The excitement of their fornication spread to Sidroc's loins, reminding him of the fair prize that awaited his pleasure. Without further delay he hurried through the crowded hall and out the doorway, where the night was cool and the fog had evaporated into the darkness. A blanket of stars twinkled from the canopy of sky stretching overhead. He could see the masts of the ships rising into the moonlight that illuminated the harbor, and in front of them the gleam of a bonfire, the sound of its crackling flames punctuated by Borstan's grunts as the Vikings beat him in their blood lust. They kicked at his swollen body upon the ground, taking their final pleasure before strapping him to the great spit and roasting him to death.

None of this interested Sidroc. Although his tired body ached all over, the throbbing in his groin led him like a beast of prey along the hillside and past the rows of crude huts dotting the harbor. As always, his senses tingled with the thrill of death, the unmistakable scent of the kill on his hands. Since adolescence he had been compelled to slaughter other human beings indiscriminately; it excited him, and never failed to arouse him sexually. Tales of his exploits following the heat of battle were already legend.

From time to time he encountered pockets of men as he continued on his way, drunken Vikings who hailed him with shouts of recognition as they downed their cups of mead. The signs of movement began to diminish as he neared the outskirts of the village. Ahead of him in the darkness there loomed a solitary hut; as he drew nearer, he could make out the forms of four large, sturdy Vikings guarding its entrance.

"Move aside!" he commanded. They backed away instantly as the Malevolent One pushed past them, gaining entrance to the hut.

The room was illuminated by the light of a candle that burned on a table along the far wall. Sidroc scanned the darkness, his eyes adjusting to the shadows, until he was able to fix on a motionless figure nestled in one of the corners.

There stood Beolinde, the most beautiful woman in Halfsfiord.

He moved a few feet to one side so that the candlelight shone more directly on her features: the cream-colored skin, full lips parted slightly, her almond-shaped eyes staring back at him, flashing with anger and fear. He watched as her breast fluttered with each intake of air, his own heart pounding like a hammer against the walls of his chest. There was no question about it; he had to have her. Without taking his eyes from her voluptuous figure, he began to remove his armor and weapons, placing them on the table behind him.

First came the great helmet, its curved surfaces glistening in the candlelight. It was followed by the weighty broadsword that had pierced Lothar's entrails, and then a hand-axe, a sharp dagger, and finally the massive war belt that held his belly in place. Soon he was clothed only in leggings, his stout torso glistening with beads of perspiration that filled the small room with an unbearable stench that repulsed Beolinde. She sidled along the wall, keeping to the shadows as if she could slip miraculously through the entrance to the hut, evade the guards and fly into the freedom of the night.

Sidroc intercepted her path and forced her back into the corner. His face erupted into a leer that exposed his sharp, broken teeth, and his thin eyes crinkled until they were mere slits etched in his face.

"Sidroc won't harm you, my sweet," he murmured. "Sidroc likes what he sees. He wants you now, tonight."

He reached down and grasped his manhood, pulling it out into the firelight, his hand massaging the hardened shaft as if he were stroking a bar of iron. He began to shuffle clumsily toward Beolinde. "Get down on your knees, pretty girl, and open your mouth..."

Beolinde spun away in disgust, ducking under his arm and scrambling across the room. But Sidroc still blocked the door, his expression creasing into a mask of anger.

"Go against my wishes, and it will be the worse for you," he hissed.

"No man but Sigli shall have me!"

"In a matter of hours your precious Sigli will be dead," he muttered, moving slowly toward her. "Withhold from me, and I'll extend his miserable existence and put him to death slowly."

Beolinde backed away as he approached until the table jutting into her buttocks prevented her from retreating further. The blood pounded in her temples as Sidroc drew near, and she reached instinctively behind her back, as if her hand could pull her across the tabletop and away from him. To her surprise, she felt her fingers close around a curved handle; she recognized it as Sidroc's dagger. She squeezed it tightly in her hand, and all the hate and defiance inherited from Lothar, her true father, surged through her as Sidroc advanced. He stepped to within arm's reach, fondling himself.

Beolinde's arm slashed forward. The dagger gleamed in the flickering light as it sliced through the air, and only Sidroc's conditioned reflexes saved him from catching the knife in the throat. He jerked his head back and evaded the brunt of the thrust, but he was unable to pull back quite far enough. The tip of the blade sheared across the flesh covering his cheekbone and gouged into his left eye, popping it out of its socket. He screamed with pain and clutched at the wound as the blood spurted in rivulets between his fingers. Beolinde leaped upon him, hoping for the chance to drive the dagger into his chest.

But Sidroc was a formidable warrior; in spite of his condition, he parried her thrust instinctively with his free arm, grabbing her by the hair and hurling her to the side. She spun around and darted to her feet, thrusting upward, but the effort left her exposed and vulnerable.

Suddenly Sidroc's great broadsword powered in a wide arc through the air, backed by all the wounded chieftain's strength. There was nothing Beolinde could do to save herself; the razor-sharp edge sliced through her throat, sending her head toppling from her shoulders and rolling aimlessly across the ground, her glorious blue eyes paled forever.

*　　*　　*　　*　　*

A light mist hovered over Halfsfiord, settling low on the water. Sigli's body ached from the ropes that dug into his flesh and bound him tightly to the mast of the dragon ship. He closed his eyes and rested his head back against the sturdy timber, feeling the gentle rocking motion of the ship moored in the harbor. Halfsfiord's fall rushed madly through his mind's eye, replaying itself again and again, and always there remained the leering face of Sidroc, raging at the center of his thoughts.

Hours had passed since the slaughter. The bonds around his limbs had tightened as the air grew damper, gradually cutting off the circulation in his extremities. He had been rocked into semi-consciousness by the sordid lullaby of Borstan's screams, as the man who betrayed Halfsfiord roasted to his death over the fire prepared for him outside the hall.

Sigli had taken a perverse pleasure in the ordeal. It was the one thing during the long night that had brought him satisfaction, a bittersweet reward that had momentarily dulled the peril of his own circumstances. But now little more than an hour remained before dawn and the harbor was silent, hiding under a brooding mantle of darkness that still enveloped the world. Nothing stirred in this, the hour of the wolf, except for the low murmuring of the two Vikings aboard the ship charged with standing watch. They crouched down in the bow, gambling to pass the time and fortifying themselves against the chill with long draughts of mead.

A low sound reached Sigli's ears from off to the starboard. Seconds later, a small craft scraped against the hull of the dragon ship, alerting the guards. One of them rose to his feet and made his way across the deck, peering over the side and down into the darkness.

"Who is it?"

"A bearer of good cheer," came a voice from below. "I'm sent by the great Sidroc, with a cask of mead to refresh you in the night."

"You're welcome, friend. Our barrel is just drained, and it's cold. Let me help you."

He reached down and grabbed the cask from the outstretched hands of the mariner, who followed by boarding the dragon ship. The man was slight of build and moved with an odd, shuffling gait. Sigli peered through the darkness, trying to make out his features, but the man's face was hidden completely by a heavy cowl.

"Break the barrel open," the mariner said, "and let us toast tonight's great victory."

The second of the guards reached for his axe and brought it down sharply on the top of the barrel. He tipped the vessel until the mead came spilling out in a thick, rich mixture, pouring until three cups were filled. "Let us drink to the last of Lothar's line," he said, raising his cup and turning toward Sigli, "Long may he live!" His shoulders shook lightly with laughter as he drew the cup to his mouth and downed its contents. His companion did the same, smacking his lips in pleasure, but the cowled messenger remained motionless, his cup brimming over.

"Why don't you drink?" the first Viking wondered.

The hooded figure said nothing, but instead retreated several steps and poured out the contents of his cup onto the deck. At that moment the Viking who had first tasted the ale uttered a horrible cry and grabbed for his throat. His partner, at last understanding the intent of the midnight assassin, reached for his weapon and took a step toward the offender. But he was too late; the sword fell from his hand and clattered onto the deck while he and the other guard sank to their knees and clutched wildly at the air. They shook convulsively for a few seconds before finally lying still at the stranger's feet.

The pain in Sigli's limbs was now forgotten. He stared in wonder as the man turned toward him and dropped the cowl masking his features, exposing a long grin that stretched across his face beneath two opaque, sightless eyes.

"Mimir!"

"Aye, child, your old teacher has come to set you free." The seer searched along the body of one of the Vikings until his hands closed around a knife in the man's belt. He withdrew the blade and shuffled over to Sigli, feeling carefully for the knots securing the warrior to the mast. "They left me alone. They didn't fear the wrath of a blind man," he murmured, cutting the bonds with a single, deft motion.

Sigli stepped free from his captivity, rubbing his arms vigorously and hopping up and down on the deck to restore the circulation in his legs. "How did you manage to secure the mead and poison it?"

"Never mind, child. I need no eyes to find my way in this harbor nor around the village."

Sigli moved forward to the bow and picked up the double-headed axe that had fallen from the hand of one of the guards, and then he turned back to Mimir, his eyes burning.

"Where's Sidroc? Take me to him!"

"You'd be a fool to seek him out," the seer said, shuffling over to him. "Your life would soon be over. He lies in a rage, wounded in both pride and body, plotting your torture for tomorrow. You'd be hacked to pieces if you were found near his quarters."

"Surely, his soldiers sleep! It's dark, and I have time. And Beolinde...I must save her from the beast."

Mimir raised his empty eyes to Sigli's face and reached up to touch the young man's cheek. "Don't throw your soul away for someone who's already gone, my child...Beolinde is dead."

Sigli staggered backward. "Beolinde....dead?" The tears immediately began to stream down his face.

He started toward the bulwark with the axe in his hand, preparing to leap overboard. But Mimir grabbed him by the arm, holding fast. "You must be strong! Mourn her, if you will, but wait for your chance!"

"Let me go!"

"Sigli!" the seer hissed, "use your wits, or you'll end up like your father and brother." His words struck a chord, and the young Viking froze in his struggle to regain control. The old man's voice softened. "Your road still stretches ahead, with many a strange turn. Accept the will of the gods, and live!"

"By Odin, I'll see Sidroc dead!"

"Your vengeance has already begun. Although Beolinde is lost forever, she didn't leave empty-handed. Your brave lover plucked Sidroc's left eye from its throne and carried it into the darkness before the Dane could force his will upon her. She died with honor, a true child to the great Lothar, the blood of your blood."

"Hate pours over me!"

"Hate, my child," Mimir whispered, "can keep a man alive." He paused and cocked his head to one side. "But now, come away. Dawn will be here within the hour; we have to hurry."

Sigli looked anxiously toward the shore. "What of my mother? Mimir, I can't leave her behind!"

"Jorda lives," Mimir said, grabbing Sigli by the arm, "but there's nothing you can do for her, not now. She's safe. Your only chance is to fly from here and seek your fortune. Remember the prophecy on the rock! Your destiny, Sigli, lies beneath the setting sun. Sidroc can only be bested by force. You're but a lone wolf, separated from the pack. Take to the open waters, child, and flee."

Sigli paused for an anguished moment, wrestling with his indecision. Finally, he took a deep breath and scrambled over the side of the ship, dropping down into the skiff moored below. He helped Mimir descend into the boat and pushed off from the dragon ship, manning the single set of oars as the seer sat opposite him, facing astern. He did not disturb the sail, using the oars to row across the harbor and through the mist that ran along the water's surface. The skiff was ten feet long with a small cabin covering the foredeck, and it glided easily through the water as it approached the low headland across from Eagle's Nest, the last barrier that separated Halfsfiord from the sea.

"I stowed weapons away in the cabin, and enough provisions to see you through several days. Beyond that, you'll have to fend for yourself." Mimir's voice was suddenly filled with an unmistakable sadness.

"We'll manage."

"Not we, Sigli...not now. You must set me ashore on the rocks, and go on alone."

Sigli dropped the oars in protest. "Mimir, you *must* come with me. I won't continue otherwise." He stared intently at the seer as the boat rocked in the light chop, drifting slowly toward the headland.

Mimir raised his face to his young charge, sighing wistfully and reaching for Sigli's hands, cradling them in his own. "Ah, Sigli...my Sigli," he whispered with deep affection. "You're a gallant and good child, and I'll love you always, beyond Ragnarok, beyond time." He paused and took in a deep breath. "But it's too late for these old bones to strike out on new adventures. The world changes, like a cliff worn away by the fury of the sea. The gods grow dim in their palace in Asgard, fading into shadows, and I fade with them. Leave me on the rock, and I'll make my way into the hills beyond the hermit's cave, so that not even the warlike arm of Sidroc can ensnare me."

Sigli began to weep, the immense sorrow of the night's ordeal washing over him in a great wave. His sobs rocked the boat. "I'm lost, Mimir...I don't know where to turn."

"Don't be afraid, for the golden dragon beckons, " Mimir smiled, his teeth shining. "He holds your destiny. Seek out his banner, and find your fortune beneath the setting sun!" He raised his hand solemnly toward the heavens.

"Go, my child, and be strong!"

Sigli continued to weep softly. He clasped the old man's hands and raised them to his lips, kissing each of them in turn. "You've always been like a father to me, Mimir. I'll miss you!"

"Don't despair, for I'll always be with you, forever. When you fall by the wayside and stagger from life's burdens, listen for me in the wind. As surely as the day dawns, you'll hear my voice and feel my soul, and you'll be revived to face your destiny. This Odin has granted."

The boat scraped to a halt, having drifted up against the headland. Mimir leaned over to Sigli and kissed him upon the forehead, pausing to stare adoringly with his sightless windows, sensing all the quiet desperation in his pupil's upturned face. "You're a man now," he nodded. "My work is done."

He stepped onto the rock from the skiff and pushed the boat away, grunting from the effort. Sigli looked sadly at him for a moment, the tears still running down his face, until he forced himself to turn away. He rowed a few strokes into the harbor, waiting for the current to grab the boat before standing up and unfurling the sail. A light breeze filled out the sheet, pushing the skiff away from the headland and across the water toward Eagle's Nest. He sat back down in the stern and grabbed the rudder, righting the boat on its course for the harbor mouth and turning once more to look at Mimir. The seer stood motionlessly, his arm raised in a silent salute.

"Goodbye, Mimir," Sigli whispered across the water. "Halfsfiord forever!"

The boat cut through the chop. The first signs of dawn appeared above the hills that loomed over the fiord to the east. Sigli glanced back over his shoulder to the rock where Mimir stood; the old man's frail arm was still raised in farewell. Even from a distance, the seer's sightless eyes burned through the gloom, two shining pinpoints of light. As Mimir's outline receded slowly into the darkness, Sigli raised his arm in a final salute. The skiff rounded land's end and shot westward into the great sea, where the waters pounded against the hull in a symphony of the primeval deep.

Now, he felt truly alone. He lifted his eyes toward the heavens and let out a long wail, a cry of despair that spiraled up and away, vanishing into the heart of the great northern night.

CHAPTER II: The Crossing

"Then rose from sea to sky the wild farewell!
Then shriek'd the timid, and stood still the brave;
Then some leap'd overboard with dreadful yell,
As eager to anticipate their grave;
And the sea yawn'd around her like a hell,
And down she suck'd with her the whirling wave."
—Byron, <u>Don Juan</u>

Sigli awoke from a deep sleep, roused by the hunger pounding at his stomach. The skiff rocked gently beneath him. He reached up and parted the covering protecting him from the elements and peered into the dawn, where the sun rose from the endless sheet of water that extended unbroken in every direction. He grabbed the roof of the cabin and pulled himself out of the shelter and into the open air, struggling to free his legs from the tangle of belongings stuffed forward. He was thankful for the provisions Mimir had stowed away; there was a barrel of water, a few days' supply of jerky, a bow and quiver of arrows, and the favored battle axe. The seer had seen to everything.

The salty air filtered into his lungs as he pulled himself up to the tiller and checked it for play, noting with satisfaction that the leather thong he had lashed between the helm and the bulwark remained taut, held in place by its tension working against the wind and waves. His course was south by southwest, running at the same angle into the sea as the night before, when he had finally grown too tired to steer the ship.

It had been a tense first day. The adrenaline in his veins had made sleep impossible as he piloted the boat away from Halfsfjord and into the uncertainty of the mist along the coastline. The same fog that had nourished Sidroc's attack hid him from pursuit as he fled, but at every moment he had expected the prow of a dragon ship to appear at his stern. He had been afraid then, filled with a fear that had not visited him even once during the dangerous hours when Halfsfiord had crumbled. With freedom finally in his grasp, the thought of losing it had become almost too much to bear. But Njord had watched over the skiff benevolently from the depths of his kingdom in the sea, and with every hour the danger lessened. By evening a light rain had begun to fall, driving him into the shelter of the cabin and a slumber so deep that nothing could disturb it.

Now it was morning again. He reached into the cabin and pulled the casket to him, grabbing for a piece of jerky and tugging on it with his teeth. He looked around as he chewed, noting a sparkling, clear sky that afforded perfect visibility. It was a brilliant summer morning. For the first time in days he felt hope, despite the fact that there could be no returning to the land of the fiords. The entire Norse coast would soon learn of the fall of the House of Lothar, and it was clear to him that the time had come to set his sights on other shores. Viking ships sailed in a steady stream to the continent; tales of the exploits of the great Rollo in the land of the Franks had reached Sigli's ears in Halfsfiord. Even more alluring was the promise of the island that some knew as England, others Britain, a land divided into many factions with no strong overlord to stave off the Viking raids that had continued for the last twenty years. A large force of men had remained on the island for most of that time, secure in the knowledge there was no need to retreat to their dragon ships for safety.

But no, he thought to himself. Not yet. There would be few men to the south and west willing to join him to return to Halfsfiord. He was convinced there was but one choice, so he grabbed the tiller and swung the skiff into the waves, heading her to the southeast in the direction of Jutland. His kind lived there, Vikings, worshippers of Odin who would understand his loss. The great king Horik had been his father's friend, ruling with influence for many years until his demise had removed the final restraints on his subjects. Without an iron hand to rule them, the Danes ranged far and wide in search of riches, no longer content to farm their small homesteads. But among those who stayed, he would discover friends. It would be a start. He would return to Halfsfiord leading a great fleet of dragon ships, seeking his revenge and the chance to place the head of Sidroc upon his war lance.

He chewed on the jerky, feeling stronger. The hunted would become the hunter. Sidroc had been sly and mighty, but despite his almost perfect conquest of Halfsfiord, the Malevolent One had made one, glaring mistake.

He had not seen Sigli dead.

*　　*　　*　　*　　*

The first mast appeared on the eastern horizon at noon. It was soon joined by a second, and then a third, until Sigli counted a score of ships bearing down upon him. It seemed impossible that they could belong to Sidroc; judging by its heading, the fleet had probably come from Jutland. But the idea of discovery by any force—even a friendly one—frightened him, and he looked about for an avenue of escape. There was no hope; the open sea stretched in all directions. He took the course least likely to arouse suspicion, maintaining his heading across the bows of the armada and hoping the small skiff would not arouse curiosity.

The minutes passed without alarm. But when it seemed as though he was about to edge away from the fleet, several of the dragon ships peeled off from the main body and bore down upon him, fanning out in a claw to intercept any course he might take to evade them. After a few moments it became apparent that protest was useless, so he dropped the sail and awaited his fate.

The three ships drew closer, allowing him to make out their features more clearly. Each was about seventy feet in length, with a single sail billowing in the wind from the mast amidships. There appeared to be approximately one hundred and fifty men aboard each of the vessels, their shields draped along the bulwarks to protect the thirty-odd rowers manning each side. The dragon ships did not draw a great depth of water, having been built primarily to take advantage of shallow coastal inlets and rivers rather than to brave the rigors of the open sea for long stretches. But despite this potential flaw, no other ships could match them; the Vikings were the undisputed masters of the sea.

The lead ship was within earshot now. A muscular Dane perched in the bow cupped his hands around his mouth and shouted across the water:

"Where are you headed?"

Sigli stood up in the skiff and pointed to the southeast. "To Jutland!"

"Who are you? Why are you alone?"

"I'm called Yodir! Son of Ankar of Lapland, from the land of the north!"

By now the dragon ship was upon him, oars raised as it bobbed in the rolling sea. The Viking in her bow regarded the single mariner with amusement.

"Well, Yodir, son of Ankar, it doesn't matter where you're from, or where you're going...you're coming with us now. You've been at sea and may have some useful knowledge. Board immediately, and we'll tie her astern," he said pointing to the skiff. "Lord Ubba wishes to see you."

Sigli knew the name well. Ubba was among the most powerful of the Danes, the youngest of the three sons of one of the most famous of all Viking warriors, Ragnar Lodbrok. The great Ragnar had been the scourge of Europe for twenty years, a raider feared in every corner of Christendom. Sigli had heard his father tell stories of the man, and Mimir had also spoken through the runes, praising Ragnar as unsurpassed in power among the Norsemen. After years of glory, the bold leader finally met with a violent end in Northumbria, where through treacherous means he was captured and thrown into a pit of poisonous snakes.

His three sons returned to Northumbria and avenged their father. Their collective might at that time was the greatest force ever to sail the northern sea; all of England and the kingdom of the Franks could have been theirs but for their petty rivalries and greed for power. While not enemies, they were far too independent and single-minded to fight together.

Sigli searched his memory. The oldest, he recalled, was known as Ivar the Boneless, so named because of an odd gristle that deformed his body. He had ravaged northern England for a while, eventually leaving for Eire to the west and disappearing into the Celtic highlands. The second son, Halfdan, reaped the richest haul from English soil, overrunning not only Northumbria, but East Anglia and parts of Mercia, so that all of England had fallen under his dominion except for the land of the West Saxons. Halfdan attempted to subjugate Wessex, but was held at bay by the forces of the young King Alfred. Tiring of the trouble, the second son of Ragnar withdrew north like his brother before him and ceased to become a factor in the plundering of England.

The reins of Viking power then fell to a Viking named Guthrum, who took over the Danish forces and skirmished with Alfred's armies for several years. Guthrum then moved boldly across Sussex to capture Wareham, the harbor fortress perched on the channel that separates England from the rest of Europe. Alfred laid siege to the Danes for long months, until Guthrum sued for peace and granted the Saxons hostages, swearing on the sacred armband of the Vikings to uphold the peace.

But Guthrum's word had merely been a ruse to hide his true intentions. The Viking army slipped from Wareham in the dead of night and cut its way through a weak link in the Saxon line, fleeing westward and taking refuge in the town of Exeter, deep in the heart of Wessex. Alfred followed doggedly, surrounding the town and waiting patiently with his forces to wear the Danish resistance down.

That was when Ubba asserted himself. Long obscured in the shadow of his older brothers and jealous of their exploits, the third son of Ragnar Lodbrok met secretly with Guthrum, agreeing to return to the Northland to raise a fleet and come to the aid of the besieged. Ubba had passed through Halfsfiord some months before, asking Lothar to lend his assistance to the effort, but the Warlord had been unwilling to offer support. There had been no animosity between the men, but Lothar's spies subsequently learned that Ubba had gone to Sidroc and struck an agreement.

And so it was that Ubba secured the necessary ships. At long last he pointed his prows for an assault on Wessex, the only obstacle lying between the Danes and complete control of England. It was now 877. Northumbria and East Anglia were firmly under Viking control, and Mercia was under the reign of a puppet ruler the Danes had placed in power to carry out their mandates. Only the West Saxons remained.

Sigli ground his teeth as he realized the import of the situation. He abandoned the skiff and climbed aboard the dragon ship, taking his place silently amidships as the rowers dropped their oars into the ocean and turned about to join the main flotilla. It was certain that Ubba and Sidroc were in league together; the question remained whether Ubba had taken an active part in the overthrow of Halfsfiord—and more important, if he could identify his new captive. Sigli had been at sea when Ubba met with Lothar earlier that year, and the two men had never been in each other's presence. He settled in silently and waited; time would provide the answers.

Almost an hour passed before the patrol ships rejoined the fleet. Mid-afternoon set in as the sun drifted high across the western sky, still a long journey from its resting place in the sea. Sigli marveled as they drew closer to the armada; what he had thought from a distance to be a score of ships revealed itself to be a good fifty vessels laden with fighting men. Ubba had done well in his recruiting efforts. The ships were strung out over the space of several leagues, the dragons on their prows leading the way on a course to the southwest.

Sigli's ship maneuvered its way through the armada until it drew alongside a formidable vessel that clearly was the flagship of the fleet. It was a magnificent piece of work that Sigli's own considerable skill at shipbuilding enabled him to appreciate. He moved to the bulwark and peered over the shields. A figure stood by the main mast; from his bearing, it could only be Ubba, an imperious man, tall and stern, with a drooping mustache and an intense, florid face. His red hair blew about his shoulders in the breeze as he looked across the decks of the approaching ships and fixed his eyes upon Sigli with keen interest.

One of the warriors threw a line to the scout ship. The Viking who had first accosted Sigli motioned him atop the bulwark, where he balanced himself between two shields and waited until the swell pitched the two vessels within a few feet of each other. He leaped out over the sea, clearing the side of the flagship and landing on all fours at the feet of the Warlord. Bounding quickly to his feet, he looked into the eyes of the Lord Ubba, third son of Ragnar Lodbrok, the self-acclaimed scourge of the Northern Sea.

"He's young and strong enough," a nearby Viking said in a low, gravelly growl. As Sigli looked toward the voice, he shuddered involuntarily; he was certain he had seen the man somewhere before.

"Not many test the great ocean alone," Ubba said, examining Sigli carefully.

"The sea has been kind, Lord Ubba. My voyage has been swift."

"And curious. Who are you, and where are you from?"

"My name is Yodir, the son of Ankar of Lapland. I left the ice and snow to seek my fortune."

"Tell me, Yodir," Ubba inquired, "what news from the north?"

"You're the first men I've encountered since I set out to sea."

"You saw no signs of activity on your voyage?"

"None." Sigli felt the eyes of the man he had recognized boring into him from behind Ubba. Without flinching, he continued. "I'm headed for Jutland, from where I gather you've sailed."

"Don't bother going to Jutland now," Ubba smirked. "Only the women and children wait there. Every man worth his mettle sails with me, to England. Two more fleets of equal size join me tomorrow. We're bound for Exeter, to rout the Saxons and lay open their lands."

"I've heard of your voyage, Lord Ubba."

The chieftain beamed. "I'm known in Lapland?"

"You're known wherever men gather and speak of great warriors," Sigli said, seizing the opening.

Ubba smiled with satisfaction. "Well, then...it's settled. You'll join me in the sack of Wessex. One of our starboard rowers took ill and died yesterday…you can replace him."

"Perhaps you would give me leave to continue my..."

"You have my leave to continue living, and row and fight in my service," Ubba interrupted. "You came to seek your destiny...? Well, you've found it. You've found Ubba."

With that he waved his hand in the direction of an empty rower's bench toward the ship's bow and turned away. The interview was over.

There could be no protesting Ubba's command. Sigli moved forward silently and assumed his assigned position at one of the starboard oars, grabbing the sturdy piece of ash and allowing it to drop into the sea. Unconsciously, he fell into the rhythm of wood against water as he pulled together with the score of warriors manning the oars on his side. Their easy motion, repeated again and again, soothed his anger as the dragon ship surged forward through the waves. After a few moments he began to feel the sweat trickling down the small of his back as his muscles responded to the rowing motion.

"Don't despair, Yodir...there are worse fates in the world."

Sigli glanced back at the rower seated immediately behind him, looking upon a rawboned face that could not hide a twinkle in the man's eye. The Viking broke into a smile, revealing a mouth devoid of all but a few sharp teeth.

"I'm known as Nari, the Open Mouth."

"And how did you win such a name?"

"Some say because of my toothless grin. Others swear it's because I can't keep a secret," Nari laughed. "Both claims bear truth."

"I have no secrets," Sigli answered smugly. "Don't waste your breath on me."

"Ah, but every man has a secret….but don't worry…I won't trouble you for yours." Nari grunted softly from the exertion of pulling on his oar. "I'm getting too old for this kind of labor. After this voyage I'll find time to rest."

"You've sailed with Ubba before?"

"Once, many years ago, not long after the three brothers stormed Northumbria. It was during the attack on East Anglia, when the Lord Ubba defeated Edmund and filled his body with arrows. I profited well from that campaign."

"What's England like?"

"I've spent the better part of the last twelve years in and around that land, my friend, with occasional raids into the kingdom of the Franks. I fought with Halfdan against the Saxons, and later took up with Guthrum in Mercia. We sail to relieve him from the siege at Exeter, where Alfred keeps him penned within the city walls."

Sigli allowed a few moments to pass as he sat lost in thought. He finally broke the silence. "And who is this Alfred?"

Nari sucked in his breath. "A man to be reckoned with. He alone holds the Saxons together. They're a wayward lot, and not a man among them can stand up to an armed Viking blow for blow. They whine like women, worshipping their Christian god—as if he can match the might of Odin and Thor! Without Alfred to lead them, they're helpless."

"One man against an army of Vikings should be of no consequence."

"Even a Viking can't catch the wind," Nari smirked. "What Alfred lacks in strength, he makes up for in wisdom and courage. He's the last remaining son of Ethelwulf, a great warrior and leader, and he's inherited the best of that man, along with a cunning that none of his brothers before him possessed. Alfred may not have the army to crush Guthrum, but he commands enough of a force to make life difficult for any Viking who dares to raid Wessex. For years now he's checked Guthrum's every advance, and Halfdan's before that. He's like Loki himself, full of deviltry...and all in a man not yet thirty."

"Then why do you sail against him, Nari? Surely there must be easier prey?"

"Because I grow old, and time escapes me. It's for the young and strong of limb, like you, to seek other adventures. Ubba is a man of might, and determined to end the game. The Saxon fields are fertile. When Alfred has been routed and put to death, there will be spoils for all, and I'll find a nice fat wife and work the land until I grow too feeble to be of use any more."

Sigli's thoughts drifted as Nari continued to chatter. Noting the young captive's inattention, the old Viking finally lapsed into silence, and they joined in with the bank of rowers, toiling on in silence. The hours passed until the light in the sky finally began to wane and the sun sank into the western sea. A light breeze stirred with the twilight, filling out the sail of the dragon ship so that the rowers were able to ship their oars, gratefully acknowledging Njord for coming to the aid of their aching backs. Sigli curled up at the foot of the sea chest upon which he had been sitting, musing on the curious twists and turns of destiny until sleep gathered him in its protective embrace.

*   *   *   *   *

A lone figure sat astride his mount, gazing silently out to sea. The still of the evening hung over the shoreline like a great, gray blanket, broken only by the flapping of wings as a hawk darted across the sky. Man and horse remained motionless, framed against the twilight. The beach where they kept their vigil was tucked into the base of a low ridge that tapered down to the water's edge, forming a protected cove that led out beyond a rocky promontory to the open sea.

Although the man was outfitted in the garb of a common soldier, there was a distinct air in his bearing that suggested higher birth, a suspicion borne out by the one incongruity in his dress, a bright ring adorning his finger that gleamed in the dusk. He was neither large nor muscled, but his presence radiated a power and authority that were reflected in even his most subtle movements. An aquiline, proud nose protruded from his beardless face. His eyes never stopped shifting across the entrance to the cove, scanning the face of the promontory, waiting.

He stirred in his saddle, prompting the horse to shake its head questioningly and paw at the sand. The stallion knew his every movement. He reached down and patted the animal reassuringly on the neck, but the beast could sense its master's concern and began to pace in a nervous gait along the beach. He reined the horse in and spoke quietly.

"Yes, you know me too well." He smiled. "I can't deceive you. But be still...the time for action will be here soon enough."

He stared into the empty horizon. How long would it remain in such peaceful slumber? In his mind's eye he could see the dragon ships, their sails filled with the wind, scudding across the sea. The heathens were coming, that he knew. When they would arrive, and in what numbers, was anybody's guess. He could sense their presence closing in upon him through the twilight as surely as he could feel the sea breeze licking at his face; that same wind would bear ill tidings on its wings.

Suddenly a sharp, excruciating wave of pain seared through his body, propelling him forward in a violent motion that nearly threw him from the saddle. He grimaced in agony and clutched at his stomach while the horse began to buck wildly. It broke into a sprint, as though it might save its master from some unseen threat. The man pulled hard on the reins with his free hand while pressing hard on his abdomen with the other, squeezing his legs through the pain and locking them tightly around the haunches of the powerful beast. Ever so slowly, he regained control of himself and the horse. The fire in his stomach gradually began to lessen, until all that remained was a dull throb in his abdomen that ebbed as the seconds passed.

The mysterious attacks had plagued him since his youth, occurring infrequently but always returning at the least expected moments. He breathed heavily and wiped the sweat from his forehead, and he felt a light shiver pass through his body with the wind; it refreshed him as he drew the reins against the stallion's neck and headed back along the beach. The pain had passed.

It was then he noticed that a small boat manned by a solitary figure had rounded the promontory and entered the quiet waters of the cove. The rider directed his horse to the point along the beach where the boat was preparing to land. He sat erect in the saddle, in command of himself again, and as the skiff drew near he was able to make out the features of the mariner.

The man was a Viking.

The keel of the skiff scraped against the sandy bottom a few feet from the water's edge. The Viking jumped into the shallow water and pulled the boat onto the beach until he was satisfied it was secure. Only then did he turn to acknowledge the rider, approaching the horse and looking up into the man's face.

"You've kept me waiting," the horseman began.

"Your pardon, Lord," the Viking replied haltingly, struggling with the Saxon tongue. "I sat in council with Guthrum, and could not break away."

"Enough, then...speak."

The Viking grunted. "Ubba sails for Exeter with over a hundred ships. They arrive within several days time, depending on the wind."

The rider let out his breath and turned to the sea. "And then?"

"Then, my Lord, Guthrum shall issue forth from Exeter, driving away the Saxons and gathering up provisions from the countryside."

"We'll see about that," the rider replied angrily, stirring in his saddle. "The men of Wessex won't break."

"Perhaps, my Lord," the Viking replied. He held out his hand expectantly.

"Ah, yes...of course." The rider winced, as if an old wound had been reopened. He reached inside his jersey and extracted a pouch, its contents jingling in the night air. "We pay you protection money, we pay you for information. When will it end?" He tossed the pouch down to the man.

"The price of blood is high," the Viking smirked. He turned on his heel and put his weight to the boat, shoving it away from the beach and struggling aboard. He settled in at the oars and began to pull away, but a second thought made him turn and call back over his shoulder.

"Don't be a fool, Alfred. Withdraw, before it's too late!"

The rider did not reply. He watched in silence as the boat receded into the darkness, feeling the weight of Christian England pressing down on his back. Above him, the rising moon shone impassively, bathing the shoreline in a quicksilver glow.

*   *   *   *   *

"Get up, son of Lothar!"

Sigli's eyes flew open to a grim awakening; there, looming above him in the half-light before dawn stood Ubba, hovering like a bird over its prey. A handful of the Warlord's fighting men stood by with weapons drawn. Rather than show alarm, Sigli allowed his body to relax, remaining prone on the deck while he assessed his antagonists. He marked them one by one until his eyes came to rest on a familiar face, framed in a leer of unbridled triumph. It was the man he had recognized the day before.

"Have you measured me, Little One?" the man cackled. "Aye...Little One. That's how they called you, just a young boy you were, playing among the ships when I returned with your father from the land of the Moors. I'm Snorri."

Sigli rose slowly to his feet, pulling himself up to his full height. "I remember you," he said in disgust, "and I remember that every man who sailed with Lothar profited handsomely from that voyage. A strange gratitude."

"Oh, I had nothing against your father," Snorri said. "He was a great warrior, and brave. But..." he paused, "Lothar is dead. The winds have changed. There's a price on your head, and I intend to profit by it."

Sigli turned to Ubba in anger. "Your treachery aided Sidroc, no?"

"Hold your tongue, boy, or I'll rip it out of your mouth!" Ubba thundered. "I bore your father no malice, but he refused to help me when I asked him for ships and men." He raised an eyebrow. "Sidroc offered me a means to that end, that's all...I can't be concerned with the consequences."

"Many are dead because of that, Ubba! My own bride was slaughtered!"

"What Sidroc did is his own affair," Ubba replied smugly. "And what he does with his share of your father's house, for that matter, is not something I care about. Thirty ships arrived from Halfsfiord in the night to join my fleet. I'm satisfied."

Sigli peered through the growing light of the early morning, able now to make out the ships on the outer edges of the fleet. There was no question the number of vessels had increased during the night. He recognized a dragon ship from Halfsfiord off to starboard, a mighty vessel that he had spent the better part of a summer building with a crew of Lothar's best shipbuilders. She was broad of beam and beautiful to behold, as fast as anything that sailed the great seas. And now she belonged to Ubba.

"May you rot in Hel, traitor."

The Warlord punched Sigli hard in the face, knocking him to the deck. He rubbed his jaw and spat a wad of blood over the bulwark and into the sea. Slowly, he raised his eyes and looked disdainfully up at his captor.

"Is that the best you can do?"

Ubba's face flushed with rage. His foot exploded into Sigli's stomach, doubling him over. "I could make you crawl on your knees and lick my feet! You'd beg for death before I was through, but you're worth much more to me alive. I'm sure Sidroc will agree!" He turned to his men. "Lash him firmly to his oar, and woe to you all if he should break free!"

A trio of Vikings pounced upon Sigli, securing him with a series of tightly drawn leather thongs. "They'll bite into your flesh as the sea weathers them," Ubba grinned wickedly. "We'll see how Lothar's pup bears up under the strain."

He turned away and swaggered aft to the helm, his laughter trailing behind him. Sigli glared at his captors defiantly, holding his angry stare until the last of them tired of the sport and left. The rage pounding against his temples would not subside; he strained against his bonds, but each effort only served to tighten the ropes and increase his frustration. Finally, he dropped his head in despair.

"It's a sad day when Viking turns against Viking," a voice observed from behind him. It was Nari. "We have enemies enough, without plotting and fighting among ourselves."

His voice suddenly dropped down until it was a mere whisper. "Don't despair…the gods smile upon you. Your father, you see, once saved my life long, long ago. I owe him still." He paused, looking around cautiously. "Before this voyage is out, you'll be freed from your bonds, that I promise you. How you fare beyond that is Odin's will."

Sigli's spirits surged back to life. "Thank you, friend," he whispered, half turning to acknowledge Nari. It was then he noticed the eastern sky blanketed in a red glow, the first sign of a coming storm. He wondered if they would beat the wind and waves to their destination, or if Thor had other plans for them while they were still at sea; to be caught in unfriendly waters when a heavy squall hit spelled danger. He turned and faced forward again, his head raised in the morning breeze, and he knew in his heart that fair weather was a friend who would not soon be calling.

The clouds gathered throughout the day as the fleet pressed on, heading into a mild wind and relying on the muscle of the rowers to propel the ships forward. By mid-day the blisters on Sigli's hands broke open, and because the leather thongs binding him to the oar did not allow him to shift his grip, he suffered great discomfort. His bonds tightened with each hour as they became wet with the ocean spray, and he continued to labor mindlessly at the oar until a cry from the watch alerted the crew that land had been sighted on the horizon. Within minutes the call rang out again, heralding the appearance of a fleet of dragon ships.

Some forty vessels lay waiting to join the armada. And the land the ships were anchored off was England—a series of green lowlands emptying down into marshy country that provided the final transition to the sea. As the fleet drew closer, the only movement along the coastline was the advance of the sails hastening to join them. The rowers shipped their oars on a command from Ubba; within minutes, the two fleets were one.

Ubba called out for Sigli's skiff to be made ready. He boarded it with several confederates and embarked for one of the ships to sit in council and decide on the armada's next move. His departure gave the men time to rest their aching muscles and collect themselves for the remainder of the day. Sigli retreated within himself and attempted to isolate the pain from his body. It was a relief to indulge in a few moments of rest, but the respite was short-lived; Ubba returned within the hour, breathing fire and exhorting the men to take up their oars and proceed along the coast.

They made excellent time for the next few hours with the wind on their starboard. Gradually the coastline began to shift, compelling them to turn into the breeze on a heading west by southwest and into the channel separating the island of England from the continent. As evening began to fall, Sigli noticed a series of white cliffs on the shore. He recognized them immediately from stories told to him by men who had navigated those waters; they called the place Dover. It was as far as the fleet would venture that day. The rowers shipped their oars, the sail was lowered, and the fleet dropped its anchors in the shallow waters off the coast and made the final preparations for the night. The men dug into their sea chests to clothe themselves and ward off the advancing chill. They refreshed themselves with water and provisions, savoring the last moments of the day before settling in for a well-deserved rest.

As darkness engulfed the fleet, a light drizzle began to fall, adding to the general feeling of ill temper aboard the ships. The men gathered in small groups and huddled around burning pots of charcoal that warmed them and helped to fend off the elements. One group gathered just forward of where Sigli was bound, enabling him to hear pieces of conversation as he rested awkwardly upon his oar, lulled by the gentle rocking of the ship in the light seas.

"Why we can't go ashore is a mystery to me," he heard one man mutter. "Any shelter would be better than this."

"You forget...we're without friends here," another offered.

"Without friends? Look around you, fool; we have enough force to beat back the Frost Giants."

"Ubba doesn't want to take chances," a third voice broke in. "I've heard that the ships joining us today didn't meet his expectations. He's beside himself with anger."

"A strange decision then, to sail to Dover," another said. "It would have been much safer to remain in the marsh country, or perhaps turn northward to Benfleet."

"Ubba would never turn away from our course. He's so close now, he can taste it."

"We're still a full day's sail from Exeter," the first complainer groused. "We could be in for trouble if the weather worsens. We'll be sailing through difficult waters the entire voyage, and things grow more dangerous with every league. The Saxons are massed around Exeter; we won't be safe until we pass by them and reach the harbor."

"They have no ships to stop us," someone said.

"That doesn't matter, if Thor and Njord decide to release their fury on the waves. The channel widens as we sail westward, taking on the smell of the Great Sea beyond, the ocean that leads to the edge of the world. When the wind is wet and blows with full force, it's strong enough to rip a mast free from the deck... I've sailed these waters before."

"Enough!" one of the older warriors protested. "You speak against us! We don't need to have our spirits doused...the rain is bad enough. Ubba's made his decision; it's too late to turn back now. All we can do is pray to the gods for safe passage, and put our backs to the task. Odin will decide the rest."

The men lapsed into silence. One by one they slid off to their posts on the deck, curling up under animal skins to snatch a few precious hours of sleep. Sigli propped his body against his oar, fully exposed to the elements. The drizzle tightened the leather thongs against his limbs, and he knew that sleep would be impossible. He concentrated on putting aside any thoughts of his predicament, clearing his mind with a meditation that Mimir had once taught him until he became suspended in a trance-like state, waiting out the night as the leather entwined itself into his flesh and squeezed his limbs until even their dull throbbing ceased.

The morning dawned thick and gray, matching the unsettled mood of the Vikings. Although the men were anxious to reach their destination, there was a general sense of foreboding among them, for the night's drizzle had dampened their enthusiasm. Even Ubba's exhortations could not quell the undercurrent of discontent; it crept from vessel to vessel, from man to man, until it seemed as though the sturdy ships could not bear up under the strain of keeping so many water-logged spirits afloat.

But there would be no turning back. Ubba had seen to that the day before with his command to push westward, and he above all others knew the fickle nature of the men he led. Vikings could never be motivated by weakness or indecision. Everything would change once they reached Exeter safely. Until then, there would be no questioning his decisions, for any man who dared raise a voice in protest faced the prospect of meeting Njord face to face at the bottom of the sea. Rising from the deck, Ubba bellowed out orders to the men, sending them scurrying about the ship while they crammed a few mouthfuls of bread into their bodies to gird themselves for the voyage. Shouts wafted through the air over the waves and mingled with the thud of oars against wood, followed by the splash of the long poles into the waters of the channel.

The drizzle disappeared by mid-morning. They were aided by a light wind that blew from the east, enabling the ships to raise their sails and supplement the efforts of the rowers. The men fell into a rhythm, chanting war songs and odes to the gods that had been handed down from generation to generation in the lodges of the north during many a long winter's night.

The coastline to the north began to change as the leagues passed. The men became aware of activity off to the starboard, first in the form of single lookouts that appeared against the sky, then in bands of horsemen that thundered along the shoreline. These new foes raised their weapons, silhouetted against the cliffs, joining their voices as one and hurling catcalls across the water. At first there was some trepidation among the Vikings, for until this altercation they had not laid eyes on their enemies. They could not know how many of the Saxons lurked beyond the crests of the low hills edging down to the sea, and the fear of the faceless, the unknown, tugged at the senses of even the most disciplined fighting man.

But gradually the alarm that had first overtaken them began to subside, and they realized that no matter how great the rival force, the soldiers were incapable of crossing the water to bring harm to them. The horsemen along the beach became abstractions, dancing figures in the mist. Mere men could not stop the ships of Ubba, who stood proudly at the helm of his flagship, gesturing derisively toward the shoreline, mocking the Saxons with shouts and challenges. His efforts inspired the Vikings; like the rushing of a great wind, their voices rolled across the water, swelling in volume as they joined him.

It was now late in the afternoon, and even the complainers among the fleet realized they were but a few hours from Exeter. There was an added urgency to their plight as the weather grew worse. The skies, already densely overcast, began to form in large, angry, gray-black balls, housing the ominous threat of Thor, the god of thunder. Rumblings could be heard to the west, directly on their course, but on they pushed, keeping to their rhythm as the Viking captains shouted out encouragement.

Soon the wind began to pick up in intensity, building foamy whitecaps atop the waves that cascaded over one another and crashed in the face of the advancing hulls. The strength of the gust made the sails of the ships useless, forcing the rowers to supply all of the power to coax the fleet forward. They weaved back and forth uncertainly through the deepening troughs forming between the waves as the ocean grew rougher with every stroke.

Sigli's motions by this time had become mechanical. The pain in his hands and limbs was replaced by dull sensations, but he kept rowing, propelled by instinct and the will to survive. The spray from the sea had drenched him through, stinging his eyes with a salty chill. When he concentrated, he could make out the labored breaths of the rowers around him as they fought to keep the ships moving forward. The going became even more difficult, and gradually the armada began to lose its form; those vessels manned by the less formidable warriors fell behind until the fleet was scattered across the channel.

Ubba's flagship led the pack into the growing darkness. The thick clouds scudded across the sky faster and faster, whipped on unmercifully by the wind that now blew directly in their faces. Pushed past the point of fatigue, the men were beginning to lose their edge. A rower positioned across from Sigli on one of the port oars slumped to the deck in exhaustion. He was relieved immediately by an alternate, but not in time to escape Ubba's wrath as the Warlord dashed forward and beat the nearly unconscious man on the back with the butt end of a spear. Seeing this compelled the others to renew their labors.

"Vikings! Pull, if you value your lives!" Ubba shouted. He pointed to a headland looming hard on the shoreline to their starboard. "Round that point lies Exeter, within our grasp! Row on! We must beat the darkness into port! Row!"

The men strained, putting their backs to the task. Their muscles screamed for release, but still they pulled, forcing the ships through the angry surf. The flagship was followed closely by the remainder of the fleet, some ships hard astern, others straggling as they fought to hold the course. In the next moment Ubba's flagship rounded the headland, and the men were met with a sight that riveted every eye among them to the coast in wonderment. A line of bonfires illuminated the cliffs, as if all of Saxon England had congregated on the bluffs to greet the fleet. Scores of enemy warriors could be seen, even at that distance, standing five and six men deep. They stretched for hundreds of yards with arms upraised, brandishing their spears animatedly and sending fear into the hearts of the Vikings.

"Forget them!" Ubba screamed over the wind and surf. "Steel yourselves! Odin favors us, and gives us hope!" He pointed directly ahead into the sea and the gathering darkness, where a twinkle of fires appeared on the far horizon. "There it lies! Exeter!"

Suddenly a jagged flash of lightning ripped across the sky, followed by a blast of thunder. The black clouds, pregnant with moisture gathered from the sea, could hold back no longer. The rain began to fall in torrents, stinging sheets of wet iron that flew into the faces of the men, and the wind howled with fury, making progress virtually impossible as wave after wave crashed into the dragon ships and spun them about in the turbulent sea. Night fell upon the frightened men with a darkness as black as the pits of Hel.

What had been a slow struggle to push forward now became a matter of survival. The storm had set a perfect ambush, falling upon them when they were so close to their destination, yet so utterly helpless in the face of the elements. The change was immediate. Thor's lightning bolts illuminated the white tips of the ocean as the waves rolled across the open horizon with frightening power. The sea began to crash over the bulwarks at regular intervals, dousing the deck and forcing the men to hold on for their lives. It was barely possible to see from the bow of the ship to the stern, and all thoughts of maintaining contact with the other vessels in the fleet disappeared.

"Keep her into the wind!" Ubba cried.

Their oars were a poor match for the powerful surf, but the men struggled to test their will against the waters. The rains pounded the deck, driven by an unforgiving wind that grew stronger by the minute. The ship was hurled about the waves like a piece of driftwood trapped in a maelstrom; to the men, Ragnorak had surely come, and the pounding of the Frost Giants could almost be heard as they strained at the gates of the Rainbow Bridge.

Thunder and lightning mixed with wind and waves in a deafening symphony of doom. A wall of water surged over portside, catching the rowers at their stations and pounding them to the deck. Sigli was wrenched against the bulwark, but the leather thongs held him fast to the oar, digging into his arms as he was buffeted about. He looked up to see the rower immediately forward swept over the bulwark and into the roaring surf; a last desperate scrambling for a foothold was not enough to save the man, who disappeared into the darkness.

A flash suddenly split the heavens, striking the mast of the ship in a loud explosion. The timber came crashing down onto the deck in burning splinters, crushing several of the crew under its main section. It was the final step into chaos; the men scampered about in terror, some struggling to free themselves from the lines and sheets that had fallen onto the deck, others cracking open their sea chests to salvage their possessions while there was still time.

Sigli felt a hand on his shoulder. It was Nari, soaked to the skin like a water rat. The old man clambered to Sigli's side with his knife unsheathed and began to cut away at the leather thongs binding Sigli to the oar.

"Your life may not last much longer tonight," Nari shouted through the wind, "but at least you won't go down to Njord's palace lashed like a dog to a tree!"

He cut vigorously at the wet leather, but the thongs did not yield easily. One by one, they gave way slowly to the blade as he struggled to keep his footing. The deck was drenched with confusion as the ship tossed about, taking on more and more of the sea. Nari was almost through when another wall of water crashed over the bulwark, sending Sigli and him to the deck. The old man struggled to his knees and resumed cutting.

But as Sigli shook the stinging water from his eyes, he looked over Nari's shoulder—there, some fifteen feet away, stood Ubba. The Warlord's face was contorted in rage as he grabbed for a lance and bounded unsteadily across the deck toward them.

"Nari, watch out!" Sigli yelled.

His warning was in vain. Ubba buried the lance in the small of the old man's back with such force that it poked through Nari's stomach, spilling intestines and blood onto the deck. Nari's eyes bulged out of their sockets as his soul flew into the storm.

The thong binding Sigli to the oar was down to a final strand. With a desperate heave he pulled against the leather, severing it completely and diving to the deck as Ubba's sword came crashing down onto the sea chest where he had been stationed a moment before. He rolled over and grabbed for a shield that had fallen onto the deck, covering himself just in time as Ubba's blade thudded into the hide-covered frame. The force of the blow, combined with Sigli's inability to grasp the buckler firmly with his blistered hands, sent the shield skidding off to the side. Ubba raised his arm to deliver the death blow, but a sudden pitch of the ship tangled him with Sigli's legs, sending him sprawling to the deck.

Sigli dragged himself to his feet, groping for a weapon. He grabbed a piece of the shriven mast and hurled it at Ubba, but the Viking fought the missile off with his sword and pressed forward. Sigli bumped into another shield as he retreated, and with a great effort he lifted it to his defense. Again and again Ubba rained blows down upon him. Sigli's legs began to buckle under the onslaught, and he could feel the fight slipping away from him after the trial of several sleepless days and nights.

Suddenly, a sickening crunch jolted the ship as a great rock pierced the hull in the darkness. Sigli was thrown off balance and hurled backward. Just as he began to right himself, a vertical wall of water flew over the opposite bulwark, catching him flush in the chest and knocking him into the side of the ship. His momentum flipped him backward head over heels, over the bulwark, overboard.

The storm dissipated into an eerie silence as he plunged beneath the surface of the sea. He thrashed madly at the ice-cold water, swallowing a mouthful of it as he struggled to break into the air. The churning current spun him in underwater somersaults until it seemed as though he would not be able to hold his breath any longer, but then his head shot above the waves, allowing him to fill his lungs again before another wave crashed down upon him and sent him back into the depths. He struggled through the darkness to reach the surface again; in so doing, his hand closed on a fragment of the splintered mast that had been cast from the ship and was floating in the sea.

He grasped the wood with the strength left to him, wrapping his body about the bark as another wave submerged him and strove to separate him from the mast. He hung on for what seemed an eternity, fighting the cold and the sea, until a powerful wave broke upon him and ripped the mast from his grip. He tumbled into the depths of the raging ocean.

But then, suddenly he felt the sea bottom scraping his back, after which the white water spit him to the surface. Another torrent of water lashed him from behind, sending him spinning madly, arms and legs akimbo, along the rough sea bottom. He regained his feet and struggled forward until the surf hit him in the buttocks, then the knees, and finally milled harmlessly about his ankles. Summoning the last of his strength, he forced his battered body onward, staggering through the last few feet of surf and onto a sandy beach.

He lurched ahead into the darkness some ten steps before crumpling in exhaustion, falling face forward into unconsciousness and onto the damp sands of England.

CHAPTER III: An Unlikely Alliance

"It is fortune chiefly that makes heroes."
—Thomas Fuller, <u>Gnomologia</u>.

"This one's alive."

The Saxon motioned to his countrymen as they rummaged through the wreckage of ships and men strewn along the beach. The half-light before dawn made it difficult to see more than a short distance, but the soldiers could not restrain themselves from filtering down the hillside to explore the remnants of Ubba's fleet. The devastation was total. Looking down the shoreline, the Saxons marveled at the destruction wrought by the night's storm. A melange of twisted spars and shattered hulls dotted the landscape. Lines criss-crossed the damp sand, snaking their way through a field of corpses caught among the shrouds that lay in soiled disarray along the beach. Out to sea a short distance, the remains of a warship jutted awkwardly from a protruding rock, the eye in the dragon's head on its prow glaring dolefully through the mist.

Over seventy-five ships had been destroyed in Ubba's mad dash down the channel. The Warlord himself escaped harm, for after his flagship foundered on the rocks he managed to reach the safety of another vessel that was able to weather the storm. It and thirty-odd ships were blown back down the channel, there to limp off into the horizon and lick the wounds inflicted by the gale.

There would be no need to reinforce Exeter now. Ubba's fleet had been the scale upon which Guthrum weighed his chances to succeed in Wessex, that last bastion of Christian England remaining independent of Viking rule. With supplies running out and no aid in sight, Guthrum would now have to negotiate with Alfred, the outcome of which was already clear. In return for safe passage back to the central Saxon kingdom of Mercia now under Viking control, Guthrum would give up his claim to Exeter.

Many Vikings had drowned in the storm, the wind and waves accomplishing what no army of men ever could have, erasing the threat of invasion in one grand gesture. Not a single Saxon perished. The men of the fyrd—the militia conscripted by King Alfred from the fields of Wessex—scoured among the spoils on the beach, celebrating their bloodless victory; the shipwrecked Vikings still fortunate enough to be alive became prisoners of the English.

"Help me, will you? He's a big one."

The Saxon bent down over a Viking who lay face-down in the sand. His cohorts crowded around for a closer look as he turned the body over. It was Sigli.

"He's alive, but looks the worse for wear," one said.

"Lift him up, and we'll bear him to the high ground," the first man ordered. "He'll revive soon, and his legs look strong enough."

Sigli awoke an hour later on top of a grassy knoll overlooking the sea and the wreckage on the beach. His limbs were trussed firmly behind him and bound around a stake wedged beneath his armpits. Some fifty Vikings were also captive, herded together where they could be kept under surveillance. Sigli rolled over, propping himself up on his knees and turning to a glum captive who sat cross-legged next to him on the ground.

"How many survived?"

The crack of a whip interrupted him. A Saxon lumbered over, gesturing angrily, and although Sigli could not understand the man's words as he spoke in the English tongue, the message was clear. The guard advanced to within several paces, his whip poised to lash out. Sigli sank onto his haunches and into silence, looking eastward down the beach where the sun had broken through the retreating clouds. The shoreline teemed with activity. A large contingent of Saxons milled about, separating the dead from the living, the useless wreckage from that which could be salvaged and put to use in English hands. There was knowledge to be gleaned from the wreckage on the beach, and with it a store of sails, lines, oars and other seaworthy gear that would prove useful.

The work continued all morning. By noon much had been accomplished, allowing a party to prepare for the journey back to the main camp while the balance of the force stayed to conclude the salvage. Most of the prisoners were collected from the beach; others were captured attempting to flee into the surrounding countryside. The corpses of those who had perished were heaped together on the sand, where their bodies would be burnt when night fell. Although it was not Christian practice to cremate the dead, the Saxons were willing to dispose of the Vikings according to heathen custom, allowing the flames to do burial work that otherwise would have been reserved for English backs.

The prisoners were herded together behind a series of oxcarts loaded high with spoils from the beach. Sigli stood among them, the hunger beginning to gnaw at his belly. He looked over his shoulder at the corpses, wondering if he would be lucky enough to have the privilege of a full Viking funeral when he died. Had his father and brother been so honored? Halfsfiord suddenly seemed far away, as if years rather than merely days stood between him and his homeland.

Waiting there with the others, he vowed again to devote his life to securing revenge, no matter the cost or sacrifice. All honor, love and birthright—all had been lost. Within a few days he had been transformed from a proud Viking prince into a destitute beggar, a slave at the mercy of a foreign hand that knew the Vikings as the bitterest of enemies. Only his hate remained to him, entwined with the burning memory of Sidroc.

They started off in a long column, heading inland along a dirt road that had turned to mud in the storm. The oxcarts labored to forge their way along the route, from time to time requiring the efforts of the Viking prisoners to help free the wheels that sank into the soft earth. News of the column's advance spread quickly through the countryside, and soon the road was lined with workers from the surrounding fields eager to get a closer look at the Norsemen. The Saxons customarily had fled their farms or locked themselves away whenever news came of a raiding party; now they had a rare chance to view their tormentors firsthand. Children peeked from behind their mothers' skirts, casting nervous glances at the captives.

But the subdued presence of the prisoners, spattered with mud as they trudged along in captivity, encouraged the crowd to grow bolder as more people joined the ranks. They directed their insults and shouts at the prisoners, hurling an occasional rock or mud ball at them from behind the safety of the first row of bystanders. The Saxon guards made no attempt to dissuade the crowd. Some of the Vikings glared angrily at their tormentors, but most kept their eyes averted; Sigli glanced occasionally into the faces gathered on the roadside, reading in their eyes a gamut of emotions ranging from curiosity to loathing. The loneliness he had experienced at sea now seemed a welcome alternative. While the burning in his hands continued to plague him, he could do nothing to relieve the pain, concentrating instead on keeping pace with the column so as not to be singled out from the other prisoners.

The condition of the road improved as they moved further inland in a circular route around and behind Exeter, and the crowds began to dissipate. In mid-afternoon the column emerged from a wood that petered out on the crest of a low hill. Below them, the marchers could make out the outlines of the camp that housed most of the Saxon army. A series of earthworks had been constructed to protect the main force from any surprise attacks, crude fortifications that stretched for miles, encircling the walls of Exeter so that the only access to the city was via the river that led to the sea some seven miles to the south.

The Saxon tents dotted the gentle slopes behind the earthworks. It appeared from a distance as though an immense force had been gathered, but upon closer inspection many of the tents revealed themselves to be nothing more than empty props thrown up to deceive the Vikings. Had the besieged garrison of Exeter seen through the ruse, it could have stormed out of the town and perhaps broken through the Saxon line. But that opportunity no longer existed, because additional troops had streamed into the camp to reinforce the core of Alfred's army in anticipation of the arrival of Ubba's fleet.

The column reached the outer fortifications and passed into the camp through a breach in the earthworks. There was little in the conduct of the Saxons within that suggested a well-disciplined or coordinated force, for the soldiers were common farmers, men of the fields outfitted hastily with a few rudimentary tools of war to staff the fyrd. It did not surprise Sigli that the Vikings had met with such success during their attacks on England; raiders striking quickly at such opposition had excellent prospects of succeeding before meeting any real resistance.

The Saxons separated the prisoners from the main column and led them into a stockade that consisted of a series of stakes driven into the ground and placed close together so that a man could not slip between them. Almost a hundred Vikings were crowded into an area only large enough to accommodate half that number comfortably. As the men entered the enclosure, a guard posted at the entrance cut their bonds, freeing their limbs for the first time since their captivity had begun. The men staked out their places within the stockade, shaking the circulation back into their arms and sitting down wherever they could, grateful to relieve their aching feet.

The mood of the prisoners soon grew boisterous and their interactions became more animated. Escape seemed impossible. The tops of the stakes that formed the stockade rose up some ten feet above the ground, their sharpened tips discouraging any attempt to scale the wall to freedom. A score of archers surrounded the makeshift prison, ready to repulse the prisoners in the unlikely event they assailed the palisade. Some of the Vikings fell to bickering among themselves; others lapsed into moody silences. Sigli kept to himself, conserving his energy in the face of the hunger consuming him as the angry mood continued to brew.

Famished stomachs were soon rewarded when a contingent of Saxons approached the stockade, swords drawn to assure an orderly dispersal of the bread, cheeses and wheat cakes that had been prepared. These guards were joined by the archers outside once the gate to the stockade swung open. The prisoners sprang to their feet and pressed forward to receive the food, grabbing their rations and scrambling off to devour them. Sigli was one of the last to be granted his share. He moved off to a corner, sat down gingerly, and began to eat.

As he devoured the food, he noticed a large, leathery Dane sitting a few yards away. The man had already finished his meal, and now his eyes darted with greedy glances back and forth around the stockade before fixing on an older prisoner eating nearby. The Dane sidled over to the man, and a few hasty words were exchanged until the old Viking, clearly at a disadvantage, handed the last few bites of his wheat cake to the Dane.

Awakened by a sixth sense that told him someone was watching, the thief looked up at Sigli with a piercing glance. Another candidate for bullying, he thought to himself, a man whose torn hands would offer no resistance. He motioned brusquely, pointing to the food in a way that made his intentions clear. Sigli averted his eyes as if to dismiss the intrusion, but he could sense the Dane approaching. A second later a voice boomed out from above him.

"Give it here, and I'll leave you alone."

Sigli remained motionless. The Dane raised his leg in anger and prepared to administer a kick to the ribs, but he underestimated his antagonist. Sigli pivoted quickly and swung his leg around, undercutting the Viking and sending him crashing to the earth. The bully reared up as if to strike but was jolted by a flying elbow to his chin that knocked him to the ground again. In desperation, he grasped at the soft earth as he fell, casting a handful of coarse, loamy sand into

Sigli's face. Enough of it penetrated Sigli's eyes so that the Dane was able to regain his balance and land a series of blows that swung the advantage in his favor.

By this time the struggle had attracted attention. The other prisoners gathered as the combatants rolled about in the dust, lashing out wildly at each other. The Saxon guards rushed into the stockade with arms drawn, and one of them separated the fighters with a few whacks from his thick walking staff. The move only served to enrage the Dane, who turned on his captor and disarmed him of the weapon, raising the pole to deliver a blow to the head of the fallen Christian.

Several arrows embedded themselves in his chest before he could bring the staff down, killing him instantly. The sudden violence sent a wave of rage through the Vikings. Scuffles broke out all over the stockade as the prisoners turned on their captors and mounted a desperate attempt to gain freedom. But the exhausted and unarmed Vikings were no match for the swords of the Saxons; several men were killed and a handful of others wounded before order was restored. As the Saxons stood before the prisoners with bows drawn, a menacing figure strode into the enclosure. He was a tall man, with a scarred face and a stony look in his eye.

"How did this all start?"

"A fight broke out between two of the heathens, Osric," a guard answered. "We put a stop to it immediately, but one of the bastards turned on us, so we killed him. It set off the rest of them."

Osric, ealdorman of Hampshire, looked the prisoners over. "We can't allow this to happen! They must be punished!" He turned to the Saxon, the same man who had been knocked down while trying to separate the fighters. "The other one involved in the fight...show him to me."

The guard eyed the Vikings as they huddled along the back wall and stared at him in sullen defiance. His eyes passed from one face to another, reaching Sigli and moving on, unsure, before returning a second time to lock decisively on him. The guard turned back to Osric and pointed.

"It's him. The tall one."

"We'll make an example of him," Osric said. "Drag him outside the stockade!"

A score of soldiers moved into the ranks of the prisoners, arms drawn, and separated the men roughly until they reached Sigli. Several of them pounced on him, expecting a struggle, but he did not resist. Within moments his wrists were bound and tied to the top of a sturdy pole sticking out of the ground at a height taller than a man, some ten yards in front of the stockade. His bonds were arranged so that the rest of his body was fully exposed, forcing him to stand on his toes to keep his arms from bearing his weight. Osric appropriated a long, lethal-looking whip from a nearby oxcart and approached Sigli, motioning threateningly to the Vikings watching from within the enclosure.

"Maybe you'll understand the language of the lash!" he bellowed. He drew the rawhide strip back and unleashed a blow that landed on Sigli's back with an angry snap, drawing with it a strip of skin and a scream of pain. Osric brought the whip down again and again. The beating continued in front of the prisoners until some twenty blows had been administered, leaving Sigli moaning, head down, back bloodied.

"You sons of Satan will keep your peace now!" Osric said. He threw the whip to the ground and turned to one of the guards. "Leave him tied there so the rest of them can see him. Don't feed him, and don't give him any water, understand?"

"And if he dies?"

"Then he dies. What should that matter, after all? One less stinking heathen for us to worry about."

He walked slowly over to the stockade and fixed his eyes on the prisoners, leaving no doubt as to the punishment they could expect if further trouble arose. They remained silent as he turned to leave, waiting until he reached a suitable distance some hundred yards away before unleashing a barrage of taunts and angry challenges.

Their calls rang through Sigli's mind in a distant echo, the hollow fragments of a fever dream.

*　　*　　*　　*　　*

Grimwald sat on his horse outside Exeter, waiting impatiently to see King Alfred. The Bishop of Winchester was almost fifty years old, wretchedly obese, and unaccustomed to traveling great distances on such short summons. It all displeased him. Even worse, he had been told to wait outside the gates of the city, denied access to the negotiations between Alfred and Guthrum. It was simply another insult he had to swallow.

And now he had to deal with the Vikings again. He was a man of the cross who had devoted his youth in the lowlands of Frisia to converting the heathen to the faith, but it was an undertaking that had grown tedious over time, driving him behind the walls of the monastery to lead a life of seclusion and tend to the vast body of translations that were the province of the Church. Over the course of a few years his knowledge increased considerably, marking him as a formidable man of letters. News of his abilities eventually reached Rome, to where he was summoned for an audience by Pope John VIII.

The magnificence of the city on the Tiber stunned him; the art, the history, the heritage—all left deep impressions. But nothing Grimwald found there was quite so alluring as the immense concentration of power, an energy that bristled everywhere in a world that was far-removed from the ascetic life of the monastery. His resolve weakened when exposed to these opportunities. As he studied the circles of influence, he became transformed into a man of politics, discovering the art of persuasion among men of position and learning how to wield the cross for purposes other than spreading the glory of God. As his influence grew, so did his coffers, and for the first time in his life he became acquainted with a life of leisure.

But Grimwald's outspoken nature and cunning deceit led him to overstep his bounds. He soon found himself on the wrong side of the bargaining table from the Pope, who waited for the right opportunity to rid the papacy of the opinionated outsider, a chance that came in the form of a plea from far-off England.

The Bishop of Winchester had grown ill with fever and died. Under normal circumstances the matter would have been resolved in local council and the vacancy filled, but King Alfred of Wessex had intervened, beseeching the Pope for a man of letters to bring learning, that most precious of commodities, to the British Isles. His Holiness met the obligation by announcing Grimwald's appointment to Winchester in front of a large audience assembled one evening in the Vatican. Before he could protest, the monk was inundated with acclaim from various well-wishers, many of them the same prelates and courtiers who had plotted to displace him. Within the month he left with a small retinue bound for Wessex, as far from the seat of power in Rome as a man of the cross could be sent.

It took Grimwald the entire journey to recuperate from the blow to his fortune. Along the way, he resolved never to allow a similar circumstance to compromise him again. His training during the three years spent in the Vatican had prepared him well, allowing him to set his machine in motion quickly once he reached England. A man of his experience had little trouble mastering the relatively staid political intricacies of the outer provinces; within two years he became a leading figure in the local religious aristocracy. But despite his success, he had yet to find happiness in the primitive environs of his new domain, where any power and wealth that could be accumulated was insignificant compared to the glory of Rome.

The greatest limits to his influence did not come from within the Church, but from Alfred himself. As a man of moral character and religious upbringing, the young king was aware of his responsibilities to the cross. He had already become a shrewd judge of character by the time he assumed the kingship, an ability that made him immediately wary of Grimwald upon meeting the monk. He would have sent the man back to Rome at once, but he knew the difficulty of procuring scholars and was intent on furthering the education of his people. He cultivated a careful relationship with the monk, involving him in certain affairs while keeping him at arm's length on other, more critical issues. If Grimwald was sly, Alfred was craftier still.

All of these issues raced across the obese Bishop of Winchester's mind as he sat astride his horse and waited outside the gates of Exeter. He tugged impatiently at the reins in his hand, glancing over his shoulder at the small company of retainers, men-at-arms and lesser prelates accompanying him. He had been summoned from Winchester by Alfred's request to be on hand to supervise matters pertaining to the cross. The king did not intend to miss the opportunity to provide the Church with the chance to baptize heathens into Christianity; it was a small bone offered to placate the order.

The thought of it all made Grimwald wince. It was an insult to be pressed into such service, a tedious business fit for a man of lesser stature. He had no use for the Vikings, dangerous barbarians whose influence could only compromise his position. He maintained a careful silence as the city gates swung open and a company of riders issued forth with Alfred in the lead. Grimwald had always found it difficult to conceal his jealousy of the man. The monk was old enough to be Alfred's father, and yet the king possessed a force, a natural charisma, that he could never hope to emulate.

The riders drew near. Alfred was engaged in a conversation with Penda, ealdorman of Devon, a trusted companion and confidant who had arrived a fortnight ago with several hundred men to reinforce the siege. Grimwald noted Alfred's dress with disdain. The king was outfitted in fighting man's clothes while the bishop, as usual, wore lavish and expensive robes. The mud that had spattered on his raiment during the journey to Exeter only added to his irritation. As the party approached, Alfred looked up and spotted him.

"Grimwald...I'm glad you've come."

"I'm honored, Sire," the monk replied, bowing from the waist while remaining in his saddle. "I wouldn't miss celebrating your great victory."

"Praise to the Lord for his watchful eye. Were it not for the storm, I'm afraid the situation would be reversed. Ride with me, for we go to inspect our hostages."

"Hostages? Since when have the heathen prisoners become hostages?"

"Since today. We've reached an agreement with Guthrum."

"I was hoping to attend, Sire. I've never met him."

"Your chance will come, I'm sure. For now, though, you must tend to our hostages. There are several hundred in our camp, I hear. Guthrum has permitted us to baptize as many as we can."

"Forgive me, Sire," Grimwald offered, a slight trace of irritation in his voice. "I don't think they'll comply unless we force them at the point of a sword. These Vikings are a barbaric lot and want no part of the one true God. They'd rather worship their pagan deities."

"Surely a man of your considerable talents can change their minds," Alfred suggested. "Or...do you balk at the challenge?"

"I'm a man of the cross, and have a duty invested in me by His Holiness," Grimwald replied smugly. "I'll do the bidding of God, no matter the obstacle. But...what about the Vikings in Exeter? What about Guthrum? If their leader's baptized, others will follow."

"That didn't come up during our discussion," Penda broke in, leaning forward in his saddle so that the monk could see his hawk-like features. "We didn't want to complicate matters at this point."

"Complicate matters?" Grimwald protested. "As a Christian it's your duty to further the Church, man!" He turned to Alfred. "I don't understand, my Lord.

We have the heathens at our mercy, and yet they're allowed to flaunt their insolence!"

Alfred shifted in his saddle and eyed the monk pointedly. "You presume too much, Grimwald. We have the Vikings at our mercy like a man adrift in the sea has sure footing." He pointed to the tents on the hillside surrounding the city. "Why else would we erect these lies, empty of men? We're barely stronger than Guthrum, and only the impossibility of breaking this stalemate prompted him to meet our demands. It does him no good to rot here. He'll leave Exeter within the week and take his force back into Mercia."

"And did you receive money from him?"

Alfred laughed softly. "My dear Winchester, I'm glad not to be paying him. Look around you. This siege has been as hard on us as it has on the Vikings. Our men have been away from their fields far too long, and the harvest is upon us. There's no way we could hope to maintain our force into the winter. It will be hard enough to rotate other ceorls from their farms in Kent to man the fyrd with a skeleton force during the next six months. I must let most of these men go home soon. Be glad you can enjoy the comforts of your abbey for another season without fear."

"And what guarantee do we have that Guthrum won't return to Wessex?"

"There's no guarantee," said Penda. "We're buying time, that's all. Besides, the Vikings don't fancy the cold any more than you do. In all these years, they've never mounted an offensive during the winter."

"That's one of the things I wish to speak to you about, Grimwald," Alfred said. "Along with rotating service in the fyrd to keep our force intact, I want to begin the task of building defensive outposts at strategic locations. I'll need the Church's help to fund the effort."

Grimwald's face grew a dark red. "Sire! I can't...."

"Not now, Grimwald," Alfred interrupted. "We can tend to these issues soon enough. But, look there...I see one of the stockades directly ahead of us. Your flock awaits."

The palisade holding the Viking prisoners came into view as they rounded a curve in the road. A number of Saxons stood vigil over the stockade, while the remainder of soldiers milled around the tents that had been erected to house the army.

"There are two similar enclosures on the other side of the river, but the main concentration of hostages is here," Penda said.

"And who's in charge of these men?" Alfred asked.

"Osric of Hampshire."

Alfred's brow creased for a fleeting second, but he said nothing. By now they were in full view of the camp, prompting shouts of recognition from the Saxons, who ran toward the column and closed their ranks around the king and his retinue. Osric appeared from among them and strode forward, bowing low from the waist as the riding party came to a halt.

"It's a good day for Wessex, my Lord. I'm proud to serve you."

Alfred raised his hand in recognition and addressed the assemblage in a clear voice. "You've all served bravely to defend our land. Wessex is indebted to you. Rejoice, men of England, for we have won! The Vikings will be leaving Exeter soon and returning to Mercia within the month."

A great cheer rose from the ranks. Alfred allowed the celebration to continue for a few moments before again raising his hand. "We'll maintain the fyrd until the Vikings have left, at which time we'll provide them with an escort through Wessex. When that's all accomplished, you may return to your lands in time for the harvest."

More shouts of approval rang out from the soldiers. Alfred turned to Osric and addressed him. "These prisoners are now our hostages. When the Vikings have reached Mercia, they'll all be set free and returned to Guthrum. Now, let me see to the Danes, for I would speak to them."

Osric motioned in the direction of the stockade. He walked alongside Alfred's horse, followed by the mounted Penda and Grimwald. The remainder of the party stayed behind at a respectful distance to observe the proceedings. Alfred examined the Vikings within the enclosure as they pressed up against the palisade; aware that it was the King of Wessex approaching, they probed him with curious, questioning eyes. As he moved closer, his attention was suddenly drawn to a prisoner hanging limply from a solitary pole outside the stockade. The man's back was stained with dried blood.

Alfred's face clouded over. "What's the meaning of this, Osric?"

"Sire," the ealdorman blurted, "a fight broke out between this man and another heathen, a ruse to draw us into confusion. When we entered the enclosure, the rest of them turned on us and tried to escape." His jaw grew firm. "I made an example of him."

Alfred dismounted slowly and walked over to the pole. It was only then that Sigli raised his head, laboring to take in air through his parched, swollen lips. His distended body hung at a grotesque angle, no longer able to hold itself erect, every fiber in his shoulders cracking from the strain. He would die if left unattended, that was clear enough. The king was struck immediately by a strange light in Sigli's eyes, a flickering flame that glowed and ebbed. He had seen it before in the eyes of men on the threshold of death. He pursed his lips and spoke in the Viking language.

"What have you done to deserve such treatment?"

"If hunger is a crime," came the faint reply, "then I'm guilty. I sought to eat my bread alone in peace...and I ended up fighting for my life." He sucked in a breath of air and continued with great effort. "I'm here in England against my will, and now I'm going to die because of it."

Alfred turned immediately to one of the guards. "Bring me some water. You others...cut this man down." Two Saxons ran over to cut the thongs binding Sigli to the post, taking care to support him from falling.

"Sire, the heathen lies!" Osric objected. "You can't permit this!"

"I'll be the judge of that," Alfred snapped. He stared at the ealdorman in a way that made Osric bite his lip. Then he took a deep breath and spoke in a measured voice.

"I'm familiar with your loss. I've not forgotten the murder of your brother and his family at the hands of the Danes. Even though many years have passed, your wounds are still open. But as a leader of men you must not allow your personal feelings to dictate your policy. This," he murmured, motioning to Sigli, "is much too severe."

"My Lord....these men are cutthroats, common murderers."

"We're Christians, Osric, men of the cross. No amount of atrocities can justify this treatment. And we must be diplomats as well...whether you take to it or not, we must live with these people. They've been on English soil all of our lifetimes. And they'll likely be here after we're gone, no matter what we do."

A soldier ran over to them carrying a bowl of water. Alfred took it and approached Sigli, who struggled to stay erect on trembling legs while supported by the two Saxons. The king lifted the vessel to the prisoner's lips. Sigli attacked it with long, breathless gulps, the excess water running down his chin and dimpling the earth beneath him. He gasped for air between swallows, looking gratefully at Alfred after he had consumed the entire contents of the bowl.

"Thank you," he whispered. "You're...you're Alfred?"

"Yes, I'm Alfred...but don't thank me. Christian or Viking, you're a man, and shall be treated as such. I don't allow anyone in my realm to be beaten like a common animal."

He nodded with a stiff smile, a diplomat's grin, and mounted his horse, turning to address the men watching from within the stockade in their native tongue.

"Vikings!" he shouted, his hand raised high above his head. "You're my hostages! You'll be fed and cared for until Guthrum has returned to Mercia! There's no need to attempt an escape; freedom awaits you soon. Let no man live in fear. Any Saxon who crosses my orders shall answer directly to me!" He paused for effect, bringing his hand down hard. "I have spoken!"

He reined his horse away from the enclosure and rejoined Penda and Grimwald, turning in the process to address Osric privately. "I don't question your loyalty, only your methods," he said quietly. "I value you and know that you'll be of greater service still. Carry on."

With a wave of his hand Alfred spurred his horse to a gallop. His companions fell in behind him and they all sped off down the road, leaving in their wake a cacophony of shouts from the Saxon faithful.

*   *   *   *   *

Summer faded from the land as the days of humid heat gave way to the first chill of autumn, and the crispness of the harvest season hovered in the evening air. The lush green of the English landscape began to soften, the forests no longer bursting in the bloom of the temperate months. Here and there an oak leaf had already turned, its dying skin transformed into a speckled palette of red and gold.

The change of seasons was marked by movement among the rival forces. The bulk of Guthrum's army had evacuated Exeter after the first few weeks, observing the agreement struck with Alfred to leave the city in stages so that no single contingent of Vikings would be large enough to threaten its Saxon escort. The invaders were funneled northward into Mercia over a period of weeks, an orderly process that encountered no setbacks. The Vikings had lost much of their aggressiveness during the course of the long siege and were clearly ready to retire from action for the upcoming winter. The Saxons, on their part, were all too happy to comply, looking forward to the disbanding of the fyrd and the chance to head for home in time to help with the harvest.

The Viking hostages remained imprisoned within the stockade at the center of the Saxon camp as an ongoing procession of their countrymen filed out of Exeter every few days to begin the journey to Mercia. Osric heeded Alfred's orders, grudgingly providing for the needs of the hostages, feeding them well and caring for those who were sick or nursing wounds. Sigli's strength grew as each day passed. His hands took the longest to heal, but within two weeks he was able to grasp objects without pain. He kept to himself during this time, preferring to avoid the company of the others, who left him alone and asked nothing of him. He made up his mind to wait out his captivity with patience until the hostages were transported to Mercia, from where he was determined to make his way into Northumbria and to the shores of the Great Sea. From there he would eventually find his way back to Halfsfiord.

What he would do once he returned was another matter. Without ships or men he stood little chance against Sidroc, but it occurred to him that if he could penetrate the man's guard for even a moment, if he had but the wink of an eye, he could slip a dagger into the Malevolent One's ribs. He spent many a night lying on his back, staring up at the stars and imagining his revenge, and the anticipation of the moment kept his spirits up. Mimir had been right. Hate, all by itself, could keep a man alive.

The weeks passed quickly. The first wave of autumn gave way to a blaze of color throughout the lands to the north. All the men in the camp grew restless, struggling with their impatience as they waited for orders to move. Their hopes were finally rewarded during the second week of October, when the last members of the Viking garrison in Exeter evacuated the town, heading off for Mercia with a Saxon escort. And then the hostages passed through the gate of the stockade and took their places in the column that started off slowly toward the north, away from Exeter and the coast. The march comprised the remainder of the Saxon army, a group of over a thousand soldiers that included Alfred and his chief companions. The Saxons already released from service had spread like seeds in the wind, dispersing in all directions for their homes across southern England.

By the third night of the journey the marchers reached the edge of Selwood forest, a thick belt of wooded country west of Devon and the marsh country of Athelney, bordering Somerset to the north. As the Saxons pitched camp, the word circulated that Alfred wanted to devote the following day to one of the court's favorite pastimes, the hunt, to be followed by an evening of celebration. The forests of Selwood were a favorite habitat of many varieties of beasts, chief among them that most sought after and prestigious of game, the wild boar.

The boar was the fiercest animal on the island of England, a bristling fury weighing several hundred pounds and capable of goring a man to death with its tusks. The danger of tracking down such quarry added an element of excitement that was missing from all the other comparatively benign forms of the hunt common to the Saxons. To corner a boar and finish it off took a special kind of courage, leading to much discussion and wagering among the elite as they sat around their fires that evening and anticipated who among them would carry the day. The prize was the hideous, glaring head of the beast, a delicacy that would grace the table of the victor.

The king and his companions normally would have employed hounds to run down their prey, but no dogs had been brought to Exeter, where the fate of a kingdom hung in the balance. Not wishing to miss the opportunity to celebrate their rising fortunes in the wake of the Viking evacuation, the Saxons latched onto a worthy substitute. All of the hostages—and many of the lesser Saxons—would be used as beaters, stationed at intervals around the forest and instructed to advance while making noise and flailing at the underbrush, so as to force the prey toward the hunters. The royal party agreed to hunt only the boar, leaving the sport of the other beasts in the forest to the men who would trail behind the main party. The day would continue until a boar had been caught and killed.

There was great activity among the tents as dawn arrived and the Saxons readied themselves for action, breakfasting quickly and organizing their ranks. Osric and his guards broke the Viking prisoners into groups of a half dozen men and rode off to various spots stationed along the edge of the wood. The ealdorman made a point of assigning himself to Sigli's group, for he had not forgotten the loss of face he had incurred, and he still harbored a grudge.

But Sigli had behaved himself as his wounds healed. He had regained most of his strength and felt whole for the first time since his wedding day, his body once again revealing the rippling muscles that were just beginning to reach maturity as he entered into full manhood. If Osric wanted to make things difficult for him, it did not matter; he knew that after what he had been through there was a light ahead waiting to illuminate his patience. And he had not forgotten Alfred's kindness in rescuing him from the brink of destruction. Something in the king's manner, brief as the encounter had been, had inspired a confidence in him.

That was not the case with his comrades. As they shuffled behind the mounted Osric and along the line of trees that marked the edge of the forest, one among them dropped back until he walked alongside Sigli.

"How goes it, big fellow?" the man offered cautiously. When Sigli failed to reply, he continued to speak. "See here, I don't care if you keep to yourself or not. None of us wants to wait any longer." He motioned to the other four men in the party. "When we get into the woods, we're going to take the Saxon."

"Why endanger yourselves?" Sigli answered, continuing to look forward. "We'll all be in Mercia within the week. If you fail, it will be the end of you."

"None of us believes we'll ever see Mercia. There's no guarantee. For all you know, we'll be put to death, or kept as slaves by the Christians."

"I've had enough trouble. I'll take my chances."

"With him?" the Viking wondered. "He nearly beat you to death. I'd think you'd welcome a chance at him. Besides...he's got the keys to free us from these irons. They're behind his saddle." He glanced down at his shackled legs for a moment. "Are you with us, or not?"

"I won't stop you, if that's what you mean," Sigli answered, looking at the man for the first time. "But it's not my affair. You'll have enough trouble in this country as it is."

"We'll make it to Mercia, one way or another. With you, or without you."

"Come on, now. Break it up!" Osric yelled at them in the Saxon tongue.

They fell silent and the column trudged on. Within a few hundred yards, Osric commanded the party to halt. The men stood on the edge of the wood poised for the hunt to begin, their leg irons allowing enough movement for the task while restricting them enough to prevent escape. Sigli looked back toward the camp, noticing other groups similar to his own, each stationed several hundred yards apart.

The sound of horns from among the main tents signaled the beginning of the hunt. Sigli watched as a mounted party issued forth from the camp, King Alfred at its head, amid great shouting and waving of banners. Within moments the riders disappeared around a curve in the forest, their hoof beats echoing in the morning air as they headed for a point where they could double back toward the beaters.

Osric gestured to the prisoners, instructing them through his actions to break off a switch from among the tree branches to use for making noise. Following the example set by the next group down the line, the men spread apart along the edge of the forest so that some ten yards separated each of them. Osric took up a position on horseback directly behind the line and motioned toward the wood.

The forest was well into the seasonal transition that would eventually leave each tree bare, stripped down until the first buds would appear again in the spring.

Although the ground was covered with fallen leaves, there was still a fair amount of foliage on the trees, which blazed red and gold during this, the peak of autumn. They could hear the efforts of the beaters to each side as the long line of men moved deeper into the forest.

Within twenty minutes the changing terrain and the difficulty of coordinating such a mass movement over wooded country separated the groups. While still within earshot, the other beaters had broken off from the original line. As Sigli's group advanced through a grove of oaks along a low ridge, one of the Vikings off to his right slipped on the damp earth and, grabbing at his ankle, winced in pain. Osric rode over to the hostage, ducking to avoid several low branches in his path.

"On your feet, man!" he gestured with his sword. "Get moving!"

The Viking ringleader who had spoken to Sigli earlier moved toward Osric and his fallen comrade from a position nearby, gesturing animatedly in protest. Osric turned toward him, at which instant the Viking lying on the ground sprang up quickly, leaving his feet and pinning Osric's arms to his sides. The ringleader reached the struggle before Osric could break free and bring his weapon to bear, and together the two hostages dragged their jailer from his saddle and onto the ground. A brief scuffle ensued, but within seconds the other Vikings had joined in, overcoming Osric and preventing him from crying out.

The ringleader grabbed Osric's sword and raised it over his head, preparing to administer the death blow. But as he started to bring his arm forward, he was apprehended from behind.

"Don't kill him! There's no purpose to it," Sigli cautioned, holding the man's arm. "If you do, and we're caught, it will mean our lives. Tie him to a tree and gag him, and we can be out of here."

"That's ridiculous," snarled the leader. "Whether we kill him or not, our lives are forfeit if we're captured. Besides, no man will take me alive again."

"But you don't know that for sure, do you?" Sigli asked, turning to address the others. "Nobody will find us here in the next few moments. Why take chances?"

"He might be right," another man agreed. "It will only take a second."

They could hear beaters off to either side, but the noise was faint enough to suggest that a fair distance separated them from discovery. One of the men grabbed the keys hanging from Osric's saddle and released himself from his leg irons, tending to the others until they were all free to go about the business of binding the Saxon and chaining his leg to a large oak. His mouth was stuffed with cloth torn from his leggings, and then the Vikings gathered up his weapons and divided them among themselves. Sigli appropriated a short-handled axe from Osric's saddlebag, a small but sturdy bludgeon that was sharpened to a fine edge.

The leader bounded up onto Osric's horse. "Since the idea was mine, I claim the steed. Our best bet is to separate and take our own chances." With that he sped off into the trees in the direction from which they had come.

The others spread out after him and disappeared quickly, until only Sigli remained with Osric. He walked slowly toward the bound Saxon, tapping the head of the axe in his hand and watching Osric's eyes grow wide. But all he did was smile disdainfully, and then he lowered the axe to his side. Osric let out a deep breath and started as if to speak through the cloth that gagged him, but Sigli turned away and disappeared into the forest.

He ran in the opposite direction taken by the other Vikings, penetrating deeper into the wood in the hope that he could get past the line of beaters and through the gap created by the absence of his group. Once past the other hostages, it would be a simple manner to outrun the advancing line, after which his challenge would be to make his way past the hunting party and off into the depths of the forest. He raced along, covering ground as quickly as he could while taking care to avoid discovery.

Within moments he heard the sound of beaters ahead. He veered to his left and down into a ravine, running laterally behind the advancing line until the sounds disappeared, and then he cut back into the forest again, hoping he had penetrated the gap.

His guess paid off. The sounds of the beaters rustled faintly off to each side as he rushed forward through the autumn trees. Soon the echoes receded behind him and he knew that he was through the line. He redoubled his efforts and sped along, his legs and lungs feeling whole, caught up in the euphoria of freedom. The yellow and red leaves exploded around him in the bright sunlight as he ran, his feet shuffling through the loose foliage covering the forest floor, his hand grasping the axe tightly.

Ahead and to his left, he heard the first sounds of the hunting horns. He angled to the right to avoid their path, trotting along for several minutes until he reached the top of a low ridge. As he started down the incline, his footing gave way in the soft earth, sending him skidding on his back some ten feet into a ditch behind a brace of trees and underbrush. Although unhurt, his lungs ached from the long run, and he paused in the ditch, breathing heavily and training his ears to catch the least sign of movement.

The forest was eerily quiet. Directly ahead, the trees funneled into a small vale, at the rear of which rose a steep wall of chalky earth. The silence in the wood was broken only by Sigli's rhythmic breathing as he struggled for air. He heard the blast of horns again, still somewhat distant; a few moments more and he would be rested enough to continue his flight.

And then he heard a muffled sound in the underbrush on the opposite side of the clearing. He crouched low in the ditch behind an oak. There was a crackling of branches and a rustling of leaves, closer now, followed by a distinct rhythm of approaching hoof beats. And then a large beast scampered into the clearing, its feet moving rapidly in a manner that belied the animal's stumpy appearance. It was a wild boar. An arrow protruded from the beast's flank, causing it to grunt in pain as it pulled up in front of the chalk wall blocking its flight. It wheeled around so that Sigli was able to study its features.

His eyes met with a sight from Hel. Weighing considerably more than a man, the boar's flanks rippled with muscles that shone through its coat of short, mottled hair. Its ears bristled atop two ferocious eyes that glistened above a long snout. A pair of short tusks protruded from its mouth, and it pawed at the ground nervously with its cloven hooves, wheezing with short, labored breaths.

As he observed the beast, a horse and rider thundered into the edge of the clearing some twenty-five yards from the boar, only a few paces from his hiding place in the ditch. It was Alfred himself, alone in the hunt. A cry of pleasure escaped the king's lips as he reached quickly into his quiver and fitted an arrow to his bow. He balanced himself in the saddle as his nervous mount paced back and forth before the wounded boar, which scurried back and forth, trapped along the chalk wall.

Alfred began to draw the arrow back, taking careful aim. Suddenly, he gasped and bent over at the waist as a sharp pain knifed through his stomach. His horse, unnerved by the boar, bucked high in the air and sent him flying from the saddle, and he crashed to the earth as the frightened animal took flight into the wood. He scrambled instinctively to rise to his feet, but to his dismay he discovered that his leg had become wedged among the branches of a fallen tree that lay in the wet clearing. He struggled in vain to free himself, still clutching at his stomach with one hand while looking anxiously at the boar as it stood poised at the opposite edge of the clearing.

The animal had watched him without moving. And now it began to paw at the earth, never taking its eyes off the king. He stared back into the furious face of the beast, and as it leaned into its charge from some twenty-five yards away, he knew he was a dead man.

Suddenly a figure leaped over him from seemingly nowhere and planted itself squarely. Alfred looked up to see the muscular back of a large man, and between the man's legs the onrushing beast, now almost upon them. The figure drew his arm back, revealing the head of an axe that glinted in the afternoon sun. His arm shot forward at the last conceivable instant, releasing the axe toward the head of the grunting beast while the man dived to the side.

The weapon caught the boar directly between the eyes, burying itself in the animal's skull at the same moment the beast's tusks shot upward, their thrust meeting nothing but air. The boar's legs collapsed and it crashed to the earth, falling a mere arm's length from Alfred, who raised his hands up instinctively to protect himself.

He need not have bothered. The boar shuddered on the ground and rolled over dead.

Alfred lifted himself up to a sitting position. The pain in his stomach had disappeared, overcome by a sense of wonder. His eyes shifted back and forth from the boar to Sigli, who now crouched over the fallen animal and inspected his handiwork. A smile flickered at the corners of the young Viking's mouth as he looked at the king, unable to conceal his pride.

"Fantastic!" Alfred spluttered. "Never have I seen such a magnificent feat!"

Remembering the language barrier, he shifted into the Viking tongue. "Please...help me out of this," he said, struggling to extract his leg from beneath the fallen trunk.

Sigli put his back to the oak, lifting it enough so that Alfred could free himself. The king got to his feet gingerly, testing his ankle.

"A close call, but no worse for the wear," he grinned. "But this..! This has won the day!" He bent down over the boar. "Good God in heaven, you buried the entire axe head!"

"I've had some practice with the weapon, Sire," Sigli bowed.

"I should say so," the king nodded admiringly. They could now hear the sound of the hunting horns blaring through the wood, accompanied by the hoof beats of approaching riders. He laughed. "The others will be jealous. All this effort, and now they must concede the head of the beast to a Viking!"

Several riders rumbled through the underbrush and into the clearing. At their head was Penda of Devon, and the puzzled expression that crossed over his features was soon repeated in the faces of the others.

"My Lord!" he exclaimed. "Are you hurt? We came upon your horse, and feared the worst!" He dismounted and approached as Alfred and Sigli remained standing over the boar.

"I'm fine, but you would have been picking me up in pieces were it not for this man," said Alfred, putting his hand on Sigli's shoulder. "It was he who killed the beast while I was trapped and helpless on the ground. I had it at my mercy, but I suffered another of my attacks and was unhorsed."

"Hunt or no hunt, you should never have separated yourself from us! What would happen to Wessex if you were to die? Think of it!"

"Even a king must sometimes be free, Penda. But fortune has smiled upon me. How this man came to be here, I don't know, but he saved my life."

Penda studied Sigli for a moment. "Unless my memory fails me," he addressed the king, "this is the same man you rescued from the whipping post that first day after the storm, when we inspected the hostages."

"So it is!" Alfred exclaimed, looking at Sigli more closely. He shifted into the Viking tongue again. "It seems we've met before, my friend."

"We have. I owe you my life."

"After today," Alfred smiled, "I would suspect the scales have balanced out."

"The question remains," Penda interrupted, addressing Alfred again, "what was he doing alone in the wood, armed and unfettered?"

Before anyone in the hunting party could answer, several riders burst into view, coming from the direction of the camp. "My Lord!" one of them exclaimed, breathless from exertion. "There's been a disturbance! One of the hostage parties rose up and attempted to escape. We caught several of them in the forest, but they tried to resist, forcing us to kill them. The others must have gotten away."

"Well, this must be one of them!" Penda exclaimed angrily. "Seize him!"

"Wait!"

The cry came from a voice from the edge of the clearing. All heads swiveled around as a figure dismounted from his perch behind a mounted Saxon guard, a shackle dangling from one of his legs. It was Osric.

"I can explain everything," he said, moving toward Alfred. "Sire, I've failed you again. I was overcome by the hostages in my party, who stripped me of my weapons and tied me to a tree. They would have killed me, were it not for this man," he said, motioning to Sigli. "I'm ashamed, my Lord, for allowing this to happen. As penance I won't remove this iron from my leg until I've acquitted myself with honor and proved myself worthy again. But this man shouldn't be treated harshly, of that I'm sure."

"Well," Alfred smiled, "it seems the heathen has done a full day's worth of good deeds. One thing, though, is certain: he who kills the boar shall feast on its head. There shall be no need for chains tonight, not at my fire. Saxons, I give you a man of mettle. All hail the mighty boar slayer!"

The men raised their weapons in a victory salute. Unbowed by the attention, Sigli put his foot on the boar's head, bracing against it as he pulled the axe from the beast's skull. He raised the bloody weapon on high for all to see, shaking it proudly above his head, a child of fortune in a foreign land.

CHAPTER IV: The Court Of The Golden Dragon

"Build me straight, O worthy Master!
Staunch and strong, a goodly vessel
That shall laugh at all disaster,
And with wave and whirlwind wrestle!"
—Longfellow, The Building Of A Ship

Sounds of merriment echoed throughout the Saxon camp that evening, borne aloft by a breeze rustling through the leaves that still remained on the October trees. A line of campfires stretched along the shadow of Selwood forest like a string of pearls, as the soldiers gathered together to raise their cups into the chill of the evening and toast their good fortune. The mead melted away the ordeals of the long campaign that had separated them from their homes and loved ones. For now, their battles were behind them.

Even the Viking hostages were in good spirits. Except for the mutineers who had fought to the death to avoid capture, there had not been any casualties during the day's encounter, and Alfred had restored order to the Viking ranks without levying the expected punishment. He even granted the prisoners a few barrels of mead for the evening, an unprecedented show of faith that amazed even the most skeptical among them.

The hunt had been generous, yielding plentiful game to the Saxons who had trailed the royal party as it penetrated the wood in search of the boar. The beast now twisted on a spit suspended over the main fire near Alfred's tent, blood dripping from its skinned flanks and spattering with a hiss into the flames. The king sat perched on a nearby stool, surrounded by his companions; among them was Sigli, who squatted on his haunches a few feet away, balancing a cup of mead in his hands and staring vacantly into the fire.

Penda stepped through the ranks clustered on the edge of the darkness and moved over to Alfred, waiting until the king finished draining his goblet before speaking.

"I've questioned the hostages, but I haven't learned much," he leaned forward and whispered. "None of them knows the man."

"Did you speak to anyone who took part in the mutiny?"

"Yes. By all accounts, the Viking was an unwilling participant."

Alfred stroked his chin. "The matter seems very strange."

"I'd advise caution. He's a heathen, no matter what happened today. He could be a spy."

"And what do we have worth discovering, Penda? Why would a man risk his life when freedom was within his grasp?" Alfred stared into the fire as a servant refilled his goblet. He took a long draught and stood to face the soldiers.

"Men of Wessex!" he shouted. "The beast of Selwood roasting before us is the work of a brave man, one who placed his body over mine when death was near! I give you a warrior...a hero! All drink to the Viking, Sigli!"

The soldiers raised their cups. Sigli scrambled to his feet, feeling the blood rush to his face as he bowed awkwardly to acknowledge their tribute. Alfred turned toward him, calling to him in the Viking tongue.

"Join at my side, friend. You shall feast on the boar's head."

The king's easy manner laid to rest any discomfort the young Viking may have had. Within seconds the steaming head of the boar was placed before them on a platter. Sigli pounced on the meat, cutting into the boar's neck and stuffing the food into his mouth.

"Your appetite seems to match your skill with the axe," Alfred smiled.

"It's been a long time since I've tasted something so sweet."

"Look there, between the eyes. As clean a blow as could be struck. You pierced his brain." The king looked at Sigli carefully. "Tell me...where did you learn how to handle a weapon like that?"

"In Halfsfiord, my home. Every boy is trained in weaponry as soon as he's old enough to pick up a sword. I learned the axe from a true master, one of my father's best warriors. By the time I was fifteen, my skill was greater than his."

"Your father is a man of holdings?"

"Was. He's dead, and my family with him."

"And how did all this happen?"

Sigli stared off into the night. "I try not to think of it, but the memory consumes me." His eyes hardened. "There's a man whose face I cannot blot out...they call him Sidroc, the Malevolent One. A fouler creature never walked the face of the earth. His treachery brought down my father's house, and with it one of the finest fleets on the northern sea. By the gods, I swear I won't rest until I've returned to Halfsfiord and claimed what's mine!"

"So, meanwhile, you decided to join Ubba's fleet to plunder England...?"

Sigli's eyes flashed. "There's no love in my heart for Ubba!"

"Then why did you come here?"

"I was taken captive at sea and forced to row with the fleet. When they found me out, I was bound to my oar. Only the storm, by Odin's will, saved me."

"And England as well," Alfred murmured. "Providence was with us."

"Ubba was a fool," Sigli smirked. "The Viking ships aren't built to forge into such a wind. He slit his own throat by sailing against the storm."

"You speak as though you've had some experience."

Sigli laughed. "I was born on the deck of a dragon ship. I've probably spent more time at sea in my life than on land, and when I wasn't on a voyage, I worked with my father's best shipbuilders. But that's not unusual for a Viking."

Alfred raised his eyebrows. "It's an art of which we in England know little. The Vikings own the seas."

"It's true. The sea is our livelihood. But a ship's design can always be improved, which is something I've long thought about. I had ideas I intended to try out in time, but now, well..." His words trailed off into the darkness.

"Time plays tricks on us all," Alfred mused. "The Lord God works in many ways not understood by men. Put your faith in him, and you'll be rewarded."

Sigli took a deep breath. "Your god may answer your prayers, but I entrust my fate to Odin."

"I don't propose to debate religion with you now," Alfred said, waving his hand. "But you must realize you won't endear yourself to anyone here with such talk."

"I'm not trying to win friends here. My mission lies before me."

"So you'll join your countrymen in Mercia?"

"I don't want to become further entangled in the web of Guthrum's power, or anyone else's." He paused, picking at the meat before him. "I don't know where I'll go next, but one thing is certain: Sidroc's head is mine."

Alfred raised his eyebrows. "Considering your straits, it might be wise for you to deliberate further before taking any action. Meanwhile, I propose that you accompany me to my estate at Chippenham, where I'll be spending the Yule season with my family and companions. Winter approaches...you'll need a rest before resuming your quest."

Sigli cleared his throat. "I'm honored, my Lord, but..."

"You've endured much, and you need time to think. Besides, there's much to be learned, and your culture and people intrigue me. I won't take no for an answer."

"Well, then, it appears to be settled," Sigli grinned. "But I may not be able to stay the whole winter."

"I'm not asking you to make any promises you can't keep," Alfred said. "Just come with me, and matters will take care of themselves. You may even find the court of Wessex to your liking." He offered his hand. "Are we agreed?"

"You're a generous man," Sigli nodded, grasping the king's hand. "I accept."

"Excellent!" Alfred smiled. "I think you'll find it to be a wise decision. But, let's not bother any more with stories of loss and revenge. Tonight we celebrate the hunt. Minstrel!" he yelled, summoning a man with a harp to sit down near the fire. "Play us a song of heroes!"

The scop bowed and took up a position near the king's feet. He plucked a few notes on the harp, gaining the full attention of the soldiers gathered around the fire. Clearing his throat, he began to sing in a sweet tenor, and within moments every man was mesmerized.

Every man but one. Alfred's mind was far away, although the expression on his face did not show it. He was skilled at the art of feigning attention while contemplating other matters, a discipline that he often found necessary given the demands of the throne. A tangle of thoughts raced through his mind as he pondered the possibilities, always the possibilities. Falling before the boar suddenly seemed to have been a very propitious thing to do.

*   *   *   *   *

Ealswith looked down into the face of her infant son as he suckled contentedly at her breast. She sat there in the day room at Chippenham, where she could see beyond the city walls, where the countryside faded into the forest.

The baby Aethelweard was an angel, a blessing sent by God in answer to her prayers. She had given up hope of ever again bearing a child after several miscarriages, but now she could rest contented, secure in the knowledge that she had given Alfred another potential heir. After having produced two sons and three daughters, she knew that her child-bearing days were over. She had done her part.

The queen loved all of her children the most during infancy, when they were totally dependent on her. It was the most fulfilling thing she could expect out of life, carrying out her duty to raise strong and healthy children who would grow to adulthood and carry on the legacy of the royal family. But the older they grew, the less influence she wielded over them. The boys would mature into men, warriors and statesmen who would never again look to her for comfort as they pursued power, that most seductive of temptations. It was something from which she could not protect them. Her daughters, meanwhile, would flower into womanhood, their bloodline marking them as attractive candidates for marriages that would secure political alliances. That was the most any woman, even one of high birth, could hope for.

Not that it was bad. Ealswith felt privileged to be the Queen of Wessex, a rank in keeping with the status of her family. She traced her lineage back through generations of the Mercian royal house, from which she had emerged as the third of three daughters. Each of the sisters had been blessed with beauty, but in that respect Fortune had been the most kind to Ealswith. Her charms attracted many suitors, but one in particular—young Alfred, son of King Ethelwulf of Wessex— had been the most ardent in his efforts to gain her hand. She even fell in love with him, a happy circumstance compared to the plight of many women who were given away by their fathers and destined to live their lives committed to a union of convenience. Genteel women of manners adjusted to their men under such conditions. For Ealswith, it had come naturally, without the slightest prodding from her father to marry into the House of Wessex.

That had been ten years ago. Three years after the wedding, Alfred ascended to the throne when the last of his four elder brothers died. As the youngest member of his family, he had overcome long odds to become king, and he lived at first under a cloud, knowing that there was no one to take his place should misfortune befall him. A king could never have too many heirs, and for that reason Ealswith was pleased to have borne her husband a second son. If Alfred's family could run through five brothers to retain the throne, what were the prospects for keeping the crown in the hands of her children? Between disease and war the life expectancy of a Saxon was far too short, and she knew that a number of Alfred's nephews, the sons of his dead brothers, waited hopefully in the wings.

She prayed to the Virgin Mary every night to preserve her husband's health, to ease the sharp stomach pains that had afflicted him since he had been a youth. The demon that lurked within his stomach would not give him peace. It could strike him at any time. None of the mendicants in England were able to help him, nor could any of them tell if the malady would worsen over time. Alfred entrusted himself to God and kept on. His eldest son Edward was still only nine years old, and it would take time before the boy would be old enough to assume the throne if his father died.

But at least the king could rest easy about the prospects of his son someday ruling Wessex with a capable hand. Edward was a born warrior, a budding leader who had managed on more than one occasion to sneak away with Alfred's fyrd when it headed off to battle. Each time the king sent his young son home, admonishing him to learn patience and his lessons, but it was clear from the twinkle in his eye that he approved of the boy's boldness. No amount of badgering could induce Edward to study his Latin, and although Alfred often despaired that the prince was unlikely to become a learned man, he recognized the importance of raising a warrior. Statesmanship and diplomacy would follow in their own time.

Ealswith shifted her body to shield the baby's face from the rays of the afternoon sun streaming in through the window. Her chambers at Chippenham were comfortable, but far from lavish. The court of Wessex maintained a number of estates spread throughout the countryside, and while the seat at Winchester was at once the largest and most centrally located, it shared its powers with the other sites. None of the manor houses could be considered a permanent residence. Perhaps because of that, each was decorated in a style that paled in comparison to the royal estates on the continent, for Alfred was not a man who placed importance on the trappings of wealth.

The queen looked out the window and beyond the town wall, fixing her eyes on the ceorls as they trudged in from the fields after the day's labors. Chippenham was laid out like most other towns spread across the southern English countryside. The main house was situated amidst a cluster of buildings comprised of smaller lodgings, stables, granaries and several spacious courtyards. This central core of structures was surrounded by a wall that varied in height, ranging from ten to twenty-five feet above the ground. In places where the wall was low or built of wood instead of stone, a ditch in front of it bristled with sharpened stakes to repel attackers.

Beyond the walls were the simple cottages where the ceorls lived, spread out over the fields that stretched to the distant forest. These free men and women supported themselves by farming small plots of land granted to them in return for their allegiance to the local lord and a percentage of their crop. They served in Alfred's fyrd when the state required an army to take the field, for while their day-to-day loyalty was pledged to their local ealdorman, their ultimate allegiance was reserved for the King of Wessex. Such respect for a central monarch was rare in Europe; once proud nations had splintered into scores of small fiefdoms dependent on local rule for survival.

Sounds of a disturbance emanated from the corridor outside her room, echoing up the winding stairway that led down to the ground floor of the building. The main house was a rarity in that age, rising a full two stories above the ground and built almost entirely of stone. Ealswith could hear laughter mingled with the patter of little feet on the stone steps, and in the next moment her daughters Aethelgifu and Aelfthryth burst into the room, followed closely by Edward. The boy put his back to the thick wooden door and swung it shut with a jarring thud.

"Children! Don't wake the baby!"

"Sshh, mother!" Edward whispered. "Don't give us away!"

The two girls, six and four, giggled as they stood off to the side holding hands. Their features were like those of their mother—round and soft, instead of the harsher, thinner lines of Alfred's blood that burst forth in Edward. The boy looked like the king, with the same penetrating eyes and an aquiline nose that, even at his young age, had begun to assert itself.

"Edward, what are you doing?" Ealswith demanded, sitting upright and shifting the baby in her arms.

"We're hiding from Aethelfled! Please, Mother, let us slip under your bed. And don't tell her where we are!"

"Very well." The queen smiled and shook her head. "I assume your lessons are completed for the day?"

"Yes, yes!" Edward answered impatiently, already busy in the act of shoving his giggling sisters under the bed on the far side of the room.

He had barely wriggled beneath the folds of the heavy bedspread that draped down onto the floor when the door to the room opened. It was Aethelfled, the first of Alfred and Ealswith's children, older than Edward by only thirteen months. The first two children had come quickly to the royal couple, before the wars kept Alfred away.

"Why, good afternoon, my sweet," the queen smiled, pretending to look surprised. "Where's your brother? And your sisters? I thought you'd be playing with them..."

Aethelfled's eyes darted around the room. "I was sure they'd be here! Edward can't fool me...he isn't clever enough to do that."

Ealswith suppressed a smile. It was like her firstborn to have said such a thing; there burned inside the girl a competitive fire equal to that of a king's champion. Ealswith could sense Edward squirming under the bed, but no noise escaped him.

"Perhaps they went down the hall. I heard footsteps, you know."

"If you say so," Aethelfled answered, unconvinced.

The queen could feel her daughter's eyes on her, and she raised her own slowly to meet them. What she saw were two large, green pools of light, almond-like in shape, almost exotic for a Saxon woman. Even at the girl's tender age, more than a year before she would experience the first blood of womanhood, it was clear that she would be a beauty. Aethelfled had inherited the best of her mother's features, embracing all of the softness without sacrificing any of the strength. Her rich auburn hair set off skin that could only be described as alabaster, so fine was its hue. And the equal mixture of her father's heritage did not render her face harsh, but framed her features with high cheekbones and proud, striking lines. It was a face worthy of a future queen, one that men would be willing to die for.

It made Ealswith once again reflect on the misfortune that her firstborn had not been a male child. Edward's protestations aside, it was Aethelfled who ran the rest of the family. She could ride a horse as well as any boy, and even Edward had to admit he faced a struggle whenever he played at war games with his sister. It was ironic to Ealswith that one so obviously destined to turn the heads of young men disdained many of the practices reserved for the fairer sex. There was still much work that had to be done to enlighten the girl concerning the responsibilities of womanhood.

"Your father should be home very soon now," Ealswith said off-handedly, changing the subject and looking out across the fields. "You must be very anxious to see him. Why don't you go find your brother and sisters? And please send in Magda when you leave. I want her to look after the baby."

Aethelfled reached out and pinched her infant brother playfully. "As you say, Mother, but Edward came by here. I can smell him...he always smells like the stables, you know." She retreated toward the door. "I'll find him and the little sisters, with or without your help!"

Ealswith looked over her shoulder and back toward the bed as Aethelfled left the room. A corner of the spread began to move, until Edward's face appeared impishly down by one of the posts. He crawled forward and emerged from the hiding place, unable to conceal his chagrin.

"Do I really always smell like the stables, Mother?"

"Of course not, Edward. She said that just to irritate you. I think she knew you were under the bed."

"Mother, little sister wet herself," said Aethelgifu, dragging Aelfthryth out into the room."

"That's what happens when you get excited like that!" Ealswith exclaimed, rising to her feet. She looked up as her chief handmaiden entered the room. "Magda, take the baby, and I'll see to the girls. It's all I can do to keep these little demons under control!"

They were interrupted by a series of shouts coming from outside the building. Ealswith, her arms now free of the baby Aethelweard, stepped to the window. She could see several people in the courtyard below pointing with alarm up toward the wall that extended away and to her left. She thrust her head out the window to see what was causing their cries, and in the next instant her heart stopped in her throat.

"Mother of God! Help us! Magda, come quickly!"

There, some ten feet away, Aethelfled stood perched precariously on a stone ledge only a few inches wide. The girl hugged the rough stone wall, holding on tenaciously, her fingertips jammed into a crevice on the face. "Don't come any closer!" the queen shrieked, looking down at the ground some twenty-five feet below them. "Go back the way you came!"

"I can't! The ledge behind me gave way!"

Ealswith could see where the stone facing had broken away from the building. Its remains lay scattered in pieces on the cobblestones below, a preview of the fate awaiting her daughter should the girl lose her grip and fall. Magda and the children crowded in next to the queen at the window, where they could see a group of people gathered below. Some of the onlookers had positioned themselves underneath Aethelfled, ready to attempt to catch her if she tumbled from her perch.

"I'll get her, Mother!" cried Edward, attempting to mount the ledge.

"Stay where you are, Edward!" Ealswith turned back to the castle wall and surveyed the ledge remaining between her and Aethelfled. It narrowed as it approached the window, but there seemed to be little choice in the matter.

"Come toward me, darling...but be careful," she urged, trying to keep her voice from trembling.

Aethelfled began to inch her way along the stone face, feeling blindly for handholds, not daring to pull her face back from the wall to watch her step. The people in the courtyard below shifted uneasily, while Ealswith strained at the window. Suddenly the section of the ledge upon which Aethelfled stood gave way. The crowd screamed. The girl scrambled wildly for a handhold on the wall as she fell, catching herself at the last instant on a stone spur that protruded from the face just below the ledge. Those in the courtyard scattered as the stones bounced harmlessly on the ground, closing ranks again to form a protective cushion underneath the princess.

Ealswith nearly fainted from shock, but she regained her composure and leaned forward through the window. Before she could advise her daughter, the girl shifted her hands and daringly reached out to grab another outcropping of stone that ran along the wall and under the window. Ever so carefully, she pulled herself along it.

"Be careful!" Ealswith gasped.

Aethelfled kept on, inching closer, determination fixed on her face. She was only a few feet away from safety, but she could feel her arms beginning to tire as she drew within range of the window. Suddenly the fingers on one hand tightened into a cramp; she fought to retain her grip, but it was no use. At the precise instant she let go and began to fall, two arms swept down from above like the wings of Providence, grabbing her wrists. Ealswith and Magda gathered her up and dragged her into the safety of the inner chamber as a few more stones broke loose from the wall and plunged earthward.

They sat there, stunned, until everyone finally realized all was well. Ealswith's panic turned suddenly to anger. "What were you doing??!!"

"I wanted to surprise you all," Aethelfled said without a trace of emotion. "I knew you were all in here, and I didn't want to be made the fool."

Suddenly, her mood changed as she remembered the events leading up to the incident. She looked defiantly at her mother. "You lied to me!"

"We were playing a game!" Ealswith admonished her. "A silly game!" She bit her lip, softening her tone. "Darling, I would never truly lie to you, you know that...but, what you did...you could have been killed! Oh, Virgin Mother!"

"I've played on the walls before!" Aethelfled protested. "And I've seen Edward do far worse." She made a mischievous face at her brother. "Do you remember the time you hung upside down from the guard tower, Edward?"

"That's enough, all of you!" Ealswith ordered. "What you did today was stupid. You didn't think when you climbed out on the wall. You must learn better judgement...do you understand me?" She looked hard at Aethelfled, and then at each of her children in turn, making sure the point was made. "Very well, then. See that it doesn't happen again."

They were interrupted by the sound of footsteps in the hallway. A page entered through the open door, unable to contain his excitement.

"My Lady, Lord Alfred and his men...they ride down from the hill!"

All eyes swung back to the window, through which they could see a body of men issuing forth from the forest. Edward burst away from them and through the door, followed by the remainder of the royal family, and within minutes they had made their way across a spacious courtyard to the main gate. There atop the wall stood Thurstan, chief steward of the estate at Chippenham.

"My Lady, please...come join me," he said, motioning to the crude ladder that led up to the parapet. One by one they ascended, until the whole family stood along the top of the wall.

"Look at them! Look at the army!" cried Edward.

By now the main body of troops had issued from the forest, and a long line of men stretched out along the road that led through the fields of oats and barley to the gates of Chippenham.

"Look at all those men walking closely together behind the main column," Ealswith said. "Are they prisoners?"

"Heathens!" exclaimed Edward. "Viking heathens!"

"There's father!" Aethelfled shouted. They could all see Alfred, riding straight-backed astride his favorite white charger.

"Thurstan," wondered the queen, "I can make out Penda, and Anarad...but who is the tall blond man riding just behind my husband?"

Thurstan squinted to make out the unfamiliar figure. "I don't know...but we'll find out soon enough." He yelled to a group of men assembled below. "Open the gates!"

The vanguard of the column paraded through a tunnel of ceorls lining both sides of the road. Fueled by the crowd, the king and his companions broke into a gallop, the banners at the head of the column whipping in the wind to reveal the golden dragon, the symbol of sovereignty in Wessex. Alfred held his hand above him as he rode toward the walled estate, the victor home at last from the battlefield. He was greeted by a trumpet fanfare from one of the watchtowers, and he thundered through the open gates as the rest of the army broke off to form camp in a large field adjacent to the walls.

Ealswith and the children hurried down from their vantage point on the parapets. Upon seeing his family, Alfred quickly reined in his horse and dismounted, opening his arms to receive their embraces.

"It will be a warmer winter with you by the hearth, my Lord," Ealswith said, addressing her husband in the formal tone she reserved for their public conversations. She turned to the king's companions as they sat mounted on their horses, bowing modestly to each of them until her eyes came to Sigli. "I don't believe I've had the honor, Sir."

"Please allow me to introduce Sigli," Alfred said. "He doesn't understand our language yet, so I'm afraid your conversation will be limited for now. But we'll be seeing much of him."

"Is he our prisoner, Father?" Edward blurted out.

Alfred laughed. "On the contrary, Edward, he holds me captive, of sorts. This brave man saved my life at a considerable risk to his own. He comes to Chippenham as my honored guest."

Sigli bowed politely from his saddle. Ealswith curtsied formally, without expression, but Edward's features lit up like those of an excited puppy. He approached and circled Sigli's horse, scrutinizing the Viking carefully from every angle. Ealswith watched her son with amusement, filled with admiration for his youthful enthusiasm, until a sixth sense made her glance over at Aethelfled. Her daughter stood in rapt attention of the handsome young Norseman, with a look on her face that Ealswith recognized instantly as she remembered her own impressionable youth.

Her daughter was becoming a woman after all. And although the queen could hardly approve of any attention lavished on a heathen, she could at least agree with Aethelfled's aesthetics; the Viking, after all, was a fine specimen. She contented herself with the thought that it would be years before she and Alfred would have to direct the affections of the young princess, hopefully toward a more suitable target.

"My Lord," said Thurstan, "you must be quite tired after your journey."

"Yes, it's time to put war aside for a while. Make sure the men outside are fed and provided for. Most of them will be leaving tomorrow to escort the Viking hostages into Mercia."

"Very well, my Lord. And Grimwald should be arriving within a few days. I sent to Winchester for him, as you requested."

"Excellent!" Alfred exclaimed. "Meanwhile, on to the house. Tonight I'll sleep in a real bed for the first time in weeks. And," he added with a wry smile, looking at the blushing Ealswith, "I shall not sleep alone."

*   *   *   *   *

"It will be magnificent. In time, Winchester will rival the great cities of the continent."

Grimwald licked the chicken grease from his fingers and reached for the wine goblet on the table in front of him. He was accustomed to eating well, and it pleased him that Alfred had seen to it that such a fine meal had been prepared for him and Werferth, the Bishop of Worcester, upon their arrival in Chippenham. Now that the Vikings had returned to Mercia and points north, the proud bishop breathed easier again; surely this delectable repast was a prelude to even better tidings.

"Do you think the king is ready to commit to us now?" asked Werferth, picking lightly at his meat. The Bishop of Worcester's eating habits matched his demeanor; he was a careful, ascetic man, plain of face and not prone to impulse. Thirty years of age and rail-thin, he was an interesting contrast to the volatile Grimwald, who hovered on the far side of obesity as he approached the half-century mark in years.

"Alfred's ready," Grimwald insisted. "Why else would he have summoned us?"

"Perhaps. But I don't think all the help should go to Winchester."

"Nonsense, man. Winchester *is* Wessex. And I," Grimwald smirked, "am Winchester."

Werferth sniffed privately at Grimwald's conceit but deferred to his superior. "Worcester is worthy of Alfred's help. I need an extension onto the monastery for the Benedictines. Don't forget the Chronicles...they're one of the king's priorities."

"I'm well aware of the work you're doing, my good Werferth, but you're still too close to danger for Alfred to devote his energies to Worcester." Grimwald smiled in satisfaction. "You sit on the wrong bank of the Severn, my friend. The Vikings could devour you as easily as I swallow this lovely chicken."

"The Vikings have left us alone. There's nothing in Worcester of value to them."

"Other than your heads. Don't underestimate the heathens. Remember what happened in East Anglia, the massacre some years ago?"

Werferth ignored him. "They've retreated to Mercia now, am I correct?"

Grimwald washed down a mouthful of chicken. "Retreat is putting it rather strongly. The situation in Exeter was a stalemate; the Vikings were paid to leave. And don't think that we were the only ones to receive hostages—it's not common knowledge, but we had to give them some of our people, too."

"Then what makes you so sure Alfred will be funding us?"

"He promised us, and he's known to keep his word."

"We'll not be kept wondering much longer," Werferth replied, looking over Grimwald's shoulder. "Unless I'm much mistaken, our summons has come."

Grimwald turned as a young page arrived at their table in one corner of the nearly deserted hall. The boy bowed in respect.

"Good day, Your Grace. Has the fowl been cooked to your satisfaction?"

"Yes, quite. Would that my own cooks were as skilled."

"I'll pass on your compliments," the page said. "Meanwhile, if you're finished, the king is ready to receive you."

Grimwald struggled to raise his corpulent body from the low bench. He rose to his full height and picked the remnants of chicken off his expensive robe. "We're more than ready to see the king. It's been a long journey."

The page nodded, turning crisply on his heel and motioning for them to follow. He led them across the stone floor of the hall and down a long corridor that opened onto the newer wing of the main house at Chippenham. They passed a series of tall, arched windows that looked out over the countryside, where the River Avon meandered through the fields. It was a bright, cloudless afternoon, and the monks could see the fields stretching for miles through the bare trees, whose spiny, leafless tips probed the sky like so many curving daggers in the waning late November sunlight. The days were short now, and all of England drew in upon itself, preparing for the onset of winter.

They walked all the way to the end of the hall and stopped in front of the last door on the left, where two armed men stood vigil outside the king's day room. The page moved to one side and motioned with an outstretched hand toward the half-opened door set in an alcove leading into the room. The two monks stepped past him and entered the chamber, where several large tables in the center of the floor were filled with charts and scrolls. Off to one side, an exquisitely carved map of the known world leaned against a wall, waiting to be properly mounted. Next to it there stood a sizable stack of bound volumes, rare works in Latin ranging from Augustine to Pope Gregory, Boethius to the Venerable Bede.

At the far end of the room, Alfred stood with his back to them in front of a large window, hunched in thought over a row of candles placed at equal distances along a narrow table. He was earnestly engaged in the act of measuring one of the burning columns, and he did not look up as the monks crossed the room and stood waiting at the end of the table.

"One more second, please...Ah, yes! There it is!"

Alfred finished his calculations and looked up at them, his thin features beaming. Grimwald and Werferth bowed.

"You probably think me mad, but there's reason behind this apparent lunacy," the king smiled. "You see, I'm attempting to develop an efficient means of telling time. A king must schedule his time wisely; there simply aren't enough hours in the day to attend to all the duties of the House of Wessex. And being away these many months hasn't improved the status of my domestic concerns.

"So, I had an idea while camped outside Exeter," he continued, warming to the subject. "It seemed to me that if one were able to determine precisely how quickly a candle of fixed diameter burned down, one could then tell time. As soon as I can calculate this rate accurately, then it will be a simple matter of fashioning candles of a length that will burn entirely over the course of, say, an hour. Light a candle for each hour of the day, and you'll be able to precisely monitor your activities, never allowing any one of them to either exceed or fall short of the time you chose to allot to it."

"Brilliant, my Lord!" Werferth exclaimed. He was a serious scholar, and his enthusiasm for this show of mettle was genuine.

"Thank you, Werferth," the king smiled, "but I'm encountering problems. Unfortunately, the least bit of air current in the room alters the burning pattern, rendering the system useless. Considering the drafty nature of virtually every building in England, this obstacle is of some concern."

"Pardon my impertinence, Sire," Grimwald volunteered, "but you only need to develop a means to shield the candles from the elements."

"Precisely!" Alfred exclaimed. "I've already commissioned an artisan to build a series of small glass cases to do just that. But meanwhile, I must continue to exist without the aid of this wonderful tool."

He stepped away from the table and moved toward the window, where several elegant, comfortable chairs were positioned to take advantage of the pleasing view across the river. He motioned toward them.

"Please...join me."

"Allow me to say, Sire, how much it pleases me to serve a king who holds learning in such high esteem as you do," Grimwald purred sweetly as the two monks moved to the window and sat down. "I think I speak for all the clergy when I say that we have high hopes for the future."

"Hopes that I'm determined to see turn into reality," Alfred nodded. "Knowledge is what separates men from the beasts of the field. But we've been remiss in cultivating it, occupied as we are countering threats from abroad."

"All the more reason to devote a concerted effort of support to the Church," Grimwald avowed. "She is our pillar of strength."

"I remain, as always, a devout Christian and a believer in the Faith," Alfred replied, leaning forward and looking earnestly at the two monks. "And I swear to you, by God and on my family honor, that I'll do everything in my power to support you, to support learning, and to further the aims of the Church." He rose to his feet and stared out the window.

A smile of anticipation spread across Grimwald's face. "The new abbey in Winchester, my Lord? You're prepared to give the order to begin work?"

Alfred turned toward him forcefully. "No, Grimwald, I'm not." He raised his hand to cut off the protest already welling in the bishop's throat. "Not yet, anyway." He began to pace back and forth. "I know I've promised this and other things to you. And so you shall have them...soon. But right now, I have other, more pressing needs."

"Such as?"

"Ships. I need a navy, and I need to begin building one immediately."

"This is preposterous, my Lord!" Grimwald exploded angrily, slapping his knee through the richly embroidered tunic covering his lap.

"Preposterous, you say?" Alfred shot back, his eyes narrowing. He thrust his finger in the air. "Is it preposterous when our enemies surround us on all sides, when the entire length of our coastline remains unprotected?"

He clenched his fists in disgust. "Were it not for the storm sent by God in His wisdom, all of Wessex would lay at the feet of the Vikings. It was a miracle that so much of their fleet was destroyed. A miracle for England, and for Christendom."

"But the Vikings have withdrawn, my Lord," Werferth protested mildly. "Their strength has been sapped."

"And so has ours, to even a greater degree. I've been unable to keep the fyrd intact; all the men have gone home. We're virtually defenseless right now."

"My Lord forgets," Grimwald gestured, "that winter is almost upon us. And never, during the nearly twenty years since the heathens first began to threaten Wessex aggressively, have they mounted any kind of offensive during the winter months."

"What you say is true, Grimwald," Alfred nodded, sitting down again, "but it doesn't set my mind at ease. I can't rest as long as we remain vulnerable. My thoughts lean toward developing a system of defense—a rotating fyrd that remains strong year-round, a series of fortresses stationed at strategic points of entry along the coastline and, above all, a strong navy."

"And who will build these ships?"

"I've found a man, someone I'm convinced has the knowledge to succeed at this undertaking. And that," he said with an air of finality, "is the reason I've summoned you today."

Grimwald and Werferth looked uneasily at each other. The Bishop of Worcester spoke first. "Forgive me, Sire, but...we know nothing of building ships."

Alfred waved his hand impatiently. "Of course not! That's not what I mean. You're here because I need your help in tutoring this man I've found. He's foreign-born, and doesn't speak our language."

Grimwald raised his eyebrows. "And where might this savior of Christendom be from?"

Alfred hesitated briefly. "He's a Viking."

"Lord God in heaven, save us!" Grimwald threw his arms in the air. "You've gone mad, surely!" He leaped to his feet, the veins in his neck bulging.

"Do you really think that a heathen can be trusted? You seek to bring a devil into our midst, after all that's happened?"

"I've made up my mind."

Grimwald stared sharply at Alfred, barely able to suppress his anger, biting his lip so as not to show further disrespect. "This man...is he the same one I've heard about, the one involved in the incident with the boar?"

"The same."

"And why has he agreed to do this?"

"He hasn't yet...but he will." Alfred leaned forward, elbows on knees, and clasped his chin in his hands. "That's why, Werferth, I propose that you stay with me for a few months. I want you to teach him our language, and enough of our ways so that he'll be capable of managing the men and money I intend to supply him with."

"What makes you so sure he'll consent?" Grimwald protested. "Why should he work for an honest wage when he can steal it? He's a Viking, and has no interest in our welfare. He can't be trusted!"

"Leave that to me, Grimwald. I requested you be here simply so you could be informed of the decision. Werferth is the one I'm asking to take on these responsibilities."

"Sire," stuttered Werferth, "while I don't really approve of such a bold scheme, I'm your faithful servant. But I personally couldn't be of much help. I can understand some of the Danish tongue, but I can't speak it. It would be extremely difficult for me to carry out your wishes."

Alfred frowned. "I thought you were fluent. But surely, you must know someone who speaks the heathen tongue?"

"Yes, there's one among the Benedictines in Worcester, a Mercian by birth named Plegmund. He's young, bright and ambitious. But he's very adept at Latin translation, and it would be a blow for the Chronicles to lose him."

"I understand, Werferth. But I'll need him only for a few months. By that time the Viking should be sufficiently versed to venture among the Saxons on his own."

"If the Saxons accept him," Grimwald smirked. "After all, he *is* a heathen."

"We must do whatever we can to pave the way for him," said Alfred. "It won't be easy."

"It will be impossible, unless he accepts the Christian faith. I, for one, won't trust him unless he agrees to be baptized. The heathens cling to their pagan deities; if his heart is true to our enemies and their gods, he won't submit."

"I agree, my Lord," Werferth added. "If, in the eyes of Wessex, the man is held to be a Christian, then you have a chance to gain the support you'll need in this venture. But I doubt many would approve if he refused baptism; I certainly would question his motives. And I would never willingly agree to spend time instructing a man who would not take to the Faith in good conscience."

Alfred stroked his chin. "Your point is well-made. I've been keeping him in quarters away from the main hall for fear of what some of the Saxons might think. We need support, and you certainly have my allegiance as far as the Faith is concerned."

He slapped his knee decisively. "I'll accede to your wishes; he'll be baptized. Send for this Plegmund right now—I'll lean on his counsel in dealing with the Viking, for he'll come to know the man well during the course of instruction."

He stood up abruptly. "Now, I must apologize to you both. I'm called upon to arbitrate a dispute that has arisen between two of my most loyal thanes, and the time," he smiled and nodded toward the burning candles on the table, "keeps me captive."

The two monks rose hastily and bowed. "My Lord," Grimwald ventured politely, "I pray you're not making a mistake."

"I pray all the time," Alfred replied, "and sometimes, even, my prayers are actually answered."

He turned so that his body faced toward the door, ending the audience. The monks bowed again and shuffled across the room, exiting through the alcove and into the hall. Grimwald shouldered his way brusquely past two men waiting to enter the king's chambers and stormed down the corridor as Werferth, scurrying behind him, struggled to keep up.

"What do you think, Grimwald?" the Bishop of Worcester smirked. "The king's song is not so sweet a melody as we would have hoped for."

"Just do as you're bid!" came the terse, whispered reply. "But I won't forget this...this treason! I'll watch the Viking, and I'll watch Alfred, no matter how long it takes." Grimwald's fleshy face tightened, and his eyes grew hard. "And God help him who first stumbles..."

*   *   *   *   *

The wood pigeon soared effortlessly over the English countryside, its wings propelling it through the crisp afternoon air. The sun was already low on the southwestern horizon, its slanting rays struggling to break through the haze that had settled over the fields earlier in the day. The perpetual grayness of winter was poised to lower its full weight on the land, but for now the sun fought back gallantly, holding onto the last remnants of autumn before its retreat and inevitable surrender.

The pigeon could see for many miles in all directions. The countryside undulated gently, its large patches of woodlands rendered transparent by the absence of leaves on the trees to protect the forest floor from scrutiny from above. The pigeon knew instinctively that to venture near men spelled trouble, so it kept well aloft after spotting a riding party on the crest of a low hill that suddenly came into view. But where men gathered, often times there was food, and the small-billed, plump bird was finding sustenance harder to come by each day. It flew toward the party, not venturing too close, alert to the presence of anything edible the men might leave behind. Seeing nothing on the first pass, it circled around and prepared to hover overhead, and as it did so it missed a quick flurry of activity on the ground as an object climbed rapidly into the sky.

The wood pigeon passed over the party a second time. It could see the men on horseback pointing up into the sky, but there were no weapons in their hands. It flew directly overhead, closer now, and scrutinized the area with a keen eye. There was nothing of interest to be found. It could see its shadow passing over the ground, and it watched the dark silhouette respond to its movements as it turned eastward and resumed its journey. It was then that a second shadow appeared, closing in rapidly on the shadow of the pigeon as it glided over the ground. Alarmed, the wood dove picked up its pace, but the second shadow closed like lightning. The pigeon only had enough time to arch its back in a reflexive action before its neck was snapped, broken instantly by the impact of a pair of talons belonging to a large peregrine falcon at the kill point of its power dive.

The bird fell lifelessly to the earth, bouncing on the hard ground. The falcon followed close behind, landing nearby and strutting proudly in a circle around the fallen dove, the bell attached to its leg tinkling in merry incongruity as it waited in a death watch for the approach of its masters. Soon a half dozen riders arrived at the spot.

"Nicely done, Sire, and on the first pass!" exclaimed Thurstan, the steward of Chippenham, as he dismounted and stood over the pigeon.

"There's not a finer bird in all of Wessex," Alfred smiled, joining the steward on the ground.

"A clean kill. The neck's shattered."

"A telling performance, my sweet," Alfred cooed to the falcon. He extended his leather-bound wrist to the bird, which latched onto it with its talons and did not protest when the king placed a hood over its eyes.

"I think that's enough for today. One must not abuse such a treasure. What do you think, Sigli?" Alfred asked, switching into the Danish tongue and turning toward the Viking, who remained mounted with the rest of the party.

"Very impressive. I haven't seen a bird quite like that before."

"Nor will you for a while," Alfred replied. "For the most part, our birds of prey are not equal to their cousins on the continent; the Franks, in particular, are expert trainers. But I would pit this treasure against the best they have to offer." He stroked the bird lovingly. "It took me many months to train her. She was captured as a wild hawk, and they're the hardest to control. But if you can master them, they're the most efficient hunters in the sky, and I like that. No wasted motion—all focused energy, muscle and purpose. Would that men were designed as well."

He extended his arm to Thurstan, who was also outfitted to accommodate the falcon on his wrist. "Remember when she would only respond to me?" Alfred sighed as the hawk switched arms. "Those days are gone now, and probably just as well. Reward her, Thurstan, and take the other men and ride off for a short distance. We'll join you soon...for now, I wish to speak to the Viking alone."

Thurstan nodded and retired with the bird, mounting his horse and motioning to the other Saxons in the party. They rode off down the hill without looking back.

"Now, Sigli...I'd like a word with you," Alfred said.

"I didn't think you asked me here merely for the pleasure of the hunt."

"You're straightforward. I like that."

"I know of no other way, my Lord. My people are direct."

"Yes, I'm aware of that...painfully so," said the king, clearing his throat. "I'm also aware of your knowledge of ships, and wish to speak more to you about them."

"It doesn't surprise me. Every time we meet, you have something to say on the subject."

"Precisely." Alfred reached into his saddlebag and withdrew a rolled parchment. "I have here some drawings I've been working on. I don't pretend to be a shipbuilder, but I've spent some time on the design of various buildings and fortresses in Wessex. It's something I wish to do more of in the future." He strode over to a large, flat rock perched atop the hill on which they stood, from where they could look out over the countryside.

"I thought the open air would provide better ideas than the stuffiness of my day room," said the king. "On an afternoon such as this, one must take advantage of the sun." He spread the parchment out over the rock as Sigli looked on. "Now, my ideas need to be refined, but here's the essence: I propose to build a ship with a keel some thirty meters or more in length—almost twice that of the most common vessels now sailing. Is it possible?"

Sigli's eyes pored over the drawings. It was obvious from first glance that the king had good instincts and a considerable feel for the engineering entailed in shipbuilding.

"The biggest problem is strength," Sigli finally replied. "Everything becomes magnified, including all the struts that run off the keel. First of all, you need to find the right timber. The keel must be one piece, and be able to stand considerable strain. It would be an interesting experiment."

"But...is it possible?"

Sigli stroked his chin. "Yes, I think so. But such a vessel would not be as maneuverable as the Viking longboats, and far less flexible in the open sea. A storm like the one off Exeter last summer would create problems for such a ship."

"That's not important," Alfred said, waving his hand to dismiss the notion. "I would, of course, build smaller ships to fulfill the needs of which you speak. But these larger vessels would have their purpose. They'd be able to transport twice as many fighting men as the Viking ships, and would be in no danger if they hugged the coastline and patrolled the many rivers that flow through our land. I see them as floating fortresses, armed for defense, blockade work and things like that."

"A very interesting idea."

"I'm glad you like it. I want you to build it for me."

Sigli's eyes grew wide. "And why me?"

Alfred smiled. "I think you know more about this work than anyone else in my kingdom. And I trust you."

"That's a lot of faith to put in a man you hardly know."

"You saved my life, didn't you? How many other Vikings would have done so?"

Sigli stood up and moved away from the rock, looking out across the countryside. "I'm flattered, my Lord, but...I have other things weighing on my mind. I don't think I can help you."

Alfred moved alongside and touched Sigli's arm. "We can help each other in this, believe me. I need a navy. You can build it for me."

"You don't understand. It would take years to build a fleet...at least enough of one to suit your purposes. The Vikings are always building. Always."

"I can supply you with the resources you'll need."

"That's not the problem." Sigli let out his breath slowly. "I can't afford to wait years. I have a man's head on my back, and I won't rest until my revenge is complete."

Alfred stood up and cocked his head to one side. "Ah, yes...Sidroc. I've not forgotten him. Where is he now?"

"I don't know. I must find him."

"And how will you do that, without any visible...means?"

Sigli's face tightened. "If I have to stow away on every raider crossing the Great Sea, I will."

Alfred began to pace slowly around the rock. "And once you find him...what will you do then?" he wondered, looking up into the air and tossing his words out as offhandedly as a child disposing of the petals on a daisy. "Will you ride into his armed camp on a white horse, and challenge him to a duel of honor? You'll both have seconds, of course...Or, will your assembled army that you'll have sworn to allegiance over the next few months meet Sidroc on the battlefield?"

Sigli's face grew crimson. "Don't taunt me like that."

Alfred wheeled and faced him. "Face the facts, man. You're no more prepared to deal with Sidroc than that dove was with my prize falcon. You're hopelessly overmatched, and until you do something to change that situation, you're lost."

The words stung. Sigli started to protest but held his tongue, knowing full well that what Alfred had said was painfully true.

"But although you're at a disadvantage, it's not an irreconcilable one," the king continued, relaxing and beginning to pace slowly around the rock again. "Look around you," he pointed. "Everything you see is mine. I'm the King of Wessex, and my seven-year reign is already longer than that of any of my four brothers who preceded me to the throne. In these dark days, with East Anglia and Northumbria settled by the Danes, and with Mercia now under Viking control, only Wessex remains. I'm the sole hope of the Saxons."

He turned and faced Sigli. "And right now, I'm your only chance as well. Listen to me: I'll give you men and money to build me a navy. Whatever you need, you'll have it. Give me three to five years, and I'll reward you handsomely."

Sigli's eyebrows arched. "How?"

"For every five ships you build, one shall be yours," Alfred replied. "The more you build for me, the more for you. And when you leave my service and set off to seek your prey, I'll match every one of your ships with one of my own, fully manned, which you may use for three months. I'll give you enough money to hire crews for your own vessels. And you'll have full privileges in all my harbors, as though you were a member of my navy. In short, I'll treat you as a valued and important ally—provided you swear your ultimate allegiance to me."

Sigli bowed crisply at the waist. "You're a generous man, my Lord. It's much to offer a man—an enemy, even."

"You're no enemy of mine. I do this because I have a feeling about you, and I trust my instincts. Honor that trust, and you'll not lack for anything."

"I understand, Sire."

"Then you'll do it?"

After hesitating for a brief moment, Sigli smiled. "I will."

"Excellent!" Alfred broke into a broad grin and reached across the rock that separated the two men, extending his arm to the Viking. "We'll both profit from this, I guarantee it. But," he cautioned, growing serious, "before I forget, there's one more thing. You must learn our language, of course. I've already sent for a scholar to come to Chippenham and tutor you over the winter months. You should be ready by spring."

"I think that's a good idea."

"Yes, but...you see, there's more. As you can understand, the political waters run deep. A great deal of animosity exists in Wessex toward the Vikings—from the common people, from the nobles and from the clergy."

"I've noticed that, my Lord. It's quite obvious."

"Yes, it is. Because of that, it's vitally important that we do everything to assure that your transition into our culture is smooth and acceptable."

Sigli frowned. "I'm not sure what you mean."

The king looked directly into his eyes. "You must agree to be baptized into the Christian Faith."

Sigli's face clouded over, and he shook his head. "I'm sorry, my Lord. That's impossible."

"And why do you say that?"

"Because I'm a Viking. I worship the Viking gods...Odin and Thor, Tyr and Njord, and all the others who live in Asgard. Put yourself in my place...what would you do if I told you that you must forsake your Christian god, and worship mine?"

"That's not the issue," Alfred said curtly. "Although I'm a devout Christian, I don't propose to debate religion with you."

"But you would ask me to disavow my gods."

Alfred shook his head. "Sigli, I have a need—and so do you. What you choose to believe in your own mind is something I can't control, and wouldn't try to. If you must worship your gods, so be it. But you must at least go through a public baptism, to satisfy the appetites of the barking dogs that nip at my heels." He stared intently at the young Viking.

"Now...will you do it?"

Sigli kept his eyes averted as his mind raced, trying to make sense of the dilemma. After what seemed an eternity, he finally looked up at the king, the disappointment clearly etched on his face.

"I'm sorry, my Lord," he murmured. "I cannot."

Alfred slapped his leg angrily. "Be damned, then!"

He gathered up the drawings on the rock and stuffed them hastily in his saddlebag, planting his foot in the stirrup and swinging his body up onto his white charger. He glared down at Sigli, the muscles in his face tightening like soaked leather around the underlying bones.

"Don't be a fool, Viking!" he hissed. "The hand of a king has been extended to you, and you refuse it! That same hand may not be open the next time it's offered!"

Alfred's horse began to buck. He reined it in with the precision of an expert, never releasing Sigli from his cold stare. "I'll give you two more days to reconsider. If you don't change your mind, then you must leave my kingdom immediately!" He smirked in disdain. "I'm sure that Sidroc will quiver in fear when he hears you're coming!"

He wheeled the horse around and dug his heels into its flanks, sending the animal galloping down the hill toward the party of men that waited faithfully for him under a brace of trees a short distance away.

Sigli let out a long sigh as he watched the king recede into the gathering darkness. And then he stared off toward the west, where the dying sun hovered in the treetops, its reddish underbelly preparing to surrender to the night.

CHAPTER V: The Flight To Athelney

"And we are here as on a darkling plain,
Swept with confused alarms of struggle and flight,
Where ignorant armies clash by night."
—Matthew Arnold, Dover Beach

Therefore it seems better to me—if it seems so to you—that we should turn into language which we can all understand certain books that are the most necessary for all men to know, and accomplish this, as with God's help we may very easily do provided we have peace enough, so that all the free-born young men now in England who have the means to apply themselves to it, may be set to learning until the time that they can read English writings properly. Thereafter one may instruct in Latin those whom one wishes to teach further and wishes to advance to holy orders.

Plegmund mulled over the words on the parchment for perhaps the hundredth time. The document bore the seal of the king, written expressly to summon him to Chippenham. After receiving it, he had left the monastery at Worcester and headed south to ford the Severn, eagerly anticipating his future.

Alfred was right. Learning had declined so thoroughly across Christendom that there were few men who could understand the divine services in English, or translate even a single letter from Latin into the native tongue. And he, Plegmund, had been chosen by the most powerful man in Wessex to help lift the veil of ignorance from the land, a veil that had remained undisturbed for centuries.

He was determined to carry out the task to the best of his abilities: along with his command of English and Latin letters, he spoke the language of the Franks, several Germanic dialects, a smattering of Italian and—most important of all to the king—the coarse tongue of the barbarians.

It had been Plegmund's misfortune to be swept up by the Vikings at a tender age. He was one of the few survivors of a violent raid on his Mercian village that had left his parents dead, and with them the quiet life in the fields that would have been his destiny. And so he lived among the heathens for several years, enduring many hardships, before he was left behind abruptly by his captors during a sudden retreat into Northumbria. For a time he scratched out an existence alone, a forgotten orphan thrown to the wind. But finally his wanderings took him to the monastery at Worcester, where the monks gathered him in and washed the dirt from his tired feet. They gave him a bed, a home and a holy book—and with it all, a purpose in life.

They taught him to love learning in a way he had never loved anything before. Books became his salvation, an escape from the mundane, and he took to their wonder immediately. Long nights spent by candlelight straining to make out every precious word before him left their mark as surely as the wax that cascaded by the hour down onto the tabletop. Countless midnight vigils passed by, until now, at the age of twenty-two, he had already attained the classical learning of many wise men twice his age.

Plegmund rose from his studies to stir up the fire. The days were short, and winter had clamped its iron fist on the land. Christmas had come and gone, as had New Year's Day of 878. It was now but a week until the Feast of the Epiphany, the closing celebration of the Yule season, and all of England warmed itself at the January hearth, consoled by the knowledge that the Viking threat lay dormant following Alfred's successful negotiations at Exeter five months earlier.

Plegmund bent over at the waist and allowed the heat from the hearth to waft upward into his face. His features were delicate, smooth and white like the finest alabaster, and the fingers on his small hands moved with the quick, precise rhythm of a spider scurrying across a tabletop. He had a light manner about him that suggested consummate agility and finesse. Although he was a genteel man of the mind, he was hale enough to have survived the rigors of life among the Vikings, and his ascetic existence within the monastery was simple and not given to the excesses of luxury. He had few wants or earthly needs, and the life of a holy man suited him well.

He sighed and looked into the burning embers below; the Viking would be along soon for his daily lessons. Alfred certainly wanted the heathen brought into the Faith, that much was clear. The baptism was scheduled for the Feast of the Epiphany, and Plegmund was satisfied that his charge had been sufficiently versed in the tenets of Christianity to make the transition. Sigli was an apt pupil who had adapted well to the exercises of the previous two months, and he showed a remarkable aptitude for the language. But the Viking's religious convictions were another issue entirely. He questioned every aspect of the Church and raised issues that sometimes left the monk on the defensive.

A knock at the door interrupted Plegmund's thoughts. He turned away from the fire and sat down at the table as the door cracked open, revealing Sigli in the hallway outside.

"Come in. We have much work ahead of us."

"I don't have anything better to do with my time," Sigli grumbled, his English halting but correct. He sat down at the table. "I'm brought here to build ships, but you and King Alfred persist in turning me into a...a bookish man."

The monk ignored him. "Let's get to work. We have much ground to cover to prepare you for your entry into the Faith." He placed his small hands on the table, palms down. "Your language skills are fine for now; we can return to those lessons after the baptism next week. Today, I want to teach you about the Holy Trinity."

Sigli shifted uncomfortably in his seat.

"The Trinity is a concept at the heart of Christian belief," Plegmund began. "By this, we mean that there are three parts of the Godhead—the Father, the Son and the Holy Spirit. When we pray, we symbolically make the sign of the cross on our bodies, starting at the forehead and proceeding accordingly," he demonstrated, moving his hands across his body, "thus assigning ourselves to God. It's an act that reminds us that Jesus, the Son, died on the cross to absolve us from Original Sin."

"Original Sin? What's that?"

"When Adam and Eve disobeyed God and tasted of the fruit of the Tree of Knowledge, they put a stain on mankind and burdened us all with the chains of carnal desires. That's what baptism is all about...as an entry into the Faith, it absolves us of the Original Sin that every man and woman is born with."

Sigli's brow creased. "We're born in a state of...guilt?"

"Yes. That's correct."

"I don't understand. Am I to be held responsible for something I never did? What's so sinful about desire? Look at nature, Plegmund; watch the animals around us—they suffer no such burden of guilt, as you would have men do."

"But man was created in God's image, and is greater than the beasts of the field. Man must rise above his carnal nature to honor and worship God. When Adam and Eve disobeyed God the Father, He became angry and filled with wrath. He waited many generations before sending Jesus the Son to atone for our sins."

"I'm confused," Sigli murmured. "You tell me there's only one God, and then you speak of the Trinity. How is that any different from Odin, the All-Seeing, and his many sons and daughters? Is it not the same?"

"No, it's not. Your pagan gods are many, and embody the frailties of men. The one true God is perfection, with many different facets. The Father, the Son and the Holy Ghost are the most obvious."

"But if God created man in His own image, then is He not flawed? Or perhaps it's the other way around; perhaps man created God in *his* own image, eh?"

"That's blasphemy!"

"Every man believes what he chooses to. Every man has his own gods, whether they be Thor and Loki, Jesus and Satan."

"Such talk is sacrilege!"

"Plegmund," Sigli replied, ignoring him, "if your God plots the destinies of men, then mine is clear."

He rose from the table. "I've had enough. I'll be back tomorrow, and you can continue to try to convince me that your many gods are indeed one." With that he turned around abruptly and left the room, closing the door behind him.

Plegmund clenched his fists in anger and brought his arms above his head before moving to the fire to warm himself. For all of his bewilderment, he could not help but admire Sigli's strength of conviction, and with it, the surprising intelligence that was housed inside the heathen's magnificent physical frame. It was a body that only God could have created. A noble savage indeed, he thought. He had been called upon to save a soul from the fires of Hell, and it was his holy duty to see the mission through.

Thus renewed he stepped away from the hearth, fell to his knees and crossed himself. And then he began to pray.

*   *   *   *   *

The horseman spurred his mount up the muddy path leading to the top of the hill, steering clear of the icy patches that lingered on the land in spite of the afternoon sun. It was a cold and clear day, the first break in an otherwise uninterrupted stretch of forlorn weather that had settled in over the English countryside. The sun reflected off the headgear of the rider as the horse's cloudy breath evaporated into the air, soon to be followed by another thick and steamy blast of vapor as man and beast labored steadily up the hill.

At long last, they reached the summit. The man peered through the tangle of bare trees that dotted the hilltop, until his eyes finally rested on a pair of mounted figures. Their backs were turned toward him as they surveyed the open fields that stretched to the south. He drew closer until the sound of his hoof beats alerted the two men, who swung around to face him. They were Vikings.

"Lord Guthrum!" announced the rider, raising his hand in salute. "The men are ready to resume the march!"

"Then give the order." Guthrum's words cut sharply through the crisp air. "We have no time to lose. The weather may turn for the worse, and we can't afford any more delay."

"As you wish, Warlord." The rider bowed in his saddle and spun his mount around, digging his heels into the animal's flanks and propelling it down the hill.

"We won't need to stop until we reach Chippenham," said old Iglaf, Guthrum's chief advisor. "The men are well-fed, and should be strong."

"With any luck, we'll dine in Alfred's hall tonight," Guthrum nodded, permitting a thin smile to appear beneath his drooping moustache. His face was stern and proud, with high Nordic cheekbones that dropped off quickly into a series of chiseled lines that had been etched into his skin by the wind and the sun over the course of many years.

"The bad weather's covered our advance," Iglaf noted with satisfaction. "I haven't seen anything other than a few peasants since we left Mercia. The scouts report no movement on the roads."

"It appears that nothing short of Thor's thunderbolts can stop us now, " Guthrum replied. "There's no organized resistance to fear." He laughed. "Everyone knows, of course, that the Vikings never march during the winter..."

"A brilliant stroke. Now, if Ubba can muster his fleet in time to cut off the southwest, Alfred will be trapped."

"Ubba's of no concern to me right now. He failed us at Exeter, and if there's a way to let us down now, he'll find it. And don't underestimate Alfred."

"He's the glue that holds the Saxons together," Iglaf agreed. "But how much damage can one wolf do, stripped away from the pack? With Odin's will, we'll catch him…and Ubba shall be left the table scraps."

"It doesn't matter. There's enough for all of us to wet our beaks. Don't waste your time worrying."

Guthrum smiled broadly and started his horse down the incline, spreading his arms wide and gesturing to the horizon. "Let cold steel and hot blood decide the issue. It's a fine winter's day, and all of England lies at our feet."

*   *   *   *   *

"The music soothes me, Penda. God was wise when he gave man the gift of song."

Alfred leaned his head back and rested it against his chair in the center of the main hall at Chippenham as the sweet sounds of a lyre wafted across the room. Every table was filled for the evening meal to celebrate the Feast of the Epiphany, and every man and woman among them gave thanks for the gifts of food and shelter they all shared.

Alfred's table stood raised above the rest, filled with an array of culinary triumphs. To his right sat Penda and other assorted nobles of Wessex; to the left were members of the clergy, each of them jealously eyeing the seat of honor that Plegmund occupied at the king's side. The remainder of the royal family was placed at a table in front of the hearth, where Ealswith directed her maids-in-waiting as they struggled to control her children, who were allowed on this special night to stay up past the usual bedtime hour.

"Music has its place," grumbled Penda, "but I'll take a good fighting man any day."

Alfred smiled. "There's time enough for fighting, my friend. Let's enjoy these moments while we have them. A kingdom must cultivate its minds, as well as its sword arms. Don't you agree, Plegmund?"

"With all my heart, Sire. I'll do everything in my power to assure that our warriors are armed with faith and learning to go along with their skills on the battlefield."

"Teach them to pray, Plegmund, so that God may hear our call and give us the strength to overcome our enemies."

"Even God would be hard-pressed to aid us now," Penda smirked. "There aren't enough armed men in the countryside to stop a band of harlots."

Alfred nodded. "At least the season grants us some respite. Come the spring, we'll muster the fyrd." He forced a laugh and turned again to Plegmund. "But come...enough of bad thoughts. Tell me, how does your work proceed?"

"Very well, my Lord. I've completed the study of the Venerable Bede and his masterpiece, *Historia Ecclesiastica*. Would you like me to begin the translation?"

Alfred stroked his chin. "Soon enough. But for the next few weeks I still want you to concentrate on Sigli's lessons. Is he mastering our tongue?"

"Most assuredly so, my Lord. As you may have noticed firsthand, his skills are already excellent. He improves daily."

"And his acceptance of the Faith?"

"It is...sufficient, Sire. He's ready for tomorrow's ceremony."

"Good!" Alfred exclaimed, pounding the table. He turned to Penda. "It will please you to know that the Viking has absorbed his lessons well. He shall enter the Faith tomorrow."

"I'll believe that only when I see it," Penda scoffed, a sullen expression clouding over his face. "I choose to remain the skeptic. The Vikings can't be trusted. Try to tame one, and like a wild animal he'll bite you eventually."

He lifted his goblet to his lips, perching his brooding face over the vessel and staring vacantly into the thick mead. As he mulled over this unsatisfactory state of affairs, an ashen-faced manservant approached quickly from the shadows and bent over to whisper something in his ear.

Alfred remained engrossed in conversation with the monk. "Returning to Bede, Plegmund, I feel his grasp of both the secular and religious issues of the last century exhibits a singular understanding of life's many conflicts. It's of utmost importance that we bring it to the English language, every bit as vital as your ongoing work in the Chronicles. I think that..."

He was interrupted by Penda, who tugged urgently at his elbow. "Lord Alfred...please." The ealdorman's face was set in stone. "You must come with me immediately."

Alfred knew Penda well enough to recognize the urgency in his voice. The two men rose and exited into a dark corridor that led from the rear of the hall. They followed closely on the heels of the manservant, walking briskly down a long, cold hallway until they finally emerged into a dim chamber, where a young man paced back and forth nervously, beads of sweat flying from his hair with each agitated step. He turned toward them, and his eyes widened as he saw Alfred and Penda. He fell instantly to a knee.

"Quick, man! What is it?" Penda ordered.

The ceorl leaped to his feet. "Vikings! Hundreds, perhaps thousands of them, two hour's march away and bearing directly on Chippenham!"

"You're sure of that? Thousands, you say?"

"I swear it, my Lord! I lay hidden in the wood and watched them pass on the road from Mercia. I slipped away and rode straight here!"

"Damned be Guthrum!" Alfred slammed a fist into his open palm. He looked up toward the ceiling in despair as the dark news wrapped itself around his shoulders. "When will it end...? When, in the name of God, will these trials end?"

He turned to Penda with a pained expression on his face. "We must evacuate Chippenham immediately. Gather together whatever forces you have and ride out against the enemy. Don't endanger your force needlessly; the night will protect you. Just distract Guthrum and slow his advance. The rest of us will need time, and you can buy it for us."

He then turned to the manservant. "Go back into the hall and bid my wife to gather the children and retire to prepare for an immediate journey. Summon Plegmund as well; I want him to escort them southeast to take refuge with Grimwald in Winchester. And bid the Viking to join us also."

"My Lord?" questioned Penda, eyebrows raised.

"Don't debate with me now, Penda. He may be of help if we should encounter the enemy. I'll accompany my family tonight, after which I'll leave them and go into hiding. We'll be forced to live like common thieves in the wood."

He shook his head sadly and then looked at each man in the chamber, his eyes piercing the smoky torchlight. "These are dark times, but we must not despair. I won't desert Wessex, no matter what the cost! Let all men you encounter know this. Tell them I'll return!"

Penda kneeled and kissed the king's hand. Alfred removed it gently from the ealdorman's grasp and turned quickly toward the winding staircase that led out of the chamber, climbing with rapid steps to gather his family about him and flee, an exile, into the uncertain darkness.

*   *   *   *   *

The cart rumbled over the frozen earth, lurching with an uneven rhythm as it encountered every bruise that winter had left on the land. The night was clear and cold, and the stars glistened against the slate sky. A full moon hung on high, bathing the countryside in a soft, eerie half-light, so that the leafless trees seemed to fade in and out of vision like silent sentinels.

Aethelfled shivered, drawing her cloak close to her body as she stared over the edge of the cart at the retreating road. Although her muscles ached from the jostling, she was too proud to complain. She turned back toward the interior of the covered wagon, where she could make out the form of her mother cradling the baby Aethelweard protectively to her breast. The younger children, Aethelgifu and Aelfthryth, were asleep. Beyond them she could see the dark back of the driver, his silhouette framed by the moonlight shining through the open flap of the cart.

She could not sleep. A nervous energy coursed up her spine as she felt the tension around her, part fear, part anticipation. She found herself looking at Edward, who was hunched directly across from her at the opposite corner of the cart. He had bundled himself in several layers of robes, leaving only his face exposed to the moonlight. She watched his eyes as they scanned the countryside; one moment they were vacant, the next rapt with intensity, searching behind every dark object that crossed their view.

He feels it too, she thought. Her brother was always ready for adventure; now, more than ever, she could sense his energy and knew that he was afraid of nothing. He stiffened her resolve. They were, after all, the royal family; if they could not set a worthy example, how could they expect the common folk to bear up under their worldly troubles? Aethelfled already understood something of the burden of empire and the life she was destined to lead, a life that could never be like that of lesser-born people.

At least they were making good time. The recent cold weather had frozen the earth, providing a firm surface for the cart and its team of horses. A party of a dozen riders accompanied the royal family; a pair of men scouted several hundred yards ahead and to either side of the cart, while two others lagged behind as a rear guard. The remaining riders hovered around the wagon, Sigli and Alfred among them. The king was dressed in the rough manner of a fighting man, wearing a shabby, nondescript helmet and carrying an unmarked shield. He did not sit astride his customary white charger, preferring the anonymity of a dark, undistinguished mount. He kept pace with the others; they all rode as one, leaning forward on their horses. The lone incongruity in the group was Plegmund, whose stiffness in the saddle was painfully evident.

Suddenly a shout echoed from the rear, followed by the sound of horses. Ealswith sat up quickly, her sudden movement awakening the children, and all eyes strained to penetrate the darkness beyond the edge of a moonlit lea that spread out behind them. It was then that one of the rear guard came into view, kicking his horse frantically in a mad dash for the cart. In the next instant they were able to see the reason for his alarm: a band of riders followed behind him in close pursuit. Two of them gained rapidly on the Saxon, and when he reached a distance of some hundred and fifty yards away from the cart, they drew abreast of him.

They were Vikings.

A sword flashed in the moonlight, followed by a sickening thump as the blade landed squarely across the back of the Saxon and sent him pitching forward over his mount. A cry of triumph sprang from the Vikings. They raised their swords and axes and thundered on toward the cart, where the escort had drawn up its defense. One of the king's men grabbed the protective rear flap that had been resting on the roof of the cart and pulled it down in a rough motion, plunging the interior of the wagon into darkness. Aethelfled reached across her body and peeled the corner of the skin back, just in time to hear her father's familiar voice.

"Arrows!" The arms of the men raised in unison and they pulled back on their bowstrings. The Vikings drew closer, until they were a mere twenty yards away.

"Now!"

A thin, hissing noise pierced the air and three Vikings were abruptly torn backward from their mounts, as though an invisible hand had yanked them down. A fourth man tumbled to the ground as his horse crumbled under him; its eyes flashed as the reflection of an arrow imbedded in its throat gleamed in the moonlight. The Saxons threw down their bows and unsheathed their swords as the first wave of Vikings descended upon them.

Aethelfled winced as a Saxon a few yards to her left was knocked from his horse. He scrambled quickly to his feet, but not quickly enough; a mounted Viking wielding a battle-axe delivered a blow that caught him flush where the throat joins the collarbone, making a sound like that of an over-ripe melon being squashed. The blood spurted grotesquely from his severed jugular and gushed into the moonlight. His scream tore through Aethelfled; she had never seen a man die before. She flung down the protective covering and hid her face in her hands. Ealswith drew her tightly in to her bosom, where the baby sisters already clung hard, searching for protection amidst the folds of their mother's robe.

Suddenly the flap was ripped from the cart and the leering face of a Viking raider peered inside. Ealswith shrieked and lifted her arm to protect her children, as the man laughed and leaned forward, sword raised. But Edward's small hand shot out from the darkness, driving home a dagger that pierced the Dane's shoulder. The intruder cried out in rage and turned to strike the young prince, who suddenly found himself staring death in the face.

But the blow never came. The Viking's eyes bulged out grotesquely as he vomited a thick stream of blood and disappeared beneath the wagon's edge. A familiar figure, grunting from the exertion, drew his battleaxe free from the man's body. It was Sigli.

Aethelfled felt as though she would become ill, but at that moment she caught sight of a motion out of the corner of her eye and cried out. Sigli whirled around and raised his buckler just in time to absorb a blow delivered by a mounted assailant. He swung his axe around with terrible force, catching the rider flush in his exposed stomach, and the man pitched backward from his saddle. Aethelfed pulled back the wagon flap as Sigli dashed off to rejoin the fight.

The sounds of the struggle continued for a few more harrowing moments. And then, all was quiet again. It was over. A stunned silence fell over the group, broken only by the sound of the wind in the trees. Alfred's anxious face appeared at the rear of the cart, relaxing noticeably when he realized that none his family had been harmed.

"Alfred! My God, Alfred!" Ealswith tumbled on her knees across the wagon. She fell awkwardly into her husband's arms, all while protecting the infant Aethelweard in her own.

"It's over. They're all dead."

Aethelfled looked past her mother and father at the carnage. A score of bodies lay sprawled grotesquely around the cart, their awkward positions describing their sudden, violent deaths. Pools of blood had collected on the frozen ground, shining in the midnight moonlight. She heard the moaning of a wounded Viking off to one side and looked toward the disturbance, only to see one of her father's men bring his sword down on the man's exposed throat, severing the head from its body. She buried her face in her hands and began to cry.

"I've tried to shield you from death as best as I could," Alfred said, caressing her head with his hand, "but now you've seen it for yourself." He turned to Edward, who sat at attention in the rear of the cart. The boy's face showed the strain of the ordeal. "And you, my son," the father murmured softly, "now, perhaps, you'll understand there's little glory on the battlefield, only blood and sorrow. Steel yourself to it."

All of the Vikings lay dead. Most of the royal escort had also perished. Try as she might, Aethelfled could not remove her eyes from the scene. Eight of the king's men had been killed, while several others had incurred wounds of varying severity. One who had escaped harm was Plegmund; he stood nearby, his face ashen. Alfred spotted him and walked over to his side.

"We've lost our driver. Can you take the reins?"

Plegmund nodded mechanically and moved in a daze toward the head of the wagon. He passed by Sigli, who was in the process of binding the wounded leg of one of the king's men. At that point the monk could no longer restrain his emotions; he fell to his knees and began to sob, his shoulders shaking from the effort. Sigli quickly finished attending to the soldier and turned to his stricken teacher, helping him to his feet and toward the cart seat. The remainder of the party mounted their horses and prepared to embark again on the night's journey.

Alfred signaled for them to move out. "God help us, but we don't have time to bury these men. May their brave souls find peace." He guided his horse toward the rear of the cart and looked in once more at his family. "We must push on now, so try to sleep. Have courage; with God's will we'll escape further danger." He grabbed hold of the rear flap of the cart and pulled it down, plunging the interior into darkness.

Aethelfled sat back against the sideboard of the cart and reached out, grabbing her sister Aethelgifu's hand to offer comfort. She could feel the younger girl's body trembling, so she wrapped her arm around Aethelgifu's shoulder and pulled her sister to her, where they sat together in the darkness as the cart lurched forward along the bumpy road. She tried to close her eyes, but the grisly images of the night kept flashing through her mind, accompanied by the screams of dying men. She fought to suppress the memory for the better part of an hour, until gradually the rhythmic rocking of the cart lulled her to sleep.

She awoke with a start. Lifting up a corner of the flap, she peered into the gray dawn, where a light morning fog lay close upon the earth. She could see the outline of a low-slung stone building located in the midst of a grove of oaks a short distance from the road. Several women stood in front of an open doorway; and she recognized them immediately by their long, flowing garments.

They had come to a nunnery.

She watched as Alfred, Sigli and Plegmund helped the soldiers who had been injured the night before; one in particular looked very weak. The nuns assisted as best they could, ushering the wounded slowly into the convent, until finally the last of them disappeared inside. Alfred and Plegmund spoke briefly to the Mother Superior, and a moment later the trio approached the wagon.

"Good morning," Alfred smiled, peering into the confines of the cart and stroking the head of the tiny Aelfthryth, whose sunny grin reconfirmed her reputation as the most cheerful of the royal children. "You won't be going any farther today, so it's time to get out of the cart."

They piled out one by one, stretching their stiff legs and walking unsteadily up and down the road. Alfred beckoned to Ealswith, who entrusted her infant son to Aethelfled and joined her husband.

"You'll be safe here, my love," he whispered reassuringly. "We put a fair distance between ourselves and the Vikings last night. I doubt they'll come this far south for a while. When nightfall comes, Plegmund will drive you to Winchester in the cart. A fresh escort will be sent to accompany you."

"And you, my Lord?" Ealswith's eyes betrayed what she already knew.

Alfred looked down at the ground. His lips tightened. "It's not safe for any of us to stay in these shires. I have to leave you for now. But I'll be with you every moment, in my thoughts and in my heart."

She raised her hand and caressed his cheek, and she laughed nervously as a tear glistened in the corner of her eye and slipped down her face. "God help us, Alfred. When will it be over? When will it end?"

"When it's finished, my love." He smiled and grasped both her hands in his. "You'll be safe with Grimwald and Plegmund in Winchester. If danger threatens, they'll make provisions for you to sail for the continent and stay at the Frankish court."

His eyes softened. Ealswith, no longer able to contain her grief, started to weep. He grabbed her in his arms and held her fiercely. "Don't let the children forget me. And be strong...!"

Sigli had been standing by a short distance away in silence. He turned as they embraced and sidled casually over to young Edward. The boy stood alone chipping away with his dagger at some loose wood on the side of the cart.

"For one so young, you handle the knife well," Sigli said offhandedly.

The boy stopped his puttering and looked up at the Viking.

"I saw the blow you struck the raider, in the shoulder," Sigli continued. "It was done with great courage. You'll make a fine warrior someday."

Edward's shoulders straightened and his eyes gleamed with pride.

"But next time," Sigli advised, "aim higher." He pointed to his throat. "Go for the kill immediately. That's why I prefer the axe...when you hit a man with one of these, it only takes one blow."

Alfred appeared at his shoulder. "It's time to go."

Sigli moved over to his horse and mounted it in an easy motion. All eyes turned to Alfred.

"I must leave you now, but I'll return, in better times," he said with a heavy voice. "Until then, heed your mother. And act with honor, as the family of a king should." A smile crept onto his face. "And you, my little fighting man," he winked at Edward, "you must protect them. You must act for me while I'm gone."

"You'll be proud of me, Father!"

"I already am. I'm proud of all of you."

He hugged each of them in turn and swung into his saddle, and then he dug his heels into the flanks of his mount, spurring the horse down the road with Sigli close behind. Aethelfled stood with the rest of the House of Wessex as the riders receded into the distance. They watched, transfixed, as the horsemen reached a point far down the road, just before it disappeared behind the trees.

The two riders paused at the bend and wheeled around, lifting their arms and waving a final time.

And then they were gone.

*   *   *   *   *

Alfred and Sigli rode west for several days. Although the weather grew warmer, the rains came, turning the newly thawed earth to mud. The two men maintained a constant vigil, moving cautiously and keeping a safe distance from any passers-by they encountered. At all times, they took great care to conceal their identities, and with good reason. Viking scouting parties continued to scour the countryside, contesting every sign of movement in the hope of capturing the Christian king. No Saxon was safe on the open road. On several occasions Alfred and Sigli spotted bands of riders and hid in the underbrush, waiting until the danger passed; their closest call came the second day, when a hostile party caught sight of them from a nearby hilltop at twilight and gave chase. But they managed to outrun their pursuers and merged, wraith-like, into the gathering darkness.

Their path took them across Hampshire and into Wiltshire. They camped one night near Stonehenge on the Salisbury Plain, another in the depths of Selwood Forest, and finally emerged onto the wild heaths of Somerset, gateway to the untamed west. As they began to cross this alien terrain, a midday storm caught them in full force, buffeting them with wind and rain. Much to their consternation, they discovered that they had now entered marsh country, where the ground became increasingly uncertain and treacherous. Stands of alders and low, tuft-like marsh plants known as sedge dotted the land, interspersed with occasional hillocks and high ground.

At one point, as they slowly negotiated their way along a series of narrow paths that wound through the marsh, Sigli glanced over his shoulder at the king. He noticed that Alfred was trembling. He said nothing but kept watch out of the corner of his eye, noting how the king's condition worsened over the next half hour.

The attack, when it came, was sudden and fierce. Without warning, Alfred gasped loudly and doubled over in his saddle, clutching at his stomach and struggling to keep from falling off his horse. Sigli dismounted and ran to the king, helping him down onto a damp patch of grass alongside the path. Alfred stretched out onto his back and began to writhe in pain. Sigli stood by helplessly, until finally the attack began to abate, until Alfred gratefully curled up in the fetal position on the damp grass, breathing heavily and trembling from the exertion.

Sigli placed his hand on the king's forehead. "My Lord, you're very sick. We must find shelter."

Alfred nodded weakly. Sigli stood up, but before he could decide on a course of action he was alerted by the sound of a bell clanging from behind a stand of alders a short distance away. He dragged Alfred back under the cover of the underbrush, from where they watched and waited.

Within a few moments a herd of cows appeared through a break in the trees, followed by a middle-aged man dressed in the garb of a commoner and bearing a staff in his hand. He moved unsuspectingly toward the bushes where the fugitives were concealed; not fearing the solitary stranger, Sigli did nothing to escape his attention. When the peasant finally spotted the tall Viking—and the body at his feet—he gasped in alarm and turned to flee.

"Wait!" Sigli cried out in English. "Please! We need your help!"

The ceorl, realizing he could never outrun the young stranger, stopped in his tracks. He began to shuffle slowly across the marshy glade, keeping behind his cows while eyeing the well-armed Viking with suspicion.

"This man is very sick. He needs help," Sigli implored. "You must believe me." With that he disarmed himself, throwing his weapons to the ground and offering his outstretched palms in a gesture of peace.

The peasant warily pushed his way past the livestock, drawing closer. He was a short man, and his face was filled with years of unfriendly weather, hard and wrinkled, like leather stretched over a barrel frame. He walked with a slight limp, his right foot dragging behind him as he hobbled up and peered into Alfred's face.

"He looks bad." He glanced up at Sigli again with a questioning look.

"My name is Sigli. And this man is Edgar, a thane of King Alfred."

The peasant was skeptical. "What are you doing in these parts?"

"The Danes have invaded Wessex. We flee south and west, in hopes of regrouping."

"You're a Viking. Why should I believe you?"

"Because a man's life is at stake." Sigli slapped his palms against his thighs in frustration. "By the Gods, if you're a true Saxon and swear allegiance to Alfred, you'll help us!"

The man's eyes narrowed. He thought things over for a moment, and finally he turned and grunted, motioning for Sigli to follow. "My home is humble...you'll have to sleep in the cowshed. That's all I can offer."

"Any shelter is welcome. You won't regret this."

Sigli helped Alfred to his feet and then up onto his mount; the king, too weak to utter even a single word, grabbed hold of the horse's neck and steadied himself as best he could. Sigli reached for the reins of both horses and led them along the path, following the peasant closely. They soon reached the edge of a small lake. In its center, rising through the mist, the outline of a low island appeared some sixty yards away. The peasant turned to Sigli and pointed across the water.

"The land is always marshy here. But during the winter, when the heavy rains come, it all floods." He looked Sigli over again carefully, as though to reassure himself one more time of the Viking's intentions. "That's where I make my home…it's called Athelney."

Sigli squinted through the mist. "How do we get there?"

"It's too shallow for a boat, and too treacherous to just walk across anywhere. If you don't know the way, it's nearly impossible. The land beneath the water is uncertain...a false step, and you'd sink deep into the earth." He hesitated. "Only I and the cows know the way."

"Listen to me, old man," Sigli reassured the peasant, "I swear to you on my father's blood, on the Gods, on the Christian God and the Holy Trinity, that no harm will come to you. I'll guard your secret and honor your generosity." He held out his hand.

The ceorl looked at it for a passing moment and then finally grasped it. "Very well," he sighed. "If you don't kill me, my wife certainly will for bringing two more mouths to our table. But I have one condition."

"Name it."

"You must help me during your stay. There's always too much work to do, and not enough hands to do it."

"You have my word, and my back in the bargain. But tell me, what's your name?"

"I'm called Meric. My wife, who lives with me at Athelney, is Ingewold."

He turned and urged the dozen-odd cows in the herd to venture into the lake. They moved some twenty yards along the bank before plunging in, immediately sinking to their shanks in the cold water. One by one they walked in single file, picking their way carefully along the unseen path that lay beneath the lake's surface, until the entire herd was stretched out, followed by Meric, Sigli and the two horses. Alfred, barely conscious, hung grimly onto his mount.

In a few moments they reached the edge of the island. Sigli looked around in wonder and admired Nature's odd creation, for they stood on a fortress that could not be breached easily. They would be well hidden here. He turned and followed Meric, who was already making his way toward a wisp of smoke that curled into the sky beyond a brace of trees ahead of them. They walked along a narrow path until they emerged in front of a hovel sitting at the highest point of the island. Behind it stood an enclosed area for the cows, with a shed at the rear to protect the herd.

"Help me get the cows into the pen, Sigli. You and Edgar can sleep in the shed. There's room near the entrance for a small fire. The nights are damp, and…"

He was interrupted by a shrill voice from inside the hovel. "It's about time you came home, Meric! My cakes are baked, and they won't wait! I…"

Ingewold stopped abruptly as she appeared in the doorway. She was a large, rough-looking woman, hardened like her husband to their difficult existence. She looked anxiously at her unexpected guests.

"Don't be alarmed, Ingewold. These men need shelter. One of them, Edgar here, is very sick. I told them they could stay in the cowshed."

"But…this one…he's a heathen!"

"Never mind, woman! Don't cross me! Viking or not, he has a broad back, and he's agreed to help me while his friend gets well. Now get back to your cakes and divide them up…I'll get these two settled."

Ingewold grimaced, but she said nothing. She turned reluctantly to attend to her duties while Meric led the cows into the pen. Sigli lifted Alfred from his horse and carried him inside the shed, laying him down on a makeshift bed of hay and then covering the king with his robe. He then followed Meric toward the hovel, remaining outside the door as the peasant entered the crude hut. He could hear Ingewold's shrill voice berating her husband from within.

"How can you allow this? We barely have enough to eat ourselves, and you bring them home!"

"Just divide the cakes and keep quiet! I can't turn a sick man out into the night. He says he's a king's thane."

"Hah! A noble wouldn't dress in such rough clothes. And as for the other one…how do you know he won't slit our throats in the night and take everything we have?"

"That's enough, woman! Heed me and attend to the cakes!"

Ingewold grumbled under her breath, ending the conversation. After a few minutes Meric emerged from the hovel carrying several warm pieces of bread. "Here," he said perfunctorily, handing the food to Sigli. "It's all I have."

"Thank you. You cannot know the good you're doing."

Meric waved his hand. "It's little enough. I'd ask you inside, but I think you'd better keep your distance tonight...my wife, you see, is a good woman—but a harsh one."

"I can't blame her. We intrude."

"You're my guests, and that's that. Now, go back and tend to your man, get some of this food in him. You'll find wood to build a fire around the back of the shed. And get some sleep; we rise at dawn. I'll make sure you earn this bread, so enjoy every mouthful. We'll sweat it out of you soon enough."

*   *   *   *   *

Several days passed. Waves of sickness descended on Alfred, fever dreams filled with aching and dread. Every few hours the king was subjected to an attack of his familiar, mysterious stomach pains; they passed as suddenly as they came. Sigli watched over him through the damp nights, leaving each dawn with Meric and returning as evening fell.

Finally, the fever broke on the afternoon of the third day. Alfred felt his mind clearing by rapid degrees, until he was able to rise from his bed of hay and leave the shed, marveling again at the small beauties of the world that are so easily taken for granted. As he looked out through the trees and over the lake, he breathed in the crisp, cold air and gave thanks to God for his recovery.

"Well...you're better, I see."

He turned around and saw Ingewold lingering near the corner of the hovel, watching him. Her hands were filled with her work; the woman was always busy, from what he could gather.

"I thought for a while you might not live," she said, "but you did. And now that you're better, you can start making yourself useful."

Alfred grinned. If only his court could see this. "What would you have me do, good dame?"

"Well, your friend was decent enough to split that wood over there." She pointed to a pile of logs near the edge of the trees. "Put your back to it and bring them over by the house." He started for the pile. "And then you can fetch some water from the lake," she called out after him. "There's a bucket by the door."

"And after that?"

"Come see me," she said, missing his gentle jab. "I'll be baking bread cakes for tonight's supper." She turned and waddled off around the corner of the house, her derriere swaying from side to side against the confines of her sackcloth dress.

Alfred hurried over to the woodpile and began loading up his arms with faggots, his breath growing heavier with the exertion. It was his first serious physical activity in days, and it felt good. He attacked the task with vigor for the better part of the next half hour. It was honest and pure, this work, and it could be measured. The sweat poured freely from his body, and even Ingewold, checking on his progress, could not help but nod to herself in approval.

She finally called out to him. "Edgar...Come inside and sit down."

He finished up what he was doing and trudged toward the hovel. Lowering his head, he stooped to walk through the open door, entering a room that was as crude within as the exterior of the dwelling was simple without. The single room revolved around a hearth aligned along one wall where an open fire crackled, its smoke escaping through a hole cut in the roof. There was a table and several chairs, a storage area designed to house various primitive domestic utensils, a bed, a pile of furs and skins—and nothing else.

"Sit down at the table," Ingewold said. He did so as she stood watching him. "So tell me the truth," she asked after he had settled himself, "you're not really a king's thane, are you?"

He smiled and shook his head. "No, not really."

"I knew it! Meric believed the heathen. Why have you taken up with him?"

"We're thrown together by Fate. When people have nothing, friendship comes easy. Fire is the test of gold, adversity of strong men."

"I know nothing of gold."

"I share in your troubles, good woman."

"And in my cakes," she observed. "But see here, I need to fetch some clothes from down by the lake. Meric and the Viking will be back before long, and we'll eat. Can I trust you to mind the cakes?"

"Yes, of course." He turned to the hearth, where a half dozen mounds of dough were baking inside a crude oven.

"They have to cook for a while, but take care; if not attended to, they'll burn and be ruined." She grabbed a basket to gather the clothes and disappeared from the hovel.

Alfred looked around the room. Despite the peasant crudeness of the surroundings, it felt good to relax in the comfort of a welcome hearth. Even a bed of hay was a fine alternative to the hard ground they had slept on for days while wandering across the countryside.

He wondered about the state of affairs across Wessex, and how to overcome the Vikings. They were not invincible; he had beaten them back before and knew it could be done again. Experience told him that the Danes tended to lose patience in a protracted struggle, when the Saxon resistance was sufficient to hold them in check. But he also knew that Guthrum was a formidable man, a crafty and experienced leader. The Danish king was not as bloodthirsty as many of his countrymen, but he was still dangerous enough. The Vikings clearly controlled

Northumbria and East Anglia, and their presence in Mercia was now stronger than ever.

He mulled over his options for many long minutes. If only Wessex could rally, perhaps some permanent agreement could be struck with the Vikings. There had to be a way to overcome the differences between the cultures, to promote a coexistence that could be managed by Saxon and Viking alike, to...

"My cakes!"

He looked up as the enraged Ingewold dropped her basket of clothes in the doorway and rushed over to the evening's meal that had been placed under his care.

"Look at them!" she cried. "They're half-burnt!" She scrambled to salvage what she could from the oven and then turned on him. "Useless ceorl! I leave you with a simpleton's task, and you fail! But you're more than ready to eat my food, to sleep under my roof, you idiot!"

She threw her hands up in dismay. At that moment Meric and Sigli appeared in the doorway, freshly arrived from the day's labors. Ingewold turned to them, holding the damning evidence in her hands for all to see.

"Look here, Meric! The fool has ruined my cakes!" She turned back to Alfred. "You and the heathen can eat the burnt portions tonight! Take them, wretch, and get out of my house!"

Alfred looked up sheepishly, noticing that Sigli could barely contain his amusement. "I'm sorry, I truly am..."

Even the patient Meric smirked in disgust. "I'm a reasonable man, Edgar, but I must agree with my wife. Take the burnt cakes and go back to the shed. I work too damned hard for this."

Alfred rose obediently and gathered up the burnt bread. Inglewold fluttered about the room like a wounded hen, beside herself with anger. "Meric, I want them gone in the morning, do you hear me?"

"I'll think about it. There's still some work to do, and…"

"Out! Out!" she cried, pointing to the door.

"Calm yourself, woman," Meric said sternly. "We'll deal with it later." He turned to Alfred and Sigli. "I think you'd better go now. We'll take up matters in the morning."

Once outside, Sigli erupted into laughter. When they reached the shed and passed out of earshot of the peasant and his irate wife, he put his arm good-naturedly on Alfred's shoulder. "You may be the King of Wessex, my Lord, but Ingewold is the Queen of Athelney!"

Alfred grinned and flopped down on the hay inside the shed, grimacing as he began to chew on the burnt bread. "A rather humbling experience, wouldn't you say?"

"I'm glad you're feeling well enough to laugh about it," Sigli chuckled. He began to gather wood in preparation for a fire. "Shall we be off in the morning?"

"I don't think so," Alfred replied, staring out thoughtfully into the evening fog as it crept in over the island. "By God's will, we've been blessed. Guthrum could never find me here."

"Nor can the Saxons. You can't gather an army by staying here."

"There's time enough for that. Let things settle for a while; until then we can stay and help Meric." The king swallowed the last of his bread.

"If he'll have us. We can only stay so long. He'd never believe you if you told him the truth."

"When the time comes, he'll believe." Alfred reached into his belongings and withdrew something. "Would a commoner be so endowed?" he asked, opening his hand to Sigli.

The Viking gasped. There, in the flickering firelight, a magnificent jewel shone forth in Alfred's palm. It was a transparent piece of rock crystal superimposed on a figurative design in cloisonne enamel and enclosed by a pear-shaped gold frame. The back of the jewel was fixed by a gold plate with basketwork hatching incised upon it; at the base, another gold extension in the form of an animal's head protruded from the narrow end of the gem. Around the edge of the frame, Sigli noticed an inscription in old English letterwork:

+ AELFRED MEC HEHT GEWYRCAN.

"It's magnificent!" he cried. "What does the lettering say?"

"'Alfred ordered me to be made.' Some of the finest goldsmiths in Wessex put their hands to the task."

Suddenly he grimaced in discomfort and clutched at his stomach. Sigli started up to assist him but the king waved him away, stoically bearing the pain and shifting on the bed of hay to find a more comfortable position. He bent over, breathing heavily, and drew closer to the fire.

"These spells you have, Sire…what causes them?"

"No medical man has ever been able to determine that. I've been plagued with the curse for over ten years now. It comes and goes at a moment's notice. I can go months and months without an occurrence, and then suddenly it returns as a daily affliction."

"Perhaps the Gods are displeased with you."

"God is good. It is man who is weak."

Sigli stared into the night. Athelney. Another exile. He poked at the fire. "Tell me…has this land ever had one king who ruled over all?"

"Yes, but for a very short time…a year or two at most. My grandfather Egbert laid claim to such dominion. 'Bretwalda,' they named him. King of Britain."

"Tell me about him."

Alfred stared out into the misty night. "Well, since there's little else to attend to, I suppose a history lesson is in order." He sat upright and cleared his throat.

"Egbert was an ambitious man, and he desired to unify all of the Saxon kingdoms under one crown. After carefully building up his armies, he challenged the king of Mercia—at that time the strongest of the sub-kingdoms in England—and defeated him decisively in 825, over fifty years ago. Within the next two years Egbert realized his goal and established himself as Bretwalda."

"Did he rule all the Saxons for long?"

"Only for a few years," Alfred said. "He was off subduing the Welsh, when one of the nobles my grandfather had deposed in Mercia regained his throne. There were too many stones to juggle; not even Egbert was up to the task. He was never able to restore the kingdom, because in 835, near the end of his reign, another force appeared on the land. Your people came."

He paused. "This was my grandfather's last great challenge. He joined forces with the West Welch and won a decisive victory over the Vikings. But his greatest triumph proved to be his last. He died the next year, in 839, and my father Ethelwulf became King of Wessex."

Alfred leaned forward close to the fire, pulling his cloak tightly about him as the damp night air descended on Athelney. He looked intently into the flames.

"My father was a great man, and a good king, " he continued. "He consolidated Wessex by defeating the Viking forces shortly after they'd wintered for the first time in England. That victory gave him the leverage he needed for the final five years of his life, and as a young boy I had the good fortune to accompany him to Rome. He had, in fact, sent me there by myself earlier, when I was only four years old. I saw the world early.

"When my father and I left for Rome, he divided Wessex between my two eldest brothers to rule in his absence. Aethelbald, the eldest, was driven by a burning ambition. He loved power, and he plotted to keep my father from regaining the throne when he returned from Rome. But he didn't succeed. My father dallied with me in the Frankish court of Charles the Bald for many months, and there he married the beautiful Judith, Charles's daughter. She was barely fourteen; my father was almost fifty. She was like an older sister to me, very kind—and yet she shared my father's bed as his queen.

"We returned to Wessex and my father took back his throne. But my scheming brother got his wish soon enough; my father died within the year, and Aethelbald became king." Alfred suddenly lifted his head and laughed. "And he took Judith, too. But that was like my brother—he always wanted everything."

"How old were you then?"

"I was nine years old. And I was eleven when Aethelbald's castle of sand slipped into the sea. He had a hunting accident and broke his neck. My next eldest brother, Aethelberht, ascended the throne, and Wessex had its third king in three years."

"And did *he* then marry Judith?"

Alfred laughed. "No, Judith went back to the Franks. She's married to a nobleman in the south of Francia, where she lives well, I'm sure. Quite a woman.

"In any case, Aethelberht was a good and just ruler. I grew to manhood during his reign, and it was a sad day for Wessex when he took ill and died in 865 after five years on the throne. I was sixteen. Aethelred, my last surviving brother, became king at the age of twenty-three.

"I loved Aethelred. And he relied on me in great measure. I had much say in the policies of state, and I saw firsthand what it took to rule a people. I came of age during the six years of his reign. And that was fortunate. Because shortly after he assumed the throne, the greatest fleet of Vikings ever to land on these shores appeared in East Anglia.

"Their leader, Halfdan, marched south with his army into Wessex in 871, just seven years ago. The events of that year caused it to be known as the Year of the Battles. And the greatest battle of all occurred during that spring, at Ashdown."

Alfred's eyes gleamed in the firelight as he relived the experience. "The armies met in the middle of the field, which was barren except for a single thorn tree. The battle raged around that tree for almost two hours. Never have I seen men fight more desperately. But in the end, we gained a decisive victory."

"Did Halfdan leave Wessex?"

"Not immediately. But he eventually withdrew into Mercia, where his army practiced extortion and sucked the life out of that defenseless kingdom. Wessex, for a time, was safe.

"But a second Viking army arrived, led in part by Guthrum—who now sits at my table this very moment, laughing at me." He poked at the fire in disgust. "Guthrum's army had the hunger that Halfdan's force was beginning to show signs of losing. In a sense, after six long years, the enemy was stronger than ever.

"And then, shortly after Ashdown, Aethelred died of fever. I was twenty-two years old, the sole surviving son of Ethelwulf, married for three years with a daughter and a son. And all of Wessex looked to me as King."

He sighed. "Luckily, Halfdan and his army withdrew into Northumbria, where most of the men have taken wives and now till fields they call their own. Halfdan died in his bed two years ago, so his force no longer appears to be a threat. The land, as it turns out, has done what thousands of God-fearing Christian sword arms could not.

"But Guthrum is stronger than ever. And Ubba lurks about, somewhere, with those of his ships not wrecked in last year's storm. And who opposes them...? A beggar king, his heathen man-at-arms, a cowherd and an old woman."

Sigli laughed. "I'd match Ingewold against any man Guthrum can field."

"I promise you this," Alfred said grimly. "Wessex shall rise and triumph. For now, we have to play a game of patience. We must wait and watch, and as God wills it, our time will come." He laughed softly, almost to himself. "Meanwhile, we must rise at dawn to milk the cows."

He pulled his cloak over himself and fell back into the hay. "It's a small enough thing...but it's a start. A warrior, my friend, must fight all battles well."

*　　*　　*　　*　　*

"Lord Earl Braggi. Tamer of the Baltic. Emissary of the mighty Haestan, pride of lower Jutland."

Braggi followed his introduction by walking briskly into the main hall at Chippenham. Anyone could see that the man's reputation was well deserved; his carriage was proud, uncompromising. Arrogant snot, thought Guthrum. A man should temper his haughtiness when he's merely the page boy to another. But it would have been too much to expect Haestan himself to make the journey from Francia; Braggi was enough.

"Remember, don't be in haste," sounded a whisper in his ear. It was Iglaf, his chief advisor. "Negotiate with care. Use judgement."

Yes, old man, you're my cart driver, Guthrum thought. You rein in my desperate moments. But we have many cards to play this time; we want his help, we want his men and ships, but not too much of him. We don't want Haestan to rule Britain. That is a prize for us.

For me.

"Welcome to Wessex, Braggi," Guthrum proclaimed, standing and gesturing broadly from behind his raised table. "Sit down by the fire. Alfred's hearth is warm."

Braggi nodded curtly and seated himself. It was late one night during the first week of March, two months after Guthrum had swept into Chippenham. Little had changed since the invasion; the Vikings still controlled the countryside, Ubba still lay holed up with his fleet in Dyfed on the southern coast of Wales—and Alfred's whereabouts still remained a mystery.

"So tell us...how goes it in Francia?" Guthrum asked innocently.

"We have our way most of the time. The plunder is good."

"How many men do you have?" Iglaf asked politely.

"That's hard to say. Various bands roam as far to the west as Normandy and Brittany. And there's always activity in Frisia and the low countries."

Masterfully done, Guthrum thought. An answer that answers nothing. "I'd heard that Sigefrith and Guthfrith led supporting forces under Haestan."

"Yes, that's true. And many others are with us. Hundeus and Baldri, Guntar and Offa, to name a few. And don't let me forget Sidroc...he joined us last year with a formidable fleet. But tell me, Guthrum," Braggi leaned forward. "We're all curious on the mainland. Just where is Alfred?" His eyes twinkled in the dim torchlight.

"I thought perhaps you might know. I'd think he'd be halfway to Rome by now."

"Then why do you need us? Why am I here tonight?" Braggi bit off his words crisply.

Guthrum was firm. "Because you have ships and men, and we have land for the taking."

Braggi slapped his knee and laughed sardonically. "But if we come, you won't be sucha rich man anymore. You'll have to divide things up into smaller pieces." His eyes narrowed. "You must be in some sort of trouble, eh?"

"This, you call trouble?" Guthrum sneered, motioning around the hall. "Look here at Alfred's hall: nothing could be more secure—and this is the door to Wessex!"

He stood up and walked around the table, his voice softening. "It's really quite simple. You raid and plunder on the continent to your heart's content; but how far can you go? The Christians are everywhere, Braggi. Where one kingdom ends, another begins, and on and on and on. Eventually your men will want to settle...you can't hope to live in a tent or on the deck of a dragon ship forever, no?"

Braggi was silent.

Warming to the task, Guthrum sat down again and stroked his chin. His voice was pure logic. "Britain is an island. There are five or six sub-kingdoms, there's Eire to the west—and that's all! That means," he smiled, pointing his finger at Braggi for effect, "that he who controls Britain has a natural defense...the sea on all sides! And the Vikings own the seas."

Braggi's eyebrows creased. "What do you propose, Guthrum? Speak plainly."

"Divert your attacks on the continent. Redirect half your men into Essex and Kent, the short sail across the channel. I already own the Thames valley and the center of the country. Ubba is poised to land with his fleet in Devon and sweep the western lands. We'll trap Alfred in our claws and crush whatever's left of his resistance."

"Ubba?" Braggi smirked. "Ubba's part of this...?" He shook his head. "I'd think he'd have fled back to Jutland with his tail between his legs after the disaster at Exeter last summer."

"Even Ubba can handle this," Iglaf said, ever ready to defray a threat to the negotiation.

"Nothing can stop us," Guthrum boasted. "Wessex is on the run. But we need your support to assure the outcome of the issue and secure a complete victory. This could all be ours, Braggi. There's enough for all of us."

"And what do we get?"

"Everything south of the Thames and east of Winchester."

"And London? Who gets London?"

"I do."

After mulling the situation for a moment, Braggi spoke out firmly. "I'm not sure Haestan would like that arrangement. And I'm not sure that Alfred is under your thumb as much as you think he is. You may be in deeper than you think. You've taken a risk and extended yourself. Your lines back to Mercia are questionable at best. Your army has been in England for seven years and grows tired. And you depend on Ubba."

He rose suddenly. "Your offer is interesting, but we have much at stake in Francia...and you have many unanswered questions. Much depends on Ubba; if he sweeps the west, well..maybe you're right, Guthrum. Maybe Wessex could truly be Danelaw. But if Ubba fails..." He left the last thought hanging and bowed crisply.

"We'll be watching with great attention, but for now, please forgive me. I must leave at once; Lord Haestan requires my immediate return."

He nodded politely to each of the men clustered by the fire, turned on his heel, and strode rapidly across the hall as the sound of his boots echoed off the thick wooden rafters overhead. A servant ushered him from the room and closed the heavy doors of the hall behind him.

Iglaf broke the silence. "Not bad, really. About what I expected."

Guthrum shook his head in disagreement. "We needed a commitment."

"You did well, Guthrum. You gave nothing away."

"And got nothing in return. Nothing for nothing." Guthrum sighed. "It's getting late. There's no point in discussing this further tonight; I'm going to bed."

He bade the council goodnight and left the hall, making his way through the dark passageways of Chippenham. The only sound that disturbed the silence was the whistling of the wind as it squeezed its way through the crevices in the estate walls. He ignored the chill, completely lost in thought as he approached his quarters.

Braggi had been right; the bulk of his men had arrived in England seven years ago and were growing tired. Decisive action was essential in order to secure Wessex. It was absolutely necessary for Ubba to come through so that Haestan would commit. That done, it would then be over for the Saxons, no matter what Alfred did. And he, Guthrum, would reign supreme in the new capital city of London.

Finally reaching his quarters, he opened the door to his bedchamber and stepped inside. He walked past the fire and over to the single window in the room, pulling back on the latch that fastened the heavy wooden shudders in place. He drew them open, allowing the moonlight to slip into the room. A cold breeze licked at his face as he looked across the river at the English countryside. Alfred was out there, somewhere. What was he thinking? How soon could he muster an army?

He shivered as the cold air continued to invade the chamber. With his head now cleared, he closed the window and stooped down over the fire, allowing the warmth of the hearth to soak through him. He removed most of his heavier clothing and crawled into the large bed that dominated the room. He nestled under the heavy covers, enjoying the comforts of his conquest, and began to fade away into his subconscious.

Suddenly a banging at his chamber door roused him. He sat up abruptly, annoyed at the intrusion, and padded across the room. He grabbed the latch angrily and swung the door open, where Iglaf stood alone in the dark hallway. Even in the dim torchlight, Guthrum could tell immediately that something was dreadfully wrong.

"What is it?"

"It's Ubba," Iglaf croaked hoarsely. "Ubba is dead."

*   *   *   *   *

Osric had already been on the road for a full hour before the sun rose to illuminate the bleak moors. It will be good to get home, he thought to himself. The west was not to his liking; it was desolate and altogether unappealing, and he yearned to see the lush fields of Hampshire again. He rolled with the rhythm of his horse. Nobody in the party of twenty-five men spoke; it would be a long day's journey, and always the threat of the enemy remained.

He looked into the sun. It hovered low in the east, directly in their path, and above it a sheet of thick clouds hung waiting to steal away its yellow heat as it rose in the sky. The way the sun shone this morning reminded Osric of two dawns earlier, at Castle Kenwith at Countisbury on the north coast of Devon, where he had found himself following weeks of wandering through the west after Guthrum's descent on Chippenham.

The Vikings had come to Devon without warning, crossing the Bristol Channel after months of feeding off the lands surrounding Dyfed in south Wales. Twelve hundred of them splashed ashore at Countisbury as two dozen dragon ships ground their keels to the leeward of Castle Kenwith. It was the remnant of the great fleet that had been wrecked in the storm off Exeter the past summer, the pincer force sent to secure the west for the Danes.

And at its head, arrogantly planted in the bow of the lead ship, was Ubba.

Overmatched, the Saxons had fled inside the walls of the castle, an impregnable fortress perched atop a promontory that jutted out into the sea. Ubba planted his forces along the neck of land that connected Kenwith to the mainland and sat his men down. If the Saxons could not be unseated by force, they could be done in by siege.

It was then that Osric's counsel carried the day. Let your stomachs growl, Saxons, he cajoled them. Feed on your anger and your hate. And while it eats away at your belly, Ubba will grow soft and sleep like a drunken sailor each morning, snoring right through the dawn as it rises in the eastern sky behind him. And that is when you shall attack, and let every man fight desperately, to the end.

Three days later, it all came to pass. The Saxons were fed, armed and ready long before the sun rose, and when it was barely light enough to see they slipped out of the gates of Kenwith, some five hundred strong. They closed in on the Vikings in a perfectly orchestrated ambush and thundered down into the midst of the Viking tents. Ubba was discovered in his bed with a woman, still besotted with the smell of mead from the night before. A stout shepherd boy from Devon found him there and ended his life with a sword thrust, and the third son of Ragnar Lodbrok died naked with his whore, choking on his blood.

The Saxons burned ten of the Viking ships as they lay moored at the shoreline; the heathen stragglers who managed to escape clambered aboard the remainder of the vessels and put out to sea. All in all, almost nine hundred Vikings lay dead. The battle in the west was over almost before it had begun. And Guthrum's master plan lay in ashes.

As he remembered all this, Osric felt a rush of freedom coursing through his veins. A great weight had been removed from the land, opening up new possibilities; now Wessex could regroup and face Guthrum. But where was Alfred? He knew that the king would not have fled like so many others to the continent; he was far too much of a man for that. And it was certain that the Vikings had not found him, for any such news would have spread rapidly. The Golden Dragon was somewhere in Wessex, hiding. He had to be found.

The land suddenly grew rough as all semblance of a road disappeared and the ground underfoot turned soft and marshy. Osric cursed under his breath. He had heard stories of men venturing into these parts who had never been heard from again, sucked into a muddy grave by the spirits rumored by local legends to abound here.

His thoughts were interrupted by a rustling sound from the wood. He reined in his horse and raised his arm to alert the others, motioning for one of his men to investigate. The Saxon disappeared into a stand of alders, returning a moment later and raising a bloodied sword for all to see.

"Over here! I've found our breakfast!"

The men urged their horses forward through the underbrush and into a small clearing on the other side of the alders, where they came upon a dead cow lying in a pool of blood.

Osric dismounted and wiped his sweaty brow. "Let's build a fire and cook it. I don't want to stay here long."

Before the men could carry out his order, they were interrupted by an anguished cry from the edge of the clearing.

"Thieves!" cried an old cowherd, wringing his hands and looking hatefully at the soldiers. "Have you no respect for a poor man's belongings?"

"Be careful, old man," Osric warned. "Show respect and hold your tongue, or you may lose it!"

"I demand my wergild, under law! As a freeman, I'm entitled to it!"

"Bring him to me, now!" Osric bristled. Two of his men grabbed the cowherd and dragged him to where their leader had dismounted. "Take back your words, or you stand to lose more than a cow!"

"Kill me if you want. I don't care," the peasant answered in sullen defiance. "My life isn't worth living anymore."

"Very well, old man. You've pronounced your own sentence." Osric drew his sword from its scabbard and raised it above him, preparing to strike.

"Hold, Osric! Stay your hand!"

Osric wheeled around. Two men stood together on the edge of the clearing, their faces obscured in the shadows.

"What insolence is this? Who dares to stop me?"

"One you know well," replied the speaker, stepping out into the light.

Osric's eyes grew wide with amazement. He dropped his sword and fell to his knees as though struck by a thunderbolt.

"King Alfred! My Lord!"

The rest of the men dismounted hurriedly and knelt in the marsh. Only Meric, the cowherd, remained standing, trembling in awe.

"Alfred?" he stammered with a quaking voice. "You...you're... King Alfred?"

"Yes, Meric. I'm Alfred, the Golden Dragon of Wessex," he smiled, advancing toward the party with Sigli next to him. "You didn't believe me when I said I was a king's thane, and you were right...I'm your king."

He turned to Osric. "This man Meric is as loyal and true a Saxon as lives. You'd have done great harm to a valued countryman."

Osric rose from his knees to face the king. "Sire, my baser instincts may diminish me, but I remain a loyal servant of Wessex. You see here, on my right ankle, the shackle I vowed to wear until I was again worthy of your praise." His eyes sparkled. "Well, the time to remove this iron has come. The West is won, my Lord! Rejoice, Alfred; Ubba is dead!"

"Ubba!" It was Sigli, his eyes gleaming.

"Ubba!" repeated Osric, raising his fist in triumph. "Ubba is dead!"

Alfred could hardly believe his ears. "God is good. Let us give thanks!"

He thought for a moment, and then he spoke to them. "It's clear to me what our course of action is. It will take some time to gather our forces. Meanwhile, we'll remain at Athelney and fortify what God has already granted us. Your men, Osric, shall ride to every corner of Wessex and spread the word of our plan. In two months, come early May, we'll meet at Egbert's Stone on the eastern edge of Selwood Forest. And we shall march forth and strike a blow for freedom!"

A cheer went up from the Saxons. The usually stoic Alfred walked among them, slapping them heartily on the backs, until finally he came upon Meric. He raised his arm to quiet the gathering and then placed his hands on the cowherd's shoulders, looking at the old man with sparkling eyes.

"For many nights, my friend, you allowed us to share your bread and sleep in your humble home. And all that time you believed we were common beggars, with nothing but our backs to offer you."

"My Lord..." Meric's voice shook, and he was unable to continue. He fell to his knees and kissed the king's hand.

"Stand, Meric, and treat me as you have all along," said Alfred, helping the cowherd to his feet. "We're equal in the eyes of God."

Meric began to cry. "My Lord, forgive my crude ways."

"Your ways are honest, and from the heart. And because of that, and the great service you've done me, I ask that you accept this." He withdrew something from his pocket and handed it to Meric. It was the jewel he had shown Sigli at

Athelney, and its appearance drew a gasp from the congregation as it gleamed in the morning sunlight.

Meric again fell to his knees, overcome. "Sire...I'm unworthy."

"No man is more deserving. You and Ingewold shall be treated with honor and shall never again need to worry about earthly wants." Alfred smiled. "But you must put up with us a bit longer; Athelney will continue to be our castle in this hour of need, until we're strong enough to meet Guthrum."

He stepped away and looked off to the northeast, in the direction of Chippenham. "Dawn has come to this dark day. Ubba is dead. Let us give thanks and move forward with courage."

And then King Alfred, the Golden Dragon of Wessex, clenched his fists and raised his eyes to the heavens.

"Hear me, all of you! The hour of our deliverance is upon us! As God is my witness, Wessex shall rise again!"

CHAPTER VI: Wessex Goes To War

"No ceremony that to great ones 'longs,
Not the king's crown, nor the deputed sword,
The marshal's truncheon, nor the judge's robe
Become them with one half so good a grace
As mercy does."
—Shakespeare, <u>Measure For Measure</u>

Many of them had been there for days. Others continued to arrive by the hour, streaming in from all points across southern England. They came alone and in groups, on horseback and on foot, some with bright swords and gleaming coats of mail, others with crude cudgels and nothing more than the cloth on their backs. They were farmers and nobles, beggars and thieves, freemen, slaves, holy men and sinners, merchants and miracle seekers. They were Saxons united in a common purpose, and more than six thousand of them had flocked to Egbert's Stone to meet their king.

The bloom of spring exploded from every leaf and blade of grass on the eastern edge of Selwood Forest. Most of the men were scattered across the broken plain that rose gently up to the edge of the wood, where it culminated in a small clearing framed by several majestic oaks. In the center of the clearing was the great stone, named in honor of Alfred's grandfather. Egbert had ordered the stone dragged there as a memorial to his victories; now, his descendants hoped to draw from its strength as they prepared to face the Viking army camped a half-day to the north on the plain of Edington.

All that was missing was Alfred.

Penda smiled as he stood among the ealdormen in the shadow of the great stone. "We've waited a long time for this. It's been a long winter," he said to no one in particular. "Now...if Alfred would only come."

He looked off to where a trio of robed monks approached on horseback, and his face tightened as he watched Grimwald, Werferth and Plegmund pick their way tentatively through the ranks massed on the slope. The two younger monks trailed behind the corpulent bishop of Winchester like bridesmaids, showing deference to his every command. Grimwald raised his hand to acknowledge the ealdormen, guiding his horse to a flat area a few feet in front of the stone and dismounting with great effort.

"A great host such as this does glory unto God," he said, motioning to the masses spread out over the plain before them. "But...where's the king?"

"I saw him two weeks ago, at his island hideaway in Athelney," Penda said. "He was in good health and swore to meet us here today. Osric of Hampshire was with him."

"Osric, eh? Has he recovered from his self-imposed exile?"

"He's well. They were all in good spirits."

"Tell me, Penda..." Plegmund broke in. "Was the Viking, Sigli the shipbuilder, still with Alfred?"

"Yes."

Grimwald sniffed. "I'd almost forgotten Alfred's pagan reclamation project. You were tutoring him, weren't you, Plegmund?"

"For several months, until the invasion."

"Strange that the king would prefer the company of a heathen to that of his thanes, don't you think? We'd all be well-served to look for opportunities to rid ourselves of this Sigli; Alfred shows him too much favor."

Several cries from the opposite side of the stone interrupted them, and suddenly a band of horsemen emerged from the thick bank of Selwood Forest that framed the clearing. Riding at the head of the party, perched proudly atop his favorite white charger, was King Alfred, the Golden Dragon of Wessex. He galloped into the clearing and slowed to a canter in front of Egbert's Stone, where he raised his sword in triumph.

A great shout arose from the host. Men grabbed each other and danced for joy; some fell to laughter, others to weeping. The king pranced back and forth on his horse across the clearing, a broad smile beaming from beneath the crown of gold that adorned his head. He dismounted with a light bound and clasped the hands of those in the clearing. And then he dashed over to the foot of the great stone and scaled it, rising to his full height atop the monument and facing the Saxon host stretched out before him. He raised his arms for silence.

"Saxons, the hour of deliverance has come! No longer must we cower in fear at the feet of our invaders! Let us unite, brothers in arms, and march to the north! And tomorrow let us bathe our swords in the blood of our enemies!" He paused for effect and then lifted his clenched fists toward the heavens. "On to Edington!"

"For God, Alfred and England!" the army shouted. "For God, Alfred and England!"

Alfred's eyes gleamed. He looked out over the Saxon army, now grown to almost seven thousand strong, and he saw a vision of destiny rising up from the vast plain before him. There was magic in the air, a strange and wonderful energy that coursed through his veins, charging him with a divine force that overwhelmed him. It was clear that God and England had entrusted him with a holy mission. He had never felt more alive.

And through it all Edington beckoned, a hot wind carrying lies. Tomorrow would tell the tale.

*   *   *   *   *

Wulfric awoke more than an hour before dawn. He had slept fitfully, tossing and turning during the night before finally rolling over onto his back, eyes wide open. His restlessness was to be expected, for he was young and had never been more than a day's journey away from his Berkshire home. The meeting at the stone had brought more men together than he had ever seen in one place before, and the thrill of witnessing the return of the king was something he would remember for the rest of his life—should, God willing, he live to tell about it.

For Wulfric had never borne arms in battle before this day.

A hollow fear nagged at his stomach as he stared upward into the darkness. He was surrounded by hundreds of men, but he felt alone, swept up in the confrontation that loomed a few hours away. He reached across his body and placed his hand on the sword and shield that had once belonged to his father, who had been killed seven years earlier at the Battle of Ashdown. He remembered that day, long ago, when the Berkshiremen had wheeled his father's body home in the back of an oxcart and buried it with honor in the fields as he, his mother and his sister looked on.

He had been the man of the family ever since. He was now nineteen years old, a freeman with his own hide of land—forty acres that he worked faithfully each day. He had no prospects for marriage, nor did his mother and sister. They were all each other had. They had begged him not to march off to join Alfred, fearing he would meet the fate of his father, but he refused to listen; he was not about to be branded a coward for failing to gather at Egbert's Stone.

He shivered from the damp spring chill in the air. As he looked into the darkness, the last lingering stars began to disappear, until finally only Venus remained, a single, frozen pinpoint of light dangling like a jewel in the eastern sky. And then the black became gray, and the first rays of daylight began to penetrate the low mist that rose from the stream at Iley where they had spent the night, just a few miles south of the Viking camp at Edington. He rose from the cold earth and shook himself, rummaging through his possessions and extracting a thin crust of bread.

"This is the day we've been waiting for, Wulfric."

He turned around to see Cutha, a boyhood friend from his native Berkshire. He forced a smile. "Did you sleep well?"

"No. I woke up hours ago...but I feel rested. Beorn is mustering the men. We'll be marching soon."

Within the hour the Saxons broke camp and formed ranks. As the men began to march northward through the lightly wooded countryside, Wulfric grasped the pommel of his sword for reassurance. He did not know how it had come into his father's possession, but it comforted him in a way that no words ever could. He glanced to his right, where Cutha marched next to him; neither of them had spoken since the ranks had formed. Most of the men remained lost in their thoughts, lapsing into long stretches of silence as they rolled, step by step, with the rhythm of the march.

Cutha broke the silence. "Do you think they know we're coming?"

"Of course they do." It was their leader Beorn, a king's reeve from their village who marched next to them a few yards away. He looked pointedly at Cutha, and Wulfric could see the hard edge to his eyes. "Save your energy, boy," he hissed. "Spill their blood. Spill their blood and bless the land."

The remainder of the march passed uneventfully into the late morning, until a stirring in the ranks ahead alerted Wulfric that their journey was about to come to an end. He strained unsuccessfully to see above the mass of men fronting him, until suddenly his detachment broke through the trees and the land dropped off, and his questions were answered. There before him to the north, less than a mile away, he could see a host of some ten thousand Vikings stretched across the broad plain. They advanced at a steady walk, shaking their weapons above their heads, their shimmering helmets reflecting the sunlight with an uncommon brilliance. Even at that distance the Saxons could hear their cries, a series of low rumbles that rolled across the grassy expanse that separated the armies.

A sudden panic surged through Wulfric, but he continued to press forward. Behind him, the balance of the Saxon army filtered through the wood and onto the open ground. Ahead, the land sloped steadily downward for perhaps two hundred yards, where it flattened out into the broad, level plain. Two low, tree-covered ridges, merging together at the southern end of Edington where the Saxons now stood, fanned northward to form a natural bowl that framed the open expanse. At the far end of the plain, behind the Vikings, Wulfric could see the low knoll on which Guthrum had pitched his camp.

A shout rose from the army, and his attention was drawn to a figure that galloped across the open area in front of the first ranks; it was King Alfred himself. The Golden Dragon of Wessex reined in his familiar white charger and looked off toward the Vikings, whose war cries continued to grow in volume as the distance between the armies diminished.

"Listen to them!" Alfred shouted, in a voice so clear and strong that every man could hear it. "Barbarians, they are! Animals! Steel your hearts and prepare for battle!"

Wulfric's hopes rose; the king was magnificent. The noon sun reflected off his armor, surpassed in brilliance only by the gleaming crown of gold atop his head.

"Hear me!" Alfred cried out. "Advance and engage them on the flat, at the base of the slope!" He pointed to the spot, several hundred yards away. "Meet them along the line...but after the battle is joined, horns will sound to order a withdrawal...give ground back up the slope, but in orderly fashion! Hold your form! And then we'll turn on them and send their souls to Hell!"

The men cheered, but Alfred's urgent motion for silence quieted them instantly.

"Saxons!" he implored a final time, raising his sword high above his crowned head and waving it at the Vikings. "They fight to eat your bread and lie with your women! But you fight for the land, for the blood of your fathers, for everything that's dear! You fight for life itself, and the one true God!" He wheeled his horse around to face the Vikings and thrust his sword into the bright sunlight.

"For God and England! For Wessex!"

The army sprang forward with a roar. Wulfric was swept forward in the great wave of flesh as the men pressed down the slope. They surged past Alfred and swarmed toward the Danes, who had advanced to within five hundred yards of them, into the narrower part of the plain. The gap between the armies began to close with frightening speed. Wulfric moved carefully, afraid of losing his footing and being trampled under the feet of his own soldiers. Despite the speed with which the two armies approached each other, everything appeared to slow down. He could now see the first wave of Vikings; their ranks formed an unbroken line of shields, beneath which their legs pumped forward like the limbs of some giant monstrosity, pounding the earth. Their babbling filled him with dread.

Closer and closer the armies drew, until the Saxons reached the flat land at the base of the incline. And then suddenly an eager soldier in the front ranks sprinted into the space between the hosts. A deafening roar shattered the air, and both armies broke into a dead run toward each other. Wulfric pounded forward, shouting with the others to release the tension, staring above the sea of bouncing heads before him. The distance between the hosts evaporated as they plummeted toward each other: fifty yards, thirty, a scream and—impact!

The front ranks began to hack desperately at each other. Behind them, Wulfric and his companions-in-arms slowed to a standstill, pressed together shoulder to shoulder, still separated from the point of attack by some thirty yards. As he edged forward his buckler jammed hard against the back of the man immediately ahead of him, and all he could see was a flurry of arms raising and lowering their weapons. He was pulled ever closer.

And then suddenly he found himself face to face with a large Dane. The man sprang upon him and swung a large axe at his head, but Wulfric parried the blow and instinctively swung his father's sword in a low arc parallel to the ground. It caught the Viking under the kidney and spun him to the earth as a bloody slash opened up along his side. Before Wulfric could follow his advantage, a Saxon standing beside him buried his blade in the Viking's chest, and a volcano of blood erupted into the air.

Wulfric felt like vomiting. He suppressed the urge and stumbled to one side, and then we was swept up in the action for what seemed like many minutes until several horn blasts pierced the air. The next thing he saw was the mounted figure of Osferth waving to the men around him to withdraw. The Saxons began to give ground slowly, pausing every few yards to blunt the enemy advance as they retreated up the incline.

The Vikings surged forward with renewed confidence, clamoring for blood. As Wulfric backpedaled furiously a few yards ahead of the pursuit, he stumbled over a body that lay on the earth behind him and fell to the ground. For a brief, sickening moment his flanks were exposed, and as he scrambled frantically to his feet he half-expected to feel an axe bury itself in his back. But he regained his balance in time to ward off a lone sword thrust and then continued to stagger up the hill.

By now the retreat had degenerated into a rout. Many of the Saxons broke into a sprint toward the wooded crest of the ridge at their rear, and Wulfric began to believe the battle was lost, that the dream had been an illusion. A great shame and dishonor had come to them all. They had failed; there was nothing left.

But at that moment, as he scanned the crest of the hill barely a hundred yards ahead of him, a strange and wonderful sight met his eyes. A lone figure— Eadred of Mercia, he was later told—stepped out from the wood with his sword raised. Immediately a long line of archers appeared, bows drawn, and as their commander brought his sword earthward, they released their arrows into the air.

The sky was filled as a blur of deadly missiles flew over the Saxons and rained down upon the enemy. A blast of horns filled the bowl of land, and the wooded ridges that framed either side of the plain suddenly erupted with men as hundreds of Saxons streamed down the hillsides on both Viking flanks. In that moment Wulfric's heart soared. As the Mercian archers in the rear continued to rain arrows into the Viking ranks, the Saxons turned again on their enemies, redoubling their efforts. Almost instantly, the momentum changed hands, and fear and doubt shifted to the Danish side. The heathens began to buckle, surrounded on three sides by Christian swords.

Wulfric and the men around him pressed ahead as the Vikings gave way. Now every man on both sides fought with a desperation that transcended anything that had already taken place on the battlefield. By now the lines had become obscured, and Wulfric found himself in the midst of chaos, never knowing at any moment whether friend or foe stood behind his back. He hacked wildly at anything that moved, and he was swept across the plain by the waves of men that collided against one another.

Gradually, inexorably, the scales tipped in favor of Wessex and the Vikings were pushed back across the plain. The Danish center had collapsed, and its flanks were slowly being pinned back. But the heathen rear guard strung the action out, leading a steady retreat until the bulk of the Vikings had drawn near the primitive palisade at the edge of their camp. The Danes closest to the knoll broke for the stakes in the hope of salvaging a defensible position, but the Hampshiremen of Osric who fought along that sector held them at bay, slowly wedging themselves between the Vikings and the outer trench that fronted the palisade.

Wulfric was among these men, for he had been swept over to the right flank during the course of the battle. As he fought alongside these strangers, he could not help but notice a tall Norseman in their ranks—a muscled warrior who swung his battleaxe in concert with Osric, the ealdorman of Hampshire. Wulfric had heard rumors of the Viking and knew that he was a favorite of the king himself, but this was the first time he had seen the man. Any of the heathens who came within his range were cut down like striplings at the hand of a master woodsman's axe.

The Danes who were pinned together in the shadow of the palisade now fought with a final desperation, knowing they would be no quarter at the hands of the Saxons. But Sigli's presence inspired the men of Wessex, and as long as he led the Saxon resistance at the trench it was clear that the Vikings would not pass.

That was when Ogrin, one of Guthrum's trusted lieutenants, took matters into his own hands. He was a grizzled, battle-hardened warrior acknowledged to have no equal in hand-to-hand combat, and he surged forward through the tangle of men until he stood face to face with Sigli. Although Ogrin was a much shorter man, his thick, stocky arms were capable of wielding a heavy broadsword all day without tiring. He weaved and ducked under the thrusts of his taller adversary, keeping up a steady flow of short, brutal strokes that forced Sigli off balance. They continued to flail away at each other for what seemed an eternity, until Ogrin closed in and managed to hook his foot behind Sigli's left heel. Leaning behind his shield, he threw his shoulder into the Halfsfiordian and sent him stumbling backward, sprawling to the earth. Ogrin pounced on his fallen prey and rained blows down upon his shield.

As Sigli struggled to defend himself, a mighty swing of Ogrin's broadsword caught his buckler and tore it from his grasp, spinning it beyond his reach. Stretched out with only with his battleaxe to protect him, his position was desperate. But as Ogrin moved in for the kill, a broadsword slashed through the air from behind and caught him squarely in the throat, decapitating him. Looking up, Sigli saw the proud figure of Osric standing triumphantly over the body.

"We're even now, Viking!" Osric shouted down at him. "A life for a life! My debt is paid!"

Paid, by all accounts, at the eleventh hour. For in the hairsbreadth of time that Osric stood rejoicing over the fallen Viking, a sword thrust caught him squarely in the small of the back. He crumpled to the ground and lay there gasping, mortally wounded, as the blood seeped through his coat of light mail. Sigli dispatched the Viking with a blow from his axe and then knelt beside Osric, resting the dying man's head in the crook of his arm.

"Are we complete?" the ealdorman whispered hoarsely, looking up into the Viking's eyes. "All is as it should be. The field belongs to Wessex..."

He began to cough violently, and a look of alarm darted across his face. He grabbed Sigli's arm with all of his waning strength, forcing his words through blood-stained lips. "Confess me!"

Sigli looked desperately around for help, but the battle had drifted farther down the palisade, leaving only a few stragglers nearby. Wulfric, by chance, was one of them. He hurried over and fell to his knees alongside the dying man.

"Confess me!" Osric gasped again.

Wulfric tentatively raised his right hand and made the sign of the cross over Osric's chest, uttering the words that he had heard the holy men use so many times before. "I absolve you of all your sins, in the name of the Father, the Son and the Holy Spirit."

Upon hearing this all fear passed from the ealdorman. A smile appeared on his lips, and the light faded from his eyes as he died on the plain of Edington.

Sigli nodded to Wulfric above the body, and then the two men turned back to the battle—or what was left of it. The fight near the palisade was virtually over, as only a few Vikings struggled to prevent the inevitable. Within moments they were killed. Only a lucky handful of the Danes on the Saxon right managed to break through the lines and join with the remainder of Guthrum's army, where they swarmed northward like a herd of frightened sheep toward Chippenham.

And then it was over.

The running stopped and the plain grew quiet. A strange, silence filled the air, and each man was overcome by the sound of his own thundering heartbeat. Wulfric surveyed the carnage around him; everywhere he looked, the grassy field was littered with bodies. He realized that the afternoon had come and gone, and the waning sun had moved into the western sky, leaving long shadows to cover the corpses strewn across the plain. He became aware of a burning sensation in his left arm and, looking down, was surprised to see he was covered with blood. But a closer inspection revealed that the wound was less severe than it had first appeared to be. He would not lose the arm.

And then as he looked up again, Cutha approached, smiling broadly. The two friends dropped their weapons and stumbled toward each other. They embraced and drew their heads back, and they began to laugh until it seemed as though their stomachs would burst—and until Wulfric noticed a strange gleam in his friend's eyes. Cutha had become hysterical. Wulfric patted him on the back, comforting him. There were others around them, men who also were too overcome for words; nothing could describe what they had passed through.

A great thing had been done that day. Against all odds, they had beaten the Vikings. It was a moment of pride and honor, a triumph beyond compare.

And as Wulfric stood there on the plain of Edington, his thoughts drifted once more to his father, and all of the afternoon's maddening passion suddenly boiled up again inside him. He shook lightly and then he, too, broke down and wept. The tears ran down his face in long, burning salt streams, releasing a spirit that washed over him. He looked up into the red of the western sky, and suddenly his heart soared. He had passed through the inferno and emerged whole, bringing great honor to himself and his family. He would always remember this glorious day; it was the day he became a man.

He smiled to himself. Beorn had said it best, after all. Spill their blood. Spill every last drop of their heathen blood.

And bless the land.

*   *   *   *   *

The Battle of Edington was one of the pivotal events of ninth-century England. It sustained the Saxon culture that had come to the British Isles some four hundred years earlier. It nurtured the flame of Christianity during the depths of the Dark Ages, when all of western civilization reeled under the weight of ignorance. And it proved that the Vikings could be held in check.

While the Norse invaders would continue to threaten Wessex and its allies for the next fifty years, never again would a Saxon king be driven to the brink of extinction by the Danish hand, forced to hide as Alfred had in the wilderness, an exile without kingdom or hope. Edington was a symbol of resiliency, a preservation of a way of life. Until it was eclipsed by the Norman invasion at Hastings in 1066, nearly two hundred years later, it was the most significant battle fought on English soil during the Saxon era. By any measure, it was the most important Saxon victory ever; without it, Alfred the Great's subsequent reign and its many remarkable accomplishments would likely have never come to pass.

No one, of course, could understand all these things in the weeks immediately following the battle. But the victory had been utterly decisive, and that was enough. Guthrum's army was shattered. Many of his men were dead, while the rest were scattered throughout the countryside, there to be hunted down by the relentless Saxons. Some would manage to reach Mercia safely, but most of the survivors fled with Guthrum to Chippenham and holed up inside the walled royal estate. Alfred camped with his army outside the gates and laid siege to the city, waiting patiently for the Viking resolve to weaken. Each day the Christian ranks swelled, as those who had been too timid to make a stand at Edington now flocked to Alfred, tipping the scales heavily against the Vikings.

The only alternative for Guthrum was to sit. And wait. And starve.

Ubba's death had effectively cut off the Viking king's right arm, depriving him of his most potent ally. Haestan, meanwhile, was now but a distant dream; a fleet of his ships had lingered off the eastern coast of England near the mouth of the Thames, but the news of Edington drove them back to the continent to join their leader in Francia. So each day Guthrum paced the walls of Chippenham, surrounded by those of his intimates who had survived the battle, stalling for a time that could not come, waiting.

Such was the general mood as Plegmund led a small train of wagons through the Saxon camp and toward Alfred's tent. He had been charged with collecting the members of the royal family from their refuge near Winchester and escorting them to Chippenham. It was a task he was more than happy to perform, considering the part he had played during the desperate flight from Alfred's estate on that memorable winter's night some four months earlier.

The party had taken several days to make the journey, accompanied every mile of the way by an escort of Saxons. Their leisurely pace had been compromised only by their desire to be reunited quickly with Alfred. And now, finally, the waiting was over. As the procession of oxcarts negotiated its way through the Saxon tents, the tired travelers were treated to the sight of hundreds of men-at-arms who lined up to greet them, forming a makeshift path that wound its way deeper into the camp and ended at Alfred's tent. The king stood waiting ceremoniously for the procession, trying his best to restrain himself. But when the lead cart bearing his family rolled into view, he broke into a run toward them. Ealswith and the children, in defiance of courtly behavior, poured out of the wagon and swarmed around him, lavishing warm, adoring kisses on his face.

Sigli stood nearby with the scores of Saxons who had gathered near Alfred's tent, watching silently amidst the general jubilation. His heart was lifted by the reunion, but the taste was bittersweet; he could not help thinking of his own family, about how such a moment would be denied them forever. As these thoughts occupied his mind, it occurred to him that no matter how much the

Saxons might accept him, he would never truly be one of them. He was a Viking—a man outside of the Faith whose slim foothold in the society was due only to his peculiar relationship with the king. At best, he would always be viewed with a degree of mistrust, as an outsider. He smiled gamely as the members of the royal family passed by, arm-in-arm with Alfred, on their way into the king's tent. And then he slipped away from the celebration and started to walk alone through the camp.

Alone, except for Plegmund. The young monk saw him moving away from the crowd and followed quickly, catching up to him within a few paces. Sigli glanced up distractedly but said nothing, continuing to walk on his way.

"You're unharmed," Plegmund ventured cautiously, keeping pace. "I'm glad. I didn't hear any news of you, and feared the worst. "

Sigli refused to acknowledge him. He pressed forward, his eyes riveted straight ahead.

"It was a great victory," the monk said, undeterred. "All of Wessex rejoices."

Sigli grunted, but once again did not look up. Plegmund's brow creased.

"Your language skills must have improved over the last few months. I would think that..."

"What is it you want of me?"

"I...I was hoping we could continue our lessons."

"I understand English well enough."

"It wasn't the language I was talking about. We must continue to strengthen your understanding of the Faith."

"The Faith! Don't bother me, monk!"

"But you must be baptized...that was the agreement!"

"Don't meddle with me!" Sigli snorted, quickening his pace. "Look to the Viking prisoners, now that Guthrum's been defeated. I've done my duty by Alfred!"

He turned and strode angrily away, ending the conversation. Gradually his anger subsided, replaced by feelings of remorse. He realized he had acted hastily and vowed that he would set matters right with Plegmund, who in spite of all his petty annoyances had proved to be a friend. He trudged along, kicking up the camp dust and wandering in the general direction of the river, until a strange sight met his eyes, recalling a host of bad memories.

There, close by the water's edge, Alfred's men had erected a makeshift stockade. Scores of Viking prisoners mingled in the cramped space inside the walls, their faces pressed against the gaps in the palisade, gazing dolefully out past the Saxon guards posted around the primitive enclosure. As he drew closer, the eyes of the Vikings inside the stockade shifted to him, their stares filled with a brooding hopelessness.

"Sigli!"

The voice sounded familiar. He scanned the sea of faces until his eyes were drawn to a man who waved animatedly to him; to his great delight, he recognized the Viking as Dagmar, a countryman from Halfsfiord. He bounded toward the stockade until only a few feet separated him from the palisade.

"By Odin, I thought you were dead!" Dagmar exclaimed. His face was drawn and dirty, but imprisonment could not hide his excitement and disbelief at meeting up with his shipmate.

"Are you well? Are they feeding you enough?"

Dagmar smiled a toothy grin. "I'm not starving, if that's what you mean. But, forget about me...how is it you're allowed to walk freely...?"

"Because I'm not with Guthrum. I'm with Alfred."

Dagmar's face dropped. "You? Fighting with the Christians?"

Sigli smiled weakly. "It's far too long a story to tell now. But I don't wish to take up arms against you—or any of Guthrum's men, for that matter. Only one thing concerns me, Dagmar..." His eyes grew cold. "Where's Sidroc?"

Dagmar looked down at the ground and shook his head. "He's somewhere in Francia. With Haestan's army, as far as I know." He glanced up tentatively, his eyes pleading. "I...I joined him at first, when all was lost. But I left him as soon as I could and came to England. Sigli...you must understand!"

"I'm prepared to forget. But you must help me."

"Anything, Sigli. You know that."

"You can start by telling me about my mother."

Dagmar let out a long sigh. "He didn't harm her, I can tell you that. But within a month after the attack, she became very ill." He hesitated. "She...she died a few weeks later."

Sigli clenched his fists, struggling for control. After a moment the anger passed out of him and his face settled into a cold, stony mask.

"We all left Halfsfiord shortly after that," Dagmar continued. "Sidroc burnt the great hall to the ground and left nothing but ashes behind him." He shook his head. "There's nothing, Sigli...it's all gone."

Sigli's eyes narrowed. "And Mimir?"

"When Mimir resisted Sidroc, the Malevolent One ordered him put to death. But when they went to the seer's quarters to find him, he was gone. They never found him...I don't know if he's alive or dead." He let out a deep breath. "In any case, I made my way to England and joined Guthrum in Mercia. That was late last autumn, after he'd been driven from Exeter by Alfred. And I wasn't the only one from Halfsfiord; at least a dozen of your father's men ended up here. Hagan and Gylfi joined the army, along with Hoenir, Bor and Leif. Unless they were killed during the battle, I'm sure they're with Guthrum, inside the city. But Sigli...can you help me? What will they do with us?"

"I can't do anything right now. But don't worry...Alfred is a just man."

"Rumor has it we'll either be executed or pressed into slavery."

Sigli shook his head. "I can't believe that would happen. But if it comes to that, I can help you. And the others from Halfsfiord as well. But if I do so, you must promise me one thing."

"Name it."

"That you and the others will join me in my quest."

"By Odin, I swear it. Had I known you were still alive, I'd have sought you out to the ends of the earth."

"I believe you, Dagmar...and because of that I'll see to it that you're spared, no matter what happens to the rest of the prisoners."

"Thank you, Sigli." Dagmar, a strong man, was on the verge of tears.

"You'll pay me back before we're through, you can be sure of that. Someday, no doubt, I'll need your sword—but for the next few years, we have ships to build, my friend! Ships that will someday sail in search of Sidroc!"

He reached through the stakes of the palisade and grasped Dagmar's hand, squeezing it tightly before turning on his heel and heading back toward the main part of the camp. The veil that had overtaken him had turned its dark attention away just long enough for a ray of sunshine to seep through. He had been uplifted by the encounter. It was a comfort to know that he was not the only orphan cast adrift in the storm that had destroyed Halfsfiord; others of his kind, men who knew and respected him, would again stand by his side.

A renewed hope surged through him. With Alfred back in power and his shipmates on hand to help, anything was possible. The House of Lothar would rise again. He would see to it.

His steps grew so light that even the camp dust remained undisturbed by his passing.

*　　*　　*　　*　　*

"Be bold, Guthrum. We have nothing to lose."

Old Iglaf's jaw was set in stone as he rode through the gates of Chippenham. He accompanied the Warlord, who that morning had finally made his decision to sue for peace. Two weeks had passed since the battle, and the men were getting hungry; they could not hide behind the city walls any longer.

So Guthrum and his advisor rode into the bright sunlight at high noon on this fine spring day, where ahead of them a lone tent rose up from the open stretch of ground between the Saxon army and the walled city. Guthrum had insisted it be that way. He was not about to ride unescorted into the midst of the Christian rabble, truce or no truce, where one false move could provoke the hostile mob against him. In accordance with his wishes, only a small contingent of Saxons surrounded the tent, for it had been agreed that all of Alfred's companions at the meeting would be men of title. The balance of the army was restricted to the main camp.

The Vikings rode forward at a slow, steady pace, in no hurry to confront the fate ahead of them. "We're bargaining for our lives," Guthrum smirked. "We can't expect much more than that." He looked over at Iglaf and smiled weakly. "After all…what would you do, if the tables were turned…?"

"If the terms are impossible, we can always fight," Iglaf shrugged glumly. "I'm not afraid to die, if it comes to that."

They could feel the cold eyes of the Saxons boring into them as they drew nearer, but they kept on until they reached the meeting place. There they dismounted and stood waiting in front of the long table that had been positioned in front of the tent. But no one moved to greet them, and they were forced to wait in awkward silence for what seemed an eternity, their eyes avoiding the sullen stares of their adversaries.

After several minutes their patience was rewarded. A fold in the tent parted, and Alfred stepped boldly into the open air, dressed in a richly embroidered robe befitting a triumphant king. The gold crown perched on his head glistened in the sunlight.

" Lord Guthrum...we meet again. Please..." The king pointed to several stools across the table. They were positioned lower than their counterparts, a subtle strategy that was not lost on Guthrum as he and Iglaf sat down. The ealdormen closed in around them like scavengers hovering over a defenseless corpse. After everyone had moved into position, Alfred took his place at the center of the table, thrusting his chin forward and carefully placing his hands face down on the table.

"Here stands the soul of Wessex," he said, looking around at his compatriots. "These are the men who stood by her in time of peril." He looked across the table at Guthrum, his pale eyes remaining neutral, uncommitted. "I hope we can understand each other...my language, sometimes, is rough. But here is one who can help us, should I falter." He pointed to Sigli, who stood off to the side a few paces away.

"We can understand you well enough," Iglaf replied curtly. "We don't need him."

"Very well, then. Let's begin."

Guthrum sat stiffly upright and cleared his throat. "I'll speak plainly, my Lord...we'll give you as many hostages as you want, and ask for none in return. Let us leave and go back to Mercia."

"Insolent wretch!" Penda shouted, bolting from his chair. But an icy stare from Alfred stopped him, and he sat down quickly, holding his tongue.

"We've always received equal hostages in the past," Guthrum continued, slowly but persuasively. "Enough men have died. Be reasonable...."

"Reasonable..?" sneered Fulric of Kent, who understood the Viking tongue. "We should hang all you heathen butchers and be done with it!"

"That's enough!" Alfred stood up in anger, his eyes flashing. Slowly, he swung his attention back to Guthrum. "You ask me to be reasonable, and yet have you ever acted so? It's not for you—nor anyone else---to tell me the way things should be!" He stood tall against the brilliant sky, the pupils of his eyes frozen. "*I* am Wessex, Guthrum. I alone shall decide your fate."

He leaned forward and placed his knuckles on the table; they grew white from the pressure of his weight upon them. "You invaded my land, the land of my forefathers. You tried to take it for yourself! I was cast out like a common beggar into the swamps, my people divided, their spirit broken. For that crime, there are some who would have you stretched out on the dry earth and left there to rot, Viking!"

Guthrum's face hardened. "We'll die fighting first."

"I have no doubt you would, and that would certainly be the case. For as sure as God in heaven watches over Wessex, you'd be crushed like a grape in the summer sun." Suddenly the king's tone softened, and he sat down. "But you're right...neither of us wants that...." Here he paused, raising an eyebrow for emphasis. "Your only reasonable choice is to accept my terms—completely."

"And what does that mean?"

"Unconditional surrender—in return for which you and all your men will be spared and set free."

A loud gasp escaped the Saxons at the table. Guthrum snuck a quick glance at Iglaf out of the corner of his eye, but the old Viking sat glued to his chair, stunned.

Alfred stood up again and raised his hands. "Hear me, all of you!" He waited until the table grew quiet and all eyes rested upon him. "A part of me cries out for death—but that's the man in me speaking. As king of this land, I must think about what's best for my people, for Wessex. And that's why I'm sparing you, Guthrum. Northumbria and East Anglia are already settled by your people; many have been there for a generation or more. It's their homeland now. No matter what happens here, I couldn't change that. Your death or imprisonment would accomplish nothing."

An uneasy murmur rippled through the Saxons.

"It's clear to me that our people must learn to live together," Alfred continued. "Otherwise, only destruction can result. And that's why, Guthrum, you must accept each of my terms."

The Warlord nodded cautiously. "Name them."

"First, you must grant me as many hostages as I choose. And you shall receive none in return."

"Agreed."

"Then, all your men must surrender their arms and issue forth from the city."

"Be careful, Guthrum," Iglaf warned. "What guarantee do we have they won't slaughter us like sheep?"

"Only my word," Alfred said evenly. "Nothing more."

Guthrum squinted up at the king. "Your word is enough. What else?"

"You must leave Wessex, of course—and Mercia as well. You must return to East Anglia and Northumbria, and never again venture into Christian England with an armed force."

"I...agree."

"You must swear allegiance to me for the rest of your life. And you must never lend support to any other Viking attack on these shores, whether led by Haestan or anyone else. If you turn against me, Guthrum, as God is my witness I'll hunt you down and destroy you!"

Guthrum, ever cautious, nodded his assent.

"And finally," said Alfred, "to seal our trust, you and your most trusted men must be baptized into the Christian faith."

"Never!" It was Iglaf who protested. He bolted from his chair in anger, his eyes blazing defiantly.

"Sit down, Iglaf!" Guthrum whispered sternly, glaring at the old Viking. He was not about to let anything stand in the way of this remarkable offer of freedom. Iglaf relented, and Guthrum again turned his attention to Alfred.

"You're a great king, my Lord," the Warlord began, "and a great statesman. I trust you. You've dealt with me today in a just manner, and as I'm a man, I won't go back on my promise." He looked forcefully at each of the ealdormen, driving his point home clearly in spite of the language barrier. Finally, he turned back to Alfred.

"You've granted us our lives, and much more. For that, I swear to never again take up arms against you, nor aid anyone else in such an undertaking." He slid from his chair and fell to his knees before the king. "I agree to all your terms, Alfred. And I swear allegiance to you, until the end of my days." He motioned to Iglaf, who knelt down beside him.

Alfred beamed. He spread his arms out and looked expansively around the table, his eyes meeting those of each and every man. "We've all done an honorable thing today," he smiled. "The war's over; our battles are ended. In three weeks we'll gather at the country church at Aller, near the swamp fortress of Athelney that served Wessex so well in her hour of need. And there, Guthrum, you'll be baptized as a Christian—as my godson—and acknowledge the one, true God."

He paused for a moment. "Thirty of your men shall join you in receiving the sacrament, as well as those heathens in my own camp..." here his eyes rested pointedly on Sigli, "...who have not yet entered the Faith. And so, God's will shall be done."

With that the Golden Dragon of Wessex turned abruptly and headed off on foot across the plain toward the main camp, effectively ending the negotiations. Every Saxon and Viking eye followed him in stunned disbelief.

* * * * *

"He'll break his promise, I tell you. They can't be trusted."

Grimwald smirked with disgust. He turned away from Plegmund and flicked the water from his fingers, reaching for a nearby cloth to dry himself. It was a distasteful business, these heathen baptisms; if only it were possible to wash his hands of them altogether. It was apparent to him that any willingness on Guthrum's part to kneel at a Christian altar was purely a matter of survival. He knew treachery when he smelled it.

"But..." Plegmund argued gently, "isn't it our holy duty to convert them?"

Grimwald scowled. "In theory, perhaps...but experience tells me otherwise. It's not worth the trouble."

He sucked in his jowls and vacantly scanned the interior of the small sacristy where they waited, tucked away in the rear of the country church near Aller. It was a warm and muggy day in early June, and the coolness of the stone church was refreshing. He could hear the Saxons gathering outside, the buzz of their conversation accompanying them as they entered the chapel.

"The heathen mind is, by nature, contrary to the Church, and must be dealt with accordingly," Grimwald continued, struggling to fit himself into his full-length white alb, "but, see here, Plegmund. Help me, will you?"

Unable to adjust the garment by himself, he turned around and leaned over. In the next moment he felt Plegmund's dainty hands moving deftly along his backside; their touch was sure and soft. He grunted with satisfaction as the alb finally slipped into place and he turned around, looking squarely into Plegmund's pleasant, smiling face. Such a pretty young thing, he thought, admiring the fair-skinned young monk. It might be better than a woman, even. He had to exercise great discretion as a man of the Church, but he was not above engaging his fancies when opportunity presented itself. Something about Plegmund appealed to him, despite—-or maybe because of—God's law that expressly forbade such an unnatural act. He had never had a boy before, but he'd often thought about it.

"Alfred has asked me to go to Wedmore with him," Plegmund said. "He'll be entertaining Guthrum and his men for a week before they leave for East Anglia. Will you be going?"

"No. I have business in Winchester...where, by the way, you should visit. You linger too long in the provincial west, Plegmund. Pay heed to where the ecclesiastical power lies."

"I suspect Alfred will send me back to Worcester with Werferth. I don't think I'm needed at the court, now that Sigli has learned the language and will be baptized."

Grimwald smiled treacherously. "You're confident that this noble savage of yours will accept the Lord Jesus into his heart?"

Plegmund averted his eyes. "He'll be baptized, like the others."

"We'll see about that. But, forget about him for now. When you're at Wedmore, I want you to petition Alfred to stay with him. He's fond of you, you know; he might be receptive if you offered to begin translating some of the classics he so reveres."

"You may be right, but...why do you want me there?"

Grimwald pursed his lips. "I need someone in the court...a watchful eye, shall we say. Alfred may be a devout man, but there are many interests that vie for his attention and his resources."

He moved closer to Plegmund, smiling sweetly. "We must ensure that the appropriate monies are continually set aside for the Church. A bright young theologian like you could have a fine future, if he so desires..." He reached out and ran his hand softly along the young monk's arm.

Plegmund shuddered involuntarily but recovered quickly, forcing a half-hearted smile to hide his revulsion. Grimwald, ever observant, had already drawn his hand back. At that moment the door behind them opened and Werferth entered the room.

"They're moving inside the chapel now," the Bishop of Worcester said. "But there's a bit of a problem."

"Oh...?" Grimwald wondered. "Is Guthrum having second thoughts?"

"No. He and his men are here. It's Sigli...he's nowhere to be seen."

"I told you!" Grimwald snapped triumphantly at Plegmund. He turned again to Werferth. "And what does the king have to say about that?"

"Nothing, except to begin the ceremony. But he appeared to be quite displeased."

"And this, pray tell, is the man who will build the Christians a navy...?" Grimwald cackled. "I should like to see how Alfred's little pet will squirm free of this one." He moved toward the door and motioned to the others to follow.

"Come. The wolves await our blessing."

As they walked through the door and onto the altar, the chapel opened up before them. From the outside, the country church appeared to be a nondescript structure of rude masonry, but the interior offered a dazzling contrast; gold and silver altar plate gleamed in chiaroscuro richness against the shadowy backdrop of purple wall hangings that adorned the chapel. The sweet, pungent odor of incense and candle wax permeated the room. Beyond the low rail that fronted the altar, a sea of faces washed across every corner of the church. In attendance were Alfred and the royal family, a large group of ealdormen and local gentry—even Meric and Ingewold, the peasant keepers of Athelney—all gathered to witness the sacred ritual.

But the strangest sight of all was Guthrum and his thirty companions, Iglaf among them, all as immaculate in their white robes as a choir of angels. Seeing these fierce barbarians gathered respectfully in a place of Christian worship was an unexpected vision, one that Plegmund realized he might never lay eyes on again.

After everyone settled in place, the ceremony began, proceeding without interruption. Alfred himself raised Guthrum from the baptismal font, standing as godfather to the old pirate and bestowing upon him the Saxon name of

Athelstan—"noble stone"—a far cry from the Warlord's Viking name, which meant "battle worm." Following anointment with the consecrating oil, the heads of the Vikings were bound with a white cloth to be worn for eight days; after that, the unbinding of the chrisms was to take place at Wedmore, concluding the baptism and marking the entry of the Danes into the Faith.

But Plegmund's mind was elsewhere. All he could think of was Sigli's disappearance, and its possible consequences. Only Alfred knew the answer. And the king's impassive features held no clue.

*   *   *   *   *

At that moment, many miles to the southeast, Sigli spurred his horse forward along the western bank of the river Avon. After slipping away undetected from the main party as it headed to Aller, he had ridden alone for a day and a half, stopping only to spend the night at the ancient Druid temple of Stonehenge. He had stared up at the starry skies and collected his thoughts. His decision had not been easy, but in his heart he knew it had been the right one. And now as he rounded a thick grove of trees along the riverbank, the familiar, salty smell of the sea greeted him. He had not laid eyes on the Great Water in almost a year, not since the shipwreck of his voyage to England.

As he approached the coast, the small settlement of Twyneham rose up ahead, near the spot where the rivers Avon and Stour emptied into the sea. He turned his back on the Avon and headed west through the trees, preferring to avoid meeting anyone on the path along the riverbank. Before long he came to the Stour, which he forded and left behind, riding the last mile or so to the south until he reached the edge of a sheltered cove located around the hook of the natural harbor that fronted Twyneham. Its waters stretched placidly toward the southeast, protected from the elements by a low headland that jutted out into the sea. He rode farther around the curve of the harbor and up onto the humpbacked spit of land, and when he reached the top of the rise he saw what he had come for.

There before him, the English Channel stretched out across the horizon in a long, low swell of windswept sea. He dismounted from his horse and sat on the damp earth, content to watch the waves scudding across his line of vision. He rested for a while, and as he did so a renewal passed through him, as though Njord had reached out from beneath the whitecaps and touched him with the hand of the gods. His resolve was strengthened, his mind made up. He could not bring himself to forsake Asgard and embrace the Christian Jesus. Let Guthrum and the others flock like sheep to the altar; it was not for him to be told what to think. He had proved himself with his sword and his intentions, and that was enough.

He poked at the soft earth and looked toward the east, where the waves hurried along the channel. He knew that Alfred would be angry. But he and the king had passed through the fire together, and that was worth something. Above all, the Golden Dragon needed a fleet of ships to be built, and he was the man to do it. It will blow over, he thought. It will be no more than the wind on the waves, guiding them but never plumbing their depths. As he stared into the dark waters, he saw the faces of his mother and father, and with them his dead brother Hathor. And then, for the first time in months, he allowed himself to think of the beautiful Beolinde. He shook lightly. The tears began to stream down his face, and soon he fell to sobbing, his heart aching for a time that was gone forever.

He forced himself to stand up and stare out into the cloudy sky on the horizon, where it mingled with the sea; somewhere past that gray mystery walked a man whom he had pledged to revenge himself on. His jaw tightened, and in his heart he renewed the promise he had made to his father. He remembered the pain and the agony of that last night at Halfsfiord, a night when the world he had known and loved had come crashing to an end. Almost imperceptibly, he whispered under his breath, so low that even Odin could not hear.

"Guard thee well, Sidroc. For I am coming."

885 A.D.

CHAPTER VII: The Lie

"Oh, what a tangled web we weave,
When first we practice to deceive!"
—Sir Walter Scott, <u>Marmion</u>

It all begins with the felling of an oak in the forest. Not just any oak, mind you, but one with a straight grain, at least two feet thick and seventy feet in length. This shall be fashioned into the keel, and from it the rest of the craft will take shape. After this first piece is cut, another of the same dimensions must be found for the keelson, which shall anchor the ribs of the vessel to the keel. Together, these two timbers form the backbone of the dragon ship, the foundation upon which all else rests.

The keel and keelson are merely the first of many oaks that shall feel the weight of the woodsman's axe; more than a dozen other trees will follow, each at least three feet in diameter and twenty feet tall. These will be quartered and cut into strakes, the thin sideboards that curve seductively along the length of a well-fashioned longship. After enough wood is cut for the strakes, two more sturdy oaks must be selected for the stem and stern posts. These will be followed by assorted other timbers used to fashion the ribs and beams, the knees and deck.

Finally, the straightest pine in the forest must be chosen for the mast. It should be some forty feet tall, and after it is felled a shorter pine should be cut for the yardarm. When the last of the trees has been cut, and all the branches are trimmed away, the logs can be muscled out of the forest and hauled down to the shelving beach, where they will be shaped with adze and axe or split with wedges into planks. Two eighty-foot sleepers will then be laid parallel to each other some sixteen feet apart, leading to the water's edge. Heavy timbers known as stocks will then be placed across the sleepers at intervals, forming a rough foundation upon which the keel may be laid.

After all of this is done, the shipbuilding may begin.

Any man with a strong back and willing helpers would be capable of felling the timber and hauling it down to the beach. And perhaps such a man would also have the good sense to store all the wood in the water, close by the place of work, keeping it soft and green so that it might be fashioned easily into its intended form. But to build a ship sturdy enough to withstand the rigors of wind and wave, a strong back and good sense are not nearly enough. Only an experienced shipbuilder trained as a master craftsman can transform the oak and pine into a seaworthy vessel. And even if he is blessed with these abilities, he must have a deeper understanding of the task. For the sea has a soul all her own; to build a ship a man must be able to peer into that soul, and fashion his fragile creation to be one with it.

Sigli knew this well. He loved the sea as much as he loved anything, and as he stood near the water's edge at Twyneham harbor he felt Njord's finger beckoning to him again. It was a fine June morning, with clear skies and high expectations, and he was filled with a quiet determination as he surveyed the modest shipyard that stretched along the beach. This was his home, as it had been for most of the seven years since Edington. To know that he would soon be leaving it left a taste in his mouth tinged with both the bitter and the sweet.

Much had changed since he had been washed ashore on English soil. It was now the Christian calendar year 885, and he was no longer a youth. At twenty-seven, he had attained full maturity, and with it a patience that enabled him to tolerate the waiting that was the only constant in his struggle to proceed with his work. Building ships should have been a simple enough undertaking, but there had been so many obstacles and detours along the way.

As expected, his refusal to be baptized with Guthrum and the other Vikings had unleashed a backlash of indignation from the Saxons. And it had visibly irritated Alfred, placing the king in a compromising position. All of these forces boiled over in a cauldron of bad feelings until Sigli, frustrated after months of bickering, threatened to leave Wessex.

But at the last minute Alfred softened. He used his considerable diplomatic skills to keep the Saxons at bay, until the debate faded and was replaced in time by more pressing matters. By doing nothing, he accomplished everything; the issue over Sigli's baptism virtually disappeared.

Meanwhile, the shipbuilder gathered together his fellow Halfsfiordians who had been set free with Guthrum's army after Edington. With these loyalists in hand, Sigli pressed the king to begin building the fleet immediately. He chose Twyneham as the site of his shipyard, lured by its protected harbor and proximity to the abundant woodlands of the New Forest. With such resources at hand, he was convinced he would be able to build as many as fifteen ships a year. But his Vikings would not be enough; he needed help from the Saxons. As long as Alfred cooperated, two to three years with such a work crew would see the job done and allow him to set sail for the continent, where he could finally revenge himself upon Sidroc.

But chaos had gripped Wessex for too long, leaving in its wake a mountain of administrative details that begged for attention. On the heels of Alfred's exile, these difficulties proved too much for the court to handle all at once, delaying Sigli's departure for Twyneham for several months. It soon became apparent that the requested labor force of Saxons was more fiction than fact, leaving only the Vikings from Halfsfiord to work on the ships. And when Sigli and his men finally arrived on the coast, they found themselves caught between Alfred's latest policies and the cold shoulders of the local populace.

The king had not stood still. With the weight of any immediate Viking threat to national security removed from his shoulders, he turned his attentions to a number of military, civil and cultural reforms. His experiences fighting the Norsemen had taught him that the most singular characteristic of the Vikings was their ability to strike swiftly, descending on coastal hamlets and river towns and then vanishing before organized resistance could be mustered. To combat this pattern, Alfred mustered the fyrd into alternating units, ensuring that enough Saxons were armed and ready to take the field at all times. While half the men were thus occupied, the rest of the ceorls were left free to till their farms, serving on a rotating basis to satisfy the needs of both the economy and the state

But it was Alfred's second military objective that compromised Sigli. The king issued an edict calling for the construction of fortresses—known as burhs—at strategic sites across the land. And while the Saxons loyally followed the reform of the fyrd, they were less than enthusiastic about leaving their fields to help build the burhs. So it was that when Sigli and his men left for Twyneham to build ships, the king had already formulated other plans. And if he harbored any doubts about his designs, they were erased by the frosty reception the Vikings encountered upon arriving at the Hampshire harbor. The small settlement of Saxons, nestled along the southern coast of Wessex between the Avon and Stour Rivers, was not overly receptive to this peaceful invasion by the heathens, and no provisions were made in the village to accommodate them.

It occurred to Alfred that he could house the Vikings, have his fortress built and placate the local populace all with one master stroke. And so Sigli and his compatriots busied themselves for the next year building a fortress instead of ships. The timber they dragged out of the forest was used for pilings and lodge walls instead of keels and oars. The labor they invested was devoted to the land instead of the sea. Despite the time lost in its construction, the Twyneham burh soon became a comfortable refuge for the exiles from Halfsfiord. There they were allowed to observe their pagan customs in peace, and if Saxon Wessex did not exactly embrace them, it tolerated their presence. And there, Sigli's word was law, enabling him to assume the power that was his right as an ally and trusted confidant of the king.

After all of this work was finally completed, Sigli and his crew labored industriously building ships for two years, helped at times by other Vikings who drifted in and out of their orbit. But the work went slowly; Alfred's wages were modest and could not compete with the opportunities on the continent, from where news filtered across the channel that was always of great interest to Sigli.

He learned that most of Haestan's raiders had settled into Flanders by 880, feasting off Ghent and the surrounding area. Shortly afterward, bands of men splintered off from the army and ranged south and west into Francia, penetrating the territories near the Somme River. Other expeditions ventured eastward into the low countries bordering Frisia, making their way as far as the Rhine and the kingdom of Lotharingia, where the Old Saxons dwelt.

Sigli heard that Sidroc was on the Rhine. The knowledge fueled his resolve, and he managed to complete eight longships during the next two years despite the distractions. But once again the specter of politics raised its ugly head, and by the summer of 882 the usefulness of his activities came under renewed attack. Grimwald, wielding religion like a hunting spear, kept the Church's interests in the forefront. And the monk's secular counterparts, the ealdormen, again began to question Alfred's commitment to the fleet, clamoring instead for his attention to be devoted to internal issues in the shires.

Fortune intervened at this point in the form of an ill-advised heathen raid along the southern coast of Hampshire. A renegade fleet of a half dozen Viking dragon ships landed near Southampton, plundering several farms and a monastery before fleeing seaward. Acting decisively, Alfred sent a large detachment of the fyrd to join up with Sigli at Twyneham. Mercenary sailors were also contracted, and the combined force set sail aboard the ships that Sigli had built to search for the offending raiders.

The result could not have turned out more auspiciously for Alfred. With Sigli and his Halfsfiordians at the helms of the ships, the unsuspecting Vikings were intercepted on the open sea. One of the enemy vessels was sunk, two others captured, and all of the prisoners were put to death as a warning to future pirates who might be tempted to threaten Wessex.

The realization that the heathens could be defeated at their own game dramatically changed the political climate, and further talk of stopping work on the fleet disappeared. Even Grimwald realized that his complaints were useless. The pendulum swung back in Sigli's favor, concluding with a recommendation by the council of Wessex to supplement his crew with Saxons from the surrounding shires. At last, he had the men he needed; his workforce more than doubled, and the masts began to rise above Twyneham harbor like a stand of pines sprouting from the sandy beach. Construction continued unabated for the next three years, during which time he kept his ears open for news of Sidroc, who still remained active along the Rhine.

But in 884, just a year earlier, his worst fears were confirmed. Sidroc disappeared.

That year the Vikings in Lotharingia were defeated by Henry of Saxony and Arno, the Bishop of Wurzburg. The survivors dispersed across the countryside, and subsequent word concerning their movements was contradictory by the time it reached England. Some sources claimed that Sidroc had sailed for Denmark; others thought he was still on the Rhine. But nobody seemed to know the truth, and for the first time since the sack of Halfsfiord doubts began to prey at Sigli. It took all the patience he had acquired to keep his mind at bay. He continued to build the fleet, holding tenaciously to his hope as he watched and waited, steadfast in the belief that the opportunity for his revenge would come.

And now as he stood before the burh at Twyneham, he knew that the time for his departure from England was drawing near. He had launched more than thirty vessels for Alfred during the seven years since Edington; completing the ones in progress would bring the number to an even three dozen. That would entitle him to ownership of seven, along with the use of seven others and their crews, as stipulated in the agreement he had made with the king. It would be enough. With any luck, after eight long years he would find Sidroc, and finally fulfill the promise he had made to his father.

He glanced up and saw Dagmar approaching from the main gate of the burh. He trusted the grizzled Halfsfiordian completely, which was more than he could say for most of the vagrants who drifted through the camp, Saxon or Viking. But as his friend drew closer, it became apparent he was upset. What could it be now?

"It's Gylfi," Dagmar said, shaking his head. "He was drunk last night and wandered into the village. There was trouble."

"What is it this time?"

"He bothered one of their women. The Saxons went after him, but he ran away." Dagmar's eyes narrowed. "They're calling for his head this morning... they say they'll petition the king."

"Damn the fool! Are you sure he was at fault?"

"Does it matter?"

Sigli fell silent. Even back in Halfsfiord, Gylfi had always been a bit of a troublemaker. He was tolerated at Twyneham for his strong back, but this latest incident was another in a long line of indiscretions. Give Gylfi a tankard of mead and he became happy; give him two tankards and he became dangerous. It was clear that he could not be allowed to jeopardize relations with their Christian neighbors, now that the Vikings were so close to completing the last few ships under construction.

"Perhaps we should punish him," Dagmar suggested. "It will placate the Saxons."

"What do you want to do?"

"I say we flog him...and let them watch."

"Is that really necessary?"

"If we don't do something, we could end up with Saxon blood on our hands. We don't have to overdo it. Just a few lashes for appearances."

"But what will the men think? It's not good for morale."

"Hagan was the one who suggested it, Sigli. And Leif and I agreed." Dagmar's voice tightened. "By Odin, I'll do it, if you want."

Sigli looked at his friend evenly and let out a deep breath. "All right, then. Send a messenger over to the village. Tell the Saxons to meet us at noon in front of the main gate."

"And the punishment?"

"Ten lashes, by my hand. Now go to it, man, and let's be done with it."

He turned away toward the harbor to look at his beloved ships once more. Trouble again, always trouble. Always something to stand in the way of a man's plans. He sighed as he stared at a particularly well-fashioned stern post that curved upward from a nearby keel; the craftsmanship and artistry at work stirred his senses, uplifting him. He knew there was no point in letting an insignificant trifle interfere with the larger concerns in his life, not when his future stretched before him like the rainbow bridge itself. It was still a fine June morning, after all.

He picked up a flat rock from the beach and idly examined it. Then he looked out over the harbor, slowly drew his arm back, and flung the stone in a sidearm motion across the water. It skipped once, twice and then a third time before disappearing beneath the light chop and sinking to the harbor bottom.

* * * * *

They would be reaching the Avon soon. Edward could almost smell the river, and beyond it the sea a few miles farther downstream. He dug his heels harder into the flanks of his mount and spurred the beast forward, urging his companions on. He was anxious to see Sigli again, anxious to renew their friendship, anxious at the prospects of what lay ahead. He had volunteered to carry his father's summons to the Viking and had fairly flown across the countryside that separated Rochester and Twyneham, stopping only long enough at Winchester to collect Ceolmund, the ealdorman of Hampshire, and then proceeding on to the coast. His mission was clear: Viking rebels in East Anglia had made trouble for Wessex, and now they had to be reprimanded. And it had to be done at sea.

That was what excited Edward; he loved ships, just as he loved everything to do with military matters. Although he was four months short of his sixteenth birthday, he had long since put aside childish things in favor of the weapons of war. Not a soul among the Saxons dared to cross his wishes, for it was clear to all of them that Edward the Elder, Alfred's son, was a born leader who someday would be a worthy successor to the throne.

"How much longer?" he shouted over to Ceolmund, loud enough to be heard above the hoof beats. Ten men rode with them.

"Be patient. We'll be leaving the forest soon."

It had been a prosperous time for Ceolmund, with little to interfere with the body politic, until a messenger carrying a summons from the king had ridden into Winchester a month ago. It seemed that a contingent of heathens had arrived in Kent from the continent, hoping to find plunder in the eastern regions of Wessex. The Viking ships had gathered at Benfleet, on the northern bank of the Thames estuary, where they were joined by sympathetic Danish ships from nearby East Anglia.

This was particularly disturbing to the Saxons, for the East Anglians under Guthrum's benevolent rule had maintained peace with Wessex ever since Edington. True to his word, the old Viking had never threatened his Christian neighbors, living the quiet life of an aging warrior who knows when the time has come to lower his sail and fold his tent.

But there was little Guthrum could do to stop the rebels. His power had diminished with each year, and tempers ran high among the East Anglian Danes, many of whom were eager to set sail against the Saxons. They joined up with the heathens from the continent and laid siege to the city of Rochester, situated on the eastern bank of the river Medway in Kent, south of the Thames estuary. The Vikings built a strong fortification outside the city gates, but they encountered stiff resistance and were unable to capture the town.

It was then that Alfred summoned Ceolmund and many of the other ealdormen of Wessex, imploring them to take up arms and relieve the siege. Responding quickly, the fyrd swung into action and marched to Rochester. The sudden arrival of the king's army forced the Vikings to abandon their earthworks and flee to their ships, leaving behind a large herd of horses, numerous stores and prisoners. Most of the renegade Vikings returned to the continent, leaving the remainder of the raiders to repair to Benfleet and points north.

Ceolmund returned to his estate outside Winchester after the Viking withdrawal, assuming that no further military actions would be taken. But only yesterday he had been roused from his affairs by Edward's breathless arrival, and he and the prince had set forth immediately to the southwest through the New Forest.

Now as he looked ahead, the ealdorman of Hampshire saw a familiar break in the leafy oaks, beyond which lay the river Avon. Praise God, he thought; the horses were tired and needed water. Soon the river came into sight, and the party rode to the water's edge and dismounted. Edward looked at Ceolmund with the same disarming stare that had continually unnerved the ealdorman for the last two days.

"How far to Twyneham now?"

"An hour, maybe," Ceolmund replied, cooling down his mount before allowing it to drink from the river. "I haven't been there in a year, at least...my memory fails me."

"You'd think you'd show more interest," Edward sniffed, looking intently downstream as the sun-dappled waters flowed around a bend in the river. "The first navy for Saxon England, and you're indifferent."

Damn young upstart, Ceolmund thought to himself. He acts as though he was already king. "We try to keep our distance, Edward. It's a delicate situation, you know."

But he could see that his entreaties were fruitless. Let the boy have his way, he consoled himself, remembering the advice of Penda and several of the other ealdormen. There were better ways to exert influence on the royal house. And so he nodded in agreement at everything Edward said throughout the remainder of the conversation, until they all remounted and headed south along the Avon toward Twyneham.

After an hour's ride the smell of the sea became overpowering, and before long they could see the outline of the burh rising above the harbor's edge. They quickened their pace and soon rode into view of the ships being built along the flat, sandy beach; the sight of them inspired Edward. But as he squinted into the sun something seemed out of place, and it suddenly struck him that not a soul could be seen among the hulls, on a day when work would almost certainly be underway. As they rounded the corner of the burh and came into full view of the main gate, the mystery was laid immediately to rest.

A crowd of some hundred people had gathered. All eyes were riveted on something Edward could not yet see, but his ears received the first inkling of what was to come. A crackling pop, not unlike the noise a flame makes as it curls around dry kindling, split the serenity of the summer morning. As the prince rode closer, Sigli came into view, wielding a whip that he brought down upon the exposed back of a man tied to the front gate of the burh. Edward could see the prisoner's face, distinguished by two steely, defiant eyes that stared sullenly into space; they winced perceptibly with each blow from the lash. The man's broad back was criss-crossed with several thin wounds, and the blood flowed from them in long crimson lines.

But the beating hurt Gylfi far less than the humiliation did.

The riding party came to a halt and observed the remainder of the flogging from a distance. Within moments it was over. Gylfi's bonds were cut, and he shot Sigli an evil look before staggering off and disappearing into the burh. The crowd began to disperse almost immediately as the Saxons shuffled off toward the village and the Vikings headed back to the water's edge to resume work on the ships.

Sigli discarded the lash and began to walk toward the ships, head down and lips drawn. But as he looked up his eyes fell on Edward, and the expression on his face turned to joy. Edward leaped down from his mount and ran to him, and the two friends clasped each other's shoulders in a show of genuine affection.

"You look well, my prince. You've grown."

Edward laughed. "I should hope so...it wouldn't do for Wessex to have a stunted king." He inclined his head toward the gate, where the flogging had taken place. "What was that all about?"

"A matter of discipline. Done to keep the peace...and punish a man who should know better."

Edward looked admiringly at his friend. The Viking had served as a role model for the young prince, who patterned himself after the shipbuilder as though he were a favored older brother. That Sigli was a pagan with the blood of the enemy flowing through his veins did not matter to Edward; the Viking had taught him to shoot a bow and arrow, sail a longboat, and ride like the wind through the forest. There was an understanding between them that transcended all else.

"The ships...how does the work go?"

Sigli laughed. "We could build them with our eyes closed by now."

He clapped the prince on the shoulders and guided him toward a nearby cauldron of hot pine tar, where several men ran lengths of twisted lamb's wool through the pitch. They then wedged the mixture between the strakes, where it served as caulking for the sideboards as they were attached to the ship. Nearby, another crew of men worked to fasten a length of strake to the arching hull of one of the longships. Clamps fashioned from white oak held the curving sideboard in place against the vessel. Pairs of men worked in concert at each of the clamps, one man pounding an iron nail through the oak while the other braced his hammer against the inside of the strake for support. Once the nail was beaten through, the inside man placed an iron washer over the protruding tip of the nail, and after his partner bucked the nail from the outside, he clinched it.

And so it went. Hammer, buck and clinch. Hammer, buck and clinch. Sweet sounds of men at work, erasing the morning flogging from their minds. This was what Sigli loved, what Edward admired, and they stood there happily for a moment, soaking in the atmosphere of the shipyard. For a moment, all troubles were forgotten.

"So why did you come?" Sigli finally asked, smiling easily at the prince. "Certainly not to stay here with me and build ships?"

"My father wants you to come to Rochester right away."

"Rochester? What for?"

"The East Anglians, Sigli. Father wants to punish them."

"What do you mean? I thought the Vikings went back to the continent."

Edward shook his head. "Most of them, but not all. A few retreated to Benfleet with the rebels."

Sigli placed his hands on his hips and walked over to the water's edge. He said nothing.

"My father wants you to sail with me to Rochester," Edward continued. "We'll gather the other ships we encounter along the way. After that, we'll sail until we find the East Anglians. And then we'll seize or sink as many of their ships as we can."

"I have nothing against those Vikings. Why should I risk my life?"

Edward's eyes hardened. "Because my father commands it."

Sigli let out a deep breath. "You don't understand, Edward. I've been working here all these years for a reason. These ships...your father and I have an agreement."

"That hasn't changed, Sigli. The king will stand by his word. But he needs you now." He paused for a beat. "And so do I."

"And the others? How can I ask them to go against their own kind?"

"They'll be paid if they choose to join us. Otherwise, they can stay here and work on the ships."

"And who commands the fleet?"

"I do." Edward's voice spilled over with pride. "With you by my side, or course. And Penda will serve as chief advisor." He moved closer and reached his hand out, and when he spoke his voice had an urgent ring to it. "Listen to me, Sigli. I can lead this expedition. I've been praying for a chance like this. And with you at the helm, well...you simply must come! You can't desert me now!"

"I remain true to you. You know that."

"Then sail with me to Rochester."

Sigli looked around at the ships rising from the beach. He shook his head with a wry smile and then, slowly, he began to laugh, telling Edward everything he needed to know. The prince of Wessex reached out and embraced him, and the two friends stood arm in arm a few feet away from the water upon which they would soon sail, laughing together.

Around them, the work on the ships clanged merrily along. Hammer, buck and clinch. Hammer, buck and clinch. The sounds echoed across the bay, escaping through the harbor mouth and wafting gently out to sea.

*   *   *   *   *

She was one of the most beautiful women in all of Wessex. It had happened quickly enough; the girl seems to remain a girl forever, until one day something changes and suddenly she becomes a woman. In Aethelfled's case, the transformation had been startling. She had been a fair enough child, but her features had blossomed into truly classic lines as she passed through puberty and into womanhood.

She was tall and proud, with a clear-skinned, dramatic face that featured high cheekbones and a wide, sensual mouth. Her aquiline nose was like that of her father's, but not as sharp; her large, green, almond-shaped eyes were those of her mother, yet brighter still. She had magnificent auburn hair, full-bodied and rich, with a natural wave that cascaded over her graceful shoulders. She had everything a woman could ask for, everything a man could want.

All this, and Aethelfled was still two months shy of her seventeenth birthday.

But beauty alone is not enough to set one woman apart from another. It is bearing that separates the spectacular from the sufficient, the exquisite from that which is merely of good quality. And bearing was Aethelfled's birthright. It showed in her carriage and her compassion; she was the flower of Wessex, and every man who saw her wanted her. They could all only imagine what delights were to be found in her embrace, for to know the daughter of the king would be to know a bit of heaven itself.

She stood alone in the small back garden of the main hall at Rochester, toying idly with a rose she had plucked from a nearby bush. It was enough that her father had asked her to go miles out of her way to see him and divert her trip to Canterbury for a few more days. That he should make her now wait like this as he attended to matters of local business was clearly asking too much. Whatever he wanted had to be of some significance if it could not wait until they both returned to Winchester in the fall.

"My lady, the king will see you now."

She rose to her feet at the urging of the young page and preceded him into the building. The hall, a single-story building made entirely of wood, was dark inside. While primitive compared to the more sophisticated architectures found in cities such as Winchester and Canterbury, it was still stately enough to mark Rochester as more than just another ordinary shire town. Her eyes struggled to adapt to the dark interior as the page escorted her down several corridors and then across the rear of a large room that served as the main meeting place in Rochester. And then it was down another hallway and through a low arch, where the boy bowed lightly and left her alone in a small vestibule, at the end of which an open door beckoned. Through it, she could hear her father's voice.

She stepped into the room. Immediately, she understood why she had been summoned.

Alfred sat behind a large, oval table made of oak. Across from him sat Eadred of Mercia, the trusted ally who had helped him at Edington and later assumed control of Mercia after the Viking expulsion. Eadred was in his early thirties, a few years younger than her father, with a handsome, bearded face and dark, thick hair. He was by all accounts a man of honor and good character who had governed his people wisely. He was wealthy and of a good family, he was the undisputed leader of one of the oldest and most prominent kingdoms of Christian England, and he had a bright future in Alfred's plans.

He was also unmarried.

"Ah, Aethelfled, my sweet…you look as lovely as ever," Alfred smiled, rising from the table. "Come, let me kiss you."

She received his affections and then bowed to Eadred. "Good day to you, Lord Eadred," she smiled graciously. "The Mercian summer agrees with you, I trust."

"Yes, my lady," the thane bowed, his eyes registering their appreciation.

"It's been a few years since you last saw my daughter, am I right?" Alfred asked. "She grows more beautiful every day."

"And to what do we owe your attentions today, my Lord?" Aethelfled smiled.

"I was conferring with your father about affairs of state and was preparing to return home when he mentioned that you frequently travel about Wessex," Eadred replied. I thought it would be a pleasant interlude for you to accept my hospitality in Mercia sometime soon."

"How generous of you, sir."

"Yes," Alfred broke in. "I was remarking how we might be spending some time in Berkshire this autumn. Mercia is just across the Thames, of course."

"There are many fascinating things to see and learn about my land," Eadred smiled reassuringly. "I'm sure we could make your stay inviting."

"That would be…lovely."

"Then you'll come...?"

She hesitated. "I'm uncertain about my plans for the fall. Plegmund has urged me to stay with him in Canterbury, and...don't forget Penda's standing invitation to Devon, father, which I've so rudely neglected."

Alfred smiled tightly, his lips drawn. "I'm sure Penda would understand, my dear. And Plegmund will certainly be back at court by then, of course."

"Of course," Aethelfled agreed grudgingly. She turned to Eadred. "You'll please forgive me if I sound distracted. My journey was tiring...allow me some time to arrange my affairs, and I'd be delighted to accept your invitation as soon as it's practical."

Eadred smiled warmly and bowed. He had heard the young woman was strong-minded, so her ability in deflecting the conversation did not surprise him. He was willing to bide his time; she was a prize well worth waiting for, and he knew the king was in his camp. Ultimately, that was all that mattered.

"I'll look forward to your arrival, my Lady. Mercia will not be nearly as lovely without you there. Now, if you'll both excuse me..." His eyes moved to Alfred, and they took on a different expression. "My Lord, I must be leaving. We shall talk, and soon." He bowed crisply and left the room.

Alfred waited until the Mercian had moved safely beyond earshot, and then he turned to his daughter. Displeasure was etched in the narrow lines around his eyes. The years since Edington had treated him kindly, but his firm grip on the throne had given him a distinct air of sovereignty that he wielded with stern confidence.

"You handled that rather evasively for my tastes," he said. "Why do you go against my wishes?"

"I don't, father. I merely postponed the visit." While she was careful to show fealty to the king in public, she was not afraid to stand up to him when they enjoyed the rare luxury of privacy.

"What's wrong with him? He's not an unpleasant sort...he's a very powerful man, you know."

"He's handsome and well-appointed, Father. But you could do me the courtesy of a consultation before forcing your plans down my throat!"

Alfred brought his fist down sharply on the table. "Consult? Since when does the king need to consult anyone?"

"I won't have it! I'm your daughter! It's my flesh you barter to secure the kingdom!"

"Then you refuse to consider Eadred as a husband?"

"I didn't say that. I just need time. Don't rush me so...and don't worry."

She moved closer to Alfred and smiled, grabbing his hands in her own. He knew what she was doing but let her do it anyway, just as he always had.

"You try my patience. You make things difficult."

"And would you have it any other way?" she teased, tossing her head to one side so that her hair swirled across her shoulders and glinted in the light. "Would you have me be some dull peasant girl, giving in to your every command? That would be unlike the House of Wessex."

"That it would," he laughed, agreeing in spite of himself. "But remember, Eadred already pledges his allegiance to me; he owes his position to my power and sovereignty. We must cement that position with our blood, our future. With you bearing his children..."

"Enough!" she laughed, placing a restraining finger over his lips. "Let me go to Canterbury, and I'll arrange my affairs shortly." She kissed him and leaned back, looking at him with bright, sparkling eyes. "I'm proud of you, Father. You'll become Bretwalda...I know it."

"Maybe so. But it will take me twice as long to unify England if I'm forced to rely on you." He pinched her playfully on the cheek. "Now, go off on your travels, and don't take too long to decide. I'll be waiting."

"Not for long...I promise you that." She kissed him again and flew out of the room, satisfied that she had at least bought herself some time.

Alfred watched her leave with mixed feelings. She would not be easy; she would not go quietly into the night. He admired her boldness and independent spirit, but he realized that they were the qualities most likely to cause him trouble. He wanted an ally who would help him to make all of Christian England his. More than ever before, he was committed to his vision of a single island kingdom, and with each year he had drawn closer to his goal. Bretwalda. King of the British. He could almost taste it.

He moved over to the window and looked outside, stroking the beard he had cultivated in his mid-thirties. His face was still narrow, his features as aquiline as ever; the relative comfort of the last seven years had not seduced him into a life of ease, the lie that injects mediocrity into the lives of great men. He was vigorously active, always attending to some detail of state, whether social, political or military. And on those rare occasions when he was master of his own time, he turned his attention to education and learning, architecture and science.

Those times were still few and far between. During the first years after Edington he had devoted himself almost exclusively to military matters, to ensure that what had happened at Chippenham would never happen again. He built burhs, he organized the fyrd, he forged weapons. And he created a navy, providing Wessex with the fleet it needed to fend off the Vikings. But one could never have too many ships, for he knew that Haestan and others like him would be back someday. When they came, he would be ready for them.

He had given Edward command of the upcoming naval expedition to East Anglia for several reasons. One was the confidence that he had in his son, and the coming of age that the expedition represented. The other was that such a move would compel Sigli to join the battle. Needing an admiral at sea, Edward would appeal to the Viking's loyalty, and Sigli would come. Otherwise, the Halfsfiordian might be inclined to excuse himself from the action and save his energies to pursue his quest.

His quest. In all his wisdom, Alfred sometimes had a difficult time understanding the Viking's obsession. This Dane Sidroc—was he even alive after all this time? And if so, what could Sigli ultimately hope to accomplish by killing him? It would not restore his father, it would not bring back his bride or his brother or his ships. It would not even gain him back Halfsfiord; there was nothing there anymore worth recovering. As far as Alfred was concerned, the Viking was unable to grasp the greater view of things. A man of vision would leave such a past behind and throw in his lot with the future. With England.

With Alfred.

He smiled and drummed his fingers idly on the windowsill. It would be in his best interests if Sigli chose to stay forever and build ships. Others could build them, of course, but not like the Viking could. It made perfect sense to let his heathen compatriot take care of everything pertaining to the navy, acting for all intents like the king's minister of defense. But beyond that, Alfred's personal interests were involved. The more secure the kingdom, the more time he could devote to affairs of state—organizing the new England, laying down laws and establishing a public system of education. And the sooner he could devote himself to those tasks, the sooner he could turn away and devote himself to the thing he loved above all else: learning.

He had yet to master Latin adequately enough to translate the great classical works into English, but it was a goal that remained foremost in his mind. He had neglected this side of his life because of the responsibilities that God and Wessex had thrust upon his shoulders, but he sensed his opportunity was forthcoming. He had already laid the groundwork for the creation of his dream by recruiting men of learning from abroad and bringing them to Wessex; one in particular, a young bishop named Asser, impressed him.

The man was a bright young scholar from St. David's in Dyfed, a remote province in the western wilds of Wales. There were others like him on the continent the king was wooing with the lure of establishing a new center of learning, teasing their appetites with the prospects of financial gain and scholarly pursuit. All of this lay before Alfred, beckoning to him as though it were the Holy Grail itself. It was the thing in his life that elevated him closest to God; it was noble, it was of the mind and spirit, it was....

He caught himself in the dream. It was all an illusion, and that was all it ever would be, unless he could solidify the national defense and put his affairs of state in order. That was why, as the king of Wessex and champion of learning, he had to keep Sigli at Twyneham. Or so the selfish monarch in him said. The man, the friend, the Christian said to let Sigli go, as the Viking would most certainly request to do when he arrived in Rochester.

Alfred had foreseen these things, and that was why he had finally decided to resort to a literal trial by combat. Let God be the judge. If Sigli, at Edward's side, led the Saxon navy to victory over the East Anglian rebels, if he captured ships and added to Alfred's fleet, then it was only fair that he be allowed to leave. But if the Saxons were to suffer a setback, then everything would change. A show of vulnerability would make Wessex that much more attractive to Haestan or the restless factions in East Anglia and Northumbria, and the king would somehow have to find a way to keep Sigli and his Vikings in Wessex to build more ships.

He heard footsteps at the door, and a moment later Penda strode into view, as taciturn as ever. Alfred had sent for the gaunt ealdorman of Devon because he was just the man to carry out a matter of extreme delicacy that anticipated every possible contingency. Just in case.

"What would you, my Lord?"

"A moment of your time. You're prepared to sail with the fleet when it arrives?"

"Yes, my Lord. We'll teach the heathens a lesson."

"And you have full confidence in my son?"

"Without question."

Alfred stepped away from the window and began to walk slowly around the table. "And Sigli?" He stopped in his tracks and looked directly at Penda. "What do you *really* think of him?"

Penda suppressed a frown; better to be honest, he thought. "Well, my Lord...I don't doubt his loyalty to you. He builds magnificent ships. And he knows how to sail them...better than any Saxon, certainly." Here he stiffened, and his voice took on an edge. "But as much as I respect him, he's still a heathen, Sire. By my rood, as a Christian and a Saxon, I bear no love for the pagans. I can't stomach them."

Alfred smiled to himself; it was just as he had thought. Penda was the right man to talk to about this.

"You asked me what I thought," Penda stammered, misinterpreting the king's silence.

"No, no...please. I have a matter of some delicacy that requires the services of a man of discretion. That's why I called for you."

Penda stood at attention, listening carefully.

"Mind you," the king continued, "there's nothing to be concerned about. Just a precautionary measure I'd like to set in motion." He sat down at the table and placed his hands in front of him. "I want you to investigate the shipbuilders, Penda. See what you can find."

"I don't understand, Sire."

"See how Sigli's men feel about him. Are they happy? Perhaps there is one among them who is less than enamored of him. There may be a grudge or two that the master shipbuilder has tendered over the years...no?"

"And you would employ this person against the Viking?"

"Not necessarily. But such a man could be useful. Even the most loyal of subjects sometimes needs to be persuaded, my friend. And sometimes the words of a king are not the best means of persuasion."

"As you wish, Sire."

"I need to know more. And that's why you must find out this information for me, and fill in the missing pieces of my knowledge." He paused and looked out the window. "Now leave me, and do what you can. We'll speak again before you sail."

He waited until he was comfortably alone before rising from the table and moving again to the open window. He did not like such covert maneuvering, nor did he condone duplicity, but no other options seemed to be available. For that matter, all of his machinations would be moot if the fleet emerged victorious. It was out of his hands now; God would decide.

The afternoon sun streamed into the room on the wings of a light breeze filled with the scent of adventure. He suddenly forgot all about the business of being king, dismissed all thoughts of Sigli and headed for the door with a bounce to his step. There would be enough time left in the day for a short hunt, after all.

*   *   *   *   *

"And forgive us our trespasses, as we forgive those who trespass against us. And lead us not into temptation, but deliver us from evil. Through Christ, our Lord. Amen."

The prayer was almost an afterthought as it escaped Plegmund's lips. He could not seem to keep his mind from straying as he knelt in solitude at the altar in Canterbury's Christ Church Cathedral, where he had slipped away to seek comfort in the familiar process of litany and ritual. He wondered just how many times he had recited the Lord's Prayer during his life. Several hundred thousand? A million, perhaps? It was almost impossible to conceive of a number that high; it approached infinity.

And infinity was a concept that Plegmund had never completely trusted nor understood.

Such an admission was tantamount to heresy for a man of the cloth. Faith was his guiding principle, a beacon that shone, however dimly, from the watchtower of God's fortress, lighting the path to righteousness and setting an example for all Christians to follow. But how could he expect to fulfill his holy duties as a shepherd to God's children, if he himself fell prey to the failings of every man? He sometimes felt as though he was unworthy of the destiny he had chosen. Although his reputation was unsullied and he was generally acknowledged to be an impeccable practitioner of the Faith, he was still plagued by private demons that whispered in his ear in relentless, dissonant voices.

He looked up at the high ceiling above the altar, renewing himself in its majesty. Canterbury was universally recognized as the center of Christianity on the isle of Britain, known far and wide to all believers in the Faith. The town was clustered along the banks of the Kentish Stour as the river flowed from a narrow valley into a marshy plain that led to the sea. The city had existed since the early years of the Roman occupation, but had flourished mainly due to the efforts of St. Augustine, who established a Benedictine monastery there during the sixth century. A few years later he founded Christ Church Cathedral in a building that had originally been used as a church by Romans of Christian belief. By the ninth century, it had become established as the most impressive place of worship in all of Saxon England.

The church was built in the fashion of the pre-Gothic architectures that characterized ninth-century Europe. It was a prime example of the classical basilica style of construction, oblong in shape and featuring a long, open nave that acted as a gathering place for the common folk. On either side of the nave, a long aisle framed by stone walls and low ceilings stretched along the length of the church. Higher up the stone gave way to wood—still the most common building material in England—fashioned into a clerestory with high, narrow windows to let in the light.

At the end of the open nave the transept rose to form the two lateral arms that characterized the standard cruciform church of the day. A fine screen hung from the ceiling at that point, separating the nave from the altar, the mundane from the divine. Immediately in front of the transept was an enclosed space, known as the chancel or choir, which housed the clergy. A few simple benches were grouped together in the center of this space, effectively directing all eyes to the altar located in the center of the apse—the semicircular domed projection at the east end of the church that gave the basilica style of architecture its oblong form.

Here, on a plain yet perfectly smooth stone table, the divine offices were recited and the Eucharist celebrated in observance of the ritual of the body and blood of Christ. The entire area around the altar was lit by candles spread around the room, their glow lending an air of piety and warmth to the rich tapestries that hung from the walls.

Such was the majesty of Christ Church Cathedral: heaven on earth for commoner and holy man alike. As Plegmund knelt alone at the edge of the altar and absorbed the grandeur of his surroundings, he felt a familiar desire welling up inside him, a desire that arose from the knowledge that all he saw before him could one day be his. He knew that he wanted it now more than ever, more than he had ever wanted anything in the world.

He had been sent to Canterbury by Alfred on a temporary assignment to assist old Aethelred, the ailing Archbishop of Canterbury. Aethelred had held his post since 870 and was known throughout Christian England as a wise and venerable man of God, fully deserving of the highest seat of ecclesiastical power in the land. But that power had become more symbolic than real over time as the old man grew infirm, and every year over the last decade had seen his influence wane, eroded by the subtle, persistent efforts of Grimwald—now indisputably the most powerful churchman in Wessex.

It would normally be assumed that the archbishopric would be passed on to Grimwald out of respect for his status, but such was not the case. Alfred had the final say as to what man of the cloth would receive the appointment, and it was highly unlikely he would choose the Bishop of Winchester. For one, Grimwald was now in his fifties and was probably too old. For another, he was too treacherous and political to suit the king, who now wielded the power in England concerning not only the state, but the Church as well. It was clear to everyone that after Aethelred died, the choice of his successor would hardly be a foregone conclusion. Many of the monks throughout England were already attempting to place themselves favorably in the path of the ultimate decision, hoping to gain the ultimate prize.

And no man among them looked upon Canterbury with as much ambition in his eye as Plegmund did.

He had reached the point in his life, as all men eventually do, when the blessings one already has in hand are no longer enough to satisfy the longings in one's heart. Power and position had taken on new meaning for the young monk. Not that he was in danger of abusing those privileges, for unlike the corrupt Grimwald, his motives were relatively pure and had not been tainted by the all-consuming fires of avarice. But in spite of this moral advantage, he was driven by his ego, and he had to admit that it was not solely the glory of God that compelled him to desire the post at Canterbury. It was the most prestigious honor he could hope to attain in his lifetime, and the thought of it seduced him completely.

He had remained in Alfred's favor, adorning the king's court like a fashionable tapestry and assisting in a variety of administrations. He had been taken into the confidence of the royal family during that time and had spent long hours educating the children in English, Latin and religious matters. Of all of Alfred's family, he had grown particularly close to Aethelfled, whose sharp intellect and humorous wit met the high standards he admired. That she would soon be joining him in Canterbury for several weeks' stay gladdened his spirits, injecting light and life into what otherwise looked to be a dull and uneventful summer.

But Plegmund's stature among Alfred's family was not nearly enough to assure him Canterbury. Still a few months short of his thirtieth birthday, he was as young for the post as Grimwald was old. He was aware of the political realities in England, and how they could very well dictate a choice that might be far removed from the king's personal inclinations. There was Mercia to deal with, and the Welsh kingdom to the west. And he knew that Alfred had expanded his horizons by inviting increasing numbers of foreign monks and churchmen to Wessex. There was Asser, the young bishop of St. David's, and several other notable religious men of quality who the king was now wooing on the continent. Any one of these new faces could in time usurp his position.

He sighed under his breath as he thought of these things. What price Canterbury? Only God in heaven knew.

A rustling sound behind him interrupted his thoughts. He turned to see a figure slipping around the corner of the screen that separated the choir from the nave, but he was unable to make out the man's face. He squinted to penetrate the shadows that fell across the room, until the figure's corpulent frame and labored movements told him everything he needed to know. A low, almost imperceptible hiss escaped through his lips as he rose to greet Grimwald.

"More confession, Plegmund?" cackled the obese Bishop of Winchester as he waddled into the candlelight. "Surely one as pure as you profess to be need not subject himself to such extended acts of penance?"

"I profess nothing more than humility," Plegmund replied, bowing stiffly. "No man is so righteous that he cannot stand to seek forgiveness from the Lord."

"Always the right answer. No wonder you've been such a success at the court." Grimwald genuflected with a grunt as he passed across the center of the altar. He squared his body to Plegmund and looked the young monk over carefully.

"I'm on my way to Rochester to see the king. But first, I came to Canterbury to confer with Aethelred concerning several matters. He's resting now, so they won't let me see him." His eyes narrowed. "Tell me...how is his health these days?"

"He's not well at all. Age is getting the better of him."

"As with all of us...but, I must say, you're looking well." Grimwald moved closer to Plegmund and smiled. "I see that Canterbury agrees with you. That doesn't surprise me, of course...."

Plegmund brushed off the insult to his ambition, but he could not ignore the invasion of his personal space. Once again he identified Grimwald's distinctive body odor, an oily smell not unlike that of fruit just beginning to rot. It never failed to repulse him.

"I'm hungry after my long journey," Grimwald continued, pretending not to notice the young monk's aversion. "Would you care to join me?"

"No thank you. I must continue my prayers."

"Ah, yes, of course..." He reached out as if to touch Plegmund but, thinking better of it, he smiled sweetly and headed back along the aisle and through the shadows. Plegmund watched his retreat, until suddenly Grimwald turned again toward the altar, his voice a soft, urgent whisper that knifed through the silence of the church.

"I could help you, you know...if you would only let me."

Plegmund stood mutely at the altar, knowing full well the intent behind Grimwald's offer. He started to speak, but could not. After a moment of awkward silence the old bishop smiled and shrugged, finally turning away and slipping around the screen that separated the choir from the nave.

Plegmund slumped down onto one of the benches in the choir, feeling the sweat trickling down the back of his neck. There was certainly nothing new about Grimwald's advances; they had been plaguing him ever since Edington seven years before. But their frequency had increased over time, and the message they contained had become more blatant with each occurrence. Plegmund was grateful that he rarely saw the old bishop; it was difficult enough to deal with the man under any conditions, but the dark shadow cast by his sexual overtures had become almost too much to bear.

It was as though Grimwald knew something about him that he himself had been unwilling to admit, a side of his carnal nature that he had buried under layers of denial. It was one thing for a man of God to desire a woman; it was another thing entirely, a mortal sin of the gravest consequences, to keep the company of another man.

But in his loins, obscured by his shame and guilt, there simmered an uneasy passion that blazed with temptation whenever Plegmund laid eyes on a well-formed man. He shivered thinking about it. A blur of images from his troubled childhood invaded his mind, as he remembered his youth spent among the Vikings after they ravaged his village and killed his parents. He had been passed around from man to man like a goblet of mead, a soft and young vessel into which they could empty their pleasure. The scars of those times ran deeply through him, no matter how he tried to suppress them.

That he could still desire a man given his experiences was the ultimate perversity. Had he been that way to begin with, or had the sodomy of the heathens formed his passion in some sick, hideous way? What was real, what was tangible, was that the desire existed. He had tried to look at women with longing, as though this lesser sin would be acceptable in the eyes of God. But always the dark thoughts returned, spurred on by the sight of firm buttocks and muscled arms, thick chests and bearded faces. And on those occasions when his lust overcame him, when he was safely alone in his chambers late at night, he would reach down and pleasure himself, his thoughts filled with strong, male bodies. The more taboo the act and forbidden the vision, the more it excited him, until his body released its lust and left him to wallow in the shame and guilt that always followed.

He had never willingly consummated his passion with another man, for lust alone could never prompt him to do that. But love was another matter; combined with desire, it had the power to send a man hurtling over the edge and into the abyss. He knew in his heart that he had been plagued with what could only be love, a love that had become the ultimate temptation. He had fought it for years and had done all in his power to deny it. He had taken great pains to avoid the object of his affection, keeping his distance and saying his prayers, but the same face always crept into his dreams, the one force on earth that was capable of unleashing his passions to the ways of the flesh.

He struggled to release himself from the spell, erasing the familiar face from his daydream and replacing it with the leering countenance of Grimwald. Grimwald, like the lowest beast of the field, violating everything that was fine and good in the eyes of God. That was a vision that Plegmund could live with, a reminder of all that was evil and wrong with his desire, a last hope for salvation and righteousness.

He rose uneasily from the bench and wiped his brow. It was clear that his evening of penance had just begun, that his prayers would be repeated again and again, until the cock crowed and his exhaustion melted away in the promise of a new morning. He staggered toward the altar and raised his eyes to heaven, and then he fell to his knees and forced the first supplicating whispers through drawn, trembling lips.

"Our Father, who art in heaven, hallowed be thy name. Thy kingdom come, thy will be done, on earth..."

*　　*　　*　　*　　*

They called the place Sheppey, "the isle of sheep." It was the largest of several low islands in the Thames estuary which were separated from the mainland by the ramifying creeks about the mouth of the river Medway, squatting like a humpbacked turtle at the point where the river empties its waters into the North Sea. It was treeless but fertile, producing grain and vegetables and serving as a plentiful grazing ground for the shepherds who tended their flocks on the low fens as their forefathers had done for centuries.

When the Vikings first wintered in England some thirty years before, they chose Sheppey as their campsite and ravaged everything on the isle. Among their targets was Minster Abbey, a nunnery founded some two hundred years earlier which few thought would recover from the damage wrought by the Vikings. But when the Danes finally sailed away, the nuns of Minster returned to restore the abbey and keep the Faith alive on their island retreat.

Alfred admired that. The life of a nun was a worthy one—if not meant for just any woman. He smiled as he tried to imagine Aethelfled ever fitting such a mold. But his fourteen-year-old daughter Aethelgifu was another story; she had been blessed with patience and an even demeanor, and had expressed the desire to devote herself to the cloth. When she came of age, he had decided to usher her into the waiting arms of sisterhood, marrying her unto the Lord. It would be a good life for her. He would build an abbey dedicated to the glory of God to honor the occasion, once again demonstrating his ongoing support for the Church.

He sighed with satisfaction as he knelt in the courtyard of Minster Abbey, facing east so that the morning sun streamed into his uplifted face. He had begun his prayers just after dawn, at the same time that Plegmund had mercifully ceased his own all-night vigil of penance twenty-five miles to the south in Christ Church Cathedral. Eyes closed, Alfred felt the warm rays seeping through his skin, bathing him in soft promises.

It had been a wise decision to leave Rochester and come to Sheppey, separated from the mainland and its endless distractions. That he had come to the island to rendezvous with the fleet was reason enough to be there, but the solitude he had gained, the stolen moments, had been truly precious. The cost of freedom was a high price to pay for a king. The time alone had enabled him to crystallize his thoughts and find the missing piece to the puzzle of his ambitions. And he knew now that he had that piece in his hand, and the hour had come to spin the web that would ensnare the final prize—London.

The city was Mercian in name only; Vikings occupied it now, as they had for decades. They had lived without incident alongside the Saxons for years, acknowledging Guthrum's benevolent reign in East Anglia and observing the Warlord's truce with Wessex. But the notion of a binding peace had been broken now that the East Anglian rebels had played their hand, leaving Alfred free to set his designs in motion.

First, his fleet would shatter the Viking resistance at sea. Provided that went well, the siege of London would begin in the autumn; otherwise, it would have to wait a year. In either case, he would be able to convince the ealdormen to follow him and take the city, for Rochester had been a brilliant, bloodless coup from which he had emerged stronger than ever. When London fell, all of Mercia under the able stewardship of Eadred would look to him as king. The Danelaw would be stripped of what had become the largest city in England and a burgeoning port of call that promised to someday play host to the world.

Bretwalda. Bretwalda. He could almost taste it.

The harsh clatter of hoof beats disturbed his contemplation. He rose to his feet reluctantly, his morning meditation over, and waited as the sounds drew closer. In the next moment a mounted rider thundered through the gate of the abbey, his sword rattling against the chain mail of his full-length hauberk as he reined in his horse and scanned the courtyard. Spying Alfred, Penda of Devon dismounted and approached the king.

"We've spotted the first masts, my Lord...off to the east. They'll be here soon."

"Very good. How many ships?"

"A score or more, at least. They're still too far away to tell."

"I'll come with you immediately."

The two men mounted their horses and set off at a brisk trot, riding through the abbey gate and into the open countryside. They could see the tents of the Saxon encampment clustered along the water's edge, and beyond them the shimmering sea as it disappeared into a vast, open horizon to the northeast. On the edge of that horizon, far off in the distance, they could make out a number of tiny objects against the clear blue sky.

"Look at those sails," Alfred said admiringly. "The breeze favors them."

"They rounded Dover late yesterday. They must have spent the night moored off Thanet."

"I hope the Vikings won't notice their arrival...with any luck, we'll surprise them." Alfred paused and leaned forward, squinting into the sun. "Any news from Ceolmund?"

"Not since he left Twyneham with the fleet. I'll speak to him immediately."

"I don't want to know any of the details, do you understand? I don't want to be involved."

"I'll take care of everything, my Lord."

A few hours later the sun hung directly overhead in the midday sky, its bright rays reflecting off the helmets of the Saxons as they stood in formation by the water's edge. A breeze filled the air, breathing life into the banner of the Golden Dragon and stretching the insignia of the mythical beast out to its fullest extension. Alfred sat tall astride his stallion beneath the pennant, surrounded by Penda, Fulric of Kent and Godwine of Sussex. All eyes looked seaward in rapt attention.

And what they saw was a glorious sight. Before them, the waters were filled with nearly forty ships that bore down on the shoreline, knifing their way effortlessly through the light chop of the North Sea. Long, low ships with high curving prows and sterns, their square, woolen sails arching with the wind and thrusting the hulls forward. Each vessel carried forty or more fighting men in addition to the sailors, their helmets visible above the shield-lined bulwarks that had been ceremonially decorated to heighten the appearance of the ships.

"Wait until the heathens see this," Fulric smiled. "I never thought I'd see this day."

"Look, there...in the bow of that broad-beamed vessel, the one longer than the others!" Godwine of Sussex shouted. "Isn't that Edward?"

"So it is!" Alfred cried. "Look at my young lion, leading the hunt!" His voice was bursting with pride. "And alongside him...that must be Sigli!"

As the Saxons lining the shore watched in admiration, one by one the sails of the armada were lowered and the shields removed from the bulwarks, replaced by long oars that slid into the sea to negotiate the final approach to the island. The first to touch keel was the flagship of the fleet. And the first man ashore was young Edward, who plunged into the knee-deep water and ran forward onto the sandy beach, there to be met by the open arms of the king.

" Look at them, Father!" Edward beamed, sweeping his outstretched arm to encompass the fleet gathered before them. "I bring you power!"

"You bring me hope...and with it, the knowledge that we can finally defend our coastline." Alfred's face lit up. "And you bring me the master shipbuilder who created this magnificence. Sigli, my friend...."

He reached out to the Viking, who had made his way onto the beach in Edward's wake. Sigli dropped to a knee and placed the king's extended hand on his forehead.

"My Lord...you do me great honor."

"We've come a long way together, haven't we?" Alfred said, raising the Viking to his feet. "Remember those stormy nights on Athelney? All this was but a dream then..." He gazed again at the ships and breathed in the salt air, smiling expansively. "But come, you must be in need of refreshment after your journey. Join me in my tent and break bread; we have much to talk about."

He put his arms around the shoulders of his son and the shipbuilder and led them through the crowd. They were the first ones to slip inside the king's spacious tent, where they discovered an assortment of breads, cheeses and freshly slaughtered lambs that had been cooked for their enjoyment. They sat down and began to devour the food, for the king had fasted at his morning prayers and the two sailors had breakfasted lightly before embarking with the fleet at dawn. Meanwhile, the tent became filled with laughter as the other members of Alfred's circle filed inside.

Edward spoke first. "Have you heard anything about the enemy, Father? The spirits of the men are high. We ought to strike soon."

"Is tomorrow soon enough?"

"Today, if we could."

"No need. They're still too far away. Here...let me show you." He grabbed a parchment from on the ground and spread it open on the table. "I commissioned this primitive map to be drawn. Here's the coastline, and here's the Thames, leading to London. This is where we are." He pointed to a round, dense mass on the parchment.

"Wonderful!" Sigli exclaimed. He had never seen such a thing before.

"Here's Benfleet, across the estuary from us," Alfred said. "You can be there in a few hours, and overrun the remnants of their fleet. But most of their ships—some twenty-five vessels, perhaps—have sailed further north. Here, by the mouth of the East Anglian Stour."

"How far is that?"

"Some forty miles. Probably six to eight hours at sea, depending on the wind."

"He's right," Dagmar concurred, having joined them at the map. "I've sailed those waters. We could be there by nightfall."

Sigli stroked his chin. "It does us no good to attack Benfleet. We'd gain little, and lose the element of surprise."

"But we'll be discovered by the time we work our way northward along the coast," Edward protested.

Sigli laughed. "Who said anything about the coast? I say we sail out to sea, away from the mouth of the estuary. We can lay offshore here," he said, indicating the open waters east of where the Stour emptied into the North Sea. "We'll be sure to wait until darkness falls, to cover our approach. We can sleep out at sea, and drift in closer during the night. When dawn comes, we'll be rested. And they'll be surprised."

"Brilliant!" Alfred exclaimed, slapping the Viking on the shoulder. "But, can you do it?"

"Why not? Dagmar knows the waters, and the weather looks good...the stars will guide us. I say we try it."

"I leave it to your discretion, then. I have complete faith in you."

"We won't disappoint you, my Lord," Sigli reassured him. He then paused, clearing his throat awkwardly. "But there are other matters, my king, that we must resolve...I've served you loyally these last eight years. I've built you ships, and I've kept my part of our bargain. Now, I must ask that you do the same. After this campaign is over, I wish to take the ships you promised me and leave for the continent."

Alfred let out a deep breath and smiled in resignation. "I gave you my word—and my word is enough. I swear that, when this is ended, you may do as you wish. Just bring home a victory."

"We'll carry the day, my Lord."

"I have no doubt that you will." Alfred raised his cup and looked back and forth from his son to Sigli. "May God protect you both, and guide you in your endeavor."

They all raised their cups, but a voice from along the back wall of the tent interrupted them.

"Before we toast our brave warriors, King Alfred, one final detail..." All eyes turned to Penda, who shouldered his way through the crowd. "You could do us a service, Sigli, which could be of great use to the king."

"Name it."

"You'll remember we took some Danish prisoners when we relieved Rochester. Many of them were from the continent. We'd like to interrogate them, but they don't trust Saxons...you understand, I'm sure." Penda raised an eyebrow. "I was thinking it would be helpful if you would leave one of your Vikings behind. He could penetrate their ranks. Much could be learned."

Sigli shrugged. "I have no objection. But I wonder if any of my men would be willing to do what you ask. What do you think, Dagmar?"

"It's not a bad idea. Maybe we could learn something that would be helpful when we sail to find Sidroc."

"But who could we leave behind?"

Dagmar thought for a moment, and then his face lit up. "I say we give them Gylfi. He's been grousing ever since we left Twyneham. I don't think he ever relished the idea of going against the East Anglians in the first place."

No one noticed as Penda's eyes darted briefly to the far wall of the tent, where Ceolmund flashed an exultant grin and silently clenched his fist in triumph.

"Then Gylfi it is," Sigli agreed. "Let us toast our coming victory."

The mead flowed freely as the room joined in salute. Penda put the drinking vessel to his lips, hiding a smile, and tilted his head back so that the rich mixture slid easily down his throat. Never had mead tasted so sweet, never had such a delicate matter been handled so smoothly. He congratulated himself and licked his lips, knowing he had served his king as a true Saxon should.

*　　*　　*　　*　　*

"I can hardly wait to see their faces. I wonder what they're thinking now?"

Edward was enjoying himself immensely. He was drunk for the first time in his life, but by God, he'd earned it.

"Fond of them, eh?" Sigli smirked, cradling a cup in his hand. "I've been warding off ealdormen ever since I first set foot in England. They're like a pack of jackals."

"Well, they'll be denied this time," Edward grinned. He swallowed another mouthful of mead and squinted through the dense fog that lay across the water. "Are you sure we're almost there?"

"We passed Sheppey well over an hour ago. There's the riverbank off to starboard. See for yourself."

Edward struggled to stand up in the bow as the ship moved steadily toward the landing beneath Rochester. A sudden rocking motion of the vessel caused him to slip and fall roughly to the deck, spilling the contents of his cup all over himself. The rowers aligned along either side of the ship burst into laughter, leaving him no choice but to join in their humor.

They could all afford to laugh, for two days earlier the Saxons had swooped down upon the rebel fleet as it lingered near the mouth of the Stour. The ships from Wessex came out of the morning sun from the open sea, following Sigli's plan to perfection and taking the Vikings completely by surprise. A few of the heathen ships managed to retreat upriver or flee along the coast, but most of the fleet was trapped along the shoreline, left to founder in confusion while its captains desperately sought an avenue of escape. Many of the Norse ships ran aground in the shallows, leaving the defenseless crewmen stranded as their hoarse cries for help split the morning air.

The battle was decisively brief. The Saxons made short work of their enemies, hacking away at the outnumbered Vikings in hand-to-hand combat over the bulwarks of the longships. The issue was decided within minutes; the fight was over almost before it had begun. Some of the retreating Danes beached their vessels and set them on fire, but the Saxons still managed to capture sixteen ships, swelling the ranks of their fleet to over fifty seaworthy vessels. The day belonged to Wessex.

And the day belonged to Edward, who would finally be able to parade his triumph before the king.

"I knew what they were saying behind my back," he smirked, laboring to raise himself again to a sitting position. "The boy king, playing a man's game. They'd love to see me fail, Sigli. It would give them great satisfaction."

"Stop complaining. You've won."

"Ah, yes. The battle won...and the victors lost at sea." Edward threw his head back and laughed. "We leave Dagmar and Penda to bring the news back to my father, and what happens? My Viking helmsman sets a course to oblivion..."

Sigli was not amused. "Only the gods can navigate the fog."

"We'd have been better off staying with the others. It's been two days now. They probably hugged the coast and beat us back to Rochester."

"Then hundreds of Saxons will be lining the streets, cheering your name."

Edward grinned. "Maybe so." He swirled the mead around in his cup and looked up at Sigli, his eyes glistening. "I've never felt this good in my life. And I could never have done it without you."

"That's just the mead talking."

"No, I mean it. You've been a good friend. A true friend. I wish you didn't have to leave."

Before Sigli could respond, a series of shouts erupted from the starboard bank. Through the fog they were able to make out the mast of a longship anchored on the far reach, and beyond it a number of shadowy figures that could be seen scurrying to the edge of the river. They all strained for a better look as their ship slid across the water and closed in on the bank. Soon a second and a third vessel emerged in the mist, a sure sign that they had reached the shelving beach downstream from Rochester. The crowd gathering to greet them began to take shape, a mass of animate forms that moved slowly, almost hypnotically, through the fog. Sigli and Edward stood eagerly in the bow as the rowers maneuvered the craft into position and shipped their oars, leaving the vessel to glide in toward the shallows until its keel finally snuggled into the soft river bottom.

Sigli recognized Dagmar in the forefront of the greeting party. With a cry of triumph, he leaped from the prow of the longship into the knee-deep water and splashed his way toward the group. But before he even reached dry land he could sense a palpable tension that crowded the still air. Every man gathered on the riverbank was eerily silent; something was wrong. He stopped abruptly in his tracks and looked into Dagmar's unsmiling eyes.

"What is it?"

The Dane bit his lip. "Well, at least you're all safe. Alfred will be relieved."

"Damn it, man! We've been drifting in the fog for two days! What's wrong?"

Dagmar cleared his throat and glanced nervously at Edward, who now stood warily alongside Sigli. "I'd hoped I wouldn't have to be the one to tell you, but so be it. After you sailed off, we gathered the ships together and started back along the coastline. The fog rolled in, and it became difficult to navigate. Late that afternoon we met up with more rebel ships...they must have come from

Benfleet. We couldn't tell how strong they were because of the mist, but we were confident after our victory, so we engaged them.

"As it turned out, there were more of them than we thought. We started to pull back to regroup, but that's when disaster struck. We were met in the rear by at least another score of ships...they must have gathered at the Stour and followed us. We were trapped." He looked up and shook his head. "It was bad...very bad."

"Good God! What happened next?" Edward's eyes bulged in their sockets.

"The first thing we did was abandon the captured ships. All sixteen of them. We didn't have enough men to defend them. They tried to surround us and cut off our escape, but we were able to break through...but not before at least ten of our vessels were sunk or captured." He let out a deep breath. "Only twenty-five ships are left."

Sigli was dumbstruck. "By Odin! How could this be??!!"

"Penda's asking the same question," Dagmar said ruefully. "He's got Alfred's ear, blaming you both for leaving him with the fleet and sailing off." He turned to Edward. "Your father will be anxious to see you. Better go to him immediately."

"But...I'm stinking drunk. I can't see him like this."

"You'll sober up soon enough," Sigli said, his eyes turning to steel. "There's no sense putting it off. I'm coming with you."

They borrowed horses from the camp and headed upriver the short distance to Rochester with Dagmar in tow. They rode in silence, stunned by the unexpected news, as though it were all a bad dream that would somehow disappear after they slept their drunk off and awoke to a new morning. But it was not to be. The fog deepened as they drew close to Rochester, which by now had received word of their approach. As they rode through the town gates, they were met by curious, searching stares from those within the city, a silent multitude that lined the muddy road like nosy onlookers at a public execution. Not a word was spoken, not a sound could be heard, except for the splashing of hooves as they sunk into the rain-softened earth. After what seemed an eternity, the three riders finally arrived at the main hall and dismounted, Dagmar remaining outside the door as Sigli and Edward entered the building.

The room was dark, illuminated only by the flickering light from the torches that lined the walls. At the far end of an open expanse, a lone figure paced back and forth across the earthen floor, looking up expectantly as the two men entered the room. It was Alfred. He turned to face them and waited, watching them intently as they crossed the hall and came to a silent stop before him.

"So. Our victory was guaranteed." His eyes bored into Sigli. "You said so yourself, didn't you?"

"We defeated them. When we left, the victory was ours."

"When you left! When you left! How could you have deserted your charge?"

Sigli raised himself to his full height, a head taller than Alfred. "We left to bring you the news, my Lord. How could we have known they could muster another force so quickly?"

"You of all people should know better than to underestimate the Vikings!"

"But we destroyed them, Father!" Edward blurted out, stepping forward impulsively. "Sixteen ships...all of them! The fleet was secure when we sailed...."

"Not secure enough, evidently." Alfred's eyes narrowed, and his brow clouded over as he looked at his son in the torchlight. "You're drunk, aren't you? A setback like this, and you come to me soaked to your eyeballs in mead...?"

Only Edward's brash self-assurance saved him from being completely humiliated. His shoulders wilted and he fell silent.

"You wrong him!" Sigli protested, glaring at Alfred. "He fought bravely. I saw him cut down more than one man with his sword. He fought like a warrior...like a future king!"

Alfred's lips twitched for a moment with unconscious pride, but then his features set themselves in stone. "A man must do more than merely fight well to be a king! He must learn to never let his guard down. Not for a moment!"

He sat down wearily on a handsome chair that commanded the open section of the hall before them. "Three dozen ships sailed from Sheppey. Two dozen came back. Whether you could have done anything to stop it is a moot point. The damage is done."

"Father, we can replace them! They can be built in a year or two."

"Oh...?" Alfred eyebrows rose skeptically, mocking the notion. "And you'll stay to build me these ships, Sigli?"

"I've fulfilled our agreement, my Lord. I ask that you give me my ships and let me go."

"How can you do this?" The king leaned forward, his eyes on fire. "You would strip me bare of what little I have left! A dozen seaworthy longships to my name? I simply can't allow it!"

"You swore it!" Sigli stepped forward angrily.

"Don't tell me what I did! You press me too far, Viking!"

Sigli paused to gather his composure, and when he finally spoke his words were carefully measured. "My Lord, I'm sorry about what happened. But it wasn't my fault. And even with this defeat, you still have more than enough strength on land to fend off any efforts by a few East Anglian rebels." He raised a finger into the air for emphasis. "But none of that should matter. By your Christian God...you gave me your word. All these years of loyal service...you simply can't discount them now!"

The two men locked eyes, their wills clashing. Edward stood by in silence, caught between the wishes of his father and his friend. Finally Alfred crashed his fist on the arm of the throne and stood up in anger, waving his hand impatiently in the air.

"Take your ships, then! Leave! And I suppose all your Viking craftsmen will go with you? How will I build my fleet again?"

"You'll manage. There are Saxons who've learned something of the trade."

"Not like a Viking. You know that."

Sigli stared at the dark earthen floor. Slowly, he raised his head, looking up until the torchlight flickered in his pale blue eyes. "If I don't follow my destiny now and find Sidroc, I'll lose him forever. On the graves of my father and mother, of my dead sister, I've sworn to have that man's head! Even if...even if you deny me so much as one ship, Alfred...I *must* leave. And it must be now. You can't deny me that."

Alfred's body stiffened and he clenched his fists, and then his mouth curled into an uncharacteristic snarl. "If I wanted to keep you here, I could. Just like I could command you to accept the Faith, when I've looked the other way all these years. But no, I won't do that. I'll ask you again, one more time, to stay."

"I'm sorry. I can't."

"Very well, then! Go! Leave me! Take your ships, you fool, and chase this...this phantom of yours, this ridiculous dream you've conjured up!" He gestured toward the door. "Now be off with you at once!"

Sigli glanced sadly at Edward and then looked back at the king. So that was the way it had to be. He turned on his heel and walked across the hall, through the door and out into the foggy night.

*   *   *   *   *

The darkness began to close in on Sigli and Dagmar as their horses plodded back along the riverbank, slowing progress and obscuring their every step. A light rain began to fall, compounding their misery and compelling them to draw their cloaks close about them. Just when victory had seemingly been in their grasp, it had been ripped away. It would have been so sweet to return in triumph, to have sailed into Rochester with the fifty ships they had left behind two days earlier. Seven for him. Another seven borrowed for a few months. And thirty-six sleek longships for Wessex, cemented by a naval conquest that would have served notice to Alfred's enemies everywhere.

Could he have prevented it? Could anything have been done? For the first time since the news had come, a sense of guilt began to creep through him. He knew Dagmar to be an able navigator, and Penda was a man who could be counted on in battle, his mistrust of all things Viking notwithstanding.

But none of that mattered now. It was time to get on with his life, to find Sidroc once and for all. He knew he had to forget the dream of an avenging armada. Even if he had to track his man alone to the most distant corner of the world, then that was the way it would have to be. Let Wessex keep its ships; to Hel with them, he thought to himself. Give me one bark, my Halfsfiordians and a few other stout hands, and that will be enough. It will be either Sidroc or Valhalla. Or both.

"So, will you come with me?" he asked Dagmar, breaking the silence as they drew closer to the camp. It was raining harder now.

Dagmar looked up as though he had been roused from sleep, so deeply had he been lost in his own thoughts. The corners of his eyes wrinkled with pleasure. "I'll go with you anywhere."

"And the others?"

"They're women if they don't. Or worse yet, swine." They both laughed.

"Well, then, we'll sail immediately."

"How many ships will we have?"

"I don't know yet. At least one; you can be sure of that. But in any case, it's on to the continent. And if it's all for naught, you can always join up with Haestan's armies."

"By Odin, that reminds me!" Dagmar sat up in his saddle, rain dripping from the hood of his cloak. "I forgot to tell you—I saw Gylfi after we made port. He's in camp, and he has news. He hinted that he could maybe help you. But, see there...we've reached the edge of the camp. Why don't you come to my tent? I'll go find him, and we can see what he has to say."

It was dry in Dagmar's shelter, and there was food for Sigli to eat as he waited under the low light cast by a single torch that hung near the entrance. As he looked out into the darkness, the rain continued to beat down on the earth, carving out a series of rivulets that streamed through the mud. He was tired from his long journey and the day's bad tidings, but he knew that sleep was still a long way away. After he talked with Gylfi he would see about gathering the rest of the Halfsfiordians. He would make his plans known to them tonight, and tomorrow they would set things in motion.

The sound of footsteps sloshing through the mud interrupted his thoughts. Soon Dagmar and Gylfi filled the entrance to the tent, shaking the rain from their cloaks and scrambling to find a space in the small enclosure. Gylfi reached out with his hand and grabbed Sigli's shoulder, grinning from ear to ear in the dim light.

"I'm glad you're alive. We were all worried."

"I'm alive, all right. And I'm ready to leave Wessex."

"Good." Gylfi was remarkably cheerful. "I'm glad to hear you say that. I'd decided to go to the continent myself, regardless of your decision. But now I'll go with you."

"So you talked to the prisoners? Where are most of them from?"

"Mostly Danes, and a few Northlanders. There's a lot going on in Francia these days. Haestan has attacked Paris."

"And Sidroc? Dagmar said you had news of him." Sigli could barely restrain his eagerness.

"Well, I think so.   I never made a secret of who I was, and word soon got out about you. Most of the men talked freely; there's no real news for Alfred about any Viking movements other than what he already knows." Gylfi squatted on his haunches and peered through the darkness. "But late yesterday, when I wandered by the stockade, one of the Danes motioned me over. He looked at me and smiled, and he said he knew all about Sidroc, and how much he meant to you."

"And....?"

"He told me that he wasn't about to talk until his release was arranged. It's his bargaining point, you see."

"Well, if that's all it is, then lead me to him. I can set him free immediately."

"Right now? But it's raining...."

Sigli stood up impatiently. "Forget the rain. Take me to him now."

They all stepped out into the night and set off briskly on foot. After a brief trek through the rain the three men came upon one of the stockades that housed the Vikings who had been captured following the siege of Rochester. It was illuminated by a series of torches posted outside near a group of tents that housed the Saxon guard. They approached the shelter closest to the stockade, where they were accosted by a man-at-arms who recognized Sigli immediately and bowed low, awaiting orders.

"We wish to see the Dane Boromir," interjected Gylfi, stepping forward.

The guard nodded and led them over to a nearby wooden gate, where they were able to peer through the slatted timber and into the stockade. Through the steady rain, they saw the outline of a crude shelter that had been erected so that the prisoners could find relief from the weather. A mass of men huddled under the eave of the dwelling, gathered in the dim light thrown off by a single flame.

"Boromir!" the guard shouted into the stockade. "Boromir! Come forward!"

There was a rustling among the cramped dugout, and then a man emerged into the rain and approached them, slogging through a sea of mud. He stepped carefully to avoid slipping into the mire, tiptoeing the last few paces and grabbing onto the wall for support. The guard raised his torch so that it shone fully on the man's face, revealing the bearded countenance of a Dane in his early thirties with round, expressionless eyes. Neither Sigli nor Dagmar had ever seen him before.

"I've brought you your man, Boromir," Gylfi said to the prisoner, motioning to Sigli.

"Say what you have to say."

Boromir pressed his face up against the palisade and smiled thinly. "A wall has a way of curbing a man's tongue," he said to Sigli. "Grant me my freedom, and I'll tell you everything I know."

"And how do I know you won't make up a complete lie, just to get out?"

"About Sidroc? Believe me, I know the man. The Malevolent One, some call him. Others know him as Old One Eye. He lost it at Halfsfiord, they tell me..."

"And how do you know all this?"

"There are many stories. I'd been plundering along the Rhine for three years, when one day Sidroc appeared. He'd had a row with Haestan, who wouldn't tolerate his insolence, so he was told to go elsewhere. I joined his raiders shortly after."

Sigli turned to the guard. "Open the gate and let him out." As the man-at-arms followed his instructions, he again spoke to Boromir. "I shouldn't be doing this...but so be it. You're on your own now."

Boromir crossed the threshold to his freedom and smiled a toothy grin that shone in the torchlight. "You're a man of your word, they tell me. So you must guarantee my safety."

"I'll do all I can to see to it. Now...speak."

Boromir took a deep breath. "I fought with Sidroc and his men against Henry of Saxony early last spring. We met near one of the tributaries of the Rhine, and we were beaten soundly. Our only retreat was to ford the river, which had risen with the runoff and was swollen with rushing water. We started across, but the going immediately became difficult. I was fighting the current and holding my own, but others were not as fortunate. More than one man was swept downstream, some still atop their mounts, others flailing helplessly as they rushed by with the current."

Boromir shook his head. "I can tell you this, I thanked the gods that I was one of the lucky ones who made it to safety."

"Hurry up with your story!" Gylfi exclaimed. "We're getting drenched!"

"We rode downstream along the far riverbank, picking up some of the men who had managed to make it ashore. But then we rounded a curve, and we came to a point where a half dozen bodies had washed up into the shallows of a small inlet. We rode closer to see if any of them were still alive, but they were all dead." He looked up uneasily, and then he took a deep breath.

"One of them was Sidroc."

"What?!! Are you sure?!" Sigli lunged for Boromir, but Dagmar and Gylfi prevented him from grabbing the Dane by the throat.

Boromir's eyes grew wide with fear. "Would I tell you this unless I knew it to be true? Would I subject myself to your wrath? You swore my safety!"

"Are you sure it was him?" Sigli croaked hoarsely.

"It was Sidroc. Knowing the man as I did...there was no mistaking him. There was no doubt that he was dead."

Sigli stared vacantly past Boromir and into the distance, almost incapable of assimilating the news. "Sidroc...dead...?"

"At least he was denied Valhalla," Boromir offered tentatively. "He died without a sword in his hand. Hel has him now. Your vengeance is complete."

"My vengeance is lost to me forever," Sigli muttered, turning away from the group and taking several uneven steps through the mud. "My life is without purpose."

Gylfi stepped forward as though to speak, but Dagmar put a restraining hand on his shoulder. They watched silently as Sigli stood alone with his back to them, his hunched shoulders pelted by a hard, driving rain that bounced off him and tumbled to the muddy darkness below.

*   *   *   *   *

Gylfi sat in the stern of the longship as it slipped down the river toward the sea. He suspected that the new day was already upon them, but the thick fog that crept along the river made it difficult to know for sure. The only sound that broke the still of the morning was that of the oars as they dipped rhythmically into the water and propelled the ship forward. He smiled and closed one of his hands around the pouch that Penda had given him, reassuring himself again that the easiest money he had ever come upon in his life was indeed real.

Like all Vikings, he loved gold. He loved it for its brilliance, its rarity, its power; he loved it for the esteem it gave him and for all the things in the world it put within his reach. It was that most sought after of prizes, one that men would gladly kill for. And now it was his. He had feared that Penda might go back on his promise and not reward him, but the ealdorman had appeared after midnight down by the river and handed Gylfi and Boromir each a bag of gold coins. And then he set them on board the longship bound for the continent, exacting their solemn pledge that they would never again set foot in England.

That was fine with Gylfi. He had tired of the staid life in Twyneham over the past few years, and he was eager to seek his fortune with Haestan's bands on the continent. The Vikings in Wessex had become like women, forsaking a profitable life of piracy to build ships for a Christian king. But what had driven him more than anything was the humiliation he had suffered at Sigli's hands during the public beating at Twyneham. It had unleashed his hatred and set it on a course for this sweetest of revenges, sweeter still than killing the man ever could have been. What he had done instead was to kill the spirit inside Sigli; he had almost been able to see it running down into the mud when Boromir had told the lie, as though a great wound had opened and the man's heart had poured out of him.

Gylfi looked forward, where Boromir's back loomed on one of the rower's benches just ahead. Where Penda had managed to find the resourceful Dane, he did not know, but Boromir had been so convincing in his story that Gylfi had almost believed him. The performance had been especially masterful considering that Boromir knew nothing of Sidroc. The fabrication had all been Penda's creation; Gylfi had been recruited to lead the unsuspecting Sigli into the trap, and Boromir had accomplished the rest.

He chuckled to himself. The Saxons had gotten what they wanted out of the affair, and so had he. A taste of vengeance and a pocketful of gold, all tied up in one tidy little bundle.

"Ship your oars!"

The voice cut through the fog. Gylfi looked forward and saw the Saxon commander of the longship rise to his feet and make his way aft toward him and Boromir. Suddenly the man stopped and pointed directly at them.

"Seize them!"

He was immediately surrounded by a group of Saxons who pinned his arms behind him and bound his wrists together with a leather thong. The same fate befell Boromir, whose normally expressionless eyes now flashed in alarm. When the Vikings were finally secured, the captain reached roughly into their pockets, withdrawing the two bags of gold that Penda had given them.

"Thief!" Gylfi spluttered, struggling in vain to loose his bonds. "You rob me, Saxon!"

"I'm no thief," the captain said grimly. "I retrieve the gold by Penda's order. But I assure you, you'll get the reward you deserve."

"What are you talking about?"

"I don't know what you heathens did, but Penda told me to tell you this: Betrayal breeds betrayal. He who would sell his brother deserves to be sold instead—to the devil!" He motioned impassively to his men. "Over the side with them."

Gylfi let out a sharp cry. He tried to resist, but the Saxons lifted him and Boromir and tossed them over the bulwark and into the river. He had just enough time to take a deep breath before he hit the freezing water and began to sink slowly toward the bottom. He righted himself and kicked furiously, until finally his head surfaced and he was able to fill his lungs with air. His wrists were lashed behind him, and the only way he could stay upright was by continuing to kick his legs rapidly, breathing in sporadic gasps as he struggled to keep his head above water. He screamed, but no one heard; already the stern of the longship was receding into the mist, leaving the two doomed Vikings in its wake.

He was vaguely aware of Boromir thrashing about in the river a few yards away, but then the Dane disappeared beneath the current, never to surface again. He continued to peddle madly with his legs, jerking his body upward to keep from sinking, and he knew that unless some miracle occurred his life would soon be over. He was a strong man and a good swimmer, but the weight of his water-soaked clothes and boots took its toll, and soon the fatigue began to get the better of him. A wild panic set in with the first unintentional gulp of water, clear and cold, choking, choking. Another thrashing of the legs, a kick in vain, and then more water into his mouth, his throat, his lungs. Fear consumed him as he fought against the river, but the icy current swallowed him up and dragged him down, down, deeper into its bosom.

And then suddenly the battle became an embrace. His fear gave way to a sense of well-being as he accepted the brilliant white light that pierced the darkness of the river. He gave himself to it completely and sank in a dream to the muddy bottom, and the secret of the lie sank with him, so deep that not even Njord could say where it finally came to rest.

CHAPTER VIII: Of Love And Lust

> *"On her white breast, a sparkling cross she wore,*
> *Which Jews might kiss, and infidels adore."*
> —Pope, The Rape Of The Lock

Old Aethelred sat up in bed and rubbed his eyes. His afternoon nap had carried well into the midsummer evening, but there was still some daylight left to him at that late hour, enough to savor for a moment before it melted away into the night. It occurred to him as he peered through the window and into the gathering dusk that his life had reached a similar point in time, that the end of his day in the sun was closing in faster than he cared to admit. There was no joy in getting old, no joy at all. Legs like lead and aches all over. The body struggling to hold out against decay, until one day it simply shuts down and ceases altogether. He had been a lucky man and had endured longer than most, but he still wanted all of life's treasures. He wanted the last drop of juice from what little fruit remained to him, hoping for more, always more.

He swung himself off his pallet with a grunt and stretched his legs, tottering over to the window and looking outside. He breathed in deeply, surprised at how good he felt. The nap had refreshed him. His head was clear and his wind was good, and it pleased him to think that he would disappoint the scavengers of the church as they hovered over him, licking their lips in anticipation. Grimwald and the others could go to Hell, for all he cared; he was still the Archbishop of Canterbury, and that was that.

He turned around and noticed a young monk standing in the doorway. The acolyte bowed respectfully and stepped into the room.

"You look well, Your Grace. Would you care for supper?"

"A few bites, perhaps, and then I'll pray. You pray more than ever when you reach my age."

"I'll bring you the food shortly. But meanwhile, Plegmund is here to see you."

Aethelred scratched his head. He'd almost forgotten he'd sent for the monk. "I hope he hasn't been waiting long. Send him in."

He had always liked Plegmund. The young man was certainly learned enough to rise as far as he wanted to in the world, and his standing in Alfred's court was impeccable, his conduct of the first order. Perhaps he was still too young to become Archbishop, but who was to say? The matter of succession would not be Aethelred's decision, but the longer he lived, the less likely that Grimwald would ever take his place. That alone was a good reason for prolonging his life.

Plegmund entered, smiling warmly. "Your Grace is feeling better?"

"Yes, yes." Aethelred waved his hand distractedly and sat down. Plegmund approached and knelt, kissing the Archbishop's ring. "You'll all have to postpone my funeral for a while, I must say," Aethelred continued, laughing at himself. "But I wanted to tell you how much I've enjoyed your stay here. I'm just sorry I've been feeling so poorly for the last week."

"Don't apologize, Father. But you speak as though my visit's over."

"It is. A messenger arrived from Rochester early this afternoon. King Alfred wants you to accompany the Lady Aethelfled back to Winchester immediately."

"So soon? Must we leave now?"

"I'm afraid so. The king will be returning to Winchester shortly. He wants to hold court and see his family again."

"I understand. But I'm going to miss Canterbury."

The old prelate squinted at him, and then he pursed his lips. "You may be back soon enough, my son. See that you remain pious and do your duty unto God. You'll have your translations to return to, I trust?"

"Yes. I've been laboring away slowly at the Venerable Bede. A few months more and I'll be finished."

Aethelred nodded his approval. "There's much intellectual activity in Winchester these days. That alone should be enough to fire your interests. Quite a scholarly lot the king has gathered." He smiled wistfully and looked out the window. "I wish I could be part of it, but I don't travel well. It would be worth the journey just to watch you all compete with each other for the king's favor."

He shook lightly with laughter, but then suddenly his brow darkened. He leaned forward and placed his hand on Plegmund's. "Whatever you do, my young friend, keep your distance from Grimwald. He can't be trusted."

Plegmund bit his lip. Old Aethelred could not know how much he feared the dangerous Winchester, nor for what dark reasons. "I'll remember your advice. Now, tell me...did Alfred provide us with an escort?"

"Several men-at-arms. The messenger himself will accompany you. He's the same Viking Alfred has long favored...you know him, I believe?"

"Sigli?" Plegmund's eyes lit up.

"Yes, that's him. He's here now, somewhere in the abbey. Now, you must swear that you'll take care of the Lady Aethelfled." He stood up and offered his hand. "I'll miss you both."

Plegmund dropped to a knee and kissed the Archbishop's ring. "Thank you for everything...your wise and kind advice, most of all." He rose to his feet. "I must be off, Your Grace; there's much to prepare for, and little time in which to do it."

Aethelred shook his head as he watched Plegmund leave, wondering to himself what it would be like to have young legs once again. But those days were gone forever. He rose with a sigh and prepared to take his supper, grateful for the appetite, grateful that God had allowed him to open his eyes again, grateful to breathe in the simple joys that still lay ahead of him.

It was another story entirely for Plegmund as he bounded across the courtyard outside the Archbishop's quarters and headed toward a larger building that housed most of the holy men who lived at St. Augustine's Abbey. Sigli was here, in Canterbury. He had not seen the Viking in years, and his excitement was enough to temper any misgivings he may have had about leaving Canterbury for Winchester. What a fine time they would have together, he and Sigli and Aethelfled; for all he knew, the Viking might even decide to stay on at the court after they arrived. He finished crossing the courtyard and entered the main hall, where several monks sat at a table in the far corner of the room.

"The Viking, Sigli...where is he?"

"He's waiting for you in your quarters, Plegmund. But I'd be careful. He's very drunk, and ill-tempered."

"Drunk? That's not tolerated here."

"Well, none of us was about to tell him otherwise. See there?" The monk motioned to a long wooden bench that had been split lengthwise with a violent blow. "One stroke of his axe. When we protested, he said he was here under orders from Alfred, and if we didn't care for his manners we could...well, never mind what he said. He took his mead with him and went to your cell."

Plegmund headed quickly down a hallway that led away from the rear of the main room, rounding several corners and negotiating another long, drafty corridor until he arrived at the door to his quarters. After hesitating for a moment with his hand on the latch, he opened the door and stepped into the chamber.

Sigli was slumped in a chair, his feet propped up on a table that ran along the far wall. In one hand he held a cup brimming with mead, in the other a greasy chicken leg. He broke into a broad grin when he recognized Plegmund, and he kicked his feet free from the table and leaned forward, raising his cup in greeting.

"Here's my teacher, come to confess me." His speech was thick and slurred. "In the name of the Father, and of the Son, and Loki and Odin and Thor."

"I'm glad you're here, Sigli." Plegmund had never seen the Viking drunk before.

"Pour you a cup, Plegmund? Oh, come on, now...You've only one God, and if he's looking the other way, he'll never know the difference." Sigli's bloodshot eyes gleamed in the torchlight. He took another gulp of mead, struggling to maintain his balance.

"What's come over you, man? Why do you debase yourself?"

"Don't preach to me! I'll drink myself to death if I feel like it."

"Why do you come to my house like this?"

"Because I don't care anymore." He stood up uncertainly and staggered along the table. "You'll be glad to know my quest is over. I can't kill Sidroc, after all...you see, he's already dead!"

"What?"

"You heard me." He rammed his cup down upon the table, spilling mead everywhere. "I've got nothing better to do than crawl back to Twyneham. I failed Alfred, you know. I lost him half his fleet. Got to build him more ships, I do." He slumped miserably back into his chair.

Plegmund moved over and placed a comforting hand on Sigli's shoulder. "It's best this way. Living your life to hunt down another man is beneath you. Evil breeds evil."

"It all seems so pointless now."

"Open your heart to God. He'll show you the meaning of love."

"Love? Love...? There's nothing left in this world to love. And don't talk to me about your God, Plegmund. I didn't come here to..." As he reached over to lean on the table he missed the edge completely, falling off the chair and onto the floor.

Plegmund bent over and with a great effort managed to help him over to the bed. "There, lie down," he urged, easing Sigli onto the pallet. "Your body rebels against the poison. You've had enough."

"Not yet, I haven't. Not until I can forget everything."

"Listen to me, Sigli...you must be strong." Plegmund took a deep breath and walked over to the lone window in his cell. He stood there for a moment and stared out into the night, until finally he spoke, without ever turning around.

"We're all challenged by God every day. He tests us to see if we can bear the misfortunes of life. Take heart in the fact that you're not alone; I'm also plagued by demons. I struggle against them every waking hour. And I pray to God to give me the faith and courage to overcome them. In time your pain will cease, and you'll find a reason to carry on, a reason to..."

He was cut short by a low, resonant snore. He wheeled around and saw that the Viking was fast asleep on the cot, his mouth open. He walked slowly over to the bed and sat down on its edge, looking into Sigli's face, exploring its every nuance. Everything about the Viking suggested vitality and robust, virile health. He was a perfect specimen, pleasing to the eye and bristling with an odd mix of untamed energy and a simple, charming vulnerability. The noble savage, indeed. Plegmund knew that a good and gallant man dwelt beneath his gruff exterior, a man who was not afraid to speak the truth in the face of hypocrisy. He could be counted on to live by his word, and that was a claim that few men of any faith could make.

But there was more. There was the matter of his own troubled conscience to deal with, for as he gazed perhaps too long and too intently at the slumbering shipbuilder, the dark specter of his desires began to take shape, casting him into an almost giddy sense of despair. The upcoming journey to Winchester would be a stern test, a battle with his soul for self-control. Only one thing in the world had the power to wreak such havoc. And here it was, stretched out before him, a gift of flesh and blood sent by fate. Desire was a ravenous beast, indeed, lying in wait to pounce at any moment.

He crossed himself and went to bed.

*   *   *   *   *

Sigli's head pounded as he sat up groggily and ran his hands through his hair, squinting at the light that streamed through the window. Too much mead again. Plegmund was right; no good could come of it, nothing of value was to be found in the bottom of a cup.

He stood up and looked around the empty cell. He had deprived Plegmund of his bed, and he wondered where the monk had spent the night. Not a very gracious way to treat an old friend, he thought to himself; he would have to make amends. But first he had to find a way to stop the pounding in his head. He walked out into the hallway and over to a large wooden door, pushing it open and stumbling into the brilliant glare of the summer morning.

No one was about. He crossed the courtyard and passed through the outer wall that surrounded St. Augustine's, stealing away from the abbey and heading toward a cluster of trees some two hundred yards away. He walked across a grassy meadow until he reached the shelter of the wood, and within moments he saw what he was looking for.

The waters of the Kentish Stour beckoned, meandering through the narrow valley of Canterbury before the river opened up into a marshy plain that led to the sea. He walked along the wooded bank until he came to a secluded spot tucked into a curve of the river, where he stripped naked, braced himself and plunged headfirst into the cold water. His senses tingled as he swam out into the middle of the stream and turned over on his back, floating with the current and watching the wispy clouds as they soared overhead.

At that very moment downstream, Aethelfled guided her horse through the trees, returning to Canterbury after her morning exercise. Every day since her visit had begun she had allotted time to be alone on these rides, to think about the forces that were acting on her life. She had mixed feelings about the upcoming journey to Winchester, for although she looked forward to rejoining her family, she could already sense the pressure her father would be exerting on her to pay a visit to the court of Mercia.

There was no arguing that Eadred was certainly handsome enough, with power and a promising future. But she did not know him well enough yet. There was only one way to remedy the situation; she would simply have to go to Mercia in the fall. She owed that much to her father—and to herself. Perhaps Eadred was a man she could be happy with, who would love her and make her feel all the things a woman could want to feel. She was still too young to know exactly what those things were, but she had her ideas—all of which left her wondering about the mysteries of love as she directed the chestnut mare down to the river's edge.

A splashing sound upstream interrupted her thoughts. She reined in the horse and peered cautiously through the heavy underbrush that lined the riverbank, where her eyes fell upon the back and buttocks of a naked man. He stood hip-deep in the Stour, throwing water on himself and shaking the river from his hair, and although she knew it was improper to look at a man like this, she could not help herself.

For what a man he was! Long, rippling muscles on both arms, attached to a broad back and shoulders, all tapering down to a waist that seemed to be narrower than that of many women. His firm buttocks appeared as though they had been chiseled out of granite. She found herself straining to get a closer look when suddenly the man turned, his hands still obscuring his features, to reveal his privates. They hung suspended like a clump of large, drooping fruit framed by a tangle of blond hair.

She had never seen anything like it. It was strange looking and even a bit ugly, but she could not take her eyes off it. So this was the instrument of love that grew large and stiff as the women-in-waiting had told her it did when excited? Her eyes wandered up the man's flat stomach and moved across the pectoral muscles that encased his chest like two thick, iron straps. And then as he dropped his hands and shook his head in the sunlight she had to suppress a gasp, for she recognized his face.

Sigli the Viking still had a magnetism that had not diminished in the four years since she last remembered seeing him at her father's court in Winchester. He had barely noticed her on that occasion. But she had noticed him, looking on with eyes that bulged with the infatuation of adolescence while she struggled to grow into herself. She had virtually forgotten about him since that last meeting. There were so many things to occupy the attention of a young woman of royal birth, so many distractions and flights of fancy. That he should suddenly appear again offered her a diversion, and her mischievous instincts took over as she noticed several articles of clothing hanging from a tree branch on the riverbank. She urged her horse forward into the clearing and plucked the garments from their perch, holding them aloft in her hand.

"These wouldn't happen to belong to you, would they?"

Sigli whirled around, flushed with embarrassment. He dropped back into the river and began to tread water in midstream, peering curiously up at the young intruder.

"They stink," she continued, making a face and holding his pants at arm's length. "You might consider washing them, as well."

"I beg your forgiveness, my Lady. You have me at a disadvantage." She was perhaps the most beautiful woman he had ever seen in his life.

"A disadvantage?" she wondered innocently, tossing her head so that her hair shone in the sun.

"I can't very well go too far without my pants, now, can I?" he laughed, swimming closer until he was able to stand, waist-deep, in the river.

"I wouldn't think that would bother a Viking. Modesty isn't a Danish virtue."

"I just don't want to alarm you, that's all."

"Alarm me...? Ha! Your axe is here on the bank. Unless you're hiding a weapon underwater, you can't very well hurt me...."

He laughed, amused by her audacity. Had she been a common woman, he might have thought about climbing onto the riverbank and taking her. But there was nothing common about this vision of loveliness, nothing at all. Judging by her dress and bearing, she was a woman of means, and he was not about to overstep the bounds of decency and possibly offend her. As he looked into her face, something in her eyes seemed vaguely familiar, but he was unable to make a connection.

"Do I know you, my Lady?"

It was the wrong thing to say. Aethelfled's eyes suddenly turned cold. "If you don't yet know me, Viking, you won't forget me soon! See how far you can get with your bare buttocks glistening in the sun!" She spurred her horse along the riverbank and galloped off in the direction of Canterbury, still clutching Sigli's clothes in her hand.

He scrambled out of the water to give chase, but when the hopelessness of the situation dawned on him he sank to his knees, pounding his palms on the damp earth and cursing under his breath. He rose angrily to his feet and watched the young woman disappear through the trees, and all he could think of was how to repay her for such a rude disservice.

But as he stood naked and dripping wet on the banks of the Stour, the humor of his predicament finally began to sink in. He started to laugh, at first lightly, until soon he was shaking so hard that it was all he could do to keep from losing his balance and falling back into the river. Never had such a ridiculous thing happened to him. He sat down on the riverbank and waited for the sun to dry his body, thinking that whatever lay ahead might somehow be bearable after all.

It was the first time he had felt anything like that in over a week, and it felt good.

*   *   *   *   *

"So let it be noted that, since the wound was inflicted where the hair will cover the scar, only one shilling shall be granted as compensation for the offense."

Alfred's verdict was final. The king had chosen on this rainy afternoon in Winchester to review any outstanding civil issues of local interest, having once again settled comfortably into the daily routine of life in what was indisputably the cultural and political center of Wessex. The main hall in Winchester was Alfred's favorite, sturdily built and fashioned mainly from stone. It could accommodate several hundred people, keeping them warm in winter and cool in summer, and it was perfect for public hearings such as the one the king had called for on this wet, misty day.

Winchester was the heartbeat to which all Saxons listened. It had been built in Hampshire on a hilly site in the wooded valley of the Itchen, lying principally on the left bank and surrounded by chalk downs that comprised part of the long ridge that crossed southern England from east to west. The city was at the center of six roads built by the Romans during their occupation of Britain eight centuries earlier, during which time it had been known by the Latin name of Venta Belgarum. The Celts had called it Caer Gwent, the White City, and it had flourished ever since. It was ideally situated; Canterbury lay a hundred miles to the east, Exeter a hundred miles west. Twyneham harbor, meanwhile, was a mere two dozen miles to the southwest, separated from the capital city by the thick woodlands of the New Forest.

"One final dispute, King Alfred," said Ceolmund of Hampshire, standing up to introduce the next issue. "Sigewulf the mason and Cedric the tanner, step forward."

Two ceorls approached and bowed. Sigewulf was a gruff, swarthy stonemason whose work was much admired around Winchester. He cleared his throat nervously and looked up at the king.

"Sire, this man Cedric has dirtied my water. He and my betrothed, Eoppa, were found together behind a closed door." Gathering his courage, he grew more excited. "I demand, as a two hundred man, that I be compensated forty shillings. And with it, the right to fight this man, when and where I choose."

Alfred pursed his lips. "The entire point of the wergild and its compensation is to avoid blood feuds. You know that."

"Yes, my Lord."

"And you?" The king looked impassively at Cedric. "How do you reply to these charges?"

"I'm innocent!" the wiry tanner bristled. "She was in my shop, it's true. But she was there conducting her father's business. As for the door, I don't know how it closed. It didn't stay shut for long."

Alfred turned to Ceolmund. "What testimony do we have?"

"The oaths," declared the ealdorman, turning to the people. "Let us hear the oaths."

An older woman of the town shuffled forward across the stone floor. Pausing momentarily to glance at Cedric with a scabrous eye, she turned to the king and swore on the blood of Christ that she believed the stonemason's accusations to be warranted. Another man followed who also gave his blood oath, and then a third ceorl did the same. When no one was left to speak for Sigewulf, Ceolmund turned to Cedric.

"Have you no one to stand up for you, tanner?"

"None, save Eoppa herself. But her father wouldn't let her come."

"Interesting..." Alfred stroked his chin and thought for a moment. "…but hardly conclusive. I'd be inclined to grant what you ask, Sigewulf, except for one thing...she's not your wife yet. You can't lay any claim to the compensation you ask for."

"But Sire! The oaths!"

"Yes, you have support, while he has none. Everyone thinks he's a rascal. But, do we have any evidence of her violation?"

Here Sigewulf reddened perceptibly, without answering.

"Well...?"

"Sire...Eoppa was not a maiden."

"I see." Alfred glanced quickly at Cedric, in time to catch the last vestiges of a smirk as it flickered across the tanner's face. Pretending not to notice, he spoke again to Sigewulf.

"That makes it rather difficult to determine if the deed was done, mason. Or if the woman in question had any objection to it, considering that she was not permitted to appear before us." He turned to Cedric. "But the oaths—as well as your reputation, tanner—conspire against you. Therefore we have no choice but to order you to undergo trial by ordeal. Your hand shall be submerged in boiling water; if the blisters heal within a week, you have our blessings and may go free. But if the healing takes longer, you shall pay the girl's father a sum that we shall decide upon, if necessary." He waved them away. "Let God be the judge...that is our verdict."

The ceorls bowed and left the hall as Alfred stood up and addressed the Witan, his ruling council. "Wessex continues to change, but our laws fail to keep pace. To that end, and with the help of my most esteemed and learned scholars," he nodded in the direction of the monks gathered in the room, "I intend to pursue this matter. Let a code of laws be put into writing, for all men of Christian England to live by. That is the first action I decree today."

He began to pace slowly, choosing his words carefully. "Of equal concern is the deplorable state of letters among our thanes and ealdormen. You would sit in judgement of others," he admonished the members of the Witan, his council, "and yet many of you here today cannot read or write. How can you mete out civil justice if you can't even understand the simplest of verses written on parchment? For several years now, the court school has flourished. Under the able administration of the Church, many of our children are reaping the benefits of learning. From this day forth, I require that all men of Saxon birth who would sit on the Witan learn to read and write English."

Several of the secular members of the council exchanged uneasy glances. Grimwald, meanwhile, smirked to himself as he examined his fingernails; let the illiterate buffoons squirm. It was only fair they be penalized for their ignorance.

"It pleases me now to introduce a matter of great significance," Alfred said. He turned and nodded to Asser, a serious-looking monk with dark hair and a full beard who fetched a wooden case and brought it over to the king.

"This is a gift sent to us by the late, great Pope Marinus in Rome," Alfred continued. "It just arrived yesterday, so I have the pleasure of surprising you all." He unfastened the clasp and raised the lid, placing his lips reverently on the contents of the box before lifting it above his head. "Here lies a fragment of the cross upon which our Lord Jesus Christ was crucified."

A gasp echoed through the hall. Grimwald leaned forward in his seat, no longer preoccupied with the state of his manicure.

"Let it be noted that on this day I, King Alfred of Wessex, decree that a nunnery shall be built at Shaftesbury in Dorsetshire. And this most holy and divine gift from Rome shall consecrate the ground upon which it is built, and anchor it in God's graces." He turned and smiled toward one of the wings leading from the hall. "When the nunnery has been completed, my daughter Aethelgifu shall take her vows and enter the Faith. And she shall become the abbess of Shaftesbury."

The hall broke into applause as Aethelgifu stepped forward and joined her father. But Grimwald was furious; he sat stiffly in his chair, grinding his teeth in anger. Why had he not been consulted? A nunnery at Shaftesbury, when he had been petitioning the king for money to build a new minster at Winchester? And why had not Alfred informed him immediately about the cross? It was *his* right, as the Bishop of Winchester, to administer the duties of Rome. He had studied and served in the Vatican, after all; what man had a greater right to act as envoy of the pope?

"That's not all," Alfred continued. He handed the box back to Asser and took his daughter's hand in his own. "To balance this most blessed day and do honor to the site of our greatest suffering, I further decree that a monastery shall be built on the island retreat of Athelney, where I hid in exile during the dark days of Guthrum's occupation. And to serve as the abbot of Athelney, I give you the most honorable John, the Old Saxon, a recent and worthy addition to us from the continent."

He raised his hand and acknowledged John, who joined him and Aethelgifu on the dias. The Old Saxon, a pious man whose gray beard made him appear even older than his forty-five years, had quickly made a favorable impression at the court and was generally acknowledged to be a scholar and Christian of great merit. Once again the crowd broke into generous applause—all except Grimwald, who was now beside himself with anger. Appointments such as those of Aethelgifu and John had always been granted only with his approval.

"Do honor unto these servants of God, as they honor us and themselves," declared Alfred. Aethelgifu and John knelt before him and kissed his hands, and then they rose and left him. He took several steps back and sat upright on the edge of his modest throne, placing his hands firmly on the rounded extremities of each arm and looking out at the large audience.

"To conclude the day, I wish to inform you all of one final decision I've made. After careful consideration, I've decided to divide the royal treasury—and all that is due me as tribute each year—into two equal parts. The first half shall be distributed to the secular interests in the kingdom. And the second half shall be granted to the Church. It shall be divided into four parts. The first part is for the poor; that needs no explanation. The second is for the royal school. The third share shall go to the new construction at Shaftesbury and Athelney. And the fourth portion shall be distributed among all the monasteries and churches of Wessex, to be used for upkeep and improvements. Let all men here bear witness under God to these things, and let them take effect forthwith."

He stood up and raised his hand to the hall. "Thank you for attending us today. May God watch over you."

He turned and exited the hall. Grimwald leaped to his feet and forced his way through the crowd, breaking through the last of the dunderheads blocking his path and scurrying across the dias in pursuit of the king. He moved quickly down a long corridor that led away from the rear of the hall, and as he passed various chambers that opened off to either side of the corridor he looked inside them, hoping to find Alfred.

He finally discovered the king washing his hands at a basin in one of the day rooms near the rear of the estate house. Gritting his teeth, he rumbled into the room, his jowls flopping back and forth with each agitated step.

"Ah, Grimwald," Alfred said cheerfully, looking up from the water bowl. "It's been a good day for progress, don't you think?"

"Progress? You call it progress when you deliberately bypass me? Those were ecclesiastical decisions!"

"I would hardly call anything deliberate. And I'd think you would support my daughter's entry into the Faith."

"It's the appointment of John to Athelney that bothers me more."

"He has the maturity to handle the post."

"But, my Lord, these foreigners already pay little enough heed to those of us in the established clergy. You dishonor me, and you tamper with the order of the Church!"

"You'd be well advised not to overstep your bounds."

"And what about the dispensation of monies?" the Bishop of Winchester continued, ignoring the king's warning. "You shower praise on Athelney and Shaftesbury, while I've been begging you for years to build a new minster here! How can you turn a deaf ear to the very place where you'll someday be buried?"

A wry smile crossed Alfred's face. "That day, I trust, won't be soon. We've more than enough time to build the minster."

"And the cross?"

"A gift sent expressly to me, to do with as I please."

"As you *please*? I must protest! You take me too lightly, Sire! Don't think that...."

"Ah, Asser," Alfred smiled, looking over Grimwald's shoulder, where the monk from Dyfed stood in the doorway. "Come in, my friend. We're just finishing here, and I look forward to your reading. We'll pursue this at another time, Grimwald. I'm sure we can arrive at a satisfactory conclusion."

Grimwald bit his lip and bowed curtly to the king. He turned on his heel and pushed past Asser, not even bothering to acknowledge the monk as he left the chamber.

"Please, Asser, be seated," Alfred said, doing so himself and motioning to a nearby chair. "I so enjoy these readings. What shall it be today?"

"I thought a selection of psalms would be appropriate, my Lord," said the studious Welsh monk. He sat down and unrolled a parchment, and he began reading from it in a soothing, melodic voice that rose and fell with each inflection of the text.

Alfred's eyes wandered to the window. Looking through it, he could see the summer rain falling on Winchester, drumming lightly on the stone sill. Let it wash away these trivialities, he thought to himself. Let it nourish the seeds that were planted today. Everything was coming together nicely, all according to plan. His policies had been announced, Grimwald was at arm's length, and Aethelfled soon would be arriving, enabling him to fit still another piece of the puzzle artfully into place.

He smiled to himself and closed his eyes. Asser's voice mingled with the rain, falling softly on his spirit and filling it with divine inspiration and thoughts of God.

*   *   *   *   *

Sigli sat impatiently on his horse, wearing a robe borrowed from Plegmund. It was several sizes too small, binding him tightly and catching in awkward places. He had torn material out from underneath the arms so that he could fit his shoulders through the sleeves, but no alteration could lengthen the robe, which dangled ridiculously at mid-calf as he sat in the saddle.

He had lost the only clothes he had thought to bring with him on the journey, and now here he was, ready to meet the king's daughter for the first time in years and looking like a complete fool. He glanced sheepishly over at Plegmund, who sat at the reins of an oxcart which had been loaded up with provisions—most of which belonged to Aethelfled.

"Too bad I wasn't a woman. She has enough dresses in that cart to clothe an entire village."

"My robe looks quite becoming on you," Plegmund said. "Just think of it as a disguise…if we're accosted by thieves, they'll never suspect the finest axe in Wessex keeps our company."

"Laugh all you want. I don't care how I look. But if she doesn't hurry up, this robe of yours just might rot on my back." He glanced impatiently over his shoulder, looking past the six other mounted members of their party.

"She's taking her leave of old Aethelred. One never knows about the Archbishop's health, you know." Plegmund bit his lip and looked wistfully around the courtyard. "Canterbury, sweet Canterbury. I'll miss it. All of it."

"And I'll miss none of it. Three weeks ago I left Twyneham a reasonably happy man. First I lose half of Alfred's fleet, then I lose my purpose...and finally I lose my clothes. What's left?"

"Your life, of course. And your soul."

"Ah, yes. My soul." He turned impatiently in his saddle again. "What's taking her so long?" He shook his head and sighed. "Tell me, Plegmund...what sort of girl is she? Isn't she the one who's going to become a nun?"

The monk laughed; nothing could be further from the truth. "No, not her. You're thinking of Aethelgifu."

"Other than Edward, I haven't seen the king's family in years. Too busy building ships." Sigli's eyebrows creased together. "So what does she look like? Got a sword for a nose like her father, does she?"

"Not quite."

"Hasn't he married her off yet? Must be something wrong."

Plegmund shifted his weight on the oxcart. "I suspect the biggest problem is that she hasn't met a man yet who can keep up with her. But see for yourself; here she comes now."

Sigli's jaw dropped. There, riding effortlessly toward them aboard the familiar chestnut mare, was the woman from the river. But of course, he thought to himself. Who else could it have been? He had been so stupid, so blind. And a fool for it twice.

"We're ready to depart, my Lady," smiled the monk as she rode up. "Do you remember Sigli?"

"All too well. That's quite a fine robe you're wearing, Sigli. Is it the Danish fashion these days?"

"Only when necessary."

"I probably should let you keep wearing it for a few days." She reached into her saddlebag and pulled his clothes out, throwing them to him. "I even had them washed—I didn't want to have to smell them for the next hundred miles."

"What's this?!" Plegmund sat upright. "Sigli, you told me a boy from the fields took them!"

"Don't worry, Plegmund," Aethelfled continued. "Just my way of introducing myself to the shipbuilder." She turned to Sigli. "And what did you cover yourself with?"

"Oak leaves. Now, if you don't mind, I'll change back into these. And then we can go."

They had to pass across half of southern England on their journey westward, through most of Kent, on across Sussex, and from there finally into Hampshire. Their path most of the way led through the Weald, a large belt of forestland some hundred and twenty miles long and thirty miles wide that stretched all the way across northern Sussex to Hampshire. While the wood was dense, a number of roads and paths had been cut through it, allowing travelers access to the shires on either side of the forest. The party entered the Weald some two hours after leaving Canterbury, and the miles passed uneventfully, fueled by a glorious day filled with the joys to be gleaned from a sun-dappled glade, a peaceful meadow, or the chirp of sparrows hidden among the tall oaks of the forest.

Plegmund and Aethelfled absorbed themselves for well over an hour discussing the virtues of Ovid and Virgil as the oxcart rumbled along at the head of the party. From time to time Sigli caught snatches of their conversation as he rode behind, until at one point Plegmund turned around and beckoned for him to come forward. He urged his horse ahead until he had drawn alongside the oxcart, where the monk and Aethelfled smiled pleasantly.

"We were discussing nature, and God's creation," Plegmund said. "Aethelfled would like to know how the Vikings, with your many pagan gods, embrace this concept."

"So you decided to consult with the king's heathen."

"No, really," said Aethelfled. "I'm very curious." She smiled warmly at Sigli. "We believe, for example, that God created the universe after a week's labors, fashioning different pieces of it on each day."

"And then he finally created man, and from man's rib, he created woman," Sigli said.

"See, I told you!" Plegmund exulted, glancing in triumph at Aethelfled before resting his admiring eyes on the Viking. "You've retained your lessons well, my friend. There's hope for you yet."

Sigli cleared his throat. "As for the Viking way, we believe the universe is made up of a great tree, which contains nine worlds. One of them is Midgard, the world of men. It was created by Odin and his brothers amidst the Yawning Void. Midgard is round, and it's surrounded by a deep blue sea."

"Ridiculous," Plegmund scoffed. "Everyone knows the earth is flat."

"Along the outward shores of the ocean, the gods gave rugged Jotunheim to the Frost Giants. Then they encircled Midgard—which they'd built using the remains of the giant Ymir—with a fortress wall. The wall was built using the Ymir's brows. His bones and teeth became the mountains, and his brains were thrown to the wind to create clouds. And after this the gods created the man Askr and the woman Embla."

"Askr and Embla," Aethelfled brightened. "Like Adam and Eve—no, Plegmund?"

"There are similarities. But the Danes believe in many deities—and not the one, true God, who is perfection."

"My people don't believe in perfection," Sigli said. "Our gods embody the frailties of men. We have many of them, each with his own personality—Thor, the god of thunder, Loki, the god of mischief, Tyr, the one-handed god of war."

"And why does he have only one hand?"

"The gods needed to find a means to enchain Fenrir the Wolf, who was born of Loki when the mischief-maker consumed the heart of an evil giant woman. It was foretold that when Ragnorak comes, when all will finally end in the consuming fire, Fenrir will devour Odin. And he in turn will be destroyed by All-Father.

"So you can see why the gods wanted to contain the Wolf. They reared Fenrir in Asgard, and Tyr was the only one courageous enough to feed him. But when they saw how strong the Wolf was becoming, they devised a fetter for him and tricked him. They suggested he might try his weight on it to see if he were strong enough to escape it. But with the very first kick the Wolf gave, he snapped the fetter."

"Why," interrupted Aethelfled, "would your gods raise the beast foretold to destroy them?"

Sigli laughed. "We often sow the seeds of our own destruction, do we not, my Lady? The gods so valued their mansions and fanes that they didn't want to pollute them with the blood of the Wolf. So they manufactured another fetter, known as Dromi, which was half again as strong as the first one. The Wolf was more wary this time, but he knew he had to risk it to enhance his reputation. And so, after a brief struggle, he shook it free and shattered it to bits.

"Ever since, it's been a proverb to 'Dodge out of Dromi' whenever anyone manages to escape from a tight spot. Anyway, the gods were now desperate. They finally turned to a dwarf who was skilled above all others, and he forged the fetter known as Gleipnir. It was made of six ingredients—the noise of a cat's footfall, the beard of a woman, the roots of a mountain, the nerves of a bear, a fish's breath and the spittle of a bird. It was soft and smooth as silk, but firm and tough beyond its appearance.

"The gods rowed out onto a lake with the Wolf and beseeched him to try his luck with the new fetter. But Fenrir immediately became suspicious, because Gleipnir looked so fragile compared to the bonds of iron he had already mastered. So he bargained with the gods. He told them that if they were determined to test his mettle, one of them would have to place his hand between his sharp fangs as a guarantee that they wouldn't betray him.

"None of the gods came forward, until finally Tyr thrust out his right fist and laid it within the Wolf's jaws. But when Fenrir kicked out, Gleipnir tightened around him. The more violently he tried to break away, the fiercer the bond bit into him, and it became obvious he'd met his match. Everybody laughed and mocked the Wolf—everybody except for Tyr, who lost his hand."

"What happened then?"

"The gods grabbed the chain attached to the fetter and fastened Fenrir to the foot of a lofty crag. And then they took an enormous boulder and drove the crag deeper into the ground. Fenrir struggled madly and tried to bite them, so they wedged a sword in his mouth, gagging him. And there bellows the Wolf, lying bound until Ragnarok comes and all is destroyed."

Aethelfled's eyes were trained upon Sigli in rapt attention. "You tell a fine tale."

"I once had a teacher, a very wise old man named Mimir. But he, like all else from my past, is gone forever."

He stared ahead through the trees, and as he did so Aethelfled's eyes lingered on him. Sigli was unaware of her attention, but it did not escape the watchful eye of Plegmund, who noticed a soft blush fill the cheeks of the princess with an emotion he had never seen before.

The remainder of the day passed uneventfully, as did the next, until by the third day they had crossed much of the Weald and drawn near the borders of Hampshire. During that time Sigli had undergone a transformation, becoming a different man from the morose creature who had arrived in Canterbury just a few days earlier. He was enjoying himself. For that matter, Plegmund was as happy as Sigli had ever seen him, and every time he looked into the monk's shining eyes he could not help but smile to himself. He had almost forgotten what good friends they had become during his first years in Wessex.

But it was Aethelfled who had really uplifted his spirits. She made him feel good about himself; she was attentive, interesting, easy to talk to and more in line with his thinking than he ever could have imagined a Saxon woman of such high birth could be. He had vaguely remembered her as a sweet young girl, but he was startled by what a formidable woman she had become, a vision of absolute loveliness.

Because he was stunned by her beauty. There were times when he looked at her that he could almost feel himself shivering. It was foolish to entertain such thoughts, he knew. The taboo of a heathen with designs on the daughter of a Christian king was more vast in its implications than the Great Sea.

But he could not help himself. He had to admit it was exhilarating to feel something again, the longing a man feels when he is excited by a woman. For the most part he had suppressed his sexual desires since landing in Wessex, consumed as he had been with building ships and seeking the revenge that had suddenly disappeared from his life. And now desire tugged at his pant leg, drawn to this new object of light that had appeared in his life.

So it was with an inescapable sadness that he stared into the campfire during the final night they would spend in the Weald. Plegmund must have felt it, too, because his voice was reflective as he broke the silence.

"So you'll be heading on to Twyneham, Sigli?"

"Alfred wants me to build ships. That's what I do best."

"Stay with us. Resume your lessons with me."

"I don't think I could do that, even if I wanted to..."

"And what *do* you want?" It was Aethelfled.

Sigli looked up and saw the firelight dancing across her face, and at that moment he knew that he wanted her, only her. He had to look away, and he stared off into the shadowy trees.

"I have this dream, many nights, that I'm sailing on the Great Sea. I'm hungry and tired and worried—about what, I don't know—when I spot land on the horizon. I set my course for the shore, but I never seem to get there. Something always happens...a storm, a fog. Sometimes the land just recedes and disappears, or suddenly I wake up."

He let out a sigh. "Someday, maybe, I'll simply coast into the beach, and the keel will slide up into the wet sand with a perfect settle, and I'll know I'm there. Really there. That's what I want." He looked up at Aethelfled and smiled. "Now it's your turn. What about you?"

She looked right into him. "Harmony and balance. The perfect union between love and duty. I want to make a difference in Wessex, to leave a mark behind me when I'm gone."

"Love and duty...that sounds like something your father would have you say."

"It's my duty to marry for the good of the kingdom."

"And so you shall," Plegmund broke in. "Eadred is noble and kind. You'll learn to appreciate him, if you give it a chance."

"Eadred? You're betrothed to Eadred?"

"In my father's mind, yes. But we'll see about that. Do you know him?"

"Yes. We fought together at Edington. But I haven't seen him in years."

"He cuts quite a fine figure," she shrugged, turning to the monk. "You may be right, Plegmund; better him than some portly nobleman from Flanders, I suppose. And what about *you*...what do you want most?"

"There are certain things I wish to accomplish...things that are quite out of my control," the monk said.

"Sometimes I think that everything is out of our control," Sigli said. "Maybe we should forget about everything, the lives we've led, the paths we've chosen...or that have been chosen for us. What do you say? We'll keep riding past Winchester, on to Twyneham, and we'll board ship and sail away."

"And where would we go?"

"Would it matter? The Pillars of Hercules, the land of the Russ...I don't care. Maybe we could just set a course west and sail off into the Great Sea, and never come back."

He looked at Plegmund and Aethelfled, and their eyes were shining. For a moment it almost seemed as though they believed him, that it all could really come to pass. He would sail with her anywhere, that he knew, to the very ends of the earth and beyond.

But then the moment faded, and in their eyes the weariness of the world again began to take shape.

"I would leave," Aethelfled sighed, "but for the responsibilities that I know await me. And both of you...you can't just turn your backs on the world."

"Very well, then," Sigli smiled. "If we can't sail off to begin new lives, then we'll just have to do something about the old ones. Here, give me your hands...."

He placed his own palm out over the fire, and Plegmund and Aethelfled joined theirs with his.

"By the gods—by any god you choose—let us enter a covenant. May the world grant us each what we most desire, whatever that truly is, and may we not rest until all three have fulfilled our pledge."

"I'll swear to that."

"And so will I."

"Look, up there!" Sigli exclaimed. They peered into the night, where a shooting star traced an arc across the sky. "An omen! So our greatest wishes shall come to pass, after all! Tomorrow, Winchester. And after that, let destiny be served."

Hands still clasped together, they sat transfixed, staring into the heavens. Each wondered what it was that he or she really wanted more than anything in the world. And all the while Desire lurked in the shadowy depths of the forest, like Fenrir the Wolf himself, driven by an insatiable appetite but bound and gagged with nowhere to go.

*　　*　　*　　*　　*

How much longer could a man be expected to wait? Plegmund tapped his foot on the stone floor, annoyed at the inconvenience. He had been in Winchester for five days, with nary an opportunity to have so much as a single word with Alfred. And now he sat here in the anteroom of the royal chambers, having waited for over an hour while the king attended to some obscure matter of state.

It had never been this way during the early years. Alfred had been hungry then, living by his wits in a world that clearly belonged to someone else. To be a part of his entourage, no matter how seemingly insignificant, had been to know the man with a degree of intimacy that had not been matched since. The king was more insulated from his people now, his every minute accounted for, his kingdom growing daily and his power on the rise. Wales had come under his thumb. Mercia, in principle an honored ally, was for all intents a puppet state under Eadred's guardianship. And whispers could already be heard, echoing through the stone corridors of the estate house at Winchester.

London, they said. London calling.

So Plegmund waited, anxious to report to Alfred on everything from Canterbury to Bede, the court school to Aethelfled's preoccupations. He had been put off by one circumstance or another, and today's chances were slipping away as evening approached, when the court would gather in the main hall for a celebratory feast honoring the appointment of John the Old Saxon to Athelney. Would he ever get to see the king?

"May I wait here with you?"

He had been too distracted to notice the approaching figure. As he looked up into his fellow monk's eyes he knew instinctively, without introduction, that the man could only be Asser. He stood up and bowed politely.

"One more person waiting could only ease the monotony; be my guest. I don't think we've met. I'm Plegmund."

"Asser of Dyfed. You've been in Canterbury, haven't you?"

"Until recently. But now I'm here, trying to see the king. Is it always this way?"

"Werferth told me he waited three hours on Tuesday before giving up."

Plegmund looked into the generous, bearded face of the Welshman, and he could not help but be impressed by its character. It was a face a few years older than his, with warm, intelligent eyes and a quick smile. A worthy candidate for consideration in any ecclesiastical matter, he thought to himself.

"Werferth has the patience of a saint. Sometimes it betrays him."

Asser smiled agreeably. "I understand you're translating Bede."

"Yes, I'm almost done. It's been quite rewarding. And you? Are you working on anything?"

"Something very exciting," the Welshman beamed. "I've begun research, after presenting the idea to King Alfred, on the story of his life and times. The work will encapsulate the struggle against the heathens, and all that's happened over the last thirty-five years."

"Incredible." Plegmund found it hard to conceal his jealousy. Why hadn't *he* thought of it?

"Quite a man," Asser shook his head. "Certainly worthy of the effort."

"Yes, of course." *The king has time for you, Asser; that's what they say.*

"And how exciting for John the Old Saxon, no? Less than a year in court, and already he's abbot of Athelney. It appears that...ah, what's this? Our wait's over."

They looked up as the door to the king's chamber opened and Alfred appeared, speaking earnestly to three stonemasons who hung on his every word. The king's eyes fell on the two monks, and he smiled broadly.

"Ah, look here. Plegmund...so good to see you." He slapped the Mercian on the shoulder, and then he turned to dismiss the masons. "Good day, gentlemen. I look forward to your next report."

The three men bowed and left the anteroom. Alfred turned back to the monks. "They're building a burh at Southampton, and there were a few architectural concerns to discuss. But, how are you, Plegmund? It's been months."

"I'm well, my Lord. I have so much to tell you...so many new developments."

"I'm sure you do." A cloud flickered across the king's brow. "But I'm afraid, my friend, that I must put you off yet again. The hour's getting late, and the feast will begin soon. I don't think I could do you justice in such a short time."

"I...I understand, Sire. Tomorrow, perhaps?"

"Yes, at the noon hour. You have my word on it." He turned to Asser. "I'd like to see you for a moment, though. We have just enough time to resolve the issue you brought up yesterday. Won't you...?"

He extended his hand toward the door. Asser smiled politely at Plegmund and brushed past the king, who again turned apologetically to the Mercian. "Once more, forgive me, Plegmund. Tomorrow at noon."

Alfred disappeared into his chambers and closed the door behind him. Plegmund stood there mutely, almost unwilling to believe his eyes. He had grown accustomed to receiving preferential treatment at the hands of the king, and he was shocked at how he had been waved off so casually in favor of the Welshman.

He had been ready to plant the seeds of Canterbury in the king's ear, to talk of old Aethelred and his continuing decline. But suddenly his ambitions weighed uncertainly on him. Maybe it wasn't the best time to bring the matter up, after all.

He shuffled off down the hall, accompanied only by his footsteps. Negotiating several long corridors, he finally arrived in front of a small door that he pushed open. The interior of the room was dark, and it took a moment for his eyes to become accustomed to the change. Moving past a row of flickering candles, he walked up a half dozen steps to a dimly lit altar, where a simple stone slab and a mounted crucifix governed the small chapel. It was one of his favorite places in all of Winchester, for few knew of its existence, and he could always count on it to provide him with the chance for private contemplation.

He centered himself before the altar and settled in on his knees, shifting rhythmically back and forth until his body was perfectly balanced. Slowly, methodically, he made the sign of the cross. It was a comforting ritual that always helped him to get in the proper frame of reference to pray; with his mind sufficiently cleared, he cupped his hands together and gazed up at the cross.

But something was wrong. He could feel it on the back of his neck, in the shadow that suddenly fell across the altar. He began to turn around when a familiar voice rang out.

"Praying won't help you now."

Plegmund rose to his feet, shuddering involuntarily as Grimwald, his prodigious bulk blocking the light in the doorway, stepped into the chapel.

"You've been avoiding me, haven't you?"

"Not at all. It's been very chaotic since we arrived."

"Yes, of course. All the time you've been spending with the king..."

"What do you mean? I haven't seen him once."

"Precisely my point." Grimwald sat down on one of the benches, glancing toward the door to make certain that no one was listening. "I'll get to the heart of the matter. I know why you're here, what's bothering you. It's bothering me, too. We need each other as never before."

"What are you talking about?"

"About Canterbury. And Winchester. And the realities of influence and power. Without them, a man might as well be dead."

He leaned forward and spoke almost in a whisper, urgent and direct. "Look here, Plegmund...even a blind man could see the changes that have come over the court in the past year. A new order, it appears. Fresh blood from foreign lands."

"Change is healthy, Grimwald."

"Did it feel healthy when Asser brushed past you into Alfred's chamber?"

Plegmund could feel the blood pounding at his temples. "How did you...?"

"I just know, that's all," Grimwald smiled thinly. "In any case, you've obviously noticed what everyone else has known for a while now. The king has new favorites. Out with the old, and in with the new."

Plegmund's shoulders slumped. "All so quickly. I don't understand..."

"This is a very serious issue, for both of us."

"I haven't given up hope. It could be a temporary thing."

"So you choose to pray to God, and hope blindly!" Grimwald slapped his knee in exasperation. "Wake up, man! God helps those who help themselves!"

Plegmund squinted through the half-light. "But what can we do?"

"We must be patient. We must watch, and wait. And we must gather information, and use it when the time is right."

"I'm not quite sure what you mean."

"Ah, my young friend," Winchester chuckled, "your naivete is as appealing as it's frustrating." He fixed his stare intently on the Mercian. "Knowledge is power, Plegmund. Knowledge of everything, all the time. Because in that vast store of information, of all there is to know about people and their lives, there's always something that a man would do just about anything to hide. Call it the stranger within."

He scratched his chin and smiled. "You're familiar with Homer, of course. Well, there isn't a soul on the face of this earth who doesn't have an Achilles heel. When a man is struck there he'll fall, and hard. Find the heel, find the flaw in the man, and you can exploit it."

"Like a parasite, you mean...? Preying on the weaknesses of others?"

"Such a vulgar image," Grimwald protested, screwing his face into an expression of distaste. "But call it what you will, it's one of the few weapons we have at our disposal to fight this rising tide of counter influence."

"So why do you need me? Surely a man of your experience has many alternatives."

"One can never have too many allies, my friend. Besides, we have much in common. Similar goals, and much the same problem."

"And what if I choose to reject this proposition of yours?"

"Then you'll never know Canterbury as anything more than a common pilgrim," Grimwald hissed, his eyes growing hard. "You may or may not be able to achieve the archbishopric *with* me; you certainly will never get there *without* me. And you'll never succeed as long as Alfred continues to court the favor of Asser, and John—and God knows whomever else. We must put a stop to it."

He rose to his feet. "I'll trouble you no more today...but think about what I've said. Be my eyes and ears, and you'll profit. Because somewhere, sometime, somebody will make a mistake. And that will be enough to hang the lot of them."

He shuffled across the chapel and exited through the narrow door. As Plegmund watched him leave, he could feel a knot forming in his stomach. Unsavory business, all of it. And yet, repulsed as he was by Winchester, he had to admit there was an element of truth in everything the man had said. He turned back to the altar, but the discomfort would not leave him. Cooperating with Grimwald was no better than dealing with the devil, that was certain; he could only hope and pray that another way could be found to loosen the bonds of doubt encircling his heart.

And still, the question burned in his mind: how much longer could a man be expected to wait? For the king, for Canterbury—for everything. How long?

*   *   *   *   *

"Smile, daughter. A long face doesn't become you."

Aethelfled grudgingly followed her mother's suggestion as they sat together at the main table in the banquet hall at Winchester. Ealswith, employing the skills she had refined from years of practice, beamed cheerfully at the ealdormen and thanes as they attempted to steal a moment with the king. Alfred sat on the queen's left, flanked by Edward, Penda and several visiting dignitaries from the continent. Winchester was alive with energy, and was clearly the only place to be on this night for anyone who cared to monitor the pulse of Wessex.

But Aethelfled found herself wishing she were a hundred miles away.

"Mother, you absolutely *must* stop telling me what to do all the time," she whispered through drawn teeth.

"Then you can start comporting yourself like the daughter of the king, instead of some petulant milkmaid." Ealswith smiled sweetly at Werferth and Plegmund as they passed by on their way to a bench off to one side of the hall that had been reserved for the holy men.

"I don't know what you're talking about. Have I done anything to embarrass you or Father?"

"Not yet. But you're acting strangely; that look on your face tells me something's wrong."

"As usual, you're reading far too much into things. Nothing's wrong."

"Then why were you so short with Magda? Surely bringing you the wrong dress was no reason to yell at her."

"I lost my temper, that's all. I apologized to her."

Ealswith fell silent. The smile that had been fixed on her face faded, but even without it she was a beautiful woman, with delicate features and a winning way. Now in her mid-thirties, she had held her form well, and she looked the part of the wife of the most powerful man in all of England. But her intuition, always tuned to a fine pitch, told her that something was wrong. She looked directly into Aethlefled's eyes.

"It's Eadred, isn't it? You're still fighting it."

"Mother, really!" Aethelfled rolled her eyes and looked off into one of the far corners of the hall. "We've discussed this before. I've agreed to go see him, immediately after the September hunt!"

"You speak as though we're sacrificing you at the altar of some heathen ritual. Honestly, Aethelfled...there isn't a young woman in all of England who wouldn't trade places with you. Eadred is a very powerful man—and pleasing to look at, as well. What more do you want?"

Aethelfled bit her lip and glanced around to make sure no one was listening. Then she turned to her mother, with just the slightest hint of defiance in her voice.

"I just don't like being told what to do all the time. It's as though I have no choice in the matter."

"And what would lead you to believe that you would? Have you looked at yourself lately? Good heavens...you're a woman! And the daughter of the king, no less!" Ealswith caught herself and sat back in her chair. Next to her, Alfred was engaged in a lively conversation with Edward concerning certain political issues in Wales; she cocked her ear briefly in their direction before turning back to Aethelfled.

"Do you think for one moment that I had anything to say about marrying your father? It was out of the question. And I certainly didn't need to be told twice what was expected of me."

"But you love him, don't you, mother?"

The question caught Ealswith off guard. "Well...yes...of *course* I do. We've been very happy together."

Aethelfled sighed. "That's just it. Everything you've said about Eadred is true. He seems to be a fine man, from what I've seen. But I don't love him, mother...not yet, anyway. And that frightens me."

Ealswith placed her hand reassuringly on her daughter's. "It will take time, that's all. I felt the same way when I was your age. I didn't know your father; I had no idea what to expect. But I learned to love him very quickly...as a matter of fact, it came quite naturally."

"But what if that doesn't happen for me?"

"Don't worry. There's no sense working yourself up over something that probably won't even be an issue. I have a feeling that all of this will resolve itself. You're about to become one of the most powerful women in all of England...I know that's important to you, to make a difference. Marry Eadred, and you will."

Aethelfled lapsed into silence. No matter what anyone said, she had her doubts, but there was clearly nothing to be done about it for now. Only time would tell. She picked at the venison on her plate, keeping her thoughts to herself.

But there was one other person in the room who was aware of her struggle. From his station on one of the long benches off to the side of the hall, Sigli could not take his eyes off the king's daughter. Ever since they had reached Winchester several days ago, he had been unable to erase her from his mind. The days they had spent together on the journey from Canterbury had affected him more deeply than even he could have imagined, and he knew—against his better judgement—that Freya had captured his emotions as she cast her love net earthward from Asgard. He was a prisoner now. He had spoken to Alfred and had agreed to leave tomorrow for Twyneham, but he knew that he would not be able to wash away the memories of the last few days. He had to speak to Aethelfled again.

"Are you ready to begin building the fleet again, Sigli?"

Plegmund's smiling face greeted him from the nearby table that the Mercian shared with the other holy men, including Werferth, Grimwald, Asser and John. Sigli collected himself and cleared his throat.

"Ah...yes, I suppose so. But I'm afraid it's going to be hard to go back to the same sorry endeavor, after all that's happened in the last few months."

"You've been through much, I know. But you must come to an understanding with the past, and look forward."

"To what? More ships? At least it will take my mind off my troubles, but eventually I'll need something...something else." He sighed and stared off into the distance, oblivious to the feast going on around him. "Perhaps an adventure might be the thing. My father told me stories of his voyage around the Pillars of Hercules. He traveled to lands where the sun burns hot all year round, and the people have dark skins."

"What good would it do you to go there? What would you expect to find?"

"Myself, perhaps."

Plegmund shook his head. "Then you'd be looking for the very thing you're running away from. This is your home, Sigli. These are your people now."

"I have neither home nor people. My life is adrift."

"Sigli, listen to me. You must look beyond your troubles. I know you've resisted before, but it's never too late to change. God is wise beyond wisdom; look to him, and all will become clear."

Sigli's eyes had a faraway expression in them as they stared off into the recesses of the hall. But suddenly Plegmund noticed a look of concern flash across the Viking's features; he followed his friend's eyes to the main table, where Aethelfled had leaped abruptly to her feet and stormed off, leaving the royal family in her wake. He could see Alfred and Ealswith exchanging worried glances, and then the king pounded the table in front of him.

"I'm sorry, Plegmund...I don't mean to be rude," Sigli said, rising quickly to his feet, his eyes following Aethelfled as she disappeared through the door leading outside. "It's just the wrong time to bring up the subject, that's all. Please excuse me."

Moving quickly, he made his way across the crowded hall, leaving by the same door through which Aethelfled had departed. As he stepped out into the warm evening he caught sight of her climbing the steps to the low ramparts that looked out over the River Itchen. He followed, mounting the steps and ascending them until he reached the top of the wall. She stood alone with her back to him, leaning against a corner parapet and looking off across the countryside. As the sun began to sink in the west, the entire valley of the Itchen glowed seductively in a lovely half-light. Sigli glanced around the courtyard below and saw that it was almost entirely deserted; virtually everyone was inside the main hall, enjoying the feast. He walked quietly along the wall, stopping when he came within a few feet of Aethelfled.

"Forgive me, my Lady..."

She whirled around, but her eyes softened the moment she realized who it was. Unsure of himself, Sigli looked down just long enough so that she could brush away a solitary tear from her face.

"I'm...I'm sorry to bother you. But I couldn't help it...I...I couldn't stay away." He looked at her, but she said nothing, waiting for him to continue. He took a deep breath. "I don't know you that well. Perhaps I presume too much..." He started to turn away.

"No, please. Don't go. I'm glad you came."

He looked at her, and her eyes almost devastated him. He felt like sweeping her up in his arms and taking her far away, where no one could find them and everything could be so simple.

"What troubles you, Aethelfled? What is it?"

A sad smile appeared on her sensuous lips. "Everything. Everything and nothing."

He diverted his eyes again. "I saw you leave the hall. And the next thing I knew, here I was up on the wall. I know it's presumptuous, after merely traveling in your party for a few days, but I..."

She raised a finger to her lips. He smiled shyly. It touched her. She had been impressed by him from the beginning and had been more than willing to admit that she was attracted physically to him; this latest gesture of faith and vulnerability did nothing to change her feelings. It only made things that much more difficult.

"I'm very pleased that you would take the trouble to think of me," she said, choosing her words carefully. "Our journey was short, but I think perhaps we already know each other better than either of us would have thought was possible." She turned again to look out across the green countryside.

"Beautiful, isn't it? I love summer evenings like this."

He turned with her and scanned the horizon. "So peaceful. But as we speak, time is slipping away. I wanted to at least say goodbye. I'm leaving for Twyneham tomorrow."

"I'd like it if you'd stay."

"Both of us know that's not possible." He noticed how the low sunlight bathed her in an otherworldly glow. It was almost enough to take his breath away. "I'll miss you, my Lady. I've enjoyed our time spent together more than anything."

"So have I, Sigli. But you musn't stay away long; surely you'll have reason to return to Winchester?"

"It's hard to say. Certainly I'll come whenever I'm summoned."

"Then consider it done," she said firmly. "I insist that you come to join in with the September hunt. You can be my honored guest. And I only hope that some other business brings you back sooner."

His eyes lit up, like those of a small boy who has just been granted a treasured prize. "I wouldn't miss the hunt for anything, my Lady. I'll count the days until autumn. Until then, I'm but a day's ride away; should you need my services, I'll be here immediately."

"God be with you, Sigli."

"And you, Aethelfled."

He bowed lightly and smiled, and then he turned and retreated with a light step along the wall. She watched his broad shoulders recede into the deepening twilight, and she could feel her heart pounding lightly in her breast, almost strong enough to make her forget what had brought her to the ramparts in the first place.

Whatever she was feeling, it felt good. And that, for now at least, was enough.

*   *   *   *   *

The last traces of summer passed benignly through Wessex, until September arrived with the first signs of the changing season. The sun began its slow decline, its rays struggling to hold on to the warm promises and long days that began to slip southward.

But the time had not passed quickly enough for Sigli. Every day seemed to drag into eternity, and even his renewed commitment to rebuilding the fleet had not been enough to take his thoughts off Aethelfled. He had not spoken about it to anyone, but Dagmar and the rest of the Vikings could tell that something was on his mind as his normal attention to detail wandered almost every day. There were times when he seemed to be a half a world away.

But all that was behind him as he stood in the courtyard of the estate house in Winchester, waiting for the dawn mist to burn away. He had ridden hard from Twyneham the day before, arriving so late that only the night watchman had been about to let him inside the silent city walls. He had not slept well, tossing and turning for hours, his mind racing as he waited for the break of day. And now he groomed his mount as Winchester came slowly to life, wondering if he should leap into the saddle and ride back to Twyneham.

Would she remember their shared trust? Had he been misled, living for a promise that almost certainly could never be kept? It had tormented him for two months. But whenever his doubts grew the darkest, he remembered the look in her eyes, the look that does not lie. That was what had kept him going; that was why he was here.

He looked across the courtyard, and his eyes met with a sight that brought a smile to his face as Edward walked toward him. The boy was a man now, with a confidence and a command to his step that marked him as the obvious heir to the throne. Sigli ran toward his friend, and they embraced in the courtyard.

"You look well, Sigli. It's so good to see you!"

"And you, my prince. Will you ever stop growing?"

Edward laughed. "Long before I ever reach your size. But I'll wager I can hold my own with you in the hunt. You're decent with an axe, but I'll bet I bring in the bigger prize."

"I'm sure of that. I learned long ago never to outdo royalty."

The prince slapped him playfully on the arm. "We'll see about that. I wanted you to ride in my party, but my sister wouldn't hear of it. She's counting on you to carry the day."

It was all Sigli could do to prevent his heart from leaping into his throat. She had remembered, after all.

"I'll do my best, of course," he stammered, "but it will be all I can do to keep up with her."

They were interrupted by a noisy bustle, and in the next moment the king's gamekeeper appeared, struggling to control a yelping pack of hounds that burst into the courtyard. By now several dozen men had assembled, tending to their horses and waiting expectantly for Alfred to arrive. Although the morning mist had almost disappeared, the sky remained dark, filled with thick, ominous clouds that moved toward Winchester from the east.

"I'm afraid we might be in for some bad weather," Edward said. "The hounds will have a hard time following the scent if it rains."

"Rain or shine, we'll get our share today. But tell me...how goes everything else?"

"Things couldn't be better. I probably shouldn't be saying anything, but it's not much of a secret anymore. We're going to move on London come spring."

"Really? A full assault?"

"I don't think anything quite that dramatic. A siege is likely; it's a Mercian town, after all. Although the Vikings still control it, I don't think they can count on much help from Guthrum in East Anglia."

"And are you back in Alfred's good graces, after what we went through?"

Edward rose to his full height, and his chest swelled with pride. "He's giving me an important command for the siege. You can be sure I won't fail this time."

Shouts erupted across the courtyard. Sigli looked up, and his heart skipped as the king rode into view atop his familiar white stallion, a falcon on his wrist and the banner of the Golden Dragon waving above him. But it was the fair form that rode beside Alfred on her favorite chestnut mare that sent a shiver down Sigli's spine. She was more radiant than ever, and even the dreary clouds overhead could not diminish her beauty. She was dressed in the rough clothes of a hunter, but nothing could hide the curve in her bosom, nor the long, tautly muscled legs that gripped the flanks of her mount beneath her.

Would that I were that mare now. He stared hard at her, until he thought she would burst into flames from the energy coming from his eyes. Somehow she must have felt it, for she turned toward him, and he could tell even from a distance that his feelings had not lied to him, not even for a moment. The wait had not been in vain. He was pulled into the crowd by Edward, and they made their way toward the king. As they drew close Alfred saw them, and he raised his hand in salute.

"Sigli, welcome! How does the fleet progress?"

"Well, my Lord," he replied, bowing from the waist. "Five more longships are nearing completion."

"Excellent! We'll be back to full strength in no time! But for now, forget the ships. My daughter is depending on you for the hunt."

Sigli turned to Aethelfled, who smiled down at him from her mount. "I won't fail you, my Lady."

"I know you won't," she laughed, tossing her hair. "Edward claims he'll bring in twice as much game today, but we'll show him."

They all dispersed to their mounts, caught up in the activity that swept across the courtyard. Sigli raised himself into his saddle and rode out with the others through the gates of the city, and within moments he had drawn up alongside Aethelfled.

"I'm so glad you've come." She smiled warmly. "I was afraid that you might have forgotten."

"I've been looking forward to this day ever since I left."

"As I have. I've missed your stories, and your laughter."

"Aethelfled, I've missed only you."

She blushed perceptibly, but was cut short by the sound of horns. The hunt was ready to begin. A moment later the hounds were set free, and they bounded toward the nearby trees, followed closely by the mounted party. At first everyone rode together, but as the party climbed the chalk downs surrounding Winchester the riders began to split apart, following each of their leaders into the heavily wooded forest.

There were a dozen hunters riding behind Aethelfled, and for the first hour they picked off all manner of game that was flushed out of hiding by the yelping hounds. But gradually the signs of wildlife diminished, and the party became separated in the depths of the forest. The day was uncommonly dark, and with each moment the storm clouds from the east drew closer, their black, billowing folds draping themselves over the earth like a great cloak. Thunder pealed in the distance, and every so often a flash of lightning ripped across the sky.

Sigli kept within view of Aethelfled at all times, one eye participating half-heartedly in the hunt while the other remained fixed on her. She was a marvelous rider and a fair shot with the bow, but all she had to show for her troubles was a lone hare that had been dutifully collected by one of the riders in the group and sent back to Winchester with the other spoils. It seemed as though Edward was destined to carry the day. But then a loud barking by the hounds alerted them to a movement in the underbrush, and they looked up just in time to see the rear quarters of a large hart disappearing through the trees.

"There's our prize!" shouted Aethelfled, looking over her shoulder at Sigli and the two other riders still with them. "You can handle yourself aboard a ship, Viking. Now we'll see just how well you can ride!"

She spurred her horse forward in hot pursuit of the hounds. Sigli kicked his mount to action, but it soon became apparent that it would be all he could do to keep up with her. He chased behind her through the trees, ducking to avoid the branches and underbrush that flew by as they sped through the forest. This went on for what seemed like many minutes, until the intensity of the barking ahead told them the dogs were closing in on their quarry. Rounding a bend in the trees, Sigli saw Aethelfled drawing an arrow to her bow, and he caught a glimpse of the hart standing on the edge of a sharp cliff that dropped away into the chalk downs.

The hounds were now almost upon the beast. The hart bounded toward the decline and, with a desperate leap, landed in a thicket growing on the opposite wall of the downs. It scrambled up the incline and disappeared into the brush, followed by the yelping dogs as they rushed into the gap and struggled to climb through the loose dirt on the hillside.

Sigli and Aethelfled both rode to the edge of the decline, but it was immediately apparent that the horses would be unable to follow; the chase was over. They sat there disconsolately as the barking sounds receded into the distance.

"I had him," Aethelfled moaned. "One more second, and he would have been mine."

"It wasn't meant to be, not this time." He looked around him, but no one else could be seen; they had lost the other riders in the chase. "We seem to have outstripped the others. It appears that...."

He was interrupted by a jagged streak of lightning, followed by a deafening blast of thunder. All at once the heavens opened up and a hard, driving rain began to pelt them. He looked around for protection and saw a large, thick oak tree whose branches curved over the edge of the downs. They dismounted and made for the cover, tethering their frightened horses to the sturdy trunk of the tree and standing under the thickest part of the foliage, which grew in a tangle together to form a natural canopy.

From there they were able to look out across the valley of the Itchen. As far as the eye could see, everything was enveloped by the storm. The wind picked up, bending the treetops as the clouds unleashed their water down on the countryside. Off in the distance, a crease of lightning cut through the air.

"There!" Sigli pointed. "It's the mighty Thor, hurling his thunderbolts!" A loud rumble of thunder filled their ears. "There sounds his hammer, Mjolnir, the Giantkiller!"

Aethelfled looked up at him, and her eyes gleamed. "And this hammer of his ...what else is it used for?"

"Bonecrusher, some call it. The guardian of the gods. Without it, Asgard lies defenseless before the Frost Giants. They actually stole it once, and even Odin shook in fear while it was gone. But that's a tale unto itself."

"Do tell it! We've nowhere to go in this downpour, and I miss your stories."

He smiled, pleased by her interest. "Well, as you like it. We may as well wait this one out." He dropped to his haunches and she sat down nearby, arranging a tuft of matted grass beneath her.

"One morning Thor woke up in Asgard to find his hammer missing. His red beard and hair stood on end in anger, and he shouted for Loki. When the Mischief Maker appeared, Thor dragged him off to the palace of Freya, the goddess of love and beauty. He asked if she would lend them her feather coat, so that one of them could wear it and fly into Giantland—for it was obvious that only the Frost Giants could have taken it.

"Loki donned the coat and flew off across the mountains. From a distance he saw Prymr, the Giant king, who sat on a mound plaiting leashes of gold for his dogs and trimming the manes of his horses. Loki flew above the Giant and demanded the return of the hammer, but Prymr laughed, boasting how he'd hidden Mjolnir deep in the earth. Only one thing could guarantee its return, the giant bellowed—Freya had to be brought to him and become his wife."

"How could the gods permit such a thing?"

"Freya wouldn't hear of it. Her breast swelled with such fury that she broke the famous necklace Brisingamen asunder. In desperation, the gods called a council and debated what should be done. It was Heimdall who suggested a plan: Thor should be dressed up as a bride, draped with a veil and with petticoats hiding his legs. Thor of course refused, crying that the other gods would call him a sissy, but Loki offered to go along with him disguised as a maid servant. Otherwise, argued the Mischief Maker, Asgard was doomed.

"The gods readied the bride for departure. They led in Thor's goats and harnessed them to his great chariot, and with rumbles of thunder and flashes of lightning, Loki and Thor drove into Giantland. Prymr heard their approach and called to his giants to set up his hall for a great feast, after which he would wed the beautiful Freya. The guests arrived amid great fanfare and after they were greeted everyone sat down at the tables. But immediately the dainty bride astonished them by devouring eight salmon and an entire ox, and washing the whole lot down with three tuns of mead."

Aethelfled laughed. "Surely Prymr became suspicious?"

"He had never seen a maiden with such an appetite. But the cunning Loki, disguised as Freya's maid servant, explained that the bride had been too excited over the past week to eat or drink. Next, Prymr decided to steal a kiss. He lifted a corner of the bride's veil, but the flashing eyes he encountered made him leap back in surprise. Again, handmaiden Loki reassured him, saying that Freya's eyes were fiery because she hadn't slept for a week.

"At last, Prymr called for the marriage to be celebrated, with Thor's hammer being laid on Freya's knee while the bride and groom swore their vows. But as soon as Thor felt Mjolnir within his grasp, he threw aside his petticoats and stood to his full height, exploding the Giant king's head into a thousand pieces with one mighty blow. And so Mjolnir was returned to Asgard, to fill these heavens before us with the power of the gods."

Aethelfled let out a long sigh. "You're such a wonderful storyteller. Would that it all was true. If only I had such a hammer...I could break free from these bonds that hold me." She looked down pensively at the dampened earth, where rivulets had formed in the mud.

"The only bonds, my lady, are those in your mind."

"Oh? And what would you do?" she glared at him. "Would you just turn your back on everything, and forsake your duty?"

"What do you mean?"

"My betrothal. I can't get it out of my mind." The frustration welled up inside her, and she sprang to her feet, walking to the edge of their natural cover and staring out into the rain. He rose and moved tentatively closer to her.

"I would follow my heart, Aethelfled. Nothing else matters."

She turned to face him, no more than a step away as the rain beat down on her delicate shoulders. Droplets of moisture glistened in her hair, and it again occurred to Sigli that he had never seen such a vision of loveliness in all his life. Her lips parted as though to say something, but she held her silence. There they stood, awkwardly looking into each other's eyes, neither one knowing what to do. Uncertain of himself, Sigli began to turn away.

"We'd better be getting back. I..."

He felt her presence close upon him, and as he turned again to face her she threw herself into his arms. Her eyes burned into his just long enough for him to see the desire there, and then she pulled him toward her, kissing him hard on the lips. Before he had time to respond she pulled away quickly, and a musical, nervous laughter trailed behind her as she bounded away and leaped into the saddle atop her chestnut mare.

One last look, eyes still aglow, and she kicked at the horse. It exploded out into the rain and sped off along the ridge. He started as though to follow her, but it was all he could do to stagger out into the nearby clearing and watch, stunned, as she receded into the distance.

The rain beat down on him, but he was oblivious to it. His body still tingled from the soft lips that had been pressed against his, months of yearning boiled down into a single moment of unguarded brilliance. Fenrir had roared; the Wolf had spoken. No storm could wash away the joy in his heart, no wind could blow him from his course. The elements did not exist for him anymore. He stood there in the rain, pounded by its relentless power, a prisoner forever to the promise of love's first kiss.

CHAPTER IX: The Wolf Comes Calling

"In this world there are only two tragedies:
One is not getting what one wants,
And the other is getting it."
—Oscar Wilde, <u>Lady Windermere's Fan</u>

"Rise for your king."

The ealdormen assembled in the evening chamber stood up as Alfred, accompanied by Edward the Elder, entered the room. The Golden Dragon of Wessex walked erectly toward the head of the large oak table around which the men were gathered, passing in front of a fire that crackled in the chimney, warming the chill of the October night.

A score of England's finest had converged on Winchester at Alfred's bidding, and now they were about to learn the reason for his summons. They had done their share of grumbling, for many of the thanes had been engaged in business of local importance, and the season was beginning to slip away. The harvest moon was already past. In a month the fields would be deserted, and life would begin to close in on itself for the long smoky silence of winter.

"You do me honor by attending my request," Alfred began. "You understand, of course, that I wouldn't have called you here unless I felt it was absolutely necessary. But something important has happened, something that will affect all of us. The Vikings have laid siege to Paris."

Stunned silence. To a man, they had believed Paris was beyond the reach of the heathens.

"I just received word a few days ago," Alfred continued. "A large force of Danes left the territory of the eastern Franks and sailed up the Seine. They've established camp on both sides of the river, near the bridge that leads to the city. The Franks are holding out behind their island fortifications."

"Is it Haestan?" Godwine of Sussex asked.

"We don't know yet. Count Odo is heading up the resistance. He's competent, at least."

"Let them have Paris. It's a waste of our time to worry about such matters." All eyes swung to Oswald of Berkshire, whose bearded, aristocratic face made no attempt to mask its displeasure. "We can't control what the heathens do on the continent. Better to let them feed their appetites there. Leave them to their designs."

"Which eventually will lead them back to Wessex again," Alfred said. "It's only a matter of time."

"So what do you propose? More fortifications?"

Osferth, the younger of the brothers from Berkshire, slapped his hand on the table. "Who has the time for that? And so much money! We're better off not rushing into anything. When they come, they come."

"Easy for you to say," said Fulric of Kent. "Your shire is landlocked. What about those of us whose villages border the sea? An invasion could come at any moment."

"We can't be responsible for that!"

"Hold on there! Enough of this!" Penda stood up and glared across the table at them. "We stand or fall together...or haven't you all learned your lesson by now? The Vikings will never defeat us, as long as we present a united front."

"Penda's right," joined in another. But someone else raised his voice in protest, and suddenly they all began arguing again.

"Enough!" The room fell silent at Alfred's command. He leaned forward and shook his head. "If they come, everyone will be affected. And perhaps you, most of all, Oswald."

"Meaning?"

"Meaning that, if I were Haestan, I'd attack the one spot in England of the greatest strategic importance. The one glaring weakness in our defense." He stood up and began to pace slowly around the table. "Where can we be breached? Well, I'll tell you: it's a place that provides access to the rest of Britain. And, Oswald and Osferth, it lies just a few hours downstream from your peaceful fields."

"Sire, please. Speak plainly."

"As you will." He stopped pacing and looked around the table. "It's London I'm talking about."

"But London hasn't been a problem for us," Ceolmund protested. He was always the least likely to act.

"As long as it remains in the hands of the East Anglian Danes, we're vulnerable." Alfred was firm. "No matter how peaceful their intentions may seem, their presence gives the Vikings on the continent access to our unprotected flank. Control of the city is vital to our defense. And to our commerce and foreign interests."

"But it's a Mercian town, after all," argued William of Somerset. "Why not leave it to Eadred to worry about?"

Alfred sighed to himself. Always looking out for their provincial interests, always placing themselves first. He had anticipated such a remark.

"Eadred will play his part. That's why our friend Wilfred, his trusted thane, is with us today." He pointed across the table at the Mercian, who acknowledged the room. "But Eadred, by himself, isn't strong enough. All of us together are."

Ceolmund shook his head. "You may be right, but is it necessary? And how do you think Guthrum will react?"

"There's nothing he can say." Edward broke in, standing up to address the room. "We have just cause. After all, the East Anglians betrayed us last summer. They deserve to be punished."

"I have more pressing affairs to consider than pursuing some vague, politically motivated revenge," another thane sniffed.

"There's more at stake than that," Penda said.

The men gave the ealdorman of Devon their undivided attention, for although he rarely spoke, his words carried weight. He smacked his lips and placed his palms down on the oak tabletop, running them slowly over the smooth grain of the wood before him.

"If we take London, we increase our leverage for the future. We show much greater strength to Haestan and the heathens on the continent. But more to the point, there's still Guthrum to consider." His eyes narrowed, and he looked up. "I don't know about each of you, but I've never forgotten Chippenham. I don't care how old the Warlord's getting, or that he's observed the peace for the last seven years. He's still there, just a day's march away. London in our grasp would effectively finish him and the East Anglians as a threat to us. We could strike a bargain that would truly be to our advantage—instead of these half-hearted truces we've been living under."

"Ah, Penda...perceptive as ever." Alfred smiled. "I couldn't have said it any better. And that's why I've summoned you all here today. My decision is made...come spring, our destiny is cast." He paused for effect, and then he looked beyond them into the dark corners of the room, contemplating a vision.

"It's London, my friends. London calling."

"London!" Edward exclaimed, raising a clenched fist.

"London!" cried Penda.

"London!" echoed Godwine and Fulric.

One by one they all rose to their feet, voicing their approval. Even Oswald and Osferth sensed the tide and relented. Alfred grinned broadly and gestured toward them with a grand sweep of his hands.

"Rest assured we'll all profit. This is an investment—for the near term, and for the future. None of you will be asked to contribute more than his fair share. Over the winter I'll devise a strategy. A siege, more than likely, and with any luck a bloodless one." He smiled and relaxed. "Now, back to your fields...and expect to hear more from me in the months ahead."

He moved away from the table, drawing the meeting to a close. As the others rose and began to break into conversation, the king prepared to leave the room. But a presence at his elbow caught his attention; turning, he looked into the face of Wilfred, Eadred's envoy from Mercia.

"A moment of your time, Sire?"

"Of course. What is it?"

"A small matter. My Lord Eadred was wondering when the Lady Aethelfled would be honoring his invitation to visit with us for a few days. He was under the impression that she would be coming to Mercia in the autumn, and....well, the days grow shorter, Sire."

"Yes, they do." A look of irritation flickered across Alfred's face. He had almost forgotten about the visit; Aethelfled had obviously allowed it to slip. He would have to see to that. "My apologies to your Lord, Wilfred. Tell him that I'll take the matter up with my daughter presently. You can expect to see her at your doorstep soon."

Wilfred bowed. "Very well, Sire. I know Eadred will be pleased."

"I'm sure he will be," Alfred smiled politely, returning the Mercian's bow. Looking up, he caught sight of his son, whose shining face was exultant in the wake of the evening's triumph. Seeing him steered the king's mind back to the business at hand, to just how perfectly all their plans were unfolding. *Yes, Edward, smile. It came easily tonight. Consensus without struggle. A few months more, just a short winter's nap, and then our time will surely come.*

He broke through the men gathered in the room and headed toward the door, with Edward closely in tow.

*   *   *   *   *

It was known as the woodcutter's hut, to those who knew of it at all. The man for whom it had been named had been dead for more than ten years, but his legacy lived on in the simple but sturdy structure that lay undisturbed deep in the solitude of the New Forest. The hut had been crafted painstakingly from a score of hearty oaks—the same trees that once stood in the small glade that the old man had carved out of the wilderness. But now the meadow, after a decade of neglect, struggled to hold back the forest. Nature wanted her plot of earth back, and she was willing to take her time to get it. And so the hut yielded ground grudgingly, waiting for a human hand to appear once again and restore it to a place with a future, instead of just a past.

That was not likely to happen soon. The woodcutter had been somewhat of a hermit, and his disdain for people prompted him to build the hut miles from the nearest village, in a spot that was out of the way for anyone crossing the forest by the usual thoroughfares. Other than the occasional hunter, no one ever stopped there at all. There was no reason for it. The place had been deserted since the woodcutter's death; it was isolation itself.

Which was precisely why Sigli waited there on this autumn afternoon, kicking restlessly at the turf outside the door and staring off into the melancholy red and gold splendor of the forest. She would be here soon. They would finally be alone, and all the waiting would be over.

He had not been able to erase her from his mind, not even for an instant, during the three weeks that had passed since the September hunt. The memory of her lingered with him; he could still feel her lips on his, warm and inviting, an all-consuming fire. Aethelfled, beautiful Aethelfled. He had whispered her name under his breath a thousand times, even shouting it out loud on a windy moonlit night in Twyneham harbor, when it was late and he was certain no one was listening. The weeks had been whittled down to days, the days down to hours, even minutes perhaps. How much longer before he finally held her in his arms?

They had arranged the rendezvous when he left for Twyneham the day following the hunt. She had come at his urgent request, slipping away just long enough from the attention of the court to exchange a few words with him. At first he noticed a reticence about her that bothered him. But it was not nearly enough to stop him; he told her that he simply had to see her again, in private, and that was enough. Whatever misgivings she may have had evaporated in the face of their shared desire. They were already imprisoned by each other, and they both knew it; there could be no turning back.

And so the hut again had a purpose in the world. It was a vigorous half-day's ride from both Winchester and Twyneham, accessible to each yet still far enough away from either to be removed from the eye of public opinion. There Sigli stood waiting anxiously, having arrived an hour earlier after riding hard all morning. The past month had given him time to think, and to understand that although he had known love before, it was been nothing like this. Knowing the impossibility of it all only made it that much more attractive. He simply had to have her. He ached from the thought, the excitement of it all, and the feeling that he could not survive so much as one more day without her.

A sound in the forest caught his ear. He leaned forward, his senses straining until...yes! A horse! He ran forward toward the edge of the glade, looking through the trees in the direction of the hoof beats. The black cloak of a rider appeared through the heavy foliage of the forest, and his heart leaped into his throat. His feet flew through the leaves that blanketed the ground, closer, closer, until he was able to make out the distinct form of a dark horse as it moved toward him through the trees.

But his heart sank the moment he saw the animal; it was not the chestnut mare. It was not her. It was Plegmund who entered the clearing, confirming his worst fears.

She was not coming.

"Sigli...hello." The monk smiled weakly.

"Where is she?"

"On her way to Mercia, most likely." Plegmund dismounted slowly and took a deep breath. "Her father ordered her to go."

"To Eadred?"

"Yes."

Sigli spun around in anger and lashed out at a nearby branch. He clenched his fists and began to pace.

"Come on now, man...what did you expect?!" Now Plegmund was angry. "What did you think could ever come of it?!"

"I don't need you meddling in this! It was our secret, damn you! It was between Aethelfled and me!"

"And how else could she have let you know? Or would you rather have waited here until the snows came...?"

The disappointment was almost too much to bear, but anger was not the answer. Sigli dropped his head and shook it sadly. "So now it's no secret anymore. Now you know the way I feel."

Plegmund reached out and touched the Viking's arm. *If only you knew the way I felt. If only you knew.*

"I've known it for a while. I'm not blind." His brow darkened. "Which is a warning to you, my friend. If I can see it, someone else could—and that would mean trouble."

"Nothing's happened. You speak as though this were a scandal."

"It would be! Good God, Sigli...it's simply unthinkable!" He glared at the Viking, but the hurt he saw told him to tread lightly. "She's very beautiful…anyone can see that. I can understand how you might feel that way toward her, but...."

"Did she go willingly?"

Plegmund bit his lip. "I told you...the king ordered her to go."

"But did she go of her own accord?"

The monk took a deep breath. "Listen to me. I bring her very words to you, and I swear on the body and blood of the Lord Jesus Christ that I speak the truth." He cleared his throat. "She sought me out, Sigli. It was hard for her...it was a confession, of sorts. We're close, she and I, so that made it a little easier." He paused and looked down at the ground. "But I must tell you this: while it's true her father demanded she make good on her promise to Eadred, she'd already decided to go, on her own. She had no intentions of ever coming here."

"I don't believe you!"

"Even while I condemn your desires, I would never say such a thing if it weren't true. Sinful or not, your lustful thoughts don't deserve a broken heart."

"But she doesn't love Eadred!"

"It doesn't matter. She can't love you. A king's daughter can't live by the same rules that others follow." The monk paused. "But that's not all. There's...there's something else." He looked down at his feet, for he could not bear to watch how Sigli would react to what he next had to say.

"She told me to tell you to banish any thoughts of her from your mind. She can't see you...not now, not ever."

Sigli began to breathe heavily, blinded by a white-hot light.

"Listen to me, please," Plegmund began, reaching out for him. "It's far better now, than later. If..."

Sigli tore himself away and ran toward the woodcutter's hut. He ripped the reins of his horse from the branch that secured them and leaped into the saddle, kicking angrily at the stallion. It sprang forward and bolted across the narrow expanse of the glade, heading recklessly for the forest. Horse and rider nearly ran over Plegmund, who dived out of the way to avoid being trampled. He rolled through the leaves as the horse sped by, and then he picked himself up from the ground and started as if to follow. But then he stopped and stood motionlessly in the middle of the woodcutter's glade, watching as the forest swallowed Sigli up, listening as the Viking's hoof beats receded into the distance.

And then all was silent. He brushed the fallen leaves and dirt from his cassock and mounted his horse, pointing the animal north to begin the long ride back to Winchester.

*   *   *   *   *

Eadred did not consider himself to be an impatient man. His rise to power in Mercia had come slowly and had been achieved thanks to a willingness to wait. He never forced anything, preferring to take advantage of each opportunity as it presented itself, and with each careful step he climbed higher on the ladder of influence. He had not been born to the first rank of nobility, and no one had ever expected him to rise to any sort of prominence, no less become the most important man in all of Mercia.

But it all indeed had happened—no small feat, considering the political climate during the years leading up to his ascension. The Vikings had found Mercia to be a plentiful hunting ground when Halfdan first occupied it following the great invasion of 865, and their power grew until they succeeded in driving the Mercian king Burgred into exile. He fled to Rome and died soon after, leaving the Vikings free to set up a puppet ruler who carried out their every request. The mantle of leadership passed from Halfdan to Guthrum in the 870s without so much as a murmur of protest from the Mercians, and it appeared as though the land would remain under the heathen yoke for a very long time.

But Edington changed everything. Alfred's great victory on the Wiltshire plain in 878 drove the Vikings back to East Anglia, restoring Mercia to Christian hands. And those hands belonged to Eadred, who had been wise enough to throw in his lot with the Golden Dragon. While he had been fortunate to rise in the attentions of the king, when the time came it was more than mere luck that decided the issue. His choice was decisive, and it was the right one. Had the Vikings triumphed, it would have meant his head, but with the Saxon victory his rise to power was assured. No other worthy thane could lay claim to Mercia, for Burgred's marriage to Alfred's older sister Aethelswith had failed to produce an heir. Eadred was Alfred's man, and after Edington all of central England looked to him for leadership.

Mercia flourished under his stewardship, picking up the pieces left in the wake of the Viking occupation and slowly becoming whole again. Farms sprang to life, families sank their roots back into the soil, and the forces of church and state resumed their duties as though the long shadows cast by the armies of Halfdan and Guthrum had never passed over the land.

In light of these successes, a more headstrong and ambitious man might have presumed to declare himself king. But Eadred was no fool; he knew he was merely Alfred's caretaker, the watchdog for a man whose powerful presence was held in great respect by even the most provincial of the locals who longed for Mercia to return to its days of glory. Now, at least, the overlord was a Christian man of the cross—even if he was a West Saxon.

Had he not been careful, Alfred could have antagonized his northern neighbors by acting with a heavy hand. But the king, always the diplomat, allowed the Mercians to govern themselves, preferring to gain their good will through trust rather than dominion. He remained a popular figure on his infrequent visits to Eadred's estates, and as long as the political situation remained stable, all was well. Given his sister's marriage to the deposed Burgred, Alfred probably had as much right as any man to the Mercian throne, but he was in no rush. Mercia was merely one step toward the ultimate goal; his quest to become Bretwalda had to be engineered carefully, and would best be served by cementing a lengthy alliance.

And marriage was the mortar that would hold the bricks together.

As he waited for Aethelfled's arrival, Eadred could barely restrain his eagerness. He sat astride his horse on a chilly, clear afternoon outside the city gates of Oxford, a modest town nestled upstream from London on the River Thames. The messengers had alerted him that she would be arriving within the hour, accompanied by her brother Edward and the persistent Wilfred, who had lingered in Winchester to ensure that the trip north would indeed happen.

Looking across the fields, Eadred could see the party wending its way along the road that led to the walled town. Even from a distance he was able to recognize Aethelfled, her auburn hair shining in the late autumn sunlight, and the thrill that shot up his spine reaffirmed once again that the proposed marriage was more than simply a matter of politics.

Like all men, he was enthralled by her. He could not believe his luck to be in such a position, to court a woman he would have desired had she been a cowherd's daughter. To lie with such a prize was all a man could ask for; that the dowry carried a kingdom along with it was simply too good to be true.

But Eadred was not blind. He realized that Aethelfled's heart still needed to be won, and that a formidable task lay ahead of him. With any other woman he would have been supremely confident, for he was much admired by the fairer sex and had mastered the subtle art of how to address a lady. His charm and social graces were attributes that had contributed significantly to his rise, but they were not enough, not nearly enough. No amount of polish and diplomacy could change his bloodline; it paled in comparison to Aethelfled's, fueling his insecurities.

No matter, he thought to himself. He would find a way to win her.

Aethelfled and her escort were just a few hundred yards away. He urged his horse forward into a canter, taking care to sit upright in the saddle, shoulders back and head held high. She had to believe she was getting nothing but the best. As he drew closer, the faces of the approaching party told him all he needed to know: Wilfred, grinning in triumph, Edward, regal and imperious as ever, Aethelfled, her reserve evident even from a distance. Time to make the distance disappear.

"Welcome to Mercia," he greeted them, his eyes coming to rest on the object of his desire. "We may not enjoy all of the luxuries of Alfred's fine estates, but you'll find us well-disposed."

"Thank you, my Lord," she bowed lightly. "We're honored."

"Not nearly as much as I am. If I didn't know better, I'd say the summer had extended itself. Your beauty is enough to warm even the dreariest day."

She smiled politely; that was all. Without missing a beat, Eadred turned to Edward. "And you, my prince...to what do I owe this unexpected honor? Or did you merely wish to provide protection for your sister?"

"She can handle herself well enough, as you may already know. I came at my father's request, to tend to matters of state."

"Nothing pressing, I presume."

"Mere formalities, my Lord," Wilfred broke in. "Certainly not worth discussing here on the open road."

Eadred smiled. "Of course...how thoughtless of me. You must all be quite tired from your long journey. Let me show you to your quarters, where you can rest and refresh yourselves until we dine tonight. I've had a special goose prepared for the occasion, which I'm sure you'll find the equal of any bird in Wessex."

Late that evening Aethelfled sat in her chamber, brushing her hair before retiring to bed. The dinner had passed pleasantly but uneventfully, and now she was tired. That Eadred was a charming host could not be denied; he clearly had taken great pains to make them all welcome. He was generous, handsome and powerful—all of which made her lingering disinterest in him that much more difficult for her to understand. She knew it would be so much easier for her if she were to give in to the wishes of her father and marry the Mercian. But every time she looked at Eadred, every time he spoke so much as a single word, all she could see and hear was another face, another voice. She could not erase Sigli from her thoughts.

It had been wrenching for her to send Plegmund to the woodcutter's hut. She could only guess at the hurt she had created, and night after night found her tossing and turning in her bed, unable to sleep. All those restless moments strung together added up to a disturbing conclusion: what she had thought merely to be an extreme infatuation, a fanciful attraction, was in truth much more.

She was in love.

A knock at the chamber door interrupted her thoughts. Before she could rise to answer it, her brother strode boldly into the room.

"Your manners, Edward, are appalling. You have no right to intrude on me like this."

"Don't speak to me about manners," he scowled. "Not after tonight."

"What are you talking about? I was perfectly polite."

He looked at her and shook his head. "Does anyone in this world know you better than I do? You may have been polite, yes...but that was all. Your lack of enthusiasm was obvious. Father would be furious."

She hurled her brush down and stood up angrily. "So that's why you came, is it? To act as Father's spy! Take care to stay out of my private affairs!"

"Private, you say? Everything you do is public; the kingdom depends on you!" He paused. "And so do I."

"Whether or not I marry Eadred should have no bearing on the matter."

He rolled his eyes and sat down on the edge of her bed. "Why are you being so obstinate? You'd think you were pledged to another, to hear you talk."

She felt a deep blush overtaking her; fortunately, he failed to notice.

"Edward, please...be patient. I know why I'm here; I'll make the effort. These things take time."

"Perhaps you should try harder, then. I've finished my business here...I'll be returning to Winchester tomorrow. At the very least you could do something to raise poor Eadred's hopes. I would think he's thoroughly discouraged by now."

"I'll be here for a week. That should be enough to placate him."

"Placate him? I can't believe what I'm hearing!"

"Edward, you simply must stop this! Have faith in me!"

He eyed her carefully, wishing to believe her but remaining unconvinced. "I'm sorry, Aethelfled. Something tells me it's not that simple."

"Love is hardly a simple matter. Least of all as far as Father is concerned. Which is why I need your support."

"Would it really make a difference?"

"What do you think?"

He shook his head and laughed. Then he rose to his feet and smiled wearily. "Very well, then. You're my sister. No matter what Father says, I'm with you. I've always been with you."

She softened. "And I with you."

"Then don't make it so difficult. I just want you to do the right thing, that's all."

She stepped forward and kissed him lightly on the cheek. "I will...I must. Now go to bed, and return to Father tomorrow. Tell him all is well."

He searched her eyes for a moment, and then he squeezed her hand and left the room, closing the door behind him. As she watched him go, it occurred to her that perhaps her brother, of all people, was the one she feared disappointing the most. She sat down again and looked at herself in the mirror, carefully scrutinizing her face. It held no answers. *I just want you to do the right thing, that's all.* Easy for them to say; just what the right thing might be was another matter entirely.

She rose from the table and blew out the candles in the chamber, and then she crawled into bed, gazing into the flames that crackled in the fireplace. Gradually her eyes grew heavy, and the world around her began to fade away. As she drifted off into sleep a handsome face appeared to her, familiar and soothing, so clear in her subconscious that it seemed as if she could almost reach out and touch it. It was the face of desire, the face of dreams.

But it was not the face of Eadred.

*   *   *   *   *

"Those were difficult days, when the Vikings were here. But we survived them, and now we prosper."

Having concluded his story, Eadred shifted in his saddle and looked out over the fields. He rode alongside Aethelfled, just as he had for the better part of the week. Each morning they had followed the same practice, exploring the surrounding countryside and enjoying the cool, clear weather, taking their time and going nowhere. The riding was pleasant enough exercise, and immune to confrontation; it suited Eadred's needs perfectly. In the afternoons there had been light lunch and relaxation. In the evenings, sumptuous dinners.

And at night, polite conversations. Nothing more.

He had thought of everything; everything except the magic words. Despite the time he had spent with her, every minute of it perfectly amicable, he still felt as though he barely knew her. She responded, but she did not lead; every conversation or gesture depended upon him.

"Have you had much experience with the Vikings?"

"Not to speak of," she said. "But I remember the invasion. I remember my father herding us into an oxcart one night. It was winter, and it was cold."

"Your father's a great man...you know that, don't you?"

"Yes. But it can be difficult, pleasing a great man."

"And how would you please him now?"

"By not riding too fast, or acting too willfully," she sidestepped. "Father says I should have been born a man."

"The world would be the poorer for it. Rather we should pluck a star from the sky."

She smiled. "You have the manners of a Frankish noble. Ever so eloquent."

"I'm afraid an eloquent man would know just what to say. Words fail me now."

"Am I that intimidating?"

He laughed. "Silence is the greatest form of intimidation. But see here...this needs no explanation." He pointed through an opening in the trees, where they could see the River Thames winding its way toward the south. "I come here often; it's one of my favorite spots."

"It's beautiful," she said, dismounting from her horse and walking over to a spot nestled beneath the leafy boughs of a large oak. He swung his body easily to the ground and followed her, stopping at a respectful distance.

"I've never been across the sea," he said. "Never to Francia, nor to Rome. But it doesn't matter; this is all the water I need to navigate. This is all I ever wanted."

"All?" she wondered, idly fingering the rough bark of the oak. "I think not."

It was the opening he had been waiting for. "It could all be yours...if you would only say the word."

She froze. Eadred had been gallant enough to spare her the abruptness of a direct confrontation—until now. The glove had finally been dropped. She struggled to think of something to say, in vain.

"Aethelfled..." he whispered insistently, moving so close behind her that she could feel his breath on her neck, "Aethelfled...why won't you open your heart to me?"

She took a step forward, keeping her eyes fixed straight ahead. "I've...I've been truthful with you, my Lord."

"Have you? Have two meaningful words passed between us?"

Suddenly she felt guilty. She turned around and looked up at him. "I've caused you some difficulty, I know. But it's...it's not you at all. It's...."

He waited, but she broke off and turned away again, moving closer to the oak. He reached out as though to stroke the back of her neck softly, but then his emotions got the better of him. He grabbed her by the shoulders and spun her around, pushing her against the great oak and pressing his body hard against her.

"I want you. I want you more than anything."

He kissed her passionately on the lips. She struggled at first, but then she relaxed and let him finish. He squeezed her waist and buttocks and tried to kiss her again, but she pushed him away, gently but forcefully, flushed from the effort.

"You musn't. Not yet."

Had she been any other man's daughter, he would have persisted and had his way with her. But he knew he could not press the issue, not with so much at stake and the glimmer of a distant light finally beginning to break through the clouds. He dropped his hands to his sides, backing off just enough.

"Someday, you'll be my bride, Aethelfled. You don't have to say yes now. Or tomorrow. But give me a sign, give me some hope."

"Just give me time. That's all I ask."

"When? When can I see you again?"

She had already thought about it, and her answer was at hand. "Come to Winchester for the Yuletide. Stay at my father's house; there will be feasting, and many people gathered from all over Wessex."

"And you?"

"I'll be there for you. I promise."

He bent slowly toward her and kissed her again, this time lightly. And then he stepped back, hands at his sides, ever the gentleman. "I can't force you to love me...that no man can do. Nor would I force you into my bed against your wishes. But I can love you, and I can wait. Because I know that someday your mind will change...and so will your heart."

Would that it could be that easy, she thought. "I pray that my heart tells me to do the right thing."

"Wish it to be so, and it will happen. Until then, I remain your faithful servant." He smiled and extended his hand. "Now, come. It's time to go back. One more evening together, and then my wait begins all over again."

He placed his hand on her elbow and guided her toward the horses. She mounted her chestnut mare and urged it forward, grateful for the reprieve but now more unnerved than ever. Eadred followed her lead and they rode through a light wind, keeping their silence, swayed by the steady rhythm of the horses' hooves beating against the ground. It was almost enough to drown out the pounding of her heart—almost. A thousand thoughts raced through her mind, a thousand dissonant rattles, each one of them posing an entirely different question, with nary an answer to be found.

*　　*　　*　　*　　*

It was late on a cold November night. All was quiet in the estate house at Winchester as Plegmund sat huddled alone in his chamber, focusing on the parchment spread out on the table before him. A single candle illuminated his labors, its flame flickering in the draft that slipped through the imperfect walls. Outside, the wind howled like a wolf caught in a woodsman's trap, whipping mercilessly through the clattering, bare trees.

It was a night for any sane man to keep indoors. But Plegmund would not have noticed had the wind blown the walls down, so completely engrossed was he in his work. Bede it was. Tonight, and every night. He had been toiling away at the *Historia Ecclesiastica* for years, picking up his quill whenever the chance arose, forever beset by a never-ending stream of interruptions. Now, finally, the end was in sight. A few more evenings, a few finishing touches, and his work would be complete.

When he had begun the translation, he had feared he might grow weary of the task and set it aside; now, he was almost more afraid of the void that would be left after it was all done. But there would be other translations, other challenges. He never tired of working with such wonderful writing. He only hoped that his efforts would do justice to the lyricism and rhythm of Bede's original, and it pained him to think that his translation might seem inferior in comparison. He knew that he could never write that well. He had to be satisfied with mimicking the great historian, breathing new life and meaning into the Latin words that seemed to leap up at him from the worn, tattered scrolls.

He was so consumed with finishing the translation that he failed to hear the light knock at the door, or to notice it crack open and reveal a face framed against the darkness in the hallway. Two large, green eyes stared into the room, watching without being watched, until their lovely owner broke the silence and knocked once again on the door, pushing it open.

Plegmund's concentration turned into delight as he looked up at Aethelfled. "Come in, come in. I'm so glad to see you."

"I'm not interrupting?" she hesitated. "It is quite late, after all."

"Nonsense." He waved his hand and ushered her into the chamber. "It's never too late for you, my Lady."

"Thank you, Plegmund. I see you're working hard. Getting much done?"

"Yes, there's been quite some progress. But enough of me...sit down, please. I'm dying to hear all about Mercia."

She perched on the edge of a sturdy, upright chair, cocking her ear and listening to the wind. "It was pleasant enough. But they don't have the culture to match Winchester or Canterbury."

"Excuse me, my lady, but I wasn't aware that you journeyed north for cultural purposes..."

She shot him a dirty look. "Oh...? Then what for...commerce, perhaps?"

He winced and leaned back. "I'm sorry. I didn't mean it that way. But, won't you tell me anything?"

"He's quite handsome. And very kind." She paused. "But I don't love him."

"Lord Jesus, save us. Be patient...you hardly know the man."

She slid her fingers evenly across her lap, studying the backs of her hands. "That will come in time," she said calmly. "I'm sure of that. But it's not why I came to see you tonight." She looked up at him, and her face grew earnest.

"You must help me, Plegmund."

He could not mistake the urgency in her voice. "What is it?"

"Go to Twyneham. Tell Sigli I have to see him again."

He shook his head back and forth and folded his arms on his chest. "It's simply out of the question! I can't do that!"

"Then I'll go myself...with or without your help."

He stood up and ran his fingers nervously through his hair. "Aethelfled, this is madness! Surely you can't be serious...the risk is too great!"

She sighed. "I've thought about all that. But I must see him. I haven't been able to live with myself, knowing how I disappointed him."

"And what would you say to him? What difference could it make?"

"It would rid me of a great burden, to know that I was strong enough to tell him myself. To know that I was able to settle my past before moving forward into the life that awaits me...as Eadred's wife."

Plegmund had never heard her speak that way. "Then you'll marry him, after all?"

"I'll do what must be done. Which is why I must talk to Sigli again, to face him...and to face myself."

"It's still too dangerous. What if you're seen with him?"

"That's why you must help me, Plegmund. You're the only one I can trust. Otherwise, I'll have to ride to Twyneham myself."

He winced. "What do you propose?"

"Ride to Sigli tomorrow. Tell him I'll meet him at the woodcutter's hut on Saturday." She waited for a reply, but the best he could do was frown in silence. She took a deep breath and gathered herself.

"Please, Plegmund. Don't refuse me."

He shook his head and began to pace the room. "By suggesting such a thing, you put me in an impossible position. If I decline, and you go through with it, it will be a disaster. And if I agree, I'll be going against everything I believe in. At the very least I must accompany you, to safeguard your honor."

"That's impossible."

"Then I can't do it! You, alone with a heathen...a man you profess strong feelings for? Who feels the same way about you? I'd be throwing you to the devil."

She stood up angrily. "You presume too much! I'm guiltless!" She glared at him, but then it occurred to her that perhaps she was the one who presumed too much. She sat back down again, the picture of distress.

"Oh, Plegmund...please. I must say goodbye to him...I simply must!"

He suddenly felt a great sorrow for her, knowing that nothing he could say would ever change her mind. He moved closer and put his hand on her shoulder.

"I know you're headstrong. But you're also forthright, and I understand your plight. If there were any way I could save you from all this, I'd do it. But I see that's not possible."

He stepped away and turned back to the table, fumbling idly with the scrolls that lay spread out upon it. "You'd go to him anyway, that I know. And that's why I'll help...out of my love for you, your father and for Wessex. But by God Almighty, you must swear to remain chaste, and be done with him!"

"I...I swear it."

He let out a long sigh and smiled weakly; he could not refuse her. "Very well, then. I'll leave for Twyneham tomorrow."

"Oh, Plegmund...!" She rushed joyfully to him, kneeling down at his feet and kissing his hand. "How can I repay you?"

"My Lady, please..."

"Of course, of course," she said, rising quickly and regaining her composure. "Well, then, I'll be going. I won't interrupt you further." She slid over to the door, leaving him with a grateful glance. "And I won't soon forget this kindness."

He smiled reassuringly as she left, but the corners of his mouth drooped the moment she closed the door behind her. It was wrong. The whole thing was wrong. Nobody would ever believe him if he claimed he was merely trying to protect her. Nothing good could come of it, nothing but devastation and ruin. But something else bothered him even more, something far worse than just Sigli and Aethelfled. He could feel the seeds of envy rooting themselves in his heart, sprouting to reveal an awful truth: he would give anything to trade places with her.

He sat down at the table and picked up the parchment again, but it was no use; Bede's prose was little more than a series of ink stains on a meaningless page. He stared off into the dark corners of the room as the wind continued to howl outside. It swirled through the cracks in the estate house walls and spiraled downward, sinking lower and lower until it rattled around at the very bottom of his soul.

*   *   *   *   *

The bare trees allowed the sky to seep through the forest and lie down, damp and heavy, atop the leaves that blanketed the ground. Sigli guided his horse through the great oaks that stood like sentinels rooted in the earth, leaning forward to avoid the occasional branch that hung down over his path. He had taken great pains to slip unnoticed out of Twyneham that morning. Nothing could be allowed to jeopardize his mission, or to give anyone even the slightest inkling of what he intended to do.

Plegmund had been firm about the matter when he appeared unannounced at the seaside burh. The news had been more than Sigli could have hoped for, but in exchange for his good tidings the monk had demanded absolute discretion, and he threatened to cancel the meeting unless Sigli swore himself to secrecy—and to protecting Aethelfled's honor.

He did not have to ask twice. But his words of warning may as well have been uttered in the midst of a raging windstorm, so little effect did they have. Sigli was blind to Plegmund's protests, and equally in disregard of the subtle longing that appeared in the monk's eyes as they stood by the seashore, buffeted by a light wind blowing in from the Channel. All Sigli could think of was Aethelfled; nothing else had existed for him since the aborted rendezvous, nothing at all.

And nothing else could distract him now as he again drew closer to his destination on a dreary Saturday in late November. He passed through a final grove of trees and entered the familiar clearing, anchored at the far end by the woodcutter's hut. He was not surprised to be the first one there, for he had left before dawn and had fewer miles to travel than Aethelfled. But he still could not suppress his disappointment, and the thought that maybe she would again fail to appear.

He dismounted and walked over to the door of the hut, pushing it open and stepping inside. The single room was deserted, bare except for a rickety table that stood in one corner. Clapping his arms to ward off the chill, he noticed a small hearth extending from one of the walls of the hut. Upon examining it further, he discovered a flint box that had apparently been left behind by one of the infrequent travelers who had passed that way. He went outside and, to his great delight, came upon a pile of wood stacked on the lee side of the hut, where it had remained protected from the weather. After also gathering an armful of twigs and dry leaves from underneath a nearby oak, he returned to the hut and built a fire.

The flames took hold immediately, warming the room and the dullness of the late autumn afternoon. Every few minutes he walked over to the door and peered outside, hoping to see Aethelfled in the clearing, but nothing met his eyes except for the bare trees of the forest. The sky was beginning to darken, and it appeared certain that rain would soon follow; he could only hope that she was drawing closer and would not get caught in the weather. One negative thought after another began to race through his mind: What if she had gotten lost, or been waylaid on the road? What if she had never left Winchester at all?

He sat down cross-legged on the earth in front of the fire and resigned himself to the wait, staring mesmerized into the flames as they licked at the oak like a serpent's tongue. There he remained, motionless and unblinking, for what seemed like many minutes, until he was alerted by the sound of raindrops beating on the roof of the hut. He rose and stepped over to the door once again, glancing outside and expecting to see nothing but the wind beating back the branches of the oaks that framed the clearing.

But what he saw brought a low cry of delight to his lips. There she sat, perched atop the familiar chestnut mare, enough of her face showing beneath her hooded cloak to tell him that it was indeed she who rode into the clearing. He threw open the door and bolted outside, oblivious to the rain that now began to fall harder. Their eyes met and she smiled, tentatively at first, until she dropped her guard with a tinkling, nervous laughter that broke through the storm.

He looked up at her, breathless. "I thought you might not come."

"It was the least I could do, after the last time."

She accepted his helping hand and dismounted. Preceding him into the hut, she pulled back her hood and lightly shook her hair so that it cascaded down over her shoulders. She was more beautiful than ever, if such a thing were possible. He took a step toward her, still unsure of himself, wishing he could hold her in his arms but unable to act out his desires.

"Does anyone know?"

"No one, except Plegmund."

"I've died a thousand deaths since we last met."

He stepped toward her, but she glided away toward the fire, extending her hands into the warmth rising from the hearth.

"It brings me great pain to know how I hurt you," she said, her back turned to him. "And as I stand here, I swear to you, were I the master of my destiny, I would fly away with you forever."

Suddenly she turned around and, summoning all of her strength, looked up at him across the space that separated them. "But it can't be, Sigli. We can't go on deceiving ourselves. You must forget me, and I you."

"I'll never forget you, no matter what happens. I love you."

"You musn't. It's impossible."

"Nothing's impossible. Not for us."

"Sigli, look at yourself! You're a heathen! For you and I to ever consider..."

"And you're the daughter of a king. I know that. But if you were the daughter of Odin himself, it wouldn't stop me."

She set her face in stone. "And what about me? What about Wessex? Think of the dishonor you would do me, and my father!"

For the first time, he buckled, stung hard by her anger. "So, you think me unworthy, do you? Am I so beneath you? Is that it? Am I some lesser form of life, some intolerable heathen beast?"

"You know that's not true." The thought of hurting him devastated her.

"Then listen to your heart...and listen to me." He moved closer. "That you came here can't be denied."

She bit her lip and took a step backward, pressing her hands lightly against the wall. "I came here to tell you goodbye."

"No you didn't. You came here because you love me. Admit it."

Her face twitched. She averted her eyes, and then she buried them in her hands and began to cry.

"Admit it! You love me, as I love you!"

He pulled her hands from her face and forced her to look up at him, just long enough for her to nod an anguished yes and throw herself into his arms, sobbing on his chest. He held her head close against him, nestling it as though it were that of a helpless infant, and at once a great sense of satisfaction mixed with despair washed over him.

"You and I were created for each other, Aethelfled. Nothing anyone can say or do can change that. Not your father, not Plegmund...not God himself."

With that he pulled back her head and looked into her eyes. And then he leaned down and kissed her on the lips. She responded, and a great warmth gushed through her. He kissed her again, and again, and then they sank down to their knees, holding each other so closely in front of the fire that nothing could have pulled them apart. He grabbed her buttocks in his hands and pressed against her, and she could feel the iron in him. And then she released the last of her protests and surrendered herself.

He pulled the cloak from her shoulders and laid it over the cold floor, and then he unloosened the dress from her lovely throat and buried his lips into her flesh, covering her with kisses. He removed the last of her garments and cupped her magnificent breasts in his hands, easing her backward onto the cloak so that she lay there before him, waiting. He slipped his leggings off and then lowered himself down onto her in front of the fire. They swayed together as the light from the flames danced across their shining, naked bodies.

Outside, the wind raged and the rain beat down on the earth. But they did not hear it. Nor did they hear another sound, muffled at first, a growl that rumbled like a low thunder through the oaks. It was the bellow of a beast, the howl of desire.

Hidden somewhere deep in the heart of the forest, the mighty Fenrir reared back his massive head and roared, unchained at last. The Wolf had spoken.

CHAPTER X: Bretwalda

"Come live with me, and be my love,
And we will some new pleasures prove,
Of golden sands, and crystal brooks,
With silken lines, and silver hooks."
—Donne, <u>The Bait</u>

Grimwald peered down into the crowded courtyard. He stood hidden in the shadows of his chamber at Winchester, from where he could look through the open window and see without being seen. There was Alfred, standing amidst his family, wearing the finest of cloaks sent to him by the Pope in Rome. In the early days of his reign the king had preferred to dress simply, but now everything was different; now he had become the Golden Dragon of Wessex, a man at one with the trappings of power.

Grimwald noted it all smugly. His eyes shifted from Alfred and focused on the two men of the cloth who stood around the king. Their backs were turned to the crowd, separating the people from their sovereign as only the Church could. Asser and John the Old Saxon, ingratiatingly smooth, willing to please, lapping like housedogs at their master's knee. Let them have their bone, he thought—but it gnawed at him that he had once stood where they now did.

His eyes swept across the courtyard until they came to rest on a rider entering through the city gates; it was Eadred, arriving on this late December afternoon to observe the Yule feast at Alfred's court. Heralds bearing the banner of Mercia followed him, holding the pennant high in the light breeze.

The ealdorman reined in his horse and dismounted, moving toward Alfred with a wide smile, and Mercia and Wessex joined hands before the cheering throng. Alfred then stepped to one side, where he grasped the waiting hand of his daughter Aethelfled and placed it in Eadred's outstretched palm. The Mercian bowed dramatically and kissed her delicate fingers, bringing a broad smile to the Saxon king's face, and with it a sigh of relief—or so it appeared to the monk.

Alfred raised his hands for silence and began to speak. Grimwald ignored him, paying no attention to the king's rhetoric and training his eye on Aethelfled instead. Her remarkable beauty and elegance were more in evidence than ever now; she had somehow blossomed over the past month to achieve new heights of loveliness.

But as the bishop watched her carefully, observing every nuance, it occurred to him that something was wrong. She seemed to be a thousand miles away. It puzzled him, for she had been noticeably cheerful of late, and like everyone else he had assumed her good spirits to be related to the planned nuptials.

His practiced eye now saw otherwise. There was a stiffness about her, the smile that did not smile, the clasped hand that did not touch. The rabble below him was oblivious to it all, of course, as were Alfred, Ealswith and even Eadred himself. But it was startlingly clear to Grimwald, as though the torch of truth now lit only her, revealing all.

All? Not so, he thought. Merely enough to cast doubts on what everyone else took for granted. He had learned over the course of his lifetime that his intuition was the one thing that did not lie; it was his most powerful weapon. And now as he watched this intriguing drama unfold below him, that same intuition dragged his eyes in another direction, to a far corner of the courtyard, where Plegmund stood alone behind the last rank of commoners watching the proceedings.

As the bishop watched, fascinated, Plegmund shifted his weight uncomfortably back and forth, wringing his hands as if to cleanse them. He was clearly agitated, and had chosen to stand in a place where he would not attract attention. Grimwald had rarely seen him during the last month, but on each occasion he had noticed a withdrawn preoccupation in the man. The bishop had not given it much thought, but this latest behavior piqued his interest, casting the matter in an entirely different light. There was something of great import that was eluding him, a twisting trail that led to a place where something of value was hidden. What could it be?

A knock on his chamber door interrupted him, and a middle-aged woman who looked much older than her years entered the room at his bidding. Her face was a picture of the hard life she lived, and she looked up at Grimwald with tired eyes that had long since resigned themselves to the conditions of the underclass. She waited in silence.

"So, we're agreed?"

She nodded without speaking.

He reached into his robe and withdrew a small pouch, from which he extracted three gold coins and placed them into her outstretched, trembling hand.

"Send the boy to the back entrance of the hall tonight, when the feast is underway. I'll meet him there."

She turned to leave the room, head bowed. But as she shuffled off toward the door, his voice trailed after her.

"Remain silent, and there will be more gold. Speak to anyone, and...."

He did not have to finish the thought. His lips curled into a thin smile as she left and he moved back to the window, drumming his fingers idly on the sill as Alfred continued to speak to his people, mouthing the same old platitudes of inspiration and hope. Aethelfled and Plegmund had not moved during the time that had passed, but the strange energy that had crackled forth from each of them was gone. The moment of clarity had passed.

He took a deep breath and closed the curtain on the scene below him. There was much to think about, but it could wait; there were other things to tend to first. The boy was young, after all, and nightfall was only hours away.

*　　*　　*　　*　　*

"It will begin as soon as the weather warms. No later."

Alfred pushed himself back from the table and looked around the crowded hall. Tonight marked the first of what would be many feasts during the Yule season, and he was pleased that everything was proceeding so well. His belly was full, his heart content, and his dreams were about to come true. London would soon be in his grasp. His daughter would cement the alliance with Mercia. What more could a man ask for?

"How many men will you need, My Lord?" Eadred, sitting next to the king, resumed the conversation.

"As many as you can spare, of course. One can never be too sure."

"To hasten the wedding, I'll see to it that every man in Mercia's there to help you."

Alfred laughed. "Be patient. You've waited this long, a few more months shouldn't matter. Once London falls, the wedding will follow soon enough."

Eadred grinned and turned to Aethelfled, who sat on the other side of him. "Your father's pressed long and hard for this union...now he postpones it."

"My Lord, one musn't go against the wishes of a king."

Alfred laughed and clapped Eadred on the shoulder. "Hard to believe, considering the source. She's made a habit of defying me since she was barely old enough to walk."

"How can you say that, Father? I've agreed to marry him, haven't I?" She smiled sweetly at Eadred.

"As any young woman of sense would be more than happy to do," broke in Ealswith, never far from the center of any conversation.

"Thank you, my Lady," Eadred nodded, "but I'm satisfied. I'd wait until the end of time to win this prize." He caressed Aethelfled's hand.

"It won't take nearly that long," said Alfred. "London will fall in the spring."

"I'm sure you're right, Father...as always." A trace of irony betrayed the sweetness in Aethelfled's voice. "And, as always, I'll be your willing servant." She turned graciously to Eadred. "And yours as well, my Lord."

"I don't want a servant. I want a wife."

"And so you'll have one. But as for tonight," she said, rising from the table, "I'm feeling rather tired. You'll please all excuse me...I'm off to bed."

Eadred intercepted her hand and pulled it to his lips, looking up at her as he kissed it. She smiled demurely down at him, and withdrew her hand with a light bow. She bent down over her father and kissed him on the cheek, and then she turned and left the hall, passing through an arch and heading down the main passageway that led to the living quarters in the estate house.

Alone at last, she let out a deep sigh. Eadred could not yet see what she feared was painfully obvious—she did not love him. There was no desire in her eyes to reassure him. She knew what it felt like to see through those eyes; it felt that way whenever she looked at Sigli. And whenever he looked at her.

They had been sneaking off to see each other over the last month, always meeting discretely at the woodcutter's hut. She was helpless to stop the fire. She knew now that it had been ignited in her as a young girl, when she had first seen the Viking ride into the courtyard at Chippenham after saving her father from the boar. Her feelings had not lied to her then; they did not lie now. She followed them and threw herself headlong into the affair, for she was completely enamored of Sigli and could not get enough of him. And although she knew she was falling deeper into the abyss, she was not about to do anything to stop it. Not yet, at least.

Only Plegmund knew their secret. His warnings and predictions of gloom were like the dull, distant roar of the sea. But they fell on deaf ears, for when Aethelfled would gallop the last mile to the woodcutter's hut, she would put the guilt behind her, and all would be forgotten the moment she found herself in Sigli's arms. They would laugh together and make love, until the day would be done and all that was left was the next time.

The flesh was powerful. She had lost her innocence, but had gained something in return, and with it the knowledge that there could be no going back. As surely as the sun rose each day, London would submit to her father in the spring, and soon afterward she would be married forever into Mercia. She would be called upon to forsake her perfect love and go live with Eadred for the rest of her life, to grow old and unfulfilled, until it was too late and all was done for.

She was trapped.

She pulled the latch on the door to her room, pushing it open and entering the dark chamber. It was cold inside. The flickering candle in her hand drew her attention to the far wall, where the shudders to the lone, tall window in the room had swung open. She shivered slightly as she fastened the window latch and shut the night out. Then she bent over and lit several other candles that stood, draped in wax, on the single table in the room. Their glow bathed the chamber in a soft light.

"Aethelfled..."

She wheeled around and caught sight of a tall man standing alongside her bed. She started as if to scream, but stopped as he emerged from the shadows.

"Sigli...my God! What are you doing here?"

"I had to see you." He bounded across the room and took her in his arms. "I couldn't stay away...knowing he was here."

"You're taking a terrible chance! What if you're caught?"

"Shhh." He kissed her once, lightly. "I'm already your prisoner, as it is."

He kissed her again, this time longer, and she responded.

"I've missed you," she whispered, taking his face in her hands and looking up adoringly at him. "Every moment without you has been an eternity."

"I can't bear it." He grabbed her hands and sat opposite her on the edge of the bed. "All alone in Twynham, counting the days, the hours...And thinking of you here, with the Mercian drooling all over you!"

"Stop it." She placed her finger over his lips. "It's nothing like that. But...if anyone were to find you here...!"

"No one saw me enter through the gates. I left my horse in the stable and kept to the shadows, until I arrived at your window."

"You climbed the wall, in this weather?"

He smiled. "I would have climbed to Asgard itself, to be with you." He looked into her face, and his eyes were gleaming.

Now *that* was the look of love, she thought. It was impossible to resist.

"Don't worry, I'll leave before dawn. No one will find us out."

"Oh, Sigli..."

She sat down on the edge of the bed beside him and threw her arms around his neck, pulling him to her and kissing him passionately. He kissed her back, and soon they were entwined, their bellies pressed together. They made love for what seemed like a long time, oblivious to the danger, until their passion reached a climax and he spent himself and collapsed into her. They lay there for a moment, breathing heavily, and then he raised his head and smiled into her eyes. He kissed her once before rolling onto his back, and they stretched out next to each other, weak in the knees, staring silently up into the darkness.

"I don't think I can go on like this," he said, finally. "We've got to find a way to be together."

It hurt to think about it. "You...you know it's impossible." She kept her eyes fixed on the ceiling.

"There must be a way...what if...what if I agreed to be baptized?"

"It wouldn't be enough. Not nearly enough. Don't you see...? It's not Eadred I'm marrying—it's Mercia."

"It won't be Mercia in your bed each night!"

"Don't say that."

"But you don't love him! Doesn't you father understand?"

"It doesn't matter. Love has nothing to do with it."

He propped himself up on one elbow and looked down at her. "Fly away with me tonight. We'll sail for the continent."

"Oh, Sigli...Can't you...won't you...understand? I could never do that. Never."

She buried her face in her hands and started to sob. It disarmed him, and he reached out and touched her. She trembled as he leaned forward and put his arms around her, and then she sighed, her voice squeezing in a weak whimper through the tears.

"It hurts me so much, knowing how this pains you...how it pains me. How we...can never...."

She started to cry again, and he felt sorry for her, sorry for them both. He squeezed her tightly and kissed her on the neck.

"I won't stop trying to find a way for us...somehow, somewhere. But if the gods are cruel, and deny you to me, well, then..." His voice trailed off in despair.

Now it was her chance to comfort him. She turned and folded his head into her breast. "I love you, Sigli. No matter what happens, we both know that. And we have each other now, tonight." She looked grimly off into the darkness. "Nobody can deny us that!"

He lifted his head and his eyes were on fire again, and he kissed her long and hard. She melted into him as he raised himself up and made love to her again. Not a word was spoken, nothing at all, as they forgot their hopelessness and stole another moment in time, sinking deeper into each other while Winchester slept all around them.

*   *   *   *   *

Guiding the quill across the smooth vellum, pen against parchment, was as pleasing an exercise as Aethelwold could ever hope to undertake. While most boys hungered for horse and sword, Alfred's youngest child never tired of practicing his letters, and at the age of eight he had already attained a level of literacy that surpassed most of the thanes and ealdormen in Wessex. He personified his father's love of learning more than any of the other royal children, rekindling memories of Alfred's precocious childhood, with its pilgrimages to Rome and study in the courts of the Frankish kings.

It pleased the Golden Dragon that it should turn out this way. While his other children had been educated, none of them was particularly disposed toward learning in a way the king would have liked. Aethelfled was versed in the classics, but had already begun to turn away from letters as marriage and adulthood beckoned. Edward was hopeless, and was clearly meant to lead men, not teach them. And the sisters, Aethelgifu and Aelfthryth, were equally indifferent; one was consumed by prayer, the other by thoughts of womanhood and marriage—after Aethelfled had spoken her vows, of course.

Only Aethelwold had inherited his father's love of letters. On this clear and cold morning he sat facing the window, his back turned toward the room so that the winter sunlight illuminated his work. Its slanting rays creased the parchment and glistened off the still-damp ink from his pen. Long, curving letters, administered with a flourish, artful yet economical. Yes, that's nice, he thought; perhaps a longer line here, and...

"So very well done."

The voice startled him. He wheeled around to discover Grimwald hovering over him, a looming, enormous hulk who seemed to fill the entire room. The Bishop of Winchester was looking intently at the parchment, and his face smiled with an insincere sweetness, all thin lips and thick jowls. He leaned so close that Aethelwold could smell him, dank and oily even in the crisp dead of winter, a ripe odor that added to the boy's general discomfort. Like most children, he was afraid of the man.

"I'm really quite sorry, child. Did I frighten you?"

"I...I didn't hear you enter the room, Holiness. I was concentrating on my lesson."

"Yes, I can see that. But what's this you're writing? Pagan letters, are they?"

The boy turned uneasily back to his work. "Just a passage from Virgil. The Aenead."

"You shouldn't be wasting your time with such heresy. Not when there are so many worthy Christian works to study."

"But, Holiness...Plegmund said I could."

"He did, did he? Well perhaps he needs to be taught a lesson of his own. Where is he?"

"He left a few moments ago. He should be back soon."

"With his arms full of heathen manuscripts, no doubt. But, enough of that for now."

Grimwald leaned even closer, his breath beating a hot wind on the boy's face. "Tell me...now that your sister readies herself to be married, how do her spirits fare?"

Aethelwold answered in a tentative whisper. "She...she's well enough, I suppose, Holiness."

"And what do you think of this Mercian, Eadred? Do you fancy him?"

"Yes, I...I think so."

"And do you think your sister feels the same way about him? Does she ready herself for Mercia?"

"Why...yes, Holiness. But why do you ask?"

"Yes, Holiness. Why *do* you ask?"

Grimwald turned toward the door, where Plegmund stood, visibly angry. He strode into the room, dumping a load of manuscripts onto one of the tables and shouldering his way between Aethelwold and the bishop.

"Rather pointed questions to be asking the boy, don't you think, Grimwald?"

"Merely an innocent conversation. But maybe I should be asking you instead...no?"

"I don't know what you're talking about. Why did you come here?"

"Now, now, Plegmund...I'm always interested in the progress of our finest minds. Even if they're studying pagan verse." He gestured toward the parchment upon which Aethelwold had been writing.

"Virgil deserves better than that."

"If you say so. But I don't propose to lecture the boy on his lessons. I was more interested in how he felt about things. It *is* his sister, after all..."

"Just what do you want, Grimwald?"

The Bishop of Winchester smacked his lips, warming to the task. "The Mercian, of course, is a desirable enough commodity. But, just think for a minute. What if...what if, by chance, she doesn't love him?"

Plegmund looked uneasily at Aethelwold. "I think the lesson is done for today. Why don't we continue again tomorrow?"

The boy did not need to be told twice. Collecting his things quickly, he slid from his chair and hurried out of the chamber, leaving the two churchmen alone in the room. Immediately, Plegmund's face tightened.

"How dare you say things like that in front of him! He's just a child! Have you no discretion?"

"When it serves my purpose. But why so agitated?" Grimwald sized up his mark. "It's true, isn't it? She doesn't love him, after all..."

Plegmund felt his face betraying him. He turned away to conceal his feelings, fumbling through the parchments on the table. "How should I know? I don't talk to her about those things."

Alerted to the scent of blood, Grimwald moved in for the kill. "You talk to her a great deal, if I'm not mistaken. I see the two of you riding off together, deep in conversation." He paused for effect, and then he probed further.

"I think you know something. Something that you're not telling."

"Why must you pry into everyone else's affairs?" Plegmund cried out in protest, keeping his back turned. "What difference would it make, even if she didn't love him? It wouldn't be the first time for a political marriage."

"Then she doesn't?"

"Don't waste your time...or mine."

Grimwald slapped his fist sharply into his open palm. "Always, you avoid me! For a man who needs friends, you make no effort to cultivate the few you have!"

Plegmund wheeled around. "Don't patronize me, Grimwald! You ask for everything, all the time, but you never give anything in return!"

"I could give you much, if you'd let me! Just tell me what you know...I ask only for the truth."

"Which you would sully with your lies and deceits!"

"Remember who you're talking to, Mercian! You step too far!"

Plegmund loathed his superior, but there was no use antagonizing him; it could only lead to ruin. "As you will," he said, looking away. "But I'll not have you slandering Aethelfled's honor. I don't know what you're talking about."

"Then where do you go, when you ride away with her for so long?"

"We ride. That's all."

"For hours on end, every week? Come, now, Plegmund...what kind of fool do you take me for?" Grimwald stared intently at the younger monk. He was so close; he could sense it. *Damn you, man, crack! Tell me what you know!*

Plegmund spoke slowly and carefully. "I keep her company...no more, no less. We've been close for years, now. You know that." He turned back to his parchments. "Now, if you require me no further, I have work to do. You've already interrupted me once...I beg you not to do it again."

Grimwald smiled thinly through his teeth and moved to the door. "Very well, my friend. Have it your way. But all is not well here. That I know."

And then he was gone.

Plegmund slumped against the table. It had been all he could do to maintain his composure; Grimwald was relentless and would not be denied. It was only a matter of time until old Winchester peeled away another layer of truth, the awful truth, plunging Wessex into a scandal for the ages. He stared into the morning sunlight that broke through the clouds, and his mind raced. It would all have to stop before it was too late.

But despite his fear and guilt, he had come to cultivate a perverse pleasure in the whole affair. Delivering her to Sigli was the next best thing to delivering himself. Afterwards, when he would return to his chamber at Winchester, he would lie down on his hassock and stare into the night, imagining himself where she had been. Rarely did a night go by when he did not let his fantasies run free. He would touch himself until the satisfaction came, followed by the inevitable tug of remorse as he felt himself plunging into the great abyss. It was as though the three of them were huddled together at the bottom of a very deep well. And above them loomed the sinister shadow of Grimwald, blocking the light, hovering like a great bird of prey as he peered dangerously down into the darkness.

As he stared off into the distant forest that led away from Winchester, Plegmund was afraid. Closing his eyes, he slipped off the chair and dropped to his knees. And then he began to pray.

*   *   *   *   *

Alfred adjusted his heavy mail coat and tightened his belt. There was a time for convenience and a time for ceremony, and he understood the value of both. It was ludicrous to be donning his armor, with no enemy within miles and all of Wessex at his feet, but he knew that his departure from Winchester had symbolic value. The message had to be clear: they would not return from London without capturing the ultimate prize.

It was late January of 886. The winter had turned mild, convincing him there was no reason to wait any longer. Eadred's pleas and his own impatience had hastened his decision, and he ordered the siege of London to begin two weeks after the Feast of the Epiphany, the closing celebration of the Yule season. He sent the word out across Wessex, alerting the countryside; at this very moment, streams of men were on the march, all moving purposefully toward the port city on the Thames. All that remained was for him to leave Winchester and set the final wheel of his machine into motion.

He reached for his bejeweled sword, housed snugly in its leather scabbard, and fastened it to his war belt. Then he moved over to a great chest that filled an entire corner of the room. Opening it, he extracted a heavy woolen cloak from within and draped it over his shoulders, clasping it on one side with an elaborate golden broach. It was the same cloak that had covered him at Edington; he had not worn it since. Then he picked up his helmet and examined it carefully. The dome-like iron headpiece was elaborately engraved, with a narrow strip of bronze bisecting the hinged faceplate and extending down to cover the nose. Two oval openings broken out of the plate on either side of the bronze served as windows, allowing him to see without exposing the upper part of his face to danger. A pair of stiff leather flaps hung down from either side of the iron head plate, covering the throat and providing the final touch to armor that was clearly too fine to be worn by anyone but a king.

He lowered the helmet over his head and strode from the chamber, walking briskly down the long hall that led to the courtyard. As he neared the final threshold, his eyes and ears were greeted by a mass of color and noise as his army prepared to leave for London. He stopped in his tracks, just out of sight of those in the courtyard. Peeking outside from the shadows of the hall, he took in the scene for a long, lingering moment, enjoying the rare chance to observe something great and glorious without being the center of attention. He reminded himself of everything that had led him to this place, every obstacle that had once seemed so insurmountable and beyond his control, and suddenly the years fell away and he felt young again.

Adjusting his armor one last time, the Golden Dragon of Wessex took a deep breath and stepped out of himself, merging into the tumult and the shouting as the morning sunlight gleamed off his helmet for all of England to see.

*   *   *   *   *

They had been riding together for several hours, and yet only a handful of words had passed between them. The only sounds that could be heard belonged to the forest: the crackle of twigs beneath the horses' hooves, a squirrel scurrying through the underbrush, the wind rattling the branches of the bare trees. It occurred to Aethelfled as she and Plegmund rode toward the woodcutter's hut that one of the true tests of friendship was silence. They could be themselves with each other, and that was the ultimate comfort.

She had always felt that way about him, but the past few months had drawn them even closer. He had willingly sacrificed himself and his beliefs to help her, and she was eternally grateful for it, even as she knew she was leading them astray. It had been weeks since they had last been to the hut, and for a moment he had begun to believe she would not call on him again. But when Eadred left for Mercia and Alfred for London, she asked him the inevitable, and to her surprise he agreed without protest. He rode the next day to Twyneham and summoned

Sigli—who by then was beside himself with longing—to once again meet them at the woodcutter's hut.

This was the first time she would be seeing the Viking since the Yule season, now that Eadred was gone and her father had finally marched on London. The thrill of it all was tempered by the knowledge that there would be no more trips to the woodcutter's hut. She now, finally, could see and accept the end.

But none of it could ease her pain, or the thought of the greater heartbreak that was sure to come. She could accept her coming marriage, she could reconcile her God and the sinful choice she had made in the eyes of the Church. But she could not face hurting him. She took a deep breath and smiled bravely.

"Thank you, Plegmund."

It was the first time that either of them had spoken in over an hour.

"My Lady...?"

"You've been a true friend. I've been guilty of abusing your trust for too long." She looked vacantly through the bare trees that stretched ahead of them. "I'm going to try to tell him today, Plegmund. I'm going to end it."

"Then why do we both ride to the hut? You could have sent me."

"I owe him more than that. This is the least I could do for him."

"Then you'll tell him as soon as we arrive?"

She shook her head. "Not immediately. I simply must see him this one more time. And I'll swear to him—and to you—that I'll see us all through this before we're done. No matter how long it takes."

The monk slapped his leg. "Believe me, my Lady, the man I summoned to the hut when I rode last week to Twyneham will never willingly accept the truth! He equates no Christian guilt with this travesty, don't you understand? He lives for one thing, and one thing only...and that's you."

"But he knows in his mind..."

"He knows only in his heart. This is a man driven by instinct, my Lady. A Viking. He's not like us at all."

"Would that we were all so pure."

"We were born into another world, my Lady. A world with rules, with a Heaven and a Hell, and the choices to be made between them. I was born to serve God. And you were born to serve England. But he carries none of that with him; the only God he's ever truly worshiped was his revenge. And that was denied him."

Her lips tightened. "No just God could condemn what we've done. Right or wrong, I feel no guilt. None at all."

He looked at her in silence for a moment as they rode along, and his eyes suddenly grew stern. "Believe what you want, but listen to me, Aethelfled. The wrath of Satan trails behind us. There's a hound from Hell on our scent!"

"What are you talking about?"

His voice quavered. "It's Grimwald, my Lady. He already suspects too much."

"What do you mean? What does he know?"

"Only that we ride together often, and are gone longer than we should be. But behind it all, he suspects the truth." Here he paused. "He knows you don't love Eadred."

She shrugged. "My father and mother both know that. So does Edward, for that matter."

"But Grimwald *really* knows. Do you understand me? He *knows*. He's the Devil himself, but even more clever and deceitful. That's why you must put a stop to this, before it's too late!"

She reached out and gently touched his arm. "Plegmund, I've wronged you. I've asked for more than anyone could ever possibly give. We ride today because I need time alone with Sigli, but I won't put you through any more of this."

"Do you swear it?"

"Yes."

He sighed. "Let us pray to God, then, and ask His forgiveness. And beg Him to let us escape without harm."

She looked ahead through the forest. "We're close now. Let me ride ahead to the hut and meet him. Please stay outside; it's not too cold, after all. And there won't be any more vigils for you...not after today."

She cast a brave smile over her shoulder and sped off into the trees. He watched her recede through the wood, feeling no better in spite of what had been said. His grief matched anything that either of them could possibly feel, for at least they had the comfort of each other. He had nothing.

He picked his way slowly through the forest, lost in his thoughts. In a few more minutes the hut would come into view and he would be left outside, braced against a tree to shield himself from the wind. That was his penance; to always be denied the warmth of true human companionship and love. So be it, he thought. That was the path he had chosen.

He mulled over all that had come to pass during the last few months as he drew closer to the familiar glade that fronted the hut, rounding the last trees blocking his view, until...What was that? He strained his ears. And then he heard it again, a low laughter coming from the hovel.

It was not the laughter of love, but a much darker sound, and when he heard Aethelfled's protests he knew they were in danger. He leaped from his horse and ran toward the half-opened entrance to the hut, leaving behind all thoughts of his own safety as he raced to her aid. The laughter rang in his ears as he reached the threshold.

There within, a large, rough man stood with his back to the door, looking down in amusement as his partner, sprawled atop Aethelfled, ripped away at her dress.

"Be sure to save some for me!" the man bellowed. "Don't take all the fight out of her!"

Plegmund stepped into the hut and grabbed a stout staff that was leaning against the wall. He swung the cudgel hard across the unsuspecting man's back, crumpling him to the ground. The force of the blow knocked the staff from Plegmund's hand, but he threw himself on the back of the second man and began to strike him as hard as he could with his fists.

The ceorl fought back, and soon his superior strength began to take its toll. They struggled for a few seconds until the man freed one of his hands; reaching into his belt, he withdrew a serrated hunting knife and slashed Plegmund's arm. The monk let out a low cry and fell backward to the ground, grabbing at his wound as his attacker advanced on him, preparing to finish the issue.

At that moment Aethelfled rose up and with all of her strength delivered a blow to the back of the man's neck, knocking him to the floor. Before she could press her attack he scrambled to his feet, joined by his accomplice. Aethelfled scurried over to the monk and pulled him with her into the far corner of the room, where they huddled together, struggling to catch their breaths.

"We'll pay you well," Plegmund pleaded. "Ransom us."

The men looked at each other and smiled wickedly. Their ragged clothes and dirt-streaked faces marked them as common thieves, brigands outside of the law.

"There's only one thing I want," the larger of the two cackled. "But first, let's finish with him."

In the next instant a shadow appeared at the entrance of the hut, followed by a loud crash as the door burst open and Sigli leaped into the room. He parried a knife thrust from one of the thieves and brought the butt of his axe down upon the man's upper back as he flew by, sending him sprawling. With cat-like quickness he pounced on the second thief, who swung wildly at him with the staff that Plegmund had dropped to the ground only moments before. Sigli ducked and delivered three blows at the man with his axe. The first two shredded the staff to pieces, but the third one found its mark, burying itself in the thief's exposed flesh where the shoulder blade meets the throat, killing him instantly. Blood spurted high into the air as the man collapsed at Plegmund's feet.

Sigli turned to the second thief, but the coward dashed out of the hut and leaped onto one of the horses tethered outside, kicking furiously at the animal and speeding off across the glade. Sigli watched as the man disappeared through the trees, and then he turned and went back into the hut, where Aethelfled leaned over Plegmund.

"He's bleeding freely," she said, looking up.

"I'll be all right." Plegmund clutched tightly at his wounded arm. The blood seeped between his fingers, sticky and wet.

"Here, let me see that." Sigli knelt down and pulled the bloodstained robe away from the monk's forearm. He frowned. "It's a nasty cut. We need to bind it immediately."

He bent over the body of the dead thief, pulled a hunting knife from his belt, and cut a long strip of material from the man's shirt and began to fashion it into a makeshift bandage. Plegmund leaned his head back against the wall and closed his eyes, grimacing in silence.

"Will he be all right, Sigli?"

"He'll be fine." He folded the cloth over in his hands and bound the monk's wound. "I've seen far worse. But, Aethelfled...how are *you*? If I'd been any later..."

"Don't worry about me. Tend to Plegmund first."

"We've got to get him someplace where he can be cared for properly."

"There's a small hamlet on the edge of the forest," she said, "about an hour's ride back toward Winchester."

"I know the one. As soon as I finish dressing the wound, we should head there. See here, Plegmund, you'll have quite the scar...something to be proud of, I'd think!"

The monk stared glumly ahead. "There's no pride in all of this."

Aethelfled reached out and squeezed his leg. "Don't say that! You were brave, and strong! You saved my life!"

He blushed for an instant, but then his lips curled cynically at the corners. "You wouldn't listen to me; I've been warning you both! It was only a matter of time before something like this happened! We're lucky to be alive!"

"There, now," Sigli said, ignoring him, "I think that should do it. It's not too tight? Good, then. Up on your feet, and let's go."

Plegmund got up slowly and moved toward the door. Aethelfled followed him, avoiding the pool of blood that had formed under the dead thief. She shuddered as she stepped over the body.

"Sigli, what shall we do about him?"

"Leave him to rot, as far as I'm concerned."

"You can't do that! You can't defile this place, not after all that it's meant to us!"

"Rogue or no, I agree," Plegmund said. "He deserves a Christian burial." He stopped and stood by the door, where the afternoon light seeped into the hut, illuminating his drawn features. "It's the decent thing to do, and besides...we can't afford to leave any evidence. It's simply too dangerous."

Sigli shrugged. "All right, then. But I've no intention of doing it now. I'll bury him on my return to Twyneham, after I've escorted you both to safety."

They stepped out into the crisp winter afternoon. Plegmund staggered slightly, weak and unsure, but Sigli was there to help him. Aethelfled brushed past them and went to gather up Plegmund's horse, which grazed quietly on the far side of the glade as though nothing of any consequence had happened. Her chestnut mare was still tethered safely to the hut, where she had tied it just before the two men appeared from the hovel and dragged her inside. But Sigli's horse was gone, leaving only two mounts for three riders.

"Plegmund's horse looks to be the sturdier of the two," said Sigli. "I'll double up with him, in case he grows weak."

He helped the monk up into the saddle, and then he swung himself easily behind and into position, putting his arms around Plegmund and grabbing the reins.

"A bit awkward, but it will have to do."

Sigli's touch sparked a warm surge that rippled through Plegmund. His misfortune suddenly seemed a small price to pay for the privilege of this unforeseen intimacy; to ride through the forest in the arms of the man he yearned for was something he had only dreamed of. The elation of actually being encircled by Sigli's arms so overcame him that he was unable to relax for the first mile, as though his body language might betray him and somehow bring an end to this sudden good fortune. The sexual tension he felt was unnerving, for he was a modest man who did not know how to deal with the strange and wonderful sensation of sharing his physical space with someone else.

But gradually he began to feel more secure, relaxing by degrees until finally his fears dissipated and his senses took over. He marveled at Sigli's rugged athleticism; everything about him was completely natural—effortless, almost, with no wasted motion. Plegmund was surrounded by a great sense of warmth that overrode the dull throb in his arm. He felt as though he could stay there forever, and all the pain and relentless uncertainty that had become so much a part of his world suddenly seemed very far away. He leaned back and wedged his buttocks firmly into the Viking, and as they swayed together with the movement of the horse it occurred to him that nothing else mattered now, nothing at all.

"How does your arm feel?" Sigli's breath beat like a warm wind against his ear, sending another chill of delight through him.

"It's not bleeding anymore. But I've lost a lot of the feeling; perhaps the bandage is too tight."

"Here, then. Let me loosen it."

Sigli let go of the reins and backed off on the pressure of the tourniquet. "I once knew a man who lost his arm because of something like this. The blood was kept from it for too long, and his flesh turned blue...we had to cut his limb off just beneath the elbow to save him."

"Don't talk that way," Aethelfled protested. She had been riding just behind them, but now she pulled up alongside as they entered an open stretch of meadow. She looked sympathetically at Plegmund.

"You look tired. We'll reach shelter before long, don't worry. But we'd better decide on a story...something to explain your arm."

"I've already thought about it," the monk replied. "We were riding through the forest when we were accosted by a lone thief on foot. He demanded our purses, but we escaped him and sped off to safety. As we pulled away, he slashed at me with his knife and cut my arm open."

"You do yourself a disservice, Plegmund," Sigli said. "Especially considering your bravery at the hut."

""No one would ever believe I was capable of overcoming an armed man by myself," Plegmund sighed. "Fleeing on horseback makes more sense...and besides, it removes you from any possible suspicion. Remember, we still have to be careful. You'll have to leave us on foot before we reach the hamlet. No one must know you were with us."

"Why all these ridiculous precautions? Do we really need to go to these lengths?"

"I've told this to Aethelfled, but now I'll tell you. We're being watched, Sigli. It's Grimwald...he keeps prying, and suspects us. There's no telling what evil the man's capable of doing, believe me. But he's still not on to you. Not yet, at least."

Sigli hissed in disgust, exchanging glances with Aethelfled.

"That's why all of this must stop," Plegmund continued, his voice rising. "Before it's too late. Before we're discovered, or our throats are cut by men like those we stumbled across today!" He half turned in the saddle toward Sigli. "Good God, man, Aethelfled was nearly violated! Surely you can't be so selfish that you'd expect her to endanger herself again, riding unescorted through the forest!"

Sigli stiffened. "If not the hut, then somewhere else! We must find another meeting place, closer to Winchester!"

"This is madness! You can't be serious about pursuing this lunacy any longer! You..."

"Don't cross me, Plegmund!"

"I won't hear of it! I..."

"I know a place." Aethelfled's voice was quiet but clear; it silenced them both. Plegmund could not believe what he was hearing, but he held his tongue.

"The tanner's hovel on the river, a mile or so upstream from my father's hall at Winchester," she continued, looking straight ahead and doing her best to avoid the monk.

"I know the one," Sigli said. He was enthralled by her, now more than ever.

"He died a month ago. No one lives there now. One week from tonight, meet me just after sundown." '

Plegmund was beside himself. "Aethelfled, how can you do this? After everything that was said, after...!"

He stopped abruptly as her eyes bored into him. Their meaning was clear; there would be no retreat. It frightened him, to be controlled and manipulated like this, and in that moment he understood the essence of her will, and the immense power of personality that she wielded. No wonder so many men loved her, he thought.

"I've made promises, and I intend to keep them all...but in their own time," she said.

She looked away from Plegmund and into her lover's eyes, and the distance between them melted away instantly.

"Sigli, today can't be helped; what's done is done. Plegmund's right. You'll have to leave before we reach the hamlet. But next week we'll meet again... if, that is, you'll have me."

"You know the answer to that."

"Then it's done. As for you, Plegmund, there won't be any need to embroil yourself in this any longer. You've already done enough."

She maneuvered her horse ahead of them, taking the lead as they left the meadow and entered the forest again. Plegmund said nothing. He was completely drained by the events of the day, but he knew instinctively that everything she had told him just an hour earlier had been obliterated by the bloodbath at the hut, no closer to resolution than ever. The affair was beyond his control now, as it was beyond Sigli's; it was clear that Aethelfled's voice was the only one that mattered. And she had spoken plainly enough.

His mind drifted away from the problem and back to Sigli again, and he savored the warmth and physical intimacy of their circumstance. Was it a reward, or a temptation? It did not matter right now. He sighed and shifted his weight so that he nestled closer to the Viking, and for a while he contented himself with the pure pleasure of riding squarely in the lap of his most secret desires.

But gradually his eyes grew heavy as he rolled with the rhythm of the horse, and the faraway ache in his arm faded, replaced by a warmth and distance that spiraled downward as he fell into a deep and merciful slumber, cradled like innocence itself on Sigli's broad chest. Next week, and all that it would bring, might as well have been a century away.

But next week never came.

Four days later, after Aethelfled and Plegmund had returned safely to Winchester, a messenger arrived at Twyneham harbor bearing a summons from Alfred. The next day Sigli sailed up the Channel in command of a half dozen longships, headed on a course around Dover and then back up the Thames, to blockade London and cast the final die that would seal the city's fate. Torn once again from the object of his desires, he pined away at the tiller of his flagship, searching the watery horizon in vain for some sign of resolution, waiting.

Things were no better in Winchester. Aethelfled suffered in silence at this unexpected turn of events, tortured by the knowledge that their difficulties were far from over. Meanwhile, Plegmund breathed a momentary sigh of relief and nursed his arm back to health, telling anyone who cared to hear the story they had fabricated about their escape in the forest. Everyone believed him without reservation.

Everyone except Grimwald. The mishap only confirmed his suspicions that something was indeed wrong, making him more determined than ever to find the truth behind all the surface lies and conceits. He brooded alone in his chamber each night, obsessed with every scant detail at his disposal, waiting and wondering.

Only time would tell, that he knew. But time wasn't talking.

*　　*　　*　　*　　*

The morning sunlight streamed in through the window, rousing Ealswith from sleep. At first she was confused and thought herself to be dreaming; the crude wooden walls and thatched roof of the farmhouse were not what her unconscious eye expected to see. But as she gradually began to assimilate the world around her, she remembered where she was and why they had come here.

Alfred had summoned her from Winchester, and when she arrived he had said something to her about their shared past, about how far they had come together. It was close now, so close, and he wanted her to be with him, to sleep beside him in a commoner's hut as they had once slept, when they were hungry and it was somebody else's world. He had wanted it to be that way, now that they stood on the threshold of a dream.

She looked at him as he slept next to her, his face a mere six inches from her own on the far end of the pillow. It was indeed a luxury to look upon him like this, when he was defenseless and could not gird himself against her or the world. For all of his charisma, Alfred was a conscious man—conscious of himself, conscious of everything and everybody around him. Free now from the burden of self-awareness, he did not look so different from the young man she had fallen in love with almost twenty years ago. The worry lines were deeper, maybe, and there were a few more of them since she had last looked closely. His skin was weathered, and there was a beard now, its dark blanket compromised by the random sprigs of white ash sprinkled throughout. But the same sharp features were still there, aging gracefully, bold and resourceful even while at rest.

Here was a man of character. A king.

He was right; they *had* come far. It was a long road that had led them here, to this simple hovel perched auspiciously near the southern bank of the Thames, nestled under a broad, spreading oak at a point commanding an ideal view of London. He had moved his siege headquarters to this spot because it allowed him to look inside the city from just across the river.

No other place offered such a vantage point, for London was surrounded on its other three sides by a wall that had been built during Roman times and refurbished in later centuries by the Celts and Saxons. It had been fortified everywhere except along the Thames, precisely where the king had determined to launch a naval offensive if the siege were to drag on, rather than force the issue by attempting to storm the strength of the defense by land.

But neither of those cases, he knew, was likely to happen. It was only a matter of time.

He had confided all this to her last night. She welcomed any news that might help resolve the siege, for she had grown comfortable with the peace they had all enjoyed over the last eight years. Once London fell, they could all go about living the rest of their lives. It would give Alfred all the power he had ever wanted, restoring him to the finer side of himself, the pursuit of law and learning. He could pass most of the kingdom's military matters on to young Edward, at once fulfilling a promise and appeasing his eldest son, who hungered for the opportunity. And best of all, the end of the siege would finally result in Aethelfled's marriage to Eadred, consummating the alliance with Mercia—and, it might be added, mercifully allowing the queen to once again sleep in peace at night.

She was the first thing he saw that morning when his eyes opened. He smiled and studied her for a moment, and then he ran his finger gently across her cheek.

"Good morning, my Lord. Did you sleep well?"

"Better than in weeks. Having you here is the best tonic of all."

She shifted her body closer to him, pleased with herself and his continuing desire for her. Last night had been their first time together in weeks, for she had stayed in Winchester during the siege and had seen him rarely since late January. They had made love before retiring—not once, but twice—and her body still tingled from the release. After all these years they were still excited by each other. She knew it was something not to take for granted; other women her age acted as though sex had to be tolerated, never enjoyed. She hoped neither of them would ever feel that way.

"I'd think you'd have some young thing here, to entertain you," she said, only half joking.

"Ah, but you please me best of all," he reassured her, running his hand along the curve of her buttocks. "You know everything, all my little secrets."

"All?" she teased. "Enough of them, at least. I can give you what any other woman can, and more. But there are still some things that nobody could ever hope to give you."

"Such as?"

"London, for one."

His eyes twinkled. "London shall not be given. It shall be taken. I'll have her soon, by God. All of her, and everything she stands for."

He sat up in bed and reached for his leggings, eager now to get on with the day. The morning chill sent a light shiver through his body.

"Well, get on with it, then," she chided him. "You've thought of nothing else for months now. It's affected everything. And everybody."

He laughed. "Why do you say that? It hasn't been that bad."

"I've a wedding to plan, Alfred. As long as the siege drags on, I can't do anything." She swung her legs over the side of the bed and began to put on her clothes.

"You sound like Eadred now," he said, cinching his belt and strapping his broadsword in place. "I'm tempted to send him back to Mercia; he can't be around more than a few minutes, it seems, without bringing up the subject."

"Can you blame him? We're all getting impatient."

"Even Aethelfled?"

She looked out the window and sighed. "I don't know what's going through her mind these days. She's been keeping to herself. It worries me."

He raised an eyebrow. "No trouble, I hope?"

"No, nothing like that. But she's certainly in no hurry to move forward. Here, help me with this, please."

She handed him an exquisite necklace imported from Rome and lifted her hair up over her head, allowing him to step behind her and fasten the jewelry in place. As he finished, he leaned over and kissed her on the back of her neck.

"My Lord, you favor me."

"One of your finest attributes," he replied, running one of his fingers along the soft nape until he reached her hairline. "It's a shame that such a delicate feature should lie hidden from the world."

She smiled. "A woman must protect her mystery at all costs. But enough of me for now. Tend instead to your business here. Finish what you've started.

And when you do, come back to me in Winchester. I don't need more than one night in a place like this to remember how far we've come."

"You look down your nose at London now, but you'll see. Mark my words: someday this city will be the greatest in all of England."

"Be sure to let me know when that happens," she said, teasing him. "Until such time, I'll suffer gladly in Winchester."

He opened the door and they stepped outside, where they were immediately surrounded by a handful of servants who had been waiting since dawn's first light, anticipating the appearance of their royal charges. By now a buzz of activity had overtaken the morning. It was impossible for Alfred to be anywhere or do anything without his retinue, and the demands of the siege had only added to the general confusion. He stepped free of the bustle and put his hands on his hips as three approaching horsemen thundered across the last few hundred yards leading up to the encampment.

"Father! Good news!" Edward reined his horse to an abrupt stop and leaped breathlessly from the animal's back, rushing excitedly toward the king. "It's Guthrum! He sailed up the Thames last night. He wishes to see you!"

"Excellent!" Alfred slapped a fist into his open palm. "Now that he's here, maybe the rest of the heathens will come to their senses! They'll listen to him."

"He's breaking his fast with the fleet, aboard Sigli's ship. They're moored just a mile or two from here, not too far downstream. Do you want to ride back with me?"

"No, I don't think so. I don't wish to appear too anxious." He fingered his chin and began to pace back and forth. "I'll wait here instead. Bring Guthrum to me, and we can meet later this morning. It will give me time to think."

He turned abruptly and strode, already preoccupied, past Ealswith and back into the farmhouse. Edward broke into a wide grin as his mother looked on appreciatively, and then he threw himself into the saddle again, motioning to his men and wheeling his horse around to return back to the ships. With a final wave to Ealswith he sped off to the northeast, in the direction of the Thames, and she watched as the horses receded into the distance, the rumble of their hooves trailing behind them amidst a tower of dust that spiraled up into the air.

*   *   *   *   *

What a difference a few short years can make, Sigli thought to himself, as the entourage of a dozen men rode toward Alfred's headquarters a few hours later. Not so very long ago Guthrum had been the scourge of Saxon England. The mere mention of his name had sent waves of fear rippling throughout the land, from Devon to Dover, Mercia to the Channel.

But now Guthrum's rule was benign and largely symbolic; with a few exceptions, there had been no organized force of Danes in Britain since Alfred's victory at Edington. In spite of all this, the Vikings had occupied London for many years and were not anxious to retreat, raising a host of diplomatic, military and practical issues. Through it all, Alfred remained determined to do the right thing.

Which was precisely why he had called on Guthrum. The old Dane had proved himself to be a loyal ally who had lived by his word, never once acting aggressively toward his Saxon neighbors, never breaking the peace. He had managed to extricate himself from the seemingly endless cycle of nomadic plunder to which others of his people were tied, and had prospered these many years with a wife of Saxon birth and a handsome estate in East Anglia. He had forsaken glory and riches for comfort, but he was still respected by his Danish compatriots, who sought his advice on many matters. He was the one man capable of influencing all those who still held out behind London's walls.

Sigli turned to his left, where Guthrum talked with Edward as the prince led the escort toward Alfred's encampment. The Dane still had the same bushy moustache, which drooped over and around his lips in a long, walrus-like arc.

The age showed on his face, but his features were as chiseled as ever, with high cheekbones and dark, piercing eyes. His years had given him wisdom, and with it temperance—two qualities that had served him well as he evolved into the role of elder statesman, presiding loosely over what remained of the great army that had first come to England over twenty years ago. He was managing quite nicely, preparing to die in a few years in the comfort of his bed with his fat and happy wife beside him. Smiling easily, the old Viking turned to Sigli and spoke in the Danish tongue.

"Strange, isn't it? Would you ever have thought two Vikings could be welcomed among the Christians like this?"

"I was never their enemy. I was brought here against my will."

"And yet you've never left. A young buck like you, with all that's going on in Francia...I'm surprised you're not off with Haestan's armies. Why do you stay?"

"I have my reasons. There's always been something to keep me here."

Guthrum pursed his lips and smiled. "There are worse fates in the world. I've got plenty of land, a nice, plump wife, two mistresses and more cows and sheep than I can count. But...what about you? You're in Alfred's good graces...surely you could turn that into something."

"An estate, you mean? I'm not ready for that. And besides...I haven't been baptized. Not like you. I'm still suspect in some quarters." Guthrum chuckled. "A little bit of water poured over the forehead doesn't change who a man is. Or what he believes in." Keeping to the Viking tongue, he glanced cautiously at Edward. "Let me tell you something, friend. I still keep the old ways. In my heart, I worship Odin and the gods of Asgard."

Sigli raised his eyebrows. "You certainly don't act that way. You'll never get to Valhalla by dying in bed, you know."

Guthrum's eyes crinkled in pleasure, and then he tapped his head sagely. "I wouldn't say that. You see, I have a blade lashed to my fingers each night. If I should die, well...I'll die with a sword in my hand, after all!"

Sigli looked incredulously at the old Dane. And then they began to laugh at the absurdity of it all.

"Come now, you two. Don't shut me out." Edward said. "Let me in on your little secret. For all I know, you've been plotting against me, speaking in your strange tongue."

"It's too late for plotting," Guthrum reassured him in English. "We were just sharing a joke. A reminder of the past."

"Save your laughter." The young prince pointed into the distance. "I see them now. Look there, in front of the hut. My father waits for you, Guthrum."

They were able to make out a small group of men standing in attendance beneath the banner of the Golden Dragon, which fluttered in the late morning breeze. Alfred was seated among them. He stood up from his makeshift throne as they approached, remaining silent until they reined their horses to a stop and dismounted.

"Welcome, Athelstan," he said. In person, he always referred to Guthrum by the Christian name he had given him at baptism. "I'm glad you've come."

"My Lord, at your service," replied the Dane, sinking down to one knee. "What would you of me?"

"Your advice. And your friendship. Now, please rise. And join me." The king pointed toward the open door of the farmhouse. "Edward, you and Sigli should attend us. And Eadred and Penda as well. Let us break bread."

Alfred and Guthrum walked ahead, chatting amiably, but Sigli never heard a word of it. His entire attention was focused on Eadred, the man who would take his woman from him, the man who would make love to her and plant his children in her belly. He had known the Mercian since Edington, but it was disconcerting to actually see him face to face for the first time since his affair with Aethelfled had begun.

Eadred was handsome enough, all right, and there was the swagger of a man in his step. Powerful, confident—he lived up to everything everyone had ever said about him. It annoyed Sigli that he had never really heard anyone speak ill of the Mercian, for he did not want to admit that anything about his rival might be the least bit attractive or appealing to Aethelfled. Everything about the matter disturbed him.

They entered the farmhouse and took their places. Alfred and Guthrum sat down across from each other at a table in the center of the room, with Edward and Eadred joining them.

"Well, I'm glad you've come, Athelstan. I would have thought this whole thing would have been over already, but it's dragged on. I have five thousand of my men camped around the city walls across the river, and I've blockaded the Thames from either direction. Nothing can get in, and nothing can get out." Here he shook his head. "And still, no word. No attempt to parlay."

Guthrum rubbed his chin. "There's no single leader among the Danes in London. By my estimate, there are at least five factions. They probably can't reach agreement among themselves."

"My men grow restless. Spring is here, and they all want to return to their fields and begin planting." He leaned forward. "Help me, Guthrum. Talk to your countrymen for me."

The Viking shrugged his shoulders. "I'm old now, and out of the hunt. Why should they listen to me?"

"Who else can talk sense into them?"

"These are suspicious men, my Lord. They don't trust each other, no less you. I imagine they fear you might butcher them all if they laid down their arms and opened the city gates."

"I've never done anything of the sort. And I've no reason to start now."

"Of course, of course. Well, they...." here Guthrum paused, "we, that is...we need assurances. And some sort of...compensation, perhaps?" He looked quietly at Alfred and waited for the king to speak.

"And what, specifically, do you want?"

Guthrum smiled. "You need me to save time, money and lives. And embarrassment, perhaps. I understand. I'll help you. But I want two hundred head of sheep, a dozen horses...and gold."

"One hundred sheep, the horses...and one hundred pieces of silver."

"Make that two hundred pieces."

"One hundred and fifty."

"Done."

Alfred smiled. "Good! Now that we're agreed, my friend, here's what I want you to do. Tell them that not only will their lives be spared, but I'll grant them land in those parts of East Anglia where I lay claim. Tell them that I'll give up my hides there, and establish a permanent border between Christian England and your land, the Danelaw. They can have it, Athelstan. They can become one with the land, as you've done. East Anglia and Northumbria are Danelaw, my friend. I lay no claim there."

Guthrum nodded, impressed by the offer.

"In addition," Alfred went on, "I want you to tell them that we'll draw up a treaty. And you'll represent them. Together, we can establish a code of laws to govern the commerce and relations between our peoples, and live together in peace."

"That's all well and good, Sire. But they'll still want to know what's to prevent your army from hacking them to pieces once they've laid down their arms."

Alfred's face flinched in irritation. "Really, Athelstan...you disappoint me. Butchery has never been a Saxon trait, only a Viking one. Kingdoms are built by persuasion and common sense as well as by the sword. I have no quarrel with those men. I have no desire for bloodshed and needless loss of life. But I *will* have London, my friend." Here his eyes blazed with conviction. "If we have to, we'll sit here all summer, until we starve them out."

Guthrum stared at him for a moment, and then he bowed his head lightly. "As you will, my Lord. I'll go into the city, and I'll tell them these things. It might take some time and debate, but be patient; their bellies already ache. The end is near. Wiser heads will prevail, that I know."

He took a deep breath and nodded, almost to himself, and then he smiled. "You want London, King Alfred? Well, then...you shall have it."

The king stood up immediately and offered his hand to Guthrum. They shook heartily on the agreement, after which Alfred turned and motioned to a servant stationed near the door.

"More mead! And let us break bread...my guests are hungry!"

The door opened, admitting more servants and a stream of hangers-on, and soon the room was alive with conversation. Sigli remained aloof from it all, watching from one side of the room as he cradled a goblet of mead in his hand. He looked over at Eadred, who talked away animatedly in the midst of the crowd, and as he did so it occurred to him that one man's loss is another man's gain. They would have their London, and all that went along with it. And he would have his despair, a lifetime of pain and denial, and none of them would ever even know what he was going through, or how they had all made it come to pass. Disgusted, he turned away from the room and stared sullenly out the rear window of the farmhouse.

"Sigli! Sigli, there you are!" He turned as the jubilant Edward approached him, raising his cup of mead. "Drink with me! To London!"

Sigli smiled weakly and sipped from his goblet. "To London."

Edward knew that it had been difficult for the Viking since the previous summer, when the fleet's difficulties in the East Anglian campaign had been followed closely by the news of Sidroc's death. Things had not gone well for Sigli, and Edward was sensitive to it.

"Now, now...look on the bright side. Not much longer and you won't have to blockade the city."

"It's all the same to me. But I'm happy for your father. He's dreamed of this for as long as I've known him."

"Yes, it's a great day for Wessex. For England, Sigli! This begins a new era for the people of our island...mark my words!"

"I suppose. I don't know if it will really change anything."

"Ha! You joke, I'm sure," Edward laughed. "I wouldn't think it would be too long before...Eadred! Eadred, you rascal!" He turned abruptly and shook the hand of the Mercian ealdorman, who had wandered through the crowd and was standing nearby. "Now, here's one man who's willing to celebrate, Sigli. After London, the next thing to fall will be my sister's maidenhood!"

Sigli winced, but remained silent. Eadred laughed, but there was a hint of embarrassment in his voice when he finally spoke. "Only a brother—and a prince—could make a comment like that, eh?"

"Well, it's true, isn't it?" Edward kept on. "You'll soon be riding bareback, my friend!" He laughed hard. "My father's devotion and my sister's hand—and everything else attached to it!"

"I'm a lucky man, Edward. It's clear that..."

"It's clear that you can't even mention her name without your pants standing up," Edward continued mercilessly. The mead was getting to his head. "I wouldn't want to be my sister that first night; she might burn herself with that hot iron poker of yours, Eadred! Why, if I..."

"That's enough, Edward!" Sigli shouldered his way roughly between the two men and headed for the door.

Edward scratched his head in disbelief. "Now what was that all about?"

Eadred shrugged. "I can't figure the heathens out, Edward. Only your father seems to have a knack for that. But never mind him." He put his hand on the prince's shoulder and turned them both toward the window. "Now, let's talk about the future. You and I...we have a long relationship ahead of us."

Outside, Sigli burst from the farmhouse and headed angrily toward his mount. He pushed his way through a group of Saxons and grabbed the pommel of his saddle, propelling his body up and onto his horse. Kicking forcefully at the animal's flanks, he sent it galloping off back toward the fleet. He rode fast, but it wasn't fast enough; he could not outrun his feelings. The hoof beats of his horse thundered under him, and his eyes began to water as the wind whipped at them and they filled with dust. But still he sped on, exerting the animal to ride at its swiftest, driven by the specter of circumstances beyond his control.

He had to see her again. And it had to be soon.

*　　*　　*　　*　　*

"This is the peace which King Alfred and King Guthrum and the counselors of all the English race and all the people who are in East Anglia have all agreed on and confirmed with oaths, for themselves and for their subjects, both for the living and for the unborn, who care to have God's favor or ours."

Asser looked up from the parchment from which he read and stopped to clear his throat. His eyes swept over the assemblage that had gathered on the banks of the Thames, and the sight of it almost took his breath away.

It was Easter Sunday, a brilliant sunny April afternoon, and it seemed as though all of England had come to London now that Alfred had secured the city. Hundreds of Saxons and Vikings had crowded together in the small, open square that fronted the river, and hundreds more had massed across the Thames, from where they could watch the proceedings. They lined the walls, they lined the streets; they were scattered throughout every cranny of the city as it strained to accommodate the press of humanity. They had all come to London to hear the proclamation of the treaty, and to see the once and future king. Asser raised his voice again for all to hear

"First, concerning our boundaries: up the Thames, and then up the Lea to its source, then in a straight line to Bedford, then up the Ouse to Watling Street."

Off to one side, Grimwald sat alongside Plegmund and observed the proceedings. It was difficult for him to watch helplessly as Asser delivered the terms of the treaty to the assemblage; not too many years ago, that would have been his right. It was just one more example of how things had changed. Never one to bear misery or discomfort in silence, he turned and whispered to Plegmund, smirking in disgust as he spat the words out under his breath.

"Look at him, so proud of himself. That could have been you, Plegmund. There stands the next Archbishop of Canterbury."

Plegmund stiffened, but he said nothing. There were too many others within earshot to pursue the conversation, but Grimwald was right; it could have been him up there today instead of Asser. Everything was unraveling all at once. He had recovered from the knife wound in his arm, but now his heart ached more than ever. Sitting here like this, so far removed from influence, was another painful reminder of how his future was slipping away from him. Through it all he had been unable to rid his mind of an even darker shadow, the one cast by his feelings for Sigli. His fantasies and idle dreams had all run together, leaving him mired in a depression from which there seemed to be no escape.

"Next, if a man is slain, then all of us estimate Englishman and Dane at the same amount, at eight half marks of pure gold; except the ceorl who occupies rented land and their freedmen...these also are estimated at the same amount, both at two hundred shillings."

Aethelfled bit her lip. London had fallen, sealing her future. She was aware of Eadred's hand on hers, but it felt foreign to the touch, as though it did not belong there. She closed her eyes and leaned her head back, and for a moment it almost seemed as though she were all alone, with no one to judge her or make demands. If only such a dream could come true.

Her thoughts drifted to Sigli. He had risked everything by leaving London a week ago and riding all the way to Winchester, where he had again climbed the wall outside her window in the dead of night and come to her. At first she had been frightened, but for him to fly to her like that was the ultimate passion, the consummate love. They had made love throughout the night, as if they could somehow make up for the long months apart, or perhaps stop the march of time and be together forever.

They had not spoken about their future at all. It was still left for her to tell him the truth, the difficult truth, and somehow finish it. That was why she had already determined to beg Plegmund to go to Sigli one more time and arrange a meeting on the eve of the first of May, at the tanner's hut upriver from Winchester.

She opened her eyes again and looked at Eadred, who sat next to her listening intently to Asser's proclamation. He smiled warmly and squeezed her hand.

"And if anyone accuses a king's thane of manslaughter, if he dares to clear himself he is to do it with twelve king's thanes. If anyone accuses a man who is of lesser degree than a king's thane, he is to clear himself with eleven of his equals and with one king's thane. And so in every suit which involves more than four mancuses; and if he dare not clear himself, he is to pay for it with threefold compensation, according to its valuation."

Sigli stood in the stern of his longship docked on the edge of the Thames, his leg propped up on one of the bulwarks, only half listening to Asser's decree. It was hard to hear from this distance, but he had wanted it that way; it would have been far too difficult to be in the square and contend with the sight of Eadred sitting beside her. He was not yet ready to confront that, nor did he know that he ever would be. He had rushed blindly to her a week ago, willing to brave any risk or threat of discovery, knowing full well what the consequences would be.

It had been worth it. He loved her more than ever now and would do anything to be with her. But as he looked over the heads of Dagmar and the other Vikings aboard his flagship on the Thames, he felt helpless, like a ship floating free with no rudder to guide it.

He suddenly wished that he could be far, far away.

"And that each man is to know his warrantor for men and for horses and for oxen."

How peaceful the moment of truth actually is, Alfred thought to himself. He sat perched on a makeshift throne, overlooking the Thames and the masses gathered here on this day. He had always thought his emotions would be beyond the bounds of control when London finally became his, but now it was all happening quietly, as though it were a foregone conclusion that everyone had always known would come to pass. Easter Sunday, indeed. In a sense he, too, had risen from the dead—or at least the ashes of his own ruin—and come to realize the promises of his forefathers, of Ethelwulf and Egbert before him.

His eyes drifted to Eadred and Aethelfled, and it contented him to know the wedding would now take place in early June, appeasing Ealswith and cementing the alliance with Mercia. But it was an alliance in name only, just as his alliance with the Vikings was nothing more than pomp and ceremony, done with a grand flourish merely for the sake of diplomacy and social order. He was lord of all before him. Not a man in all of Britain could now dispute that.

He glanced to either side of him, where Ealswith and Guthrum sat. They both nodded their respects, and he smiled to himself, the smile of a satisfied man

who knows that he has won. He turned his attention back to Asser as the monk
concluded the formal portion of the treaty.

*"And we swear that no slaves nor freemen might go
over to the Danelaw without permission, any more than any
of the Vikings may come to us. If, however, it happens that
from necessity any one of them wishes to have traffic with
us, or we with them, for cattle and for goods, it is to be
permitted on this condition: that hostages shall be given as a
pledge of peace and as evidence whereby it is known that no
fraud is intended. So it shall be written on this day under
King Alfred of the Saxons, in the Year of Our Lord, 886."*

Asser rolled up the parchment in his hand and stepped back toward the
platform upon which the king and his immediate entourage were seated. There
was a moment of silence, punctuated only by a soft rustling among the crowd, and
then all eyes were drawn to a lone figure who leaped atop the low wall drawn
along the Thames and drew his broadsword, raising it high for all to see.

"Friends! Saxons and Vikings!" Penda shouted, his voice carrying across
the open expanse. "I give you peace! I give you order! I give you a king among
men, born to greatness!" Here he turned, and his eyes met those of Alfred's. He
smiled fiercely, and he thrust his sword toward the heavens.

"I give you Bretwalda!"

The crowd erupted into a roar. The men assembled drew their swords as
one and raised them into the air, shaking them so that the sun reflected off the
naked blades in a thousand glimmering points of light. Through it all Alfred sat
there silently, like a great rock nestled against the sea, taking in the rolling wave of
emotion that now, finally, washed over him. For one, shining moment, everything
in him was whole and complete. He felt as good as a man can possibly feel.

He was the Chosen One. The King of Britain.

Bretwalda.

CHAPTER XI: Iscariot Speaks

"The sun no longer shows
His face; and treason sows
His secret seeds that no man can detect;
Fathers by their children are undone;
The brother would the brother cheat;
And the cowled monk is a deceit."
—Walther Von Der Vogelwilde,
Millennium

Darkness, fog and drizzle. Any one of the three would have been difficult enough for Plegmund to contend with; together, they slowed his progress to a crawl. The forest, recently in bloom, faded into the gathering gloom as the mist crept in from the south and swirled through the oaks. What had been clear and crisp was now indistinct. The day had been mild enough, but as the still of the evening set in, the darkness and the mist and the light rain conspired to obscure all. It was enough to sink the spirits of even the best of men.

Such was the monk's plight on this late April evening as he rode through the forest, bound for Twyneham Harbor and one last rendezvous with Sigli. He cursed the poor planning that had delayed his start. He had left Winchester late in the day, and now he was paying the price, rushing to find the banks of the Avon before the elements closed in. He pulled his cloak around him to ward off the chill, straining his eyes to stay on the path. He would have thought himself capable of navigating the road to Twyneham in his sleep, so many times had he made the journey, but now he was unsure of himself. Within moments it would be too dark and misty to continue, and he would be lost.

But then he saw it through the gloaming, so low along the ground that even the fog could not obscure it. The river! He breathed a sigh of relief as he drew closer to its marshy bank, and then he turned his horse to the south, toward the sea. Within a few moments the twilight became virtually impenetrable, but it no longer mattered. He knew if he kept the Avon hard on his right it would lead him close by the Viking burh that Sigli had built overlooking the harbor. There would be a roof over his head tonight after all.

His mind drifted to other things; unlike the weather, they were issues that would not soon pass. Part of him had not wanted to come. He had fought against Aethelfled, refusing her more than once, but she had insisted that it really would be the last rendezvous, and something in her eyes told him that this time she finally meant it. For his own good, he knew that the less he saw of Sigli, the better. It was just another temptation that could only lead him astray.

He was a desperate man whose life was falling down all around him, and he did not know where to turn. The events at London had convinced him once and for all that Grimwald was right. It was true; Asser was Alfred's chosen one. In less than a year the newcomer from Wales had wedged himself firmly under the king's wing, succeeding at every turn and building a barrier that no other churchman could hope to breach. Choosing to chronicle Alfred's life had been a brilliant stroke. Asser was the darling of the court, and with old Aethelred largely confined to his bed, he had now become the obvious heir to Canterbury.

Merely thinking about it turned Plegmund's stomach. He knew it was beyond him to change anything, beyond even the devious Grimwald to alter God's will. He had stood by and watched helplessly as his influence waned, and now the last threads were unraveling before his eyes. Devoid of Canterbury, life somehow did not seem worth living.

He rode into the fog for the next hour, pushing his horse to cover the distance and escape the weather, when suddenly the ground beneath him turned to sand. Within a few more yards the sound of waves lapping lightly at the shore confirmed his suspicions; he had ridden too far. How could he have missed the burh? It occurred to him that the rain would have extinguished any torches the Danes might have lit along the walls—assuming a fire could even pierce the gloom over the harbor. He turned his horse around and to the left, urging it forward as the rain came down harder.

He debated whether to cry out in the hope that someone would hear him. But then he looked up, and there before him the low walls of the burh emerged from the fogbank. He rode beneath the palisade, inching along it slowly until he came to the main gate. It was closed. No one was stirring about. He drew his cloak closer around him to ward off the weather, and then he cupped his hands around his mouth and shouted up into the darkness.

"Hal—l—l—ooo!!"

Silence.

"Hal-l-l-ooo!! Is anyone about? Open the gates!"

A voice rang out in the Viking tongue. "Who goes there?!"

"It's Plegmund!" He spoke in Danish. "I've come from Winchester to see Sigli!"

A low grumble slipped over the wall, and then the sky above the burh was dimly illuminated by the light from a single torch. He could hear the man cursing under his breath as he struggled to negotiate the distance through the mud to the gate. The Viking reached the barrier and fumbled at the latch for a moment, and then the gate swung open, leaving Plegmund face to face with one of Sigli's men.

"What are you doing out on a night like this?"

"I got off late. I was slowed down by the weather."

The Viking waved at the darkness. "You're lucky you don't have to sleep somewhere out there tonight."

He motioned for Plegmund to follow and turned toward a building that rose up, taller than any other structure, in the middle of the burh. "Your timing's good. We killed a deer this morning. Can you smell it?"

"Yes. I can almost taste it."

The monk looked around the inside of the burh in the dim torchlight. The enclosure was no more than fifty yards on a side, with walls ten feet high and a number of small huts wedged together surrounding the hall. They walked across the mud to the door of the main building and the Viking guard opened it, releasing a tide of warmth, noise and light that poured out to greet them.

"It's the monk, Plegmund!"

Sigli was in the process of devouring a steaming piece of venison at the far end of the table. He dropped the meat onto his plate and stood up, grease dripping from his fingers.

"Plegmund! Welcome! There's plenty of meat and mead...come warm yourself by the fire!"

Had there not been a fire in the room, Sigli's presence would have been more than enough to dry the monk's robes and raise his spirits. He moved quickly toward his friend, stepping out of his wet cloak as the others settled back into their conversations.

"Well? Well...??!!" Sigli leaned forward.

"Well, what?" Plegmund rubbed his hands and sat down, looking around the room for the meat platter. It irritated him that she was all the Viking could think about.

"Surely you didn't ride all that way in this weather just to visit me, now, did you?"

That would have been more than reason enough, Plegmund thought to himself.

"Really now, Sigli...you could at least let me catch my breath, and have a sip or two of mead, no?"

Sigli snapped his fingers impatiently. One of the Vikings passed a cup filled with the thick liquid over to them, followed by a plate with several pieces of meat on it. Plegmund stuffed some of the venison into his mouth, chewing away gratefully and washing it all down with a long gulp of mead. Not very dainty, perhaps, but when one ate with the barbarians, one might as well eat like them.

"You're trying my patience, Plegmund! What did she say...?!"

It pleased the monk to actually have power over someone else for once. He savored the moment, stretching it out for as long as he could.

"The evening of the first of May, next week." He looked around just to ensure that no one was listening. "At the deserted tanner's hut near Winchester, the one we talked about before you were summoned to London."

"I know where it is."

"Be there by dusk. She can't stay too late."

Sigli's eyes drifted off. He was so easy to read, Plegmund thought, so direct.

"This is it, you know," he said. "This will be the last time."

"There is no last time. There's no such thing. It doesn't end—not just like that. It will live on." He shook his head wistfully and turned his full attention back to the monk. "But never mind that for now. It's late, and I'm tired."

"Where shall I stay?"

"You can sleep here in the hall if you want, or you can stay with me. I've got an extra bed in my hut."

Later that night Plegmund stretched out on his back, staring into the night. They had retired hours ago, but he was unable to sleep; there was too much going through his mind. The steady drumbeat of the rain on the roof failed to provide any rhythm to his thoughts. He turned his head and looked across the room toward the dim outline of Sigli's body, but it was too dark to see anything.

No matter—he did not need eyes. The sound of heavy breathing told him that the Viking was fast asleep. He sighed to himself and sat up in bed. Reaching for the tinderbox from a nearby table, he struck a match and lit a wax-encrusted candle that soon bathed the chamber in a soft half-light. Now Sigli's profile came into full view—the noble cut of the brow, the robust health that fairly burst from every pore. Plegmund sat there motionlessly for several minutes, mesmerized by the gentle rising and falling of the Viking's chest with each breath.

At last he rose to his feet and crossed the room, sitting gingerly on the edge of Sigli's bed and staring down into his face. He reached out to touch the Viking, but thought better of it. Instead, he passed his hand lightly over his own groin, his misgivings falling away in the face of the heat that tingled through him. He knew he was venturing into dangerous waters, but he did not care. If he could not have Sigli, if Canterbury was beyond his grasp, at least he could have this moment, and the forbidden pleasure that it promised.

And then Sigli's eyes opened.

"Wh...what's going on here?"

Plegmund stiffened, fumbling to remove his hands from himself. "I was...I couldn't get to sleep." His face flushed, and he began to sweat.

"What's wrong?" Sigli sat up in bed and reached out to him. "Are you all right?"

"I...I don't know." Plegmund shuddered involuntarily, wringing his hands.

"You're trembling. Are you ill?"

"No, no...I..." He could not control himself, and began to weep.

"It's the strain we've put you through, isn't it? We never should have involved you in all this!"

"It's not that. It's...it's..." He could not say the words.

"What? What is it?"

"Oh, Sigli..." Plegmund sobbed. Breaking down, he suddenly threw himself into the Viking's arms. "Would that I were made of stone, and could bury these...these feelings, this...this curse!"

"What are you talking about?"

"About *my* secret. The one I've kept shamefully to myself these many years."

A sudden rush of emotion surged through him, obliterating the last barrier between his inhibitions and the truth. He sat back and looked into Sigli's eyes, and the words poured from him in a great release.

"I love you, Sigli! I love you!"

Sigli was stunned.

"There! I said it! All this time, watching you and Aethelfled together, wanting desperately to take her place, to be held and loved by you..." He paused, his voice choking from the strain. "God and the Church be damned! That's the way I feel!"

Now Sigli understood. He thought himself to be in some sort of dream, perhaps, but the trembling man in his arms told him otherwise. And then his disbelief turned to an involuntary revulsion. He dropped his arms and pushed himself away from Plegmund, and then he swung his legs to the floor and stood up, backing away from the bed.

"Sigli, no! You musn't...! You, you...."

Plegmund's voice trailed off as he sank to the earth on his knees, arms raised, clawing at the distance that separated them. His heart boiled up, and as he fought through the tears his folly became clear to him, so painfully clear, filling him with the greatest sense of shame he had ever known. He jumped to his feet and ran to the door, bursting out into the dark, rainy night before Sigli could stop him. He raced through the fog, through the open gate of the burh, and out into the unknown. He tried to run faster, but he stumbled and fell hard, landing on the drenched earth. As he lay there, the misery of it all overwhelmed him completely, and he pressed his forehead into the mud and began to sob.

The rain beat down in stinging pellets upon his back for what seemed an eternity. But gradually his senses returned to him, and as they did the instinct to preserve his miserable existence gained strength. He rose to his knees in the mud and sat back on his haunches, staring vacantly into the gloomy mist.

The night was dark and dangerous. *He* was dangerous; yes, he knew that now. And in that moment a strange sense of clarity came upon him, something cold and hard from within that had been released with all his other repressed emotions on this stormy night, something that he had never before dared to contemplate or consider.

As the fog closed in on him, he set his jaw and made up his mind. He knew now what must be done. What he had to do.

He knew.

*   *   *   *   *

Alfred was already bored. Only a few weeks had passed since the fall of London, and now the long, arduous process of codifying the law had begun. It was an administrative challenge rather than a creative one, and while he was an astute manager, he preferred working on a conceptual level. He was a thinking man first.

The last week had been more taxing than he ever could have imagined; long hours spent debating the merits of every proposed law, working daily with his ealdormen to define every last detail. At first he had led the discussions, but gradually he stepped to the rear and allowed his nobles to take the floor, followed by a slow succession of thanes and ceorls. It ensured that the common people had a voice, but it ran counter to his natural inclination to move forward quickly and get things done.

"Here's my proposal then," proclaimed Ceolmund, standing alone in the middle of the open floor. "If anyone fights in the house of a ceorl, he's to pay six shillings compensation to the ceorl. If he draws a weapon and doesn't fight, it should be half as much."

"Wait, wait," Penda interrupted. "No action, no crime. You can't penalize a man for what he hasn't done."

"Hasn't done? Unsheathing a sword in another man's house is a serious offense. There's intent involved."

"But what if the perpetrator is the ceorl's lord? What then?" asked Anared of Dorset.

Ceolmund rubbed his chin. "You have a point."

"Compensation should be due if he fights. But if he merely draws his weapon...."

"Let's not forget the motivations involved," said another voice. "Where do we establish the boundaries of just cause?"

And so it went, on and on, hour after hour. Tedious work, but necessary. The laws of the land were poorly documented, and the changes throughout Wessex over the last fifty years cried out for legislation. All of Christian England was now under the rule of one king. Not since Alfred's grandfather Egbert had laid claim to Bretwalda some sixty years before had such a situation existed, and even then his sovereignty had been all too brief, compromised by the first serious Viking invasions. With Mercia independent in name only and the Danelaw little more than a vassal state in the shadow of Alfred's newly centralized power, the time had come to lay down the law for all to understand and obey.

That was where the problems started. For many years the concept of Saxon law had been grounded in the notion of the wergild, a system whereby dependents with cause or complaint were compensated monetarily for damages. The wergild had been instituted as a measure to prevent blood feuds that had caused an undue share of death and social disorder over the years. But while the system had largely been successful, it left much to be desired; all too often crimes were committed with no precedent to guide the sentencing. The adoption of a primitive jury system of peers had proved adequate for determining guilt or innocence, but the penalty structure was all too fragile to sustain a satisfactory outcome in many legal matters.

And so every crime of consequence had to be defined, along with its specific wergild. How much should a man be compensated for the loss of a limb, as opposed to a simple blow to the head? What should his family receive if he is killed? Rendered a cripple? Distilling these abstractions into a structure based on silver and gold was an enormous task that required patience and meticulous attention to detail. It was a formidable process further complicated by matters of class and culture. By any measure it was tedious and plodding, like a lame horse.

Unable to contain himself any longer, Alfred rose and walked over to a window that overlooked the courtyard; immediately the room behind him fell silent. He turned around and saw that all eyes were trained on him.

"Don't mind me," he said with a wave of his hand. "I'm still listening."

Some of the time at least, he thought to himself.

The discussion picked up again. Outside, the rain that had been falling for several days had finally stopped, but he could see a low mist beginning to creep into the river valley, blanketing the earth in a cloak of gray. Maybe it was the weather that was depressing him. He turned back toward the room and his eyes fell on the row of churchmen who sat along the far side. Plegmund was among them. The king noticed in the waning daylight that the Mercian monk looked uncommonly pale and drawn, that perhaps the fellow had been working too hard and needed a rest.

His eyes drifted further along the row, to where Asser and John the Old Saxon sat paying close attention to the proceedings. Asser in particular had exceeded his expectations; it delighted him that the young Welshman had undertaken the writing of his biography, and in all other respects the monk had proved to be an exemplary addition to the court. He had already made up his mind to appoint him as Aethelred's successor in Canterbury when the old man finally passed away.

And then his eyes came to rest on Grimwald. As if on cue, the disagreeable Winchester looked at him sullenly before turning away.

Alfred harbored few regrets from the early years of his reign, but Grimwald was clearly one of them. He had granted the monk far more power than he ever should have, and he and the Church had been paying for the mistake ever since. He knew the Bishop of Winchester hated him, but he didn't care; with a bit more effort, perhaps he would be able to remove him entirely from the complicated matrix of church and state in Wessex.

He shifted his attention back to the rest of the room and discovered that he and Grimwald were not the only ones who had become bored by the ongoing debate. Edward yawned conspicuously. Old Guthrum, meanwhile, had fallen fast asleep, his lower lip vibrating lightly with each intake of breath.

Alfred suppressed a smile, turning away again to stare out the window. As he watched the mist thickening along the banks of the river, his attention was drawn to a lone horse and rider who cantered across the courtyard, heading for the city gate and the open countryside beyond.

He immediately recognized the cloaked figure as Aethelfled. How strange she would be going out at this late hour, with the weather closing in. But he had learned long ago not to question his daughter's independence; she had willingly agreed to take Eadred as a husband next month, and that was more than enough to satisfy him. As he watched her spur her chestnut mare into a gallop, he realized he had not spent much time with her over the past few months. He would have to change that, especially now that she would soon be leaving his house forever.

"Well, then, if one should fight in the house of a six-hundred man, then the compensation is to amount to three times the compensation due to a ceorl," Ceolmund's voice droned on in the background. "And if this should happen to a twelve-hundred man, then the compensation should double again."

He turned suddenly toward the window where the king stood. "What do you think, Lord Alfred?"

The sound of his name snapped the king back to his senses. "What's that, Ceolmund? My mind had wandered."

"My recommendation, Sire, is to triple the wergild of a ceorl in the case of what is due a six-hundred man when someone fights in his house. And to double that again in the case of a twelve hundred man. And then, I think, we should adjourn for supper."

"An excellent idea!" the king trumpeted enthusiastically, stepping back toward the center of attention. "An excellent idea, indeed!"

*   *   *   *   *

Aethelfled's spirits were low as she left Winchester and rode upstream along the River Itchen toward the tanner's hut. She longed to see Sigli, but she dreaded what had to be done. She had carefully rehearsed what she would tell him, anticipating every objection, but no matter what scenario she envisioned, the result was always the same—heartbreak and despair. Plegmund had been right; the Viking would never accept it.

Was there any other choice? She had been weak and indecisive for not ending it sooner, and she felt an overwhelming sense of guilt for allowing things to come so far. Not for her own feelings, for she was strong and would manage; *he* was the one she worried about. He was not the kind of man who could simply turn away and wash his heart and mind of the affair. How could she ever forgive herself for hurting him?

She passed by a cluster of huts that housed the ceorls who worked the nearby fields. Although it would not be dark for at least an hour, the fog was heavy enough to shield her on this final journey, and everyone had retired indoors to escape the light drizzle that misted down from the skies. The weather had closed in to where it would have been difficult to find the tanner's hut had she not known the way. She panicked for a moment, suddenly wondering if perhaps Sigli might have gotten lost; such a misfortune would only postpone the inevitable one more time. But as she rounded a bend in the river and emerged from the bank of trees that sheltered the hut, her fears were allayed. There was the hovel. And there was his horse, tethered outside.

She rode up to the door and dismounted, but before she could enter the hut he appeared on the threshold, his eyes shining, and he took her in his arms and covered her face with kisses.

"I was afraid, my love," he panted, pausing long enough to speak. "I was afraid you wouldn't come."

"Nothing could have stopped me."

"It's happened before. Your father, perhaps, or..."

"I'm here tonight. Just for you."

He smiled the smile of love and swept her up into his arms, carrying her across the threshold and inside the hut. The single room was bare except for a pile of straw in one corner; he headed right for it, sinking down onto his knees and nestling her gently atop the makeshift bed. She could see his eagerness in the dim light shed by a candle that he had placed a few feet away on the floor, and she let him consume her and have his way. It was her way also. She clutched him tightly, wanting to make this last time the best time, the most perfect of all, wanting to always remember the way it felt and make him hers forever.

When it was over she stroked the back of his head and held him close to her.

"I love you, Sigli."

He kissed her, and then he pulled himself away and rose to his knees. For the first time, she felt alone, and a shudder passed through her body. He offered to cover her with his cloak, but she shook her head, and he knew instantly that something was wrong. He started to speak, but held back. Instead, he stood up and put his leggings on, and then he walked across the room to the single window, his back gleaming in the candlelight.

"I know how you feel. I know it's difficult. But I can't live without you."

She had put her dress back on by now, and she sat upright in the straw. "Oh, Sigli...Sigli, can't you see? We've run out of time!"

He whirled around. "Never! I won't give you up!"

She stood up, unsure of herself but determined to see it through. "You have no choice! Nor do I!" She stepped forward tentatively. "We can't go on anymore, Sigli! I've been trying to find the courage to say this to you for weeks. Don't make it harder than it already is..."

She weakened, and he bounded across the room to her, grabbing her by the arms and searching her eyes. "You don't mean that! You love me...I know you do!"

"Of course I love you, but..."

"Then nothing else matters! Nothing!" He squeezed her tightly. "Oh, Aethelfled...we were made for each other! You musn't talk of such foolishness, ever again!"

She pulled away from him. "Sigli, listen to me! In one month I'm to be married to Eadred. Nothing can prevent that. He'll take me to live with him in Mercia, and I'll be gone forever!"

"I'll follow you!"

She rolled her eyes. "Oh, will you? And what would you do, hide in some hovel for months on end, hoping to see me? Or would you expect me to sneak away at night, and somehow keep it all from my husband?"

"I can't allow that to happen! I...I...you can't do this!"

"I'm the daughter of the king, Sigli! I'm bound by the laws of my forefathers, of generation upon generation of Saxons before me! No matter what happens, I must live up to my duty!"

He stood there and stared at her, and then the words she dreaded to hear slipped from his lips. "Then your duty is more important to you than our love?"

She looked away for a moment, and when her eyes met his again he became aware of a tangible distance between them. It was as though someone else stood before him now instead of the woman he loved. He spoke again, but more tentatively than before.

"Aethelfled, answer me. Is your duty more important to you than I am?"

She looked through him, and her heart broke as she said it.

"Yes."

He clenched his fists and struggled to control himself. "All right, then! Go to your Mercian! Lick his hand like a faithful lapdog! Go on...go to him!" He raged about the room, back and forth, and then he stormed over to the door and yanked it open.

"Go on! Leave! You've used me up..now, leave me!"

She buried her face in her hands and began to sob. "Oh, Sigli...! Sigli, no! Don't!""

Go on! Go!"

"Sigli, I...I love you! Don't say those things...!"

He breathed heavily, and then all the indignation began to leak out of him, until there was nothing left. He looked at her evenly, trying to retain his dignity.

"You'd better leave now."

She removed her hands from her face, shaken by his sudden calm, and for the first time it really hit home that it was over. They were done. She ran to him and threw herself into his arms, but she might as well have rested her head on the chest of a stone statue.

"I love you! I'll love you forever!" she cried fiercely.

She grabbed his face in both her hands and kissed him hard, almost hurtfully, on the lips. She pulled back to look at him one more time, and then she tore herself away and ran through the door, looking for her chestnut mare. She swung herself onto the horse and kicked it hard, galloping off without looking back.

Sigli stood alone outside the hovel. As she receded into the distance he broke down and began to weep. He leaned against the door and cried, feeling as though he could die then and there, and he let his emotions carry him away. He had never, ever cried so hard in his life.

Several long minutes passed until, finally spent, he wiped his face and stepped back into the hovel. He gathered up his cloak and blew out the candle, and then he closed the door behind him and swung himself up onto his mount. Casting a last look around, he turned his horse in the opposite direction from Winchester and rode off into the darkness.

The night was quiet again. But the old owl that had stayed in his nest waiting for them to leave did not venture forth. Neither did the fox, nor the stoat, nor the other creatures of the night. They all waited patiently, until the other intruder, the heavy one with the foul human smell, led his horse out of the thicket alongside the tanner's hut. They watched from their hiding places, as he had watched from his, and had they been able to study his face they would have seen a great, leering smile of triumph, so complete that it threatened to illuminate the night.

Grimwald laughed low to himself. He turned and placed his foot in one of the gleaming silver stirrups that hung decorously from its saddle and proceeded to drag himself laboriously up onto his horse. Breathing heavily, he turned the animal back toward Winchester and began to ride slowly along the river, until finally his large, baggy form dissolved into the mist.

*   *   *   *   *

Alfred looked at the stack of parchments piled on the writing table and let out a long sigh. It would take days to sort through the mess and restore order to the affairs of state that now demanded his attention. In the euphoria following the unification of England, he had overlooked the vast workload that lay ahead of him, and his preoccupation with the lawmaking process had further diverted him from the daily responsibilities of running a kingdom.

Where to begin? At least a dozen land disputes among the thanes of Berkshire stared him in the face. There were the plans for the latest series of burhs to be fortified along the south coast. Border issues between Christian England and the Danelaw had to be resolved. And then there was the wedding, now only a month away.

And so he had come to his dayroom on this bright May morning, determined to seal himself off from the world for a few hours and tend to a few things. Soon enough, it would be over. One year, maybe two, and the deluge of details that confronted him would be sorted out. All laws would be set, all disputes settled, all delicate issues put to rest and assimilated into the grand scheme that he had first dreamed of some fifteen years earlier when he had become king.

And then, after all was fixed in place, he would finally be able to turn his attention to his real interest in life, the translations of the great Latin classics.

He reached out for the topmost parchment on the table and unrolled it. He spread the document out before him and was just about to begin reading it when a knock on the chamber door interrupted him.

"What is it?"

The door opened and a manservant entered. "Excuse me, my Lord, but it's Grimwald. He requests an audience."

"I'm busy now. I don't have time to see him."

"He claims it's urgent, my Lord. He says it can't wait."

Alfred sat back in his chair and threw up his hands. "God help me, that I should be a slave to so many masters!" He waved his hand impatiently at the manservant.

"Very well, then. Show him in. But I don't intend to see anyone else today. Tell them whatever you have to...tell them I'm hunting, if you must. But no one else is to bother me...do you understand?"

The man nodded and left the room. Alfred turned his attention back to the parchment, not bothering to look up when the sound of shuffling feet and closing doors told him that Winchester had entered the chamber. He remained buried indifferently in the manuscript, making no attempt to hide his displeasure at being interrupted.

And yet, Grimwald did not speak. A full twenty seconds went by. Irritated by this show of gamesmanship, Alfred shuffled the parchment absentmindedly and finally looked up. The expression of mild amusement on the overripe pumpkin that was the bishop's face annoyed him even more.

"Well...? What is it, then?"

"Excuse me, my Lord," Grimwald began, purring sweetly out of the side of his mouth. "I know your time is valuable. I would hate to compromise it."

"You already have. What do you want?"

The monk smiled. "Oh, it's not what *I* want, my Lord." He turned toward the window and began to walk idly toward it. "Rather...it's more about what *you* want."

The arrogance of the man astounded Alfred. "This isn't about the minster here in Winchester, is it? We've already discussed that."

"Oh, it's that. But it's more. Much, much more."

"You're wasting my time. Speak plainly."

The monk moved in front of the window and then turned back to Alfred, his enormous bulk blocking much of the light from entering the room.

"I have some...information, shall we say. Something that may be of great interest to you, I would suspect. In fact, I imagine it would be of great interest to many people, come to think of it."

"Namely?"

"It pertains to your daughter."

"Aethelfled?"

"Yes, Aethelfled. England's jewel, and Eadred's prize. And a fine one at that, even if some of the luster is lost."

Alfred grew wary. "What are you talking about?"

"Just this, my Lord...just this. The bloom is off the rose, I'm afraid. Your lovely daughter has been, shall we say...compromised?"

Alfred leaned forward, gripping hard at the pommels of his chair. "What's the meaning of this, man??!!"

Grimwald's eyes gleamed with excitement. "I saw her myself! I saw it all with my own eyes! Aethelfled has taken a lover, Alfred!"

The king exploded to his feet, clenching his fists. "Insolent wretch! Liar!! I'll have your tongue ripped out for this!"

"I speak the truth, Alfred. Believe me."

"Prove it!"

"I followed her the other night. It was foggy, and she couldn't see me. She rode upriver, to a deserted hut—the one the old tanner used to live in, remember him?" He nodded soberly. "That was where she met him."

"Who? Who are you talking about?"

Grimwald eyed the king evenly, reveling in the moment. "It's the Viking, my Lord. *Your* Viking."

Alfred's brow clouded over in disbelief.

"I told you years ago that no good would come of him. I warned you."

Alfred began to tremble. He swept his arm across the table, knocking most of the parchments to the floor and sending them clattering across the stone surface in all directions. He proceeded to kick them about the room, thrashing this way and that like a madman, until finally he spent himself and stood there, shaking his head.

"It's...it's impossible! Absolutely unthinkable!"

"Unthinkable, but true."

"I'll have his head! And I'll make an example of her, for all to see!"

"I don't think that would be very wise, my Lord. To see everything you've worked so hard for ruined in the blink of an eye, well..." Grimwald left the sentence hanging. "Don't forget...the scandal hasn't been exposed to the public. Not yet, at least."

"What are you saying?"

"Simply this. Do as you wish with Sigli, but don't call the marriage off. No one needs to know the truth."

"What about Eadred? Surely, he'll protest!"

Grimwald smiled. "And cut himself off from the reins of power? I don't think so. He'll swallow his pride and keep his mouth shut. Mark my words."

Alfred's eyes narrowed. He walked up to Grimwald, invading his space and studying him carefully. "Surely you're not telling me all this out of the goodness of your heart. What do you want?"

"Ah...so perceptive, even in this most difficult of moments," the monk chuckled lightly, his eyes crinkling into slits. "You'll agree, I'm sure, that knowledge of this sort is highly valuable. The good news is that the secret is safe with me—provided, of course, you meet my conditions."

Here his face grew hard, and he looked directly into Alfred's eyes. "Because if you don't, as God is my witness, I'll ruin you, your house, your kingdom and your future!"

"Traitor! That's blackmail!!"

"Such an unsavory term," Grimwald murmured, backing away from the king and casually examining his manicured fingernails. "I prefer to think of it as insurance...for both of us. A man must protect his interests, after all."

"You presume too much. Don't think yourself safe from me!"

"Really, now," the monk smirked. "You disappoint me with such vulgar threats." He began to pace idly about the room.

"Do you think me such a fool to expose myself so thoughtlessly? If anything should happen to me, there are documents—duplicates, in fact, all hidden away in separate, safe places. They'll be recovered by my designates, their seals broken, and their shared secrets spread to a waiting world."

He stopped in his tracks, and his eyes laughed at the king. "You really have no choice, my Lord. You must deal with me. On my terms."

The thought of it made Alfred sick. But he gathered himself together and spoke slowly.

"Name your conditions."

"First of all, the restoration of all my previous rights, both formal and unspoken. That means I'm to be consulted on all ecclesiastical matters, and have the final word on behalf of the Church. All appointments, all decisions—all must have my consent. And all expenditures are to be under my jurisdiction, starting with the long-promised minster here at Winchester."

"You would bleed me dry!"

"Not so, not so. In terms of the Church, I'm more interested in power than money. As for myself, however...well, that's another matter. There are some lands that I fancy to the east, on the edge of the Weald. Grant me that estate, along with three hundred pieces of gold a year for my own coffers, and my lips shall remain forever sealed."

"And what guarantee do I have of that?"

"My life truly wouldn't be worth much if the secret were out. But neither of us wants that, of course."

"You disgust me, Grimwald...everything about you! I should have banished you and your treachery long ago!"

"But you didn't, did you?" The bishop smiled in triumph. "Yes, my Lord, you've pushed me farther and farther away from the light for years, but that's over now. I've returned. But I'm a reasonable man, after all. Meet my terms, and I'll consider our account settled."

Alfred was powerless to refuse. His lower lip quivered, and his nostrils flared as he spoke.

"All right, then! I consent. But don't push me too far, or I'll wring your worthless neck myself, and drag you down to Hell with me!"

"One final thing," Grimwald replied, ignoring him. "Just so we fully understand each other. When I said I wanted the right of approval in all ecclesiastical appointments, I meant *all*. That means when old Aethelred dies—as he surely will before long—I shall be the one who names his successor at Canterbury."

"Under no circumstances could I ever allow you to sit in that position!"

Grimwald laughed in amusement. "Really now...you underestimate me, my Lord. I have no desire at all for the post; too much work, and far too much visibility. No, I would prefer to remain behind the drawn curtain, to enjoy my prosperity in peace. Call it power without presence, if you will. But understand one thing: I'll name the next Archbishop, and it certainly won't be your pet Asser!"

"Get out of my sight!" Alfred screamed, pointing toward the door. "Leave me at once, or by God, I'll cut you in half!"

"Are we agreed then?"

Alfred had never felt this way before, not in any battle nor any conversation, not even in the hard months of exile at Athelney so many years ago. And never before had he been so thoroughly beaten, so utterly incapable of commanding his own destiny. He swallowed and looked hard at Grimwald, vowing that someday, somehow, the monk would pay.

"We're agreed. Now leave me at once."

Grimwald bowed lightly and turned for the door. Even from behind, Alfred could see in his mind's eye the leering grin of triumph on the monk's face as he departed and closed the door.

Alone again, he slumped back against the table amidst the carnage of parchments strewn about the room. *Aethelfled, my Aethelfled, why have your forsaken me?* The thought burned through him. And so he did the only thing he could think of to release the pain, the only thing that might restore some order to his universe. He began picking up the parchments, one by one, as though he could put everything back together the way it had all been before. He stacked them all neatly on the table, not stopping until he had picked up every last one, and then he walked over to the window and looked up into the morning sun.

It was then, and only then, that he buried his face in his hands and wept.

*　　*　　*　　*　　*

"My lady looks so beautiful. As fresh as a spring flower, ready to be plucked."

Magda the handmaiden smiled approvingly and watched as Alfred's eldest daughter sat brushing her hair in front of her mirror. The girl had been ill for several days, her spirits as low as Magda had ever seen them, but now the worst seemed over. It had been the strangest affliction; there had been no fever or obvious physical disorder that could be diagnosed and treated. There had only been a listless depression, marked by hours and hours of sleep. But now Aethelfled was finally back on her feet again and showing signs of recovery, making Magda feel better and opening her eyes again to the future. Perhaps now they could get on with planning the wedding.

"Poor health hasn't bothered your hair any," she said admiringly as she straightened things up in Aethelfled's chamber. The late afternoon sunlight invaded the room, bouncing off the girl's auburn tresses. "I've never seen it so full-bodied and alive."

Aethelfled smiled. Finally. "Oh, Magda...you always say such nice things. What would I do without you?"

"You'll find out soon enough. One more month, and my little baby will be gone forever."

She saw the reflection of Aethelfled's eyes in the mirror, and knew immediately that she had said the wrong thing. The girl's shoulders sagged perceptibly.

"Oh, there, there..." Magda murmured, walking over to her charge and stroking her hair. "I'll come visit you in Mercia whenever you want."

Aethelfled turned around in her seat and hugged the old woman, wrapping her arms around Magda's familiar midriff.

"I'm scared, Magda. I don't know if I can go through with this."

"Nonsense. There's nothing to worry about." She continued to stroke Aethelfled's head. "It's perfectly natural for a young woman to feel that way before her wedding."

Aethelfled said nothing. She remained there in her nurse's arms, not wanting to let go.

"You've much to look forward to, my Lady."

"My Lady. It sounds so strange when you call me that."

"But you *are* a lady now. A woman, in every sense of the word."

In more ways than even Magda knew, Aethelfled thought. She pulled back from the old maidservant and smiled bravely.

"I'm going to miss you very much."

"And I'll miss you, my dove. Remember how I used to call you that?" Magda smiled and removed herself gently from the embrace. "So very long ago. But enough of that—be happy, and make Eadred the envy of every man in England. Your mother left yesterday, you know, to meet with the Mercians and plan the wedding. She's a bundle of nerves these days, poor woman." She shook her head and returned to her duties. "Meanwhile, I've got to attend to your things...I'll be back shortly."

She loaded her arms with a bundle of nightclothes and disappeared from the room, leaving the door slightly ajar behind her.

Aethelfled turned around on the stool and resumed brushing her hair, relieving it of every snag and rough spot, grateful to be alone again. The past few days had been brutal. There seemed to be no hope in this heartbreak, no relief to the crushing weight and hurt she was feeling in the wake of her final meeting with Sigli three nights ago. Time would be the only answer. It would have to be.

And so she had begun the slow healing process, putting on her bravest face and trying her best to look ahead. She belonged to England now, to the future. As she brushed her hair she felt better, as though she could comb out her old habits and cleanse herself for the new life that lay ahead. She would have to be patient and allow her emotions to collect themselves, to return again to the way things had been before. It would not be easy, but at least it was a start.

Her thoughts were interrupted by the sound of a creaking door behind her. Assuming that Magda had returned, she spoke without bothering to turn around. "So...when will Mother be back?"

There was no answer. She shifted in her seat. "Magda...? What do you...?"

She stopped abruptly. Her father stood there in the doorway, his face pale and gaunt. But his eyes were on fire, and the heat in them filled her with alarm. She rose slowly.

"What is it, Father? What's wrong?"

He moved into the chamber and closed the door behind him, never once removing his eyes from her. And yet he said nothing. He just stood there, staring at her.

"Why do you look at me like that?" She was standing on the threshold of her worst nightmare. "What have I done?"

"You know very well what you've done!" he finally said, his voice escaping in a hiss from behind drawn lips. "You've shamed me, your mother, and your people. You've dishonored everything I stand for!"

She dropped her brush onto the floor and stood there, terrified. "How could you??!!"

He stamped his foot on the stone floor and bristled with a raw fury. "You defy the laws of decency! To willfully give yourself away, out of wedlock like this!"

He began to pace back and forth, never taking his eyes off her. "You sin against the Church, and against the throne! You mock the good name of Eadred, the man who is—who was, for all I know now—to become your husband!" He stopped and eyed her coldly.

"And you defiled yourself with...with him! With a heathen!"

Her pride overcame her fear. She looked hard at him for a moment and then blurted out her feelings.

"I love him, Father!"

"Love??!! Love??? What does love have to do with it??!!" He threw his arms up into the air. "You're the daughter of a king, foolish girl! You'll learn to love the man you're given to, when you're given to him! But no....not you! Instead, you drag the House of Wessex through the mud, carrying on like a common whore!"

"That's not the way it was! That's not the way it was at all!"

"Oh?? And what do you call it, rooting away on the floor of a deserted hovel like an animal?"

"Father...please!"

"You were seen, Aethelfled!"

"By whom?"

"By Grimwald!!"

The name slammed into her with a dull thud. Plegmund had warned them about the treacherous Winchester, but they had ignored him. And now it was too late.

"Grimwald, you say? And who else?" She caught her breath in fear.

"No one, that I know of. But Grimwald is enough. You're going to cost me a fortune with that man! I must pay dearly to keep him silent!"

It was enough to send Alfred spiraling out of control once again. "How could you...? How could you, with one of them?? A Viking!"

"I told you. I love him." She was suddenly calm, now that all had been revealed. "I'll marry Eadred, or anybody else you want me to marry. But I love Sigli, Father. Nothing can change that."

"You've deceived me! You've made a fool of me!"

"Only of myself."

"Your senseless lust has compromised our house!"

"My senseless lust?" She became indignant. "And what about you, Father? I've heard the stories. I've heard about your dalliances with other women, about the consorts you keep. You're no better than I am, after all!"

He struck her hard in the face with his open hand, knocking her to the ground. She looked up at him with fear, guilt and loathing in her eyes, and he felt his fingers beginning to tremble. He had never hit her before. Edward, many times—but never her. A wave of sadness washed over him, but he did not allow those softer feelings to deter him. Instead, he looked down impassively at her as she lay there on the floor in the light of the afternoon sun, a thin trickle of blood on the corner of her lips.

"Understand this: you'll be married to Eadred, and soon! I'm moving the wedding up, as early as next week. How you choose to tell him about all this is your affair, but I intend to say nothing. Not to him, or anybody else. Your wretched secret is safe with me."

Another thought crossed her mind, the only thought that mattered now. "What about Sigli? What will you do to him?"

"I haven't decided yet. He probably should be put to death."

"You can't even think about that!"

"He defiled my flesh! A heathen, even thinking about such an outrage!"

He served you well! He gave you years and years of his life, building your ships, standing by your side! It's not his fault...it...it was mine!"

"This is how he repays my generosity!"

"He saved your life once...have you forgotten? And don't tell me you didn't use him, for your own designs!"

Inwardly, Alfred cringed. It was true enough; he *had* used Sigli. He had lied to him, keeping him building ships while living in a prison of deception, just another mere playing piece in the grand game of state. And now it had all turned for the worse. The bad seed had taken root, infecting his precious daughter and choking him with his own self-serving designs.

She dragged herself over to him and clutched at his leg. "Blame me! Hate me, if you must! But spare him...please! If you don't, by God, I won't marry Eadred! I swear it!"

"Don't threaten me, girl...I don't know what I'll do!"

He breathed heavily, knowing that he had wronged the man in the eyes of God, and that it was all coming back to him. But he was still overcome by his anger.

"No matter what, you're never to see him again! Never! Now let go of me before I hurt you again! It could never be one tenth the hurt and harm you do to me!"

He pulled himself violently away from her and staggered out through the open door, slamming it in his wake. She watched him leave, unable to move, until finally it overwhelmed her and she burst into tears. She buried her face in her arms and remained there on the floor, sobbing uncontrollably, needing someone to turn to. And then she thought of him, her closest confidant, the one man who knew the whole bitter story.

She had not seen Plegmund since he had gone to Twyneham to arrange the final rendezvous with Sigli, but she was almost certain he was in Winchester. He simply had to be. She rose to her feet and collected herself, wiping the tears from her face and the blood from her lip, and then she raced through the corridors of the estate house until she found herself in front of his chamber. She knocked sharply on the thick door.

"Who is it?" The voice sounded distant and hollow, as though it came from the bottom of a deep well.

"It's Aethelfled."

There was a moment's pause. "I'm not feeling well. Could you come another time?"

"I must see you, Plegmund! It's urgent!"

More silence, and then finally an answer. "Come in."

She pushed the door open and entered the room. Plegmund sat at a table by the window, poring over several parchments that were unrolled before him. He was pale and drawn, with two baggy circles perched beneath his washed-out eyes. He looked as though he had not slept or eaten for days, and his normally thin face was stretched tightly against his skull, giving him the appearance of a much older man.

She did not notice. Instead, she ran to him and threw herself at his feet, burying her face in his lap.

"It's over, Plegmund! Father knows! We've been discovered!"

He looked out the window and off into the distance. Reaching out with his hand, he stroked the back of her head as she cried in his lap, and then he let out a long, quivering sigh.

"It was only a matter of time. We all knew it would happen, my Lady."

"What will I do, Plegmund? My life is over."

"Your life is just beginning."

"I've dishonored my family, betrayed my father," she went on, ignoring him. "And I've broken the heart of the only man I'll ever love...."

"Had I not consented to help you both, this never would have happened." He shook his head sadly. "I've been preparing for this moment ever since you first took up with him. I share your grief. But you must go on, and put it all behind you. In time, your father will forget and forgive."

She wiped her eyes and stood up, gathering herself and staring out across the countryside through the open window. It seemed odd that the sun would be shining at such a hopeless moment, but there it was, glistening in the afternoon sky like a magnificent jewel. It felt like the end of the world—but the world still existed, oblivious to her grief, going about its business as though nothing at all had happened. It made her feel even more alone now.

"What am I to do, Plegmund?"

"What you were born to do, my Lady."

She turned and walked toward the door, pausing just before she opened it. "You're right, Plegmund. It's over. But I'll marry Eadred as an act of duty, not of penance. I'll never feel sorry for what I did…what we did. Never. And if that path leads to Hell itself, then so be it."

She slipped out of the chamber and closed the door.

It was only then that he looked up, his eyes filled with regret, and as he sat there alone he began to tremble. And then he buried his face into his hands and began to sob, his shoulders shaking from the strain.

My God, my God, what have I done?

He cried for a while, until his tears were drained, and then he finally stood up from the table and moved toward the far corner of the room, pulling his robe back from his shoulders as he walked. The sun was low in the sky, but its last rays penetrated the room, illuminating his back and the angry red scars upon it. He reached behind a drawn curtain and withdrew a bundle of thorns that was tied together at one end, its thistles fanning out in a long, menacing sweep at the other. He raised the lash before him, closed his eyes, and began the ritual he had been following every day without fail since he had spoken to Grimwald, bringing the thorns hard over his opposite shoulder and onto his unprotected back.

Swish, thwack, grunt. Swish, thwack, grunt. The pain came in waves, but it wasn't enough; no amount of self-flagellation could ease his guilt. He was a part of their agony, feeling the remorse of his decision, condemned to face himself and what he had done. Judas lives, he thought. Iscariot speaks.

Swish, thwack, grunt. The sun went down, plunging the chamber into a darkness so deep that not even a thousand candles could have illuminated the path to salvation.

*   *   *   *   *

It had been a long day in the saddle, but Sigli didn't care. He was going back to Winchester, back to her, and the thought of it enabled him to shrug off the fatigue and press onward. He did not know why he had been summoned, or why Alfred had sent an armed escort all the way to Twyneham to accompany him. It did not matter. He would have walked every last step of the way just to be near her, with or without an invitation; that the king himself had sent for him was merely another sign that her path and his were still intertwined.

He had not been able to erase her from his mind, no matter what had been said and done. She had told him it was over, but he didn't believe it for even a moment. All he could think about was how to change the inevitable and convince her to fly away with him. He was not given easily to defeat under any circumstances, and he could not see simply turning his back on the woman he loved without at least mounting one, final effort to somehow win her hand. He had resolved to do something about it—if not now, then soon—before the Mercian Eadred laid claim to her and took her away from him forever.

As the mounted party thundered out of the forest and into the Itchen valley, he could see Winchester rising before him. There was hope in that fair city, embellished by the scent of late spring in full bloom. For the moment his heart felt light, uplifted by the possibilities. The last remaining mile evaporated beneath their hooves, and soon he and the party of Saxons rode through the gates of the city. No one was there to greet them except for a few stable boys who rushed out of the shadows to attend to the sweaty mounts; perhaps the court was dining in the main hall. There had to be a compelling reason for his summons, because every time he had requested they stop to rest the Saxon in charge had insisted they press on, riding even harder. Why the hurry? If Alfred thought it was that important, he would have been in the courtyard now to meet them, instead of the eerie silence that greeted him.

It was then that Penda emerged from the gathering darkness. Alfred's watchdog, Sigli thought to himself—that alone was enough to make him uneasy. Even after these many years, he did not feel comfortable with the ealdorman of Devon, and as he dismounted there was nothing in the Saxon's manner to suggest those feelings might suddenly change.

"The king awaits you in his chambers," Penda said brusquely. "He'll see you immediately." He turned to the mounted escort. "You can wash and have something to eat inside, but don't stray too far. You'll be riding off on fresh mounts before long."

"What's this all about? Why the sudden hurry?"

"I have no idea, Viking. You can ask the king for yourself." Penda turned toward a side door in the estate house and motioned for Sigli to follow. "He's been pacing about his room all day, so it must be something important."

Sigli knew better than to try to force a conversation with the austere Saxon; instead, he followed in silence, watching the man's shoulders roll from side to side as he strode through the halls of the estate house. They finally mounted a stone stairway that led to a corridor at the end of which there was a single door, guarded by two men who stood in the flickering torchlight. Penda nodded and pushed past them, opening the door and standing to one side. He motioned to Sigli to enter the room first. The Viking did so and turned to speak when, to his surprise, Penda closed the door behind him, leaving him all alone in the chamber.

And alone he was, for there was no sign of Alfred. He looked around the room, noticing the parchments that were stacked high on several tables and thinking what a long way the king had come since their days of exile in Athelney. It suddenly made him feel proud to have been there and taken part in the building of a kingdom during a time when many of even the most loyal Saxons had given up hope and abandoned Wessex. He smiled as he sat down in Alfred's great chair, running his fingers along its smooth arm and remembering the wrath of old Ingewold when the king had burned her cakes. Only eight years had passed since those days; in his mind it might as well have happened a lifetime ago.

He failed to notice a movement of the curtain at the rear of the room, nor did he see Alfred step silently into the chamber. The king watched him without speaking for several moments, until Sigli finally raised his head. The shock of realizing he was not alone jolted him from the throne.

"My Lord...you startled me." Embarrassed, he rose quickly from the chair. "Excuse me for taking your seat."

Alfred glowered back at him. "Would that it were all of mine you presumed to take."

"Sire?" It was hard for Sigli to see Alfred in the dim candlelight, but he could feel the tension.

"I laid a kingdom at your feet, Viking," Alfred said, drawing closer. "I gave you life, I gave you purpose. And now you stain my house and name with this...this barbarous treason!"

"My Lord, I...I don't understand..."

Alfred brought his fist crashing down upon the table before him. "Wretched ingrate! Don't presume your innocence, after all that you've done!" His face was hard and edged with a steely resolve. "You laid with my daughter, as though she were some common scullery maid, and then you have the cheek to suggest ignorance...?"

It took Sigli's breath away. He stepped backward, his face flushed, and his heart began to pound wildly.

"Ah, yes...there it is, in your face! The truth comes out! I should separate your head from your shoulders now, and be done with it!"

And now, exposed, Sigli tightened his jaw, stood tall, and told the truth. "I love her, Alfred. I love her more than life itself."

"Then be prepared to forfeit your life!"

"Do what you will with me. I'd die gladly for her!"

"How could you do this? How could you even think about such treachery?"

Sigli took a deep breath. "The only betrayal would have been to my heart, my Lord. And to Aethelfled's. Never once have I conspired against you. I've served you these years, with never a thought for my own desires."

"Until now!"

"Until now. We were made for each other, Alfred. By Odin, I..."

"Silence! Don't insult me, or invoke the name of your pagan gods!"

Alfred's eyes narrowed, and he took a step forward. "Now listen to me, Viking. You've built me ships, a mighty fleet. You've fought by my side, and stood by me during the dark times. And you've saved my life, probably more than once. But all that's behind us now. What you and my daughter have done cannot be tolerated. It defies my laws, and those of God. Were you any other man, in any other circumstance, I'd have you put to death!"

"I have nothing left to live for."

"Then I'd end it now, but I can't allow that kind of attention to be brought on you. There must be no questions asked. That, and Aethelfled's pleas on your behalf, compels me to spare your miserable existence. But I banish you from England forever! If anyone asks, they'll be told you left of your own accord. And if you dare to ever set foot on these shores again, I'll hunt you down and hang you. Do you understand me?"

Sigli remained silent.

"You may take one—and only one—of the longships at Twyneham. And take your Vikings with you; they've been a thorn in my side, with all their carrying on over the years. If they choose not to go with you, then they'll be escorted to the Danelaw by armed guards and delivered over to Guthrum. The choice is theirs. In any case, you have three days to set sail. If you're still on English soil by sundown on Saturday, as God is my witness I'll have you put to death, no matter what kind of stir it causes!"

With that he averted his eyes and turned away. "The guards outside my door have been instructed to deliver you back to the escort. You're to ride to Twyneham immediately, without delay. Now leave me...and God help you if I ever set eyes on your face again!"

"Alfred, I..."

"Go at once!" the king commanded, clenching the fingers of one hand into a white-knuckled fist. "Before I change my mind!"

There was nothing left to say. Sigli took a deep breath and turned away, and then he began the long, lonely walk across the room. Without looking back, he pushed the door open and took the final step across the threshold, walking out of the chamber and into the night, out of Alfred's sight and into exile.

*   *   *   *   *

"Dominus vobiscum. Et cum spiritu tuo."

Grimwald smiled as the evening mass droned on in the background. It was all coming together so perfectly; tonight would add the last delicious touches to a triumph that was almost complete. It was turning out to be a brilliant coup, a resolution that was all the sweeter in light of the years of struggle that had preceded this final, unforeseen turn of events. He had persevered and won, and the look on Alfred's face had said everything. He had never seen the king so defeated and heartbroken.

For now, there was one final piece of business to wrap up, the last link in the chain that would truly crown his triumph. His eyes wandered across the darkened sacristy, discarding all other distractions until they came to rest on the profile of Plegmund as he knelt in rapt attention. It was the first time Grimwald had seen the reclusive monk since the confession; at last, the game was afoot again.

He smiled to himself. They all start out that way, burdened with remorse and riddled with guilt at the thought of what they've done. At first even the most venial sin takes on the specter of something much greater. But the sinning gets easier, and gradually a man learns that lightning will not strike him dead every time he strays from God's will, until even the most mortal of sins becomes venial, and all becomes lost.

That was the way of personal power and profit. He did not give a second thought to the consequences of such an apparent fall from grace, for he no longer believed in God. And because of that disbelief, he had no particular issue with guilt nor conscience, no concern for any of the excess baggage that weighed down most men. An opportunist cannot afford such weaknesses. An opportunist cannot wait.

He rose from his knees and moved to the center aisle, genuflecting while facing the altar and then walking between the ranks of holy men and acolytes assembled in Winchester for the evening mass. Pausing at the rear of the darkened chapel, he sidled up to a young page standing by and whispered in the boy's ear.

"Do me a service. Tell Plegmund that I wish to see him immediately in my chamber."

He left the chapel and made his way down the corridors of the estate house until he reached his room, which he had decorated with the finest of tapestries and comforts imported from the continent. He had never forgotten the time he had spent as a young man in Rome; it was a place that understood the trappings of power like no other and knew how to use them to best effect. Winchester paled in comparison to the glory of the Vatican, and if nothing else he was determined to remind himself of the way things could have been—indeed, the way they now might be—by recreating the opulence of Rome within his own four walls.

He stepped over to the open window and looked outside, where the green of the countryside had taken on a grayish hue now that the sun had disappeared over the horizon. He stepped back into the chamber and lit the candles spread around the room, bathing the walls in a soft, comforting light. Ambience was everything, considering the delicate task that lay ahead. He started to arrange the curtains to his liking when he was interrupted by a sharp knock. He walked over to the door and opened it, consciously twisting his mouth into a wide, generous smile.

"Ah, Plegmund...I'm so glad you're here. Do come in."

The monk stepped past him and walked over to the table in the center of the room, where he stood stiffly with his arms at his sides.

"Please...sit down," Grimwald continued, motioning to a large, stately chair. He sat himself down nearby, close enough to afford intimacy, far enough to avoid discomfort.

"I'm surprised I haven't seen you since our last discussion. I would have thought you'd be keenly interested in the details."

"I haven't felt well. I've stayed in bed."

"You certainly don't look to be in good health. A bit of fever, perhaps?"

"A fever in my soul, Grimwald. I've had second thoughts."

"About Canterbury...?"

"No, not about Canterbury. About what I've done to gain it."

Grimwald shook his head and laughed softly. "My dear boy, don't be foolish. Every end has its means."

"Including betrayal?" Plegmund's face was deathly pale in the candlelight.

"Don't torture yourself. You did the right thing. It was only a matter of time before the secret was revealed, and it would have been far worse later on. By speaking up when you did, you prevented a major scandal."

"That's not why I spoke up, Grimwald. You know that."

Grimwald rose to his feet and gestured to the room at large. "So you had an ulterior motive? Why not? There's nothing wrong in profiting from the affair—which you certainly couldn't have done if someone else had discovered the truth first."

"That doesn't make things any easier. I've had to face myself these last few days, and I haven't liked what I've seen."

"Get used to it, man. You made a decision; now you have to live with it. There's no turning back."

Plegmund sat staring glumly into the corners of the room, until finally a sigh escaped his lips. "Very well, Grimwald...as you will. So tell me, then: is Canterbury mine?"

"Yes, of course. Provided you cooperate..."

Plegmund's brow creased with sudden suspicion. "What do you mean?"

"Well, you see...it's a very complex matter," Grimwald said, running his fingers idly across the tabletop as he paced slowly back and forth. "I had to be careful with Alfred. I didn't want him to suspect the identities of anyone else involved in the agreement."

"So you didn't discuss Canterbury?"

"Now, now...I didn't say that," Grimwald smiled. "It was part of the bargain. In return for my silence, Alfred gave me the right to name Aethelred's sucessor at Canterbury when the old man dies. That was the extent of it."

Plegmund leaped to his feet in anger. "That's no guarantee! What's to prevent you from naming someone else when the time comes?"

"Ah, you're so perceptive. I like that. You'll go far in this world, Plegmund." He moved closer and reached out for the young monk. "Which is why you must continue to cooperate with me."

"What more do you want, Grimwald? What can I give you that I haven't already...?"

But he knew the answer as soon as the words escaped his lips. He knew it by the way Grimwald smoothed his robes, by the lascivious look on his face, dripping with desire. Stunned, he took a step backward.

"Yes, I see. You do understand. I've asked for your friendship and favors these many years, and you've refused me at every turn. Now I require something more, something intimate."

"Never! Never could I sink to such a base level!"

"Oh, couldn't you now?" Winchester sneered. "It seems to me you already have. You've played your hand, Plegmund. And unless you meet my conditions, you risk losing all, with nothing to show for it."

He paused for effect. "The choice is yours."

"You disgust me."

"You disgust yourself, foolish boy! You've already sold your soul; your body may as well follow!"

"Oh, what a foul, foul thing this is," Plegmund moaned, his shoulders trembling lightly. "You deceive me...as you deceive everyone!"

"No, Plegmund. I merely protect my interests, and profit accordingly. But come," Grimwald beckoned, his voice sweet and low, "treat me well, and you'll prosper. You're young, and strong. Let me feel that strength..."

This was everything Plegmund had feared, his worst nightmares come to life. How naive he had been, to think that he could outfox the fox himself. And now he was caught in the jaws of an iron trap, like a frightened beast forced to gnaw away at its own leg to keep the dream of freedom alive. Would he give up the limb? Or would he merely give up, and risk losing everything?

But he had already made the decision long before this moment. Grimwald was right; he had come too far to turn back now. He maintained his steady stare into Grimwald's eyes, until finally he turned away from the light and loosened his robe, allowing it to slide from his shoulders. It fell to the cold, stone floor in a disheveled heap, revealing all.

*   *   *   *   *

Dagmar stood at the water's edge at Twyneham harbor, looking out over the sea and taking in the last sunset he would ever see at the place that had been his home for almost eight years. The single longship had been loaded with provisions, and all was ready to set sail with the dawn's first light. Where they would go, he did not know; Sigli's dark mood had discouraged any discussions about the matter, and it was anyone's guess if he had even thought about setting a course. But they were all going with him, every last man among the Vikings who lived at Twyneham, for it was clear they were no longer welcome in Wessex.

Dagmar did not know exactly why this sudden banishment had come to pass, but like the rest of the Vikings in Twyneham he had his suspicions. No one ever talked much about Sigli's frequent absences over the past six months, but they all assumed they had something to do with this latest crisis. His moods had swung wildly between two extremes—long periods of dark depression, broken by sudden, intense turns of what could only be described as euphoria.

Dagmar knew it was best that they were going away, the farther the better, for there was something in England that was eating away at his friend. He checked the ship one more time to make sure all preparations were in order, and then he started back for the burh, trudging across the beach. He was just about to pass through the gates of the enclosure when a movement along the edge of the forest caught his eye; looking up, he spotted a rider emerging from the trees.

It was Edward.

He waited until the king's son rode up to him, and then he bowed respectfully. "My Lord...what would you of me?"

"I've come to see Sigli. Where is he?"

"He sits brooding in his chamber, waiting to set sail tomorrow."

"Tell him I want to see him."

Edward dismounted from his horse as Dagmar bowed and left. He smoothed the sand idly underfoot, turning to look at the harbor and the sea beyond. A light breeze blew in from the water, and for a moment he wished that he were sailing tomorrow, bound for some mysterious adventure to an unknown, distant shore. But that was impossible, and would always be so; his life and responsibilities lay before him.

As he pondered these things, a sixth sense suddenly told him he was no longer alone; turning around, he found himself face to face with Sigli. The Viking was standing just outside the gates of the burh, watching him silently. They looked at each other for a moment, neither man smiling, neither knowing what to say, until Sigli finally spoke.

"So, you've come to finish your father's business? You know about everything?"

"Yes, I do."

"Then you must hate me. You must hate me very much."

"I don't hate you. I hate what's happened to you...and to Aethelfled."

"I love her, Edward. You must understand that."

"I understand one thing. You'll be leaving England forever, and taking your secret with you. It's over now...no one else can ever know."

"So you came all the way from Winchester just to tell me that?"

Edward kicked at the sand, and suddenly all the anger he had been holding in exploded.

"How could you let this happen??!! How could you do such a thing, with all that's at stake?"

"I told you. I love her."

"If you loved her, you never would have put her through this!"

"Damn it, Edward!" She loves me, too!" Sigli threw his hands up and started to pace back and forth across the beach. "I'd give anything...anything in this world, just to see her one more time!"

Now that he was in the presence of his friend, it was clear to Edward that Sigli meant everything he said. It made him feel better; he knew he had done the right thing in coming. He pursed his lips and spoke softly.

"She's here, Sigli."

"Here...? What do you mean?"

"She's waiting in the forest. She's...wait, not yet!" He reached out and restrained the Viking, who had already started for the trees. "You can't go now...not while it's still light. No one else must know. I'll bring her to your quarters after dark."

Sigli was stunned. "Why are you doing this?"

"Because she asked me to. And because I...." Edward looked away awkwardly for a moment, and then his eyes swung back, dancing around Sigli before finally coming to rest on him.

"You've been like a brother to me, Sigli. And as for Aethelfled...well, we've always been as close as a brother and sister could be. I was heartbroken when I first heard the news. I was angry at both of you for allowing it to happen, furious, really. But then, when I thought about it, about you, about what my sister is being forced to do against her will...."

He stopped, finding it difficult to continue, but then the words spilled out of him. "I wish I could do something to change all this, to somehow grant you Aethelfled's hand!"

They stared at each other for a moment, and then the space between them evaporated. They embraced each other, and then Sigli clapped Edward on his back and pulled away, measuring the young prince at arm's length.

"Say it isn't so. Say it can still happen..."

Edward looked down at the damp sand. "You know better than that. It's over. Tonight you can see each other one last time. I suppose it's due to you, for better or worse...at least that's the way I see it. That's why I consented to do this. But after tonight no man in England has the power to save you, Sigli. You must leave. And she must marry Eadred. Nothing can change that."

Sigli smiled in spite of it all, even as his heart was breaking. "Edward... I owe you my eternal thanks, and the promise that I'll always remain true to you and your house. For as I'm a man of honor, and truth, I swear that all I've done has been done out of love. If that's a crime, then so be it! I'm guilty of loving too much, and too long."

"I'll return after dark...with her. And I'll see you off in the morning. But as God is my witness, Sigli, you'll someday return to Wessex! When I'm king of this land, years from now, I'll rescind my father's command! I swear it!"

They clasped hands, and then Edward mounted his horse and rode slowly off toward the dark line of trees at the edge of the forest.

Within two hours the night had set in. Sigli sat on the edge of his bed, staring out through the open door and into the darkness, filled with anticipation. He felt the same disorientation and sense of living in a vacuum of time and space that he had experienced during the fall of Halfsfiord nine years ago. Two episodes in his life: one forever to be left unresolved, the other resolved for him before its time. His family was long dead, his memories of them dimmed by the years. Only his failure to find Sidroc and revenge his father's house had remained to him from those days, like a wound that would not heal. And then that wound had been compounded by a new one, every bit as painful, every bit as permanent.

He had lived for nothing but revenge until a year ago, and then for nothing but love since; both had betrayed him.

His eyes strained to pierce the gloom outside the door, and in that moment he mercifully saw a bit of heaven, the last rose in the vanishing garden of his promised land.

There she stood, framed by the doorway, as the light from the single candle in his room illuminated all of her exquisite perfection. She was a vision of clarity and light, and all he could do was look at her mutely and try to capture the moment for all time. She stood there silently as well, taking every bit of him in, until finally they both stepped together into the center of the room and embraced each other.

"What's become of us?" he said finally.

"What we always knew would. It never could have really ended, not until someone else put a stop to it."

"It never will end. Not for me."

She loved him now more than ever. "Nor for me. Not in my heart. But our course is set...we can't change that."

He moved over to the door of the hut, closing it to ward off the night, and then he turned back to her. "It was dangerous for you to come."

"My father went to London; I felt I could do it. I had to."

"But why did you enlist Edward? Why not Plegmund?"

She sat down on the edge of the bed. "Plegmund didn't want anything more to do with it. He's crushed...he feels as though he was responsible. As for Edward, he found out from my father. He came to me, as angry as I've ever seen him. But when I told him everything...how I was determined to see you one more time even if I had to do it alone, he agreed to escort me."

He moved to the bed and sat down next to her. "So when will you marry Eadred?"

"In less than two weeks," she said painfully. "Father ordered it."

"And how will you explain everything to...to your husband?"

"He'll never know. I'll never tell him."

"But...how can you possibly...you're not a virgin, after all."

"I'm a horsewoman. Hard riding can have the same effect, you know. But that doesn't matter," she said, holding her head high. "He won't ask. If he suspects anything, he wouldn't want to find out the answer. More than me, he needs my father. The marriage will give him that."

She winced. "Let's not talk about it any more. I came tonight for you, to be with you one more time. And to tell you that I'll always love you."

He looked at her in the candlelight, realizing once again how beautiful she was. "A year ago, I wanted to leave England more than anything. And now I can't bear the thought."

Her face grew sad. "Where will you go, my love?"

"East, at first. After that, I don't know."

She reached over to him and grabbed him gently by the chin, pulling his face toward her. "Oh, Sigli...Sigli. I'll never love another like I've loved you."

He slipped his arm around her waist and pulled her to him, and she came easily, without reservation. He kissed her and she kissed him back, and they embarked on their last voyage together. In the heart of darkness there shone a light that surrounded them and protected them, and for once they took their time with each other, without fear or guilt. They made love until the first faint glimmer of dawn broke through, until they could love no more. And then, exhausted, they fell asleep in each other's arms, naked and innocent to a world that had betrayed them.

He awoke first and looked at her for long minutes as she lay there, beautiful in slumber, and he did not have the heart to rouse her and force himself to say goodbye. It was simply too much to bear. He lingered there for a while until finally he pulled himself away, dragging himself out into the sunlight and on into the future.

They were all waiting for him at the ship, even Edward. He walked across the beach and embraced the prince a final time, and then he pulled himself over the bulwark and on board the largest, finest dragon ship he had ever built. For it was indeed a dragon ship, outfitted with a Viking prow; he and his men had long ago fashioned it in anticipation of this day. Several of the Danes put their backs to the stern and shoved the bark away from the shore, jumping on board as the others sank their oars into the water and propelled the craft out into the middle of the harbor. The men amidships raised the lone, rectangular sail, which filled immediately with a favoring wind that pushed them toward the sea.

Sigli stood in the stern, his eyes fixed on the shore. He watched as Edward's form diminished on the beach, receding into the distance with each minute. And then he saw another figure join the prince on the shore, and he knew it was her. He raised himself to his full height in the morning sun, and he waved his arms back and forth. He saw her doing the same, but she became smaller, ever smaller, until finally the ship rounded the spit at the harbor mouth, and she was gone.

He slumped down at the tiller and stared ahead into the horizon. It was done. Over. And all that was left to him was the restless motion of the dragon ship's hull beating itself against the sea.

* * * * *

And so a great scandal was averted as Sigli sailed far away, disappearing into the great northern sea.

Ten days later all of Christian England turned out for the wedding of Aethelfled and Eadred, and there was great rejoicing as Wessex and Mercia were finally joined. Nobody celebrated more heartily than Eadred, who was already well in his cups by mid-evening when he finally escorted Aethelfled to their bridal chambers. He plowed her with wild abandon, a happy man, and even had he been sober he might not have noticed her fallen maidenhead, so great was his lust.

Freed for the first time from the constant burden of worldly affairs, Alfred turned to his translations, setting the monks of England to work and even trying his own hand at the Latin classics. The age of learning took root. Amidst that learning Grimwald prospered, to the dismay of churchmen and nobles alike. At the powerful Winchester's urging, Alfred sent Plegmund to Canterbury to attend to old Aethelred as the old man's health continued to decline. Within two years he would be dead, and Plegmund would be anointed the nineteenth Archbishop of Canterbury at the tender age of thirty-four.

It was a tender age all around, with peace and prosperity settling in on the land. The realm was secure, the harvest was good, and hope was in abundance. And then in early February of 887, not even nine full months after the wedding, all of England rejoiced at the news that the Lady Aethelfled of Mercia had given birth to a baby girl. The child was exceedingly fair, more so even than her mother, with rich blonde hair and eyes so blue they shamed the sky on a brilliant summer's day.

She was the pride of her grandfather Alfred and the fruit of the land, a symbol of all that was right in England. She was the tie that binds.

They named her Elfwyn.

892 A.D.

CHAPTER XII: Old One Eye

"'Tis all a checkerboard of nights and days,
Where Destiny with men for pieces plays:
Hither and thither moves, and mates, and slays,
And one by one back in the closet lays.
—Edward Fitzgerald, <u>The Rubaiyat</u>
<u>of Omar Khayam</u>

"Shake the ice from your bones, Aelfric. If that's the way you move when you chase after Edith, you'll never catch her."

The others chuckled at old Edmund's humor, but Aelfric was not amused. It all seemed like such a ridiculous waste of time. Romney Marsh was probably the last place on earth that would ever come under attack, and yet here they were on a balmy mid-November day, building a burh while their workloads continued to pile up in the fields. Winter would soon be here, and there was much to be done.

"You're wrong, Uncle," Aelfric replied. "I've already caught her."

And so he had. Edith was a rather plain girl, but she was enough for him; beautiful women were not among the things a ceorl of rural Kent could hope for. They lived in a world where everyone worked hard, from dawn until dusk, six days a week with only the Sabbath for rest. And the work took its toll, turning a young girl into a matron well before her time. Perhaps there were genteel women somewhere in England, with unlined faces and smooth hands, but they were not to be found here.

"Then you won't keep her long, boy," Edmund scolded, shaking his head. "If we don't finish this work by Yuletide, we'll be hearing about it. Fulric will skin us alive."

There was a general grumbling, but all of them knew better than to protest. Better to save their energy for other things. They were men of the earth, and only a few of them had ever been outside the borders of Kent. Their village, Appledore, was far removed from the halls of power in Wessex, tucked away some twenty miles southeast of Canterbury on the edge of the Weald. The village rose up from the banks of the Limen, a sluggish stream that crept out of the Weald and emptied into the marshland south of the village, from where it meandered into the sea just a few miles away.

The ceorls tilled their fields in anonymity, ignorant of the greater world around them and more than happy to keep it that way. But they were not oblivious to the change in their lives; like all of Christian England, they were grateful for the order Alfred had brought to the land. It was now 892, six years since the king had annexed London, and Vikings had not been seen in force throughout Wessex for the better part of a generation. Kent had not felt the heathen hand for almost thirty years, and it had been even longer for the people of Appledore and Romney Marsh. Even Edmund had been too young to remember anything more than the stories.

And yet the men slaved away, sweating in the unseasonably warm weather as they built an unmanned fortress to ward off an unseen enemy. The burh was located on the edge of the marsh a mile and a half south of Appledore, at the tip of a thin promontory surrounded on three sides by the Limen. The single landward approach led up into the forest, hiding the earthworks from view as the river wound its way through the marsh and toward the sea. Less than twenty of them labored today while the other ceorls of Appledore worked the fields and gathered provisions for winter. The log they were moving was long and cumbersome, and it took all their efforts to mount it in place atop the low wall that fronted the river. With a final heave of their shoulders, they wedged the long timber into place.

"You men there, nail her in place. The others, mix us up some mortar." Edmund breathed heavily as he looked around him. "And Aelfric...grab the axe and cut us another big oak from the forest."

Aelfric picked up the long-handled axe and started for the trees. At least he'd be out of sight, free from his uncle's watchful eye.

"You'll have to go deeper into the wood, up to the grove we looked at this morning," Edmund called after him. "They're the only trees big enough to make the span. Do you hear me, now?"

Aelfric waved his hand over his head without looking back, annoyed at being told the obvious. That was just the way it was when your uncle was the village elder. Someday it would be his role, he thought, as he trudged through the low underbrush and into the wood. He breathed in deeply as he climbed the gentle incline and worked his way through the rotting autumn leaves that covered the ground. Soon the bare, spiny limbs of the trees enveloped him, and he quickly found himself out of sight and sound of the burh.

Within a few moments he came to the grove his uncle had talked about. Yes, there was one, a tall oak that would do the job. He walked up to it and set himself, and he swung the axe in a long arc behind his head, bringing it hard across his body until it embedded itself in the trunk of the tree. The impact was hard. It felt good, and so he threw himself into the work, taking satisfaction as chunks and slivers of bark flew in every direction.

But the oak was large, and would take time. The sweat spread across his back as he labored steadily for the next fifteen minutes until, drained of energy, he let the axe drop to his side and stood there breathing heavily. By God, there was still more than half the tree to go! He slumped down to the ground and leaned his back against the oak.

To hell with Edmund. He needed to rest.

He looked through the trees and over the marshland to the south as the sweat cooled against his body. The grove where he sat commanded an expansive view of the bog and the river, which meandered by him several hundred yards away through the sedge and rushes. He could smell the sea, obscured by the tangled marsh that led off into the low November sun. Ah, what a day it was. His thoughts turned to Edith, and her warm arms that would be reaching for him when the day was done. He could barely wait until spring, when they would be married and finally free to lie together under the same roof. She would bear him strong sons, that he knew. And in a few years he would have his own land— several hides, if he was lucky—and the right to sit at his uncle's councils. There was much to anticipate.

He closed his eyes as a comforting breeze drifted across his face, and he let the sun soak into him as he leaned against the oak. It felt good to steal these few moments of rest. Against his better judgement, he kept his eyes closed, and he allowed himself to slip into a rhythm of regular breathing. It all felt so pleasant, so warm, until the light rustling of the branches above him faded into the background and he fell asleep.

He awoke with a start. He had no idea how long he had napped, but his attention was drawn to a series of strange noises coming from the river. He shook the sleep from his eyes and looked through the trees. He saw nothing. It was time to get back to the burh. He stretched his arms. He brushed himself off and started to get up from the ground.

And then he froze.

There before his eyes, drifting suspended some ten feet above the river, a gleaming, carved dragon's head floated across his view. It glided through the trees and underbrush, its baleful eye seemingly trained on him. He heard the sound of oars scraping against bulwarks, and with it the guttural, incomprehensible tangle of men speaking in a foreign tongue. He crept behind the trunk of the great oak and peered cautiously to the south, and to his horror all suddenly became clear.

The Limen was clogged with a line of Viking ships that stretched as far as he could see, their masts bare like the autumn trees as they inched up the river toward the burh.

He had to warn the others. He crawled away, scurrying across the ground until he had backed down the incline and was safely out of view. Grabbing his axe, he scrambled to his feet and hurried back toward the burh, warding off the branches that whipped into his face as he ran through the forest. Each step seemed to take an eternity. He pushed himself forward until, looking ahead, he recognized a familiar low brace of underbrush, around which the trail bent down to the burh some fifty yards below on the promontory. Knowing they could now hear him, he filled his lungs and prepared to cry out.

But God stayed his breath and saved his life. For as he reached the bend in the trees, Aelfric skidded to a stop, and he swallowed the cry in his throat.

He was too late.

All around the burh, the Limen was clogged with a single file of dragonships, stem wedged against stern in the narrow stream. He crouched down behind a low, thick bush and watched in stunned silence. He could see a half dozen vessels surrounding the fort, sails and oars drawn, each carrying around fifty fighting men. A score of Vikings stood atop or inside the halfhearted walls, raising their swords in celebration. What must have been a short and decisive struggle was now over; the floor of the fort was covered with bloody bodies, several of which still writhed in their death throes. Almost all of them were Saxon ceorls. His friends. Boys he had grown to manhood with, played with in the fields.

My God, my God...how can this be? In that moment the sounds of the world faded away, replaced by an all-consuming emptiness. His eye was drawn to Udric, one of his closest friends. What was left of the poor fellow now lay arched back against the wall, spread-eagled with outstretched arms, looking sightlessly up toward heaven. His chest was bathed in a sticky, wet crimson splash.

Couldn't they have escaped? Wouldn't they have seen the masts in time? And then his eye wandered off to the side, distracted by a piece of woolen tunic that had been ripped off and had caught on a nearby branch. *Lord Jesus, they came through here. They snuck through the trees and surprised us.*

Fear overcame him. He looked over his shoulder, half expecting to see a band of Vikings descending upon him from the trees. *They passed right by me. Right over me.*

The sweat dripped from him. His breath escaped his body in gulps, and it was all he could do to force himself to raise his eyes again and look back through the underbrush toward the burh.

Suddenly a group of the Danes clustered together in a corner of the fort turned toward him, and in their midst there stood a man whose hands were bound behind his back. It was Edmund. Aelfric's grip tightened around his axe, and for a moment he contemplated plunging rashly down the trail and throwing himself into the midst of the invaders. But there was nothing he could do. He watched as the Vikings dragged his uncle into the center of the burh and then turned their attention toward the ships. Suddenly they began to shout, raising their voices in throaty, dissonant bleat.

"Jalkrtyr vollu sporna harbardsljod! See--drak! Old One Eye! See-ee-draaack! Old One Eye! Par munu dyggvar ok of aldrdaga yndis njota! See—e-draack! Old One Eye!"

Old One Eye. It was the one thing Aelfric could understand. His eyes were drawn to the nearest ship, and he squinted to see through the brush as a mass of Vikings standing just outside the burh separated to let one among them pass. They lifted their arms and shook their weapons as a helmeted figure made his way between the ranks and strode toward a gap in the unfinished fortress wall. As Aelfric watched, the man came into full view.

What he saw made him shake involuntarily, and then release the breath from his body in a long, low hiss.

The man was not particularly tall, but he was much broader across his shoulders and chest than any of the other Vikings. He looked to be over forty years old, but there was nothing in the way he carried himself atop his churning, bulky legs that suggested anything other than absolute strength and power. His exposed upper arms revealed two thick, muscled hams that were almost completely covered with dark hair. A broadsword dangled from his belt, housed around a waist that was thick without being fat, rock hard despite its girth. A gleaming helmet sat atop his head, sprouting a tangled mass of black and silver hair that shot out in all directions, reaching down to his shoulders and covering his bull-like neck. He was filthy and unkempt, with a dark, matted beard that left only his lips, cheeks and lower forehead visible.

And what a face it was! Even from that distance Aelfric could make out the man's gruesome complexion, his skin pockmarked with a thousand scars. He was incomparably ugly. But there was something even more disturbing—for there, outlined in the curve of his face where his left eye should have been, a long, red, angry scar glared defiantly out at the world with a disarming vision all its own.

It was a face from Hell. Old One Eye, indeed.

All this young Aelfric saw, as Sidroc the Malevolent One set foot on English soil for the first time.

"Berserkr Odin! Vindkaldr! See-dra-a-akkk! Old One Eye! Si-dr-o-c!"

Their voices died down as the Viking took the last steps up into the burh, where he stopped before the bound Edmund. A thin trickle of blood streamed down the side of the prisoner's face. Sidroc looked him over, turned to one of his men, and said something that Aelfric could not quite hear. The man then addressed Edmund, speaking in perfectly understandable English.

"How far to the nearest village?"

"Many, many miles. At least several hours march," Edmund lied, standing tall and unbowed.

"Where's your king, Alfred?"

"Winchester. But he'll be here, within two days. And he'll push you back into the sea!"

"Where are your nearest stores of grain? Your livestock?"

"Not where they'll do you any good!"

The Viking shrugged his shoulders and turned back to Old One Eye. The Warlord listened as his interpreter spoke, all the while looking intently into Edmund's eyes. When the translation was complete, he barked out something unintelligible and then turned and headed back toward the ships.

The meaning of his command became disturbingly clear when a Viking standing behind Edmund raised a wooden cudgel and brought it down squarely across the Saxon's back. As Aelfric watched in horror, his uncle collapsed to the ground. The other heathens stood over him and began to beat him, the thumping sounds of their weapons mingling with the jeers of the army. A groan echoed up from the earth, followed by a sickening, squishing sound like that of a rotten melon exploding as one of the Danes brought his club squarely down on the Elder of Appledore's skull.

Aelfric backed away from the underbrush and struggled to his feet, leaving his axe behind him as he stumbled away from the burh and hurried into the trees. But he was unable to run more than a few yards before he became violently ill. Dropping to his knees, he sagged visibly as a hot stream of vomit erupted from him and poured out onto the damp earth. He gagged over and over again, his eyes blinded, trying not to make too much noise for fear that it might carry down to the burh.

Could they hear him? Would they race up the slope and beat him to death, as they had done to his uncle? He struggled to his knees and wiped away the spittle from his face—and with it, the last vestiges of the simple, unburdened life he had known until now. Things would never be the same. His world, and that of all the people he knew and loved, would be changed forever.

Summoning all his strength, Aelfric grabbed a nearby branch and pulled himself to his feet, and then he started off through the trees toward Appledore, running as fast as his fear and his legs could carry him.

*   *   *   *   *

"I, Alfred, honored with the dignity of kingship through Christ's gift, have clearly perceived and frequently heard from statements in holy books that for us, to whom God has granted such a lofty station of worldly office, there is the most urgent necessity occasionally to calm our minds amidst these earthly anxieties and direct them to divine and spiritual law. And therefore I sought and petitioned my true friends, that they should write down for me from God's books the following teaching concerning the virtues and miracles of holy men, so that, strengthened through the exhortations and love they contain, I might occasionally reflect in my mind on heavenly things amidst these earthly tribulations."

Werferth let out a sigh of satisfaction and looked up from the parchment spread out before him. "Thank you, My Lord. It's a wonderful preface you've written."

"It's a wonderful piece of work," Alfred smiled. "Ever since I finished translating Gregory's *Pastoral Care*, I've been hoping someone would do the same for his *Dialogues*. Now you've done it."

Werferth beamed. It was honor enough to be lauded by the king; to be praised in the presence of his peers was the ultimate compliment. Alfred's day room at Winchester was filled with holy men. Asser was there, of course, and so was Plegmund, Archbishop of Canterbury. Also on hand were a number of the leading members of the Church, along with a handful of lesser prelates and acolytes. The king had called them all together on this day to celebrate their accomplishments and discuss the future.

"We've all much to be satisfied about," Alfred said from his place at the head of the table. "Over the past several years many of my dreams have been realized; Werferth's latest translations of Gregory add one more jewel to our credit. These moral teachings are words that all men can profit by."

"We've you to thank, Sire," said the bearded Asser from his seat alongside the king. "Your own treatment of *Pastoral Care* set a standard for the rest of us to follow. It gave us the courage to trim some of the cumbersome Latin and tailor it more effectively for English-speaking people."

A few places away at the table, Plegmund could not help but smirk to himself. If one thing surpassed Asser's obvious brilliance, it was his pandering to the king's every wish. How Alfred could not see beyond it amazed the Archbishop; it certainly never failed to irritate him.

"Ah, thank you, Asser. You above all others have been patient, distracted from your biography of me these last years. But I do believe your work—and that of so many of you here today—in translating Orosius's *Histories Against the Pagans* was well worth the effort. It's far more important than my story."

"Don't underestimate yourself, My Lord," said Werferth, still basking in the warm glow of attention. "Without your support, none of this could have ever happened."

"Perhaps...thank you. But look, all of you!" Here he ran his fingers across a thick, bound parchment that lay open on a reading stand behind him. "The history of Orosius, here brought to life, from ancient times to this modern, graceless age. Here you can read about Hannibal and Alexander, Pyrrhus and the Caesars of Rome! This is a priceless treasure, a history of the world as we know it, preserved in English now for posterity!"

Alfred's eyes shone as he looked through the narrow windows that arched up the facing wall, revealing a view of the limestone cliffs across the river that led up to the rim of the Itchen Valley. He was forty-three years old now, still strong and energetic despite the infirmities and stomach pains that continued to plague him from time to time. Above all, his mind was clear. He had never felt so alive as during the past few years, ever since London and the matters of unification had been resolved and he had been able to turn his attentions toward learning.

It had been nearly five years to the day when, in mid-November of 887, he had interrupted Asser's reading and asked the Welshman to record a particularly compelling quote on parchment for him. It marked the beginning of a tradition; ever since that time he had continued to amass certain words of wisdom that intrigued him, recording them in what became known as his enchiridion, or handbook. He kept it by his side night and day, referring to it whenever he was in need of inspiration, and in time the simple volume began to approach the size of a psalter. From this humble beginning he embarked on a series of scholastic adventures, mastering both the skill and the subtle art of translating Latin with his own hands and mind—a discipline that resulted in the successful completion of Gregory's *Pastoral Care* some two years later.

That same devotion manifested itself in the energy he spent directing his monks. Orosius had been a great accomplishment by all of them. But in his heart Alfred knew that it had simply been a matter of commitment, all quite achievable considering the lack of distractions at home or from abroad. England had enjoyed peace and prosperity for some time now. The unification of all points south and west of Watling Street under one Christian crown had gone smoothly, aided by the cooperation of the Danelaw in abiding by the treaty the Vikings signed at London. Even when old Guthrum died in 889 in the comfort of his bed, a sword lashed to his hand to secure his entry into Valhalla, the peace was maintained.

Guthrum's passing was the end of a life, but not the gains it had wrought. Christian England and the Danelaw managed to coexist peacefully, profiting mutually from a slow but steady stream of commerce that evolved as the two cultures grew accustomed to each other. But there was still a lingering mistrust that could not be erased in such a short time. And no one was more aware of these differences than Alfred, who had never forgotten his own tribulations at the hands of the Vikings. He kept one eye on the Danelaw and the other trained on the continent, mindful of the heathen horde that continued to ravage Francia and wary that Haestan and his lieutenants would one day set their sights on England.

When that day came, England would be prepared. He had made great progress in fortifying the burhs dotting the coastline, and the fyrd had been molded into a swift and formidable fighting machine. He had further strengthened his position by subduing the Welsh to the west and working with Eadred of Mercia to secure his borders on the north. To his delight, the Mercian had proved to be a strong and dependable ally, thanks in no small part to his successful marriage to the Lady Aethelfled. By now Alfred had forgiven—if not forgotten—the sins of his daughter, and the pain she had caused him more than six years ago.

All this gave him the opportunity to pursue learning, the true love of his life. He knew that time was now more of an adversary than an ally; he would not live forever, and it was important that he accomplish as much as possible in the years that God in all His wisdom had granted to him. And so he had put his hours to good use, forging ahead in the quest to advance the cause of scholasticism.

His translation of Gregory's *Pastoral Care* had been a monumental achievement, carried out almost single-handedly with a flair for the work that even his most ardent supporters would not have believed possible. The collective efforts of the monks in translating Orosius's *Histories Against the Pagans*, along with their continuing work on the Chronicles and Werferth's latest triumph with Gregory's *Dialogues*, were testimony to the fact that Wessex was not merely one of the places in Europe for a serious scholar to be. It was the only place.

"There's a greater significance to the completion of Orosius," Alfred continued, warming to the task. "It fills a gap in our library. Plegmund's fine work on Bede's *Historia Ecclesiastica* provided us with an accurate history of England.

And now we have a representative history of the entire western world. But all this is a mere prelude to the future."

He rose and began to pace the room, growing more excited with each step. "I want to go far beyond what we've done. I want to set a precedent that will last for generations, to stimulate learning so that no wave of barbarism can stamp it out. I've thought about it, and I want to start as soon as possible on Boethius's *Consolation of Philosophy*."

A murmur rippled through the chamber. "Sire," said Wulfsige, "do you really think that's the best choice? After all, it's not an overtly Christian work."

"It's one of the most important and influential books of the Latin tradition. And Boethius, despite being a Roman, was most definitely a Christian."

"I concur," Asser chimed in, agreeing as always. "His view of Providence is certainly compatible with a Christian viewpoint."

"I also approve, but for different reasons," Plegmund added, not to be outdone. "Boethius wrote *Consolation of Philosophy* while in prison, awaiting his execution for supposed treason. It's a rite of passage. One can see the transformation in the man as he proceeds from reflections on injustice and misfortune to a true appreciation of the role of fate and Divine Providence in the universe. Given these times we live in, I think it's appropriate."

"Exactly!" Alfred exclaimed, quickening his pace. "Well put, Plegmund! And for that reason, I believe it to be the right thing to do. But it's just the beginning...I see other possibilities, other works that need our attention. St. Augustine's *Soliloquies*, for example, works on the art of medicine, the psalms of the Psalter, to name a few. And after that…"

Suddenly he doubled over in pain, clutching at his stomach. The holy men jumped to their feet in alarm, and several of them rushed over and helped him into a nearby chair as he gasped for breath. His face contorted into a mask of pain as he held his belly with both hands and wheezed from the effort.

"Get the leecher! Hurry!" One of the acolytes sprinted out of the chamber.

But there was nothing anyone could do; they all knew that. None of the court physicians had ever been able to diagnose the king's mysterious infirmity, which had now been plaguing him for twenty-five years. Some thought it might be connected to nerves, for it had eased up slightly over the past few years, during a time when the kingdom had been free from strife and political stress. There were many theories, but no cures. The attacks were always difficult to contend with, for no one could ever be sure whether matters might escalate to the point where no man's help would be enough. The beast might disable, or even kill.

They looked on helplessly as Alfred writhed in his chair like a stuck pig, until the court physician rushed in and began to apply pressure to the king's left side. The attack continued for the better part of a minute until, mercifully, Alfred finally began to breathe more regularly. He shook lightly as he looked into the faces of the crowd hovering over him.

"Are you all right? Can you speak?" the leecher asked.

"Yes...yes. But I'm...I...I feel chills."

The physician felt the king's sweaty forehead. "A fever as well, perhaps. Is the pain in the usual place?"

Plegmund watched as Alfred nodded uncomfortably, until he became aware of someone at his elbow. Turning, he looked into the face of a young man-at-arms who stood on tiptoe trying to see over the heads of the churchmen.

"Is he all right?"

"Yes, I think so. The worst seems to be over."

"Good...but there's a messenger outside to see him. What should I do?"

"He can't be bothered now. Bring me to the man."

The guard bowed and led Plegmund out through the chamber door as the others continued to huddle around the king.

"You should lie down, my Lord," advised the doctor. "You've had enough for today."

"Very well…but, please... help me up." Holding the left side of his lower stomach, Alfred rose painfully to his feet. "I'm afraid you'll have to excuse me...but, do carry on. Perhaps...maybe I can join you later."

The physician and several of the priests led him away slowly through a side door, attending his every step. Werferth pursed his lips as the rest of them moved back around the table and sat down.

"Strange, how he's been plagued all these years. Early in his life it was piles. They would come upon him so badly that he would bleed and have to stay off his feet, sometimes for days."

"His infirmities don't seem to stop him."

"Nor should they stop us," said Asser, trying to restore direction to the meeting. "Perhaps we should pick up where we left off. Weren't we discussing Boethius?"

"Yes," Wulfsige said. "And I was saying that there might be better choices. After all, with all the work that lies ahead of us, well...let me put it this way: I think the king should be more selective, and maybe, perhaps, even...."

Suddenly he stopped, and his forehead creased as he looked toward the chamber door. "Plegmund? Plegmund…? What is it?"

All eyes swung around to where the Archbishop of Canterbury stood, his face pale, looking past them as though he had seen a spectral vision.

"I wouldn't worry about Alfred's next translation," he said quietly.

"What do you mean? What's wrong?"

Plegmund stepped into the room. "Two hundred and fifty Viking ships have landed in Kent. Above Romney Marsh, in Appledore." He took a deep breath and looked at all of them.

"My friends, the days of Boethius and Augustine are over—for now, at least. Time to put down the pen and pick up the sword. It's war."

* * * * *

Ride like the wind!

Flying over ditch and dale. Speeding across the open meadows on the wings of angels. Racing against time itself, and winning. That's what it felt like to her as she put the chestnut mare through its paces, both horse and rider testing their limits. Squeeze and roll, squeeze and roll. Yes, this is what it's all about—being alive, leaning over the neck of the beast until you can whisper in its ear, becoming part of the surging muscle and bone. Flying. Yes, flying! That's right, wheel around here, let's conquer that fence, and…steady, now...*up* and over! Good girl! Good, good girl!

Aethelfled leaned into the wind and spurred her horse across the final mile of open fields leading to Oxford. She was more in touch with herself during these moments than at any other time, completely alone and freed from the web of obligation and responsibility that dominated the rest of her life. Here it was different. She could do what she pleased, without restraint or the fear of being judged; she could be herself. And she could certainly ride a horse. Her control of the beast was so complete that she was more like an extension of the animal than merely its rider. It responded to her every movement, to every subtle flick of the wrist, every minute pressure from the knees.

Now they were in the straightaway, and the horse's hooves seemed to barely touch the ground as they raced home. The wind brought tears to Aethelfled's eyes, and her auburn hair trailed behind like a colored streamer blowing in the breeze, her own fiery flag of indomitability. She was a much-admired figure throughout the midlands, for the people of Mercia had gladly opened their arms to her when their ealdorman rode home with her six years ago. Like Eadred, they felt themselves to be the proud recipients of Alfred's finest treasure. Even now, at the mature age of twenty four, she was still easily the fairest woman in all of England, a woman of breeding and grace whose stunning beauty was merely one of her many attributes.

She was the Lady of Mercia, and she belonged to them.

She slowed the mare to a canter as she entered Oxford, the bustling town that was Eadred's principal residence and seat of power. She rode through the main square, acknowledging everyone she met, and then she dismounted and handed the reins off to a waiting attendant. Brushing the dust from her riding clothes—her servants always protested, but she insisted on doing it herself—she entered the simple wooden estate, smiling the smile of the madam of the house as she made her way to her quarters. She liked it here. She had grown to appreciate the beauty and tradition of her adopted home, and after six years of living in Mercia she no longer pined for Wessex and everything that it had once meant to her.

It was all one England, anyway. Her father had seen to that.

He had forced her into a difficult situation, but she could not ultimately fault him for his decision. She had always known it was the prudent one—if not the passionate one—and she had no regrets. Eadred had been good to her. He was an attentive husband, a strong and respected leader, and an ardent lover. She had been patient, and over time her mother's simple advice had turned out to be true; she had learned to love him. Not in the way she had loved Sigli, but more like a slow and even stream that widens as it draws near the sea. It was a measured affection, and it surprised her that she could be so content with a man for whom she did not ache every waking moment.

That passion was more reserved for affairs of state. She wanted to make a difference, to lead people, to make decisions that would have positive effects. The blood of kings flowed through her veins, a sweet elixir of willpower and desire, and she needed all of it and more to cope with living in what was clearly a man's world. She usually deferred to her husband in public, using her influence behind the scenes to gain her desired ends. And while those ends were usually reached, the indirect means she was forced to use left a sour taste in her mouth that would not wash away as the years passed.

Someday, she hoped, her time would come.

She stepped through the doorway to her chamber and then stopped, shaking her head and smiling. Her daughter Elfwyn was busy admiring herself in a looking glass, spinning around so that her brightly colored dress twirled around her legs in a smooth, circular motion. Her face was transfixed with delight.

"Look, Mother!" she said, her attention still fixed on the mirror. "Isn't it beautiful?"

"Yes, my sweet. But don't you think you're spending a little too much time looking at yourself? This is the fourth change of clothes you've made today."

The girl looked up, puckering her little face into a mask of protest. "But, Mother...the other dresses didn't feel right today. And this one is so, so pretty!"

Such a social little animal, Aethelfled thought. Her daughter was disarmingly articulate, having already mastered the language far more effectively than many adults could after a lifetime of trying. Her precision with words was a talent that was complemented by an underlying sensitivity that sometimes astonished Aethelfled. You had to be careful what you said around the girl; her perceptions were remarkably acute. She was capable of reading meaning into even the most passing, casual references. And with that sixth sense came a natural inclination toward what was *not* said, the underlying truth at which words could only hint. Still three months shy of her sixth birthday, Elfwyn had already become a formidable little lady.

"Did you ride well today, Mother? Did you go fast?"

"Yes. I went very fast."

"Well, then...have you sent a message to Plegmund yet? Have you arranged my visit?"

"I sent the message."

That was another thing about the child—she never forgot anything. Every little promise was followed up, every pledge resolved to her satisfaction. That would make this all the more difficult. Aethelfled cleared her throat as she continued to remove her riding garments.

"Elfwyn, I have to tell you something. We're going to have to wait a month or two before sending you to Canterbury."

"Why, Mother? You promised I could go before the Yuletide!" The girl loved her yearly visits to the Archibishop of Canterbury. He was so attentive and smart; they had so much fun together.

"I know. But...you see, it might not be very safe right now. Some very bad people have come to Kent, a whole army of them. They're not really very far from Canterbury, and it could be dangerous there."

"You mean Vikings, Mother? Are they Vikings?"

How did she know about that? They had said nothing around her since word had reached Oxford a few days ago.

"Yes...they are."

"Are they bad, Mother? Are all Vikings bad?"

"Well...some of them. These Vikings are bad. But how did you know it was them?"

"Well, um, because you said bad people...And I know that Vikings are bad people. Everyone says so. Father says so."

"Not all Vikings are bad, my sweet. They live in the Danelaw, you know. On our borders. And they're really quite peaceful and decent."

"Do you know any good Vikings, Mother?"

"A few."

"Who?" Elfwyn stood right next to her now, her little hand on her mother's knee as Aethelfled sat at her dressing table.

"Oh...just some...people. No one you know, my sweet."

She smiled to mask her discomfort, but as she glanced into the girl's large blue eyes she saw *him* again. A familiar, dull ache returned to her, as it always did whenever he crossed her mind. She could not look very long or very deeply into Elfwyn's eyes without seeing him there; as far as she knew, she was the only one in the world keeping the secret. She was the only one who understood that the girl had not been sired by Eadred. It had occurred to her that Plegmund might know—even Edward might suspect, after all—but neither of them had ever said anything. That was enough for her. It was not a secret to be taken lightly, nor to be revealed.

If Eadred had any inkling at all of the way things were, he had never let on to her. His drunken joy on their wedding night had blinded him to the possibility that there had ever been another before him; for all he knew, Aethelfled had been his alone. He certainly loved his daughter as only a father could. There was no betrayal in his smile whenever he sat the girl on his lap and stroked her blonde hair and fair skin, talking softly to her and laughing under his breath. She had been a joy and a delight for him, and his affection for her was genuine, given unconditionally.

But whenever Aethelfled looked at her daughter, it was obvious to her who was the real father of the fair young jewel of Mercia.

"Who, Mother?" Elfwyn persisted. "Who do you know that's a good Viking?"

"Really, now, child...I don't even remember. It's not important." She brushed her hair back. "But don't worry. You'll only need to wait a bit, until after the Yuletide, perhaps, to visit Plegmund. Your Uncle Edward is gathering an army together to face the Vikings, and I'm sure he'll have things under control in a few months. It'll be safer then. In fact, Uncle Edward is coming here to see us...he should arrive later today."

"Oh, good! I'll put on my special dress for him! The red one! And, Mother...can I wear your earrings?"

Aethelfled laughed. "We'll see about that, my sweet. Now, leave me in peace for a few minutes so I can dress. Go change again, why don't you—it's only noon, after all, and your closet is still full!"

Several hours later, Eadred sat astride his horse outside the walls of Oxford, watching intently as the column of riders approached. His eyes strained to penetrate the gathering autumn twilight, struggling to make out the dusky faces of the men as they crossed the fields leading up to the city.

Despite the darkness, his attention was drawn to one figure in particular. It was Edward, all right; he could tell by the jaunty angle at which the cap was perched upon the lead horseman's head. No one could accuse Alfred's son of lacking confidence. But there was something about the young man that made Eadred uncomfortable, a forcefulness of purpose that fairly crackled with energy, threatening to consume everything in its path. He stayed out of that path whenever possible, because Edward's fire grew ever more hot and dangerous the closer one got to the source. A man could easily be burned.

"Here rides the boy who would be king, Wilfred," he said to his trusted confidant, who waited on horseback alongside him.

"Now, now, my Lord," the pinch-faced thane replied, cautious and calculating. "There rides your future—and that of England."

"I have no doubt about that. But at least he could wait until he sits on the throne before giving orders. His father's still very much the king; he could stand to remember that more often."

"He's his father's son."

"Edward! Greetings! I'm so glad you've come!"

The heir to the throne of England lifted his arm in acknowledgement and then dug his heels into the flanks of his magnificent black stallion. The horse sprang forward into a bold trot, raising its forelegs ceremoniously. It was so like Edward, Eadred thought to himself; the boy king loved pomp and ceremony.

Everything about him was honed to a razor's edge. His thin, intense features were more sharply defined than ever, and at the age of twenty-three, he was handsome in a harsh, striking kind of way. He was darker than his sister, with eyes that darted ceaselessly beneath a pair of high, arching eyebrows. Tall and wiry, his stride was as quick as it was long, and he was capable of great bursts of energy that dominated everything around him. Impetuous, charismatic, a tad arrogant, perhaps—Edward the Elder was all these things and more.

And someday, he would be king.

"I was hoping Lord Alfred could accompany you," Eadred said, offering his hand.

Edward allowed it to dangle in the air briefly before extending his own, subtly conveying his displeasure. It was just like his brother-in-law to cast him offhandedly in his father's shadow; the remark was seemingly innocent, but it annoyed him.

"He's not well these days...the attacks, you know. But he's feeling better lately, and should be ready to ride soon."

"Your journey was uneventful, I presume?"

"Quite."

Edward had long been aware of Eadred's feelings about him; they shone through even the thickest of smiles. While he respected his sister's husband as both a man and a kinsman, there was a distance between them that he was not necessarily compelled to close. The Mercian was almost old enough to be his father, and he knew that the man had to swallow hard as he acquiesced to every request from the south. No matter how loyal Eadred professed to be, Edward suspected that his brother-in-law sometimes had to squirm under the weight of Wessex that constantly hung over him. He knew he would feel that way, were their positions reversed.

"I imagine your men are hungry," Wilfred said. "I think we've prepared enough food for tonight, at least. Some of them can stay in the town, but the remainder will have to pitch their tents outside."

"They're prepared to live off the land, if need be," Edward replied as the three of them rode through the gates of Oxford. "But thank you for your kindness...in a matter of days we'll be in Kent, after which...why, what have we here?"

He smiled broadly as Elfwyn raced across the open square toward him. Bending low, he scooped her up in his arms and raised her into the saddle.

"Such a pretty little thing!"

"Uncle Edward! Mother says you're going off to fight the Vikings! Aren't you scared?"

He laughed. "No, not at all. Not with men like your father to help me."

"Father...? Are you leaving, too?"

"That I can't say, my dear," Eadred smiled, dismounting and handing off his reins. "Only your uncle and your grandfather know the answer to that."

"You'll know soon enough, Eadred. For now, some meat and mead are in order."

There was a hint of fatigue in Edward's voice, but it disappeared as he turned his attention to Elfwyn once again. "And you, my precious fawn...what have you been up to?"

He tickled her mischievously, and the girl giggled as she writhed in his arms. She was a little beauty, all right. When he looked hard enough he could see some of his sister in her, the same intensity and independence, the same spirit of adventure.

But nothing about his niece reminded him of Eadred, nothing at all. In the back of his mind there still lurked a question that he had never dared to ask, nor most certainly ever would.

"Edward! Edward!"

He looked across the courtyard and into Aethelfled's shining face. He loved his sister more than anyone in the world, and the ties that bound them were strong. They had grown up together learning to cope with the burden of responsibility, and with that shared experience had come the knowledge that no one else could ever duplicate the special relationship they had. These were the bonds that uplifted him now as he handed Elfwyn to her father and dismounted, breaking into a smile and running across the courtyard into his sister's arms.

A short time later they all sat gathered around a table in the main hall, finishing off a supper of venison, freshly baked bread and mead. Having been patient long enough, Eadred turned to his daughter and smiled.

"It's time for bed, child. Give us a kiss and leave us."

"Must I, Father?" she begged, screwing up her tiny face. "It's early."

One firm look answered her question. She moved obediently to her father and kissed him, and then she smiled knowingly. "You're going to talk about the Vikings now...aren't you?"

Before he could answer she moved along the table, stretching out her time and making a grand show of her exit. One by one she kissed the adults, fussing over each of them before finally leaving the chamber with one of the waiting handmaids. The smiles of the room trailed behind her.

"She knows how to get her way, that one," Eadred laughed, sharing his pleasure with the others. "So, Edward...what shall it be? Do we march with you to Kent?"

"No. But I'll need several hundred of your men immediately, provided you can spare them. Otherwise, we've raised enough of the fyrd in Wessex to hold the Vikings. We won't need you in the south...not yet, anyway."

"But the heathens are gathered in force, aren't they?" Wilfred asked. "Are you sure you won't need more men right now?"

"I don't think they'll be straying too far. Winter's almost upon us, and we're mobilized on all sides of them. I plan to take up a position on the edge of the Weald, where I can keep an eye on them. If they venture too far afield, I'll cut them to pieces."

"Why not let us march with you? We can overpower them!" Eadred exclaimed.

"It's not that simple. They're already entrenched in Appledore, and it's a difficult position to attack. Besides, Eadred...the king is concerned about East Anglia and Northumbria. He and I both feel you should arm yourself and watch your own frontiers. We need you to protect us from any flank assaults the Vikings might mount. I'm not sure the heathens who've landed in Kent are all we'll have to contend with before this is over."

"You may be right," Wilfred said. "It's been quiet for years to the north and east, but I hear rumblings. Northumbria in particular has seen some activity." A thought came to him, and a light appeared in his eyes. "In fact, I've recently heard some interesting rumors. Do you remember your father's shipbuilder, the heathen?"

Aethelfled had been working on a handsome quilt, keeping to herself at one end of the table, but she froze perceptibly upon hearing Wilfred's words. The needle slipped from her hand and fell to the floor. She reached down for it, gathered herself, and then rose and resumed her work as though nothing had happened.

But Edward had noticed. "Do you mean...Sigli?"

"Yes, Sigli...that was his name. One of my thanes told me he thought he was the one. It seems he's taken up residence high on the north coast, where he keeps a few ships."

"He disappeared rather suddenly some years ago, didn't he?" wondered Eadred. "Considering his skills, I was surprised Alfred allowed him to leave."

"They had a...a bit of a difference," Edward said. "I don't remember the details, but my father banished him. He's not to set foot on English soil again." It hurt him to say it, for Sigli had been one of his few true friends.

"Then maybe he'll join his countrymen in Kent, now that they're raising such a stir," Wilfred wondered out loud.

"I should think not." Aethelfled's voice had an edge to it. "He would never raise his hand against my father." Her nostrils flared slightly, and she leaned forward. "I simply can't believe that would happen."

Suddenly she realized how odd she must have sounded, reacting so strongly to such a minor piece of news. She relaxed her shoulders, gathered her quilt up and rose to her feet.

"If you'll excuse me, it's getting late. I think I'll retire."

She kissed her husband and then Edward, squeezing her brother's hand lightly. Then she turned and walked across the hall, and as the prince watched her leave he thought about the way things had once been, and how sad it all was, after all. But it was far behind them now. He turned to Eadred, remembering the words his father had said to him: be a diplomat first and a warrior second. He cleared his throat and began to speak, and as his voice filled the room he was surprised at how easily the sweet talk and half-truths of statesmanship poured out of him. Maybe his father was right; maybe it wasn't such a difficult thing to do, after all.

And as the men spoke of strategy in the main hall, Aethelfled stood alone on the other side of the estate house, shivering slightly as a cold wind poured through her open bedroom window. She stared out over the fields and into the distance, straining to see what was not there, until her eyes grew tired and the vague outline of the forest faded into darkness, melting away into the night.

*   *   *   *   *

Sidroc stared sullenly into the half-empty cup of mead. Laughter and noise engulfed him in the small meeting hall at Appledore, mingling with the smoke from the fire that burned in the center of the room.

But he heard none of it. Had Ragnarok, the Crack of Doom, been roaring around him, he would not have noticed.

His mood and Appledore were the same: cramped and close, littered with boredom and a dense, all-consuming ennui. The Vikings were hemmed in by the elements and the enemy, condemned to play a waiting game. The weather and the Saxons had proved more difficult than any of them could have imagined, and they were gathered here on this late December evening as they had been every night for the last few weeks, drinking themselves into oblivion.

But even the mead would all be gone by the New Year. What then?

Sidroc's one good eye remained fixed on his cup, unblinking, the lone point of light on an otherwise dark and brooding mask that grew more surly with every gulp. He sat slumped over a table, tree-trunk legs askew, his hairy arms draped over the hardwood like two densely forested ridges rising up from a broad plain. It tore at him to waste away like this, for he was a man of action, and it was more than he could bear, watching helplessly as another missed opportunity slipped away.

They had been in England for almost a month, but their hopes had turned into slush, soaked by the frozen rains that had poured from the sky for days on end. The balmy weather of November was gone and winter had closed in, chilling the heart of even the hardest of them. But the weather was the least of their problems. The Saxons had mobilized swiftly and fielded an armed force that stretched for miles throughout the Weald. At first the Vikings had pillaged the surrounding countryside without fear, scavenging the hard-earned harvests left behind by the fleeing peasants. But the people had been alerted in time to take much of their food, livestock and belongings with them, and soon there was nothing left to pillage.

The few raiding parties that ventured too far from Appledore suffered a rude fate. Instead of ragtag bands of farmers armed with sickles and scythes, they met up with well-trained, disciplined fighting men who operated efficiently and cut off their every avenue of escape. Many of the Vikings had fought in England during the campaigns of Guthrum—and before him Halfdan and Ivar the Boneless—but none could remember ever encountering such organized resistance. And so almost ten thousand Vikings rotted in Appledore, waiting for the weather to clear, contemplating other arrows in their quiver for the attack on England.

The first of these was the Danelaw. With Guthrum now dead, the invaders looked toward the Norse settlers of East Anglia and Northumbria for support. Even a shadow force along this corridor would create enough pressure on Alfred's flank to open things up in Kent. But it would take time to mobilize any kind of resources from the north, and no help could be expected until spring at the earliest. Many in Appledore doubted that anything at all would come from their tame cousins; after just two generations of settlement, the melting pot had already begun to boil, and the Danelaw had lost its teeth.

The other arrow in the quiver was Haestan, the most powerful and aggressive Viking alive, and the only plausible heir to the status that the legendary Ragnar Lodbrok had once enjoyed. Ragnar's sons Ivar the Boneless, Halfdan and Ubba were all dead. So was Guthrum. And while a number of influential leaders clung with iron grips to the rung just below Haestan on the ladder of power, that rung was far removed from his lofty perch. No one was even so much as a vague threat to Haestan. He was the only one.

He had long been plotting the invasion of England, but the ripe harvests of the continent had provided a well-stocked table for the past fifteen years that no glutton could afford to ignore. The inevitable finally became a reality when a famine raged in northern Francia and the low countries during the first seasons of the 890s, compelling Haestan to finally set his great wheel in motion. The two hundred fifty Viking ships that invaded Kent were merely the first wave of the offensive, a prelude to another force that would land with the Warlord himself near Rochester and Milton, creating a giant pincer that would surround and annihilate the Saxons.

But not a word from Haestan or the Danelaw had been heard in Appledore. How much longer would they have to wait?

Sidroc was not a patient man. His voice was the loudest of all in the war councils, urging the Danes to forge out into the countryside again in spite of the opposition they would encounter. But he had neither the power to make such decisions nor the might to change his circumstances. The Vikings in Kent were led by Hundeus, a loyal favorite of Haestan's who followed the Warlord's orders explicitly. He was an older man who had grown conservative and was not prone to impulse, and he had commanded his lieutenants to forego the raids until word of Haestan's departure arrived from the continent. It was anybody's guess when that time would come.

And time had become Sidroc's enemy. Age had begun to drape itself over his shoulders like a dark, heavy cloak, and as his dreams of conquest and power continued to fade, his bitterness grew. The sack of Halfsfiord fifteen years earlier had been his crowning achievement, a bold coup that had landed him on the threshold of greatness, ready to take the final step. But he had never again been able to duplicate that stunning victory, and all of his impassioned attempts to leverage his power into something that would play on a grander scale always ended in the same bottomless pit of frustration. Those same qualities of his that turned hearts to jelly on the battlefield inevitably turned ears to stone in the meeting hall; he was a vulgar man without subtlety, blind to manipulation and the art of consensus.

He was regarded warily by Haestan's circle—feared and mistrusted, even—for his successes had been gained by a savagery that was extreme even by Viking standards. Haestan had always used him in ways that played to his strengths, wielding him as he would a blunt object to hammer away at the opposition. It had worked for a few years, and all of northern Francia and the low countries had paid the price. But the two men repeatedly clashed wills, stretching their patience to its limits, until the Malevolent One finally tired of doing the Warlord's dirty work. He left Haestan to seek his own destiny to the east, crossing the Rhine and invading the lands of Saxony and Lotharingia.

At first the gods smiled upon him, but eventually his weaknesses caught up with him and he had to swallow his pride and return under Haestan's wing, once again serving as little more than an instrument at the beck and call of another, greater man. He plodded on, disillusioned by the growing suspicion that he might never get to where he had always thought he wanted to go. Driven by inadequacy, he resorted to even more extreme acts of brutality, alienating himself from all but the most radical and bloodthirsty elements among the Vikings. This lunatic fringe of berserkers was comprised of desperate men like him, men without conscience who shared his disdain for even the most basic forms of civilized behavior. And as long as he commanded their respect, he remained a force to be reckoned with.

That made him a very dangerous man. To Haestan and Hundeus, to the Saxons, to everyone.

He scowled over his cup and stared morosely into the dark, smoky room. Suddenly the door to the hall opened, and several men entered, led by Hundeus. So, she had decided to come out from behind her quilts and silks, had she? He knew that Hundeus had been ill—he looked pale, even in the murky light—but he was of the mind that the man had lost more than just his health. He had lost his nerve, and long ago at that, as far as Old One Eye was concerned.

Hundeus was fifty years old, with long, streaming red hair streaked with gray. He was a hard man who had profited all of his life by living off the labors of other people, and he was not about to change. He moved slowly toward the center of the crowded room, for he had indeed taken to his bed over the past week with a high fever and was just beginning to feel like himself again.

"Vikings!" he bellowed. "I'm whole again. And like you, I have the future to look forward to. England lies at our feet, waiting to be taken!" There was a general murmur of approval. "And this land shall be taken, by the time we're finished. But it will take time. We can only be patient and wait."

Here a grumble or two slowed his pace, but he kept on. "I'll be straight with you: get used to the waiting, because more of it lies ahead." And then he paused. "I just received word an hour ago from Francia; Haestan won't land in England for at least two or three months."

A groan rose throughout the hall. And then there was a great howl and a crash, and all eyes turned to where Sidroc had swept the mead before him onto the floor with his hairy paw. He was very drunk, and he glared at Hundeus.

"You think I'm going to stay chained in this hole, do you? Well, you can think again! The rest of you can sit here, mending your leggings!"

"That's not for you to decide!" Hundeus growled back. "There's a time to make war and a time to wait!"

"And who's to say I can't go out and take my chances in the forest? Many here would follow me!"

A low rumbling in the room bolstered his confidence, and he staggered toward Hundeus. "As soon as the rains let up, I'm going out! And you can't stop me!"

"If you go out, then you go out alone! I can't allow any others to go with you. It's stupid right now, considering the obstacles."

"Only a woman would stay here and rot, Hundeus! Or a coward."

"Don't bully me! I've enough blood on my sword to drown you; everyone knows that!"

Hundeus turned to the room, and his voice grew persuasive. "Nor will you dispute me, once you hear what I have to say: time is on our side. Because Haestan has assured me he *will* come, no later than the spring. This winter has already been the coldest in memory, and it grips Francia as it grips us. And besides, the ships need work; some hundred or so will sail, and half of them need restoring before crossing the Channel.

"So, we have two choices. The first is Sidroc's way: storm out like wild men in the rain and snow, against an organized force in its own territory, an army that probably outnumbers us right now. The other way is Haestan's—and mine, and everyone else's, for that matter: wait until the sun shines again and our forces are doubled, and then crush these Christians like insects!"

He paused for effect, and then he turned to Old One Eye, unable to resist the moment. "It's a question a fool could answer, Sidroc. Even a drunken one!"

Sidroc snarled and took a step forward, reaching for his war belt. But his sword wasn't there; he had left it next to his bed. He staggered forward anyway, but he was immediately set upon by a handful of men, who pinned his arms to his sides and struggled to control him. He thrashed about and gave them all they could handle until finally the entire mass of bodies collapsed to the ground, and they pinned his arms and legs to the earth, where he lay there helplessly.

Hundeus stepped forward, unable to contain his annoyance. It would have been so convenient to bury his sword in the Malevolent One's throat and end things once and for all, but he knew that Sidroc was too valuable to waste. It was trying for him to deal with such an animal. He looked in disgust down at the mead-infested mass of perspiring flesh below him, and he shook his head in frustration.

"Enough, Sidroc! I'm not your enemy, man! Save it for the Saxons! "

There was a glint of recognition, a resigned shudder, and then Old One Eye grew still.

"Let go of me, then," he hissed. "I won't provoke anyone!"

The men loosened their hold and he sat up, grimacing, looking around with disapproval and embarrassment. Once again he had suffered the role of the fool. To Hel, with them. To Hel with them all. They'd just go back to their drinking, and all would be forgotten in the morning. He scowled long and hard at

Hundeus, dragged himself to his feet, and then he strode forward and pushed his way through the door, stepping out into the freezing rain.

It was all he could do in his stupor to find his way through the darkness, slipping and sliding down the muddy lane that led to his quarters. He had chosen one of the more comfortable huts on the edge of the village for his own, and no one had dared stop him. But the distance to the hovel now took its toll, soaking him thoroughly as he cursed the gods under his breath with every stumbling step. At last he came to the darkened outline of the hut. He shook the rain from his hair and beard and then he opened the door, bending down and stepping into the warmth of the candlelit room.

She sat perched stiffly on the edge of the bed, just as he had expected she would be. He caught her eye for just a moment before she looked down at the ground, and in it he saw a mixture of sorrow, loathing, regret—and absolute fear.

No matter, he grunted to himself. It would do. He began to strip the wet clothes from his body, and as he did so she lied down on the bed, covering herself and facing away from him. She was not a beautiful woman, but her looks exceeded her luck; she had been one of the few who had not escaped when the Vikings had swept into Appledore. Old One Eye himself had killed her husband as the poor ceorl fought to defend his home, and he claimed the peasant woman for his own, intending to let the others have her when other women turned up in the camp. But with no raids there were no women, and until further notice the ceorl's wife was his.

He stood naked in the cold room, eyeing the curve of her body beneath the heavy blanket. He lumbered over to the side of the bed and pulled the cover from her. Reaching down, he pulled her over onto her back and spread her legs, kneeling down between them and stroking himself. Never once did she look at him. He lowered his body onto her, already hard with excitement, and she cried out briefly as he thrust forward and penetrated her. He rocked his bulging groin back and forth, harder and harder, and he began to sweat profusely as the poison of the mead released itself from his body. She kept her eyes closed tightly, moving only to hasten his completion and finish the ordeal, and he pummeled her until finally he exploded with a shudder that took the strength from his knees and the sting from his heart.

He sank down on top of her, breathing heavily, and then he rolled over onto his back. She rose from the bed, slipped her crude dress over her head and disappeared through the door, running out into the rain and back to one of the other huts in the village.

He lay there listening to the sleet as it beat a pattern on the roof, and it occurred to him that, except for the moment he had entered the room, she had not looked at him at all. Not once. None of the women ever did. That no longer surprised him, for he knew he was an ugly man, but he also knew there were others in the world not particularly fair to look at who still managed to keep a woman happy. What he did not know was how they went about doing this; he had heard of this thing called love, but he had never experienced it. To him, it was a mere illusion.

He had never experienced love in the arms of a woman, and certainly not in the arms of his mother. She had been stolen from her Frisian home and carried off to Jutland by Danish raiders, who kept her as a slave and passed her from man to man. She had turned to mead to ease her sorrow, gravitating to anyone who would give her a roof over her head, her body serving as the barter to secure the bare necessities.

There had been nothing left for him in this sad shuffle. He did not know who his father was; he had many fathers, after all, and none of them ever cared at all about him. The best treated him with indifference; the worst simply mistreated him, mocking him for his ugliness and beating him for their misguided pleasure. When his mother finally died, a drunken whore, he left the village of his youth behind forever, ten years old and scarred for life.

And still, so many years later, he had never known anything resembling love. It had made him a bitter human being; it had created the monster that men knew as the Malevolent One.

He stretched himself out on the bed and stared up into the darkness with his one good eye. It saw more of this sorry world than he really cared to see. He could close it, of course, but that never seemed to help. Because when he did, the visions returned, taunting him with the specter of a life that sometimes did not seem to be worth living. Night after night he wrestled with his demons as though he were Loki, chained in Niflheim for eternity, condemned to flinch as every drop of poison from the grinning mouth of the Serpent of Hel burned deep into his soul.

CHAPTER XIII: Voices In The Dark

"Revenge is a luscious fruit which you must leave to ripen."
—Emile Gaborial, <u>File 113</u>

"If I died today, Plegmund, would I go to Heaven?"

The question caught the Archbishop of Canterbury off guard. He looked up distractedly from the parchment he was studying and was immediately swept into Elfwyn's fair, upturned face as it hovered over her calligraphy lesson. Her features were soft and reflective, bathed in an innocence that was capable of shedding light without dispensing heat.

He had once approached life that way, but now his light shone like a burnt offering, scorched by the coals of political intrigue and self-interest. He had long ago given up on the notion of Paradise. He was a prisoner to his ambition, and while he had learned to live with his mistakes, he had never been able to reconcile them. For now, it was a blessing to replenish himself with the girl, and forget the mass of tangled contradictions that crowded his life.

"Now, why would you ask such a question?"

She answered without hesitation. "Because I don't want to go to Hell."

He laughed. "I'm sure you don't have to worry about that...unless, of course, you've committed some horrible sin you haven't told me about...?"

"Well...what if you die, and...and you've committed some *little* sins...not really bad ones?"

"Then you go to Purgatory."

"Purr-ga-tory?"

"Yes, Purgatory. It's like Hell, I imagine, except there's an end to it."

The irony was not lost on him; it sounded just like life.

"Your soul does penance by suffering until all your sins are cleansed. It prepares you for Heaven and eternity. That's the road for all of us who are baptized into the Faith."

"But...what if you haven't been baptized?"

"Like a baby, you mean? A little baby who dies? Well, an unbaptized child goes to Limbo."

"Lim-bo?" she sang out, taken with the melodious sound of this new word. "How do you spell it?"

"L-I-M-B-O."

He watched with interest as she earnestly began to ink the letters on the parchment before her. He loved being with her like this and looked forward to all of her visits. She came to him at least once each year, sometimes for as long as a month, and he felt in every way as though he were an extended parent.

But if he loved the child for who she was, he loved her even more for the sake of the woman who had brought her into the world. He had wronged Aethelfled for his own gain, exposing her to treachery and blackmail, and he had been dragging himself slowly back up the dubious road to salvation ever since. It was one of the two great sins in his life—the other being his debasement at the hands of Grimwald—and he knew there was no room for a third. If betrayal is the greatest sin a man can commit, then he had already sinned enough for two lifetimes, and he was determined to devote the rest of his days to making things right.

His actions had certainly not caused Aethelfled any lasting harm, and she still had no idea that he had been the instrument behind her discovery. At least Grimwald had remained silent about that. But while he had managed to satisfy himself about her, he could never quite come to grips with what had happened to Sigli. He had willfully hurt his friend and caused him great pain, and he had sent him spinning out into the great unknown forever. It continued to haunt him, and he was reminded of it every time he was with Elfwyn.

Nothing had ever been said to him, no one had even so much as hinted at the truth, but he knew. He knew when he looked into the child's eyes. It was as though loving her could help blot out the betrayal of her father, and it was all that was left to him.

"What's Limbo like, Plegmund?"

"I don't really know," he said, scratching his head and walking over to her. Yes, she had spelled it perfectly, with exquisite penmanship. "It's much like a state of nothingness, with no pain or joy. Or anything else, for that matter."

"But the little babies...who takes care of them?"

"God looks after all of his children, Elfwyn."

She looked through the window of the small anteroom of Christ Church Cathedral and into the cold drizzle outside. It was late February in the Year of Our Lord 893, and she had been in Canterbury a week. Her mother and father had given in to her wishes, satisfied that all was safe in the face of the ongoing stalemate with the Vikings in Kent. The invaders had now been camped there for more than three months, but the long shadow cast by the Saxons under Edward's watchful eye had kept them confined largely to Appledore. They were a mere half-day's ride to the south, but it seemed as though they might have been a thousand miles away.

"What about the others, Plegmund?"

"What others?"

"The others who haven't been baptized...where does God put them?"

"I'm not sure what you mean, child."

She squirmed in her seat. "Well...I mean...what about the Vikings? They don't believe in Jesus, and they haven't been baptized. Where do they go when they die?"

She *would* have to ask that. He had no idea where they went.

"I guess they probably go to Hell…especially if they're sinners, and heathens."

"But Plegmund…Mother says they're not all bad! What about a really good Viking, a friendly one, who's nice…what happens to him if he dies and hasn't been baptized? God wouldn't send someone like that to Hell, would He?"

He had contemplated that very same dilemma many times without ever resolving it; it was too logical for any thinking person to miss. He took a deep breath and placed a hand on her shoulder.

"I think, perhaps, that someone who hasn't been exposed to God's teachings can't be penalized for it. The bad Vikings go to Hell, just like bad Christians. And the good ones probably go to a place like Limbo, where they remain suspended."

"With the babies? You mean there are babies and Vikings in Limbo? And dark skins, too?"

He chuckled lightly. "Yes, Elfwyn…I guess there are all sorts of strange souls there, all shapes and colors. But for Christians, the choice is clear: do good unto others, and you'll join God in his heavenly kingdom. Stray from that path, and…."

"And you'll burn forever alongside Satan in the fires of Hell."

Plegmund never failed to cringe at the sound of Grimwald's voice. He turned around, and there the man loomed in the door, a hulking, obese presence. Thick folds of flesh draped themselves over his collar, hanging from his cheeks as though they were the gills of a fish. A few isolated wisps of hair protruded from his head, which otherwise was bald and wrinkled at its crest. He was old now, and his movements were labored, but the twinkle in his eye revealed a mind as sharp and penetrating as ever. He waddled into the chamber.

"Excuse me, Your Ho-li-nessssss," he smiled, drawing out Canterbury's formal title with a barely concealed sneer. "I wouldn't normally interrupt you like this, but the debate interests me. Particularly when it's directed at such a sweet young thing. You don't mind...do you?"

Plegmund grimaced. He had submitted to Grimwald's every wish for more than two years as he waited for Aethelred to die and Canterbury to be his. They were two years of Hell, with his body the payment and his soul the price. When the day of his ascension to the archbishopric had finally come, he had thrown off the yoke of captivity and slowly, painfully, set about the process of rebuilding his battered self-esteem.

First he stopped allowing Grimwald to have his odious way. Then he stopped his nightly self-flagellations, gradually piecing his life together and becoming his own man again. He did it by devoting himself to a higher purpose, using his official capacity within the Church to foster good deeds and effect positive changes. And in time, his efforts were rewarded, for while his actions to achieve Canterbury had been of low character, his performance after attaining the post had been worthy of great praise. He was the man who made the chief ecclesiastical decisions in England; Grimwald no longer had a hold over him. The old prelate could hardly afford to expose his own sordid part in their intrigue, and so at long last Plegmund was free.

But the sly old fox had never allowed him to forget how Canterbury had been won. It was a matter of pride, a sword that always dangled over him.

"I was merely explaining a few things to the girl. But I'm sure your vaunted knowledge of the scriptures has enabled you to long since resolve such trivial issues." He smiled thinly at Grimwald, making no attempt to hide his disdain. "Now, to what do we owe this unexpected visit?"

"I had some business in Rochester, and thought I'd stop by on my return to Sussex Downs," the old monk sniffed. "It's rather quiet there, you know, and I sometimes tire of the loneliness. I need to reassure myself that the Church is in good hands."

"You doubt me?"

Grimwald smiled transparently. "Now, Plegmund...don't be so defensive. And don't be so quick to forget your old friends."

"I would never forget a *true* friend."

"My, isn't he the sensitive one, child?" Grimwald purred at Elfwyn. "And with such a short memory. Why, I can remember at least one occasion when true friendship proved to be a rather inconvenient obstacle." He looked harshly at Plegmund. "You would do well to keep that in mind, Your Ho-li-nessssss."

They stared silently at each other. Grimwald's triumph had assured him of all the power and profit any man could desire, and he had gorged himself until even he had become sated. He certainly had no use for more land or money, and all of his desires concerning the Church had been achieved with spectacular results during the first years following his grand coup.

And that was the problem: there were no worlds left to conquer. He was old and had little energy left for the intrigues that had once occupied so much of his attention. Issues of church or state rarely interested him any longer. Time and age had conspired to do what kings and archbishops could not; he was no longer a dangerous man.

In the twilight of his life, Grimwald had become rather ordinary. And that was the one thing he could never accept.

"What is it you want of me?" Plegmund finally asked.

"A little respect, perhaps, to begin with. But that would be a minor miracle...so for now I expect nothing. Other than a simple crust of bread and a place to sleep tonight."

"That I can certainly give you."

"At the very least, I should think, in spite of all that's happened between us. But never mind that...there's one other thing, one piece of advice you'd do well to heed."

"And that is...?"

"Look outside." Grimwald pointed out the window. "It's a cold rain right now, but in a few weeks the buds will be on the trees. Spring will be here."

"I'm aware of that."

"Then be aware that springtime is a dangerous time, whenever the Vikings are concerned. Mark my words: as soon as the weather clears, they'll be on the march."

Plegmund shrugged. "With Edward standing by, there's little to fear."

"Perhaps. But if the Saxon line fails, you'll be in the path of danger. The Danes will point to Canterbury, I'm afraid."

"And what about you? Sussex Downs isn't all that far from Appledore...what makes you so sure you're any safer than we are?"

Grimwald smirked. "Why would the heathens bother with an isolated estate in the middle of the great Weald when they can have the gold and the glory of Canterbury? Don't hesitate. Be prepared to fly when they march."

"And why this sudden concern for my welfare?"

"Because *you* are the Church now. And while you may find it hard to believe that I could care at all, I don't want to see so much of what I've devoted my life to torn apart with a few simple sword strokes." He smiled down at the girl. "Nor should I want to see this vision of loveliness compromised, and with it the future of Christian England."

He turned and walked toward the door, pausing at the threshold. "Contrary to what you're thinking, Plegmund, for once in my life I have no ulterior motives. Life is a strange journey indeed, don't you think?"

He left the room, and Elfwyn was the first to speak.

"He's so fat…"

"Yes, child. He certainly is."

"And smart, too."

"Yes. Too smart for his own good, I should think."

There was a moment of silence, and then she spoke again. "You don't like him very much, do you?"

He cocked his head. "Now, child...what would make you think that?"

She picked up her quill and returned to her calligraphy. "Oh, I just know, that's all. You don't like him, Plegmund. I can tell."

He said nothing, sighing to himself as he watched her concentrate on her letters. *Don't be too perceptive, child; it can only do you harm. For if you knew all the things I know about Grimwald, you wouldn't like him, either. You wouldn't like him at all.*

Ten days later, on a crisp morning during the first week of March, the waters of the Thames Estuary off Rochester and Milton bristled with sails. Before any resistance could be mounted, almost a hundred Viking ships ground their keels on the north coast of Kent. A panic rippled through Wessex, all the way to Winchester and beyond as Haestan, Warlord of the Vikings, set foot on the damp sands of England.

Grimwald was right. Spring had come.

*   *   *   *   *

Alfred looked into the dark corners of his bedchamber at Rochester and drummed his fingers on the tabletop before him. The only light in the room flickered from the candles that surrounded the parchment upon which he had been writing. As he waited for the ink to dry, he reflected on the shadows that danced across his vision, waving in the wind that slipped through the cracks of the walls.

He had known it would come to this. He had never allowed himself to be drawn into a false sense of security during the years of peace and prosperity that England had enjoyed for most of the last decade. While others had scoffed at the possibility of another invasion, he remained vigilant, watching and waiting.

And now the inevitable had happened, forcing him to put on his armor and wear his war helmet once more. He believed that bloodshed could be avoided, but he was prepared for the worst. He had marched hurriedly from Winchester with several thousand men, a force that doubled in size by the time he reached Rochester, swelled by a long column of soldiers that arrived with Eadred from Mercia. It was enough to keep Haestan at bay—for now, at least—as the Viking watched warily from nearby Milton on the estuary and marshaled his forces. How much longer could the stalemate last? When would the heathens play their hand?

He would soon find out. Straining in the half-light, he leaned forward over the parchment, blowing on the damp ink and reading what he had written once more to satisfy himself that his message was complete:

Edward, my Son:
May these words reach you before the heathen moves upon us, or we upon him. We have drawn our lines up at Rochester and have shown the enemy our might, and for now, by God's grace, it has stayed his hand. Our strengths are nearly equal, but I believe that our position is defensible, and the Danes would be foolish to attack us at this time and place.

We must take nothing for granted, however, nor can we overlook any possibility. I say this because I have met with Haestan and already know him to be as dangerous and cunning an adversary as any Viking we have faced. Not since the days of Halfdan and Ivar the Boneless have we come up against such a formidable man. We met for an hour in the open country between here and Milton, each of us accompanied by a score of men, and the moment I looked into his eyes I knew that what lies before us will not be simple to conclude.

He is a man of presence, a few years older than I am, with long white hair and beard, and a cruel mouth that chooses its words carefully. We spoke of peace but thought of war, for as the Lord God is my witness, I can think of no other reason for his coming to these shores, armed with the knowledge that an even greater number of his people wait in Kent, ready to move upon you the moment he gives the word. He has brought horses and cattle with him, and there are women and children in his camp, so I must conclude he intends to stay and has prepared himself for a long and protracted struggle.

I could see all this in his eyes as we met, and I take solace in knowing that he understands who and what I am, and what I have done to guard England against him and his kind. We are strong now, unlike the dark days when I was a boy king with nothing more than faith to survive against the heathen onslaught.

We shall persevere and triumph, but it will take time. For now I have a strategy that I would impart to you. Tomorrow I will meet again with Haestan and give him gifts of gold and silver, in return for which he has agreed to let his young son be baptized into the Faith. I will serve as the boy's godfather, and so there shall be a bond between us that only war and bloodshed can break. May God in Heaven grant that it not be so.

I am convinced that the real danger is not Haestan's army, but the greater force that you now watch to the south. And so I ask that you send an emissary to them and arrange for a meeting. Guard yourself well, for the heathen is treacherous, and is not above deceiving you and trying to take your life. Talk to their leaders and discover what you can. Look for signs of disagreement, which you can use as a wedge to drive between them. Ask them to leave Wessex in peace, although I hold little hope for that now. And above all, give them no money, as it will not solve the ultimate problem.

There is nothing else I can tell you now. You are my son, a brave and true guardian of the realm, and I am proud of you and know that your sword will strike swiftly when the moment comes. Trust in me, as I trust in you, and let us

*pray to Almighty God for strength and purpose in these
trying times.*

Alfred, the King

He rolled up the parchment and grabbed one of the candles, allowing its wax to drip across the edge of the scroll before sealing it in place with his ring. And then he stood up from the table and walked across the room, opening the door that led into a long hallway. A man-at-arms hurried over to him.

"Go now and summon Penda for me."

The man nodded and trotted down the hallway, disappearing into the darkness. Alfred turned back into his chamber, moving over to a shuttered window and opening it. The cold night air rushed into the room, clearing his head and filling his senses.

If it all ended tomorrow, he could take pride in knowing the journey had been worthwhile. For as he grew older he had begun to sense his mortality, to feel the slow ache that sometimes chilled his bones, to grudgingly accept the lengthy recoveries from ills which not so long ago would have cured themselves in days instead of weeks. He was now forty-three years old, and he was no longer a young man.

But he was by no means old, and there was still much work to be done. For all of his accomplishments, he knew that only the time ahead of him mattered; without goals and a sense of hope, no man can endure for long. He took a deep breath and looked up into the stars, feeling as though he could almost reach out and touch God and the universe. There was so much left to learn, so much to be thankful for in life. And so much left to prove—to Haestan, to Edward, to everyone who looked up to him as Bretwalda, the Golden Dragon of Wessex, the great king of England.

"What would you, My Lord?" It was Penda.

"Come in, my friend. I have a mission for you."

He watched the Saxon as he entered, and he could not help but notice the lines that now creased the back of Devon's neck, snaking along his skin like fissures in a weathered rock. It comforted him to know he wasn't the only one getting old.

"This Haestan troubles me, Sire. He won't be easy to solve."

"I have a plan." Alfred stepped over to the table and picked up the sealed parchment, handing it to Penda in the flickering light. "At dawn I want you to ride south and give this to Edward. And then I want you to stay with him...counsel him. I want you both to meet with the Vikings, and it's important that Edward keep his head and think clearly." He smiled apologetically. "My son has few equals as a soldier, but his statesmanship still leaves something to be desired. I trust that you'll curb his, shall we say...more impulsive tendencies?"

"You can rely on me, My Lord."

"I know I can. But remember this: if words fail, don't hesitate to let him run free. Show them no mercy, Penda. Spill their blood."

"Nothing would give me more pleasure, My Lord. You know how I feel about the heathens."

"So I do." He smiled encouragingly and offered his hand. "Now go, and may God protect you."

Penda returned the handshake and bowed, and Alfred was alone again. He removed his boots and heavier clothing, and then he blew out the candles on the table, plunging the chamber into darkness. He felt his way along the wall until he came to his bed. Kneeling down beside it, he prayed briefly, and then he rose and laid himself down upon the simple mattress, stretching his body to its full length and staring up into the night.

Within a few moments his eyes grew heavy, and he had barely closed them when he fell into a deep, dreamless slumber. It was the contented sleep of a man at peace with himself who does not worry, a man who knows that his day has been well spent and he has done all that a God-fearing Christian can be expected to do.

*   *   *   *   *

"He says he doesn't care about hostages, My Lord," Werferth translated. "All he wants is gold."

Edward smirked as he looked into Hundeus' eyes. The Viking returned his stare evenly, leaning his head back as if to suggest that there was no room for compromise, no point at all in bothering to negotiate. Not that Edward was prepared to bargain; his father's instructions had been clear, and Penda's counsel had filled in the blanks. There would be no capitulation, no display of weakness or indecision.

"No gold," Edward said brusquely, never taking his eyes off Hundeus. "Tell him those days are over. But if he isn't willing to exchange hostages, then how can we trust him to keep the peace?"

Werferth of Worcester nodded, shuffling his feet as he stood alongside Edward and the score of Vikings and Saxons in a meadow at the edge of the Weald. Despite his fluency in the Danish tongue, it had been many years since the monk had been in the presence of the Norsemen, and their scowling, warlike faces unnerved him. He was now of the age when a man prefers to sit by the hearth and contemplate his life instead of placing his body in harm's way.

But there was little he could do about that now; clearing his throat, he passed Edward's words on to Hundeus, who shook his head and laughed before barking out his reply. Werferth listened carefully and then turned to the prince.

"He answers your question with one of his own, Edward. He wonders: what was it that led you to think the Vikings ever intended to come here in peace?"

Edward struggled to maintain his composure; he could not let the Danes see how much their disrespect irritated him.

"Insolent wretches, aren't they?" he said with a chameleon smile, speaking to Penda beside him. "I should pull my blade out and lop his head off, the filthy pagan."

"Be careful. One of them might understand."

"As you say, Penda. But it's all for no use."

He turned back to Werferth. "Tell him we're strong and determined. We can follow him all over England, if we have to, and not let up until we've pushed him back into the sea. Ask him if he's willing to pay that kind of price."

Edward watched the Vikings carefully as Werferth translated. First he observed Hundeus, but it was hard to read the Dane. The heathen had mastered the art of listening to contrary news without showing signs of displeasure, a lesson that Edward realized he still needed to learn. His eyes darted around the table, making a note of the other Vikings who had accompanied their leader to the negotiation. They were a swarthy lot, rugged and rough-hewn, and he realized why the people of Wessex and Mercia were so afraid of them. Without exception, they appeared to be men of action, men who were not likely to lose heart or courage at the first sign of opposition. One by one he marked them, fixing them in his memory.

And then his eyes fell on a face so hideous that it could only have sprung from Hell. How he had missed the man when they had all approached the meeting place was beyond him; he must have been so intensely focused on Hundeus that he had shut everything else out. But there was no ignoring the Viking any longer. His large head, matted hair and beard, pockmarked face—and, above all else, the expanse of scarred flesh where his left eye should have been—marked him as perhaps the ugliest man Edward had ever seen.

Somehow the Viking must have sensed he was being observed, for his lone eye swung around and fixed hard on Edward, and his face lit up in a cruel sneer. A lesser man would have looked away in fear, but Edward stared calmly back at the Dane, measuring him carefully.

You're dealing with the son of a king, heathen. The House of Wessex does not scare that easily. Why, if you....

Penda was nudging him. He snapped to attention as Werferth's voice droned on beside him.

"...doesn't seem to matter, My Lord. The decision, ultimately, is Haestan's. Hundeus is pledged to follow his Warlord. But his men are restless."

"Then tell them that Haestan consented to have his son baptized. It's done. Tell them that my father, King Alfred, stood yesterday as the boy's godfather. What is such a ceremonial act, if not an act of peace?"

Hundeus listened impassively as Edward's words were translated. It surprised him that Haestan would submit to such a ridiculous ritual, but he was undaunted. Perhaps the Warlord needed more time. Perhaps he merely wished to observe the Saxon king more closely and maybe discover a weakness. In either case, Hundeus knew the Vikings paid little attention to such conversions, nor compromised their belief in Odin and the gods of Asgard. No mere sprinkles of water on the forehead could change a man that easily.

The message from Haestan had been clear: hold fast in Appledore until the Warlord made the first move. If Haestan sensed he had the advantage, he would attack the Saxons immediately near Milton, and the force in Kent could then move on Canterbury. But if he felt there would be a struggle, he intended to repair north to a position in Benfleet on the shores of East Anglia, across the Thames Estuary from Kent. In that case, Hundeus was to feint toward Canterbury, send his ships to join Haestan in Benfleet, and then set out with his army toward Winchester and the west. Such a move, Haestan hoped, would extend the Christians and create new opportunities for all of them.

"Tell the young prince that no god—not even the weakling Jesus—ever stood between men who meant to make war on each other," Hundeus said to Werferth, taking particular satisfaction in the insult.

He smiled as the Bishop of Worcester stiffened, and then he turned his attention to Edward. The boy king had courage, of that there could be no doubt. But did he have the cunning to withstand them, the experience to know when and where to play his hand? If not, they would destroy him. They would drag him from his horse and cut him into pieces, stripping him of his armor and leaving his body for the dogs.

"No gold could ever guarantee that you'd leave England," Edward replied coolly. He decided to give the negotiation one more try. "Think of all the needless bloodshed, all the Vikings and Saxons who will die for no reason. All of that can be avoided, if only you would say the word."

Hundeus was still fashioning a reply when a thick, angry protest sounded to his left.

"A Viking welcomes war!"

All eyes swung to the voice. It was Sidroc. Before Hundeus could stop him, the Malevolent One stood up and shook a massive fist at Edward.

"If your knees quake like a woman's at the thought of blood, then name yourself a champion, Christian! Your gold against our retreat! Feed the lamb to me, and let me see what he's made of! If he kills me, then we'll leave England...but if I win, then you'll pay the price!"

Werferth looked at Hundeus, not knowing if he should proceed with the translation. But the Viking chieftain stood there silently as a sly smile spread across his face. And well it should have, for he had never seen a man stand up to Old One Eye and live to tell the tale—not that he would have minded ridding himself of Sidroc if such an impossibility were to happen. Either way, he could not lose. He laughed and nodded and then he spoke to Werferth, knowing that the bargain meant nothing to him and he would never leave England, regardless of the outcome.

"The Viking proposes a challenge," Werferth said uneasily, explaining the terms of the offer. With each word that escaped his lips, Edward's mood grew darker. "And for his champion," the monk concluded, "Hundeus chooses the one-eyed heathen. His name is Sidroc. They call him the Malevolent One."

Edward was stunned.

He stared at Old One Eye, who grinned satanically back at him. The Viking's ham-like forearms bulged as he clenched his fists in anticipation, and it was all that Edward could do to contain his excitement. Sidroc! The name and the man came together all at once, and as he looked into the Viking's face he saw all the horrors that Sigli had described, painted in every pockmarked hollow, dripping from every matted strand of his beard.

"Penda! Did you hear that??!!" he whispered, stone-faced. "Sidroc!"

"I heard."

"I thought he was dead! Killed on the Rhine!"

"Evidently not," Penda said dryly, remembering his own part in the great lie.

Sidroc pointed a gnarled finger at Edward. "Perhaps the Saxon boy king would show himself to be a man and take up the challenge himself," he smiled, "...or do his tender little balls not have any hair on them yet?" The other Vikings roared in laughter.

"What did he say, Werferth? What did he say?" Edward's face turned bright red as he leaned forward. Upon hearing the monk's translation, he started to reach for his sword, but Penda's iron grip closed on his wrist.

"Don't be a fool, man! Think, for once!"

"He mocks me, Penda! I'll have his head!"

"Or he'll have yours."

Edward hesitated. "Would you allow me to dishonor myself like this, in front of our men?"

"There's no dishonor in discretion," Penda cautioned, speaking slowly and carefully. "Think about it: do you really believe the Vikings would keep their word and leave if you were to win? And what if you were killed? What do you think that would do to the men? What about your father, and the throne? Is it worth it, to be lured into such a simple trap by these vermin, all because of some misplaced sense of honor?" Here he paused, letting it all sink in. "I think not, My Lord. I think not."

His words had their desired effect. Edward collected himself and resumed his dialogue with Hundeus as though nothing had happened, and when he saw the disappointment on the Dane's face, he knew he had done the right thing. So be it, he thought. The talking is over; let there be war.

But as he accepted that truth and the meeting wound down, he became aware of Sidroc's single, loathsome eye, which remained trained on him. Every few seconds he stared back into it defiantly, holding his ground, wishing that Sigli could somehow be with him and see what he was now seeing.

And then it was done. They all bowed stiffly to each other, and the Vikings mounted their horses and rode off slowly toward the trees behind them. Sidroc was the last to leave. Edward watched the Malevolent One as he retreated, his broad back swaying side to side as he sat upright in his saddle. Just as he was about to enter the wood, the Viking turned back toward them, shouting across the open meadow. He bellowed away for a few seconds, concluding with a final, obscene gesture and then turning and disappearing into the trees.

"What did he say, Werferth?"

Werferth cleared his throat. "He said, My Lord...he said that Alfred's son is no son at all, certainly not one sired by a king. He said your father must be an imposter...or else you...you must be a fatherless whore-child, sucking at the teat of the she-goat that bore you."

Edward clenched the pommel of his sword until his knuckles turned white.

"Don't worry, My Lord. You'll get your chance at him." Penda said. "But I can tell you this: your father will be proud of you. You showed great restraint, when it was called for. You did the right thing."

It occurred to Edward that he had. And as he stood there, his eyes still fixed on the distant forest, he realized what now had to be done. It was the right thing, the honorable thing. It was the *only* thing. Never before in all his life had he been so certain of himself.

He turned and walked toward his horse, his mind made up. Let the serpent devour its tail, let the circle close in upon itself. Let Destiny be served.

*   *   *   *   *

The fog crept in from the North Sea, billowing over the still waters of the harbor. Not a sound could be heard from the cluster of huts tucked into the hillside above the crescent-shaped cove, high up on the lonely Northumbrian coast. The hour was late, and if not for the gentle lapping of the waves against the hulls of the three dragon ships moored in the harbor, the midnight silence would have been complete.

A lone figure sat on a large rock that protruded into the cove, watching the fog and listening to the sea. He cradled a cup of mead in his hand, and the sweet brew rushed to his head, filling him with longing. It all reminded him of home, long ago and far away, a dream that had faded for him as the years slipped away. Unable to sleep, he had climbed out to the rock to stare into the darkness and think, to brood in his cups and once again reflect on what a sad and lonely thing it all was.

He shivered as a blast of wind crossed the harbor. Death in life, that's what it felt like. Cynical, drunk and left to drift without a rudder, he found himself wondering if there was any purpose at all to carry on.

Sigli had seen the world, and yet he had seen nothing. The almost seven years since he had been exiled from England had been filled with wandering, across one sea and over another, looking for something, looking for It. Like his father before him, he sailed south through the Pillars of Hercules, to faraway lands inhabited by dark-skinned people who spoke in strange tongues. It was not there. He dared the unknown and went back through the Pillars and even further south, hugging the damp, close west coast of Africa, finding nothing but hot nights and untamed savages. It was not there, either.

When he reached the windless doldrums and could go no farther, he pointed his prow northward again, but still he did not find It. He visited Francia and Jutland, the island kingdom of Eire and the low countries of Frisia. He sailed east, to the land of the Russ, and then farther north than perhaps any man had ever gone before him, along the shores of the Arctic Sea. He sailed almost everywhere in the known world, but there were two places he did not go. One of them was England, and the other was Halfsfiord. Silence and ruins, exile and burial bairns.

There was nowhere left to go.

Nowhere but west, into the endless sea that stretched into the horizon. He wanted to sail there now, but the others were against it; they feared it would take them to the end of the world and crash their ships against the rocky coast of Jotunheim, where the frost giants waited to devour them. It would not have bothered him at all. He tried to convince them to sail with him, but even Dagmar had been against it. They were all he had, and he could not bring himself to part with them, and so he listened and stayed, with no place to go.

The fog surrounded him now, and the night grew colder. He struggled to his feet and lurched forward, spilling his mead and nearly falling as he stepped off the rock and onto the path that led up to the huts. His breathing grew heavy as he labored up the hill, and his head began to spin. Too much to drink tonight, more than usual. He was still fit and in good health, but the nightly bouts with mead had taken their toll. He breathed a little bit more deeply these days than he would have liked to admit, but by now his youth was behind him. He was thirty-five years old.

He kept climbing until the outline of a hut loomed before him in the mist. A few logs slapped together to ward off the wind, a leaky roof that kept most of the rain out, but at least it was his. Such were the privileges of leadership. Most of the others slept in a cramped hall up the hill where the meeting fire burned, a smoke-filled room that even he reluctantly resorted to during the coldest nights. Thank Odin that spring was on the way. He pulled aside the animal skin that covered the door and ducked inside, and then he crawled into his bed, a heavy bearskin that lay draped over a pile of straw. He rolled over onto his back and stared up into the darkness, his head spinning as the fog seemed to swirl into the room, and then he did what he always did, every night.

He thought of her.

She was the only one, even if she was just a memory. Because loving a memory was better than loving nothing at all. He still clung to the slim hope that he would someday see her again, if only just to lay his eyes on her one more time. It was all that was left to him. He often wondered what it was like for her, living in Mercia with Eadred, and he wondered if she ever thought of him, of the way it had been between them. She was etched like a flawless jewel in his mind, and he knew she would always stay that way, beyond the reach of time. It was more than he could bear to think that she might not love him anymore, and so he remembered the way they were, and took what comfort he could in it.

Her face melted into the mead as he closed his eyes and drifted away. The night grew distant, and soon he found himself suspended in a dreamy semi-consciousness, neither asleep nor awake. He could feel his body floating, until by some trick of the gods he was uplifted into a standing position, and his furs fell from him into a heap upon the earth. The mist clogged the room, close and impenetrable, and he felt a great need to escape the hut for the open air. He tried to step forward but could not. And then a great force pulled at him, like a powerful magnet, and he glided effortlessly toward it, passing through the animal skin across his doorway and out into the night.

He found himself standing in the center of a great flat rock surrounded on all sides by the mist. The air was still, framing a silence so deep that even when he clapped his hands together he could neither hear nor feel anything. His being was numb; he could not move his legs. As he stared straight ahead, the fog pulled back from what he had thought to be an outcropping in the rock, revealing a hooded figure dressed in a long black robe.

He tried to run away, but could not. And then the apparition took a few steps toward him, raising a bony finger and pointing it at his face, and he felt his stomach begin to tumble. He cried out, but no sound escaped his lips, and just when the silence seemed unbearable, a sharp, familiar voice cut through the air:

> *"Hearken to me, Lothar's child; your teacher speaks again,*
> *From dark and dreary Niflheim, deep in Loki's den."*

Suddenly the cloak fell away to reveal a thin, ascetic man gnarled with age. Sigli gasped as he stared into the man's sightless eyes, two opaque windows to the world that saw nothing, yet understood everything.

"Mimir!" he shouted, noiselessly.

The old seer smiled the same wide, toothless grin that Sigli had known and loved so well, and then he reached out with his bony hand and beckoned. The same force that had pulled Sigli from his hut now yanked him forward once again, closer to Mimir and near the edge of the rock, and suddenly he had the power to raise his arm and reach out for the old Halfsfiordian. But he was still not close enough to touch him; he strained and strained, extending himself until his joints ached and his fingers were mere inches from Mimir's, and then the seer stepped forward and locked hands with him. His grip was icy but firm, and Sigli felt himself being lifted up and pulled over the edge of the great rock as they leaped headlong into the fog.

He closed his eyes and tried to scream, and when he finally had the courage to look, a brilliant sky had replaced the swirling mist. Its blue backdrop was broken only by a series of cotton-shaped clouds that reflected the rays of the sun. He and Mimir now stood together on the edge of a large field of grain that shone like pure gold in the sunlight, so bright that it almost hurt his eyes. The silence was complete again, suspending them in a vacuum that made everything that much sharper to the eye, almost surreal. The field stretched to the distant horizon, its thigh-high stalks bending in the wind and rolling in a great wave as though the grain was the sea itself. It was indescribably beautiful to look upon.

Mimir took him by the hand, and to his surprise he found he could walk. They plunged into the field, neither their steps nor the rustling of the grain against their legs making even the faintest noise, and they began to make their way slowly toward the horizon. He became aware of something moving in the grass in front of him, and suddenly he could see a small child, a girl of perhaps five or six whose head and shoulders extended above the waving wheat thirty yards ahead. As they drew closer he could see that she was naked. Her blonde hair and blue eyes blended perfectly with the field and the sky, and he could feel her power, at once innocent and sensual. There was something about her that he found irresistible. He quickened his pace through the wheat, filled with a great delight.

When he had closed to within ten yards the girl turned and began to run through the field, moving just quickly enough to stay ahead of him. Sigli kept his eyes focused on her, trying to run and moving just fast enough to track her. She darted back and forth, as carefree as a child can be, and she was a joy to behold. He followed her like this, mesmerized, until finally he looked up and saw a man watching them from a short distance ahead of the girl. She ran and hid behind the man, who was ashen-faced and cheerless, one of the walking dead.

As Sigli drew closer, he gasped; it was his father, Lothar.

He was overcome by the sight. He felt a hand on his shoulder; it was Mimir again. The seer smiled and spoke in a voice that crackled with energy as it punctured the silence:

> *"Your passion now has run its course, your seed has skyward sprung.*
> *And all your life seems over—but all is not yet done!*
> *Remember now your lifelong pledge; take up your father's sword*
> *And strike a blow for honor. Forsake not Halfsfjord!"*

With his heart pounding, Sigli turned back to Lothar, who reached stiffly into his belt and withdrew a gleaming broadsword. The blade flashed in the sunlight, a thing of power and beauty, compelling him to step forward. He stopped in front of his father and reached out, closing his fingers tightly around the hilt and raising the sword above him.

At that moment a blinding flash of lightning tore through the sky, striking the blade and igniting it into a brilliant, white-hot fire. A crash of thunder shattered the silence, echoing across the field and causing the earth to tremble. And suddenly the fleecy, powder-puff clouds were gone, transformed into an angry mass of dark thunderheads that scudded across the sky, gathering in intensity and hurling the wheat field into chaos.

Sigli looked around in a panic. As the wind screamed in his ears, he saw the little girl running toward a dark mass of trees that bordered the field. Something about the forest alarmed him terribly, so he broke into a sprint after her, sword in hand. She reached the edge of the field, turned to look back at him, and then disappeared into a break into the trees. He ran toward the spot, but when he reached it he found that the forest had somehow grown over in a deep tangle of underbrush and thorns. He began to hack wildly at the foliage, sweating profusely, but with every stroke that ripped away at the thorns it seemed as though twice as many brambles appeared to take their place.

She was gone, vanished in the forest.

He leaned on his sword, breathing heavily, and stared into the impenetrable mass before him; to his surprise, his eyes were suddenly filled with a vision from somewhere deep within the tangled wood. A lone figure, burly and broad-backed, sat brooding under the shadow of a great oak. The man faced the opposite direction, obscuring his features, but Sigli could tell that he was a Viking. A war helmet was perched on his black-maned head, while a menacing battle-axe leaned against a nearby rock; he appeared to be a man of great strength.

But something was wrong. The man struggled to hold something close to his chest, enveloping it in his hairy, muscled arms so that Sigli could not see what it was. There was a cry, and then suddenly the man swung around, his one good eye leering wickedly as he clutched the fair little girl to him.

It was Sidroc.

The Malevolent One howled with a murderous laughter that sent chills up and down Sigli's spine. His heart stopped, and he could not breathe. He felt himself begin to stagger.

And then the leering eye transformed itself into two familiar, sightless windows. Mimir's cold hands cupped his face, and he was vaguely aware they were no longer in the wheat field, but had returned to the rock and the mist. He felt himself flying into the seer's eyes, those wild eyes, and he heard his old teacher's voice ring out again, beating a hot breath against his face:

> *"The Beast of Blood has shown himself, the Hel Hound is revealed.*
> *Sigli's bane, the one-eyed Dane, lies lurking in the Weald.*
> *Blood be spilled and blood be saved, by Odin's prophecy.*
> *Seek out now the twilight hour, where vengeance waits for thee."*

Mimir dropped his hands to his sides and began to glide ominously backward, surrounded by silence and the swirling mists. Sigli tried to cry out as the seer began to fade away, but he could not. Mimir was now at the edge of the rock, the dark robe once again draped around his shoulders, and the fog closed around him until all that remained were his two sightless eyes, burning like twin coals. The old man whispered, fainter now:

> *"Blood be spilled and blood be saved, by Odin's prophecy.*
> *Seek out now the twilight hour, where vengeance waits for thee."*

And then he was gone, swallowed up by the fog. Sigli tilted his head back and screamed out.

"M-I-MMMMM-I-RRRRR!"

He awoke sitting upright on the floor of the hut, sweating profusely. The room was deathly quiet, but much brighter than before; the fog had disappeared, replaced by a full moon that shone through the open space between the animal skin and the frame of the doorway. He trembled, and a wave of claustrophobia washed over him, and he felt a great need to escape the hut. He stumbled to his feet, tearing at his clothing to let the cool air dry the sweat from his body, and then he burst through the doorway and onto the hillside.

The night was clear. He stood in the crisp air, struggling to compose himself, but he could not seem to make sense of anything. The dream began to replay itself again, filling him with a great fear and uncertainty. He was consumed by a vast sense of loneliness. As he stood there, shaking in a light breeze that swept across the headland, he suddenly became aware of activity on the hillside above him. It came from the path leading to the main lodge at the crest of the incline. He heard footfalls, and turned to see several of his men hurrying toward him, Dagmar in the lead.

"Sigli! You're still awake! By Odin, you won't believe..." Dagmar stopped abruptly. "Are you all right, man? You look terrible."

Sigli waved him off as the other men hurried forward. "No...no...don't worry. It was just a dream. You can go back, now...I'll be fine, really."

"You don't understand!" Dagmar's eyes gleamed in the moonlight. "News has come, from the south! By the gods, there *is* justice in the world, after all!"

Sigli had never seen Dagmar so excited, not even in the heat of battle. The other men bristled with the same strange energy.

"Come forward, man!" Dagmar shouted. "Here's the one you seek!"

The Vikings parted, and a man Sigli had never seen before stepped toward him. His dress and bearing immediately identified him as a Saxon. The fatigue on his face and his damp, mud-stained robe made it obvious he had been riding for some time and had just come off the road. He eyed Sigli carefully.

"It's you, all right," he nodded, convinced. "They said you might be the one who was moored here. I remember you, from years ago…although you don't know me."

"What do you want?"

"I'm sent by Edward the Elder," the man answered, more formally now, "with a message. My Lord bids me to tell you that what you're about to hear is neither a reprieve, an end to your exile, nor a call to action. It's the truth— nothing more, nothing less. What you do about it is your business."

"Get to it, man! What is it?"

The man cleared his throat. "Lord Edward has met with the heathen invaders in Appledore. He's seen them with his own eyes. One among them, he thinks, is of some importance to you."

Here he looked directly into Sigli's eyes, and the Viking somehow knew what he would say before he said it.

"His name is Sidroc, the Malevolent One. Old One Eye, some call him. He's very much alive, and he invades Wessex as we speak."

CHAPTER XIV: The Valley Of The Shadow

"Come in under the shadow of this red rock,
And I will show you something different from either
Your shadow at morning striding behind you
Or your shadow at evening rising to meet you;
I will show you fear in a handful of dust."
—T.S. Eliot, <u>The Waste Land</u>

How long he had been asleep he could not tell, but Alfred knew it had not been long enough. At first he could not find his bearings, but the creaking of the ship as it rolled in the light sea refreshed his memory, if not his spirits. The night had been cold, and he moaned as he sat up in the pre-dawn darkness, all aching joints and stiff muscles. It was bad enough that a man his age had to sleep in a strange bed; doing it aboard a ship, propped up against the bulwark like a damp sack of grain, was almost intolerable.

But such are the fortunes of war. He had known the time was near when the Viking ships left Kent, bound around Dover and then north to join Haestan. The bulk of the Danish army, meanwhile, stayed behind the fleet in Appledore. He believed the heathens were preparing to advance northeast on Canterbury; it was the only explanation that made any sense. Edward had positioned his troops between the Vikings and the Kentish Stour, leaving Penda and Fulric of Kent in command and hastening west to Winchester to raise another army. With the long winter of inactivity coming to an end, every man in Wessex capable of bearing arms had to be summoned into the field.

The king rose to his feet, steadying himself against the bulwark. Most of the men were asleep on the deck, and as he looked astern he could sense the first signs of dawn in the air. A morning mist lay over the sea, making it difficult to see more than a few yards in any direction. There were other Saxon ships out there somewhere, but how many or how close they were he did not know; they would all gather together to assess matters when the day broke.

He wondered if he had made the right decision, sending for the fleet. It had been moored on the lee side of the Isle of Thorney, poised to meet the Viking ships from Kent before they could join with Haestan. But there were over two hundred dragon ships in the heathen armada, and he did not want to take the chance that his navy might be broken in an all-out battle. He had sent word for his ships to retreat ahead of the advancing heathens and descend on Haestan's rear from the sea. He would attack the Warlord in concert from the land, surrounding the Viking and crushing him before the reinforcements from Kent could arrive.

But the crafty Haestan had taken matters into his own hands and launched his own attack against the Saxons the day before at dawn. After an initial disadvantage, the English had gathered to counterattack, but the Vikings withdrew as suddenly as they had come and fled to their ships.

It was only then that Alfred realized the ruse. Haestan had packed everything up and readied his fleet to sail during the night; all his horses, his livestock, his fighting men—all were prepared to slip away from Milton. The attack at dawn had been a distraction to cover his retreat, and when the last of the Vikings finally clambered aboard, every last vessel put out to sea and headed toward the northwest, closer to London.

Alfred's own fleet arrived just a few hours later from Thorney. After replacing his tired sailors with fresh men, he boarded one of the ships and immediately set off in pursuit of Haestan, dispatching the rest of the army to London to fortify his defenses. He had hoped his adversary would sail for the city, for he would have been able to follow the Viking and cut off his escape to the sea.

It would then have been a simple matter to advance upon them with his navy, his army from Rochester and the Mercian force under Eadred that was now bearing down from the northeast.

But once again Haestan had been too clever to fall into the trap. Feinting toward London, he turned back to the northeast and the open sea, crossing at the widest part of the estuary and heading for Benfleet on the East Anglian coast. There he could expect to find a warm welcome from the Danelaw. There would be food and supplies now that spring was here, and with Guthrum dead and his restraining hand no longer a factor, Haestan's ranks would undoubtedly grow stronger.

Even with these latest setbacks, Alfred was undeterred. He could feel his spirits rising despite the dampness of the morning; the sun would burn off the remaining mist, and then they could regroup. They would have to bypass Benfleet and fortify themselves to protect London, from where he had access to all of Wessex, Mercia and East Anglia. He was confident it was a position he could hold indefinitely. Even the combined Viking fleet would not be powerful enough to disturb him there. And with his army in Kent facing off the heathens in Appledore, soon to be fortified by Edward and the western fyrd, he felt prepared.

Shouts rang out from somewhere in the mist ahead. He stood at attention, peering out over the bow and across the dark waters, but it was still impossible to see anything. The yells grew louder, and he could hear the splash of oars. It awakened the others, too, and soon the deck was alive with men. He ran forward, squinting through the fog, waiting, wondering. Suddenly there was a loud crash, the unmistakable sound of two ships colliding. They could hear men swearing angrily. And then, knifing toward them through the fog, the prow of a ship suddenly appeared no more than twenty yards distant, its deck lit by the torches. It was a Viking dragon ship, flying the banner of the Raven.

"Arm yourselves!"

The ship was heading directly toward them. They would crash; it was inevitable. But then Alfred saw the helmsman swing the tiller hard to one side, acting in perfect harmony with his port oarsmen as they pulled through the chop. The starboard rowers lifted their own blades out of the water, and the dragon ship changed course sharply, veering hard to the right. It was deftly done, magnificent, even—but it was still uncertain if they would avoid a collision. The Saxons readied themselves as the dragon ship swung lazily toward them in a long arc, straining against the sea. And then the helmsman righted the tiller while barking out a command. Both the starboard and port oars pulled in unison, and the ship surged safely forward.

There was noise and yelling and an awful clatter, and the torches on the deck of the Viking ship now illuminated the faces of the men on board. Some of the Saxons scrambled to their oars, while others armed themselves as the dragon ship began to slice past them, no more than a few yards away. Alfred's eyes were drawn to the helmsman as the Viking stern slashed by through the water, and at that moment the man looked directly at him. Their eyes locked.

It was Sigli.

Alfred fell back against the bulwark, stunned. The dragon ship churned forward and began to slip away.

"Man the oars! After them!"

The Saxons leaped to their positions and brought the vessel about, and soon they were moving forward through the water, still within sight of the fleeing dragon ship. They pulled together on their oars, and the craft responded, knifing through the sea in pursuit. But it wasn't enough; they continued to drop farther behind. By now the dawn was breaking, and with each minute the mist continued to recede, ensuring that the dragon ship would remain in view. Alfred looked all around him, where he could now see the two Saxon ships that had collided, along with several other vessels that had joined in the chase; none of them were as close to the Viking as he was. It was up to him.

Suddenly the dragon ship turned hard to port, angling across his bow on a course that would bring it back within reach. He shouted to his helmsman, who adjusted the ship's course to cut off the heathens. The rowers attacked their oars with renewed vigor and the ship picked up speed; surely it would only be a matter of minutes before they caught up and were able to engage the enemy.

As he watched the dragon ship, he suddenly understood why Sigli had veered back into his path; there, materializing through the dissipating mist, he could see at least a half dozen of his own ships bearing down on the heathens from the starboard.

"We've got them now! Row, by God!"

He looked astern, where several more Saxon ships continued to cut through the water hard in his wake. He felt a breeze begin to lick at his face from behind them west, a following wind that would help propel them along their course, and then he looked ahead and to starboard again, where the Vikings were raising their sail. He yelled to his men to do the same, and they lost precious seconds fumbling with the rigging, but soon the sheet was up. It filled with the breeze, accelerating the ship through the light chop, and the Saxons went back to their oars.

The sun was now up in the east, directly in their course, and Alfred could see a familiar spit of land jutting into the estuary ahead of them. They had to catch Sigli before he rounded the point and reached the open sea. It was up to them now, for most of the other pursuers had dropped off, struggling to hoist their own sails and rejoin the chase.

But there was no way Sigli could avoid them, no escape. He could not veer off back into the other Saxons, he could not bear too hard to port and risk the danger of running aground in the shallow waters off the spit. He had no choice but to take his chances and run with the wind. It began to blow harder, filling the sails of the two ships as they sped over the water, the rowers straining to the exhortations of their masters. The Saxons had now angled to within fifty yards and were closing fast, and several of them had taken up a position in the bow with grappling irons, waiting for the chance to board.

Sigli barked out an order, and several Vikings surged to the bulwarks with bows in hand. Each placed the tip of his arrow in the torches that burned in the breeze, and the cloth-wrapped barbs immediately burst into flames. Drawing their bowstrings back, the archers took aim, and one by one they unleashed their fiery missiles in high, sloping arcs toward the Saxon ship. Some of the shafts fell harmlessly into the sea, while others landed on the deck and were quickly extinguished by the rowers.

The ship surged on, now within thirty yards of the Danes. But the first salvo had shown the Vikings the range. They refitted their bows with flaming arrows and let the missiles fly. This time five of the shafts found their mark, ripping into the sail of the Saxon ship. Despite the dampness of the morning, several of the arrows were fanned by the wind, and in the next moment a section of the sail caught on fire. There was nothing the Saxons could do to arrest the flames without slowing down, so they kept rowing, hoping to close with the heathens before it was too late.

But then a tongue of fire raced along the seam of the sail, splitting it in half, and the race was over. The Saxon ship stopped dead in the water as the rowers threw down their oars and scurried about to control the flaming sail.

But Alfred paid them no heed; he could have been surrounded by the fires of Hell and would not have noticed. He only had eyes for Sigli, who now glared at him in triumph from the stern of the retreating dragonship. The other Saxon vessels were now coming up from the rear, but they were too late and too far behind to catch the escaping heathens.

It was over.

Alfred watched the dragonship as it rounded the promontory and shot into the open sea, running before the wind and picking up speed. He brought his hand angrily down on the rail atop the bulwark, and he swore loudly at his bad luck.

And then the Vikings were gone.

Above him, a flock of seagulls soared effortlessly over the estuary. They could see the lone Viking ship scudding off to the east, and behind it a score or more of Saxons vessels converging on the fire at sea. But none of it mattered to the birds; they were intent only on finding their breakfasts. It was a fine spring morning, after all, and the fish would soon be jumping.

*   *   *   *   *

There is no greater lie than the lie of security. It was an irony that Plegmund contemplated yet again as he packed his belongings into an oxcart outside Christ Church Cathedral. He had always thought that Canterbury would be the answer to his prayers, that it would provide the final piece to the puzzle of his master plan. But Canterbury had merely been a symbol that, until it was achieved, had obscured the larger issues in his life: peace of mind, self-realization and that most elusive of all pursuits, happiness.

When he had achieved the Archbishopric, the temptations of the world had faded in importance, only to be replaced by metaphysics. And metaphysics were intangible; you could not touch them, breathe them, or acquire them to show off to your peers. Being at one with the greater universe was a state reserved for God—and for those who were destined to be at one with Him for eternity. For Plegmund, that was the most uncertain destiny of all.

He only knew that he was preparing to flee a place and a position that had meant everything to him. Oh, the time would pass and he would return, but Canterbury was no different than any other place. Might made for right, and brute force would always gain the upper hand. He had learned that hard fact again the night before, when a rider arrived from Alfred to warn him that Haestan was on the move and there was no one left to protect the northern and eastern approaches to Canterbury. Edward still remained between them and the heathens in Kent, but they could no longer remain along the banks of the Stour and be secure.

Because there was no such thing as security, after all.

"I'm ready now, Plegmund."

Elfwyn walked into view, a perfect little angel, reminding him of the real reason he had decided to leave.

"You look refreshed, child. Did you sleep well?"

"Very well, thank you. But when do we leave? And do I get to ride my own horse?"

"Part of the time, at least." He crammed another bag filled with parchments into the cart; one could never have enough writings on hand for an extended absence. "And part of the time you can ride with me, and drive the cart."

"Oh, but those oxen are so fat and slow." Her face screwed up into a contorted little knot. "I like horses better."

"Like your mother. She would approve."

"Here, Plegmund," Elfwyn said, extending her hand to him. "I drew a picture for you last night."

"Oh, did you? Let me see!" He was delighted to receive her attention. Unrolling the parchment, he peered down at it. Two stick figures rode on horseback, outlined in several brightly colored inks that vaguely defined their bodies in a crude but compelling vision. It was irresistibly charming.

"That's us, Plegmund," she laughed, pleased with her handiwork.

"I'm the tall one, I suppose," he chuckled. "But, who are all these dark figures, the ones here in the background?" He pointed to a tangled mass of ink on the edge of the page.

"Oh, those are the Vikings."

"Vikings? What do you mean?"

"They're chasing us."

"And why would you have them doing that?"

"Because they're out there, and they're chasing us. That's why I drew us on horses, Plegmund...so we can get away."

"You have an active imagination. You shouldn't even think such thoughts." He reached out and stroked her blonde hair. "We're just taking a trip west, that's all. It's springtime, and we should be thinking about getting you back to your mother and father."

"But why don't we go through London, like always?"

"It's not such a good time to go that way right now, Elfwyn. Besides, it's so pretty this time of year in the Weald. All the buds are opening on the trees, and soon the forest will be like a great green blanket. We'll head west, toward Winchester, and either cross the Thames later to get to Mercia, or wait in Hampshire until someone comes for you. Now, why don't you look through your room one more time, to make sure you have everything. What about that bonnet the Sisters made for you...have you forgotten that?"

She dashed back through the door that led to her quarters, consumed with this latest matter of importance. It was a good thing that she kept her mind on such banalities, he thought to himself. They had to move quickly to get beyond harm's way. He looked around at the score of armed men who would accompany them and nodded in satisfaction. There were enough soldiers to protect them, but not too many to slow them down. They could be in Winchester in several days, as long as the weather held up.

And as long as they avoided danger.

He looked again at the parchment, and his eyes drifted to the dark stick figures scribbled along the margin. There were always the scribbles to account for; a man could never afford to lose sight of that.

*   *   *   *   *

Just before dark that evening, Penda of Devon rode into Canterbury at the head of a long column of men. His orders from Edward had been clear: the city had to withstand an attack at all costs. That morning a detachment of Vikings had broken away from Appledore and headed across the countryside as though they meant to take a direct route toward the city. Fulric had fallen back to block their path, but from that point on their movements had been difficult to track. Penda had left with a larger force for the city itself, anticipating that the main Viking army would double back and try to swing wide around the Saxon right flank, approaching Canterbury from the Weald.

And so they did—or so it seemed. But just an hour ago he had received word from his scouts on the perimeter; the Viking forces were now heading west, moving directly away from Canterbury and through the Weald. None of it made sense, unless they were planning an assault on Winchester—unlikely considering their strength and the reinforcements the Saxons could expect from the west. But Penda had learned never to attempt to divine the inner workings of the heathen mind. They were unlawful savages, men without a cross, and they could never be trusted or understood.

It was just as well, he thought to himself, as he rode into the main square in front of Christ Church Cathedral. His men could rest in Canterbury tonight, finally escaping the tedium and discomfort of the provinces. He could feel his stomach grumbling in anticipation of the evening meal, so he called a ceorl over to him.

"Go summon Plegmund for me, will you, man?"

"I'm sorry, My Lord. He's already gone."

"Gone? Gone where?"

"He left this morning, My Lord, with a score of men. He's heading west, he is, through the Weald and toward Winchester. And the girl's with him."

"Elfwyn, you mean? Alfred's granddaughter is with him?"

"That she is, My Lord."

"Damn!" Penda slapped his palm against his leg. "Go summon some of the monks for me, will you?"

He dismounted from his horse as the ceorl bowed and scurried away, and he barely even noticed the other Saxons as they rode into the square. There had been a miscommunication. Plegmund should never have left. With the redeployment of the Saxon forces, there was no safer place to be right now than Canterbury. He shook his head and let out a deep breath as the darkness descended over the banks of the Stour. He would set out after them tomorrow, with enough men to withstand anything he might encounter on the road.

Until then there was nothing to do but wait. And that was the hardest part of all.

*   *   *   *   *

The dragon ship crawled slowly up the Limen and through the sluggish waters. The river was not much wider at that point than the ship itself, a disadvantage that was not lost on the men. There was little room to maneuver—barely enough to even turn around, for that matter—and they would be virtually defenseless if attacked from either bank. They knew they could expect little mercy at the hands of the Saxons; the narrow escape in the Thames Estuary the day before had proved that. And they were clearly in Saxon territory now, with the marshy countryside of Kent seemingly merging into their bulwarks as they rowed on, heading deeper inland with each stroke of their oars.

Sigli stared ahead from his post at the tiller. There could be no turning back now. At any minute he half expected to encounter Hundeus' army, and the thought of actually seeing *him*, of finding Sidroc after so many years, was almost more than he could bear. He wondered if he would be able to contain himself, if the element of surprise would be lost to him because of his excitement, for he doubted that Sidroc ever thought of him or suspected that his quest was still a living thing after sixteen long years.

But his desire for revenge was stronger than ever. Mimir had been right that night on the rock at Halfsfiord; hate can keep a man alive. The news of his enemy's reappearance had come to him like a dark blessing, a welcome gift from the gods. For the first time in many years he had something to live for, and he was grateful for it.

They had sailed south from Northumbria for Kent when word reached them that Haestan was planning to establish himself in Benfleet, so they headed immediately for the East Anglian harbor and arrived in port a few hours before the Warlord. Sigli had hoped that Sidroc was with Haestan, but the arrival of the Danish fleet dispelled that notion.

With Kent still foremost in his mind, he shoved off in the middle of the night and sailed directly into the teeth of the Saxon blockade. He had known it would be a great risk, but he was unwilling to stay and take the chance they might be confined to Benfleet if the Saxons could hem them in. Only quick thinking and skill had enabled them to evade the Saxon ships, but they had still paid a serious price. Alfred had seen them and now believed they were part of Haestan's invading force. It was just one more thing working against Sigli; he was a marked man.

Later that day they met up with the Viking fleet from Kent as it rounded Dover, and they learned that Sidroc had wintered in Appledore and was preparing to embark with the rest of Hundeus' army on a massive raiding expedition into the heart of Wessex. And so they sailed on through the night, reaching the mouth of the Limen by dawn and heading inland on what had turned out to be a bright spring morning.

Now they rounded a bend in the river and came upon a partially built fortress, nestled in the shadow of the forest that crept down to the edge of the marsh. It was the same Saxon burh upon which the Vikings had advanced the autumn before. Not a soul could be seen stirring about the crude earthworks. As Sigli stared across the marsh, Dagmar made his way through the banks of rowers, passing by the bare mast amidships and finally leaning against the port bulwark near the tiller.

"I don't like it. I don't like it at all," he finally said. "If they were still here, we would have seen signs."

"We haven't reached Appledore yet. We'll have to wait and see."

Dagmar leaned forward. The sunlight glinted off his beard, illuminating each speckled grey hair as though it were a strand of fine silver.

"I'm worried, Sigli," he whispered so the others could not hear. "I'm worried about the men."

"What do you mean? What's wrong?"

"We're vulnerable here, you know, and if Hundeus has already left, the countryside could be crawling with Saxons by now. We don't have a very defensible position here."

"What's there to defend?"

"Their lives are at stake, after all, and it will only get worse once we reach Appledore. What do you intend to do about the ship?"

"I haven't thought about that."

"But what if no one's there? Will we turn around and put out to sea again?"

"We're not going anywhere, Dagmar. There's nowhere left to go. If the army's left Appledore, then we'll have to abandon ship and follow them."

"That's madness! The ship would fall into Saxon hands, and we'd be stranded!"

"There are ten thousand Vikings out there somewhere. It's not as though we'd be completely alone."

Dagmar shook his head. "I don't think any of us wants to side with either Haestan or Hundeus. We don't want to make war on Wessex. And besides, what can we expect from the Danes when it becomes clear that you want to find one of their leaders and kill him?"

"I couldn't care less. Whether you and the others come along is something you'll have to decide for yourselves, but I'm committed. Nothing can change that. Now...are you with me, or is this our final goodbye?"

Dagmar shook his head and broke into a pained smile. "I'm with you, Sigli, until the end. You know that. But the others, well...I'm not so sure."

"We'll worry about them later. But for now, take heart. And thank you."

They continued to row silently up the Limen as the sun beamed down upon them, and their fear subsided as Appledore finally appeared within view. They could see two dragon ships moored at the edge of the village, and there were signs of activity on their decks as a number of Vikings loaded the vessels. They rowed steadily closer, until finally one of the Danes loading the moored ships turned and hailed them.

"Halloo, there! Why are you returning? Is something wrong?"

"We're not from the fleet!" Sigli shouted. "I'm looking for a countryman of mine…his name is Sidroc! Do you know him?"

"Old One Eye, you mean? I know him, all right...and I'm just as glad to see him gone!"

"Where did he go?" By now they had pulled alongside the dragon ship.

"There," the man answered, pointing northwest past the village, where the forest crept down to the edge of the fields. "They all left two days ago—Hundeus, Sidroc, all of them. How far they've gone I don't know, but I'm not about to stay any longer to find out. We were left to take care of a few last details, but we'll be sailing down river within an hour to join the rest of the ships. Did you meet them at sea?"

"Yesterday, around the tip of Dover. But tell me...where is Sidroc going?"

The Viking shrugged. "West for now. That's all I know. You're too late. Take my advice and sail with us; the Saxons will be here before long, and they'll be ready for blood."

"I'm afraid that's impossible. Are there any horses around here we might have?"

"Not that I know of. Hundeus took them all. It will be almost impossible for you to find any...either we took them before winter, or the Christians ran away with them. But look, man...I've got to finish here. Are you sure you won't sail with us?"

"I'm sure."

"All right, then…it's your neck." With that he clambered ashore to continue loading the dragon ship with the others in his crew.

Sigli turned to address his men. "You heard him," he said, looking each one of them in the eye. "You know as well as I do the way things are. But my mind's made up; I'm not going back. I have no use for this ship anymore, so if any of you don't want to go on with me, well...do what you want with it."

He threw his cloak over his shoulders and leaped over the bulwark into the shallows, plowing through the knee-deep water until he reached the shore. Finally, he turned to face them.

"All those who want to come with me, decide now. As for the rest, may Odin be with you. Someday, perhaps, we'll meet again."

The men looked back and forth at each other, hesitant to make a move. Finally Dagmar broke the awkward silence. "I'm a fool, I know it...but I'll be a Halfsfiordian until the day I die. That's all that matters."

He jumped into the Limen and waded ashore. At first no one moved to follow, but then Leif slid over the bulwarks, and after that Hagan. The last to leave the ship were Bor and Hoenir, until finally all five of the original Halfsfiordians who were still with Sigli stood on the riverbank.

But that was all; none of the other men on board stirred.

"So be it. It's done," Sigli said.

He turned and began to walk through Appledore, followed by Dagmar and the others. They trudged silently down one of the narrow lanes in the village, stepping over the uneven furrows that had been carved into the mud by the wagon wheels. No one looked back as they headed for the open field, and beyond it the thick line of trees that marked the edge of the Weald.

Leaving the last huts behind, they crossed over the damp, heavy grass and climbed the slight incline that led to the forest. Soon they reached the trees, and it was only then that Sigli stopped to look behind him. His eyes wandered past the village, where he could see his ship already making its way back downstream, followed by the last two Viking vessels to finally evacuate Appledore.

They watched until the masts of the dragon ships disappeared from view, and then they turned away and entered the forest.

*   *   *   *   *

At that moment some twenty miles northwest of Appledore, Sidroc signaled for his men to water their horses in a stream that meandered slowly through the Weald. They were tired. They had been wandering through the forest for two days without any sense of where they were going, and it was beginning to wear on all of them. At first they had ridden toward Canterbury as though to attack the city, after which they had doubled back toward the west with the intention of spreading confusion throughout the heartland of Wessex.

But until now most of the confusion had been self-inflicted, and no one was more frustrated than Old One Eye himself. He felt as though he had been sent, armed and ready, into the middle of nowhere. He had urged the council for months to move on the enemy, and just when it seemed as though they would have the chance to storm Canterbury, Hundeus had pulled back. The order was passed for the army to splinter into mobile raiding parties and sweep through the

Weald, finally uniting again on the plains of Hampshire after looting everything in their path.

There was only one problem with that strategy—there was nothing in their path. Hundeus and his favored lieutenants had pursued the more fruitful course along the southern edge of the Weald, leaving Sidroc to clean up what few table scraps were left in the more heavily forested north. His raiders had spent all their energies fighting the wilderness instead of the Saxons. They were unfamiliar with the paths that crossed through the thick forest, and more than once they doubled back on themselves. There was little satisfaction to be gained from burning the few hovels they encountered along their way, and it seemed as though they might wander until Ragnorak without meeting another living soul.

Sidroc comforted himself with the knowledge that, when the time for bloodletting arrived, their eagerness would be at a fever pitch. He looked forward to that moment, anticipating the adrenaline of the fight and the chance to wet his sword with Christian blood. That was what they were here for, after all. There were countless riches to be won in this country, a sense of possibility that had lured them from the continent. After being confined to Appledore all winter, the last thing they needed was to wander aimlessly through the wilderness, moving forward into nowhere while Hundeus had the pick of Sussex at his disposal.

It irritated Sidroc to think about it. He had lost all patience with Hundeus; the man spent most of his energies currying favor instead of making decisions. He was like all the rest of them, just another in a long line of lapdogs fawning at Haestan's feet, wagging his tail every time the Warlord turned his attention on him.

Sidroc spat in the stream, disgusted. He knew that no man could ever command his loyalty that way. You looked out for yourself in this world, and damned be the rest. You lived like a man, not a dog, commanding fear and respect, and you backed it up with iron instead of words.

He sank down to his knees and leaned over the brook, and he could sense the eyes of his men on him, waiting for him to give the order to ride on. There were at least two hundred Vikings in his party, and if he suffered the disfavor of the general war council, he knew that he had the last word now, alone here in the wilderness.

Let them wait, he thought as he shook the stream from his face, and as he did so he could see his reflection in a standing pool of water that had collected in the earth. Yes, they were right to think him ugly. There was no denying it. He had always used his ugliness to spur him on, as though he could somehow make up for the inequities of nature and emerge a new man, fine-featured and whole. But always the face remained, taunting him. It would be the last thing some unlucky Saxon would ever see, he assured himself, as long as he and his men kept moving toward the open lands to the west. Maybe this time would be different. Maybe this time the ultimate victory would be his.

He rose to his feet and looked at the Vikings gathered around. To Hel with them, he thought, sneering at no one in particular. To Hel with Hundeus. To Hel with them all.

*   *   *   *   *

When Aethelfled learned of Haestan's decision to evacuate Milton for Benfleet, her first instinct had been to send word to the stables at Oxford to have her chestnut mare saddled. She did not have to be told that the Viking's action was a prelude to war, and it did not surprise her when news of Alfred's refortification of London reached her on the open road. She had already anticipated the obvious and was well on her way there, following hard on the heels of Eadred, who had left the day before at Alfred's request with several thousand Mercian soldiers. He had kissed her goodbye thinking he would not see her for quite some time, but he should have known better; she had existed on nothing but nerves and feelings ever since Elfwyn had been cut off in Canterbury. Nothing could stop her from flying to her daughter now.

They should never have allowed Elfwyn to leave the safety of Mercia. Aethelfled had scolded herself mercilessly every night since Haestan's arrival in England, and more than once she had been on the verge of riding to Canterbury to retrieve the girl. Her logical mind told her there was nothing to fear, that the armies of her father and brother were enough to keep the Vikings in check. But all the while her heart had whispered other, darker feelings of dread into her worried ear, drowning out the reassurances of the others who claimed to know better. She did not care that the Saxons in Kent were falling back to protect Canterbury; all of her father's soldiers and spears could not counterbalance her intuition, and so she sped off to London.

These were the demons running through her mind as she rode through the Watling Street gate and into the city on the Thames. Darkness was beginning to settle in and a light drizzle was falling, and she was anxious to find Eadred and refresh herself after her journey. They had left Oxford early that morning, and she was tired. But no fatigue could dull the ache of uncertainty that plagued her, and she knew she would not be able to lay her fears to rest until Elfwyn was safely in her charge again.

It began to rain harder as they made their way through the muddy streets of the town. At long last they reached a low-slung hall on the north bank of the river, and she shook the water from her cloak and waited impatiently inside the entrance to the building as one of the attendants hurried off to find Eadred.

The man returned before long, smiling apologetically. He beckoned for her to follow him down a series of dark corridors that led finally to thick door. He opened it and stepped aside, and as she entered the room she could see her father and husband sitting at a low table. They rose to greet her, and she could immediately tell something was wrong.

"Aethelfled," Eadred said, advancing toward her, "you shouldn't have come." He embraced her, but she could feel the stiffness in him.

"I couldn't stay away, not a moment longer. And I refuse to sit by while Elfwyn is in Canterbury. I'm going there tomorrow, no matter what you say."

Eadred started to turn toward Alfred, who was standing by at the table in the semi-darkness, his face obscured in shadow. Thinking better of it, he stopped and took a deep breath, placing his hands gently on her shoulders.

"My love, Elfwyn and Plegmund have left Canterbury already."

"Are they coming here?"

It was hard for him to look at her. "We don't know, Aethelfled. We don't know where they are."

She swooned slightly, but he caught her in his arms. Alfred stepped forward uncertainly, trying his best to remain calm.

"Don't think the worst," he reassured her. "We've no reason to think any harm has come to them. They left yesterday, heading west, and as soon as Penda heard about it he set off to find them. For all we know, they could be safely in his protection now."

Her eyes welled up with tears, and then she began to sob uncontrollably. "I knew it!" she choked. "I knew something was wrong! Eadred, we must find them! God save us!"

She tried to break away from him and run for the door, but he held fast to her, folding her head protectively into his chest and stroking her hair. Alfred stepped away and bit his lip. Why God had chosen to afflict them like this he did not know, but it was clear they were being tested. They would have to summon all their strength to persevere. He left the chamber, and the two grieving parents in it, and he prayed in his heart that he could somehow have enough strength for them all.

Later that night Eadred lied awake in bed while Aethelfled mercifully slept beside him. He had already steeled himself to what faced them; there was nothing they could do to change it now. His first reaction to the news had been to gird his men for action and prepare to march south immediately, but Alfred had forbidden it. To leave London would be to run the risk of exposing all of England to Haestan's advances, and it did not take much persuasion on the king's part to convince him of the greater responsibility that rested on his shoulders. At least they had the comfort of knowing that all efforts were being made to locate Plegmund and the girl; if anyone could find them, it was Penda.

He looked at the outline of Aethelfled's face in the darkness. Even in the night, he could see that she was still a beautiful woman. He had sensed her reticence about him when they were first married, but the years proved to be a wonderful ally, and he felt as secure about her love and respect as a man can feel. If those issues had once been in doubt, they had gradually eroded with the birth of their daughter. She was the foundation upon which their love rested, and it was an ugly feeling to know that it could all come tumbling down around them now.

Merely thinking about it made him sick. He tried to blot the fear from his mind, but it rattled around his brain as the night dragged on. He endured like this for what seemed like hours, until at last his fatigue overcame him and he drifted off into sleep.

He awoke just before dawn. The fear and uncertainty still weighed upon him, perched on his chest like some monstrous vulture. He sat up and tried to shrug it off, but when he looked through the darkness his heart sank even further, and a shudder ran through his body.

Aethelfled was gone.

*   *   *   *   *

Plegmund also awoke before dawn that morning, but his spirits were considerably higher than Eadred's. He was oblivious to the disturbance his disappearance was causing; he only knew that the first day of their journey had passed without incident. They had covered over twenty miles after leaving Canterbury, and by late afternoon they left the fields of Kent and entered the Weald. At first their progress had been excellent, but then he made a bad decision and took a wrong turn in the forest, leading them astray. He had hoped to find suitable shelter for the night, but when the darkness descended they were still wandering in the woods, with no choice but to pitch camp and wait until morning. The weather was already beginning to turn with the arrival of spring, and they passed a comfortable night in the forest under a canopy of budding branches and clear skies.

And now, as Plegmund lay on his back looking straight up into the sky, he could see the stars beginning to fade with the first signs of the new morning. Everyone else was still asleep. He glanced to his left, where the tiny figure of Elfwyn lay bundled up on a patch of grass under the shelter of a large oak; that she was safe and warm was all he cared about. They would get an early start after breaking their fast, and with any luck he would soon regain his bearings and restore them to the main trail that led west through the Weald toward Winchester.

They had only met up with a few woodsmen after entering the Weald, and it seemed unlikely that any of the Vikings could have penetrated this far into the wilderness. He had been right to fly; they had not left Canterbury a moment too soon. They were safe here, hidden in the forest, and in his mind the conflict that was poised to sweep across England might as well have been part of another world. For all he knew, a major battle had already been fought, or perhaps was about to be joined. He prayed silently to God, beseeching Him to prevent the heathens from breaching the Christian line of defense and destroying all that he held dear.

Suddenly the bundle on his left began to move, writhing about like some strange creature trapped under the earth and struggling to break free. In the next instant the apparition transformed itself into a vision of loveliness as Elfwyn's little face popped out from beneath the layers of blankets and peered around the clearing. When she recognized Plegmund, her eyes took on the glow of the familiar and cleared up with relief. She struggled to her feet and walked over to him, wrapping one of the blankets tightly around her to stay warm.

"Good morning, child. Did you sleep well?"

"Mm-hmm," she nodded, rubbing her eyes.

"Good. I was worried you might get cold. But don't worry...I shouldn't think you'll have to sleep on the ground anymore." She was looking vaguely past him, and he watched as her face gradually sank into a worried frown.

"What is it?" he asked. "What's the matter?"

"I want to go home, Plegmund."

"Now, now...don't be upset. That's where we're going."

"I want Mother..." She started to cry.

"Come here, child," he said, drawing her to him. She buried her head on his shoulder with a soft whimper.

"I know it's not much fun stomping through the forest like this, but the worst is over. It's going to be a fine day, and we should make excellent progress. We'll find you a nice warm bed somewhere tonight, and before you know it you'll be back in Mercia."

"But you don't know where you're going, Plegmund."

"We'll just watch the sun and keep heading west, and everything will be all right. You'll see. Just because we got lost yesterday doesn't mean it will happen again."

She looked suspiciously at him. "Do you promise?"

He laughed. "Yes, I promise. Now, go get yourself ready for breakfast. The others are beginning to stir, and we'll want to be off soon."

She turned away and headed back toward her blankets. What a sad little figure she cut, he thought to himself. It made him all the more determined to see them all to safety without further delay. He stood up and brushed the night from his robes, stretching his limbs in the cool dawn air. He felt a great sense of optimism and faith rising inside of him as he moved to a dry spot near the edge of the clearing and knelt down to say his morning prayers. The light was beginning to break in the east as the sun rose to greet them. It was the first day of April, and everything hinted that it was going to be a good one.

And so it was. They soon located the main trail through the forest, and by late afternoon the party had traveled many miles to the west, still in the Weald but with excellent prospects to exit the wilderness the next day. Everyone's spirits were high. Other than the occasional woodsman, they failed to encounter anyone, and there seemed to be little reason to worry about anything more serious than where they would spend the coming night.

As they passed by a number of familiar landmarks, Plegmund was flooded with memories of the fateful trip he had made with Sigli and Aethelfled eight long years ago, the beginning of the dangerous liaison that would have such a profound effect on their lives. He remembered how they sat around the campfire sharing their dreams, still innocent and untouched by all that was yet to come, and how they had thought their fondest wishes would be realized when they saw a star shoot across the heavens.

The star had lied; he knew that now. He had won Canterbury, true enough, but at what cost? Aethelfled had gone on to fulfill her destiny as Eadred's bride, but only when no other choice had been possible. Whether or not she was happy with her life was something he did not know.

And then there was Sigli. He still thought about the Viking often, never failing to pray each night for his friend, hoping that he among them had perhaps found peace—if such a thing did indeed exist.

As always, the memories depressed him. He tried to replace them with cheerful thoughts. But he was reminded again of his sins when they passed by a trail that veered from the main path and led to the north, where it eventually emptied into a long valley bordered by hills that kept much of the sunlight out. It was known to some as the Valley of the Shadow, but for Plegmund the name had taken on a deeper meaning. That was because the countryside between the forested ridges was dominated by Sussex Downs. And that was where old Grimwald had lived for the last five years.

There had been times before he had achieved Canterbury when Plegmund had been called to the Valley of the Shadow and asked to humiliate himself, to engage in shameful acts all for the sake of his blind ambitions. While those days were over, he had not forgotten them. Simply looking down the trail and knowing he was within a few miles of Grimwald's lair sent a shiver up his spine. He turned to Elfwyn, who rode next to him in the oxcart.

"Are you feeling better now? You have much to be happy about."

"Yes," she sighed, "but I'd rather ride a horse. It's so much more fun."

After so many hours spent bouncing around on the hard wooden seat, he had to admit the idea sounded appealing. He turned to two of the men-at-arms who rode alongside them, requested they trade places, and as soon as the switch was made, Elfwyn's mood brightened. Plegmund marveled at the way she handled herself on the mount; clearly her mother had taught her well. To see someone so delicate comporting herself with such command amazed him.

"Can't we go faster, Plegmund? It's so boring to just sit here in the saddle!"

"Now, restrain yourself," he laughed. "We have to stay with the others in our party...you wouldn't want to ride through the forest without them, would you?" The men around him laughed in amusement.

It did not amuse her. "I could beat any of you in a race! I know I could!"

"It wouldn't surprise me at all, bright eyes," one of them chuckled.

"Don't take her up on it," Plegmund advised, fighting back a smile. "If you won, she'd be upset for days. And if you lost, you'd never live it down. Either way, there's no profit." They all laughed again.

"You think it's funny, do you?" she protested. "Well, I'll show you!"

She dug her heels into the stallion and sent it bolting forward down the trail. She could hear the men shouting for her to stop, but she urged her horse over the hard earth as though it had wings on its hooves. The faster she went, the better it felt. She looked over her shoulder and laughed as several of the Saxons chased after her, and then she faced forward and prepared to negotiate a bend in the trail ahead.

She leaned into the turn and was just about to spur the horse on again when she saw something that filled her with fear. A number of rough-hewn, dangerous-looking men clogged the trail ahead of her, some on horseback, others on foot. They saw her the moment she rounded the trees and reined in her horse, and they all shouted and started toward her. She froze for a dangerous moment, but then the shock of the truth hit home. These were the dark shadows she had heard so much about, the nightmarish visions from which mothers protected their children with the sign of the cross each night. These were the men she had been warned about.

These were the Vikings.

She wheeled her horse around and bolted back around the bend toward the Saxon party, never looking back. The men-at-arms who had been chasing her appeared on the trail as she retraced her steps, but she raced past them, shouting to warn the main party of the danger ahead. She rode up to the oxcart and reined in her horse, and she and Plegmund huddled together as the men collected themselves and formed a crude line of defense.

The quiet of the afternoon was shattered by the shrieks of the Vikings as they barreled around the bend in the forest trail, waving their weapons menacingly above them. There was nothing the Saxons could do other than to stand their ground and cross themselves as they waited for the first wave of attackers. The Vikings swarmed over the last few yards of open ground and crashed into them. At first the Saxons held their ranks, but gradually they were forced back down the trail, giving ground grudgingly as several of them fell and were trampled underfoot.

Plegmund and Elfwyn stood by as the fight surged toward them. The Archbishop looked beyond the front ranks of soldiers, where he could see scores of Vikings now streaming down the trail and through the woods; it was then he realized that all was lost. One of the Saxons turned toward him and cried out.

"Fly, Plegmund! Ride for your life!"

The man started to turn back to the fight when suddenly he lurched forward, his eyes bulging out of their sockets as a Viking broadsword caught him flush across the back. He crumpled to the ground.

That was enough for Plegmund. He grabbed Elfwyn's reins and wheeled both of their mounts around just as several Vikings broke through the ranks and started toward them. They flew back down the trail as fast as their horses could run, spurred on by an all-consuming fear. He looked over his shoulder, where he could see several mounted men following in close pursuit, but it was all he could do to keep up with Elfwyn as she sped down the path ahead of him. Kicking his mount furiously, he pulled alongside her just as they turned another bend in the trail that led to a long straightaway heading east.

But instead of an open road, they saw another party of Vikings blocking their way. They were trapped.

Spotting a small break in the forest to his left, Plegmund waved for Elfwyn to follow, and without slowing they pointed their horses toward the narrow opening and disappeared into the trees. There was the hint of a path through the underbrush, but it soon evaporated into a general tangle of bushes and heavy growth. The going became difficult, forcing them to dodge all manner of obstacles while keeping up their speed, and all the while they could tell by the thrashing sounds behind them that they were being followed. They fought desperately through the underbrush, guarding their faces from the lash of the stray branches that whipped past them, pushing their horses relentlessly for several long and fearful minutes.

Gradually, the sounds of pursuit faded behind them, but they did not let up. It was only when they had burst out onto a well-worn path that led toward the north that Plegmund finally had the nerve to look behind him again; to his relief, no one was in sight. He glanced over at Elfwyn, who despite the ordeal seemed in control of herself. For the first time in his life he understood what it meant to be graced with royal blood; no other child could have possibly stood up to such a demanding task. Seeing her like this renewed his strength.

"Are you all right?" She was wide-eyed and a bit frightened, but she nodded to him. "Good, then! But we can't afford to stay here...I'm sure they're still after us. Follow me!"

They made their way northward along the trail for the next hour and a half, and with every mile Plegmund began to feel a bit more confident about their chances. The late afternoon began to darken as evening approached, and soon the sun disappeared completely from sight behind a long ridge to the west as they entered the Valley of the Shadow. Plegmund knew it would be futile to ride on much longer; there was really only one logical thing to do, one place to go. Swallowing his pride, he set their course slightly to the west, heading toward the last spot on earth he would have chosen to spend the night had any other option been open to him.

The twilight fully enveloped the valley when they rode into view of Sussex Downs. It was a substantial estate that had belonged to one of the king's thanes for many years, but it had reverted to Alfred with the death of the final surviving family member, and the king had passed it on reluctantly to Grimwald as payment for the treacherous old monk's secrecy. The estate was comprised of a gathering of hovels clustered alongside a winding creek that gurgled through the valley, surrounded in every direction by farmland that filtered through the trees and spread outward, disappearing finally into the hillsides that led up from the valley floor. These holdings fanned out from the centerpiece of the estate, the main house and its associated buildings, which hovered over the rest of the grounds on a flat piece of land framed on either side by two rows of tall, stately oaks. Plegmund noticed as they rode closer that a large wooden cross had been erected in front of the building, dominating the approach.

"We'll be safe here, Elfwyn. And you'll have a bed tonight, after all."

She did not smile this time; she was obviously tired. He reached out and stroked her shoulder to comfort her, and then they rode the last quarter mile in silence, stopping finally when they reached the great cross. It loomed above them, overpowering the main square fronting the estate house, and from its base they could see clearly up and down the valley, which now lay completely in shadow as the evening approached. He dismounted and helped the exhausted child from her saddle, and then he walked over to the massive front door and banged on it.

No one answered. He knocked a second and a third time, and he was just about to give up and walk away when the door swung open, revealing a familiar face inside. It was old Valeric, the crippled chief steward of Sussex Downs, a man who had lived in the Valley of the Shadow as long as anyone could remember.

"Why, Your Holiness...what a surprise!" The old ceorl bowed low to the ground and then moved instinctively, the way the best servants do, to Elfwyn's aid. "My, what a pretty little one you might be! And so very tired, I see."

"We both are, Valeric. We were attacked by Vikings several hours ago in the Weald. Thank God we managed to escape, but I'm afraid the others in our party were not so lucky."

"Then it's true," the steward said, shaking his head sadly. "There was talk of how they might be coming this way. Almost everybody has left the Downs already and run off north."

"What about Grimwald?"

"The Master's still here. But it's just the two of us. He yowled and screamed, said he would see to it everyone was sent to the devil...but it didn't take with them. They all left anyway, yesterday morning."

There was a resignation in the old man's eyes, as though he had seen more than his share of bad times, but he quickly masked his feelings and placed his hand gently on Elfwyn's head.

"Don't you worry, child. I've some hot broth for you, and a warm bed. Come now, both of you...I'll take you to the Master, and then I'll tend to your horses."

He grabbed a burning candle from a ledge near the door and turned down a long corridor, motioning for them to follow. He walked with a pronounced limp, dragging one of his feet behind him in an awkward shuffle that echoed eerily off the dark walls, heightening the sense of loneliness and depression about the place. Plegmund held Elfwyn's hand as they made their way slowly down the hall, squinting as the light from the candle cast long, elusive shadows that darted from floor to ceiling like a serpent's tongue, dancing before their eyes. Finally they came to a thick door, which Valeric opened. He poked his head inside.

"Master, we have visitors. A familiar face or two, to join your supper."

"Visitors?" wondered a voice from within. "And why would someone come to the Downs now?"

"Vikings, Grimwald," said Plegmund, brushing past Valeric and leading the girl into the chamber. "We're all in danger."

"Well...what have we here?" grinned the old monk, leaning forward in his chair, a cup of mead in his hand. "Such a pleasant surprise...the lambs come to their shepherd, after all."

"More like lambs to the slaughter, Grimwald," Plegmund replied in disgust. It was bad enough to see the obese old lecher again; that he was drunk only made things worse.

"You shouldn't be so cynical, Plegmund. Not with the Jewel of Mercia at your side. Come here, child; sit down beside me and eat."

Elfwyn moved over to him and pulled herself up to the table as Valeric immediately tended to her, placing a steaming cup of broth between her hands. She sipped mechanically at it, too tired to do anything but suck the warm soup into her mouth.

"I don't think you heard me the first time," Plegmund said, glowering at Grimwald. "The Weald is crawling with heathens! We were lucky to escape them...for all we know, they could be heading this way now!"

"Ridiculous!" Grimwald raised his cup and drained it. "This is probably the safest spot in all of England!"

"Believe me, as long as we stay here our lives are in danger. We should probably saddle fresh horses and leave right now!"

Grimwald waved his hand. "I simply won't hear of it."

"That's because you can't! You're incapable of reason, you drunken old fool!"

Grimwald's eyes were laughing as he sized up Plegmund. "I may be drunk, but I'm not stupid!" He motioned to a nearby window. "It's already dark outside, and there's a valley mist beginning to roll in. We'd only end up riding around in circles if we left. And besides, the child is exhausted...would you drag her out into the night after all she's been through?"

Plegmund's eyes drifted to Elfwyn, who now lay curled up in a little ball on her chair, fast asleep. Grimwald was right; they could go no farther today.

"All right, then...we'll stay the night. But we'll want to be off at dawn, so be sure that Valeric has provisions packed and our horses ready. And if you know what's good for you, you'll come with us."

Grimwald laughed openly at him. "Why, of course, Your Holiness-s-s-ss. A man of your stature deserves the best, knows what's best...how could anyone ever disagree with you?" He leaned back in his seat. "Pull up your chair beside me and share some of this mead. We have so much to talk about..." here his voice took on a derisive tone, "and so many wonderful memories to relive."

Two hours passed, and the night settled in. Unwilling to disturb poor little Elfwyn, Plegmund allowed her to sleep unmolested in her chair. Meanwhile, he refreshed himself with the fine table of meats and cheeses that Valeric had laid out for him, tolerating Grimwald's presence and struggling to shut out the constant monologue that droned on from across the table. He had nothing to say to the man, nothing at all. He counted the minutes to himself as they crept along, waiting impatiently for the chance to finally steal a few hours of sleep and then be off with the first light.

Grimwald had no such intentions. He remained glued obstinately to his chair, oblivious to the possibility that the Vikings actually might stumble across Sussex. There was simply no point in leaving; this was his home, and here he would stay.

He was too old to search for any new worlds to conquer. His life had been a long and prosperous journey, and he took great satisfaction in knowing he had achieved virtually everything that had been important to him. Power, money, influence—he had tasted them all. He had been to Rome. He had risen to the top of the ecclesiastical ladder in Wessex, amassing a small fortune in the process. He'd had everything and everybody at one time or another. He had even been hailed as a learned man once, so very long ago, and he could still hold his own with the most accomplished minds in all of Christiandom on subjects as diverse as science and history, Latin or philosophy.

But there was one thing he still lacked, one thing that had eluded him all these years, and he did not have the slightest idea how to go about attaining it. That thing was friendship. He had never learned the meaning of the word. And now, as the curtains began to close on him and the lights grew dim, he realized that he was a very lonely man. It had never mattered before; there had always been more important diversions to occupy his attentions. But with no apparent purpose each day other than to rise, eat and drink, defecate, count his money and then go to bed, for the first time in Grimwald's life the idea of companionship appealed to him.

He had finally begun to realize all this just yesterday, when the locals had fled Sussex Downs and left him and the faithful Valeric behind. They had deserted him, all right, leaving him there to rot, and he knew that even the old steward's loyalty was more inclined toward the house and its heritage than to him. The notion that his passing would not particularly affect anybody was unbearably depressing.

Oh, they would all come back, eventually. But for now he was alone—which was why the prospect of engaging Plegmund for the evening had come as such a welcome diversion. Here at last was someone of equal mettle, a worthy foil for his attentions. Fueled by a belly filled with mead, he regaled his former protege with all kinds of observances, ranging far afield and whiling the night away with idle chatter. But every time he attempted to spark a response, he was met by an indifferent silence—or at best, a cursory reply.

"You dishonor me, you know," he finally snapped, his voice taking on an icy edge. "You show me no respect at all."

"That's because I despise you. You, and everything you stand for."

"Oh, do you now...? And why, pray tell?"

"Do you even have to ask? After all that you've put me through?"

"Whatever you did, you did of your own will. You're a hypocrite to think otherwise."

"You took advantage of me, Grimwald! Instead of helping me, when I most needed it, you used me! In the most disgusting way, for your own ends!"

"And you...? You didn't use me?"

"I submitted to you. I had no choice. But at least I did no one else any harm."

"Not to me, perhaps...but your damage was already done," Grimwald sneered. "You betrayed the lovers, remember...? All for your benefit! Don't deny it!"

"I spoke out against something I knew was wrong! If anything, I sinned by not stopping it earlier! And if I profited from it, it was for a worthy end, rather than the evil, self-serving motives that will see you rot in Hell, you foul deceiver!"

"Rail on all you want, Your Holiness-ssss," Grimwald smiled, pleased by the turn matters were taking. "You and I, you see—we're the same, after all. Neither of us was ever good enough on our own merits to warrant attention; we had to bend the rules to get what we wanted for ourselves. But that's the way of the world, my friend. That's the way it is for everyone. Alfred, even. Only a fool would think otherwise."

"What you say is against everything the Church stands for, everything I've sworn to uphold."

"The Church! The Church! You and your lofty attitude, as though you're so much better than anyone else! You point your finger at me, but what's the difference? You extort, I extort. We both profit. And then you have the nerve to blame me!"

"It's not for that I blame you most!"

"What is it, then? The buggery? Is it the buggery? Yes, of course it is!" Grimwald sneered, watching the truth reflect in Plegmund's eyes. "Don't like it when another man has his way with you, do you? Well, let me tell you something: yes, you have a pretty enough arse, all soft and pink, but that's not what I wanted. No, not that! I could have had any young thing who suited my fancy."

He leaned forward, his eyes crinkling with anticipation, and he smiled in triumph. "What I wanted most was to let you know just who was the master. *Your* master. And that you were nothing without me! You were mine, Plegmund! Body and soul! You were mine!"

"You foul, filthy thing!"

"And so it ever shall be!"

"Wretched, hateful..."

"And so it ever shall be!"

Plegmund jumped to his feet, and in that moment he was capable of murder. He might even have done the deed, gladly, even as his beloved Elfwyn laid there asleep in the room, had not the door suddenly swung open. He and Grimwald both looked up; it was Valeric. The steward's eyes bulged wide, and he entered the room without bothering to ask for permission, dragging his bad leg behind him.

"They're here!"

"Here? What do you mean, man?"

"The Vikings! They're here! I saw them outside, gathered beneath the cross!"

"God save us!" Plegmund muttered. "What can we do?"

Grimwald was stunned. "It's too late to run. Even if we could slip out the back, we couldn't make it very far."

Valeric pointed toward the corridor. "The cellar! You can hide down there!"

"Yes, the cellar!" Grimwald exclaimed. "It's hard to find, and very dark. It's worth a try!"

Plegmund gathered the sleeping Elfwyn in his arms and followed close behind Valeric and Grimwald, one limping and the other waddling, as they hastily left the dining chamber and entered the dark corridor. They scurried down the dimly lit hallway until they came to an alcove that led into a narrow pantry with storage bins lining the walls on both sides. They stopped to listen, but all was silent; if there truly were Vikings on the grounds, they had not entered the house yet.

Near the back of the pantry there was a break in the racks. Valeric placed the candle on a ledge above them and stepped forward until he stood in front of a dark, nondescript door. He pulled hard at it, but it would not open. He applied his full weight to it, wrenching at the protesting latch, until finally he broke the seal that had formed between the wood and the wall in a bond that only occurs when a door has been closed for a very long time. The panel groaned free, and they peered through the opening; there was nothing but darkness inside.

Turning back toward them, Valeric gave the candle to Grimwald. "Off you go, Master...you and His Holiness. And the girl."

"Come on, now, Valeric," Grimwald motioned impatiently. "Take the candle and lead the way. Go on, now!"

But the steward did not move. He looked down, and when he spoke there was a slight stammer in his voice.

"No, Master...I cannot go. The candles are lit at the Downs. The food, it's on the table. They know someone's here, that's for certain." His eyes were filled with a quiet resignation. "It might as well be me."

Grimwald peered curiously at him in the half-light. "Well done, then, man. Well done. May God bless you, and good luck. Maybe you can get away."

But they both knew better. Grimwald brushed past the steward, with Plegmund and the sleeping girl close behind him, and before they had the chance to reconsider, the door shut behind them. They found themselves alone at the top of a stone landing that led down into the darkness below. Grimwald held the candle aloft and slowly began to descend the damp, slippery steps, taking care not to lose his footing and plunge down into the black hole beneath him. Above them loomed the dark underside of the main floor of the house, and as they stepped down farther into the bowels of the estate Plegmund understood why the cellar was not a place often visited. The air was cool and moist, and a dank sense filled his nostrils, filtering all the way back down his throat and growing more overpowering with each step. He shuddered slightly but kept on, clutching Elfwyn close to him.

They negotiated the dozen or so steps that curved along the cellar wall until they reached the bottom of the stairs and found themselves on an uneven stone floor. Breathing deeply, Grimwald took several steps forward, and then he stopped. He turned toward his right and disappeared into a shadowy crack in the wall.

"This way," he whispered. "Over here."

Plegmund followed, and as he slipped through the narrow opening he could see the outline of a large wooden cask that lay on its side. Old Winchester motioned to him, and they both edged around behind the cask, where there was just enough room for all three of them to huddle together on a bed of straw that lay gathered up against the wall. Grimwald was the first to sit down, and Plegmund maneuvered the sleeping child so that he was able to sink to his haunches and slip his legs beneath him while keeping her curled up in his arms. The straw was damp, but it was better than the cold stone.

"This house goes back to Roman times," Grimwald whispered, placing the candle on the floor in front of them. "They used to store wine down here." He said it as though they were conversing casually over a goblet of spirits. But then his voice turned serious.

"I'll leave the candle lit, as long as no one enters through the doorway above. But if we hear anyone, then we'll need to put it out. Don't worry...I have a flint with me, as well as some other candles. We'll need to burn several of them until dawn, at least. Maybe then we can have a look upstairs."

"That might be too soon. They'll likely spend the night here, don't you think?"

"Perhaps. But we'll have to surface eventually."

"Do you think Valeric could have been mistaken? After all, we never saw them."

Grimwald shifted his immense bulk. "Valeric doesn't make mistakes—other than to have been here tonight, that is. But if you don't believe him, then go see for yourself. Just make sure to shut the door behind you."

Plegmund sat there in silence, resigned for the moment to their fate. Mercifully, for the first time that evening Grimwald also had nothing to say, and not a word passed between them as they huddled together in the darkness. Every sound that penetrated the deep cellar, no matter how subtle, rang so loud and clearly that they might as well have been sitting in the midst of a raging storm. The slow drip over stones, the hiss of their breaths in the dank chamber, the rustling of the child in Plegmund's arms—each noise jolted their senses.

How strange Fate is, Plegmund thought. Here he was, cast into a dismal hole with perhaps the basest man in Wessex, all to avoid an even greater evil that clawed the surface above them. He could feel Grimwald's fear in the darkness, he could hear it in the old man's breath, could almost see it in the mist that formed in the dim, flickering half-light as the air escaped their lungs in uneven rushes. Yes, he was afraid, too. More for the child, who still slept undisturbed in his arms, than for himself. More of the unknown, of the whole obscenity of being trapped like this in the bowels of Grimwald's lair, than of anything that could happen to him.

And then they heard it. Voices. Muffled and distant, but distinct. Voices shouting. Thumping, bumping sounds. Heavy footsteps racing above, penetrating through the dark rafters that separated them from the intruders.

"My God!" Plegmund whispered.

But Grimwald was silent, save for his shaking breaths.

"Is there no way out of here...??!!"

More silence next to him. And then, feebly, "No."

Minutes passed as they squatted under the shadow of fear in a handful of dust. The Valley of the Shadow, indeed. More thumping, running. More madness.

And then the door opened above them with a wrenching, jarring thud.

Grimwald's hand snaked out and snatched the life from the candle. Now they were in utter darkness, save for the gleaming torchlight coming from around the corner and up above them, out of sight. They could hear the Viking voices, gruff and excited, rolling in the thick Danish tongue that both of them understood well.

"Down here! Look!"

There was an excited mumbling, and then another voice. "Go on down! Maybe the gold's there!"

Plegmund and Grimwald sat frozen in the antechamber, hidden in the darkness behind the cask, helpless now as a half dozen Vikings descended the steps amidst a clatter of weapons and feet against the stone floor. The light from their torches bounced off the rafters above, and as the men drew to within a few feet away, separated only by the cask and the opening that led into the main cellar, Plegmund said a silent prayer. And then, suddenly, the light burst into the antechamber.

"What's in there?"

"Oh, nothing but a big old rotten barrel."

And then, just as suddenly, the glare grew dimmer as he returned to the cellar. "Let's go. There's nothing here."

Plegmund's heart pounded with joy. They had not been discovered! He could even hear the first of them starting to ascend the steps; yes, it was true! They were going to make it.

"What's down there?" The voice was sudden, and carried the unmistakable ring of authority. It thundered down from above, from the threshold at the head of the stairway, and it froze the other Vikings in their steps.

"Just an empty old cellar, Warlord. Not worth the trouble."

"Let me see."

Plegmund's heart pounded again, but this time it was the hot breath of fear that beat down upon him as a single set of footsteps descended the stairwell.

"Let me have that!" And then the light returned suddenly to the room with a naked glare, and Plegmund could feel a great, dark presence immediately on the other side of the cask. Seconds passed. And then,

"Curse the gods!"

Plegmund could feel the presence turning away, turning, turning. But just when it seemed they would be miraculously saved a second time, Elfwyn awoke in his arms and cried out.

All was lost.

The light returned, this time moving back into the chamber with a grim purpose. As Plegmund looked up in horror, the blazing torch appeared around the corner of the cask, followed immediately by a large, burly man. And then the three of them were naked, bathed from head to toe in a harsh, unforgiving light, and when the Viking saw them an exclamation of triumph escaped his lips.

Plegmund let out a gasp of fear and clutched the girl to him, burying her face in his robe. Grimwald whined, terrified.

And well he might have been. For there before them leered the most gruesome face either of them had ever seen.

Rearing back his shaggy head, Sidroc the Malevolent One laughed so loud and deep that it seemed the cellar walls would cave in and bury them in utter darkness.

CHAPTER XV: A Gathering Thunder

"If I cannot bend Heaven, I shall move Hell."
—Virgil, The Aenead.

It seemed to Elfwyn as though a horde of monstrous, shaggy bears had crashed through her dreams, snorting and carrying on as though they had stumbled upon a nest of hornets. Although she had never seen a real bear, she had heard stories about them from her grandfather. She had imagined them to be just this way—hairy and coarse, larger than life, filled with a looming menace. So these were the bears, she thought; these were the Vikings. She did not even have time to cry out, so quickly did they fill the tiny antechamber, dragging her and the two holy men into the main cellar.

A large, filthy Dane swept her up in his arms and began to ascend the stairway, and she was overcome by the stench from his sweaty body. Up ahead, the heathens dragged Plegmund over the stone landing, while behind her she could see them rolling Grimwald upward, one slow step at a time. They bolted out of the cellar and swept into the dark hallway, and all she could see in the torchlight was a series of bouncing heads around her, until the entire buzzing mass poured into the main hall.

Yes, this was where she had fallen asleep, was it not? But the room was different now than when she had left it, filled with loud and dangerous men who ringed the perimeter, chanting for them, chanting at them. And then she saw Valeric. The poor old steward was strung with his hands bound and raised above him by a rope that had been wrapped around the rafter above and then drawn down to stretch his limbs skyward. He had been beaten severely. His back was covered with long, angry slashes of blood, and even she could tell that he would not live long. But his eyes were still very much alive, and in them she could see a distinct sadness, now that he realized they all had been discovered.

They were set out in front of their captors, and Plegmund folded her head protectively into his robe, as though he could block out the awful truth. But she looked up anyway, and the first thing she noticed was him. *Him.* Simply the most amazing face she had ever seen, so inhuman that it hardly seemed real. In spite of his hideous features, she was unable to take her eyes off him. He sat there bent forward at an odd angle, his hairy forearm resting on the table like a large ham, a formidable bulk of a man. But he had no interest in her; instead, he looked Plegmund and Grimwald over carefully, his single eye darting back and forth between them.

He raised his arm off the table and grabbed a large gold medallion that hung around his throat, shaking it vigorously at them and grunting in labored breaths. Neither Plegmund nor Grimwald moved. He shook the gold again, his terrible face filling the room, but still the Saxons remained frozen in place, waiting. The Vikings surrounding them crowded in closer, dangerously closer, as though in the next minute they would tear the prisoners apart.

And then Plegmund spoke. "If it's gold you want, I can't help you. The girl and I are not from here; we were simply passing through."

Sidroc sat straight up in his chair, as surprised as the rest of them. "Where did you learn our tongue?"

"I was raised by Vikings. Halfdan's army took me in."

"And now you wear the cross?"

"I'm a man of learning, Sidroc. The church affords me that luxury."

Old One Eye leaped to his feet. "How did you know my name?"

Plegmund collected himself; this would be the most delicate part of all. He had known who Sidroc was the moment he first laid eyes on him. There could be no mistaking it, not after all he had been told about the man. The knowledge he had might be enough to save their lives.

"I've known about you for a long time. No one is more feared by the Saxons than Sidroc, the Malevolent One. Old One Eye. Lothar's bane, the conqueror of Halfsfiord."

The Viking's face lit up, and his head jutted forward. He closed in slowly, looking Canterbury over with great care. "Who are you?"

"Plegmund of Mercia."

"Who told you of me?"

"Many people. Your fame as a warrior is known all throughout England."

Sidroc grunted. He looked down at Elfwyn. "And her?"

"An orphan in my charge."

Now Old One Eye's gaze turned to Grimwald, who had been standing by silently, sweating freely and breathing in short, agitated gasps.

"And what about you? This must be your house, then... no? Tell me where the gold is! Tell me!"

Grimwald pretended not to understand, even though he knew what Sidroc had said.

"Too bad for you, then. We'll wring it out of you all the same." He waved to his men. "Seize him!"

Several Vikings pounced on Grimwald, but the old prelate squirmed away from them, squealing like a stuck pig.

"No! No, don't! I can help you!" he protested in the Danish tongue. "I can help you more than you ever believed possible!"

"Another one, eh?" Sidroc laughed. "I suppose you were raised by Vikings, too?"

"No, but I've dealt with you and your kind before," Grimwald said, collecting himself. "And I know you'll always listen to a worthy proposition."

"Then tell us where your gold is."

"I have no gold. I'm an old, lonely man on a meager pension, with nothing but this house and the land under it." Here a devious gleam lit up his eye. "But spare me, and I can promise you more gold than you ever dreamed of!"

"Why should I bargain with your life, when I can beat the truth out of you?"

"Because you'll need me. To effect the negotiation."

Sidroc stared intently at him. "Speak, then. I'll spare you if your secret's good enough. But I warn you, Christian...try to deceive me, and I'll tear you limb from limb!"

Grimwald pursed his lips, and then he turned toward Plegmund. "This man lies to you. His name is Plegmund, all right... but he also happens to be the Archbishop of Canterbury. He'll bring you a pretty price, I'll warrant."

The room gasped collectively. Plegmund stiffened.

"But all that's nothing," Grimwald continued, warming to the task. "Nothing, compared to the riches that will be showered upon you when you loose me on Alfred of Wessex. I shall be your agent. For I've no love lost for the king, believe me. And it will give me great pleasure to see the look on his face when I tell him that his prized granddaughter is in your clutches!"

Plegmund leaped at Grimwald, groping for his throat, but the Vikings pulled him away from the old man.

"Wretched, disgusting worm! To betray an innocent child...!"

"We all have something to barter," Grimwald replied indifferently, rearranging his robe. "Such is the cost of the negotiation."

Sidroc merely smiled, his eye now having wandered to Elfwyn. He approached her and dropped to one knee.

"Such a pretty little thing, you are. And the blood of a king, besides..."

He reached out a finger and ran it across her smooth face, but she neither recoiled from him nor showed the least sign of fear. Although she could not understand anything he said, she somehow knew that this strange, terrible man would not hurt her. And then she did something totally unexpected. She grabbed Sidroc's meaty finger in her small hand and laughed.

It took him completely by surprise. He started to pull away, but she held on, continuing to giggle. Finally the absurdity of it all moved him as well, and a low snicker escaped his lips.

"She has spirit, this child. They usually run and hide from me."

"Sidroc, do with me what you will," Plegmund implored, "but spare the girl from harm. She's a special child, and my responsibility. I'd do anything to guarantee her safety!" And then he turned to Grimwald again.

"You'll burn in Hell for this, Grimwald! You betrayed your king and your country. And your God! If I only knew where your gold was hidden...if only I could betray you!"

The voice that interrupted him was weak but distinct. "By the Lord God, I'll help you, Your Holiness..."

All eyes turned to poor Valeric, hanging limply and bleeding off to the side. The old steward forced a smile, obviously in great pain.

"The Master deserves it, he does, turning on you like this," he gasped in English through drawn lips. "He was lying about the gold. Lying! But I'll see justice done, by God. Yes, I will!"

He turned his head in the direction of the door. "Go back down to the cellar and break open the old cask...You'll find what you're looking for."

"Ingrate!" Grimwald screamed, his eyes bulging. "You've betrayed me!"

"You've betrayed yourself," the steward answered, turning his eyes away.

Plegmund wasted no time in translating Valeric's message to Sidroc. The Viking's face grew brighter with each word, and when Canterbury had finally finished he let out a cry of delight and urged his men down into the cellar once again. They raced out of the room and tumbled down the stone steps, and after smashing the cask open their efforts were rewarded. They found a number of bulging chests in the womb of the old barrel, and it took several strong men to drag each of them upstairs. The chests were laid out in a row before Sidroc, who waited until the last of them was in place before ordering them all to be opened simultaneously. When the lids were thrown back, not a man in the room could control his wonder.

There was precious plate, and all manner of silver. Exotic jewels from the lands at the end of the inland sea, coins from every known kingdom under the sun. Pearls, silks, rubies and emeralds, studded crowns and richly adorned belts.

And above all, gold. More gold in one place than anyone in the room had ever seen.

"By Odin...by the gods!" Sidroc cried in disbelieving rapture, running his fingers through the treasure. The other Vikings joined him, pressing the bounty to their chests and laughing giddily at this sudden good turn of fortune.

"And this foul creature would have had you believe he was penniless," Plegmund smirked, pointing a damning finger at Grimwald.

Sidroc's eye lit up with terrifying joy. "Yes! So he did, didn't he?"

He rose from the treasure and allowed the last bits in his hand to drop to the stone floor; they clattered ominously, scattering over the hard surface. Mindful now only of the lie, he beckoned to the quivering Grimwald, who was dragged forcibly before him.

"I warned you, priest! Choose the manner of your death!"

"No! No! Please don't kill me! You need me! You need me to negotiate with Alfred!"

"If that's what I need, then Plegmund here can do it just as well, no?" Old One Eye grinned maliciously.

Grimwald sank down sobbing to the stone floor and began to grovel at Sidroc's feet. "Oh, please, Warlord! Spare me! By God in heaven, spare me!"

Old One Eye kicked him away. "Your God can't help you now. No one can!"

And then an idea occurred to him, and a smile of wicked satisfaction crept across his face. "Since you would not choose the manner of your death, I'll choose it for you. I think it might please you, in fact...after all, it would be a great honor to die the same way your Christian god did, would it not?" He raised his arm and pointed toward the front of the estate.

"Take him outside, to the giant cross! Raise him up on it and lash him there...crucify the dog!"

A great shout exploded in the room; now, at last, there would be blood sport. The men descended on Grimwald and hoisted him above their heads, passing his body across the room and toward the door over a sea of outstretched hands. As he was swept out of his hall at Sussex Downs for the final time, Plegmund saw in his eyes a look of terror that he had never seen in all the years he had known the man.

And in that moment he decided once and for all that God was good, God was great. Justice did indeed exist on this wretched, unforgiving earth after all.

* * * * *

Elfwyn was the first to awaken the next morning. She and Plegmund had been shunted off to a private sleeping chamber late last night, there to grab a few hours of sleep while the heathens caroused wildly throughout the estate house, draining its tankards of every last drop of mead they could find. How long the Vikings celebrated she did not know, having retreated into the deep sleep that is the exclusive territory of a tired child, even in the most trying of times. But it was very quiet now, as the sun began to rise in the sky.

She rubbed her eyes and looked at the cot next to her, where Plegmund was stretched out asleep. She had no way of knowing that he had laid there awake until dawn, tossing and turning in the dark as the muffled celebration of the heathens slipped through the chamber walls. He had even ventured toward the door at one point, thinking perhaps the Vikings would be too drunk to maintain their watch and hoping for an opportunity to sweep her up and steal away. But he had been greeted instead by the leering face of a chamber guard, already deep in his cups and in no mood for trouble, and so he had returned to his cot, where he continued to toss until finally he fell asleep.

Elfwyn rose and walked across the room. She opened the door and stepped over a bearded Viking who snored fitfully beneath her, and she walked down the hall until it turned to the left, leading to a doorway that opened up into a small, central courtyard. Catching a glimpse of the bright sunlight that flooded the far wall of the house on this early April morning, she walked toward the open doorway, pausing in the shadows on its threshold.

There he sat, all alone but for a chest at his feet, admiring in his outstretched hand a gleaming amulet of gold that shone in the sunlight.

Him again. Sidroc, they called him; that was his name.

She stood there for a few seconds, watching from his blind left side where he could not see her. She found once again that she could not take her eyes off him. He was so strange looking that his ugliness ceased to be frightening, and he almost did not seem to be real. He appeared more like a character drawn from some bedtime story than an actual person of flesh and blood. She was completely fascinated by him.

And then he turned his head, and his lone eye gathered her in. They stared at each other for moment, until finally he swung his massive, swarthy body around and beckoned for her to come closer. Without showing the slightest bit of apprehension she walked over to him, the sunlight glistening off her brilliant blonde hair. He looked at her without saying anything, savoring the chance to observe something so beautiful, so precious, at such close range.

"I'm hungry," she said, squinting her eyes and tilting her head to one side.

Without understanding her words, he knew what she meant. "So am I, little one," he said in Danish. "But you and I are the only ones up. The rest of them sleep like old dogs."

She bent down and picked up a brilliant sapphire from the treasure he had carried outside for inspection. The sunlight bounced off it and reflected the blue of her eyes as he watched her.

"It's pretty. I've seen one once, but never like this. My father says they come from lands far away, beyond even where the sun rises in the east."

He was charmed by her innocence. It did not matter what she was saying; that she was talking to him at all astounded him. A king's granddaughter, indeed.

"I like the rubies even more," she said, reaching for the chest. "I think that...."

"Elfwyn!"

Plegmund burst into the courtyard, ready to defend her with his life. But as soon as she turned toward him it became apparent she was there of her own free will. Her attitude disarmed him just as it had surprised Sidroc; he slowed and approached her with caution.

"Elfwyn, be careful. You shouldn't be with him."

"Speak so I can understand, priest!" Sidroc grunted angrily, his back arching.

"What you can understand, she can't," he replied in Danish. "I have no choice."

"Very well, then. Take her under your wing. And care for her well...she's the only reason you're still alive. That, and the ransom you'll bring."

"What about the others?" Plegmund put his arm reassuringly on Elfwyn's shoulder. "What's happened to them?"

"Never mind them. Just take care of her, and get her fed. It's time for my men to wake up now, lazy bunch of jackals. I want to be out of here and heading west within the hour."

Plegmund grabbed Elfwyn and hurried back into the estate house. He busied himself attending to her as the Vikings began to rise, struggling to shake the previous night's mead from their groggy heads. When he was confident that she was safely engaged in a breakfast of biscuits and fresh goat's milk, he slipped off and made his way to the main chamber, in hopes of offering poor Valeric comfort.

But when he arrived in the room, he found the old steward dead, his body hanging limply from the same rope with which he had been bound the night before. He untied the cord and lowered the old man to the floor. Kneeling over the body, he made the sign of the cross and offered up a silent prayer for the man's soul, content in his heart that the steward's lifetime of loyal service would be enough to guarantee his place in heaven for eternity. Valeric's troubles were over; theirs were just beginning.

An hour later he and Elfwyn were finally led out to the front of the estate, where the Vikings were completing their preparations to leave. His eyes were drawn immediately to the giant cross, and the wretched figure of Grimwald stretched out upon it. Holding onto Elfwyn's hand, he led the girl across the large square that fronted the house. Finally they arrived at the foot of the cross, and they looked up at the sagging form above them, silhouetted against the bright blue morning sky.

Grimwald had been lashed tightly to the cross by a series of ropes that held his extremities firmly in place. But the rest of his body hung there grotesquely, its cumbersome weight thrusting it forward and dragging it down with gravity's pull. The distended angle of his shoulders bore witness to the strain being put upon them, but after having hung in place all night he was in shock, well beyond the great pain to which he had been subjected. His head drooped to one side, its parched mouth open, eyes gazing dully off into space. He had suffered mightily, and now the end was near.

Plegmund stood gazing silently at the dying man, and the sight of it all sent an involuntary shudder through him. Somehow, it was enough to break through the spell of Grimwald's trance; the old man's head swung around, and his bloated eyes came to rest on the two pilgrims beneath him. He took in a deep, labored breath.

"So," he whispered. "You've won, Plegmund. You've triumphed over me...after all."

"No, Grimwald. This is no triumph."

"I am...undone." He breathed heavily. "But I feel no more pain...just a great numbness. Had I known before what death was...perhaps I would not have feared it so much in life."

Plegmund remained silent, staring up at him.

"And now, you...you must do your duty unto God, Plegmund," Grimwald croaked in a hoarse whisper. "You must confess me!"

Plegmund could feel his right hand raising itself and his mouth uttering the familiar Latin words: "In nomine patri, et file, et spiritu sanctu...." His absolution droned on, until finally he finished the prayers. Only then did Grimwald avert his eyes, allowing his head to fall back on his shoulder and lapse again into semi-consciousness.

They were distracted by loud shouts as a score of Vikings raced from the house, waving burning torches in the air. Already a few ominous tongues of flame had begun to lick at the walls of the estate through an open window. As the fire gathered strength, a Viking rode over to them with a pair of saddled horses and gestured for them to mount. They did so, and were swept along in a mass of men, oxcarts and horses as the Vikings, some two hundred strong, pushed off down the long stretch of land that fronted the estate.

There was a great commotion among them as they rode, but Plegmund remained silent, his eyes fixed forward. After a few more moments, the cavalcade reached the end of the open country and prepared to turn west onto a trail that led through a dense belt of trees. It was only then that he finally turned, looking back over his shoulder one last time.

There in his wake he could still make out the giant cross, and Grimwald protruding from it. Behind the cross the main house of Sussex Downs was completely ablaze, its gables having succumbed to a great wall of flames that crackled skyward. Valeric's funeral pyre, he thought to himself; the old steward might have appreciated it, had he not been such a devout Christian.

But there was no redemption to be found on this day. There was only a great cloud of soot and smoke that floated above them and across the Valley of the Shadow, as years worth of work and life and memories were destroyed in the blink of an eye. A wrathful eye, belonging to an angry God.

Crossing himself, Plegmund turned from the destruction and stared blankly down the trail ahead. It wound through the trees and disappeared into the wilderness, leading them away from the smell of burnt offerings.

*   *   *   *   *

All Huda could do was stand there and shake his head. He, his wife and the boy had never seen anything like it. The western Weald was rough country, heavily forested and lightly trafficked, and any man who lived in those parts was either home-bred, dangerously stubborn, or just plain disinclined to be around other people.

Huda was all three. He had built his hut in a quiet meadow tucked into one of the remotest parts of Sussex, far from the nearest village, with little to disturb him other than the odd wild animal preying upon his livestock. Weeks could go by without a single stranger passing through.

So it was that the parade of bodies crossing his land during the last two days had been most unusual. He stood outside his hovel with the Saxon advance scouts, watching scores of men emerge from the trees and into his meadow, and he prayed under his breath that this would be the final invasion of his privacy for a long time to come.

"See the tall one who rides stiff-backed in his saddle?" one of the Saxons said to him. "That's Lord Penda."

Huda scratched his head and glanced over at his wife and son. The boy was a level-headed sort who was unlikely to look any farther than the edge of the meadow for his life's answers. And that was a good thing. Because all the other young men wanted to go to Winchester, to Canterbury, to London. Or to war. Always somewhere else; that was the way. There was so much work to be done, and he didn't want any of that fanciful rubbish entering *his* boy's head, not at all.

"Lord Penda, eh?" he wondered. "I don't think I'd be shook now if King Alfred himself rode this way, by God, what with everyone else who's stepped on me land since yesterday."

By now Penda had drawn close. He reined in his horse and looked down at them. "You've something to tell us, I hear?"

Huda bowed stiffly at the waist. He had never spoken to an ealdorman. "My Lord, I can tell you only what my own two eyes have seen the last two days. If that be of substance for you, than so the better." He squinted up at Penda, blinded by the bright sun.

"All news is useful. All news matters."

Penda dismounted and handed his horse to an aide. He shook the dust from his cloak, and then he accepted a gourd of water from the ceorl's wife, who bowed and retreated hastily back into the shadow of the hovel. He drank long and hard from the vessel, sighing in satisfaction and wiping his beard with the back of his forearm, and then he sat down upon a low stool that had been placed outside Huda's front door.

"Sit down, man," he said, motioning to a nearby pile of logs that had not yet been cut up for firewood, "and tell us what you have to say."

"Well, My Lord, the family and me...we're simple folk, you see. We don't bother no one; we work the land, and graze the few cows we own, and that's that.

Nothing ever happens here, and nobody comes this way. Until yesterday morning, that is.

"I was chopping away at this woodpile, I was, when me boy comes hurrying out of the trees, driving our cows before him, and I could tell right away that something was wrong. So he comes running over to me, all out of breath and the like, and he starts babbling on about all these men, strangers with a strange tongue, all heading this way. He'd seen them without them seeing him, and he hurried back here to warn us."

Here Huda paused to wipe his chin. "Well, My Lord...I may not be a much-traveled man, but I knew right away it was the Vikings. Had to be. I knew they'd landed in Wessex again, but I hadn't thought much about it…like I said, no one comes here, so it didn't much seem to matter. But I'd heard all the stories about them, I had, about how they'll burn you out and take everything. And I didn't much want to have the last thing I ever saw before I died be a stampede of godless heathens straddling me old woman, plain thing that she is, and torturing me poor boy. 'Cause that's what would happen; aye, I'm most certain of it.

"Well, I weren't about to stand here idle and all, so I gathered up the whole lot and headed into the trees there," he pointed to the south. "Me and the woman and the boy, and our two horses and our cows. The trees are thick, and there's a trail that a man could never find unless he stumbled on it. You go in a quarter mile or so, and there's a little dell carved out of the earth, all covered round by brush. I sent the woman and the boy in there with the cows and horses, and I laid up back in those trees, on a low branch, so I could see the whole meadow.

"I weren't there long when, sure enough, they come flying through the forest there to the east, yelling and making these God-awful horrible noises. Soon as they saw the hut, they went right for it, and they didn't waste no time breaking in and ransacking the place. But there was no great worth here, poor sorts that we are."

He laughed. "When you have nothing, what's to lose? " And then he shuddered. "But all I could think about was what would've happened if we'd been there. I was sweating in the trees, by God.

"Anyway, soon the meadow filled with them…about eight, ten score." He looked around him now. "Well, I can tell you that I never seen such a sight in all me life, that I have not. These heathens, they look bigger to me than Saxon folk, God help us. And so I'm sitting there watching all this, and I'm ready to jump down and run back if they decide to turn me way, when finally I see this man ride into the meadow, and I knew right away he was their leader. They all stopped and looked to him, and I swear, even from off in the trees, I could see he was the ugliest, scariest man I ever laid eyes on, big and strong, like he could break an ox in half with his own hands. He only had one eye, too, and well…I thought I'd just about seen it all."

"Sidroc," Penda muttered under his breath, remembering the negotiations at Appledore.

"What's that, you say?"

"Never mind. Continue."

"As you wish, My Lord. As I was saying, I thought I'd just about seen it all. Until the priest and the little girl come riding into sight, that is."

Penda stiffened and leaned forward. "The girl! God save us! Was she fair, about six years old?"

"That she was. And she rode that horse of hers better than I can ride, I can tell you that. Better than the priest, it's fair to say."

"Were they safe? Had any harm come to them?"

Huda shrugged. "They looked fine to me, but what do I know? They weren't tied up, not anything like that, they weren't. And no one seemed to bother them at all. For the life of me, I couldn't figure it out."

"Go on, then. What happened next?"

"Well, nothing, really. They stayed for a while, and drank from the well, and that was that. Didn't bother to torch me hut...couldn't care less, I'll warrant. Took a few things with them, and by noon they headed off that way." He pointed to a well-worn trail that led to the west. "I waited a piece, until they were all gone, and then I ran back to the dell and gathered the family up again. When we got back here, I sent the boy out to make sure...but they were gone."

Penda took a deep breath and stood up. "Well, thank you, then. It's not what I was hoping to hear, but at least we're on track." He turned to one of his aides. "Water the men and horses, and then...."

"Pardon, My Lord," Huda interrupted, "but I'm not finished."

"Not finished?"

"Not by a long measure. I haven't even come to the best part."

Penda sat back down on his stool "Please...continue."

"Very well, then. Me and the boy go back to our woodpile, and just before nightfall we're about to call it a day, when we turn around, and there no more then twenty feet from us there's five of them standing there. Five heathens, big, rough-looking men. And the biggest one of them all, a head taller than any man here, he takes a step forward, and he's carrying this war axe with twice the heft to it of me simple tool, and, well...I just looked up to heaven and I started in with me prayers."

He sat back now and slapped his thighs, and he laughed. He was enjoying this rare attention. "Well, God in heaven must have been turned me way, because I'll be damned if the Viking didn't stop right there in his tracks and raise his hand, and he says in perfect English, clearer than I can even say, 'Don't worry, friend. We won't hurt you.'

"So one thing led to another, and he and his friends asked to stay the night. Said they'd pay us, in fact." He shook his head. "One minute I'm worried for me neck, and the next I'm filling up me pocket, eh, what? Well, they were staying whether or not I let them, so naturally I said yes, and the whole lot of them trooped into the cottage and broke bread with us. Never bothered my woman, never took a thing. They all spoke the language, they did; said they'd lived down in Twyneham for some years. The big fair one, he had nothing to say, just sat there…but the others talked. So naturally, when we felt better about them, I finally told them about the other Vikings who'd been here that morning. I figured they were from the same bunch, but the way they were acting it seemed like maybe they weren't. But they wanted to hear about it, all the same.

"So I started in by telling them about the priest and the girl, you know, seeing how that was the strangest part of all, and they seemed interested, of course. But when I finally got around to the one-eyed Viking, well, it was like the big blonde one came alive. He jumped up, and his eyes got real wide, and he made me tell him everything, just like I'm telling you now. And all the while he's rubbing his hands, and his friends are slapping each other on the backs, and…by God, it was like they'd found a treasure chest in me hovel, instead of a few scraps of bread."

"Sigli," Penda said quietly. "It must have been Sigli."

"Sigli, you say?" Huda wondered. "Was that his name? Funny, he never told me. But anyway, we all went down for the night. They slept on me floor inside, for it rained early on, as you probably remember, and I swear, I couldn't get to sleep because the big blonde one, he kept tossing and turning, and mumbling things in the Viking tongue that I couldn't understand.

"But finally dawn broke, and they got right up and packed a few cakes with them. And the big one called me over, and he told me that he was also bent on taking me two horses with him, seeing as how they were all on foot. Now, I started to complain, for they was all I had, those two old nags, pitiful as they might have been, and that just goes to show you how easy I felt around the Vikings, when they could have had me head, and been done with it. But the heathen went into his pouch, and he gave me this."

Huda reached into his pocket and withdrew a gold coin, which he proudly displayed for the Saxons. "Worth a lot more than two horses and the bread, I'll tell you that."

What he didn't tell them about were the three additional gold pieces the Viking had given him, all of which were safely hidden beneath a loose board next to his bed inside the hovel.

"Well, that was that," he continued. "The five of them were off a minute later with the two horses, heading west, just like the others. Me and the boy went back to work for a few hours, and the next thing we know, all of you come into me meadow." He shook his head. "The day's still young, after all...God knows what tonight'll bring."

"There may be others passing through here," Penda said, rising, "but no one that should cause you any worry. There's half an army a day or so behind me, all heading west, all chasing down what you saw in the last two days. But I must ask you one more thing. I need you to sell me your cows. Food is hard to find for so many men, and you'll be doing a great service for your king and your country."

"Well, of course, My Lord," Huda stammered. "But they're all I have now, you know, and..."

"Say no more." Penda extracted a handful of gold pieces from his pouch and handed them over to the ceorl. "Once again, you'll find you're getting more than your animals are worth, but you've earned it. And you've told me what I need to know. It's a bargain both ways, no?" He turned to his aides. "We're off. The game is afoot."

He and the others left Huda in front of the hovel, where he stood fondling the latest addition to his coffers. Along with what Sigli had given him, he now had enough to buy twice the livestock he had previously owned, and the wherewithal to do nothing more than sun himself in the meadow for the next year without so much as lifting his hand to do a single day's work.

He jingled the coins in his hands and laughed. He was beginning to like these interruptions; maybe an invasion of his privacy every few years wasn't such a bad thing after all.

*   *   *   *   *

Pro-pitty, pro-pitty, pro-pitty. Pro-pitty, pro-pitty, pro-pitty.

Property, indeed, Alfred thought, listening to the drumbeat of his charger's hooves on the road to the southwest. There were several hundred Saxons with him, but he rode alone just ahead of them to better focus on his thoughts.

He had been unable to stay in London any longer. Matters with Haestan had reached an impasse, with no indication that the stalemate would soon be broken. Haggard from several sleepless nights following the disappearance of his grandchild and daughter, he had risen at dawn and ordered his personal guard into the saddle. He left strict orders for Eadred to remain in London while he was gone, making sure to be on the road before his son-in-law was given the news; it would not do for both of them to turn their backs on Haestan. Someone had to stay behind to protect the one spot that held the key to all of England.

Pro-pitty, pro-pitty. He sighed as the hoof beats drummed on. It had been too much to ask for, to expect the remainder of his days to be free from strife. It was not the war that troubled him, for England had never been better prepared to defend herself. It was standing by and watching the time slip away that was the worst thing of all. Because time was no longer an ally, and he had become extremely protective of it. And now it was filled with distraction.

Pro-pitty, pro-pitty, pro-pitty. He had more property than any man in England—more than just about anyone in the world, for that matter. He had powerful allies, the good will of the Pope and the devotion of thousands of Englishmen. But none of it could prolong his days or buy him time. How fleeting it all was! His children were grown now. His youngest, the scholarly Aethelweard, was fifteen, and seemed set on a lifetime of study. His daughter Aethelgifu had been the Abbess of Shaftesbury for five years, and Aelfthryth would soon be leaving for the continent to marry Baldwin II, count of Flanders—willingly, thank the Lord! And Edward, of course, seemed well on his way to establishing himself as a force in England, a worthy heir to the throne.

And then there was Aethelfled.

Pro-pitty, pro-pitty. No, Aethelfled had never been his property. She had a mind of her own and had never hesitated to use it; of all his children she was the one most like he was, that he knew. But her fierce independence had always meant trouble. As proud as he was of his eldest, her headstrong ways had always cost him, one way or the other. Always.

She should have been born a man, he thought to himself for the thousandth time.

Thinking of her like this again led his thoughts to Sigli, to a man he had trusted like a son. He had never been able to come to grips with what had happened between them; the banishment had failed to resolve anything. He had wronged the Viking, lied to keep him in England against his will, and it eventually had come back to haunt him. They had betrayed each other, in the end. But none of that mattered anymore; he could not forgive Sigli's return to England under the banner of the Raven. He was one of *them* now. He was the enemy. It was a dirty enough business without friends turning into foes. He would simply have to destroy everyone and everything that took up arms against England, and damned be the personal cost.

That was all there was to it. Sigli's fate was just one more thing to think about, another intangible. Another twist of fate to complicate his life as he sped to the southwest, searching.

Pro-pitty, pro-pitty, pro-pitty.

*   *   *   *   *

"Did you ever wonder what it would have been like, had Borstan not betrayed your father?"

Sigli stared into the flames of the campfire. "That was sixteen years ago, Dagmar. A long time."

"Ah, but think of it. The ships...Halfsfiord...the way the sun would set over the harbor…Do you remember those days? It was all ahead of us then, Sigli."

"Yes, it was."

A low breeze moaned through the trees. Sigli looked over at the sleeping bundles that were Hoenir, Leif and Bor, and he sighed. "You know, I thought of my brother Hathor today. About how we'd hide under the furs in my father's lodge when the elders would meet, trying to keep from laughing, knowing we'd be paddled if we were found out." He shook his head. "Ah, Hathor...I remember how he was always running, trying to catch me. But I was always just a little older and stronger, always a step ahead."

Dagmar grinned. "He was a bold one, he was."

"Yes, a bold one, all right. My brother. He was just seventeen when he was killed."

"I haven't forgotten."

Sigli fell silent. A flood of images washed over him, all the little particulars that give a time and place its own special identity. The mist over the fiord at dawn. The majestic sheer walls of rock, rising like towers from the water's edge. The mournful sound of Hrothgar's horn when the dragon ships would slide into view around the harbor mouth.

And then he thought of Beolinde, the first love of his life. His *sister*. Beolinde, by Odin! Beolinde!

And Aethelfled. Beautiful Aethelfled.

As he sat there staring into the fire, he realized that love was one of the only things ever really worth being lucky in. Everything else was tangible.

Everything else could be achieved, if you really wanted it. But of all things, love and health were all that mattered, and a man had precious little to say about either one.

No one seemed to have it all. Not even Alfred, of all people. What had happened? What did it all mean? What was he chasing? He felt that old familiar weight on his chest, the one that pounded away with a dull ache, and right then he wanted to see her again, if just for a moment.

"What is it we do, Dagmar? What are we looking for?"

"Whatever's left."

"Whatever's left?"

"Yes…come on, now. You've said it yourself many times. There's nowhere left to go. And that's why we do what we do, what you've led us to do these many years. That's why we hunt Sidroc...because it's all that's left."

Sigli nodded. "All that's left."

Dagmar stood up, shaking the loose earth from his leggings. "Go to sleep, Sigli...I'll keep the first watch. Tomorrow we'll get up and do it again. Because tomorrow could be the day."

It was true; tomorrow *could* be the day. Too tired to even be depressed any longer, Sigli turned over and fell asleep.

He awoke with a start. The first thing he saw was Dagmar staggering toward him, mouth agape and looking down in disbelief at the feathered shaft protruding from his chest. The blood had already formed an expanding circle around the wound, and it glistened in the moonlight. Sigli sat up and reached for his war axe, but it was already too late. The clearing was filled with a score of Saxon archers, their bows trained on him and the other three Vikings who had been asleep while Dagmar stood watch. All he could do was attend to his friend, who had dropped to his knees in front of him, gasping for air. He pulled the

Halfsfiordian to him and cradled him in his arms, and then he put his axe in his friend's hand to deliver him to the promise of Valhalla.

"Finish it," Dagmar whispered up to him. "Finish what we started." He shuddered and died.

"We wouldn't have killed him, but he resisted." Penda stepped forward from the ranks of the Saxons and into the firelight.

"You would have killed him, anyway. You've no love lost for the Vikings."

"That's right, Sigli," the ealdorman said. "You come here to kill, rob and plunder. You rape our women and destroy our churches...why should you expect anything less?" He turned to his soldiers. "Bind them, and make sure they're securely fastened. Tie them to each other so they can't escape."

"What will you do with us?"

"Nothing...other than slit your throat if you make any trouble. Alfred will decide your fate, now that you've disobeyed him and returned from exile under the enemy's banner."

"I come alone! I'm not your enemy!"

"You conspired with Haestan at Benfleet!"

"That's a lie!" Sigli grimaced, restrained by his captors. "We're here for one reason, Penda...the same reason that brought me to these damned shores sixteen years ago! The Dane Sidroc is in Wessex now, and I intend to kill him!"

Penda eyed him carefully. "I can tell you that Sidroc is indeed alive and in Wessex," he finally said. "I saw him myself just a month ago, when Edward and I parlayed with the Vikings."

"Then release me, Penda! I swear I won't harm any Saxon or his possessions! All I want is Sidroc...nothing more!"

"I can't do that. Only Alfred has the power to release you. When he saw you at sea off Benfleet, he issued orders for your capture, alive or dead. The choice is yours."

"By the blood of my father, by Odin, I swear we'll fight at your side! Release us!"

Penda merely shook his head. "It's impossible. But there's something else. I also pursue Sidroc...but for different reasons. Reasons even more important than those that will put your neck in the hangman's noose. Old One Eye holds Archbishop Plegmund of Canterbury hostage—and with him Elfwyn, the daughter of Aethelfled and Eadred."

The news sent a jolt through Sigli. He struggled against his bonds.

"That settles it, then! You have no choice but to release me and allow us to help you. By your God, Penda...please listen to me!"

"I can't help you. But content yourself in knowing that you draw closer to Sidroc. For as God is my witness, we'll find him, and deliver his head to Alfred!" Having said his piece, he turned to his men. "Let's return to camp now; we'll need to get some sleep. And woe be to him who allows any of the heathens to break free!"

He turned on his heel and stepped over Dagmar's body, his sword jangling against his hauberk as he strode off into the darkness.

*   *   *   *   *

For the first time in a very long while, Sidroc was pleased with himself. He smiled as he sat along the left bank of the River Tarrant looking downstream and idly sharpening his sword against the rocks at the water's edge. He and his men had emerged from the Weald into West Sussex that morning, and there was nothing left to do but wait for the arrival of Hundeus and the rest of the Viking Warlords. At that very moment, according to his scouts, they were coming up from the southeast to meet them.

Wouldn't they be surprised, the insolent fools, when he showed them what human treasures he had found in the wilderness? What had started out as a disaster had turned into a great triumph. Yes, it would serve them right, to look on in envy at the good fortune that had attended him. They had laughed behind his back when the lot he had drawn consigned him to the Weald—it had all been arranged against him, of course—and congratulated each other for their cleverness.

Send Old One Eye into the wilderness, they snickered. Let him get tangled up with himself, lost and frustrated, and maybe luck would have it he'd never come out of the forest alive, and they would be rid of him once and for all. That's what they had been saying to themselves, yes, that was it. He had seen it in their eyes, behind their self-satisfied smiles, and it had stung him.

Well, there would be no more of that. He did not intend to tell them about the fabulous store of Grimwald's gold, having already sworn his men to secrecy and hidden all the gold and jewels at the bottom of the oxcarts he had confiscated from Sussex Downs. No, the priest and the girl would be more than enough. The Archbishop of Canterbury and the granddaughter of Alfred were a fine catch if he ever saw one, and would command a handsome price. He would keep the lion's share of it, as was his right, and then after that…well, anything was possible. Perhaps he and the entire Viking army could turn on the Christians and storm Winchester itself, now just a day's march to the west.

And yet, he had second thoughts about relinquishing his prisoners right away. As long as they were in his possession he could rest securely; the Saxons would not dare to attack him. He could choose the time and place for action, and until then get whatever he wanted—all as long as he maintained control over his precious captives. That was the logical explanation, at least, and the one he would offer up to anyone who chose to confront him. Because in his heart, he knew that he really did not want to let go of the priest and the girl at all. Oh, the priest, maybe; he was dispensable, no matter how valuable his translations.

But not her. Not the girl.

He looked up from his work and there she was, the sunlight shining in her blonde hair as she watched him from the edge of the bank, twenty yards downstream. Those eyes again, looking not so much at him as through him, a translucent blue that was brighter than the sky at noon. He had only been around her for a few days, and yet he found that she had touched a part of him that he had not even known existed.

It had made him uncomfortable at first, but then the pure seductiveness of it all began to take over, and he found himself drawn to her, wanting more. It was not a sexual thing—no, nothing of the sort—so much as a warming of the soul, a slow heat that he found indescribably pleasurable. When he looked at her, they connected in a way that he could not even begin to explain but found irresistibly compelling, having never known such pleasure before amid the pathos of his life. There was something in her that tamed the beast in him, and he liked it.

He looked back at her now, just the two of them, enjoying the fact that the attentive priest was not hovering around her like a hen doting over its chicks. He beckoned to her.

"Hey, there, girl...come here."

She walked toward him, and he studied her carefully as she picked her way along the bank. Such a delicate little creature, so perfectly made. The gods had been kind to craft such a fair thing to look upon, so very pleasing to the eye. He drank her in to his great delight until she came within a pace of where he sat, so close that he was able to reach out and touch her soft little arm with his weathered hand.

"When will I see my mother again?"

He said nothing, but merely watched her. Her skin was smooth and perfect, like the alabaster surface of a gleaming pearl.

"Do you know my mother?" she asked, undeterred in spite of the language barrier. He started as though to answer, but a voice from over his shoulder interrupted him.

"She wants to know when she'll see her mother again," Plegmund said.

Sidroc grimaced, displeased at having his private moment with the girl invaded. "Tell her I don't know. I don't even know who her mother is."

"Having once laid eyes on the Lady of Mercia, you wouldn't be able to forget her. I can guarantee you that."

Old One Eye laughed bitterly. "Then perhaps a trade would be in order. The girl is sweet, but something a bit older might be even more to my liking."

"Thank the Lord Jesus she can't understand what you said!"

"Careful, priest…I've slit men open at the gut and fed them to the crows for less!" And then he looked at Elfwyn and he softened, as though a cool breeze had washed over him. "I think you underestimate her. I think she knows me better than you could ever imagine."

"How your sword shines!" Elfwyn suddenly exclaimed, reaching out to touch it.

"Be careful!" Sidroc shouted, pulling it back protectively. "It would slice your finger before you even felt it!"

She stood there watching him, and she laughed. And then she asked him the obvious question, one that had been forming in her mind ever since she had first seen him.

"What happened to your eye?"

Plegmund hesitated before translating her request. At first Sidroc pulled back, but then, finally, he raised a hand to his face and rubbed his fingers over the angry scar in the socket where his left eye had once been. "It was a dagger, and a sharp one at that. I never saw it coming."

"Who did it?"

But he did not answer her. Instead, he looked down at the ground, lost in thought.

"It was Beolinde of Halfsfiord," Plegmund blurted out.

Sidroc glared at the Archbishop, and the muscles in his face tightened. "How did you know that?!"

"Because I once knew someone who knew both of you, and was consumed by his memories. Someone who was like a brother to me during the years when he lived in Wessex, building ships for the king."

"And who was this man?"

"Sigli, son of Lothar."

Sidroc flinched. "Sigli! All these years, I've wondered what happened to him..." He leaned forward. "Do you know where he is now?"

"I don't know if he's alive or dead. He and Alfred became at odds seven years ago, and he left England." He sighed. "For all I know, he may be at the bottom of the sea."

"Which is where I would have sent him, had he not escaped," Sidroc said, his voice suddenly thin and shrill. "After so many years, he must be dead...otherwise he surely would have found me by now."

"He longed for nothing so much as to feel his fingers around your throat, to repay his family's blood debt. But long ago, even before the siege of London, he heard that you were dead. Because of that, he stopped looking for you. If only he had known...."

"Dead? Ha!" Sidroc laughed. "There are more than a few men who wish such a thing were true."

He stared out across the river, and his brow clouded over. "But Sigli...he was the one that got away. For the longest time I waited for him, looking over my shoulder, expecting him to try to do what any Viking worth his manhood would do. It was his duty to avenge Halfsfiord. And do you know something, priest? I wanted him to do that. I wanted that day to come. I wanted to face him, to show him that it was no accident that I took his father's ships and laid with the women of his village. I wanted to tear his heart out with my fingers and crush it!"

"I wonder if you could have stood up to him, man against man."

"You fool!" Old One Eye hissed, rising to his feet in anger. "No man has ever yet gone against me in combat and lived! No man!"

"No man has ever had such just cause as Sigli did."

"There wasn't a Viking in all of Jutland and the north who didn't celebrate the sack of Halfsfiord. Lothar wouldn't cooperate. Not with me, not with Ubba, not with Guthrum. Not with anyone! He deserved his fate; if it hadn't been me, someone else would have done the same, I'm sure of that!"

"Don't try to justify the slaughter of innocent men and women."

The Malevolent One sneered. "Yes, that's right; I almost forgot. You Christians turn the other cheek, don't you? Well, if a man turns his cheek to me, I'll drive my fist right through it. Like I'd do with Sigli, if I ever met him again!"

"I'd give anything to have him here right now. I knew him well, and loved him. He bore a great love for the woman who is this child's mother, in fact. As I do also."

"Ah...so it is, then," Sidroc nodded, able somehow to read into the monk's remark. "All entwined together, separate strands in the same rope."

His eyes wandered to Elfwyn, who had turned aside and was playing on the bank. Once again, his spirits lightened. "And here before us, one of the knots. The tie that binds, no?"

He watched her as the sunlight continued to play tricks with her hair, as she crouched at the river's edge and ran her fingers through its cool waters, the very essence of innocent youth. Her spell was hypnotic; he was entranced.

Plegmund looked on as Sidroc eyed the girl with this strange and unexpected display of tenderness, brutal and gentle all at once. For such a creature to show such emotion seemed too strange for words, so unlike the man and his reputation that Plegmund could not fathom it, nor even begin to figure out what potentially sinister direction its affections might take.

And that was the thing that bothered him the most.

*   *   *   *   *

At that moment a day's march to the west, Edward the Elder rode into the valley of the Itchen at the head of a force of fifteen hundred men. Below him he could see the king's main estate at Winchester, where he knew that Ceolmund waited for him. He had left it to the ealdorman of Hampshire to gather up as many men as he could from the city, while he had ridden hastily off to Dorset and Wiltshire and managed to raise the soldiers who now accompanied him. It felt good to finally be heading east; that was the only way to go now, back into the jaws of war. He was tired of administering to details, tired of negotiating. Tired of waiting. The time had come to put aside words and take up arms.

There had been moments during the last few months when he had feared it would all pass him by and fate would leave him with no war to fight. Such an alternative was simply unacceptable. He knew that to truly be considered great, a king at some time in his life had to lead his people into armed conflict, just as his father Alfred had done at Ashdown and Wilton during the Year of the Battles twenty-two years ago. He had been a baby in his mother's arms then, and Alfred had been a mere boy himself, younger even than he was now, ruling a kingdom under great duress.

In an odd way, it made Edward envious. He sensed that nothing he could ever do in his military career would ever measure up to his father's accomplishments, if for no other reason than the times in which his father had lived. The Golden Dragon had made England strong; soon, it would be up to him to maintain and advance that strength. How to do it? As he rode closer to Winchester, waving his hand to the ceorls that looked up from their plows in the fields, he knew it was up to him to create his own opportunities, to make his own destiny. No one else could do it for him. He resolved that he would move relentlessly forward; no matter where the Vikings ran, they could not hide. Whatever it took, he would find them.

He saw a horseman riding hard toward them up the winding road that led to the city, and as the rider drew closer he could tell by the long, flowing hair waving in the wind that it was a woman. A few more seconds passed, and then his eyes lit up with delight when he recognized his sister Aethelfled.

What was she doing here? Why wasn't she in Mercia, or with her husband in London? As she approached him, she looked haggard and drawn, unkempt in a disheveled way that was quite unlike her.

"Aethelfled! Why are you here?"

She reined in her horse. "For the same reason you are, Edward. Are these men fresh enough to resume their march after a short rest?"

"You look terrible...what's wrong?"

"Elfwyn has disappeared. Haven't you heard?"

He hadn't. His mouth dropped, and he sat speechlessly on his horse as she told him what she knew.

"I've been on the road for two full days, now," she finally concluded, "and I don't know where else to turn. When I failed to encounter anyone directly south of London I came here, hoping for some news. But nothing...nothing at all."

"Don't worry. I'm sure we'll hear something soon. For all you know, they may be safe in London right now."

"No, Edward. I fear the worst. Their route placed them in the path of the Vikings. Something dreadful has happened...I just know it!"

"There, there," he reassured her. But he was also afraid. "Who would have thought they would have marched so far west? It makes no sense."

"They wouldn't hurt her, would they? What would they do with a harmless child?"

"Aethelfled, take heart. You're going to drive yourself mad carrying on like this. Now, don't worry...help is on the way. You just came from the city; did Ceolmund raise many men?"

"Close to a thousand, he said."

"Excellent! Then we've more than enough to make trouble for any Viking force. Listen to me, sister...we've got them now! If Penda trails behind them, then we'll trap them between us. There's no way they can escape!"

"But there are so many of them, Edward."

"And more than enough of us to beat them back. We've got them in the open country now, far from their ships or their allies!" He rubbed his hands in anticipation.

"But Edward! If they have Elfwyn...what can we do?"

"We can't assume that. And if they do have her...no matter. We'll buy her back, and when she's safely in our hands we'll fall upon the heathens and carve them up into so many pieces that not even the birds will bother to feed on them!"

"You give me faith. There's no one I'd rather have by me in these times than you."

He flushed with pride. "I'll never let you down...know that now, and forever. I've been waiting for this chance all my life, and I'm not about to stand by and watch it slip away!"

"Good! Then we'll leave Winchester immediately?"

"We? I...I think not, Aethelfled. This is no time for you. Stay behind; there's no reason to endanger yourself."

She turned on him with a splendid, impassioned fury. "Are you mad? My child is somewhere out there, and you expect me to stay behind in Winchester with all the other gentlewomen?"

"War is man's business."

"Show me one horseman in this entire force who can outride me! You yourself still can't, by God!"

She was right, of course. But still he resisted.

"You and I both know you're not the type to hang back. You'd be right in the front lines. And neither Eadred nor Father would ever forgive me if anything ever happened to you."

"And I'll never forgive you if you try to make me stay behind! You can't stop me, Edward! No one can!"

He looked at her, and then he shook his head and laughed. "You're right. It's useless to try and tell you what to do. I don't know why I bothered in the first place." He stared ahead, where towering clouds had begun to form in the eastern sky.

"Then so be it. Let's have at them, then, Aethelfled! To war!"

"To war," she echoed quietly, and they rode forward as the dust from several thousand hooves trailed behind them, the only blemish on a day that otherwise was most excellent and fair.

*   *   *   *   *

Hundeus sighed. It was getting late, and he was tired of hearing his war council arguing about the army's next move. Some of his men wanted to turn back toward Kent and take their chances with the Saxon force that followed them; others wanted to do nothing, preferring to wait on the banks of the Tarrant until the enemy arrived.

And then of course there was Sidroc, who now loomed before him in the light of the campfire, exhorting the council to continue west and attack Winchester. Managing such a beast was sometimes more than he felt like doing. He found himself longing for the old days, a simpler time when his decision had been the only one that mattered, when the fate of merely a few dragon ships rather than an entire army rested in the balance. But as he sat stroking his beard and nursing a cup of mead, he realized that those days were gone forever.

"It's Winchester, I tell you!" Sidroc shouted out, casting his eye at each of them for effect. "Winchester is the heart! The key to all of England!"

"That's not what Haestan thinks," one of the Viking earls said. "It's London that he has his eyes on."

"London will fall in time," Old One Eye replied. "But the Saxons are well-fortified there. If we can strike quickly and take Winchester, it will throw them into disarray. They'll be forced to weaken themselves on Haestan's front in order to send reinforcements our way. And that will open up the whole countryside to attack!"

"It's too risky. I say we stay here and fortify ourselves."

"Not here! We're vulnerable. I say we turn back and face our pursuit!" cried another.

"Stupid fool!" a third man urged, "Our best opportunity, by far..."

"Quiet, all of you!"

All eyes turned to Hundeus, who raised his hand in command. "I've heard enough! We can't stay here; we'd eventually be trapped. Turning back makes no sense; there's no plunder in the shires we've already crossed, and we'd be marching right into the Saxons, on their terms. And forging ahead to Winchester is too great a risk." Here he looked at Sidroc. "We don't know what we'd encounter, and heading that far west would put us dangerously out of touch with Haestan."

"Out of touch! Do we need Haestan to make our every decision, as though we were incapable of thinking for ourselves? You defang us, Hundeus! You take away the bite, until only the bark remains!"

"There will be time enough for biting, Sidroc."

"You've been telling us that now for months!"

"As I'll tell you again. Wait."

"Then what would you, Hundeus?" asked one of the others. "Does that mean we stay here?"

"No. It means we march north tomorrow."

A murmur swept through the council. "Why north? To what purpose?"

Hundeus stood up and spoke in a clear, stern voice that left no doubt as to whom was in command. "From the very beginning, Haestan planned our movement as a diversion, hoping Alfred would deplete his ranks in London. As far as we know, that hasn't happened."

He paused and began to walk slowly around the circle, measuring his words. "Either way, our orders remain the same. We'll march north, into Berkshire, and cross the Thames just west of London. At that point, we'll either turn on the city, or continue through Mercia to rejoin Haestan in East Anglia."

"More delay! More of nothing!" Sidroc protested, facing off against Hundeus from the opposite side of the fire.

"We'll fight soon enough, Sidroc. As long as we stay on the march, the advantage is ours. A moving target is hard to hit."

"Winchester! It's Winchester, I say!" Old One Eye shouted.

But as he looked at the other Viking chieftains, he could see that the consensus had shifted against him. Sheep, he thought to himself angrily. Bleating, shaggy-faced sheep! And as the murmurs started, and a smirk began to form on Hundeus' face, he knew that the time had come to play his hand. He turned toward the darkness behind him and beckoned imperiously.

"Bring the prisoners before us!"

Several figures emerged from a nearby dark grove of trees, and a ripple passed through the council as Plegmund and Elfwyn stepped into the firelight.

"What's the meaning of this?!" Hundeus thundered.

"This," Sidroc sneered triumphantly, unable to conceal his arrogant pride, "is our shield! And my salvation. You would have all wished me to meander lost through the Weald, but this is what I found instead. The greatest prize of all—the Archbishop of Canterbury and the granddaughter of Alfred the king!"

The council erupted into confusion. It was just as Sidroc had hoped; he had them now. He grasped the pommel of his majestic sword, a blade half again as heavy as those wielded by most other men, and he raised it into the air, his one eye gleaming with satisfaction.

"With these captives in our possession, we can do anything we want! It's Winchester, I say! On to Winchester!"

The babble continued, until Hundeus stepped forward and raised his hand. He waited until he had everyone's attention, and then he spoke, directing his words at Sidroc.

"What you've done is a worthy thing. You've given us another potent weapon, indeed. But my mind is unchanged; we're still marching north."

"But the prisoners!" Sidroc gasped. "You relinquish our advantage!"

"The fate of these hostages is for Haestan to decide."

"Haestan! To Hel with Haestan! These are my hostages! I captured them!"

Hundeus shook his head. "It was long ago agreed among us that all significant booty would be gathered together and shared accordingly. This, you may remember, was done by the will of a general council, headed up by Haestan himself." He nodded toward Plegmund and the girl. "These two are certainly important enough to warrant such treatment. They'll be turned over to Haestan when we rejoin him."

"Impossible!" Sidroc spluttered, the rage welling up inside him. "I won't allow it! The girl and the priest are mine!"

"Not yours, Sidroc. Ours. And just to make sure you don't stray from my order, I'm taking them away from you. They'll remain in my custody."

"Wretched schemer!" He brandished his sword menacingly and took a step toward Hundeus. But before he could get within ten feet of the man the rest of them interceded, drawing their swords and demonstrating their loyalties once and for all.

Sidroc's rage gave way to caution; now was neither the time nor the place to go against the council. He glared at each of them, barely able to control his anger, until finally he slid his blade back into its scabbard and stalked off toward the darkness. He paused near the edge of the firelight long enough to point a threatening finger at Hundeus.

"I won't forget this! By Odin, I won't forget!"

He veered off into the night, shoving rudely past the others and heading along the bank of the river. He picked his way through the remaining Viking campfires until he was beyond the last of them, breathing heavily and grinding his teeth in rage. The fools! The insolent, cowardly fools! He had thought that his prize catch would net him an advantage, but it had all turned against him. His precious treasure had been stolen from him; the girl was gone.

A heavy mist hung in the air as he staggered forward, flailing at the stray branches and underbrush that blocked his way, until finally he smacked his head by accident against the trunk of a tree. He bellowed in pain and grabbed at his head. How it ached! How it stung! And then a frenzy overwhelmed him, and with a cry of rage he pulled his great sword out of its scabbard and began to hack wildly at the tree. He rained blow after blow down upon it, grunting and swearing from the effort, venting his anger against the splintering bark as though it were the head of Hundeus himself. By now the mist had turned into a drizzle, but he did not relent. He continued to slash away at the tree until the sweat and the rain had soaked him completely through.

At last, a crackling noise signaled the only triumph he would enjoy that night. The tree groaned and began to give way, finally surrendering itself to his will and toppling over with a crash. It was only then that he leaned on his sword, his rage spent.

But no amount of fatigue could dull the hate in his heart. He stood there in the rain, breathing heavily, until finally a whisper hissed from his lips.

"Blood will spill for this! And by the gods, I'll be the one to spill it!"

* * * * *

It was drizzling when Sigli woke up at dawn. He shivered as he huddled beneath an animal skin with his hands tied behind his back, lying in the shelter of an oak. He had slept poorly during the night, afraid to stir for fear his movements would disturb the skin. First a leg had been exposed, then his head, and finally his back; no position offered the least bit of relief. His body was stiff from the hours of confinement. As he peered forlornly across the drenched meadow that stretched before him, he was an utterly defeated man, one whose life had come full circle. He had arrived in England sixteen years ago in the same condition he now found himself: a bound captive, prisoner to a people and culture he understood no better today than he had then.

Thinking about it devastated him.

He remembered how Alfred had saved his life on the plain near Exeter as he had baked in the sun, and he found himself thinking that it all should have ended then and there. Would that the king had never come along that day and prolonged his agony! Would that he had just died, another nameless, faceless casualty of war.

And so as he sat up in the drizzle, as depressed as a man can be, he barely noticed that the camp had begun to stir. He did not bother to acknowledge the other prisoners as they grunted their good mornings in dull monotones and rose stiffly from their beds. He just stared ahead into the gray dawn, seeing nothing. They were all thrown a morning ration by their captors, who laughed contemptuously as they stooped forward on their knees, hands bound behind them, and buried their faces in the stale hunks of bread scattered on the wet ground.

Twenty minutes later the four Vikings found themselves strung together by a long rope that entwined itself around each of their wrists, still bound behind them, making an escape impossible.

The army marched northwest at a brisk pace. The countryside was open compared to the wilderness of the Weald, and they made good progress during the next few hours over the rolling hills and fields. They finally paused at mid-day to rest and refresh themselves, and the Viking captives slumped on the muddy ground, grateful for the respite. The drizzle had continued all day, and Sigli sat cross-legged in it, eyes closed and face uplifted toward the heavens. He remained that way for a few moments, his mind drifting, until he became aware of a presence looming over him and opened his eyes.

It was Penda.

"Tell me what you know about Haestan."

"I don't even know the man."

"Will he persist? Does he have enough sense to know when he's met his match?"

"Has he? I'm not so sure you can say that yet. But I told you, Penda, I don't know anything. Haestan's concerns don't matter to me...nor do yours. What's between you has nothing to do with me." He looked down into the mud. "My cause is no one's but my own."

"Such a pity. He who is friend to neither is an enemy to both."

"I have no quarrel with you, Penda. Nor with Alfred."

"You shouldn't have come. You shouldn't have ever come back to England."

"I shouldn't have come here to begin with, but what's done is done. Would that I had never set foot on this wretched shore!" His back stiffened, and he leaned forward. "Release us, Penda! Release us, and I swear on my father's grave not to raise a hand against you!"

The Saxon shook his head, and for a fleeting instant Sigli thought he saw a hint of compassion in his captor's eye. But then the stare returned, and the two of them maintained their distance, worlds apart.

"You know, I pity you in a way," Penda finally said. "I pity you, because I believe you. I've no doubt you speak the truth, and any man is to be commended for that. But your truth and mine are different. And mine is the will of Alfred."

They were interrupted by a crescendo of shouts that rolled across the camp. As they looked up, the Saxon ranks parted to reveal a lone rider galloping toward them through the army. The scout negotiated the distance between them and finally thundered to a stop in front of Penda, leaping breathlessly from his horse and bowing.

"My Lord, we've sighted them! An hour or so away, heading for Farnham!"

"Farnham!" Penda clapped his hands together in glee. "We can be there by late afternoon!" He raised a closed fist and shook it in the dank, misty air.

"Mark me, Saxons! We'll ride them down before the day is done! The eyes of England are upon you!"

CHAPTER XVI: The Battle Joined

"There is no love in war, but there is a lot
of war in love."
—Katji Michael

Plegmund brushed Elfwyn's hair as they sat together in Farnham town, sheltered in a hut near the River Wey. It was a dreary afternoon, and a light rain fell outside, its staccato beat rattling off the roof above them. Although more than four hours remained before sunset, the day was suspended in a perpetual twilight, enough to sink the spirits of even the most cheerful soul. Plegmund was as depressed as a man could be, weighed down by the gloom and fearful of what lay ahead. But at least the girl was safe.

Such softness, he thought as he stroked her blonde locks, such gentility in these barbarous times. It eased his nerves. He thanked God that she was spared the terror of knowing what could befall them; she was not yet capable of understanding the politics of atrocity. If it came to that—the unspeakable, the unthinkable—he did not know what he would do. Perhaps the merciful thing would be to take her life himself, should it come to that, for he knew what the Vikings were capable of doing. But to take anybody's life, even with good reason? No, as a man of the cross he could not do it. It was sacred and in the hands of God.

"Ouch! Plegmund, you're hurting me!"

"I'm...I'm sorry."

His hands recoiled momentarily and then resumed combing. He looked out the window of the hovel and into the gray afternoon, where the River Wey rushed by, its usually torpid current now swollen from the spring rains. The water level was higher than usual, a tumbling mass of dirty, turbulent wash. Most of the time it was easy enough to ford the river anywhere along the bank, but the flooding had limited its crossing to a single rickety bridge that spanned the river at the south end of the village. He could not help but wonder how sturdy the structure was as he watched it wobble lightly back and forth from the pressure of the Wey.

"Thank you, Plegmund. That's enough."

He stopped and handed her the brush, admiring his work. Her hair was absolutely angelic. As he watched her, she turned to look out the window, and suddenly her eyes took on a strange expression. When he turned to see what had alarmed her, he understood why. Sidroc filled the window. The Viking's lone eye was fixed on Elfwyn, gleaming brightly in the gloom, hypnotic and terrible all at once. For the first time, it scared her. Plegmund reached out protectively and glared at the intruder.

"What do you want, Sidroc?"

"How are you, my sweet?" Old One Eye smiled at the girl, ignoring him. "Are you well?"

She looked back at him uncertainly.

"Go away! Leave us alone! Can't you see she wants no part of you?"

"Shut your mouth, priest!" the Viking snarled. And then his eye narrowed and took on a cruel glint. "Or are you afraid I would dote only on the pretty little one, and not offer you any? Yes, you know what I mean, don't you? You're such a pretty boy, so fair-skinned and soft…"

Old One Eye began to laugh, but then he heard shouts coming from the north end of the village, where Hundeus and the other Viking earls were headquartered.

"Don't worry...I'll be back," he sneered. "That I promise." His face crinkled in delight as he turned back to Elfwyn. "Yes, Sidroc will come for you, my sweet. Yes, he will. And soon you'll again be mine."

He disappeared from the window.

"What did he say? What did he want, Plegmund?"

"Oh...nothing, nothing at all. Never mind, child. Pay no attention to him."

She shuddered. "He's scary. I didn't think he was so scary before, but now I do. I'm afraid."

"Don't be," he answered softly, trying his best not to show alarm. And then he stared glumly out the window, watching the river race by.

Sidroc strode briskly toward the war council's lair. The shouting grew louder, and as he drew nearer the edge of the village he recognized a familiar energy that now fairly crackled in the air. He did not have to look between the huts and over the heads of the men to see what he already knew was there. He did not have to see it at all, or even hear it. He could smell it. Because there was nothing at all like the smell of war.

"See here, Sidroc!" Hundeus shouted to him from among the Viking earls. Off in the distance to the north, a long line of Saxon horsemen had formed along the river. "No need to go out of our way to find the enemy...they've found us! And if that's the lot of them, then they'll pay dearly!"

Sidroc became aware of a stirring in his loins, and to his great delight he realized that he was as hard as iron, his member swollen in a way that not even the most beautiful woman could inspire. By the gods, he felt alive! Invincible! And he realized again in that moment that he lived for the thrill and the adrenaline of battle, for the outrageous intoxication of it all, the ultimate confrontation. Nothing could duplicate the feeling.

"Vikings!" Hundeus boomed out. "Here, along the river on our left, we'll fight them on foot. Hold this line, where their horsemen will try to penetrate. Sidroc, you and your berserkers shall man that flank, in front of the town!" His eyes gleamed. "I'll command the center. We'll strike at the Saxon left, away from the river." He then turned his attention to several of the other earls. "You men, meanwhile, gather our horse and remain hidden here in the village. When I give the signal, circle around hard to our right, flank them and roll them back to the river. We'll surround them, and cut every last man to pieces!"

Shouts of approval greeted his words; it was a good idea. Sidroc was beside himself with excitement as he bellowed out orders to his berserkers. But they needed no encouragement; like him, they were restless and ready for the confrontation. The Viking ranks formed, men pressing against each other in a line that stretched from the river across the entire front of Farnham town. They began to bang loudly on their shields and cry out in a discordant din that rattled like thunder across the valley. Louder and louder it grew, and the earth under their feet began to tremble with the stomping and pounding of their feet.

And then Hundeus, positioned in the center of the Norse line, raised his sword and pointed it north toward the Saxons. The Vikings plunged forward.

*   *   *   *   *

No one gathered at Farnham that day was more restless with anticipation than Sigli. And no one was more helpless to do anything about it. He and the last of his men—Bor, Leif and Hoenir—had been sequestered in a small grove of trees along the riverbank, strung together behind the Saxon line. An ill-tempered guard stood over them, angrily pacing back and forth, displeased at having to stay behind his countrymen as they went into battle. The hardness in his eye made it clear that escape was futile; they could expect no mercy from him.

They stood there grimly, all roped into the same line, and watched as the horse soldiers ahead of them waited for the order to advance. The tension in the air was oppressive, sticky and hot even in the damp April afternoon. As Sigli looked toward the huts of Farnham in the distance, he could see and hear the Viking army as it stretched out across the meadow before them. It was a formidable host, and an intemperately loud one; the beating of their shields reverberated through the dull air, enough to unnerve even the bravest man.

But if the Vikings outnumbered the Christians, they lacked mobility. All of them were on foot. Anxious to exploit this advantage, Penda rode back and forth in front of the Saxon ranks, shouting encouragement to the men and holding them back from breaking ranks.

"Let them come to us! Let them advance until they're free of the village, where we can have at them in the open country!"

They did not have long to wait. The Vikings suddenly advanced with a great shout, banging their shields and waving their weapons in the air. They chewed up the distance between the two lines, until Penda raised his sword in the mist and spurred his horse forward, followed by the entire Saxon line as it thundered across the meadow.

A few frantic moments passed as the men rushed headlong toward each other, until at last the armies met with a great crash that echoed over the surrounding hills. Metal against metal. Grunts and groans, howls of pain, anger, dismay, fear, tension and release all at once. At first the Saxon horse had its way with the Viking infantry, and it appeared as though the heathen line would break. But the Danes remained massed and determined not to buckle, and gradually they reformed their ranks, absorbing the Saxon charge and swarming around the attackers. Neither side gave way as the fighting raged up and down the line, but finally the Saxons began to push the Vikings back toward Farnham. Penda's plan was working.

His moment was short-lived. For as Sigli and the others all looked toward Farnham, a large mounted force of Vikings suddenly issued from the town and raced to encircle the Saxon left, away from the river. It caught Penda by surprise. He tried to reinforce his unprotected flank, but before long the Viking horse was in position, peeling back the Saxon line like the skin of an overripe onion. It was a bold maneuver, and a successful one; the Saxons had no choice but to fall back toward the river and fight for their lives. The tide had swung; the Vikings now advanced on all fronts with renewed determination.

"Great God in heaven!" the Saxon guard exclaimed hoarsely, dismayed by this sudden turn of fortune. He looked again at his captives, and his eye gleamed with fear. Around them, the fighting grew closer on all sides. The Viking horse had rolled the Saxon left back upon itself, and the men were now reduced to a desperate mass of heaving, retreating bodies, giving ground generously and falling back toward the grove where the prisoners were bound.

In that moment of reckoning the guard's nerve broke.

"I'll be damned in Hell if any one of *you* survive this day!" he cried, and he leaped upon them. He severed the defenseless Bor's head cleanly from its shoulders with a long, sweeping blow from his sword. Blood spurted in all directions as the Viking's body sagged against the rope, dragging the others down with him. They could do nothing more than close their eyes and turn away as the Saxon resumed his murderous attack, and soon Leif and Hoenir were hacked to death. Now only Sigli was left, and as he struggled to regain his feet in the muddy earth the guard advanced upon him, raising his sword to finish his bloody work.

"Hold, man!"

The voice stayed the guard's hand. There above them loomed Penda, peering down from his horse, covered with sweat and blood from the battle. He pointed to the ranks. "Join the others...you'll have chance enough to use your sword now!"

"Shall I finish this one?" the man asked, his voice trembling.

"No. Leave him to me! Now, go!"

The guard raced off into the battle, leaving Penda alone with Sigli. Blood dripped from a wound on the ealdorman's leg. "The day goes against us…but if we can't win, we'll at least die fighting!" he snarled. "But before I die, I'll deal with you!"

He raised his bloody sword above him. Sigli closed his eyes and shuddered, waiting for the impact, but the blade whistled harmlessly by his ear and cut cleanly through the rope that bound him. He was free.

"Let God decide your fate now, " Penda said, glaring down at him. "But I warn you: the next time my sword swings in your direction, it will be to kill!" He turned his horse back into the battle, shouting encouragement and rallying his men.

Struggling to free himself from his dead comrades, Sigli unloosened the last knots that restrained him and rushed forth into the chaos that raged all around.

*   *   *   *   *

In another part of the meadow, close upon Farnham, Sidroc bent over the body of a dying Saxon, resting for a moment as he stripped the man of a bright amulet that hung around his neck. He had already killed more than his share of the enemy, sapping even his prodigious energies, and as he paused to refresh himself the battle surged ahead of him, rushing forward alongside the river. He collected himself and looked around, and he was just about to rejoin the carnage when a rider from the village came thundering up behind him.

"Sidroc! Sidroc! The Saxons are attacking from the rear!"

He craned his neck toward the village. There to the south, still some distance beyond Farnham, he could see a column of mounted soldiers riding from the trees.

"How many?"

"Too many to count!" the rider replied. "I'm off to warn Hundeus!"

Sidroc knew what he had to do; it was everything he had prepared for. He turned immediately and ran back toward Farnham, away from the battle, breathing heavily as he picked his way through the dead and the dying that littered the meadow. When he finally reached the village, his handpicked escort of almost a hundred fighting men was already saddled up and waiting for orders.

"Quickly...to the bridge! Everyone across it, and save the wagon for last! You men, there," he motioned to a handful of Danes, "attend me!"

He dashed among the huts, bearing down on the one that held what he was looking for. He could see the Saxon reinforcements thundering toward them from the south, but it would be several minutes before they could reach Farnham, leaving him just enough time to ford the Wey to safety.

He and his men hurried through the village until they reached the hut that contained Plegmund and Elfwyn. He brought the pommel of his sword down hard on the door, throwing the barrier open and clearing the way to enter.

Plegmund huddled with Elfwyn in a corner of the room. Heedless of his own safety, he raised his hand against Sidroc, who swatted him away as though he were a child. He fell to one side as the Malevolent One groped for the struggling girl, but he rose quickly and threw himself on the Viking, pounding on the Dane's back with his fists. Sidroc turned and brought the butt end of his sword hard against the side of Plegmund's head. The monk crumpled into a heap on the floor, clutching at his temple as blood streamed through his fingers.

His head throbbed unmercifully, blinding him, and by the time he could see again, the hut had emptied. He looked outside through the door, where he saw Sidroc swinging himself into a waiting saddle, holding Elfwyn close to him. Grabbing onto the leg of a nearby table for support, he raised himself and staggered out of the hut. But the Vikings were gone, already riding rapidly toward the bridge at the edge of the village. A number of them were already thundering across the rickety structure, which bowed noticeably from their weight as it swung back and forth over the river.

Plegmund knew he had to get across that bridge. He began to run toward it, the blood from his head soiling his robe, but he had barely gone a dozen steps when he was overcome by a wave of dizziness. He leaned against the wall of one of the huts along the river, too dazed to continue, when suddenly a riderless horse came bounding along the muddy village path.

Summoning all of his flagging strength, Plegmund reached out and grabbed hold of the bridal of the terrified beast. He was able to calm the animal and mount it, and suddenly the pain and fear washed out of him. He dug his heels into the horse and galloped toward the bridge, and before he had any time to think about what he was doing he thundered over the span. He could feel the bridge giving way beneath him, swaying back and forth as though it would collapse at any moment, but then his horse bolted forward onto the opposite bank, and he headed toward the mass of men that had gathered around Sidroc.

Old One Eye sat imperiously on his horse with his arms tightly around Elfwyn, his attention completely focused on the bridge. Turning behind him, Plegmund saw why: on the opposite side of the river, a Viking sat atop a single oxcart loaded down with booty.

It was Grimwald's hoard. The treasure of Sussex Downs.

The man screamed at the team of horses hitched to the wagon, urging them to move onto the bridge and cross the rushing river. But the animals were afraid and refused to obey; only when he reached for his lash and began to whip them did they finally take their first tentative steps forward. The wagon lurched ahead onto the bridge, which groaned audibly from the tremendous weight of its burden, swaying back and forth as though it were an old withered tree being whipped by the wind.

Meanwhile, the first of the onrushing Saxons from the south poured through Farnham, streaming into the village as the battle continued to rage in the meadow north of town. Some of them yelled and pointed toward the bridge, and now there was the very real possibility that they would be able to cross it and engage the Vikings.

But then Plegmund heard a snapping sound, like that of dry twigs being crushed underfoot. As he looked on with amazement, the bridge supports shuddered and gave way, and the span collapsed into the river. The oxcart plunged into the current, and its priceless contents spilled into the turbulent waters and disappeared.

The treasure was gone.

There was no way to recover so much as a single gold ingot, nor was there any time to even think of trying. By now the first Saxons had reached the opposite bank, where they shook their weapons at the Vikings. But there was no way they could cross.

Sidroc was beside himself. He swore loudly and stood up in his saddle, but it was done. Clutching Elfwyn to him, he wheeled his horse around and pointed toward the rolling countryside to the north, urging his mount forward. The Vikings took off at a gallop behind him, despondent at the loss of the treasure but happy to be alive. Plegmund rode with them, and no one in the party wasted any time looking behind them as they fled Farnham.

Had they done so, they would have seen Edward's fresh recruits from Winchester streaming on horseback from the south through the village, hastening to relieve the Saxons. They would have also seen another advance from farther to the east, where Penda's lagging foot soldiers were now arriving on the battlefield in the enveloping twilight, further sealing the fate of Hundeus and his Vikings. And just to the north of the village, amidst the battle itself, they would have seen a lone figure hurling his body mindlessly into the rushing river, fighting against the current to ford the rapids.

But the Wey was too swift even for Sigli's resolve. He could make no headway, and after a brief struggle he gave up trying to cross and stood waist-deep in the river, screaming at the top of his lungs, his words drowned out by the river and the fighting and the bedlam all around him.

But he was oblivious to it all; he only had eyes for one man. For he had watched as the adventure at the bridge unfolded, and a great jolt of adrenaline had surged through him when he saw, for the first time in sixteen years, the beast he had vowed to kill.

Sidroc!

In the flesh, so close that he could practically reach out and touch him! And yet so far, separated by a surging mass of water that could not be breached. He stood shivering with excitement, almost unable to believe his eyes, until Sidroc finally disappeared into the trees off in the distance, followed closely by Plegmund and the rest of the Viking party.

He remained standing in the shallows of the river for a moment, stunned by what he had seen, until finally he whirled around and struggled through the torrent, clambering up onto the bank and back into the melee. But the battle he rejoined was far different than the one he had left behind; already the main Viking army was beginning to buckle, pressed by the Saxons on all sides. The only escape was to the northeast, away from Edward's horse and into the gap that still remained between Penda's force and his foot soldiers now arriving from the Weald.

Sigli could think only of finding a horse to carry him away from the battle and in pursuit of Sidroc. He raced through the stragglers and the wounded, spurred on by his magnificent obsession. He ran like the wind, almost young again, and the ground flew by under him.

And then, suddenly, he stopped.

A group of Saxons huddled around a prone figure whose head was propped up against one of the soldier's legs. The man's body was covered with blood, and he clutched at an ugly wound in his side. As he lay there in the mud he confessed himself and prepared to meet his God.

But at that moment he looked up, drawn by instinct, and his eyes came to rest on Sigli. One of the Saxons raised his sword and prepared to attack, but the man lifted his arm weakly and cried out.

"Hold! Let him be!" he gasped, breathing heavily.

And then, exhausted by the effort, Penda slumped back into the arms of his lieutenant, clutching again at his wound as he lay there in the trampled grass of Farnham meadow.

"So I'm done, Sigli," he sighed with a wan smile. "And so, at my final hour, I must confess myself...to you."

"I'm not your God, Penda. Speak to Him."

"Ah, but I've wronged you, you see. I've sinned against you..." He coughed, a long, low gurgling sound, and then he beckoned weakly. "Come closer," he whispered.

Sigli knelt over him, so close that he could feel the dying man's breath on his cheek.

"We lied to you," Penda wheezed. "At Rochester."

"Lied? What do you mean?"

"Do you remember...the...the Dane who swore…that Sidroc was dead? Do you?"

Sigli nodded.

"It was a lie...we...I arranged it."

"Why? I don't understand."

Penda smiled. "To keep you building ships...to keep you here. To...keep you."

"You said we! Who else?"

The ealdorman shook his head. "I'll confess to my own sins...but not to those of others." He looked up at one of his men. "How goes…the battle?"

"The day is ours, My Lord. We shall win."

Penda's eyelids fluttered. "Then my death has not been in vain."

He turned back to Sigli. "I set you free...to absolve myself. Don't waste the chance! Hunt him down...the girl, Plegmund...hunt him down and kill him! Kill him!"

Suddenly his body grew stiff. The air released itself from his lungs in a long hiss, and he laid his head gently back down into the waiting hands of his countrymen and died.

*   *   *   *   *

Aethelfled's heart had pounded with anticipation from the moment she rode out of the forest and saw Farnham in the distance. An hour later, her pulse rate was still alarmingly high, fueled by the excitement and frustration of the battle. While some of the Saxons had seen Elfwyn and Plegmund whisked away by Sidroc across the river, the news had not yet reached her. She rode back and forth across the meadow, her eyes straining against the twilight, hoping to catch sight of her daughter while all around her the fighting continued in pockets.

She had no regard for her safety. It was just as Edward had feared; she would have suffered a thousand deaths merely for one glimpse of Elfwyn. At first he kept his eye on her as they thundered through the muddy lanes of Farnham and into battle, but soon the greater duty of his command captured his attention, and he threw himself into the fight. It was everything he had waited for, everything he had dreamed of. He was not about to let the moment pass him by, and so he raced around the battlefield with a courage and leadership that would be talked about for years to come.

Left to her own devices, Aethelfled encircled the battle lines time and again in search of Elfwyn. Her skill as a horsewoman saved her life more than once, as her chestnut mare carried her faithfully out of harm's way whenever danger threatened. More than one Viking made a serious attempt to reach her, for she stood out among everyone on the meadow, and it was an affront to the Danes to think that a woman could have the courage to face them in battle. Even as they fought desperately for their lives, many among them watched her, ready to expose themselves to even greater danger for the chance to unhorse her.

But she was too quick and eluded their every effort. And all the while she exhorted the Saxon forces to press forward, doing her part to bring the action to a close. It was getting late now, and although the rain had stopped, the twilight made it difficult to see very far. A panic began to fill her breast as the encroaching darkness threatened to cut short her search, and morbid visions of Elfwyn began to race through her head. Driven by the fear that only a mother can feel for her child, she bolted toward the center of the retreating Viking army.

Although she did not know it, she was now heading squarely into the jaws of Hundeus' main guard. The Vikings were doing their best to maintain their ranks and carry out an orderly retreat; it was the one spot along their line that had not caved in. It was also where the battle raged the fiercest, and she found herself drawn toward it, into the vortex, as if all the forces of nature were pulling at her. She rode hard ahead, swept along by the moment, surrounded on all sides by Saxons and Vikings whose shouts pierced the air as the battle raged on.

And then everything changed. She looked all around her and suddenly realized that her compatriots were nowhere to be found. She had slipped into a swale that abutted a low line of underbrush, hemming her in and hampering her maneuverability. And every face she now looked into was a Viking face, filled with hatred.

Fear raced up her spine. She kicked wildly at her mare to climb the embankment and escape from harm, but the way was blocked, and suddenly they were around her on all sides, hacking blindly away. She parried the blows, keeping her horse always moving to force them to give ground, but there was no relief. The roar of the surrounding battle filled her ears, and then she felt hands on her body, felt them dragging her down, down, until her shoulders thudded into the sopping wet earth and they were on top of her. She struggled as one of the

Vikings wrestled with her in the mud while two others dropped their belts and pulled something ugly and dark out into the twilight, and oh, God, please no, please not this way I don't want to end this way. My God, this cannot be....

And then she heard screams coming from somewhere behind the Dane who straddled over her and blocked her view. The two Vikings who had begun fondling themselves suddenly lurched forward, exhaling blood from their mouths and chests as they crashed into the mud. The man on top of her managed to raise himself to his knees before he, too, was swept away by an axe that cut into him in a long, sloping arc, knocking him forward a full body length and into the next world.

She sprawled there helplessly in the mud, and in the gloaming she was dimly aware of the hulk of a large man bending over her and raising her up again to her feet. And then everything was quiet, as though the battle around her had dissipated, and at that moment she knew she surely must be dead. For there in the meadow of blood and destruction she stood looking into the face of the one man she had truly loved ever since she had been a child, when life had still been a great, gleaming possibility that seemed to stretch forever.

And as she and Sigli looked once again into each other's eyes the world stopped, and there were just the two of them standing there together in the gathering darkness, as though all that had come before had been just a prelude to this moment of sweet redemption.

*   *   *   *   *

The skies finally cleared as night closed in over Wessex. A full moon shone down from above, its pale gleam bathing Farnham meadow in a glistening and mysterious half-light. The battlefield was strewn with bodies, corpses frozen in place where they had fallen, arms and legs akimbo against the backdrop of the dark, blood-drenched earth. All was silent except for the occasional groan from one of the wounded stretched out on the field. The dogs were already out, sniffing among the bodies. The birds would arrive at dawn, and before them a few of the more daring and curious of the local folk, who would flit among the corpses to loot them under the cover of darkness. But for now, an hour or so before midnight, the meadow was deserted.

It was across this desolate wasteland that a small patrol of Saxons reconnoitered the battlefield. The mission displeased them, for the day's work was done. Far better to be in Farnham celebrating with the others than here among the dead and the dying, whose bodies dotted the meadow in random, dusky lumps that rose into the moonlight.

"I've had enough," grumbled one of the men. "Can't we go back now?"

"We've almost reached the outer edge," said another. "A little while longer, and we can head toward the river and work our way back to Farnham." He looked over his shoulder, where the torches from the village beckoned through the darkness.

"It makes no sense to be out here. There's nothing we can do."

"Be glad you weren't here today," one of the older men in the patrol admonished him. "You might be laying face down in this mud instead of slogging through it. And besides...you won't be on duty tomorrow. It'll stink to high hell once the sun comes up."

"All right, then. But I want to march with the others tomorrow. I want to chase after the heathens; let someone else clean up this mess."

"Don't worry, the townspeople will do that."

"It's a lot of grave digging. A lot of work," another man muttered, stepping carefully to avoid a corpse in his path. "Do you suppose they'll bury the heathens, too?

"I'd leave them for the dogs, if it were up to me," said the older ceorl. "But if it's bad enough, they might just gather them up in a big pile and burn them. It's faster that way."

They all fell silent. And in the quiet of the moment a sound broke through the night, low at first but gathering in intensity, the sound of approaching horsemen.

"Look! Over there!" pointed one of the Saxons. "Do you see them?" A dark mass of silhouetted riders appeared in the moonlight, heading directly toward them.

"My God! What if it's the heathens? They'll cut us to pieces!"

"Quick! Everyone get down! Maybe they haven't already seen us!"

They all dropped to the earth, shivering quietly on the damp ground as the riders drew closer. The first of the intruders reached the edge of the battlefield, where he slowed down and shouted back to the others. They gathered round him one by one, reining in their mounts and staring in wonder at the carnage before them. An excited babble ensued. And in the midst of that confusion the men in the patrol smiled and breathed a great sigh of relief, for the riders spoke in the familiar rhythm of the Saxon tongue.

"Here! Over here!" one of them shouted, standing up and waving his arms to attract the attention of the horsemen.

Several of the mounted party rode toward them, and by the time the first of the newcomers had arrived, the men in the patrol were able to make out what seemed to be at least several hundred Saxon horse in the moonlight. Before anyone could speak, the riders parted on either side to reveal a lone figure on a stately white stallion, heading briskly and confidently toward the patrol. The moonlight reflected off his helmet, brighter than that of anyone else, and it was clear from his fine cloak and armature that he was a man of importance. He drew closer and stopped, peering down at the Saxons in the darkness.

The old ceorl in the patrol was the first to recognize him. His eyes grew wide, and he fell immediately to his knees. "My God, it's Alfred! It's the king!"

The others quickly dropped to the earth, heads bowed.

"Get up, all of you. What happened here?"

"A great victory, My Lord!" blurted out the first young ceorl, now suddenly delighted to be wandering in the darkness on the edge of Farnham meadow. "Your son Edward has carried the day! The heathen army was routed!"

"Edward? My son has done this?" The king's voice betrayed his pride.

"Yes, My Lord! He rests now in Farnham, celebrating the day's work!"

"And Aethelfled? Has there been any sign of my daughter?"

"She's with him, My Lord. And by all accounts safe and unharmed."

The king let out a great sigh. "God be praised! Then tell me...how did the day go? Where are the Vikings?"

"Their force is broken," said the older Saxon, stepping forward. "Many were killed or taken captive. Their leader, Hundeus, escaped to the northeast with the main body of his force, but he was badly wounded and was carried from the field. They're all heading for the Thames now, to cross and somehow retreat to East Anglia, I would think. But no matter...they can do us no more harm in Wessex. The war in the west is over!"

"You make me a happy man, my friend," Alfred smiled, his favored white stallion prancing lightly about. But then he reined in the animal and leaned forward. "And what of Plegmund, and my granddaughter? Any news of them?"

"Yes, My Lord," the Saxon mumbled uncertainly, looking down at the earth. "They're still in heathen hands. A small detachment of Vikings managed to cross the river and destroy the bridge before we could follow. They rode off in that direction," he said, pointing due north. "The Archbishop and the girl were with them."

Alfred slumped back in his saddle. "Then...our work is not yet done. So be it." He let out a deep breath. "Any other bad tidings to tell me? Get it out now, man, and be done with it."

"Only this, My Lord. Penda of Devon is dead. He died a hero on this day, fighting nobly in your service."

"Ah…faithful Penda," Alfred whispered, staring off into the moonlit meadow. "God speed your soul." And then his eyes sharpened again, and he addressed the men around him.

"What's done is done. Thank the Lord God that those who died today didn't lose their lives in vain. But enough for now...come, all of you! It's on to Farnham, to raise our cups to my valiant son!"

*   *   *   *   *

It took Aethelfled and Sigli a while to work their way back to Farnham amidst the tangle of the evening. Her identity made it impossible to return untended, and soon they were surrounded by well-wishers eager to engage the Lady of Mercia. Some of the Saxons had seen the adventure at the bridge, and it was not long before she learned of the fate of her daughter. The news threw her into a deep depression, and even Sigli was forgotten as she retreated into her grief, raising a wall around herself that effectively shut out the rest of the world.

But no matter where she rode, she remained the center of attention. It was novel enough to have an armed woman on the battlefield, but to fight alongside the beautiful and much-loved daughter of the Bretwalda himself was something no Saxon there on that day would ever forget. She had been magnificent, one of them, and had earned their respect forever.

And so they sidled up to her, men from Sussex and Somerset, Berkshire and Dorset, Hampshire and Devon, hoping to take something back to their ordinary lives and boast of their acquaintance, however fleeting, with royalty. They thronged around her every step of the way back to Farnham, virtually ignoring Sigli as he walked in silence alongside her, tripping over themselves to edge just a little bit closer to the Lady of Mercia.

Night had fallen by the time they arrived in the village. The tension that had preceded the battle was gone, and the men were ready to celebrate, even though the heathens had drained Farnham of every last drop of mead that the fleeing townspeople had left behind. But that didn't seem to matter; most of the Saxons were already drunk on the heady wine of success, while others were simply exhausted and drained of emotion. And so it was—jubilation mixed with ennui, emptiness filled with hollow glee—and Aethelfled and Sigli were swept along in it by the unending flow of men and beasts, until they were finally deposited at the doorstep of the hovel Edward had chosen for his headquarters.

There was a great sadness in Aethelfled's heart as she left the cheering fyrd and stepped inside the hut. At first Sigli hesitated, but then he followed her. A feeling of desperation suddenly overcame him, and he had to suppress the urge to take her in his arms and hold her close to him once again. It was hot and stuffy in the crowded room, and as he shouldered his way into the hovel his eyes were immediately drawn to Edward.

The young prince stood talking animatedly to Ceolmund and several other thanes in a corner of the room, his face flushed with excitement. He was still clearly swept up in the events of the day and the great success for which he could now take credit, filled up with the honor of it all. His eyes shone in the dim torchlight; they were the eyes of victory. But the light in them softened as they came to rest on Aethelfled.

"Thank God you're safe!" he cried, stepping free from his thanes and reaching out to her. "I was afraid...so very afraid something had happened!"

"Edward, we must mount a party now! We must chase after them!" She was frantic, on the verge of tears. "They have Elfwyn!"

"I know. I know all about it. But there's nothing we can do tonight."

"Don't tell me that! They have my baby!"

"They're safe, Aethelfled. They were seen riding away unharmed."

"By God in heaven, Edward, how can you expect me to stay here when I know we're so close? We must follow them!"

"And so we shall," he said firmly. "We'll head north at first light and ford the Wey as soon as we can. We'll run them down tomorrow. As I'm standing here, I swear that... " Suddenly he stopped in mid-sentence, and his jaw dropped.

"My God…I don't believe it!"

His eyes fell on Sigli, standing just inside the door, and for a moment Edward remained frozen in place, unable to move or speak. And then he broke the spell by leaping forward with outstretched arms, and he and Sigli embraced.

"I'd heard you'd returned, but I never thought I'd see you again!" Edward held the Viking at arm's length and admired him. There were lines in his friend's face that he had not seen there before, the slow drip over stones that marks the erosion of a man. But none of it mattered now. After so long a separation, the moment was sweet indeed.

"I remain your faithful servant, My Lord."

"God is good. God is fair, to return you safely to these shores."

Edward's eyes were gleaming. He had already forgotten his sister in the excitement of seeing Sigli, and as he continued to give the Viking his complete attention she pushed through the assembled thanes and left the hovel, disappearing into the crowded lane outside. Sigli's eyes followed her, even where his feet could not.

"I still can't believe you're here!" Edward continued. "You look well, even after all these years!"

"And you…you're a man now. The boy I left behind for exile is gone forever."

"Many things are gone, Sigli. But I've...I've seen him! I've seen Sidroc!"

"I know. I owe you everything for having sent word to me."

Edward looked cautiously around the room. "That must remain our secret. If my father ever knew..."

"How is he, Edward? How is the king?"

"He's well. But never mind him! I tell you, I saw the Malevolent One! I saw Sidroc! I met with the Viking chieftains at Appledore, and he was among them. He was everything you'd ever said, Sigli! The moment I laid eyes on his face, I knew it had to be him!"

"I saw him today at the bridge, but I was too far away to make him out well."

Edward's eyes narrowed. "He's a dreadful man. Tomorrow we'll set out after him. And God protect him if any harm has come to Elfwyn or Plegmund."

"We'll track them down," Sigli smiled weakly, placing his hand on Edward's shoulder. "The gods have brought me back for a reason, and by Odin, I won't disappoint them! We'll do what we must do tomorrow. But tonight...right now...I must find your sister!"

Edward sighed. "Do as you will...I can't stop you. Nor have I ever tried to stand between the two of you, even when perhaps I should have."

"There's nothing you could have done, Edward; you know that. But you've always treated me as a friend, and for that I love you like a brother and shall always do you honor."

He threw his arms around the prince and embraced him again, and then he turned and pushed his way through the crowded room and toward the door of the hovel. The air was overpoweringly oppressive. He hurried to escape the stuffiness and the stench of men's bodies, most of them still covered with sweat and dirt and blood, until he burst through the door and into the clear night, into the roar that filled up the streets of Farnham.

Men were dancing with each other, waving torches in the air above them, hopping from foot to foot with mindless abandon. Someone grabbed for him, but he shook free and pressed forward. He ran down the bustling lane, weaving back and forth between the hovels and through the crowd, until gradually the din and the numbers of men and the torchlight subsided, and he found himself alone near the riverbank, standing under a full moon.

He walked instinctively downstream, and as he did it all began to come clear to him: all of this was meant to be. His entire existence had been controlled by destiny, and if there was one thing that he felt about himself deep in his heart, it was the conviction that he had always been a victim. There had been very little that he had hoped for in his life that had actually come to pass. Unlike others he admired and envied, he had never been able to force the way of the world to his will. No, that was for other men, the Alfreds and Edwards and Eadreds. The Haestans and Grimwalds and Guthrums and Ubbas.

But now he felt as though his time had finally come. Aethelfled and Sidroc, in one day.

It had been seven years since he had seen her, and sixteen since he had last laid eyes on the Malevolent One. And yet today he had crossed both their paths. As he looked up above him at the incandescent moon there was no loneliness in his heart anymore, only a clarity and enlightenment that urged him on, pushing him forward. The truth was out there somewhere; he could feel it. And so it drew him a few more steps along the river, around a brace of trees and into a clearing.

And there he saw it on the edge of the meadow, saw the truth shining like a halo over the head of Aethelfled, who stood gleaming like a milky white statue in the moon.

She turned at that moment and looked at him, and the sadness in her eyes took his breath away. By the gods, she's perfection itself, he thought to himself. She's the most beautiful woman I've ever laid eyes upon, and how have I managed to live my wretched life all these years without her? He staggered lightly and lurched forward, and he stopped in the clearing a few feet from her, sensing her uneasiness and not wanting to trespass on it. He sighed audibly, and as he looked into her face the moonlight revealed every nuance, every subtle turn, rendering even the shadows magnificent.

"You know," he said slowly, clearing his throat, "when I was a boy I always thought it would be so simple. I would live like my father before me, and like his father before him, and I'd find a woman, and that would be that. And you know, in many ways, when I was young I didn't really want that, because it all seemed so...so ordinary."

The sense of weariness and resignation in his voice was overpowering. She stared sympathetically at him, her face streaked with dried tears, but she said nothing.

"And so I went along, and it all seemed so predestined, but then in the space of one night my life changed forever. Suddenly all the things I had taken for granted simply disappeared. And somehow, because of it all, I became the one thing that I feared the most...I became ordinary."

He looked into her eyes now. "I lost something then, Aethelfled, and I've never gotten it back. Never, that is, except for those few brief, shining moments when I had you."

He felt something breaking up in him, felt his hands beginning to shake, but he fought it back and continued. "And now I see you here again, and your heart is breaking because your girl is in trouble, your daughter. And my heart is breaking too, to see you like this, to have you but not to have you at all, to be...."

His shoulders trembled violently and he began to sob. It was then she stepped forward and took him into her arms, cradling his head to her breast, and she began to cry as well. They stood there in the moonlight, holding each other for what seemed like the longest time until finally, mercifully, the tears stopped.

They hobbled together toward the river and sat down on a nearby log. She wiped her eyes and held his hand, and as she looked at him in the moonlight she managed a wan smile.

"You look well. Tired, but well. How have you kept yourself these years?"

"Poorly. Far too much mead. But I'm a healthy sort, at that. It would take a lot more than just being miserable to kill me."

She smiled now in spite of herself. "And...have you kept good company?"

He shrugged. "Men like myself."

"No...I didn't mean..." She paused. "Have there...have there been others?"

It surprised him. "And why would you want to know that?"

She blushed.

He smiled, happy that she cared to ask. "No...or at least none that mattered, anyway." Here a mischievous grin spread across his face. "And you? What about you?"

"What do you take me for?" she cried in mock protest.

"You laid with me, didn't you?"

"That was different. That was because I..." She stopped.

"Because...?"

She hesitated. "Because I loved you."

"And now? Do you love me still?"

She looked into his blue eyes, glistening in the moonlight, and she wanted to say yes. But he wouldn't understand, couldn't understand, because it was through their daughter Elfwyn that she loved him the most, and somehow she could not bring herself to tell him about that now. He sensed her hesitation, and so he asked a different question.

"Then...do you love him?"

She paused for just a moment, and then she nodded. "Yes. Yes, I love Eadred."

He studied her carefully. "In the way...you loved me?"

And now she looked directly at him again. "No. I'll never love anyone the way I loved you."

He sighed and looked off across the meadow, awash like quicksilver under the moon, and he shook his head.

"There's a part of me that would fall down on my knees right now and beg you to fly away with me, to leave all this behind, but I know now that life has passed us by, you and me. For so long I dreamed that we could be together, that somehow it could all be different. That I could somehow sleep where Eadred sleeps, instead of waking up the next day condemned to my pointless existence.

"But now, finally, I know it doesn't matter. Even the gods can't take away what I feel for you, something that will never fade or grow old. Because when I look at you now, and whenever I've thought of you these many years, I still see the young girl who loved me. And that will always remain."

As she watched and listened the familiar ache returned again, the ache for him and for Elfwyn, for the daughter she saw in him whenever she looked into his eyes. She started to cry again. He held both her hands in his, and she realized how good it felt to be with him.

"I do love you, Sigli," she whispered.

She put her arms around him and squeezed him tightly, but then the moment passed and just as suddenly she shuddered and broke away, possessed again by other thoughts. She stood up and took several agitated steps toward the river, tense and ill at ease.

"Elfwyn is out there somewhere, out there in the darkness with that animal!"

Sidroc. Always Sidroc. He stood up and clenched his fists.

"I'll have him, Aethelfled! I'll do whatever I must to save your daughter, but I'll have him, by Odin! He'll be mine!"

He could feel the energy coursing through him, and he realized that in his own perverse way he actually loved the idea of Sidroc, needed him to desire something with passionate conviction and want it more than anything else in the world. And then he felt another strange sensation, something that she also evidently felt, because they both whirled around and looked behind them, back in the direction of Farnham.

A lone figure stood in the shadows on the edge of the clearing. Even from that distance his rage crackled through the air, and although he was alone he might as well have been thousands, so powerful was his presence. The man stepped forward at that moment into the moonlight, and they both gasped in shock as Alfred the King pointed an accusing finger at Sigli.

"You! You dishonor me like this, pawing at my daughter like some beast of prey!" He advanced toward them, his hand reaching for the sword that hung from his side.

Sigli stood his ground. "I dishonor no one!"

"I sent you away from England on the pain of death if you ever returned! And so you shall die!"

He rushed forward, but Aethelfled threw herself between them, grabbing Alfred and preventing him from drawing on Sigli. "Father! My God! Stop it!"

"He's against me, child! Let me go!"

"Father! Father! Father, for God's sake, stop it! He saved my life today, father!"

It was enough to sidetrack Alfred's rage. He shifted his angry eyes to her.

"Yes, that's right! He risked his life to save mine, and he killed the very men you would kill, Father! Merciful God, you must honor him for that. You must!"

Alfred took a step backward. "You were with Haestan in Benfleet!" he shouted at Sigli. "I saw you with my own eyes!"

"You saw me, all right! Me and twenty of my men, sailing under no one's banner but our own. Escaping Haestan, escaping you. I have nothing to do with your enemies, Alfred. I have only one enemy, and that's the only reason I'm here tonight!"

"A king's word is law! By returning, you've disobeyed me! I could have you put to death for coming back!"

"You killed me a long time ago, Alfred. You beat on me as though I were a drum. You used me, used my back and my head and my heart, drained every last bit of me as though I were a fruit to be devoured and cast away by the side of the road!"

Now Sigli was angry, his blood boiling, and he could not stop himself from blurting out what he had learned that day.

"And if I've caused you any pain, then you have no one to blame but yourself! You kept me here against my will, against everything you swore to me by your God...You lied to me, Alfred! You lied!"

The king stood there in mute silence.

"That's right!" Sigli trumpeted self righteously, pacing back and forth before the king, Aethelfled still between them. "You lied to me! You and Penda, your faithful hunting dog, leading me to believe that Sidroc was dead!" He spat into the dark earth. "If I've dishonored you, or your daughter, then you've gotten what you deserve. The gods see all, Alfred!"

"Such insolence!"

"Insolence or not, I'm going after Sidroc tomorrow! No one can stop me!"

"I'll stop you, if I want! You dare to flaunt me like this! I'll have you trussed up like a pig, I'll..."

"Father, stop it!" Aethelfled shouted, grabbing at his arms again to restrain him.

"Let go of me, Aethelfled!"

"Only if you let him go! Tomorrow, you must let him ride with us! It's only right!"

Alfred glared at her as he struggled to free himself. "So that's it? So you too would dispute me, shame me for the decisions I've made for the good of the state, for England? Is that what you would do?"

"Father, stop it! You're not making sense!"

"Oh, I'm not, am I? Then tell me, why should I let this heathen chase after Elfwyn, this exile whose countrymen now have your child? Tell me why I should spare his head!"

The roar of the river seemed to drop away until there was nothing but silence and the three of them there in the moonlight. She felt her throat constricting, as though she would choke, but then the secret came tumbling out.

"Because...because all of our blood is mingled, Father." She turned to Sigli, who stood clearly illuminated in the moonlight before her.

"As God above is my witness, this I swear is the sacred truth. Lord Eadred is not Elfwyn's father. You are, Sigli."

Sigli's heart started to race in his chest. Alfred staggered several steps backward. The king reached out and grabbed a tree branch to keep from falling, and then he leaned against the trunk and stared blankly ahead.

"The last time we met, when I sent for you...that's when it happened," she said, speaking clearly and calmly. "I already knew I was with child when I first lay with Eadred, but I said nothing. After all, why should he be hurt? Why should Mercia be dragged into it? And the scandal of it all…there was no reason to let the secret out."

She took a deep breath. "Eadred still doesn't know. Nor does anyone else…although if they ever saw you and Elfwyn together, I hardly see how they could think otherwise. She looks so like you—her eyes, her hair—she's yours, Sigli. She's ours."

She turned away from him and faced Alfred, who still leaned in a daze against the tree. "So now, Father, you understand. I made many mistakes in my youth, but I've never thought that Elfwyn was one of them. And now her life is in danger. It's only right that her father, a good and brave man, should have the chance to save her from the foul creature that holds her in his power. After everything Sigli's been through, after so much pain, it's only right."

Alfred shook his head in disbelief as the truth slowly sank in, and for the first time he began to see that everything that had happened was far beyond even his control, possessed of an energy all its own. There comes a point in every man's life when his pride must bow to the greater force that rules the universe, when he must come to terms with his own insignificance in the face of all that is around him. And in that moment Alfred could now see all things clearly, and he felt ashamed that he could have been so filled with pride to believe he was above the will of God. He had thought himself capable, in all of his vanity, of directing the course of others' lives.

It was all such folly; he had been so blind, such a fool.

"You're right, Sigli...God sees all," he finally sighed. "What you say is true. I did indeed conspire against you, to keep you in England building ships. Not maliciously, not ever—for all I knew, this man Sidroc *was* dead. But I did keep you, when you would have left these shores, and all that has come to pass since can be laid on my head, by God. So be it."

He waved his hand in resignation, and then he raised himself to his full height and drew his shoulders back. "Nothing can erase the fact that you both sinned. It hurts me now as it hurt me then. But in my heart, Sigli, I do believe you. And as much as I wish none of this had happened, I understand that what you both meant to each other then was a powerful thing...too powerful for me or anyone else to prevent. Elfwyn is the result, and never could a grandfather love flesh and blood more. That is the only thing I know, the only feeling I'm left with in the end. And so it shall be my guide in all that follows.

"Your secret is safe with me. No one will ever know on my accord. And as for this great rift that has separated us these many years, Sigli, well...enough of this blood debt. You've never deserved my ill will; no, in truth, all this time I should have been honoring you for the great love you've borne me. Let us be done with it. Let us go on."

Here his lips tightened, and the moonlight glinted off his pale, thin features. "But tomorrow we must finish what we started. Tomorrow you ride with us."

He turned and started back along the river toward Farnham, leaving them standing on the edge of the meadow. The rushing waters of the Wey drowned out his footsteps, and soon all that remained was the sight of him flitting through the trees like a gaunt specter, exposed to them under the benign and impassive face of the moon.

CHAPTER XVII: Twilight On The Thames

"Even so my bloody thoughts, with violent pace
Shall ne'er look back, ne'er ebb to humble love,
Till that a capable and wide revenge
Swallow them up."
—Shakespeare, <u>Othello</u>

The dawn was fair, for the storm clouds had begun to dissipate the moment the battle had been decided, and barely a trace of gray remained in the sky by the time the sun rose. There was clarity in the Saxon camp as well, for the victory at Farnham had answered many questions. Down to the last soldier, every ceorl and thane now felt a great sense of confidence about the war and the men who led them in it, and if there had been any doubts about their prospects before the battle, they had been decisively erased by the outcome.

Farnham had been the first engagement of any consequence since the Vikings had landed in Kent five months earlier, and it affirmed that England was prepared for anything. Alfred's strategy of national defense was proving to be even more effective than anyone would have imagined. The fyrd was armed and ready on all fronts, thwarting every move the Vikings made, and although Haestan still posed a threat to Mercia and London from Benfleet in the east, the shadow of a multi-front war no longer loomed above England.

By evening the last of the Vikings not killed or captured would be across the Thames and out of Wessex, bearing the wounded Hundeus on a litter as they fled through Mercia toward East Anglia. The west was won.

But if the ranks were buoyant, the mood was noticeably grim among the king and his advisors. Any joy they may have felt following the battle had long since been forgotten, and all attentions were now focused on recovering Elfwyn and Plegmund. Alfred was up with the first light, busily engaged in marshaling a force of several hundred men—Aethelfled and Sigli among them—to ride with him in pursuit of Sidroc. Edward, meanwhile, prepared to march northeast in pursuit of Hundeus, hoping to spread confusion among the Vikings before they could reorganize and again pose a threat.

The prince had second thoughts about not being included in the quest to regain Elfwyn. But it was clear that someone had to look after the national interest, and his victory at Farnham had established him as England's next great field general and the man of the hour. And so he bid them all a hopeful goodbye as they mounted their horses shortly after dawn and headed north along the riverbank, waving to them as they receded into the distance. When they finally disappeared he turned his attentions again toward the army, and within a few moments he had completely forgotten about the others, barking out orders with his usual forcefulness, ever the impetuous one.

For the king's escort, every hour was precious; the longer it took to catch Sidroc, the better his chances of escaping. Alfred pushed them hard, still a powerful figure astride the saddle, as energetic now as on the day of his first great victory at Ashdown half a lifetime ago. He led them at a brisk pace along the river, and not a word was spoken in the ranks as the Saxons rode on.

Within fifteen minutes they received their first good omen of the day; one of the men sent ahead to reconnoiter returned to report of a bridge a few miles upstream that would allow them to ford the river. Soon they were across it, heading due north into Berkshire and toward the Thames, their scouts fanning out ahead of them to scour the countryside.

For Sigli, it seemed that life had begun all over again. Everything that had come before this moment had been nothing more than a long prelude that now led him to his ultimate reason for being. He rode in a daze, glancing Aethelfled's way every few minutes and then looking to Alfred, as if to reassure himself that everything he was seeing was more than just a dream. A thousand different thoughts tumbled through his mind as he rolled along, enjoying the rhythm and the power of the horse beneath him, the ground flying by, the freedom.

It had all come down to this. The very man he most hated and feared in the world once again held him by the throat, unwittingly possessing the means to do him the ultimate harm. Sidroc could not know that *he* was the girl's real father, did not know or have any idea that *he* was again in England, could not yet feel that it was *his* hot breath beating down his neck hard in pursuit, mere leagues behind and closing fast.

And yet it was all true, every bit of it, and it made him feel alive in a way he had forgotten it was possible for a man to feel. He allowed the lushness of the spring to intoxicate him. An overwhelming bloom pervaded the trees and the meadows, the deep kind of green that marks England's seasonal metamorphosis, filling the air with promise and possibilities. Yes, it was all possible for him now; he could redeem himself, fulfill himself, do that which the gods had clearly laid out for him to do.

The truth had changed everything: he was a father now. And his child was in danger.

The brooding self-absorption that had plagued him for sixteen years had vanished, leaving him truly and completely whole for the first time since the fragile moments of joy he had felt before the fall of Halfsfiord. Now he had something to live for, something good that was beyond the boundaries of his own pathetic concerns. He knew in his heart that nothing but Elfwyn mattered as he leaned into the wind, eyes ahead, chasing after her.

And chasing after him.

*   *   *   *   *

The sun beat down hard on Sidroc's shaggy head, soaking his matted hair in sweat, but it failed to slow him down at all. He pressed on like a salivating dog, urging his broken band of Vikings relentlessly forward. Although he had not stayed in Farnham long enough to know exactly how the battle had turned out, he was convinced the Saxons had carried the day and would soon be on his trail. He had ordered everyone into their saddles early that morning and then headed north without delay, not knowing what was behind or ahead of him, and not all that anxious to find out. Only one thing was certain: the entire countryside would now be up in arms, thirsting for Viking blood.

Anything less than an organized force would not be able to stop them; if they could cross the Thames into Mercia before day's end, the worst would be over. Every hour that passed without incident improved their chances. Yes, Sidroc thought, there would be recriminations. There would be those who would point their fingers and accuse him of deserting the cause at Farnham. But he could argue that his position, caught between the converging Saxon forces, had given him no alternative other than to fly and fight again another day.

Of course, he had left the field for reasons that had little to do with the battle or his men and everything to do with his own selfish motives. He would not have believed the gold and silver from Grimwald's coffers could have existed had he not seen it for himself. And if he still possessed any of the booty, he would have understood why his countrymen might have looked at him with suspicion when the subject of Farnham came up.

But the treasure was gone forever. There was no reason for anyone to know about it.

And then there was the girl. No matter what he had lost, he still possessed her. No Saxon would dare harm him as long as she remained in his power. He glanced behind him and could see her and the priest riding together in the middle of the party, doing their best to maintain the pace. They looked tired, and when he turned forward again and saw a small watering hole just ahead beneath a small grove of trees, he knew it was time to stop and rest. He raised his ham-like forearm in the air and motioned for them to rein in their horses, and soon the entire party had dismounted.

For Plegmund, the reprieve came not a moment too soon. He began to rub gingerly at his tailbone as soon as his feet hit the ground, for no matter how often he rode there was something about a horse's back that did not agree with him. He moaned and shuffled about, but despite his discomfort he never once took his eyes off Elfwyn, who approached him after quenching her thirst from the pond.

"How do you feel, child?"

"Do we have to keep going? Can't we stay here for a while?" The heat and uncertainty had drained her.

"I know it's hot, and it's so dusty riding in the middle of everyone. But at least you know how to handle a horse. Be glad you don't ride like I do; my back feels like it's breaking."

"How much longer, Plegmund? When can I go back to Mercia?"

"That's where we're headed now, at least. But I don't imagine we'll be free to do as we like. Be patient, girl...I suspect your Uncle Edward has won a great victory and is bearing down upon us as we speak. We'll be rid of this menace before long."

It was as though his words had summoned the beast itself, for as he looked up, Sidroc approached them. Plegmund moved over to Elfwyn and placed his arm protectively around her.

"You don't need to hide her from me, holy man," Old One Eye scowled, resentful of Plegmund's familiarity with the girl. "Here...let me see her."

He reached out for Elfwyn but she shrank from him, clearly frightened. He left his outstretched hand dangling in the space between them, giving her the opportunity to reconsider his advances—all to no avail. Disappointment flickered across his face, replaced immediately by the mask of anger with which he always faced the world.

"You've turned her against me!" he snarled.

"Leave us alone, Sidroc! She wants no part of you!"

"Liar! It's all your fault!"

"You can't control what she thinks! You can do with us what you like, but there's no way you can make her come to you if she doesn't want to. Can't you understand that?"

"I don't believe you! You've turned her against me! She came to me of her own free will, until you filled her head with evil!"

Plegmund stared at the Viking in disbelief. "She may be just a child, Sidroc, but she can see what sort of brute you are! No honorable man would even think of abducting us like this, unless he were a filthy, godless heathen, a base creature without heart or soul!"

With each word he heard, Sidroc's eye narrowed with anger. Unable to restrain himself any longer, he lurched forward and brought the back of his hand hard across the monk's face. The blow tore Plegmund free from Elfwyn and sent him sprawling to the ground. Sidroc bounded forward to pounce on the Archbishop, but at the last instant Elfwyn threw herself in front of him.

"No, please! Don't hurt him!"

Her courage distracted him and he froze, looking her over carefully and grinding his teeth. All the Vikings watched them, fully expecting him to brush her aside and strike Plegmund again. But nothing happened. Slowly, almost painfully, he regained control, never taking his eye off her until he finally spoke.

"Very well, little one. Have it your way…this time."

He turned to the men. "Hurry up and finish tending to the horses! It's time we were out of here!" He glanced back at the girl once more, and then he strode briskly off in the direction of his own mount, the fury rolling off his hunched shoulders and evaporating into the air.

"Plegmund...oh, Plegmund," Elfwyn cried. "Are you hurt?"

He sat up and rubbed his jaw, spitting out a thin stream of saliva and blood. "I'm all right. Don't worry about me."

He stroked her hair and summoned a weak smile, hoping to hide his anxiety. He watched the hulking form of Sidroc move through the heathens, and he could feel the fear expanding inside him. If Old One Eye had once seemed vaguely capable of acting like a rational human being, those illusions had long since faded.

The beast was on the verge of breaking. And someone was going to pay for it.

*   *   *   *   *

If London was quickly becoming the heart of England, then the Thames and its tributaries were the veins that fed into it. During the Saxon rule the river had served as a natural border between Wessex and Mercia, which had vacillated over the years between uneasy friendship and hostility and had come to blows as recently as the reign of Alfred's grandfather Egbert. Mercia had been the stronger of the two for hundreds of years, but now the situation was reversed; Wessex was the protector of its northern neighbor, which had long suffered the brunt of the Viking invasions.

Now the Thames was more of a link than a border. It gathered all kinds of people from central and western England, some of whom traveled downstream to London, others who journeyed to the continent beyond. Just before it flows through the city, perhaps a day's ride west, the river passes through a particularly beautiful part of Berkshire, where the country stretches placidly for miles. Here was where the Vikings finally reached the Thames, as the brilliance of the afternoon faded away and the shadows began to lengthen.

Sidroc craned his neck in either direction, hoping to see a way to cross over into Mercia. Instead, nothing but trees and river met his eye, backed by a low chalk down that rose up from the riverbank and was topped by a thick brace of oaks that obscured whatever lay behind it. Wanting desperately to leave Wessex before nightfall, he dispatched riders in either direction along the river and ordered the party to dismount and take a few moments to break bread. Not only were they running out of time, they were running out of food; it was the last of their provisions.

He sat down by himself under the leafy bows of an oak. On the run again, he thought gloomily. Either on the run or on the prowl—that's the way it always seemed to be. It was all that his life had ever been; just one extended confrontation, with someone trying to take advantage of somebody else. And now they were the ones dangling on the end of the stick, wondering how much longer they could evade pursuit.

He looked over at Plegmund and Elfwyn, who were resting by an oxcart the Vikings had recovered that afternoon during their flight. Any problems he may have had keeping them under his control were nothing compared to the ones he would face in the days ahead. He had become aware of a grumbling in the ranks; there was no mistaking it. The men knew that while their prisoners afforded them a certain safety, they also brought with them more than their share of attention, more than anyone needed at a time like this. They could not care less about the ransom; they wanted only their freedom and their lives.

And Sidroc wanted only Elfwyn, and all that she could provide.

His thoughts were interrupted by the sound of hoof beats. Everyone in the camp looked up as one of the Viking scouts approached rapidly across a long expanse of open meadow. He was riding too fast to be bearing anything less than important news, and Sidroc's heart sank as he anticipated the worst. His fears were realized as the scout thundered over the last hundred yards to the river's edge and leaped from his horse.

"Saxons! Bearing down hard upon us!"

They all looked up again, and at that very moment they could see a large body of men riding into view over a swale to the southeast, still some distance away but now clearly within range. With no immediate means of fording the Thames, they were trapped. Fear rippled through the men, and the camp was thrown into chaos as they scurried about. And then the shouts began.

"The girl! Give up the girl!"

"Ransom her! Buy us our freedom!"

"You must give her up, Sidroc!"

"The girl, Old One Eye! Give up the girl!"

Sidroc shouldered his way through them and strode purposefully toward the oxcart where Plegmund and Elfwyn sat. With a powerful thrust of his leg he pulled himself up and stood imperiously with one foot perched on the wagon's rickety wooden side, every muscle in his body bristling with authority.

"Now is not the time for fear! If I didn't know better, I'd think you were all Christians…pathetic Jesus-loving vermin who scurry for cover at the least sign of danger! Look at yourselves—look at who you are! In all the years since we set sail, have we ever been defeated? Have we?"

He paused for effect, his eye scanning the two hundred faces before him. The sun broke briefly through the clouds as it dipped toward the horizon.

"From Frisia to Francia, from the Rhine to the great western sea—there lives no man as terrible as a Viking in battle! Listen to me! You've yet to meet your equal! No man can stand up to you! Even if we were to take ship and sail over the wide ocean to Jotunheim, to make war on the Frost Giants, you wouldn't find your match. By Odin, you're the best! Each one of you is worth four of the enemy. And I can already see, looking at the Saxons, there aren't four of them to your one!"

The mention of the riders made every man turn to the southeast. True to Sidroc's words, the enemy numbered only perhaps twice as many soldiers as they did. But the Vikings were still at a disadvantage, with no hope of reinforcements, and their resolve was weak. At that moment the sun disappeared behind the clouds, further darkening their spirits, but before the gloom completely overwhelmed them Old One Eye's voice rang out again, strong and clear.

"Don't waste your time looking at them! What difference does it make if they're four hundred or four thousand? Don't you see? Here beside me I have that which makes their numbers useless, that which turns their swords into harmless sticks. They have an army...but we have their heart and soul! A girl and a holy man! The most renowned of their priests, the most precious of their heirs!"

He looked down at his prisoners, who stared helplessly at him, and he could not stop from leering in triumph. He raised his fist and turned back to the Danes.

"Not so much as one drop of your blood will be spilled as long as these two belong to us!"

"Ransom them! Buy us our freedom!"

"Time enough to do that! Would you have me hand them over now, while we're on the wrong side of the river, and then watch as the Saxons fall upon us?"

"He lies! It could never happen!" Plegmund shouted out. "No God-fearing man of the cross would go against his word, against his faith, and stoop to such common butchery!"

But no one listened to him; they were all swept up by Sidroc's persuasion.

"Now isn't the time to give up our hard-won treasures!" he cajoled them. "Let us talk to them, let us negotiate. But I say we gain safe passage into Mercia over the Thames first, and *then* give up the girl and the priest!"

This latest proposal met with murmurs of general approval. Sidroc studied the men as they warmed to the idea, each of them seeking the approval of the others, until soon every head in the meadow was nodding in agreement. As he looked in each of their faces, he knew he could bend them to whatever he wanted them to do. Perhaps he could not only wriggle free from his difficulties, but he even perhaps could have his way without making the slightest compromise.

Because under no circumstances was he willing to give up Elfwyn. Not yet. Not without escaping and having it all, on his terms. He had already decided that.

Looking up at Old One Eye in his moment of triumph, Plegmund also now somehow came to understand the truth. An overwhelming despair rose up inside him, and he glanced down at Elfwyn. Her upturned face looked to him with all the hopeful innocence of youth, clear and flawless. Good for her, he thought; she was unable to understand Sidroc as he manipulated the men in the coarse, unintelligible babble of the Viking tongue.

And in that moment of clarity he made his own decision, one that went against every instinct he had cultivated over a lifetime of avoiding things, of failing to come to grips with his own manhood. Because everything now boiled down to the bare business of being a man.

He raised his eyes to heaven, and any sense of God was blocked out by the shadow of the monster looming over him, as though Satan himself had taken hold. Yes, that decided matters, all right; there could be no doubting himself now. The time had come to stand up. He steeled his nerves, said a silent prayer, and decided once and for all what he would do.

When Alfred saw the Viking party gathered by the Thames, he knew that the search for Elfwyn and Plegmund was over. Even from a great distance, he knew they had found what they were looking for. Sigli and Aethelfled also knew it, and were beside themselves with eagerness to plunge forward and conclude the chase. But of course that would not do; now was a time for caution. There had been very little discussion among the Saxons as to what would happen when they finally caught up to the Vikings, so now everyone looked to Alfred.

"Spread out in a long line, parallel to the river!" he shouted to the men, as they slowed their horses to a canter and fanned out behind him. "They must not be allowed to escape along the bank! We'll close them in!"

Satisfied that the troops had been properly deployed, he turned to Aethelfled and Sigli, who rode on either side of him. "We have them now."

Before he could say anything else, Aethelfled gasped and clutched at her breast. Alfred and Sigli followed her eyes, where they could see the oxcart at the rear of the Viking party, close by the Thames. A robed figure stood on top of it, leaning against one of the sides, and next to him at a height no taller than his waist they could see a head of bright blonde hair gleaming in the late afternoon sun.

"There she is!"

Alfred looked on without expression, studying the ranks intently, but Sigli was completely entranced by the sight. He had never seen his daughter. He had no frame of reference by which to gauge her. The distance that separated them made it impossible for him to get anything more than a vague sense of what she looked like. But he recognized Plegmund immediately, and his thoughts turned to memories of friendship, to all the fine moments they had shared together during days long gone by. It had never occurred to him that the monk could possibly have been involved in his exile from England; he had always remembered him with fondness. He had heard Aethelfled say how close Elfwyn and the Archbishop had become, and it made him all the more determined to recover both of them safely.

And then his eyes were drawn farther along the Viking line, until they came to rest on the threatening figure of the man he had been seeking for sixteen years. There could be no mistaking him. Even at a distance, the Malevolent One carried himself with an air that clearly indicated he was the one, the man himself. His size, his bristling arrogance, the sheer animal presence—all of these things crackled through the air. Sigli could not believe he was finally looking at his obsession, in the flesh, and he silently gave thanks to Odin for rewarding him at last.

He was so wrapped up in his thoughts that he never noticed the lone Viking who rode slowly forward toward them, his arm upraised in a gesture of peace.

Alfred turned to Osferth of Berkshire, in whose lands they now rode, and pointed toward the Dane.

"You speak the heathen language, don't you? Go see what he wants."

The ealdorman rode forth into the open space between the two forces and spoke briefly with the Viking before wheeling around and returning. He reined in his horse and backed in carefully next to the king, waiting until he was settled in position before speaking.

"The heathens request a meeting, My Lord. They know what we want, and who you are. They're willing to discuss terms of ransom. They wish to meet on horseback between the armies, no more than six men to a side. And all weapons shall be left behind."

"Don't trust them!" one of the Saxons yelled out from the ranks. "Beware of treachery!"

Alfred waved away the protest. "Treachery will only end in every last one of them forfeiting his life, by the sword or the hangman's noose. But we'll keep our wits about us."

"All I care about is Elfwyn," moaned Aethelfled, struggling.

"Don't worry; we'll get her back."

"Don't pay them so much as one gold coin!" Sigli cried. "It's unthinkable to allow them to profit from this outrage!"

"You've marked your man," Alfred said. "He won't be able to escape you much longer. But, here...he approaches us now, unless I'm much mistaken."

They looked toward the river, where a half dozen Vikings rode slowly toward them across the meadow. Sidroc was in the lead. Plegmund and Elfwyn remained behind in the oxcart, watched closely by several of their captors, and Alfred never once took his eyes off them as he spoke to Sigli and Aethelfled.

"You may accompany me, but you must restrain yourselves. Any kind of altercation will endanger our mission. Now, leave your weapons behind," he said, unbuckling his sword and handing it to an adjutant, "and ride forth with me. Osferth, join us also, along with two of your men."

They started across the meadow and headed for the Viking delegation. Sigli exchanged glances with Aethelfled, and then he focused his complete attention on Sidroc. As they drew closer, he got his first good look at the man since that fateful evening long ago. Yes, he was as grotesque as ever—the matted hair, the cruel, sinister mouth, the pock-marked face, the threatening presence. But there was something new, for he had last seen the Malevolent One an hour or so before Beolinde had defiantly left her mark upon him. He was not quite prepared for the missing eye and the pink vacuum that now occupied its socket. It was the perfect touch, the crowning flourish to what could only be described as a vision of evil.

Beolinde, I've not forgotten you. It will be more than my hand that strikes the final blow.

The delegation rode forward until it drew within some thirty feet of the Danes, and the king raised his arm and signaled for the others to stop. It was Osferth who spoke first, in the Viking tongue.

"Here rides Alfred the King, the Golden Dragon of Wessex. Bretwalda, Ruler of Britain—and all men of the cross in her who believe in the one true God!"

The Malevolent One eyed his adversary without bowing, or bothering to show even the least sign of respect.

"I am Sidroc," he finally said. "I have no title. I have no lands. And I have no men, other than what you see before you. But I'm known all across the northern sea. No man has ever bested me in single combat, and no force has checked my will. It would be foolish for you to try."

"Force is the last resort of a wise man, and the first instinct of a fool," Alfred replied calmly, unimpressed by the Viking's posturing. "What a man carries in his head, he doesn't need to haul on his back. Experience, I'm sure, has taught you at least that much...which is why I believe we can come to a sensible agreement."

Sidroc snickered. "That may well happen, but your load will need to be lightened—no matter where you carry it."

"Enough. I didn't chase you down to match wits; it's the girl and Canterbury we want." Never taking his eyes off Old One Eye, Alfred turned toward his daughter.

"This is Elfwyn's mother, the Lady Aethelfled of Mercia."

Sidroc shifted his attention to her. His lone eye glistened as it contemplated the fine, exquisite figure of womanhood before him. He made no attempt to curb his lecherous instincts; he regarded her with a leer, provoking a universal disgust among the Saxons. Alfred especially was revolted by this crude show, but he pressed on.

"With me also is Osferth, ealdorman of Berkshire, and two of his men. And finally," he added, pausing ever so slightly, "here's someone I believe you know, someone you may be interested to reacquaint yourself with. Allow me to present Sigli of Halfsfiord."

Sidroc leaned forward in his saddle, his body stiff with excitement.

"You!"

"Yes, Sidroc! It's me!" Sigli cried out, barely able to restrain himself. "I've waited for this moment for more than half a lifetime, you filthy beast! You escaped me once, but I promise you...vengeance will be mine!"

Old One Eye reared back his head and laughed hoarsely. "I escaped *you*? As I remember it, *you* were the one who fled into the night after I had my way with your father, your brother, your mother! Your bride! Your everything!"

Sigli stiffened in his saddle, but Alfred restrained him.

"That's right, boy," Sidroc grinned with evil satisfaction, relishing the chance to taunt his opposite. "Sit there and swallow. Because if you so much as lay one finger on me, the girl and the priest will die!"

Aethelfled let out a low, anguished moan, infuriating Sigli even more.

"Coward! You hide behind your hostages, as you once hid behind your treachery! Without your schemes and lies, you're nothing! If you were a real man, with real courage, you'd meet me alone here on the field, and let the gods be the ones to decide. Where's your honor, Sidroc?"

"Honor? Honor, you say? What does honor have to do with anything? Why should I sacrifice my advantage to satisfy your whining complaints? So you've chased me all these years, dreaming of me night and day, living your life for the moment when you could gain your precious revenge...? Well, let me tell you something, son of Lothar: I've hardly thought of you at all these many years. I didn't even know who you were, other than some spineless Christian lover, when you rode up to me...that's how insignificant you are!"

He laughed again, delighted at the effect his words were having.

"Laugh now, Sidroc, but you're mine! I'll see you dead!"

"Not likely. Because if you're unlucky enough to face me alone, you'll meet the same fate as all the others. I'll kill you and put your pretty head on my standard pole!"

"Enough!" Alfred silenced them. "Your private arguments don't concern England. What do you want, Sidroc? What will it take to recover our charges?"

"Gold and silver. More of it than you can imagine...or possibly supply."

"I have an active imagination," the king answered dryly, "and ample coffers. But be reasonable. There's more than your purse to consider...your own life hangs in the balance."

It rankled Sidroc that the Saxon king could remain so calm. Clearly, he was not a man to be bullied or pushed into rash acts. He felt a sharp needle pricking at his insides, increasing his irritation.

"Don't threaten me, Alfred; I'm afraid of no man. Not you, not your Saxons—and least of all, not your Halfsfiordian suckling boy!" He allowed a smirk of satisfaction to cross his face. "Just give me your gold."

"You'll get your gold. Now, release Elfwyn and Plegmund to us, and you have my word that you can return to East Anglia in safety...at which time an agreed upon sum of ransom shall be delivered to you."

Old One Eye shook his head. "What kind of fool do you think I am? We'd be dead before we even made it across the river. And if we did escape, the gold would never follow."

"He gave you his word of honor!" Sigli shouted angrily.

Sidroc spat onto the ground in front of him. "Shut your mouth! My business isn't with you!" He turned sourly to Alfred. "Here are my terms: you and your men will retreat, and give the order for no one to obstruct us on our way to rejoin Haestan. Once we're safe, then we can talk again about the gold."

He had no intention whatsoever of surrendering Elfwyn, not yet. But the king did not need to understand that.

"I want the prisoners now." Alfred was firm.

"No, that's not possible. I'd be completely at your mercy."

"Perhaps you'd consider other hostages in return, as a measure of my good faith?"

Suddenly something occurred to Sidroc. Yes, of course; why hadn't he thought of it sooner? A wicked sneer flickered across his face as the idea took root. "Here's what I propose. We'll keep the girl until East Anglia, and you keep the gold until then. But I'm willing to make an exchange right now. I'll give you the priest..." Here his eye swung slowly to Sigli, "if you give me the Halfsfiordian."

Sigli glared at him, and then he bit his lip. "Include the girl, and I'll consent."

"No! You for the priest...that's all!"

"Nonsense," said Alfred. "Utter nonsense. I'd be sending him to his death. I'll deal with you in silver, not in flesh."

And then, suddenly, a cry of dismay broke out in the Viking ranks. Everyone looked back toward the river, and what they saw threw the negotiation into another dimension, rendering Sidroc's plans impotent, Alfred's entreaties useless and Sigli's offer meaningless. No more words needed to be spoken, no more insults traded. What they saw changed everything.

As he sat there in the oxcart watching the negotiations from afar, Plegmund knew that things were not going well. He had seen Sidroc's fascination with Elfwyn during the week of their captivity, and he no longer trusted the Viking's intentions. Old One Eye's interest in the girl had even outstripped his greed for gold and silver; no good could possibly come of it. Plegmund knew that matters had reached a critical juncture. He had never been a man of action—all of his machinations had been, like those of Grimwald, clandestine in nature—and he had always envied people like Alfred and Sigli who were unafraid to confront life directly. Now he was being called upon to do just that.

It would not be easy. But the Vikings guarding the cart had shifted their attention to the meeting, and all of their faces were turned toward the south, away from the river. Only a single guard sitting on the driver's seat still attended to them, but his back was turned as he craned his neck to see over the others and watch what was happening on the meadow.

Plegmund looked down at the floor of the oxcart and saw a stout club that lay behind the front seat. He eyed it nervously, shifting his attention back and forth between it and the Vikings, and his hands began to tremble. Three times he made up his mind to pick it up, and three times his nerve failed him. He could not overcome the fear; he was incapable of doing the thing that had to be done.

And then his eyes fell on Elfwyn. She was sitting on the floor of the cart, next to the club, and she was looking up at him. The sun was beginning to sink in the west, its slanting rays illuminating her face and bathing it in a warm glow. Her blue eyes sparkled in the light, and the expression in them was one of hope and trust, of indisputable faith. He felt his heart surging out to her, pounding in his chest.

Thump, thump, thump. He looked at the Vikings. Thump, thump. He eyed the back of the sentinel's head, and then he glanced down at the club. Thump, THUMP, THUMP. And then he looked once more at Elfwyn, and he felt his heart rise into his throat as though it would strangle him. THUMP, THUMP, THUMP.

He reached across the girl, raised the club over his head, and brought it down hard on the back of the Viking's skull.

The impact sent the man slumping to one side, but his weight still held him up against the front of the cart. He shuddered convulsively and started as though to recover his balance, but Plegmund swung the club hard against his exposed collarbone, once, twice, knocking him from the wagon. He threw the weapon aside and grabbed the reins of the cart, and he slapped at the horses that were hitched up to the wagon. They reared, startled by the shock, and then they burst forward, dragging the cart noisily ahead.

Plegmund tried to head the cart toward the Saxons, but the Vikings blocked his way. He veered the horses sharply to the right, throwing Elfwyn against the floor as the wagon groaned in protest, but it responded and sped away from the mass of men, some of whom had to leap to the side to keep from being trampled. One of the Vikings grabbed hold of the rear of the cart, running in step as he tried to pull himself up onto it, but he lost his footing and tumbled onto the meadow. The cart careened away to the west, racing some twenty yards parallel to the Thames as the cries of the Vikings rang out.

Sidroc was the first to react when they all saw the oxcart break free. He reached behind him and withdrew a dagger he had hidden along the base of his saddle, and with a sharp kick at the flanks of his horse he headed for Alfred, raising the knife and aiming a blow at the king's unprotected face. But Alfred slid quickly down and away from the blade, using his horse's neck to shield him from danger as the dagger hissed harmlessly through the air. Sidroc let out a cry of disgust and thundered past the king, never stopping as he swung his horse around and galloped back toward the Viking camp.

Sigli's first thought had been to get to his nemesis, but he had to deal with another Viking who rushed at Aethelfled. He intercepted the man just as he was about to close with her, landing a hard punch that caught the Dane in the temple and knocked him from his horse. He wheeled back around and caught sight of an arm descending toward him from behind, and he reached up just in time to parry a knife thrust intended for him. His assailant drew back his arm and delivered another blow. He thwarted it by grabbing the man's wrist as they were thrown together, their horses spinning furiously. The attacker's momentum pulled them out of their saddles and sent them crashing to the ground, and the impact of the fall knocked the wind out of the Dane. Sigli struck him twice in the face, knocking him unconscious. He took the man's dagger and thrust it into his own belt, and then he looked around to regain his bearings.

The Saxon force was rushing past him toward the Vikings, who had taken up arms and were now closing their ranks. He looked into the onrushing masses of men and was relieved to see that both Alfred and Aethelfled were unharmed. The king directed the movement of troops as they streamed toward him, while Aethelfled strained to see over the heads of the Vikings, having lost sight of the fleeing oxcart. Sigli grabbed for the bridal of his horse as the beast wandered nearby and swung himself up into the saddle in one powerful motion. He dug his heels hard into the flanks of the horse and headed off through the midst of the gathering melee,

Sidroc, meanwhile, had thundered immediately after the priest and the girl. One of his men came running from the edge of the Viking ranks holding his leader's familiar, massive sword in his outstretched hand, pommel extended. Old One Eye headed for him, leaning out and snatching the blade without breaking his horse's stride, and then he veered westward in pursuit of the retreating wagon.

He could see Plegmund urging the oxcart forward several hundred yards ahead of him. The rhythmic pounding of the hooves beneath him renewed his confidence, driving him onward and into a heightened sense of exhilaration. All thoughts of his men, of Alfred and Aethelfled, of the strange reappearance of Sigli and the danger he was now in—all evaporated into the encroaching twilight as he rushed forward.

If Sidroc was swept up by the moment, Plegmund was terrified by it. The sudden rush of adrenaline that had catapulted him into action still raced through his veins. But fear and doubt had already begun to creep back into him. He looked down at Elfwyn, who clung tenaciously to the side of the cart as they bounced along, crying out. And then he looked behind him, and instead of seeing the Vikings receding in the distance he saw Sidroc, whipping his mount on and gaining ground fast. Terrified, he snapped wildly at the reins, screaming at the horses, pleading with them. His eyes began to fill up with tears as the wind whipped into them, making it harder to see as he glanced over his shoulder every few seconds.

And then Sidroc was right behind the cart. At first he thought to ride up and decapitate Plegmund with one clean blow, but then he decided against it; the wagon might spin out of control without someone to guide it. He thrust his great sword back into his belt and spurred his horse on, overtaking the cart from the left and pulling alongside Plegmund. The monk looked over at him in terror, his face completely drained of blood as he continued to lash furiously at the horses.

Sidroc measured his pace against that of the cart, leaned toward it, and suddenly lunged for the nearest handhold. In the same motion he disengaged his legs from his horse, and for an instant it appeared that neither the animal nor the wagon would be able to accommodate him. But his prodigious strength proved to be enough as he swung his body over the abyss to safety and clambered aboard the cart.

Plegmund turned and began to strike Sidroc with his whip, but the weapon was of little use. The Viking yanked it from his hand as though he were relieving a child of a toy, and had the wagon not been on the verge of tumbling out of control he undoubtedly would have drawn his sword then and there and killed the Archbishop. Instead, he threw a thundering right hand that exploded into Plegmund's jaw, catapulting the monk backward over the edge of the cart and onto the meadow. Sidroc then grabbed for the reins as the wagon bumped along furiously, and gradually he was able to regain mastery of the horses, pulling them neatly back under control without slowing the cart down.

He looked back over his shoulder, where he could see the receding form of Plegmund rising laboriously to all fours on the meadow. It irritated him that the monk was still alive, but there was no time for him to do anything about it; he had to ride ahead and ford the Thames to avoid capture. In the distance behind him he could see the struggle underway between the Saxons and Vikings, and he became dimly aware of a few scattered figures on horseback that had broken free and were beginning to follow him.

Then he looked down at the object of his desire. Elfwyn sat huddled and shivering on the floor at his feet, clinging in fear to one of the poles that rose up to form the sides of the cart. Her little face was filled with terror, but none of that mattered to him now. She was his again! All his! Let her cry; he would make things right later on. The treasure, the men, the glory—all faded away in the face of his instinct to survive, to have her with him as he crossed into Mercia and found his way back to Haestan's camp.

And then, as he scanned the meadow over the bouncing heads of the horses, a wonderful sight met his eye. Three ceorls had landed in a small boat along the riverbank and stood alongside it, looking his way as he thundered toward them. Clearly, the gods were with him. The three men were armed, but it never occurred to him that the odds could be anything but in his favor; he simply headed the cart directly at them and whipped the horses on with a loud cry.

The ceorls jumped out of the way as he rode past, and they drew their weapons as he reined in the horses and brought the wagon to a halt. They advanced toward him with a confident shout, unaware until it was too late that the apparent mismatch in their favor was in fact a fatal error in judgement.

Sidroc leaped down from the cart and drew his sword, wading directly into them. He swung the blade with such force that it tore downward through the futile defense of the first ceorl, shearing through the man's body at the point where the neck meets the collarbone. The blow severed the poor wretch's shoulder and arm from his body, and the blood spurted grotesquely in every direction, spattering them all.

Sidroc stepped over the man's wriggling torso as the other two Saxons took a step backward. He hacked wildly at them, alternating his blows with a rapid, powerful fury, swinging the heavy blade first at one man and then at the other. It was all they could do to protect themselves, and they gave ground before his relentless advance. Finally, one of his blows met with flesh instead of steel; it was enough to throw Sidroc over the edge and into a frenzy. With a single-minded purpose that all but ignored the second attacker, he leaped upon the wounded Saxon and hacked him to pieces, until the man was a writhing, pulpy mass of blood.

The last of the peasants threw down his sword and ran away. Sidroc let out a low grunt and paused to catch his breath, when out of the corner of his eye he caught sight of a movement behind him. He wheeled around, where Elfwyn was lowering herself down from the cart. She began to run away, crying out in fright, but he bounded after her across the meadow and grabbed her from behind.

"I won't hurt you!" he cried, trying his best not to sound threatening. But she screamed and tried to wrench herself free, her golden hair tangled with sweat and heat and fear.

"Stop it!" he cried out. But her resistance only increased. He dragged her toward the riverbank and the waiting boat that Odin had so generously bestowed upon him.

"You're hurting me! Stop!" she screamed.

But his hand remained clenched tightly around her arm. She stumbled along behind him, her face crimson. He wrestled her to the riverbank and then swung her over the side of the boat, depositing her in its belly. She grabbed hold of the gunwale as though to struggle back onto the bank, but he shoved her so that she fell backward, bruising herself against the hard bottom of the skiff as he pushed it out into the river and clambered aboard. He fumbled with the oars for a moment before dropping them into the murky water and propelling the boat toward the opposite bank of the Thames.

While this was happening, Plegmund knelt on the ground downstream, trying to clear his head. He had landed in a soft patch of grass, and no bones were broken. His jaw pounded and his back ached, but already he was beginning to recover. He remained bent over, massaging his jaw, and as the veil that had cloaked itself over him slowly began to lift, he became aware of the sound of approaching hoof beats. He raised his head and looked up as a lone rider reined in his horse and called down to him in a breathless, vaguely familiar voice.

"Plegmund? Are you all right?"

Plegmund squinted up at the face above him, and his jaw dropped. He could not believe his eyes.

"Sigli...? Sigli? Is that you?"

"Where are they? Where's Elfwyn?"

"They...I think they...Lord God in heaven, Sigli...is it really you?"

"Yes, Plegmund! But for the love of God, where are they??!!"

The monk looked upriver, where the sun now lay hidden behind a swarm of angry clouds, hastening the twilight and throwing a mantle of gloom over the river valley. But even in the gloaming, Plegmund could see the wagon through a thin brace of trees that marked a bend in the river ahead.

"There!" he pointed, attempting in vain to rise to his feet. "It's him, Sigli! By God, it's him!"

Sigli dug his heels into the horse and surged forward. He raced along the riverbank, straining unsuccessfully to see through the trees, until finally he rounded the bend and breathed a great sigh of relief. He could see Sidroc dragging Elfwyn out of the boat and onto Mercian soil on the opposite bank of the river. He rode along the Thames and past the deserted oxcart, urging his stallion forward and plunging madly into the stream.

"Elfwyn!"

Sidroc and the girl turned and stared at him from across the river, a mere fifty yards away. But no matter how he tried, he could not make the horse swim out into the Thames; the beast protested and spun out to one side, throwing him from its back into the shallows and scrambling up onto the bank. He stood up in the hip-deep water and looked across the river, where he could see Sidroc gesturing at him and jeering derisively, all the while clutching onto the girl. Finally, Old One Eye turned away and raced onto a path that disappeared into the forest, where it led up along the face of the tree-lined chalk down.

Sigli struggled to free himself from his heavy chain mail shirt, and after a few frantic seconds he managed to tear the weight from his shoulders and cast it away. He was about to plunge forward into the river when he remembered that the dagger in his belt was his only weapon; turning around, his eyes fell upon the bodies of the two Saxon ceorls who had fallen near the cart. He splashed through the shallows and clambered up onto the bank, sprinting to the nearest body and taking the sword that still rested in its bloody hand. He shoved the blade into his belt before racing back into the Thames and diving headfirst into its brisk waters.

The iciness of the Thames in spring jolted through him as he kicked forward. He was an excellent swimmer, and despite his leggings and the sword that encumbered him he was able to make rapid progress through the light current. With every stroke the electricity surged through his body, wave after wave of tension exploding with an adrenaline high. By the gods, he was alive! Alive! He had waited all his life for this moment, and now it was here; there was no way Sidroc could escape him this time. He felt a giddy satisfaction that was completely unique to his experience, a feeling that he had never felt before.

And so when Sigli of Halfsfiord scrambled up onto the northern bank of the Thames and set foot in Mercia, he was a happy man.

Ahead of him, Sidroc struggled to make progress along a steep path that tunneled its way upward through the trees. When he had first left the riverbank, he had been confident he would be able to escape. But the girl had been reduced to a tearful mass of nerves, and while she did not try to thwart him, she was in no condition to do anything other than be dragged about, as though she were a load of bricks. He finally swept her into his arms and ran up the incline, attempting by sheer strength of will to escape and set them free.

But he was no longer a young man. His wind and his legs were not what they used to be, and running uphill in full battle gear with an extra fifty pounds in his arms was more than even he could do. Everything depended on the curve in the trail ahead. The path tunneled through the dense trees to a point where all he could see was the nothingness of the broad twilight sky, and then it broke off sharply upward and to the right. If the ground leveled off there, if by some miracle a horse had wandered off untended, if...

He churned on up the hill, sweating profusely. But when he finally reached the end of the chute his questions were still unanswered. Below him the Thames Valley stretched to the west, and he could see upriver for many miles. To the right, the path flattened out, leading to a series of stone steps that had been cut out of the hillside.

Beyond them and facing out over the ledge was a carefully sculpted Roman portico, now covered with moss and in a state of disrepair, its roof long since collapsed into ruins. The portico led up several more steps to a circular area with a fountain in its center that commanded the best view of all. It appeared to lead to another path beyond his line of sight that evidently went straight up and over the top of the chalk ridge, from where a row of tall trees now peered impassively down at him, silent sentinels in the twilight.

He walked toward the portico with Elfwyn in his arms. The sight of the ruins somehow calmed her, and at long last her sobbing stopped. There was the sense of something old here, something that had come and gone long before their time. The Romans had disappeared from England over six hundred years earlier, but their influence still remained. As Sidroc walked through the portico his eyes were drawn to the elaborate fountain that commanded the center of the circular space a few steps ahead, and the strange and powerful statue on top of it that stared down at him with a bemused smile.

It must be one of their gods, he thought to himself; only a god could look like that.

And so it was that as he climbed the steps leading to the fountain with Elfwyn still in his arms, he was completely absorbed by the grandeur of what lay before him, crumbling and overgrown but majestic nonetheless. Life was a ruin, the world was a ruin. It was only when Sidroc reached the base of the fountain and looked up and to the right that he realized the smiling god was something more. It was just another of Loki's cruel tricks, the Norse god of mischief in one of his many disguises, laughing in his face and mocking him for his stupid folly.

For as Old One Eye looked on in dismay, he saw that the entire side of the cliff had caved in, leaving a tangled mass of broken trees in its wake. There was no way to get to the top of the ridge. There was no way out.

His eye alternated between the cliff and the pseudo Roman god's face—Loki's laughing face—once, twice and then a third time, before he turned and looked back down the portico, toward the bend overlooking the Thames where he had first emerged from the trees. He put Elfwyn down and started back toward the steps, walking in the same direction from which he had come.

And at that moment Sigli stepped around the corner of the trees and into full view, stopping in his tracks and staring down the length of the crumbling portico toward them.

Sidroc hissed in disgust. So it had come to this, after all. He reached into his belt and withdrew his massive sword, the same one he had carried with him since his very first raiding expedition over thirty years ago, and he raised it high above his head in a gesture of supreme defiance.

"You want me, Halfsfiordian?" he cried out, his voice ringing off the steep down. "Then come! Come to me, foolish boy...come to your death!"

Sigli walked forward slowly, moving up the light incline and across the cracked stones of the portico until he reached a point some twenty feet from the base of the steps that led up to the circular area around the fountain. That was where Sidroc stood, holding his broadsword in one meaty hand and Elfwyn's arm in the other. Sigli now looked fully into his daughter's face. It was too beautiful and perfect for him to have ever possibly imagined, so exquisite were its lines, so bright were her eyes, even in this moment of oppressive terror. And in those eyes he saw himself, saw his father Lothar, and he knew then that everything Mimir had long ago foretold was true, and had always been so.

He looked with pride and self-assurance at the beauty and the beast before him, with the strange, laughing Roman god presiding over all. And he heard himself muttering the words Mimir had recited to him so many years ago, on the rock above his father's great hall on the banks of the fiord:

> *"Thunder, lightning, woe and worry, strife in Halfsfiord!*
> *He who lurks in Loki's womb shall conquer by the sword.*

> *Lothar's pride shall rise again upon a distant shore,*
> *To flourish in the setting sun, yet return...nevermore!*

Next to greatness, Sigli, stand! The dragon wields your fate.
Lured by love of sovereign seed, yet driven hard by hate

Your vengeance at the twilight hour lies in wait for thee,
Beneath the golden dragon's banner, far beyond the sea..."

And now he only had eyes for the Malevolent One. "The time has come, Sidroc."

"Fool!" Sidroc cried. "You think to frighten me with verse, do you? Well, all the fine words in the world won't help you now!"

He continued to clutch Elfwyn tightly, gradually moving toward the low stone wall that overlooked a drop of some forty feet of cliff that fell away from the base of the portico and fountain.

"I don't need words any longer. Or prayers," Sigli began to mount the steps. "All my prayers have come true."

"Don't come any closer!" Sidroc hissed, pulling Elfwyn to him and heading for a break in the wall. There was a gap of some ten feet where the stone had crumbled over the years and released itself to the will of the cliff. He positioned himself so that he stood between the girl and the sheer drop into nothingness, and he stared menacingly at Sigli.

"If you value the child's life at all, keep your distance!" He placed the blade over her tender throat and clenched his teeth.

"Let her go, Sidroc," Sigli replied evenly, mounting the last step and drawing to within a few paces. "She's innocent of all this."

The Malevolent One laughed nervously, not wanting to betray his bluff. "There's no such a thing as innocence in this world!"

"She doesn't belong here. She has nothing to do with what's between us."

"Then if I slit her throat and let her bleed to death here in front of you before I slice your own head open, it shouldn't matter, should it?" Sidroc taunted him, knowing full well that it was the very last thing in the world he would ever do.

Elfwyn was afraid, but her attention was now locked on the marvelous blonde giant who stood before her. She felt in his presence something far more powerful than a mere man of flesh and blood. And he felt it in her. She was an absolute jewel, a treasure that shone as the twilight deepened.

"Even you couldn't destroy such a rare and beautiful thing." Sigli raised his sword and took a step forward. "Cast her aside, Sidroc. And let the gods be our judge."

Sidroc knew his bluff was over. But if he could no longer use the girl to shield him, she could still help him kill the Halfsfiordian. His eye gleamed with hate, and he raised his sword above him.

"Cast her aside, you say? Very well, then, son of Lothar...as you wish!"

He dragged Elfwyn across his body and sent her careening toward the gap in the portico wall. Without hesitation, Sigli lunged forward and grabbed her with his free hand, just in time to prevent her from plunging into the abyss. But the effort left his body momentarily exposed.

Sidroc swung his broadsword around in a reverse arc that avoided Elfwyn, bringing the blade down hard and with expert accuracy. It sheared into Sigli's side in an explosion of steel and blood, knocking him to the ground. The Malevolent One raised the blade with a triumphant leer and prepared to deliver the death blow to Sigli's head when a frightened cry distracted him.

He looked up, and to his horror he saw Elfwyn dangling over the edge of the precipice, hanging tenaciously from one of the marble columns as she struggled to gain a foothold. He leaped forward and lunged for her. His hand closed around her tender, white arm just as the section of wall she was holding onto broke free and tumbled down the side of the cliff, and with a great sigh of relief he drew her up toward him and onto solid ground.

It was then that a hot fire invaded his belly, a sensation unlike anything he had ever felt before. It was not until he turned his head and stared wide-eyed into Sigli's face, now only a few inches from his own, that he realized his stomach had been torn apart. The dagger that one of his men had treacherously brought to the parlay with Alfred was now embedded in him, with the Halfsfiordian grimly attached to its handle, rotating it in his belly. He dropped his sword and grabbed for Sigli, trying to crush him in his massive arms, but his bear hug proved to be nothing more than a futile embrace.

The two men remained locked together dangerously close to the edge of the portico, holding each other up in a macabre dance. Neither had the power or the strength to stand up alone. Their chins practically touched as they clasped onto each other, and Sidroc's lone eye bulged out grotesquely as he stared into the face of the man who had done what no one else had ever been able to do.

It was not possible; it could not be. But the fire in his belly did not lie.

"Vengeance is mine! At last!" Sigli gasped, half-delirious with pleasure and pain. "For Lothar! For Hathor and Beolinde! You're mine Sidroc...mine forever! For Halfsfiord!"

With his last remaining strength he pulled upward on the handle of the dagger, dragging the blade through the Malevolent One's intestines and all the way up into his rib cage. Sidroc gurgled in dismay as he felt his sphincter emptying. Summoning the last of his will, Sigli pushed the foul object of his obsession away from him and collapsed to the ground.

Sidroc took a final, uncertain step and toppled backward over the edge of the precipice, his muffled scream echoing out over the valley. By the time his body finally came to rest at the base of the chalk down, he was dead.

At that moment a handful of Saxons appeared at the bend of the trail, led by Alfred and Aethelfled. The Lady of Mercia, seeing her daughter safe and unharmed at the base of the old Roman fountain, let out a cry of relief and sprinted the length of the portico. She gathered the girl up in her arms and showered her with kisses. The others followed close behind, and Alfred was the first one to climb the steps and tend to Sigli. One look at the gaping wound in the Viking's side told him everything.

"Sigli...Sigli," he said, kneeling over him and clasping his hand. "How can we ever..." And then his voice choked, and he had to fight back the tears. He placed his sword in the Viking's hand, opening the gates to Valhalla.

"It's done," Sigli whispered in a faltering voice, looking up through the dull mist that was already beginning to cover the world. "My quest is over...my life...complete." He turned his head as Aethelfled fell to her knees beside him.

"My love...oh, Sigli!" she cried out, lifting his head up and cradling it in her lap. She wiped the sweat off his brow and caressed his forehead. "You've saved Elfwyn, given her life...you've..." Her voice broke and she began to weep quietly, continuing to stroke his head with trembling fingers.

Sigli looked up into her eyes, and then into Alfred's. He smiled weakly. "All my life, I've wanted to...to belong," he whispered. The faces above him were fuzzy, and he was no longer able to feel his legs. "You're the ones I love...have always loved. To leave the world like this..."

He looked past them and up into the cloud-covered sky. He felt a vague, burning sensation in his side, but it did not bother him; instead, he was consumed by the heavens, infinite and eternal, as they stretched above him. He felt a great sense of acceptance, an understanding of everything and all things that he had never known before. It all seemed so simple, and as his mind drifted from cloud to cloud he wondered to himself why he had never been able to see things the way he was seeing them now, no longer obscured by the futility that had always seemed to fill up his life.

As he stared up into the benevolent, eternal sky, he saw a vision carved out of the twilight; it was the spectral figure of his old benefactor Mimir, reaching out to him. The seer was smiling, and Sigli felt himself flying upward toward the clouds and Mimir's gleaming, sightless eyes.

And then a voice pulled him back. "Oh, Sigli...Sigli," it sobbed. "Forgive me, please! By God in heaven, can you forgive me?"

He turned his head with a bemused expression and looked directly into Plegmund's sad eyes as the monk knelt weeping over him.

"Forgive...?" he muttered, in a delirium that possessed a clarity all its own. "There's nothing...to forgive. There is nothing..." All he saw when he looked into their faces was love, and the high clouds in the sky above them. And then he heard Aethelfled's voice again, as though it was echoing down a long, smooth tunnel.

"Elfwyn," she said softly, melodically. The very name itself was music to his ears. "Come to us, Elfwyn. And look upon the gallant man who gave you life."

As his eyes swung across their blurred faces, the girl stepped into his vision, silhouetted by the benevolent sky. At that moment the sun slipped below the clouds and rested on the horizon, and its dying rays shone directly on her, illuminating her cheeks in a warm, golden glow.

By Odin, she's a vision, he thought. More wonderful than anything I've ever seen. She smiled from above and knelt down beside him, all innocence itself, and in her sparkling blue eyes there was an understanding that transcended everything. She was the love itself, and in that delirious moment he knew that she knew, that there were no more secrets, nor anything else left to be sorry for. He felt his heart embracing her and all those he loved around her, and in that instant she leaned down over him and kissed his cheek.

It was as though a gentle feather had stroked his skin, and as she raised her smiling face and wise, understanding eyes back into the infinite sky, a cool breeze drifted over his lips. He felt his soul racing into those eyes, into the gleaming tunnel of light that led through them and into the eternal beyond. He smiled the smile of a man who knows all.

"Life is so beautiful," he whispered. And then he died.

They all gathered him in their arms and wept, knowing that something wonderful had passed from the world and was gone. No one spoke for several moments, until finally Alfred stood up and looked off to the west, where the bottom of the orange sun was beginning to sink into the trees.

"Let us pray to the Lord God in heaven for the soul of this man," he said, bowing his head as the others knelt around Sigli's body and crossed themselves. "Let us give thanks for having known him...for as I stand here before God, never have I met a man more gallant, more true, more selfless and honorable. If this is what a Viking is made of, then I say, let us embrace them. Let us make war no more. For here lies a better man than I, a noble creature made in the image of God."

He raised his head again and looked down over the valley. "We shall honor our friend by burying him in the style of his ancestors, as he would have us do. Give him a Viking funeral, I say. Let all men know of our trust and love, and let us all remember him, and keep his love alive. For we shall always keep a place in our hearts for Sigli of Halfsfiord, son of Lothar, the last of his line. The last Viking."

Off to the west, the sun sank beneath the horizon. A faint thunder rumbled in the distance as a bird flitted by them in the twilight, hastening homeward to its nest. It raced to beat the darkness, flapping its wings one last time and then gliding into the dusky trees, there to hide itself away for a few sheltered hours from the all-consuming loneliness of the night.

EPILOGUE

> *"I heard the dead cry;*
> > *I was lulled by the slamming of iron,*
> *A slow drip over stones,*
> > *Toads brooding in wells,*
> *All the leaves stuck out their tongues;*
> *I shook the softening chalk off my bones,*
> > *Saying,*
> *Snail, snail, glister me forward,*
> > *Bird, soft-sigh me home,*
> > *Worm, be with me.*
> *This is my hard time."*
> —Theodore Roethke, <u>The Lost Son</u>

Richard of Dover sighed as he peered through the dim candlelight that illuminated his chamber at Canterbury. There was so much work to do, so many details. Outside, he could hear the winter wind whistling through the trees, rendered impotent and distant by the crackling fire that warmed the room. Yes, he should be thankful for his lot, he thought to himself. No matter how much work remained to be done, he was lucky to be sitting here, warming himself at a hearth to which every holy man in England aspired.

It was January of 1175, and Richard had been appointed the forty-first Archbishop of Canterbury just a few months earlier. There had been much ado among the clergy concerning just who would be named to the post, for the seat of Canterbury and everything it stood for had become more desirable than at any time during its long and distinguished history as the ecclesiastical heart of Christian England. All of this was because of the previous Archbishop, Thomas

Becket, who four years earlier on a dark day in December of 1170 had been assassinated in the great Gothic cathedral by a band of renegade knights, men sympathetic to Henry II and his growing discontent with Canterbury.

The foul murder had turned Becket into a martyr and Canterbury into a shrine. Pilgrims now flocked to Kent from all over England, France and even Rome itself to worship God and pay homage to the man they called St. Thomas. A successor had not been named to his seat for so long simply because no one could have possibly taken the great one's place amidst the emotional and political unrest that his death had spawned. King Henry suffered greatly during this time, for he and Becket had once been inseparable, and their falling out and its consequences had weighed heavily on the king's conscience. No matter that the knights had acted on their own resolve; whenever Henry looked at himself in the mirror, he saw the face of the man indirectly responsible for Becket's death.

And so, just a few months earlier, the king had come to Canterbury to do penance, entering the town barefoot and clothed in a monk's crude cassock, the rain soaking him through every pore as though it might wash away all his sins. Henry had walked through the mud and come to the cathedral, where he fell on his knees before Becket's tomb and was symbolically flogged by dozens of holy men belonging to England's ecclesiastical order, Richard among them. And God spoke out, for shortly afterward the King of Scotland was captured as he invaded England, which many attributed to St. Thomas' intercession following Henry's penitent gesture.

That was proof enough to everyone that Becket did indeed sleep in the lap of the Lord.

And so Canterbury was elevated to new heights, a lofty perch to which Richard ascended when he finally emerged as the choice to succeed St. Thomas after four tempestuous years had passed without an Archbishop in place. He was a lucky man, indeed.

But there was so much to be done! First and foremost, it was his responsibility to maintain the otherworldly sense of sacrament that now pervaded Canterbury. Nothing could be allowed to compromise that vision. He above all had to protect it, to retain the lofty hand of God that rested on his shoulder, while at the same time tending to everyday business and restoring the administration of ecclesiastical duties to an efficient and workable order. The parchments and papers stacked on the table before him would have been enough by themselves, but there was more, always more. The fire had seen to that.

Just a few months earlier the choir of the cathedral had burnt down, as though God had decreed that one final penance was due to purge the great crime that had been committed there. Amidst the tangle of paperwork and pilgrims and politics and religion, the house of God had to be rebuilt. William of Sens, the French master mason, had been brought across the Channel to oversee the task. His laborers were just now clearing away the last of the debris in the choir, preparing for the new to supplant the old, to build something worthy of God in His infinite glory that would rise out of the ashes and inspire men everywhere.

And so when a knock at the door disturbed Richard late on this midwinter's night, he was not surprised. He looked up wearily and bade the visitor to enter, and he laid his quill down on the table as one of William's foremen, a Gascon laborer with dirty, calloused hands and a lined face, opened the door and stepped into the chamber. The man bore a small, finely crafted wooden box in his hands.

"What is it, Gilbert?" the Archbishop asked, leaning back with thinly veiled irritation.

"I...I beg your pardon, Holiness. We found this today while digging. It was underneath the stones, in a hollowed-out place. There's a parchment inside it, but well...none of us can read, Your Holiness, so we thought you should have it." He stepped over to the table and placed the carved box before Richard, who reached over and gathered it in.

"Thank you, Gilbert. That will be all."

The man bowed awkwardly and backed away. Richard turned his attention to the box, and it was not until he heard the sound of his chamber door closing and Gilbert was gone that he opened the lid. A rolled-up parchment was inside, so old and brittle that he marveled it was still in one piece. Handling the document with great care, he rolled it out gently on the table before him and pulled the candle closer. The flickering light revealed a faint but discernible writing rendered in ink, clearly legible in Latin. Richard leaned over the parchment and began to read:

Here under the eyes of God I, Plegmund of Mercia, the nineteenth Archbishop of Canterbury, do prepare to take my leave of this world. I am an old man, and my time is nigh, and before I go to my grave there are things I would say, some of them never having been uttered to any man—no less God in heaven Himself.

Much have I seen in my time, and not all of it righteous and of good faith. But there has still been much to rejoice about, many worthy things that shall be recorded in the annals as works of honor that do justice to both man and God. For I have been lucky to have lived during the reign of England's greatest king, Alfred of Wessex. Some call him Alfred the Great, with ample reason. I have seen with my own eyes how he united this land under the cross, Danes and Saxons alike, living together in peace and harmony.

My King Alfred took his place alongside God some twenty-four autumns ago, dying in the Year of our Lord 899 at the age of fifty. Let it be said now that no man ever ruled as wisely, nor did so much good. And let us thank God for leaving the great man in peace for the final five years of his illustrious life, so that with his own hand he was able to craft many wonderful and lasting translations, turning words of wisdom from Latin into English, so that all men may partake of them and rejoice.

And the Lord blessed England with Edward the Elder, who still reigns on the throne, master of all Britain. He has pushed our fair boundaries far to the north, for now the kings of Scotland and Strathclyde do acknowledge him as father and lord, as does Raegnald, the Viking king of York, and Ealdred, the English lord of Bamburgh, and all Northumbrians do likewise pay him homage. A greater general in the field no man of our generation has seen.

And I have had the joy and privilege of knowing Edward's sister and Alfred's daughter, Aethelfled, the Lady of Mercia. When her lord Eadred died in 911 she took up arms and horse, riding with her brother to the north and subjugating the peoples there. Leicester surrendered to her without a drop of blood being spent, and the Danes of York swore their allegiance to her when threatened by a foreign hand from across the northern sea. My Lady passed into the arms of God five years ago, during the summer of 918, and never was there a more blessed ruler in the land—neither man nor woman. So I say to you now, it is true.

And so I write these final words, lest the secret shared between the Lady Aethelfled and myself die with me, and never be uttered. For it was I who served as the liaison between my lady and the man she loved, the very man I too have loved before all others these many years. Sigli of Halfsfiord was his name, a Viking by birth, and he was the most kind and gallant man I have ever known. It was I who enabled them to lie together under the disapproving eyes of Alfred and God. And it was I who betrayed them, when the noble Sigli rightfully turned away from me when I would have had him take my own body and make it his.

I plunged him into exile, and Aethelfled into grief. I have confessed this to no man, just as I have not spoken of my greed for Canterbury, and how I debased myself forever in the eyes of God. Yes, I sold my soul and my body for personal gain, allowing the unspeakable to happen so that my own ends could be met. I am forever unworthy, even as I love Aethelfled and Sigli still. And even as I love their secret, the child Elfwyn, born out of wedlock to them and now grown to fair womanhood. God at least smiles on her, not blaming her for the sins of others! She lives now as a ward in Edward's court, and as I have seen her I have seen *him, the one I loved most and for whose sake I allowed myself to commit so many grievous sins.*

I am old now. The lights grow dim. How is it that I have survived all these others, now faded memories no more distinct than the summer twilight? Who can predict the hand of God, and all His wondrous gifts? For no gift is as wondrous or terrible as the gift of life. Would that I could have lived it more fully, when it was mine and the world stretched out before me.

The time has come to join my departed comrades. I grow tired and weak; my hand trembles. There is only the strength left to confess myself, a coward to the end, unable to utter these words to those who surround my bed. I only hope that someday a better man than I shall discover what I have written, and see it in his power to grant me the salvation I so long for—and yet have not the courage to seek out as one who has wronged his fellows, his God, and himself.

Good night, England, and farewell! I pray the next world will be a better place than the one I leave behind. May the Lord God in heaven hear my prayers, and forgive me for my sins.

> *Plegmund of Mercia*
> *2 August*
> *The Year of Our Lord 923*

Richard let out a deep breath and stared into the fire. He shuddered, as though he could feel Plegmund's spirit in the room, hovering above him in the heat that gathered against the darkened ceiling. Two hundred and fifty years had passed since the words before him had been written; Alfred the Great and his Saxon kingdom were already the stuff of legends. And yet it was true, all true! Here was the proof of that dark and distant age, a proof to be celebrated all across England.

But instead of feeling the exhilaration and joy of discovering something precious, Richard was ill at ease. He began to pace back and forth across the chamber as the wind howled outside, and with every step the weight he felt in the room began to press more heavily upon him. No, it would not do. No one else could be allowed to see the parchment. With all that had happened during the last few years, nothing could be permitted to mar the good name of Canterbury, no matter how distant or vague its calling.

Here was a sinner, confessing acts of treachery, adultery and unspeakable lust, all of which could be laid on the head of the Archbishopric. No, Richard thought—that was not what Becket had died for. And that was not why Plegmund had chosen on his deathbed to commit his final secrets to pen and paper.

His mind made up, Richard stepped over to the table and picked up the brittle parchment. He walked over to the hearth and stood before the fire, lost in thought as the orange and blue flames sent their flickering light dancing into the far corners of the chamber. He let out a deep breath and looked into the darkness above him.

"Your secret shall remain safe with me, Plegmund. By the power invested in me by the Lord God, I do hereby acknowledge your confession and absolve you of your sins. In the name of the Father, and the Son, and the Holy Spirit. Amen."

With that he crumpled up the parchment and threw it into the flames. It caught fire immediately and began to crinkle, turning black first at the edges and then throughout, until the paper was nothing more than an indistinct mass. And in that moment there was a sudden draft in the room, an unexplained gust of wind, and Richard felt the heaviness pass over his shoulder and into the flames.

As he watched, the last remnants of the parchment disappeared and transformed themselves into ash. Something else mingled with the smoke, turning it for a fleeting instant into a strange, otherworldly vision, and then the entire mass floated up the chimney. Upward, ever upward it climbed, until it finally escaped into the night and was swept away into nothingness by a cold and cleansing wind.

FINIS

Acknowledgements

While *The Last Viking* is a work of historical fiction, I took great pains to be true to the recorded history of the era—a period that was mired in the depths of the Dark Ages, when learning and scholarship were in short supply. Although we do have access to the history of 9th century England, by any estimation the sources are sparse. Most notable are *The Anglo-Saxon Chronicles* and Asser's *Life of King Alfred*, the latter biography written by a monk who was a contemporary of the king—and who dutifully appears in *The Last Viking*. I also cobbled together various encyclopaedic entries, along with a few other collected sources, and I personally explored all the sites in southern England that are mentioned in the book, and where the story unfolds.

The beauty of this thin fabric of recorded history is that it provided me with a great deal of freedom and license to inject my fictional characters into the actual events that we know happened. Sigli and his family, as well as Sidroc the Malevolent One, are fictional characters. So is Grimwald. But all of the battles, the chronology of events, the movement of troops, the storm that destroyed the Viking fleet near Exeter, the various naval encounters—all are historically accurate. I wrote the story to fit into the history of the times.

Beyond my main protagonists, all other principal Vikings, as well as the entire Saxon royal family and most of the Saxon nobles, were real people whose acts reflect the history we know. King Alfred remains to this day the only monarch in English history accorded the title of "The Great." And Plegmund was indeed the nineteenth Archbishop of Canterbury. I humbly request his forgiveness if I have taken undue liberty with his behavior and actions.

Last but not least, Aethelfled did indeed have a daughter, apparently sired by Athelred of Mercia—whose name I mercifully changed to Eadred to avoid needless confusion with the similarly named eighteenth Archbishop of Canterbury (it seems that every third person during that day and age was named Athelred).

So, to conclude, it must be said that it is extremely unlikely that a Viking named Sigli built Alfred's navy—although Alfred is indeed credited with creating that entity, along with so many of his other outstanding accomplishments that are recounted in the book. It's also unlikely that a Viking named Sigli accompanied Alfred on his famous flight to Athelney, fought at the king's side, and was exiled from England, only to finally return to consummate his vengeance.

And it's also unlikely that a Viking named Sigli fell in love with Aethelfled and became the father of her daughter.

But then again, maybe he did.

Jon Rant
February 2016

Made in the USA
Monee, IL
13 December 2019

18556833R00352